ALSO FROM JOE BOOKS

Disney Frozen Cinestory Comic

Disney Cinderella Cinestory Comic

Disney 101 Dalmatians Cinestory Comic

Disney Princess Comics Treasury

Disney•Pixar Comics Treasury

Disney Darkwing Duck: The Definitively Dangerous Edition

Disney Frozen: The Story of the Movie in Comics

Disney Big Hero 6 Cinestory Comic

Disney•Pixar Inside Out Cinestory Comic

Disney•Pixar Inside Out Fun Book

Disney Gravity Falls Cinestory Comic Volume One

Disney•Pixar The Good Dinosaur Cinestory Comic

Disney•Pixar The Good Dinosaur Fun Book

Disney Zootopia Cinestory Comic

Disney Winnie the Pooh Cinestory Comic

Disney Descendants Wicked World Cinestory Comic Volume One

Disney Descendants Wicked World Cinestory Comic Volume Two

Disney Alice in Wonderland Cinestory Comic

Disney•Pixar Finding Nemo Cinestory Comic

Disney Star vs the Forces of Evil Cinestory Comic

Disney•Pixar Cars Cinestory Comic

Marvel Thor: Dueling with Giants

Don't miss our monthly comics…

Disney Princess

Disney Darkwing Duck

Disney•Pixar Finding Dory

Disney Frozen

GRAVITY FALLS

CINESTORY COMIC

VOLUME 2

JOE BOOKS LTD

Copyright © 2016 Disney Enterprises, Inc. All rights reserved.

Published simultaneously in the United States and Canada by Joe Books Ltd,
489 College Street, Suite 203, Toronto, Ontario, M6G 1A5

www.joebooks.com

No portion of this publication may be reproduced or transmitted, in any form or by
any means, without the express written permission of the copyright holders.

First Joe Books Edition: July 2016

ISBN: 978-1-988032-91-7

Names, characters, places, and incidents featured in this publication are
either the product of the author's imagination or are used fictitiously. Any
resemblance to actual persons (living or dead), events, institutions,
or locales, without satiric intent, is coincidental.

Joe Books™ is a trademark of Joe Books Ltd. Joe Books® and the Joe Books Logo are
trademarks of Joe Books Ltd., registered in various categories and countries.
All rights reserved.

Library and Archives Canada Cataloguing in Publication
information is available upon request

Printed and bound in Canada
1 3 5 7 9 10 8 6 4 2

For information regarding the CPSIA on this printed material, call:
(203) 595-3636 and provide reference # RICH - 613704

CINESTORY COMIC

VOLUME 2

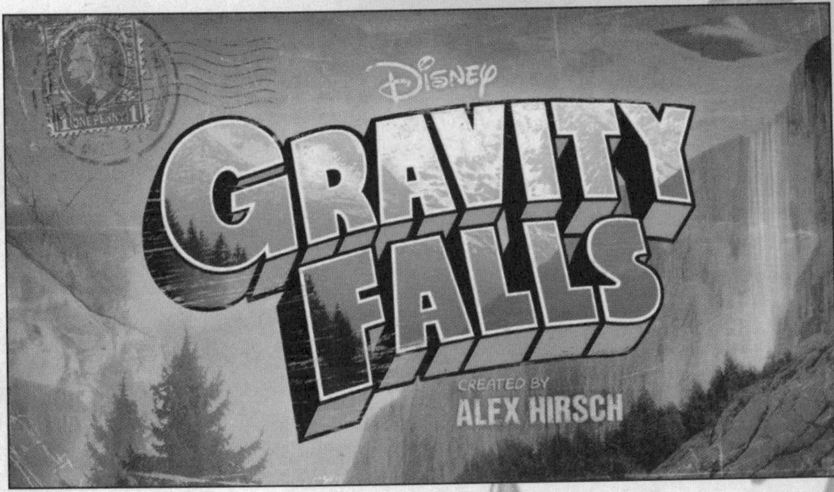
DISNEY
GRAVITY FALLS
CREATED BY
ALEX HIRSCH

THE HAND THAT ROCKS THE MABEL
EPISODE 4

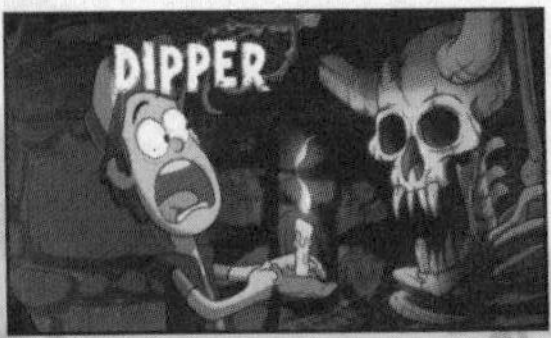
DIPPER

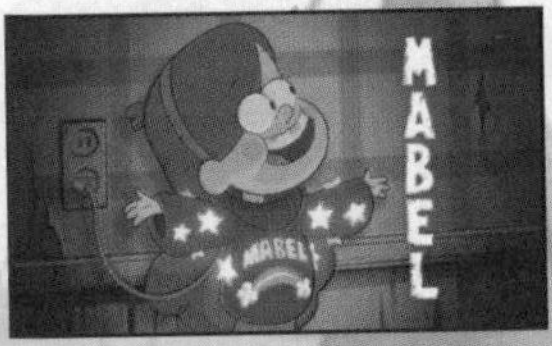
MABEL

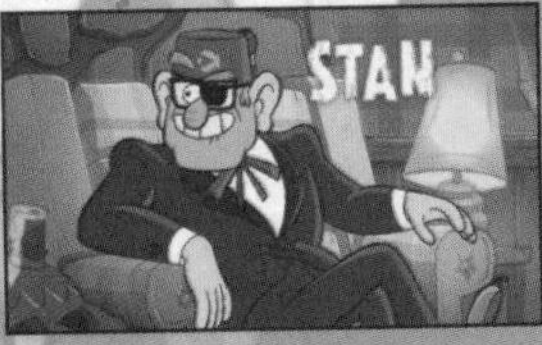
STAN

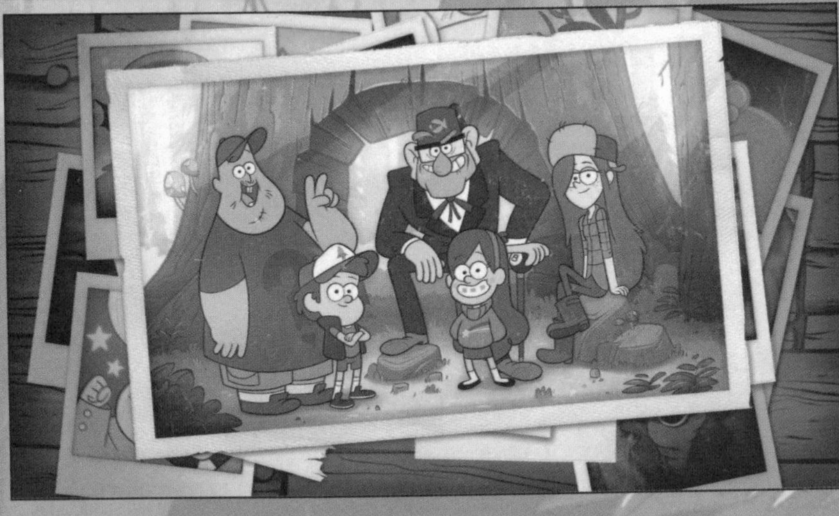

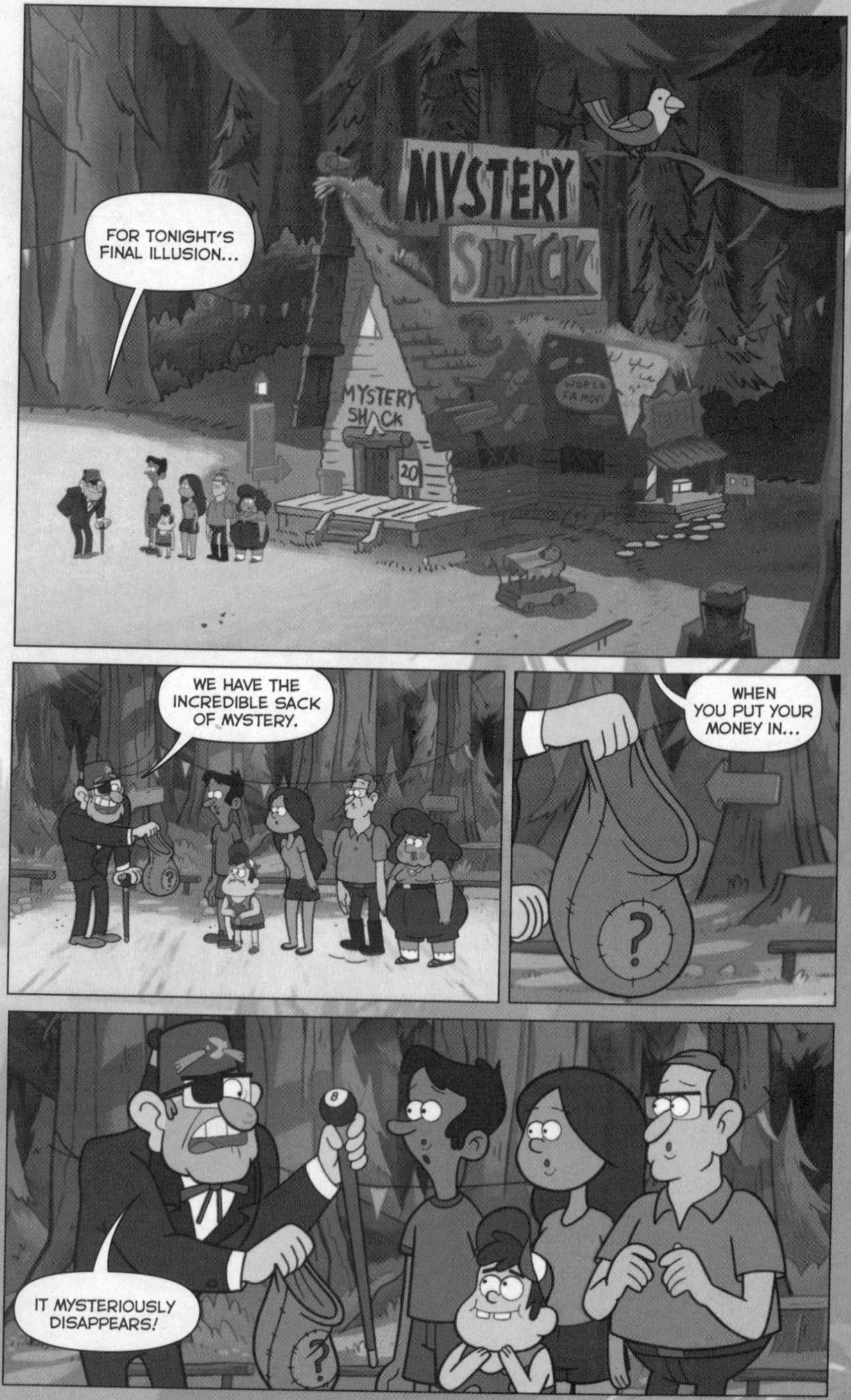
FOR TONIGHT'S FINAL ILLUSION...
MYSTERY
SHACK
MYSTERY SHACK
WE HAVE THE INCREDIBLE SACK OF MYSTERY.
WHEN YOU PUT YOUR MONEY IN...
IT MYSTERIOUSLY DISAPPEARS!

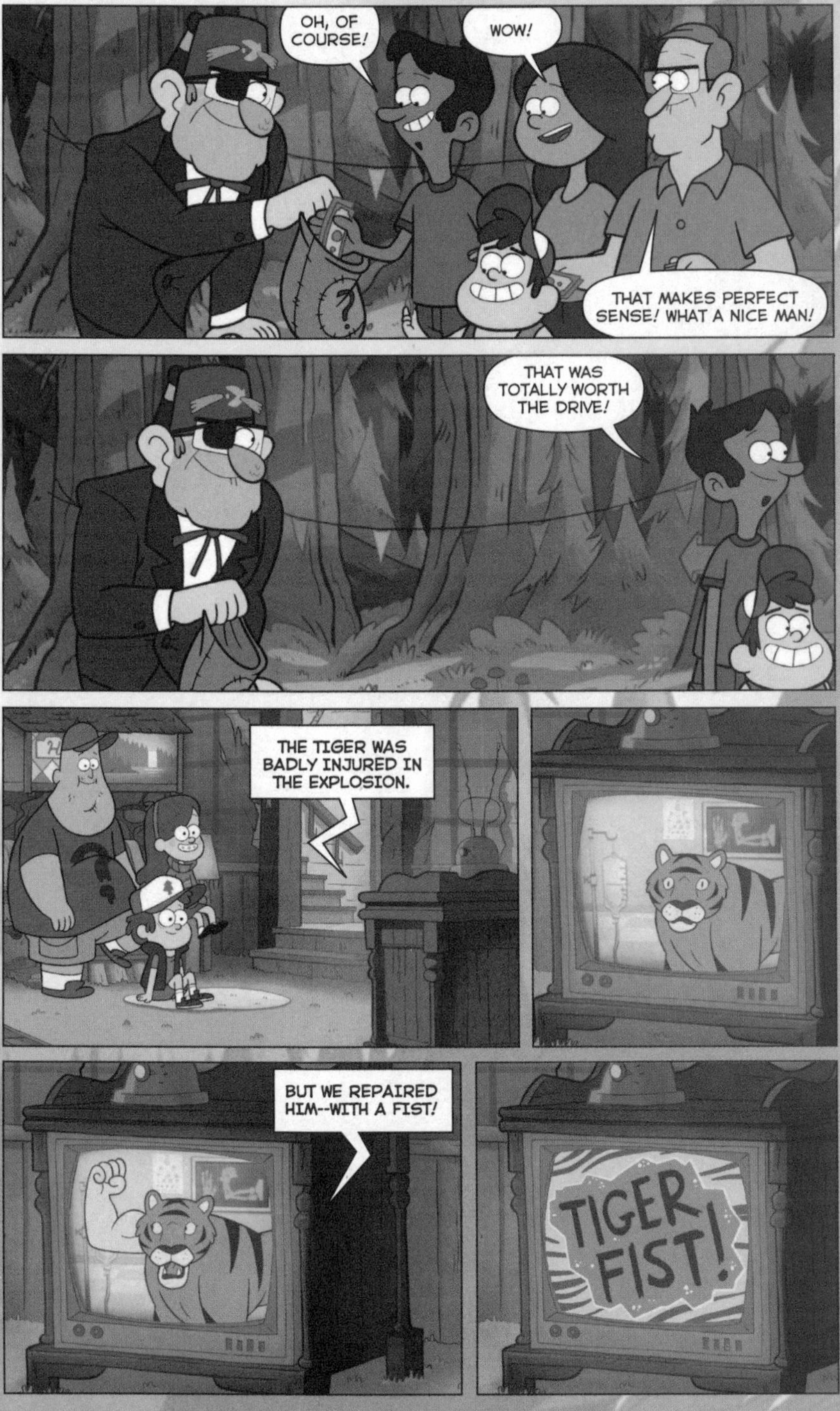
OH, OF COURSE!
WOW!
THAT MAKES PERFECT SENSE! WHAT A NICE MAN!
THAT WAS TOTALLY WORTH THE DRIVE!
THE TIGER WAS BADLY INJURED IN THE EXPLOSION.
BUT WE REPAIRED HIM--WITH A FIST!
TIGER FIST!

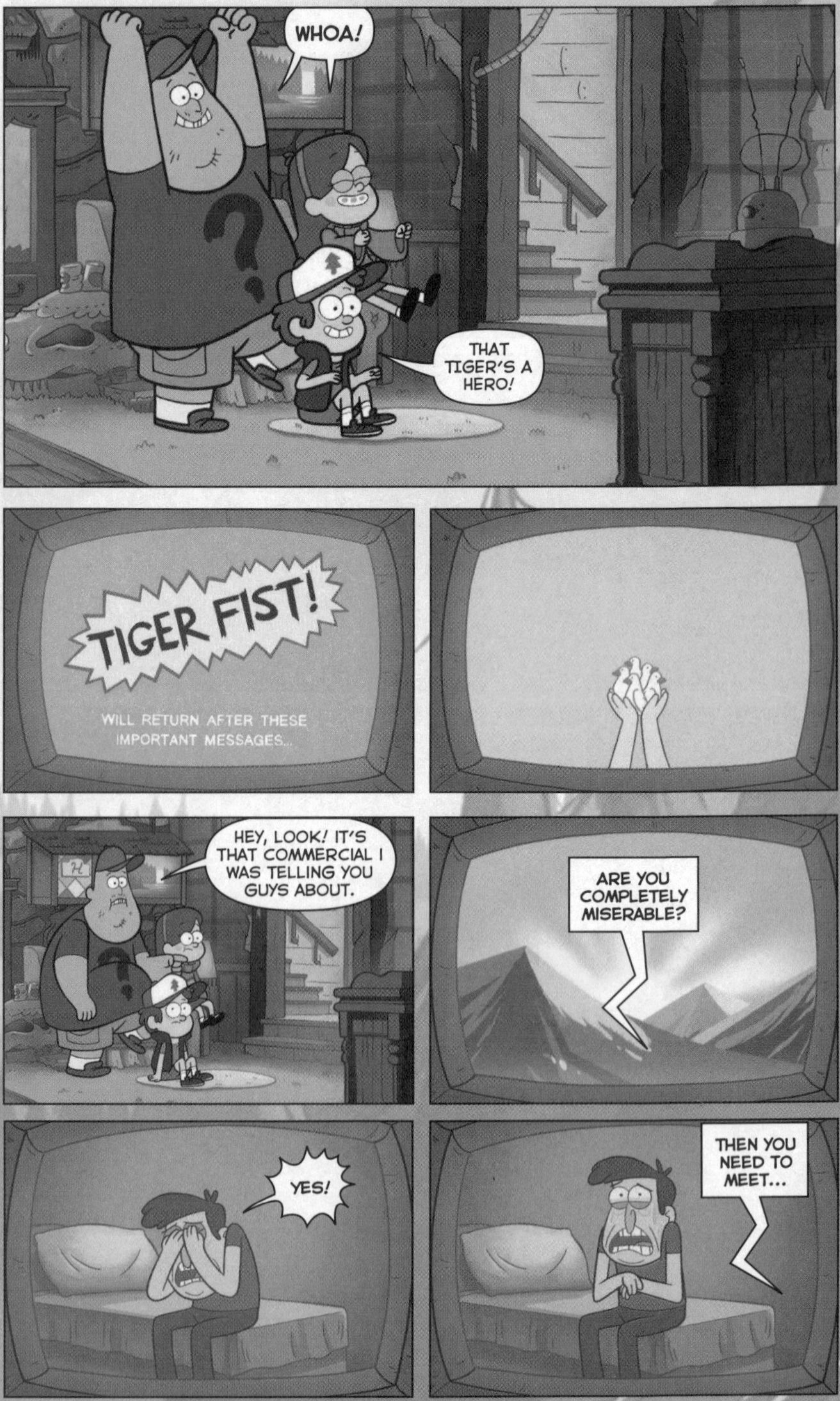
WHOA!
THAT TIGER'S A HERO!
TIGER FIST!
WILL RETURN AFTER THESE IMPORTANT MESSAGES...
HEY, LOOK! IT'S THAT COMMERCIAL I WAS TELLING YOU GUYS ABOUT.
ARE YOU COMPLETELY MISERABLE?
YES!
THEN YOU NEED TO MEET...

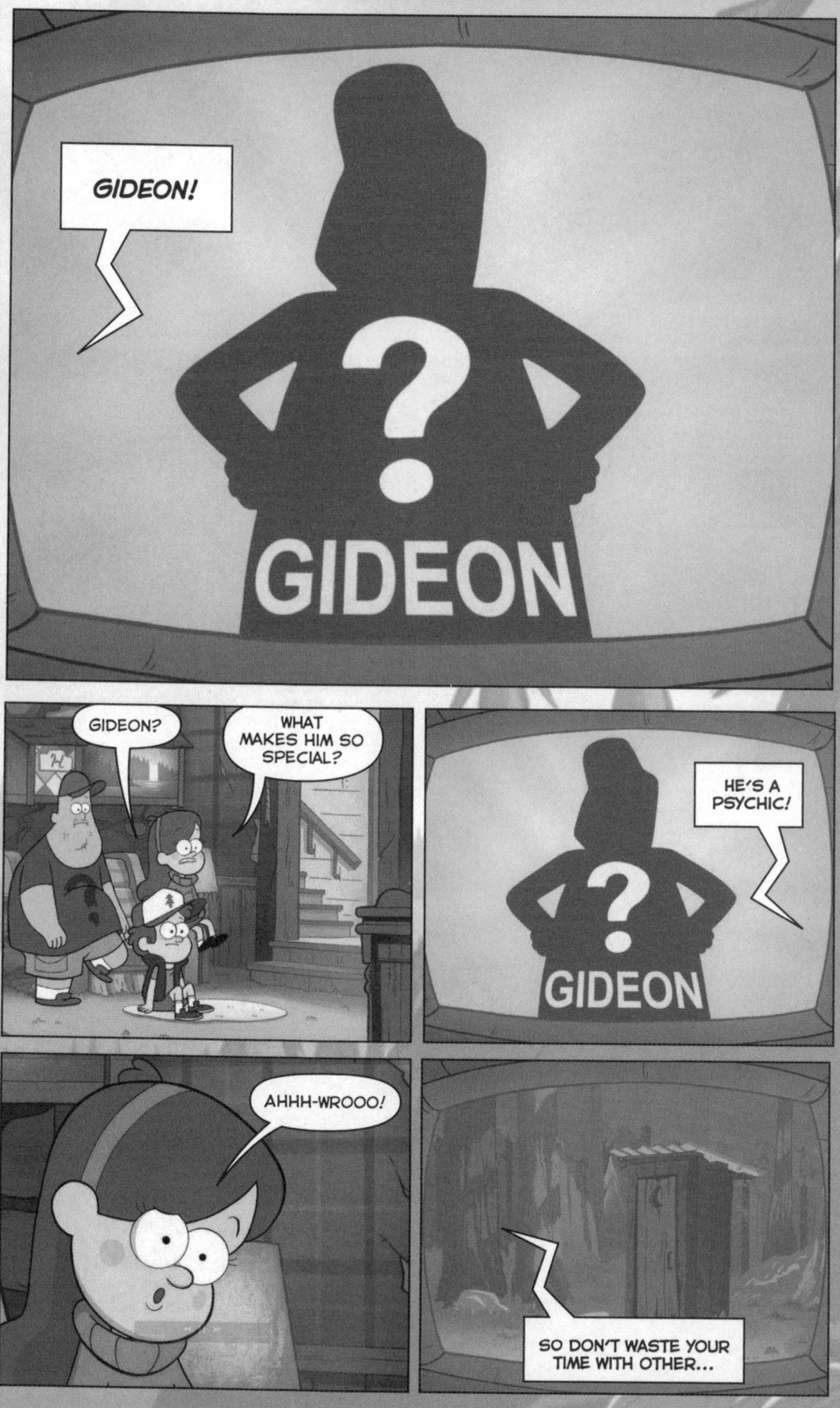
GIDEON!
GIDEON
GIDEON?
WHAT MAKES HIM SO SPECIAL?
HE'S A PSYCHIC!
GIDEON
AHHH-WROOO!
SO DON'T WASTE YOUR TIME WITH OTHER...

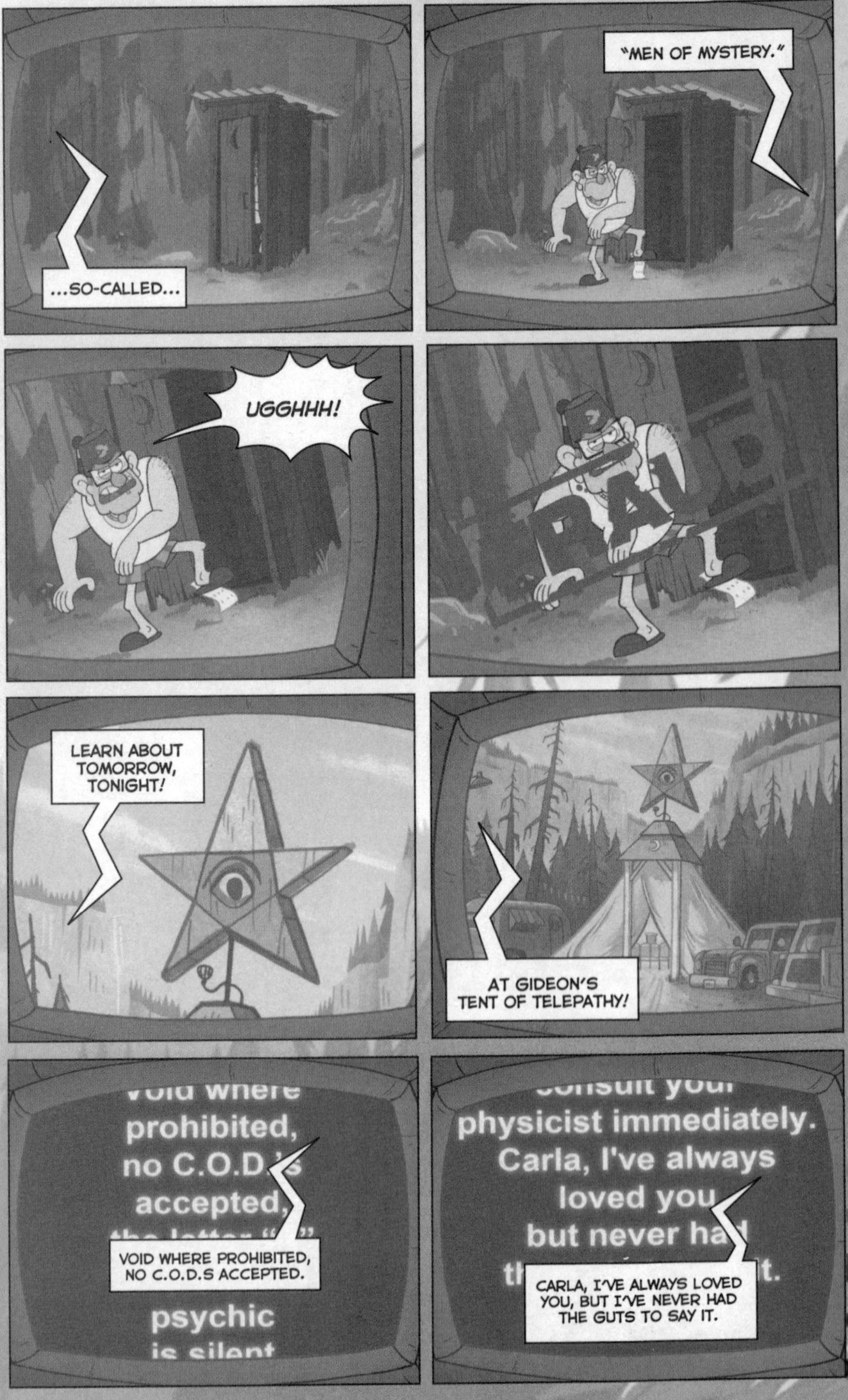
...SO-CALLED...
"MEN OF MYSTERY."
UGGHHH!
LEARN ABOUT TOMORROW, TONIGHT!
AT GIDEON'S TENT OF TELEPATHY!
prohibited,
accepted,
VOID WHERE PROHIBITED, NO C.O.D.S ACCEPTED.
psychic
physicist immediately.
Carla, I've always
loved you
CARLA, I'VE ALWAYS LOVED YOU, BUT I'VE NEVER HAD THE GUTS TO SAY IT.

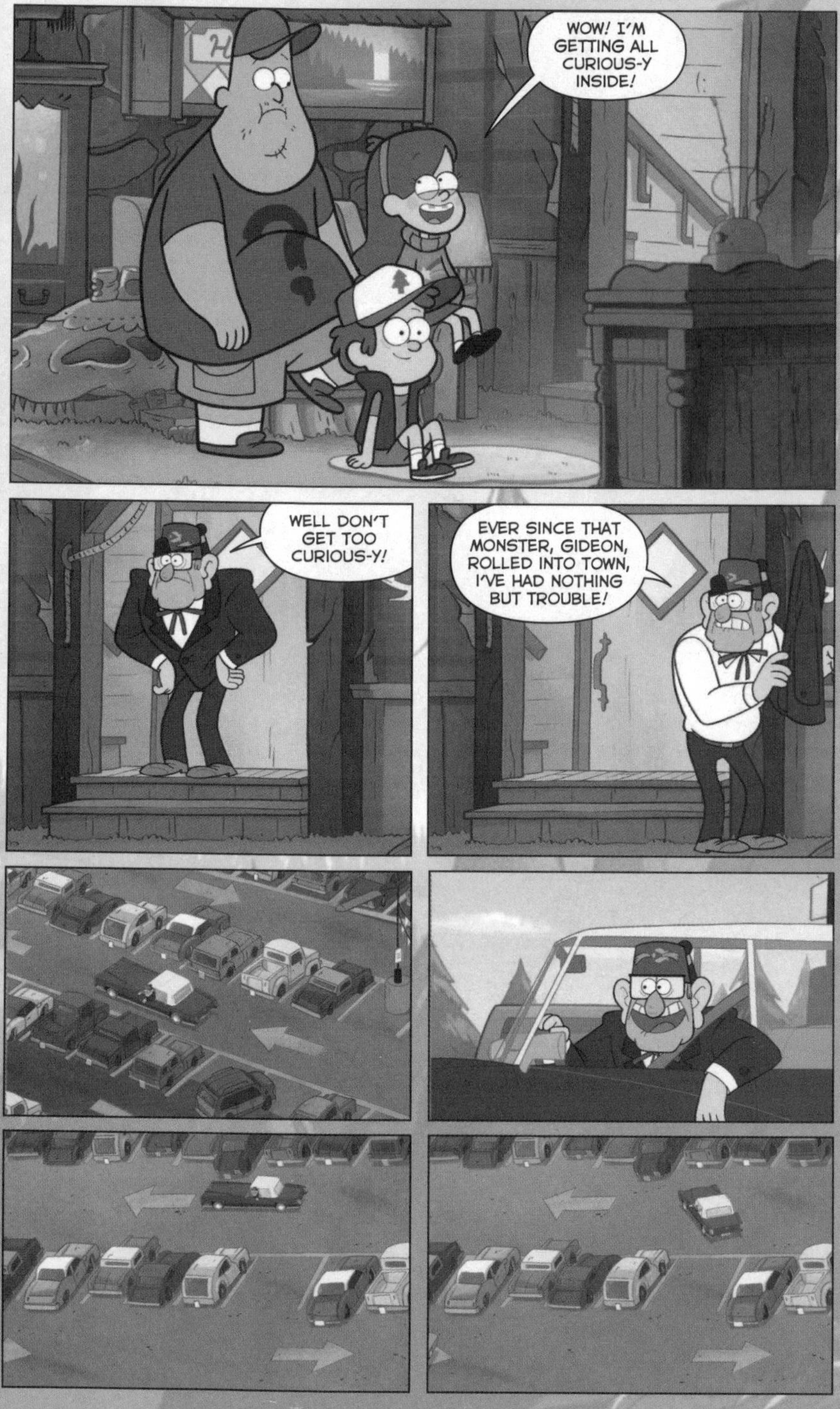
WOW! I'M GETTING ALL CURIOUS-Y INSIDE!
WELL DON'T GET TOO CURIOUS-Y!
EVER SINCE THAT MONSTER, GIDEON, ROLLED INTO TOWN, I'VE HAD NOTHING BUT TROUBLE!

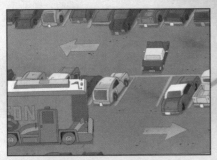

CHEER
CHEER
CHEER
CHEER

GIDEON

GIDEON!

WELL, IS HE REALLY PSYCHIC?

I THINK WE SHOULD GO AND FIND OUT.

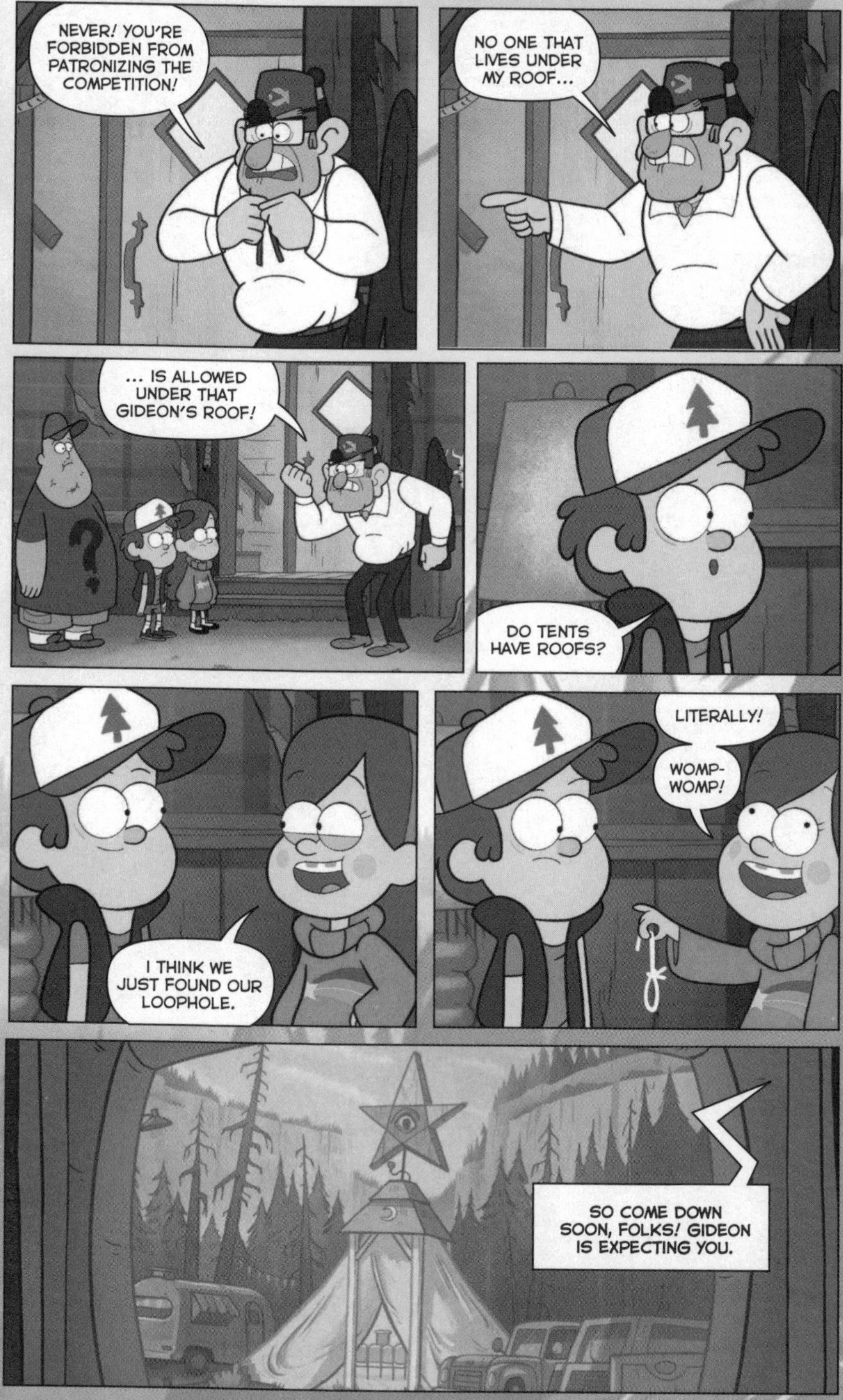

NEVER! YOU'RE FORBIDDEN FROM PATRONIZING THE COMPETITION!
NO ONE THAT LIVES UNDER MY ROOF...
... IS ALLOWED UNDER THAT GIDEON'S ROOF!
DO TENTS HAVE ROOFS?
I THINK WE JUST FOUND OUR LOOPHOLE.
LITERALLY!
WOMP-WOMP!
SO COME DOWN SOON, FOLKS! GIDEON IS EXPECTING YOU.

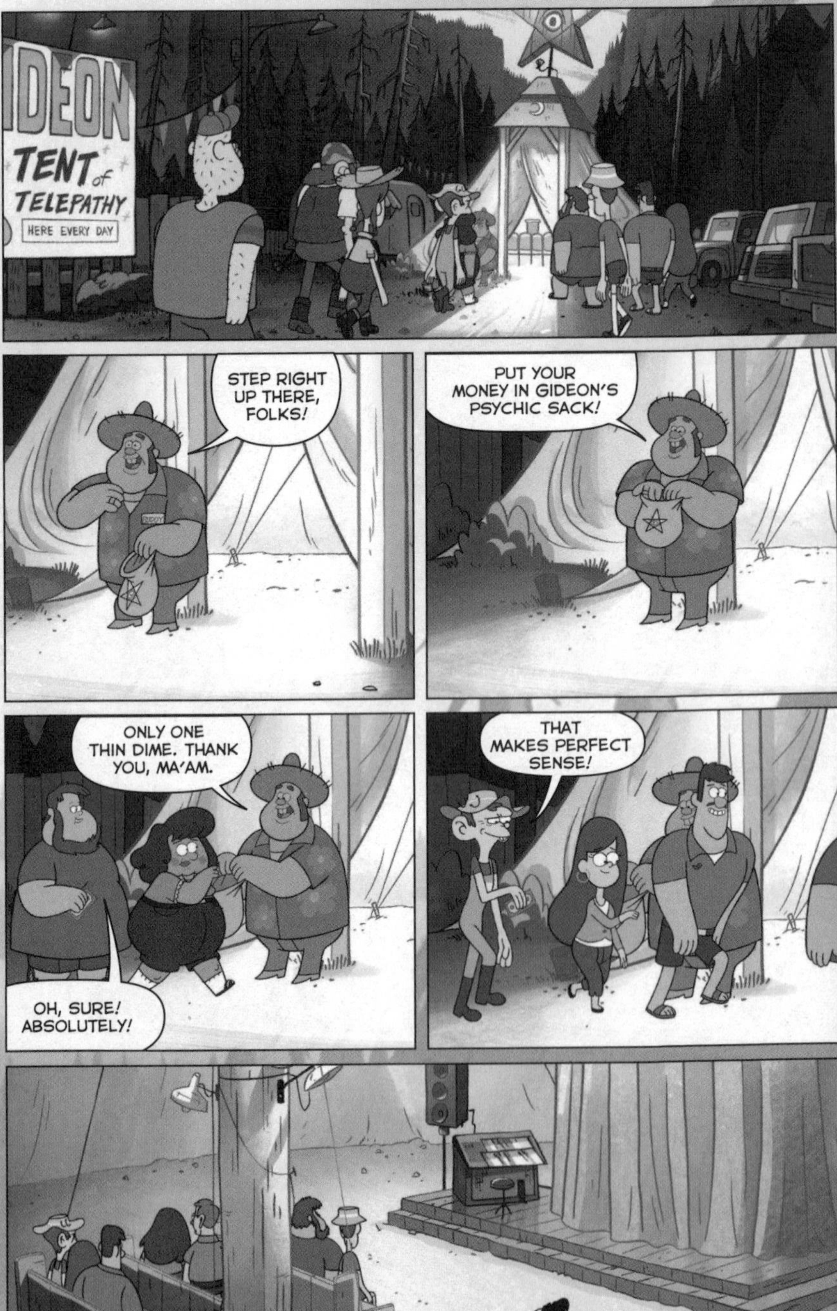
IDEON
TENT of TELEPATHY
HERE EVERY DAY
STEP RIGHT UP THERE, FOLKS!
PUT YOUR MONEY IN GIDEON'S PSYCHIC SACK!
ONLY ONE THIN DIME. THANK YOU, MA'AM.
OH, SURE! ABSOLUTELY!
THAT MAKES PERFECT SENSE!

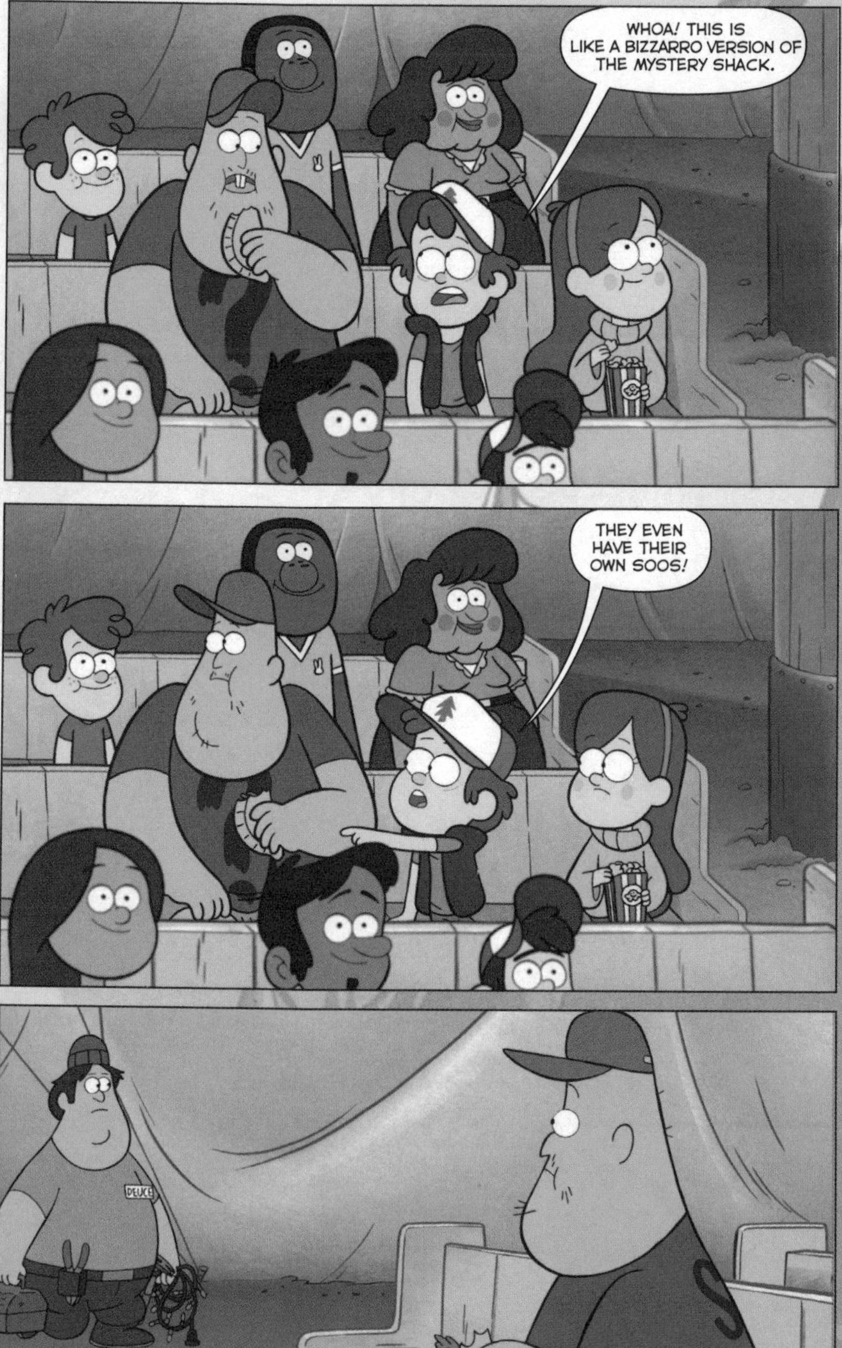
WHOA! THIS IS LIKE A BIZZARRO VERSION OF THE MYSTERY SHACK.
THEY EVEN HAVE THEIR OWN SOOS!
DEUCE

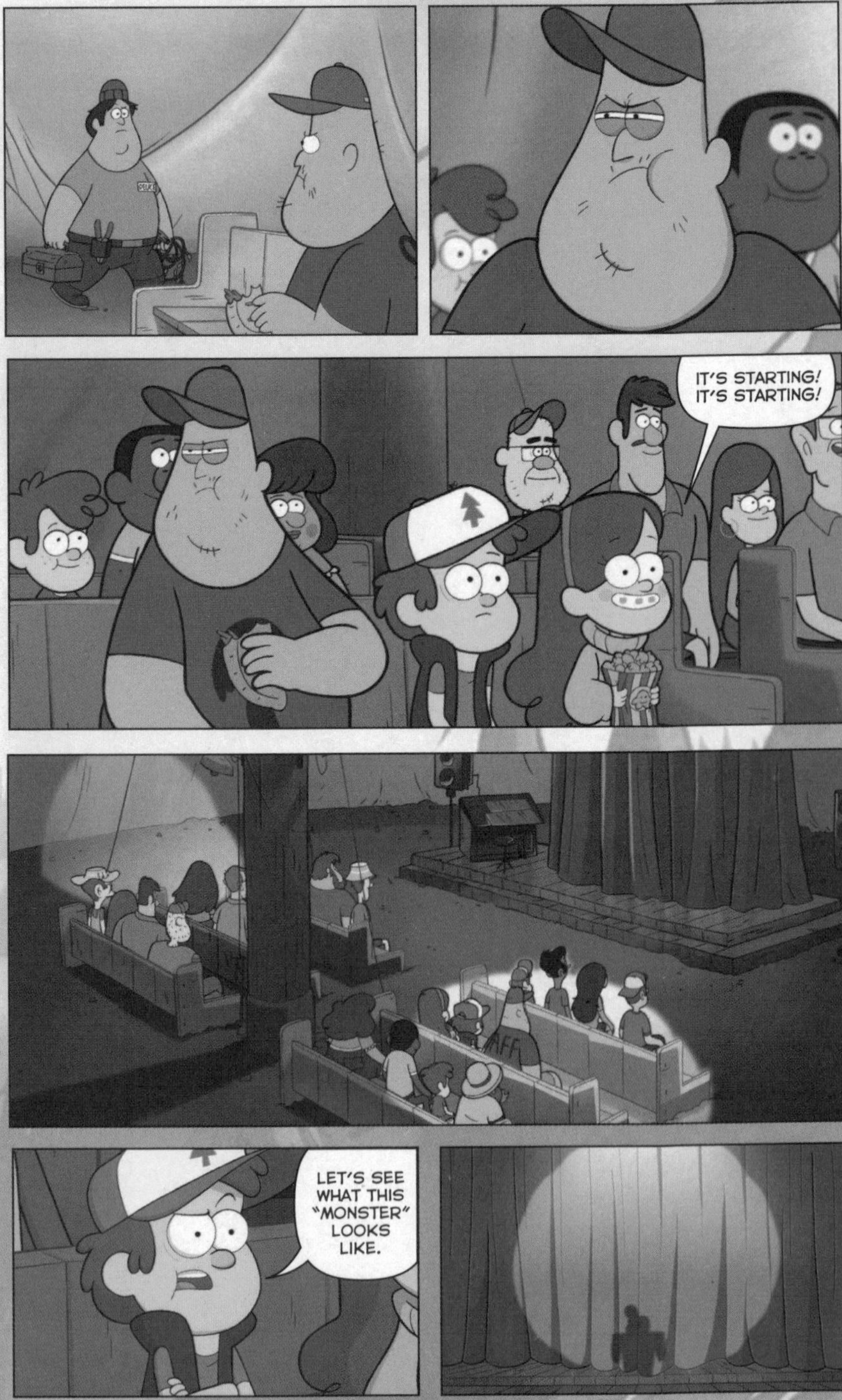
IT'S STARTING! IT'S STARTING!
LET'S SEE WHAT THIS "MONSTER" LOOKS LIKE.

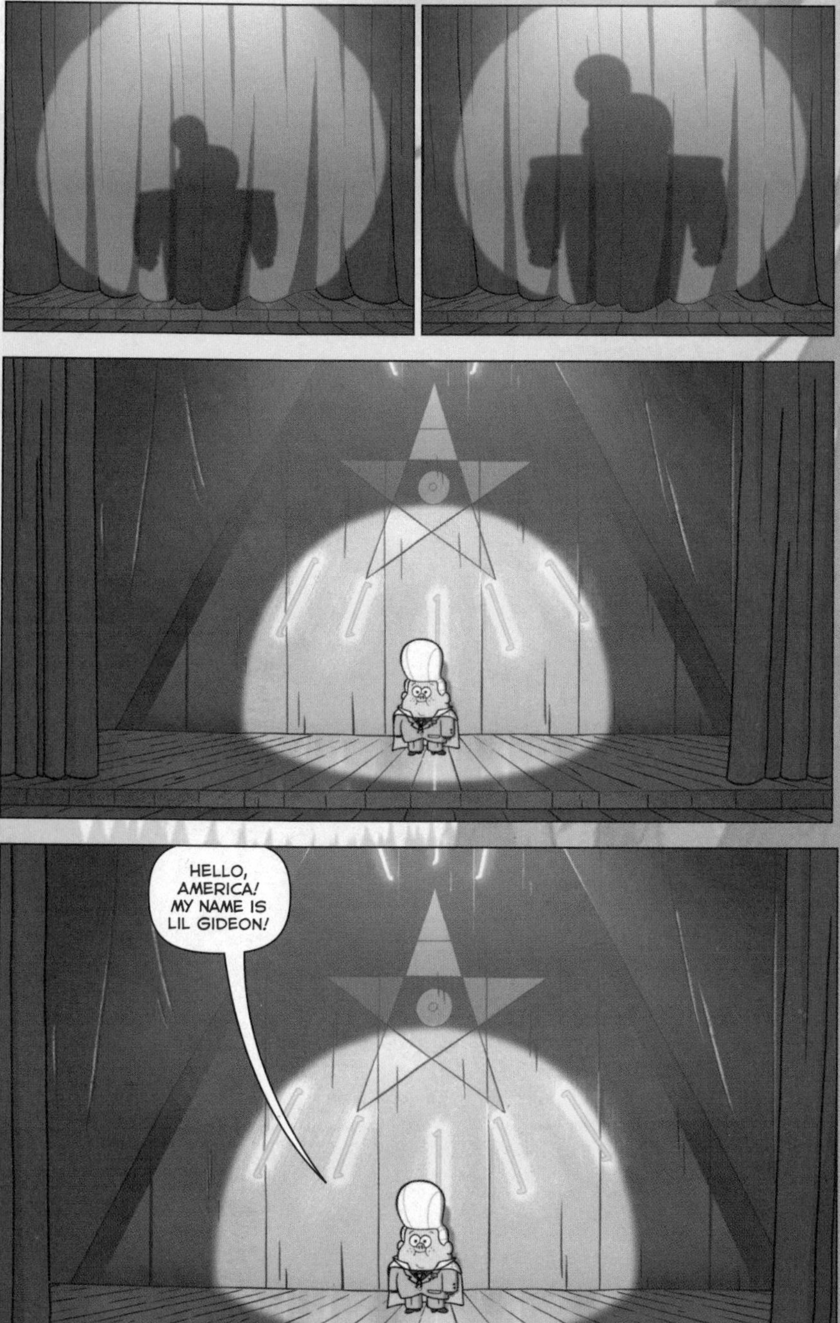
HELLO, AMERICA! MY NAME IS LIL GIDEON!

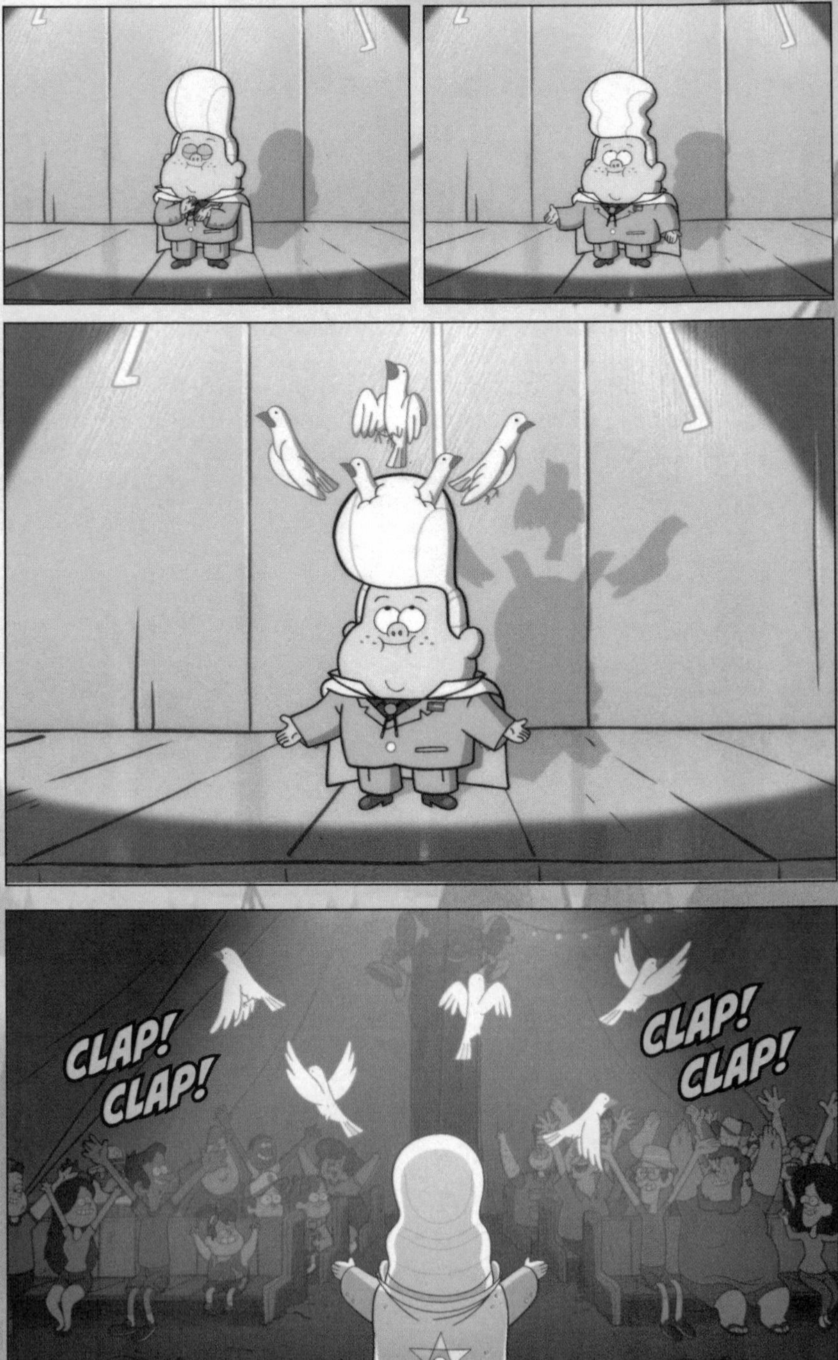
CLAP!
CLAP!
CLAP!
CLAP!

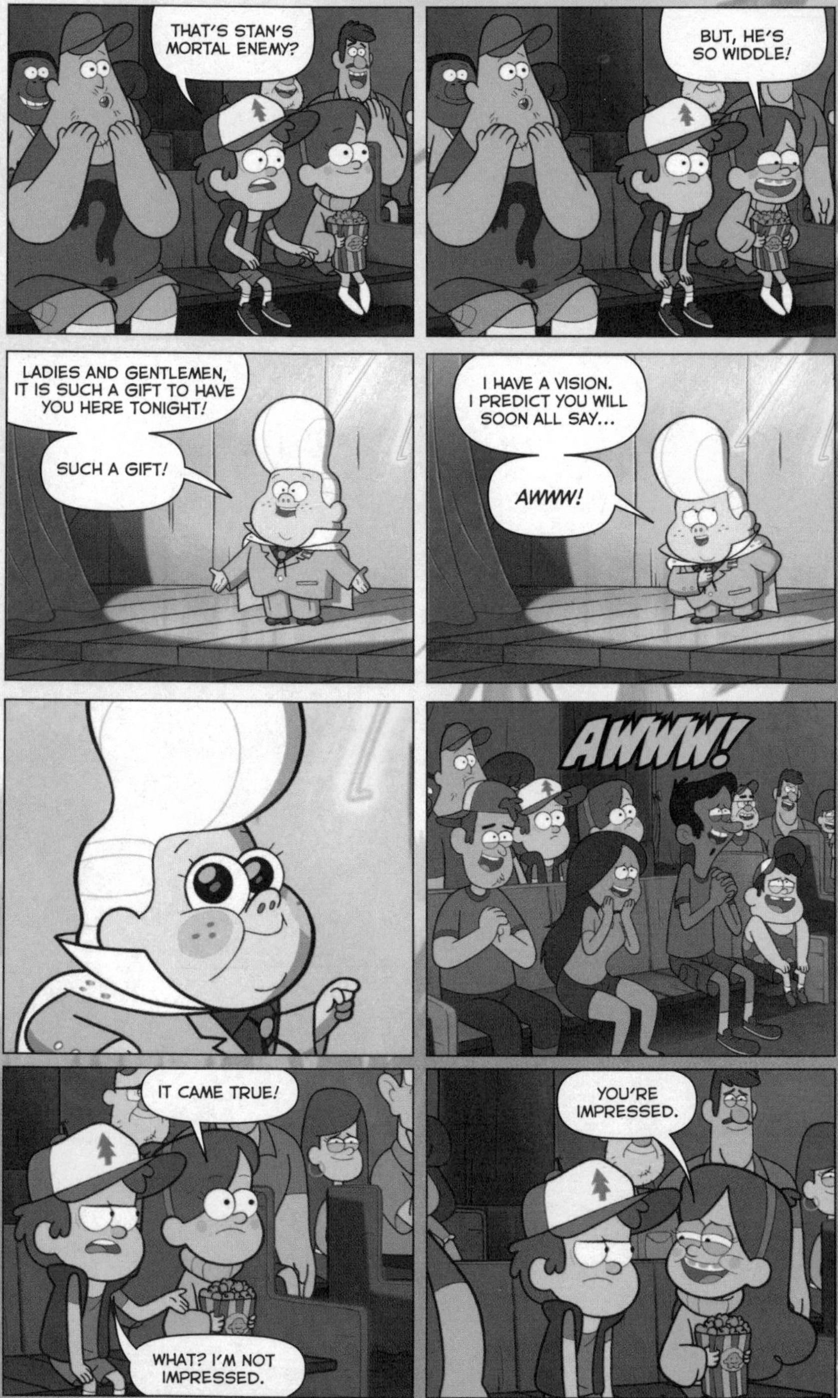
THAT'S STAN'S MORTAL ENEMY?
BUT, HE'S SO WIDDLE!
LADIES AND GENTLEMEN, IT IS SUCH A GIFT TO HAVE YOU HERE TONIGHT!
SUCH A GIFT!
I HAVE A VISION. I PREDICT YOU WILL SOON ALL SAY...
AWWW!
AWWW!
IT CAME TRUE!
WHAT? I'M NOT IMPRESSED.
YOU'RE IMPRESSED.

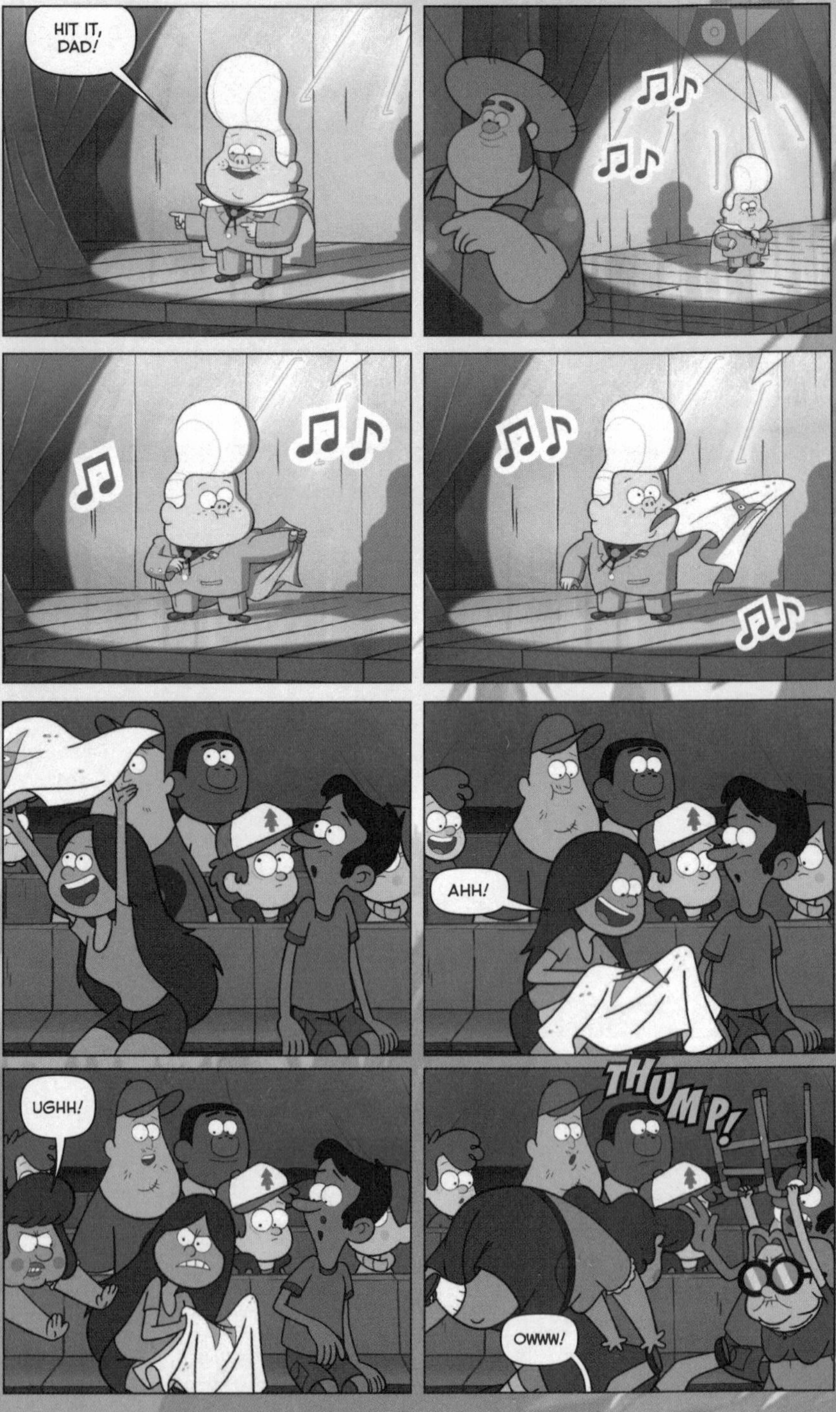
HIT IT, DAD!
AHH!
UGHH!
THUMP!
OWWW!

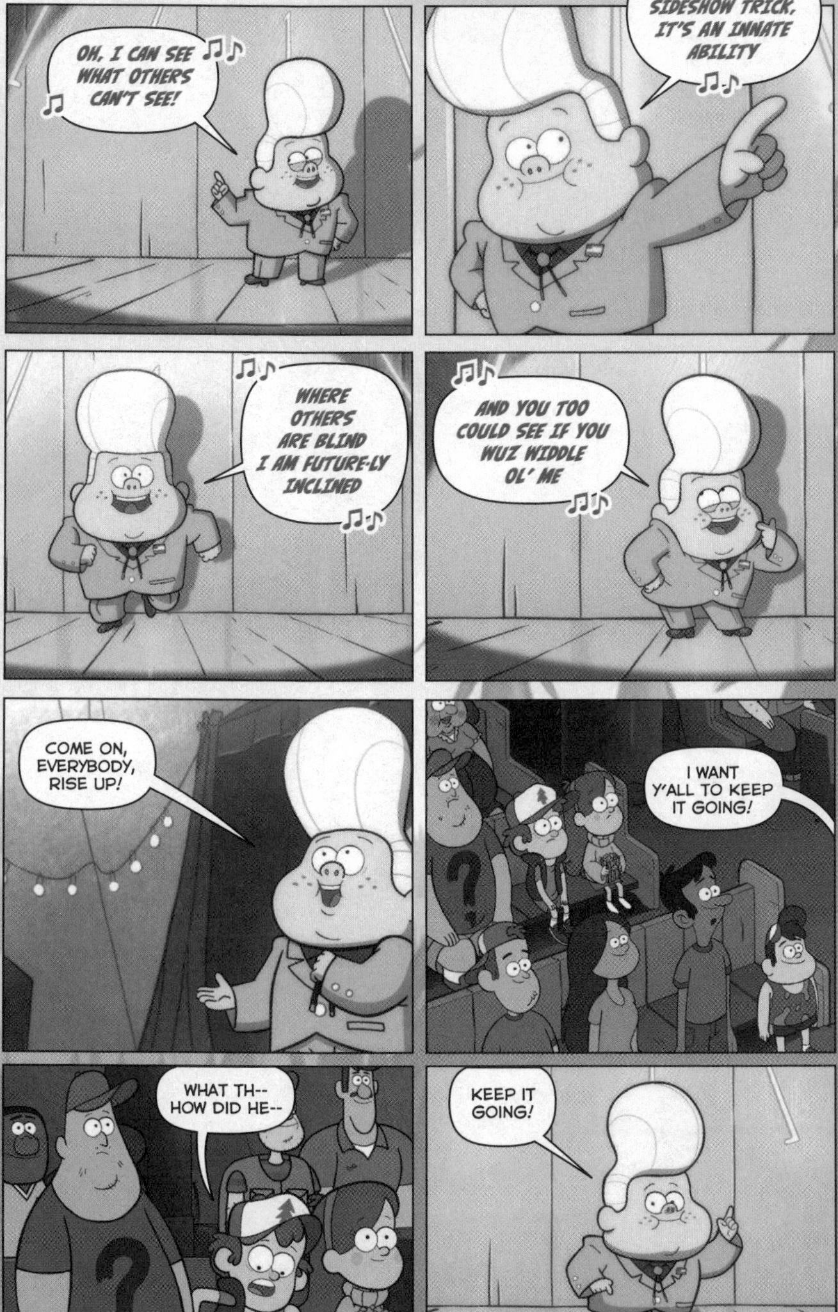
OH, I CAN SEE WHAT OTHERS CAN'T SEE!
IT AIN'T SOME SIDESHOW TRICK, IT'S AN INNATE ABILITY
WHERE OTHERS ARE BLIND I AM FUTURE-LY INCLINED
AND YOU TOO COULD SEE IF YOU WUZ WIDDLE OL' ME
COME ON, EVERYBODY, RISE UP!
I WANT Y'ALL TO KEEP IT GOING!
WHAT TH-- HOW DID HE--
KEEP IT GOING!

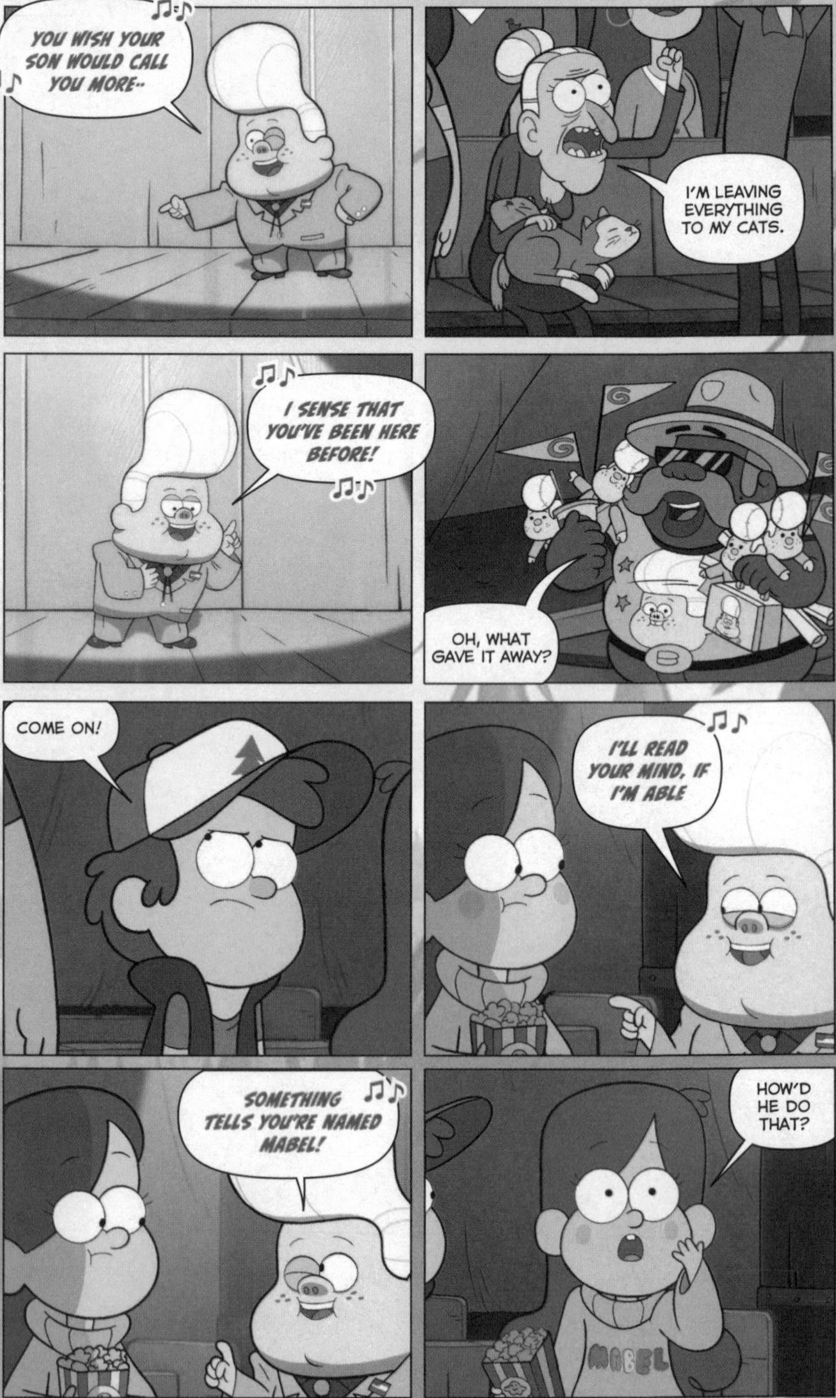

YOU WISH YOUR SON WOULD CALL YOU MORE..
I'M LEAVING EVERYTHING TO MY CATS.
I SENSE THAT YOU'VE BEEN HERE BEFORE!
OH, WHAT GAVE IT AWAY?
COME ON!
I'LL READ YOUR MIND, IF I'M ABLE
SOMETHING TELLS YOU'RE NAMED MABEL!
HOW'D HE DO THAT?

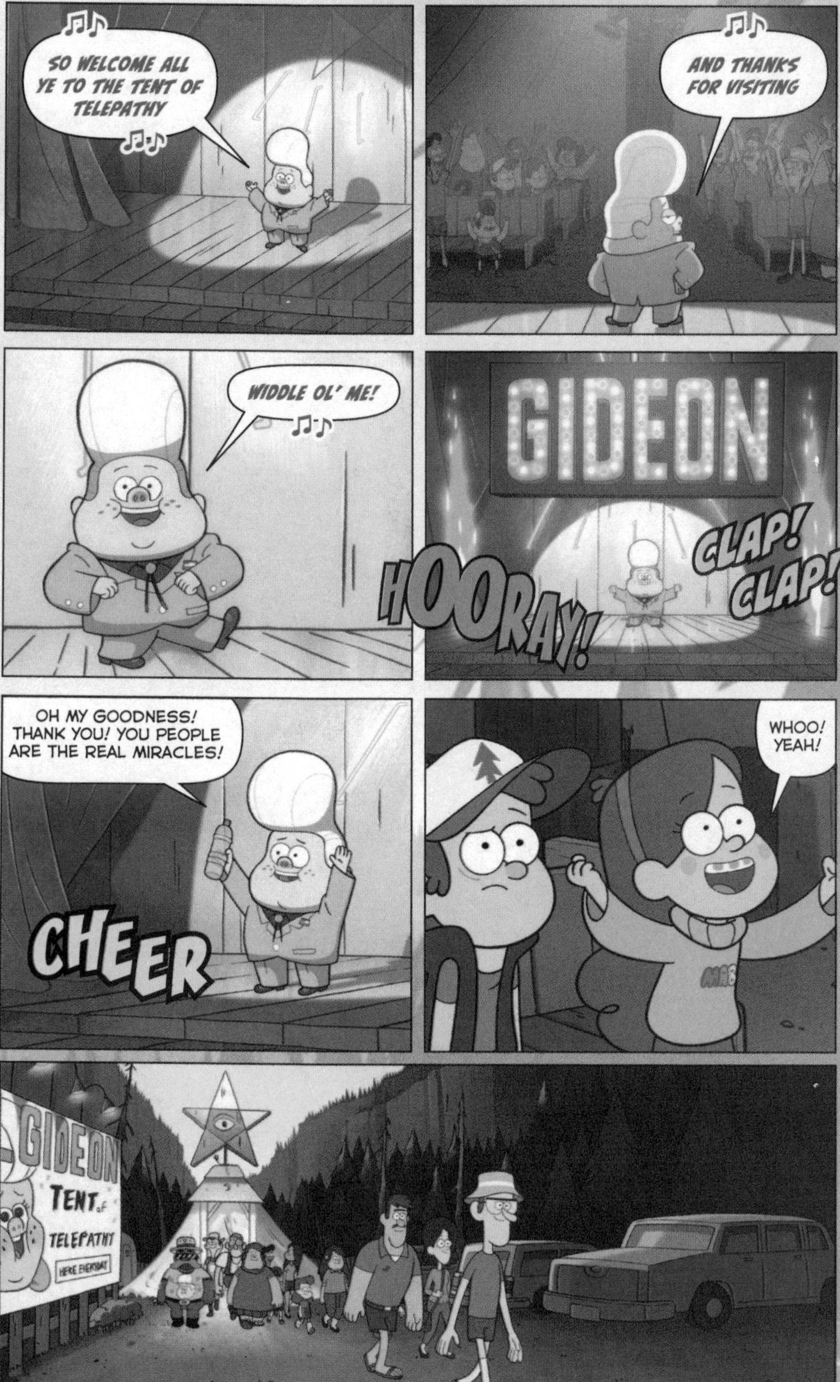

SO WELCOME ALL YE TO THE TENT OF TELEPATHY
AND THANKS FOR VISITING
WIDDLE OL' ME!
GIDEON
CLAP! CLAP!
HOORAY!
OH MY GOODNESS! THANK YOU! YOU PEOPLE ARE THE REAL MIRACLES!
CHEER
WHOO! YEAH!
GIDEON
TENT of
TELEPATHY
HERE EVERYDAY

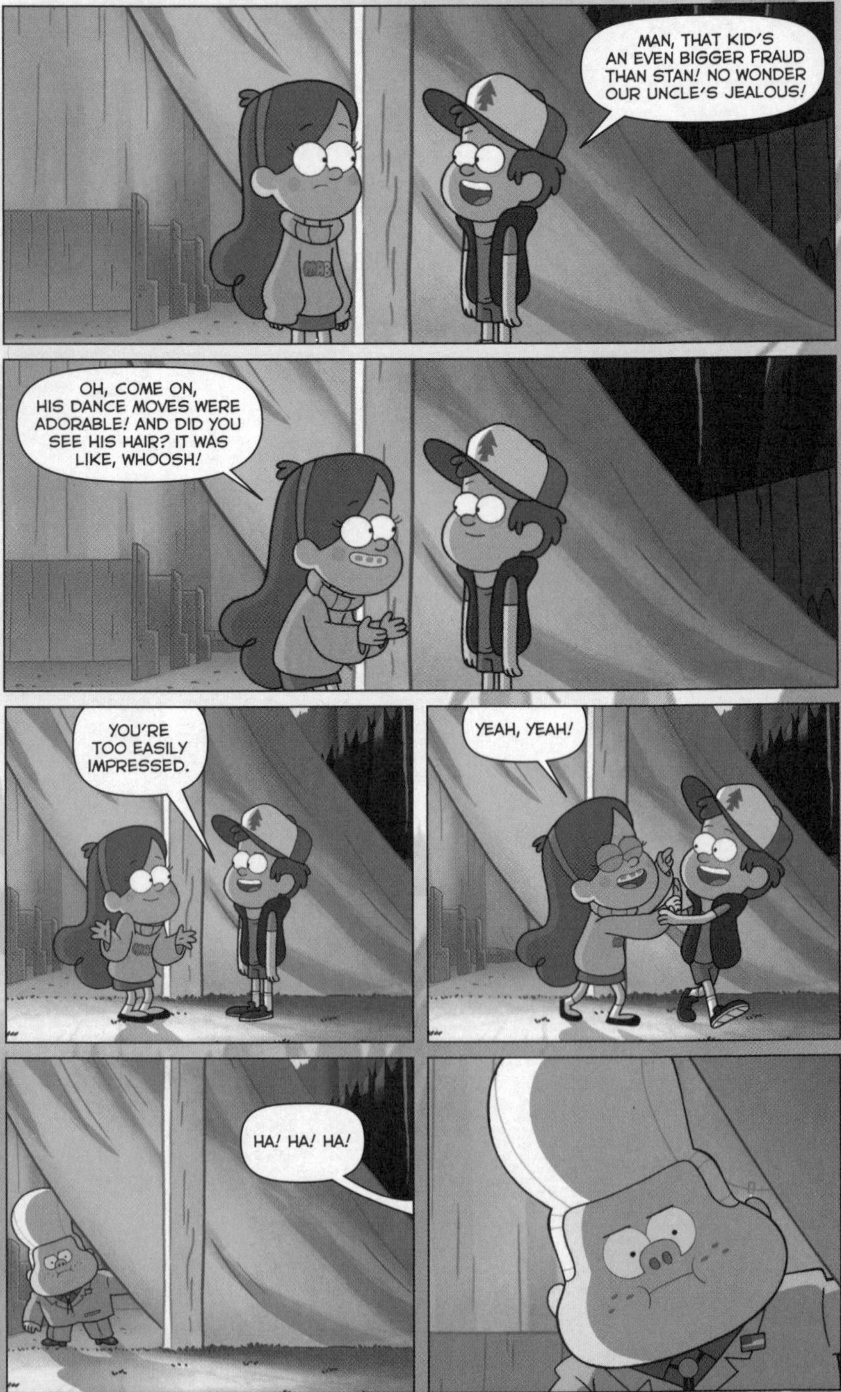
MAN, THAT KID'S AN EVEN BIGGER FRAUD THAN STAN! NO WONDER OUR UNCLE'S JEALOUS!
OH, COME ON, HIS DANCE MOVES WERE ADORABLE! AND DID YOU SEE HIS HAIR? IT WAS LIKE, WHOOSH!
YOU'RE TOO EASILY IMPRESSED.
YEAH, YEAH!
HA! HA! HA!

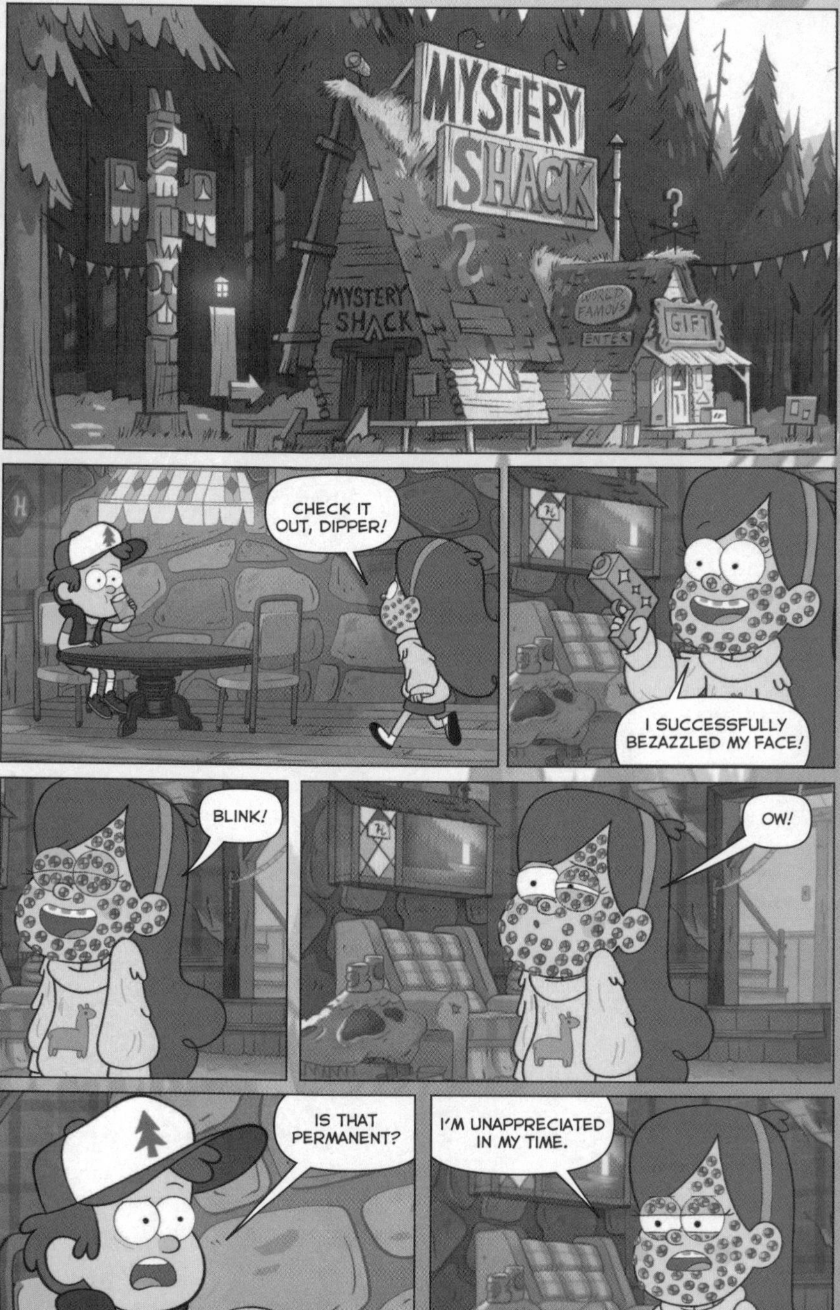
MYSTERY
SHACK
MYSTERY
SHACK
WORLD FAMOUS
ENTER
GIFT
CHECK IT OUT, DIPPER!
I SUCCESSFULLY BEZAZZLED MY FACE!
BLINK!
OW!
IS THAT PERMANENT?
I'M UNAPPRECIATED IN MY TIME.

DING-DONG

SOMEBODY ANSWER THAT DOOR!

I'LL GET IT!

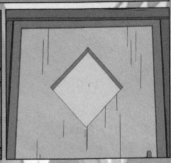

HOWDY.

IT'S WIDDLE OL' YOU!

YEAH, MY SONG'S QUITE CATCHY.

I, I KNOW WE HAVEN'T FORMALLY MET, BUT AFTER YESTERDAY'S PERFORMANCE...

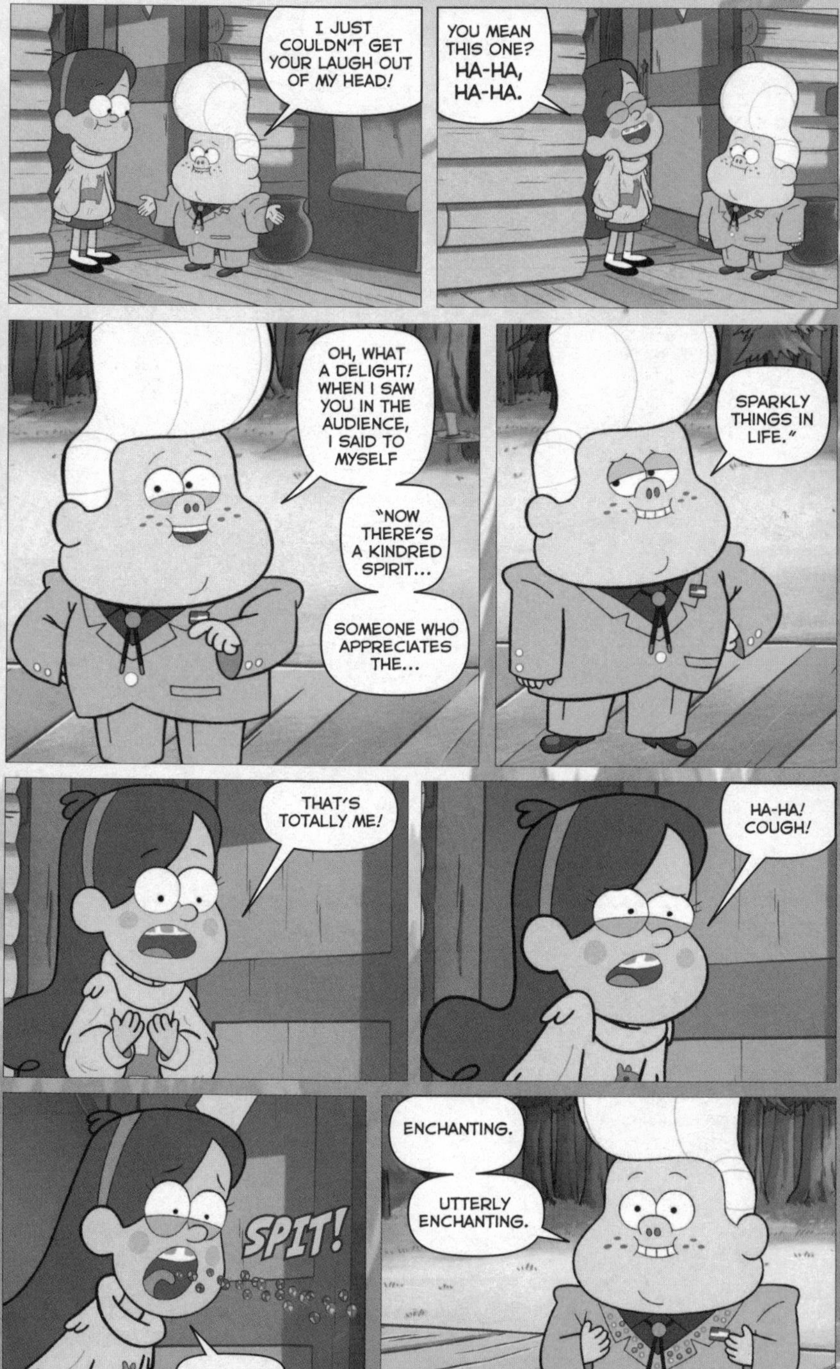

I JUST COULDN'T GET YOUR LAUGH OUT OF MY HEAD!
YOU MEAN THIS ONE? HA-HA, HA-HA.
OH, WHAT A DELIGHT! WHEN I SAW YOU IN THE AUDIENCE, I SAID TO MYSELF
"NOW THERE'S A KINDRED SPIRIT...
SOMEONE WHO APPRECIATES THE...
SPARKLY THINGS IN LIFE."
THAT'S TOTALLY ME!
HA-HA! COUGH!
SPIT!
UGGHHH.
ENCHANTING.
UTTERLY ENCHANTING.

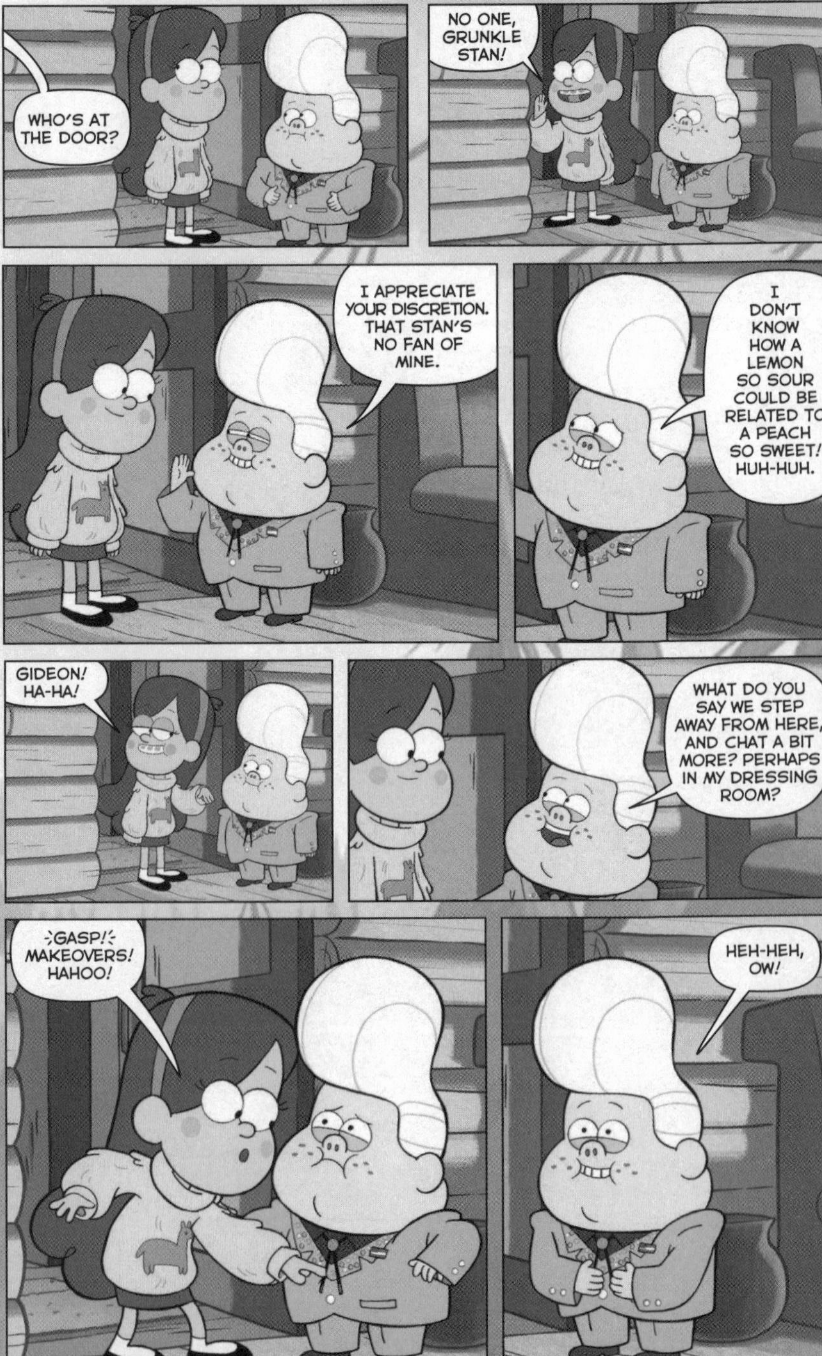
WHO'S AT THE DOOR?
NO ONE, GRUNKLE STAN!
I APPRECIATE YOUR DISCRETION. THAT STAN'S NO FAN OF MINE.
I DON'T KNOW HOW A LEMON SO SOUR COULD BE RELATED TO A PEACH SO SWEET! HUH-HUH.
GIDEON! HA-HA!
WHAT DO YOU SAY WE STEP AWAY FROM HERE, AND CHAT A BIT MORE? PERHAPS IN MY DRESSING ROOM?
GASP! MAKEOVERS! HAHOO!
HEH-HEH, OW!

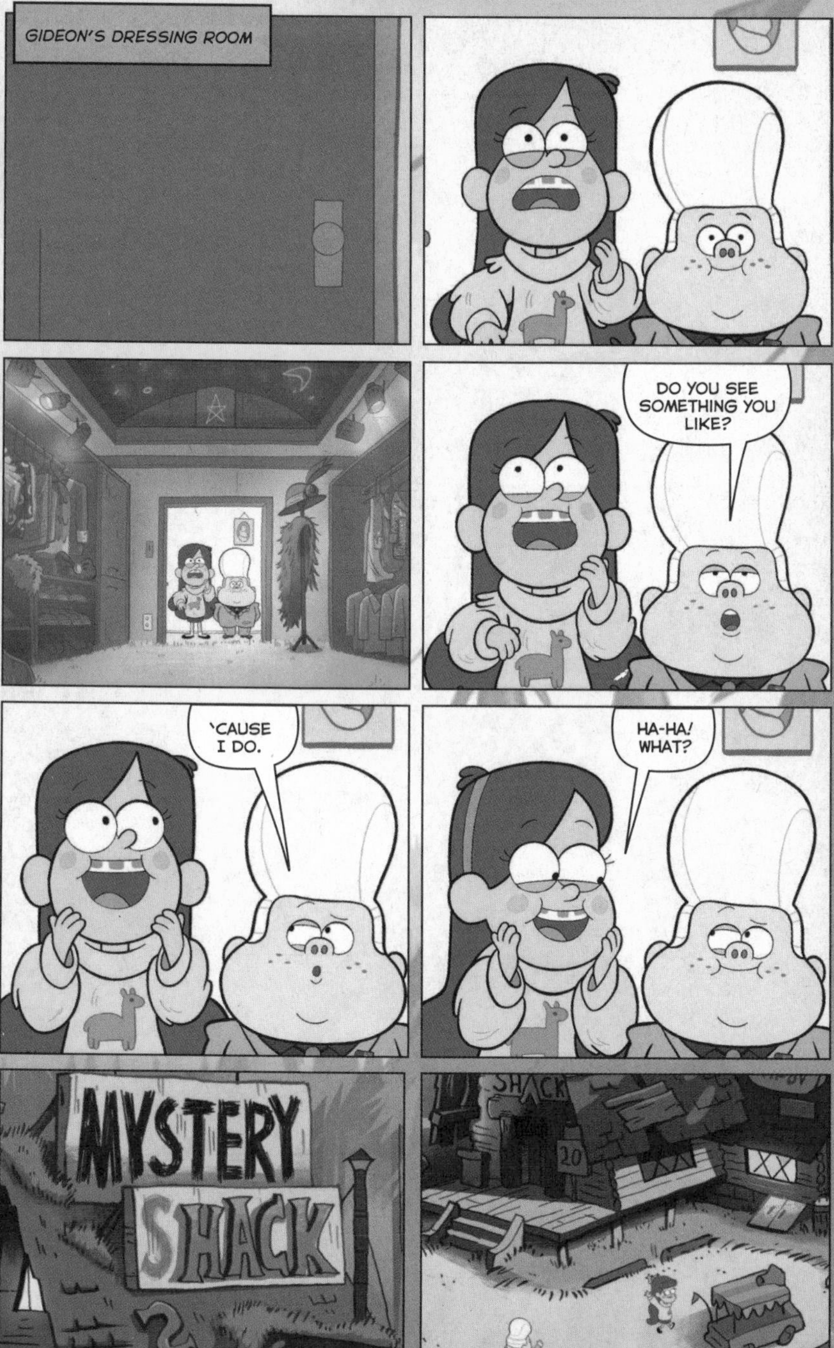

GIDEON'S DRESSING ROOM
DO YOU SEE SOMETHING YOU LIKE?
'CAUSE I DO.
HA-HA! WHAT?
MYSTERY
SHACK

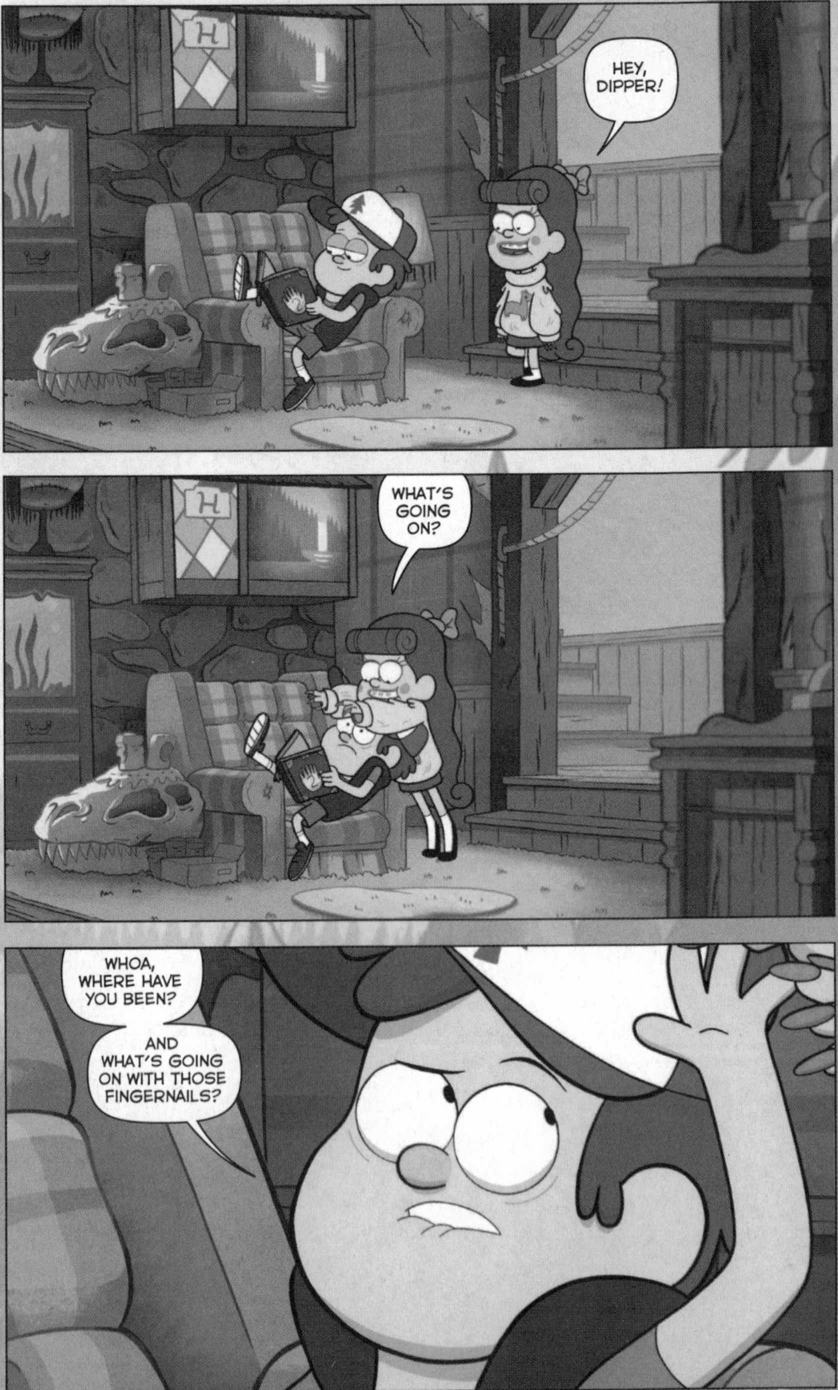
HEY,
DIPPER!
WHAT'S
GOING
ON?
WHOA,
WHERE HAVE
YOU BEEN?
AND
WHAT'S GOING
ON WITH THOSE
FINGERNAILS?

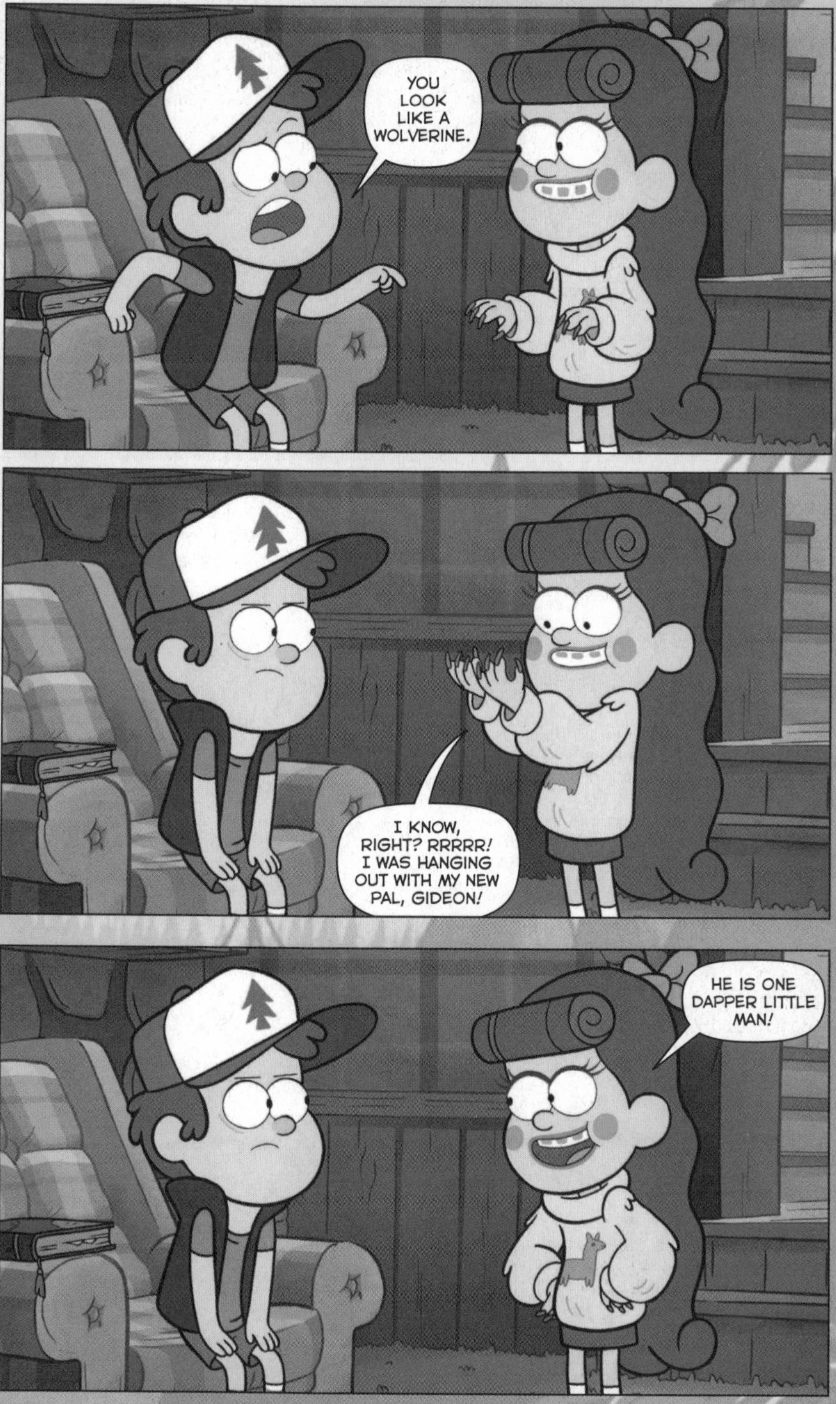
YOU LOOK LIKE A WOLVERINE.
I KNOW, RIGHT? RRRRR! I WAS HANGING OUT WITH MY NEW PAL, GIDEON!
HE IS ONE DAPPER LITTLE MAN!

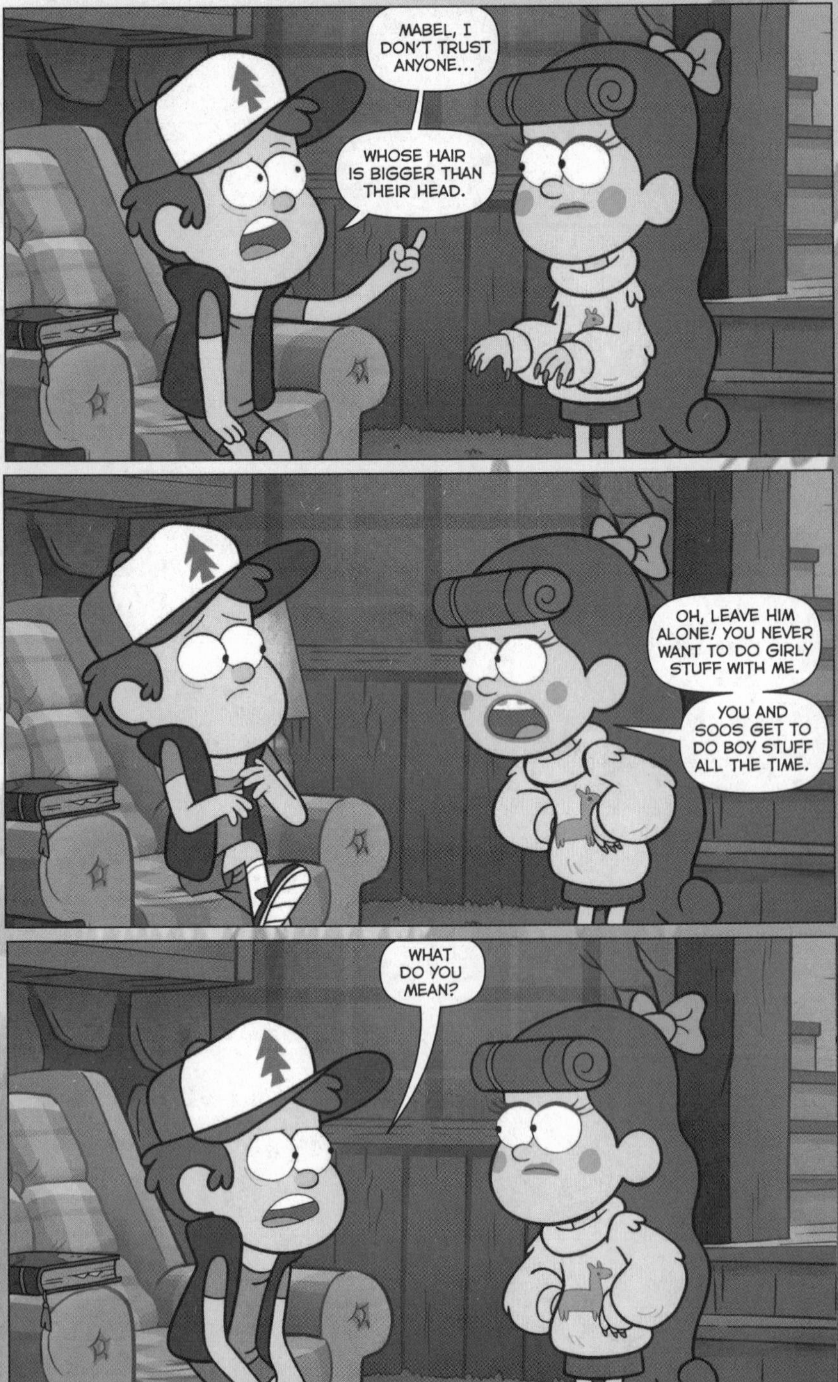
MABEL, I DON'T TRUST ANYONE...
WHOSE HAIR IS BIGGER THAN THEIR HEAD.
OH, LEAVE HIM ALONE! YOU NEVER WANT TO DO GIRLY STUFF WITH ME.
YOU AND SOOS GET TO DO BOY STUFF ALL THE TIME.
WHAT DO YOU MEAN?

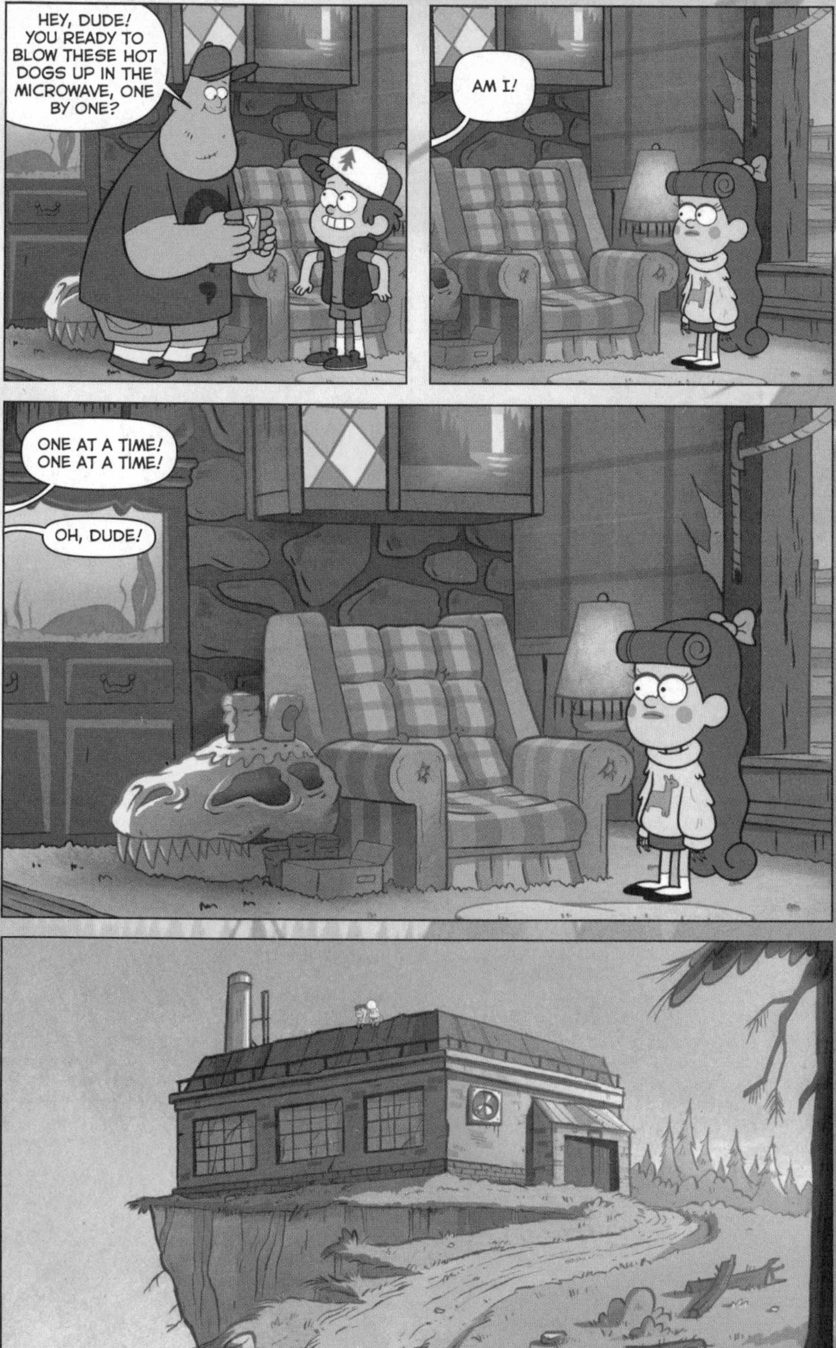
HEY, DUDE! YOU READY TO BLOW THESE HOT DOGS UP IN THE MICROWAVE, ONE BY ONE?
AM I!
ONE AT A TIME! ONE AT A TIME!
OH, DUDE!

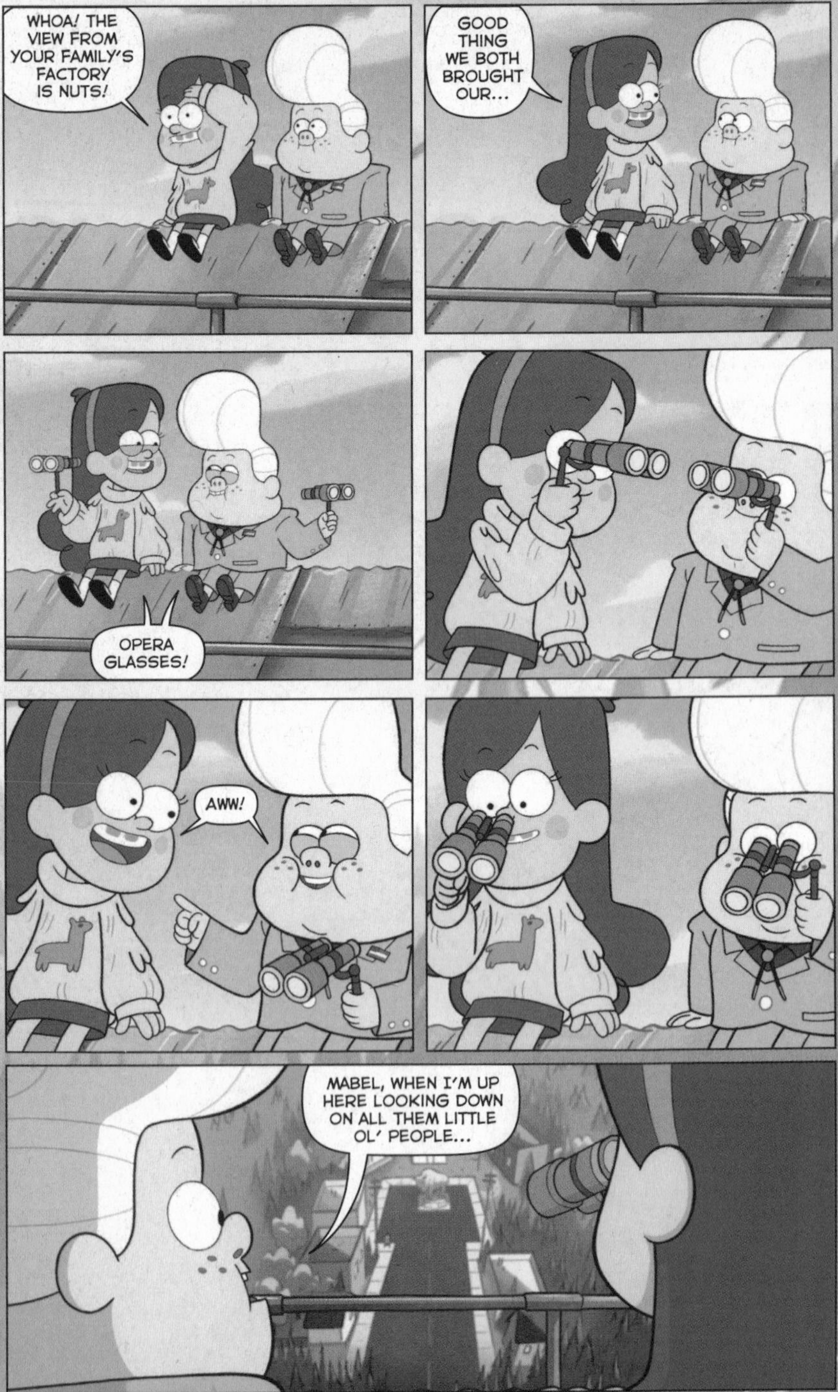

WHOA! THE VIEW FROM YOUR FAMILY'S FACTORY IS NUTS!
GOOD THING WE BOTH BROUGHT OUR...
OPERA GLASSES!
AWW!
MABEL, WHEN I'M UP HERE LOOKING DOWN ON ALL THEM LITTLE OL' PEOPLE...

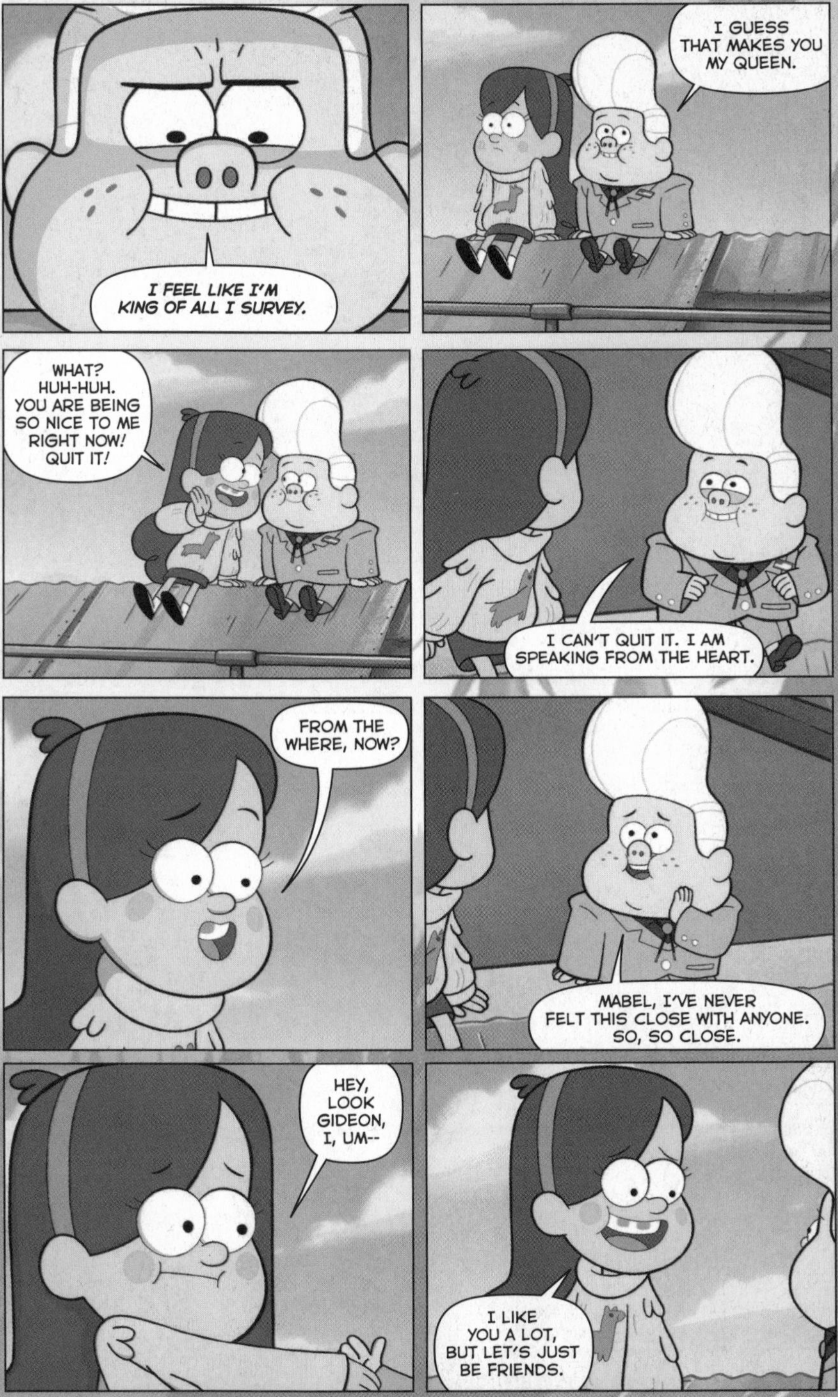
I FEEL LIKE I'M KING OF ALL I SURVEY.
I GUESS THAT MAKES YOU MY QUEEN.
WHAT? HUH-HUH. YOU ARE BEING SO NICE TO ME RIGHT NOW! QUIT IT!
I CAN'T QUIT IT. I AM SPEAKING FROM THE HEART.
FROM THE WHERE, NOW?
MABEL, I'VE NEVER FELT THIS CLOSE WITH ANYONE. SO, SO CLOSE.
HEY, LOOK GIDEON, I, UM--
I LIKE YOU A LOT, BUT LET'S JUST BE FRIENDS.

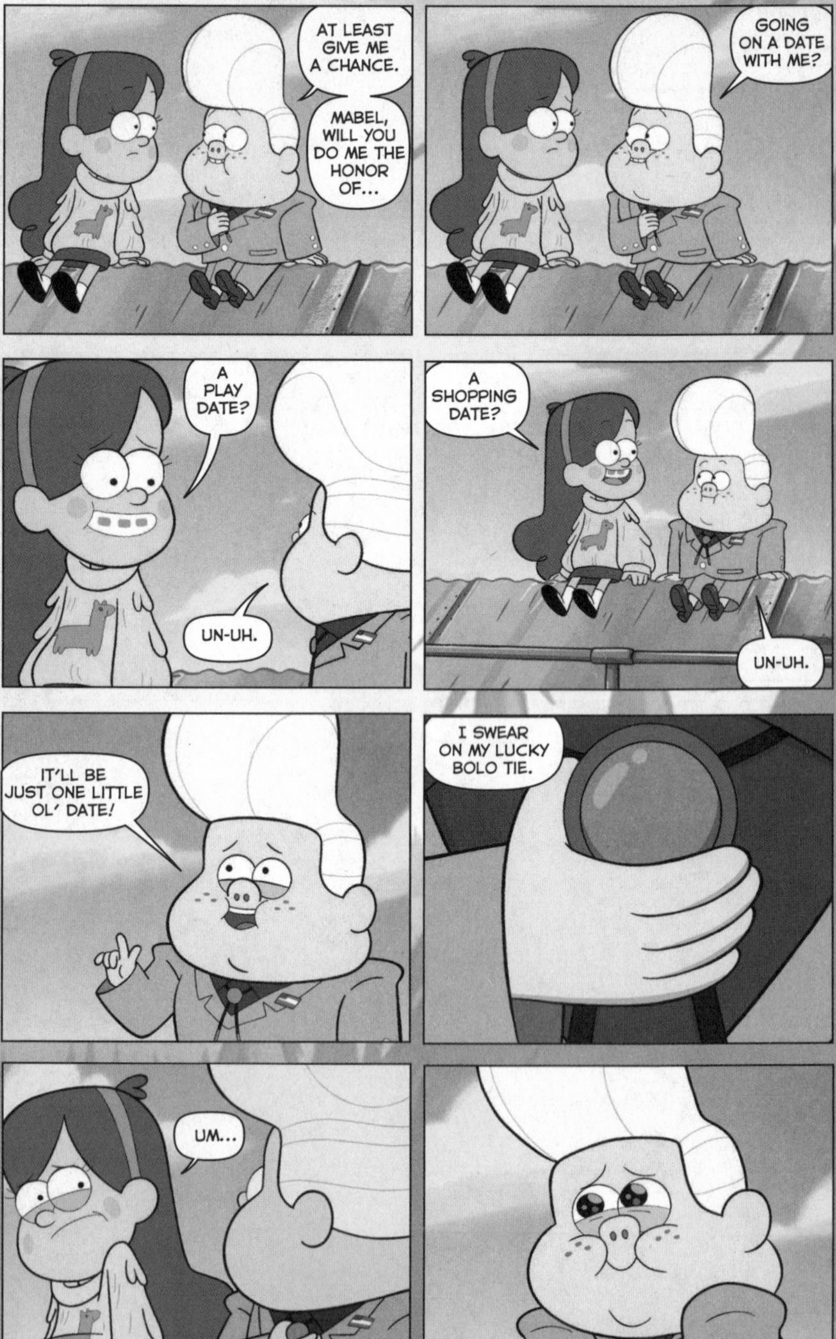

AT LEAST GIVE ME A CHANCE.
MABEL, WILL YOU DO ME THE HONOR OF...
GOING ON A DATE WITH ME?
A PLAY DATE?
UN-UH.
A SHOPPING DATE?
UN-UH.
IT'LL BE JUST ONE LITTLE OL' DATE!
I SWEAR ON MY LUCKY BOLO TIE.
UM...

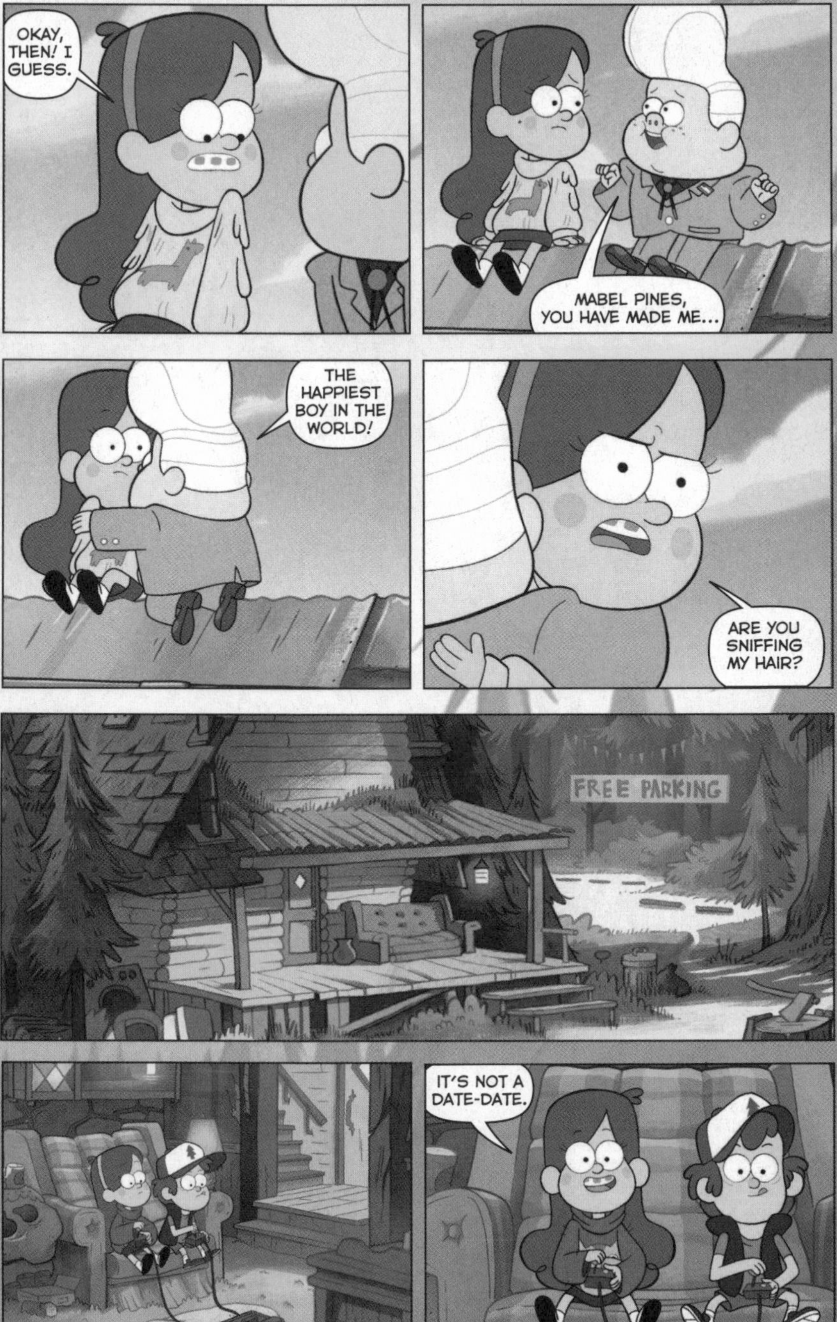
OKAY, THEN! I GUESS.
MABEL PINES, YOU HAVE MADE ME...
THE HAPPIEST BOY IN THE WORLD!
ARE YOU SNIFFING MY HAIR?
FREE PARKING
IT'S NOT A DATE-DATE.

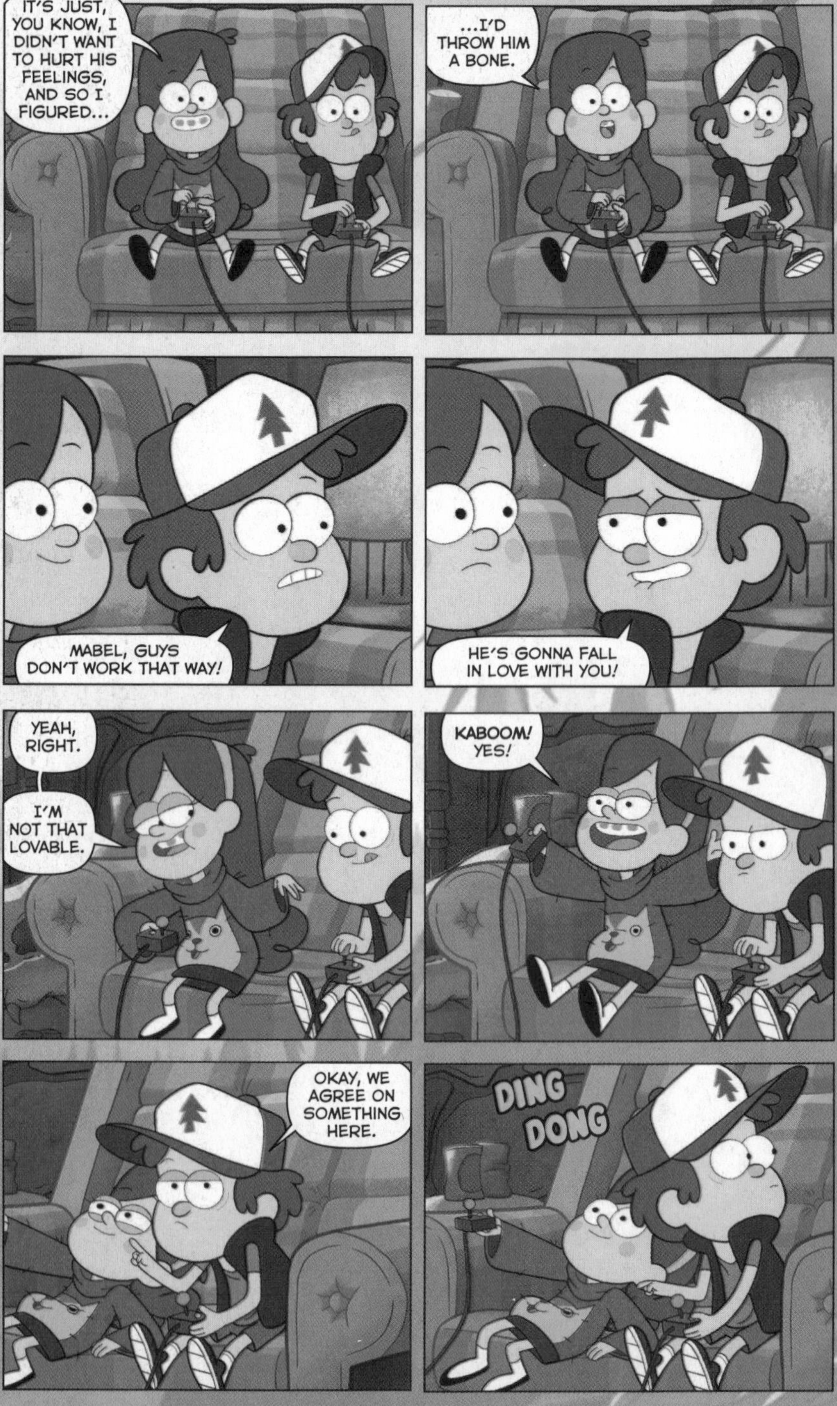
IT'S JUST, YOU KNOW, I DIDN'T WANT TO HURT HIS FEELINGS, AND SO I FIGURED...
...I'D THROW HIM A BONE.
MABEL, GUYS DON'T WORK THAT WAY!
HE'S GONNA FALL IN LOVE WITH YOU!
YEAH, RIGHT.
I'M NOT THAT LOVABLE.
KABOOM! YES!
OKAY, WE AGREE ON SOMETHING HERE.
DING DONG

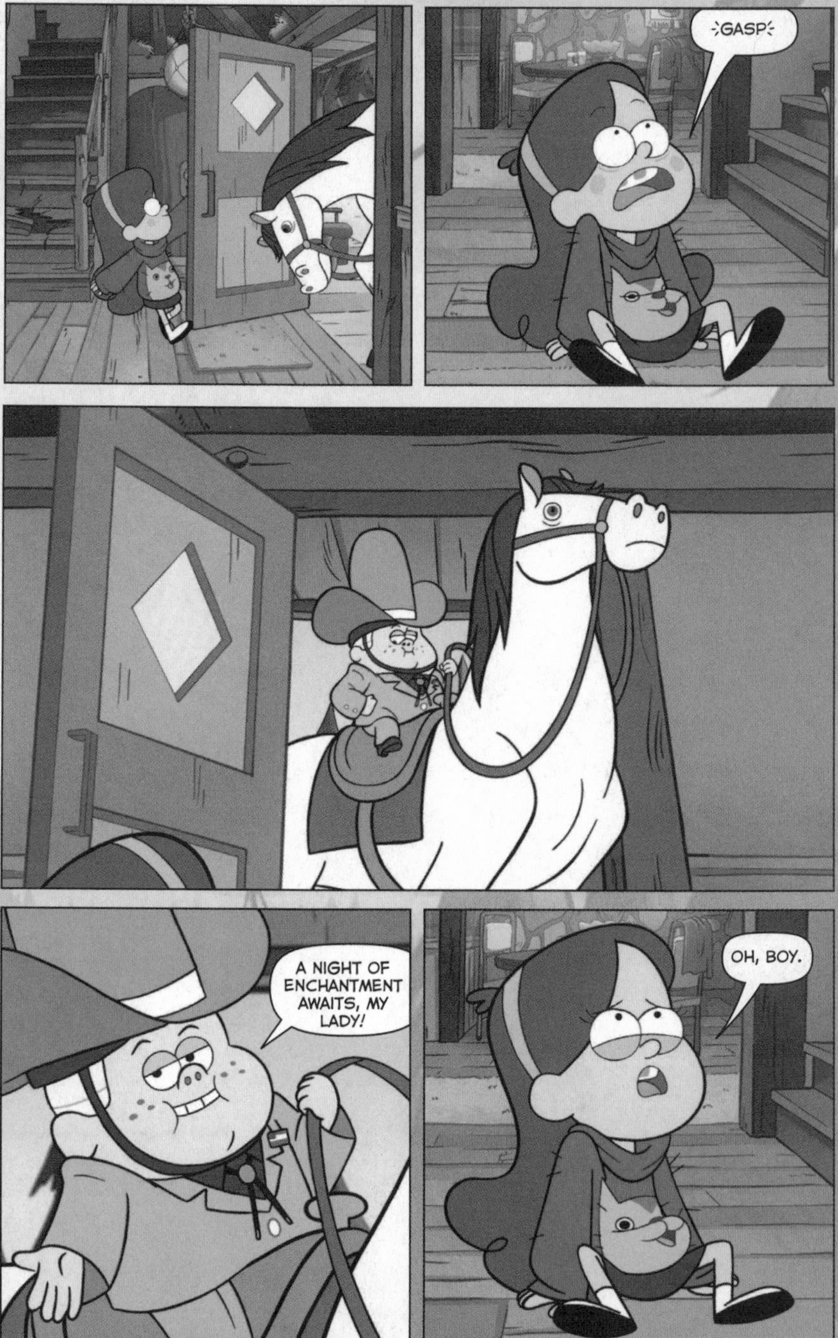

GASP
A NIGHT OF ENCHANTMENT AWAITS, MY LADY!
OH, BOY.

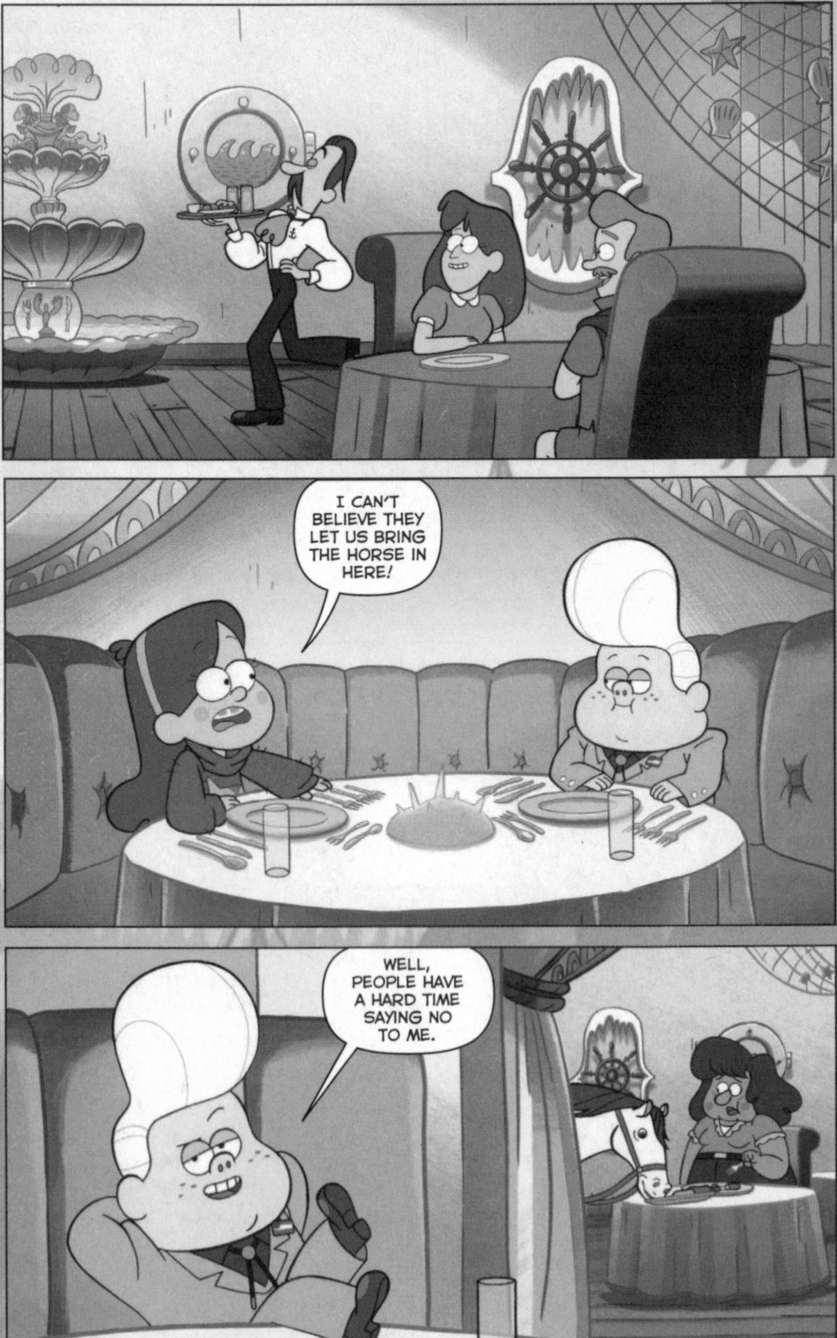
I CAN'T BELIEVE THEY LET US BRING THE HORSE IN HERE!
WELL, PEOPLE HAVE A HARD TIME SAYING NO TO ME.

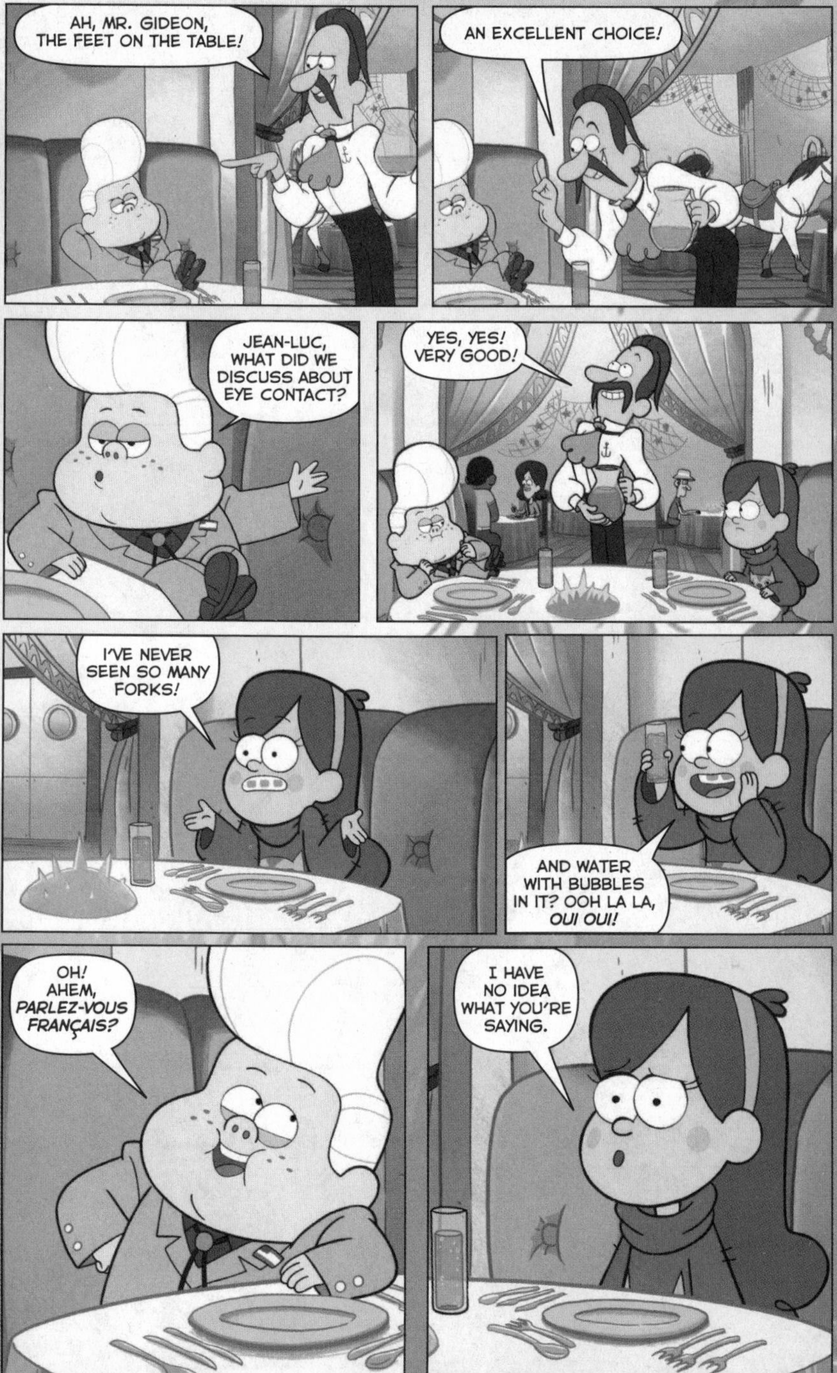
AH, MR. GIDEON, THE FEET ON THE TABLE!
AN EXCELLENT CHOICE!
JEAN-LUC, WHAT DID WE DISCUSS ABOUT EYE CONTACT?
YES, YES! VERY GOOD!
I'VE NEVER SEEN SO MANY FORKS!
AND WATER WITH BUBBLES IN IT? OOH LA LA, *OUI OUI!*
OH! AHEM, *PARLEZ-VOUS FRANÇAIS?*
I HAVE NO IDEA WHAT YOU'RE SAYING.

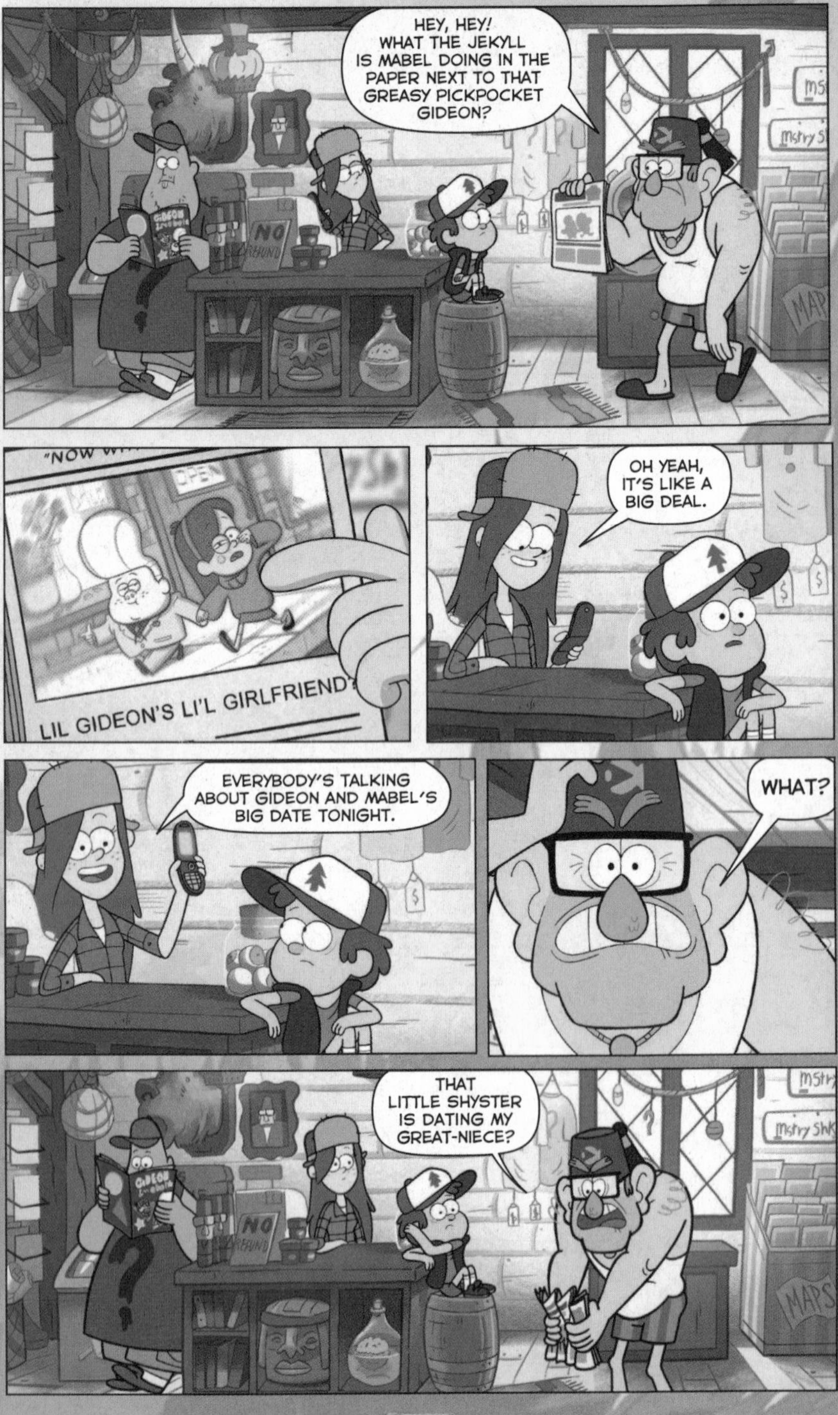
HEY, HEY! WHAT THE JEKYLL IS MABEL DOING IN THE PAPER NEXT TO THAT GREASY PICKPOCKET GIDEON?
NO REFUND
MAPS
"NOW WH
OPEN
LIL GIDEON'S LI'L GIRLFRIEND?
OH YEAH, IT'S LIKE A BIG DEAL.
EVERYBODY'S TALKING ABOUT GIDEON AND MABEL'S BIG DATE TONIGHT.
WHAT?
THAT LITTLE SHYSTER IS DATING MY GREAT-NIECE?
NO REFUND
MAPS

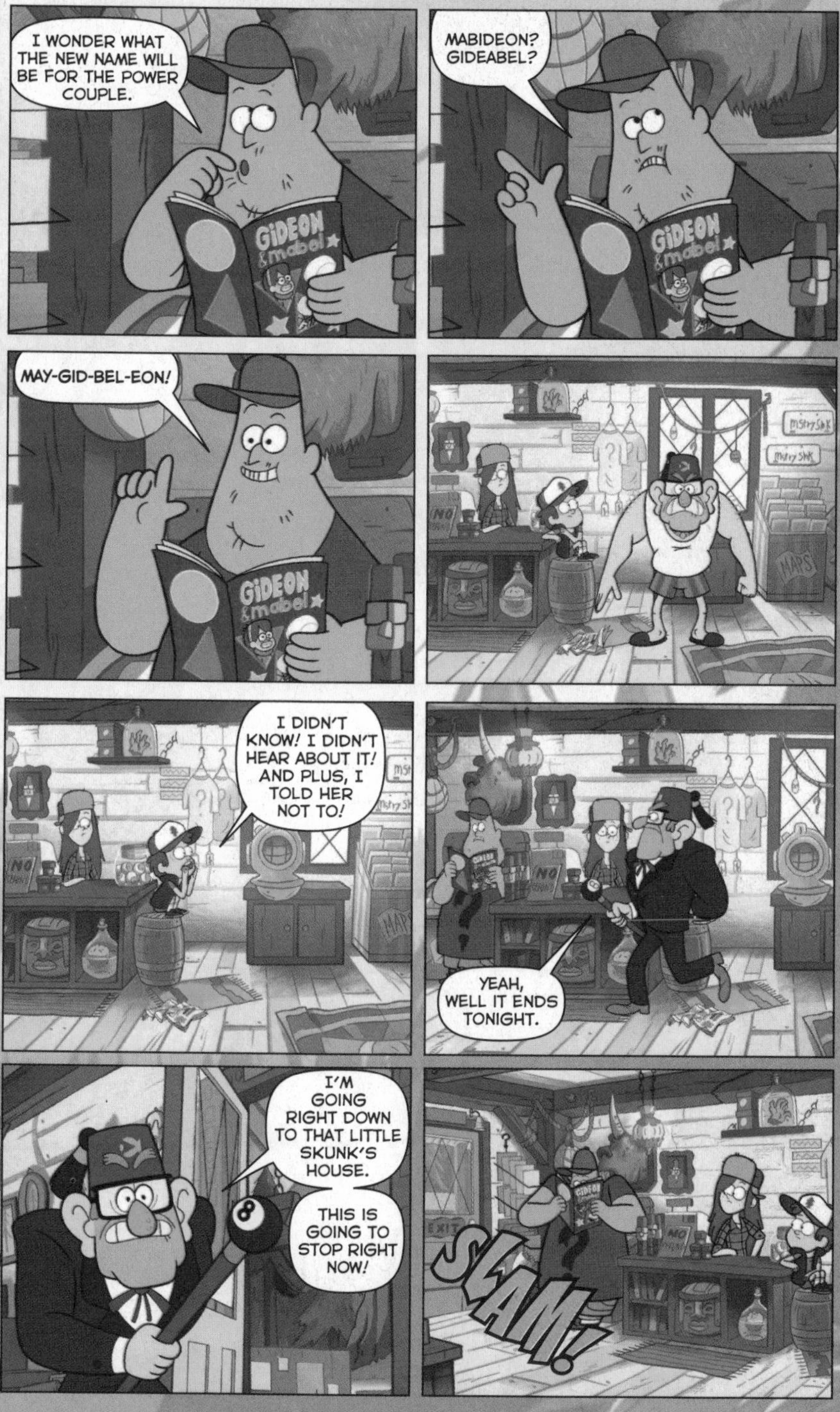
I WONDER WHAT THE NEW NAME WILL BE FOR THE POWER COUPLE.
GIDEON & mabel
MABIDEON? GIDEABEL?
GIDEON & mabel
MAY-GID-BEL-EON!
GIDEON & mabel
NO
MAPS
I DIDN'T KNOW! I DIDN'T HEAR ABOUT IT! AND PLUS, I TOLD HER NOT TO!
YEAH, WELL IT ENDS TONIGHT.
I'M GOING RIGHT DOWN TO THAT LITTLE SKUNK'S HOUSE.
THIS IS GOING TO STOP RIGHT NOW!
EXIT
SLAM!

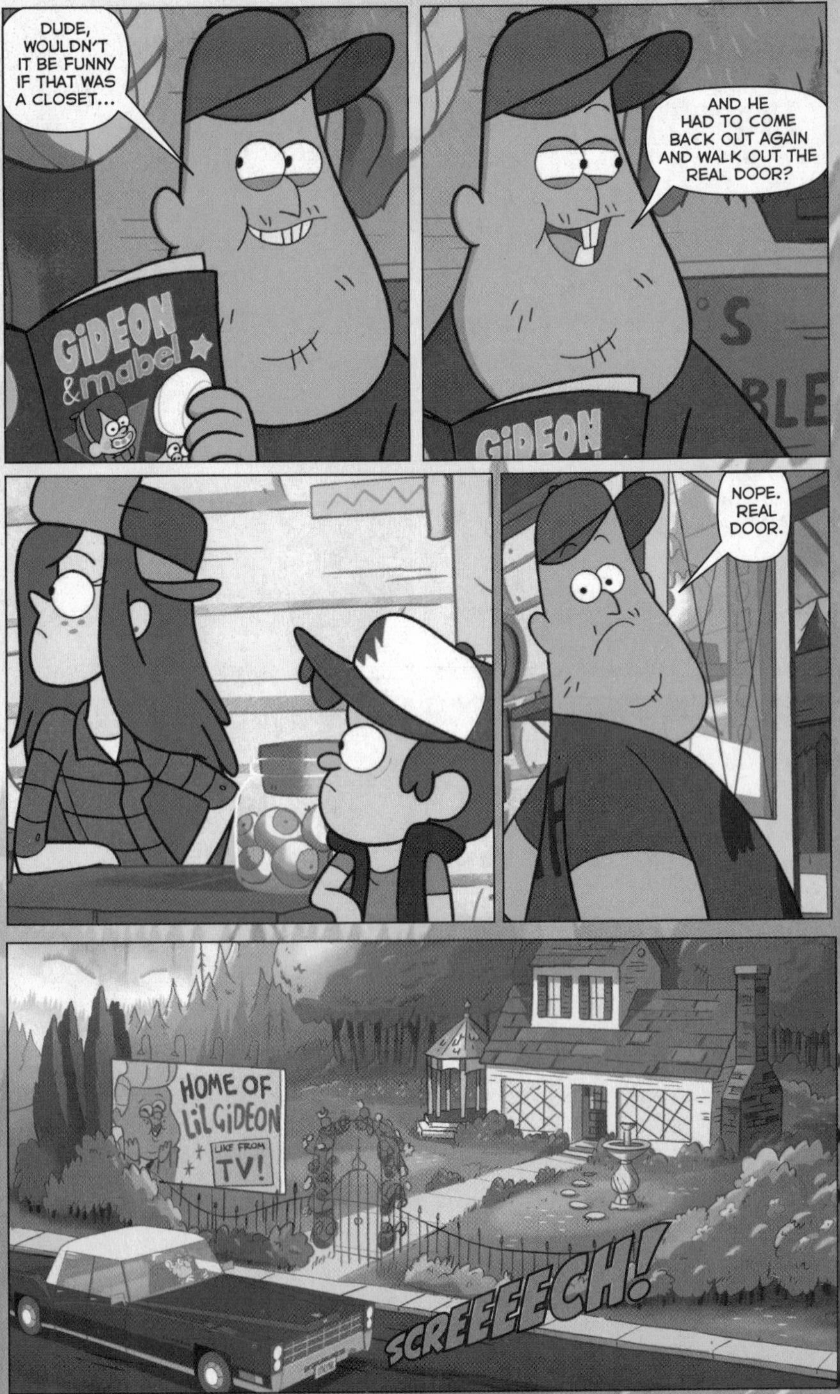
DUDE, WOULDN'T IT BE FUNNY IF THAT WAS A CLOSET...
GiDEON &mabel
AND HE HAD TO COME BACK OUT AGAIN AND WALK OUT THE REAL DOOR?
GiDEON
NOPE. REAL DOOR.
HOME OF LiL GiDEON
LIKE FROM TV!
SCREEEEECH!

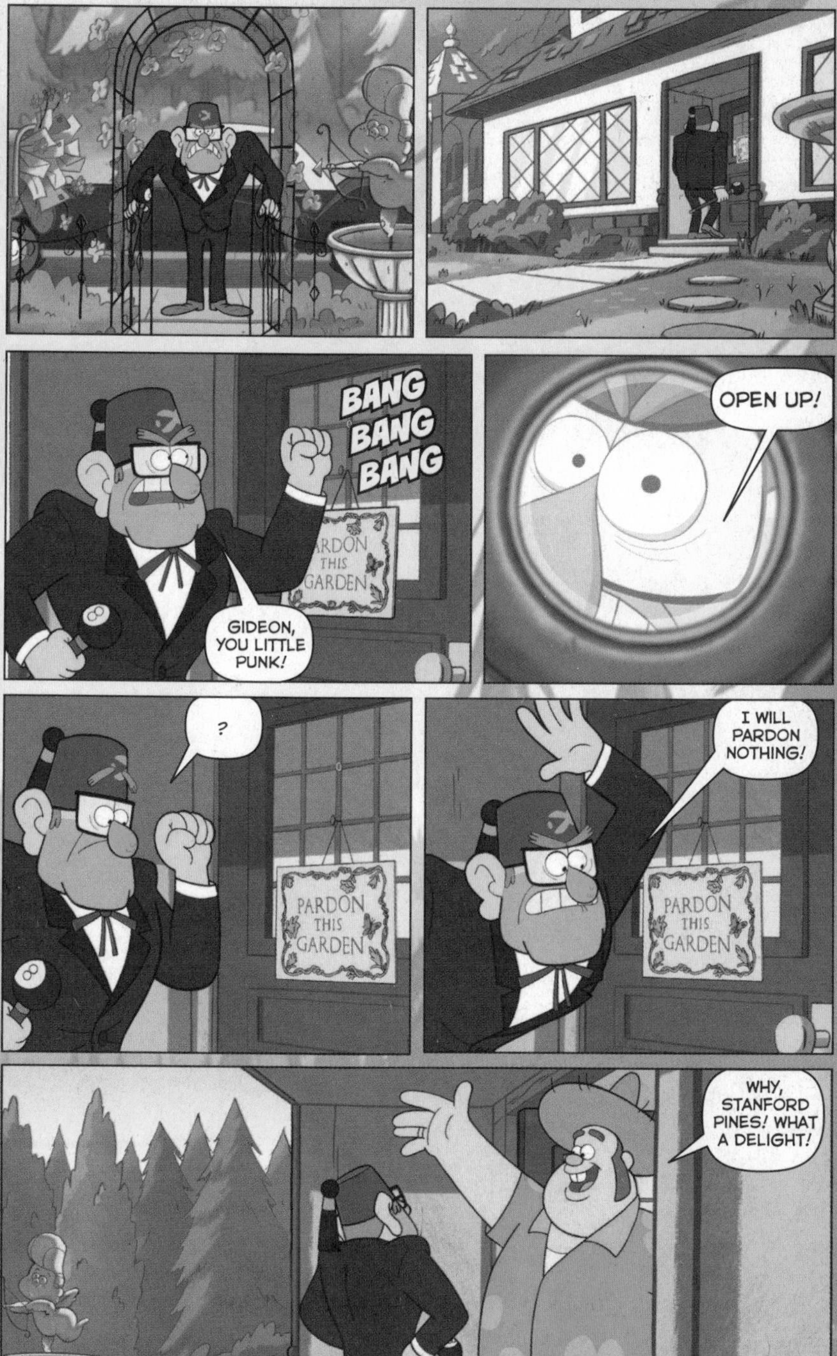
BANG
BANG
BANG
PARDON THIS GARDEN
GIDEON, YOU LITTLE PUNK!
OPEN UP!
?
PARDON THIS GARDEN
I WILL PARDON NOTHING!
PARDON THIS GARDEN
WHY, STANFORD PINES! WHAT A DELIGHT!

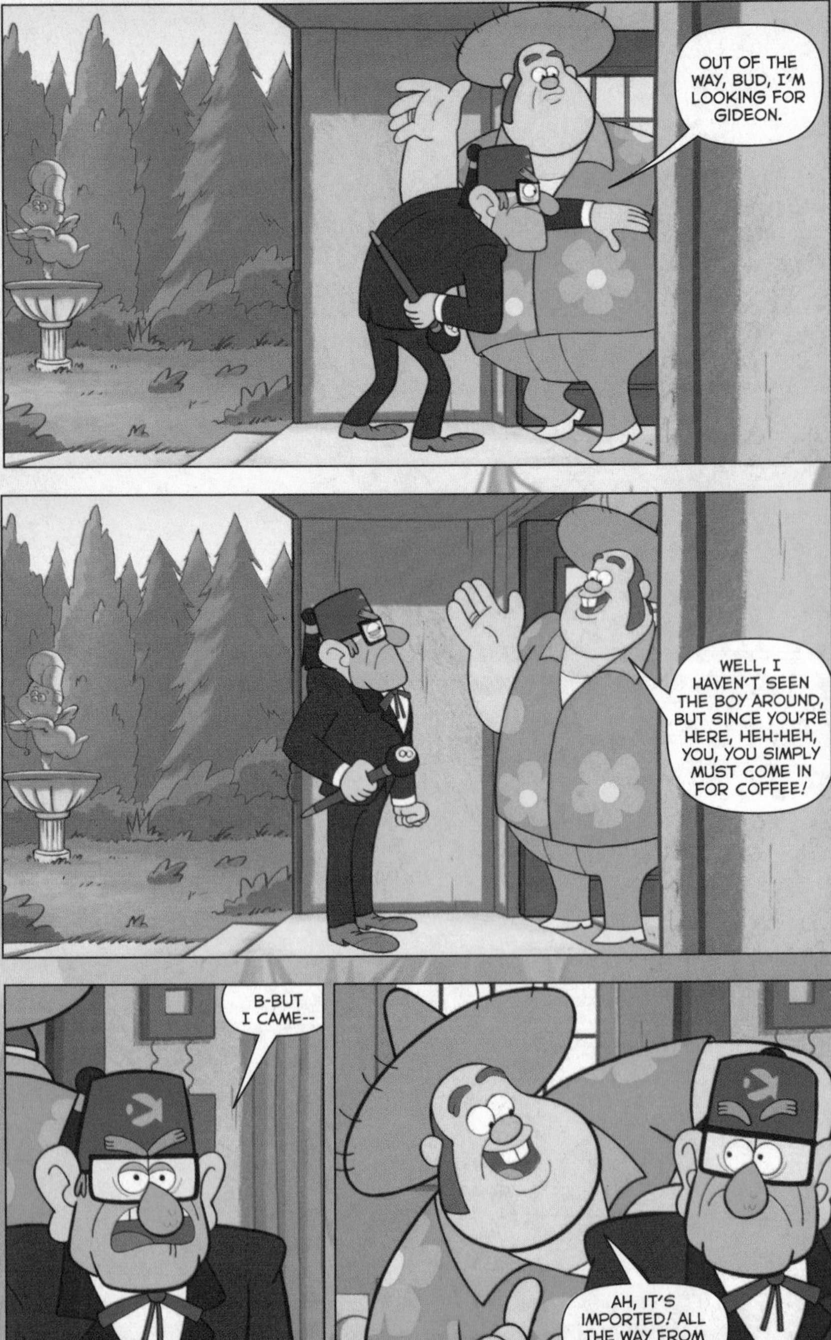
OUT OF THE WAY, BUD, I'M LOOKING FOR GIDEON.
WELL, I HAVEN'T SEEN THE BOY AROUND, BUT SINCE YOU'RE HERE, HEH-HEH, YOU, YOU SIMPLY MUST COME IN FOR COFFEE!
B-BUT I CAME--
AH, IT'S IMPORTED! ALL THE WAY FROM COLOMBIA!

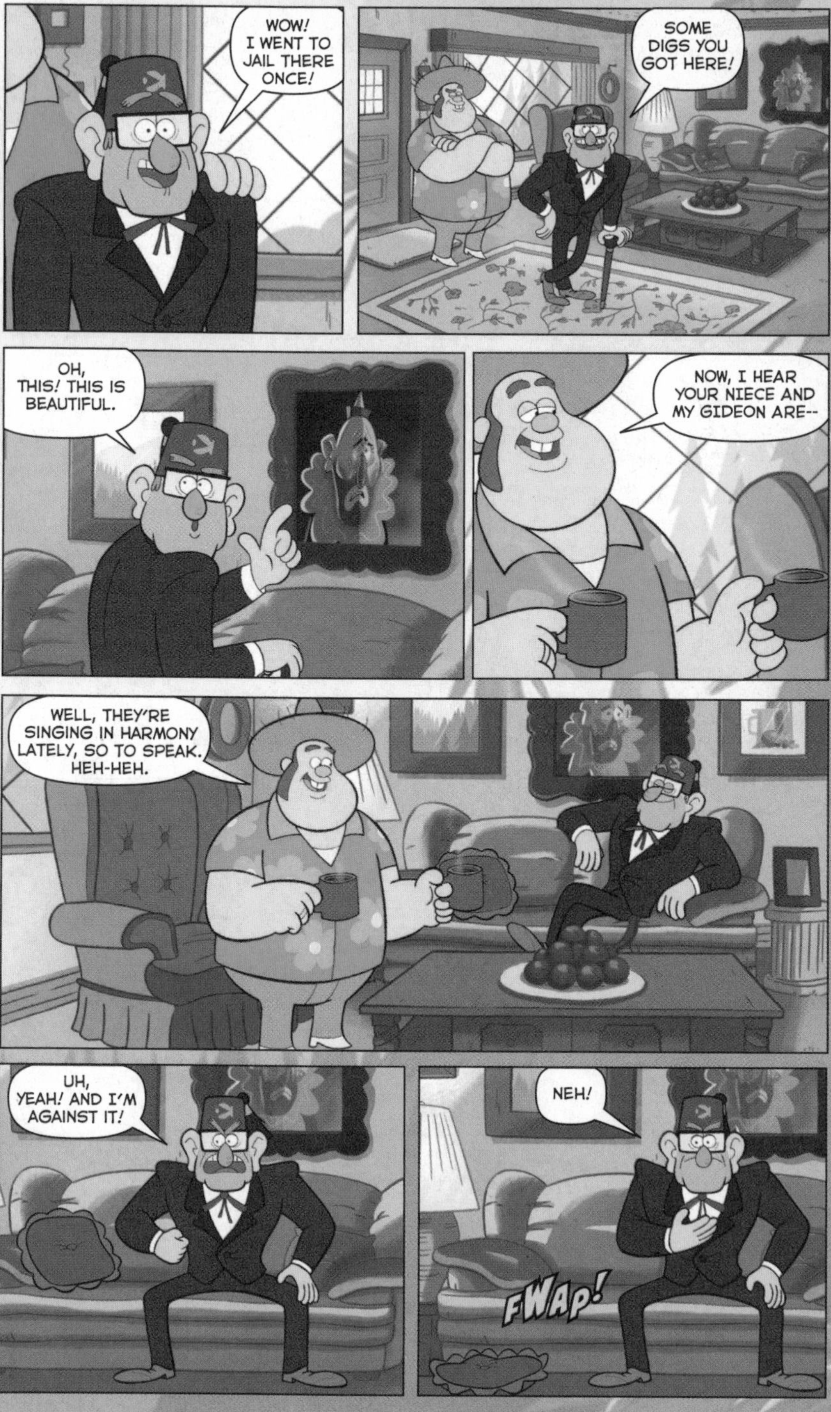
WOW! I WENT TO JAIL THERE ONCE!
SOME DIGS YOU GOT HERE!
OH, THIS! THIS IS BEAUTIFUL.
NOW, I HEAR YOUR NIECE AND MY GIDEON ARE--
WELL, THEY'RE SINGING IN HARMONY LATELY, SO TO SPEAK. HEH-HEH.
UH, YEAH! AND I'M AGAINST IT!
NEH!
FWAP!

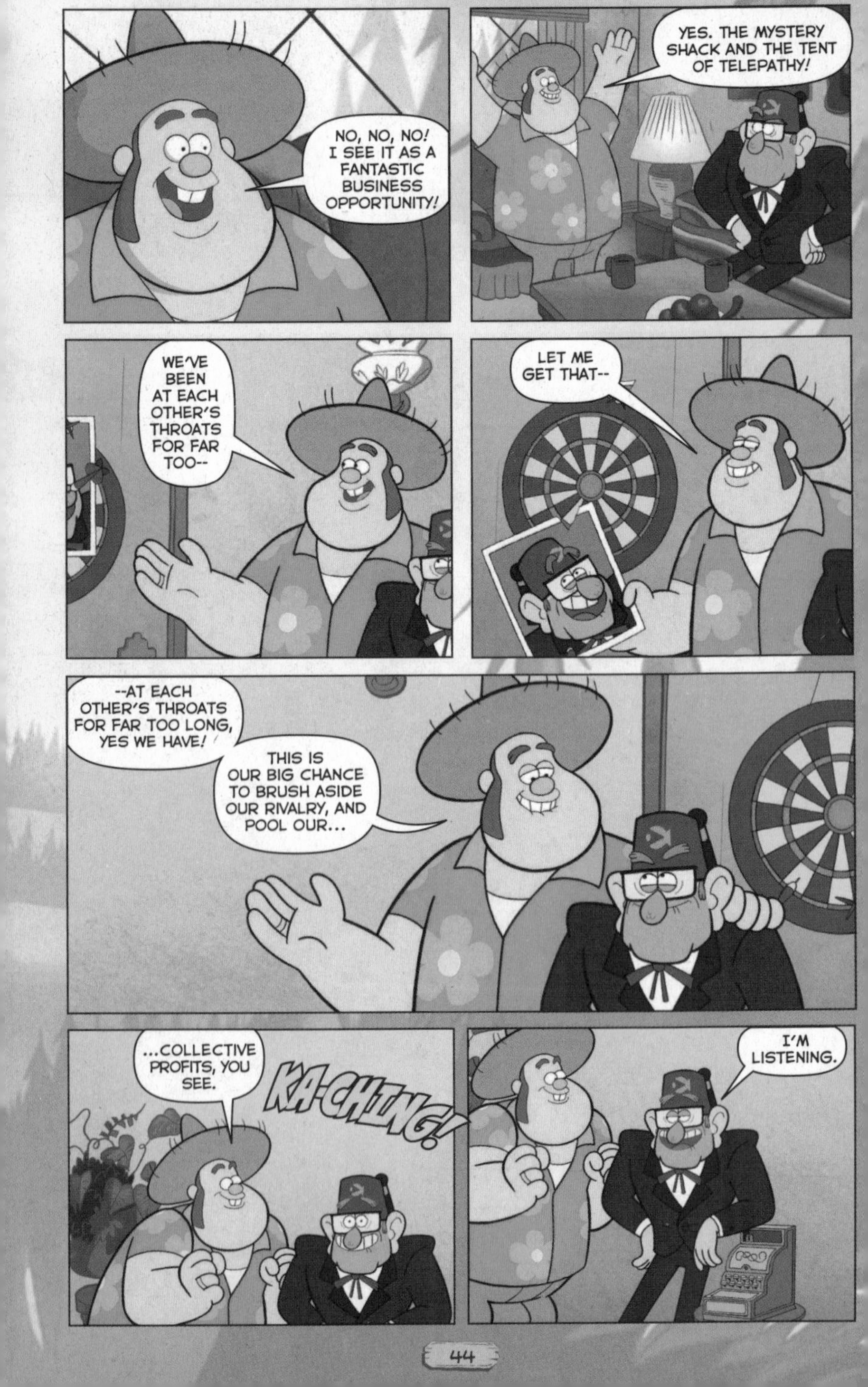
NO, NO, NO! I SEE IT AS A FANTASTIC BUSINESS OPPORTUNITY!
YES. THE MYSTERY SHACK AND THE TENT OF TELEPATHY!
WE'VE BEEN AT EACH OTHER'S THROATS FOR FAR TOO--
LET ME GET THAT--
--AT EACH OTHER'S THROATS FOR FAR TOO LONG, YES WE HAVE!
THIS IS OUR BIG CHANCE TO BRUSH ASIDE OUR RIVALRY, AND POOL OUR...
...COLLECTIVE PROFITS, YOU SEE.
KA-CHING!
I'M LISTENING.

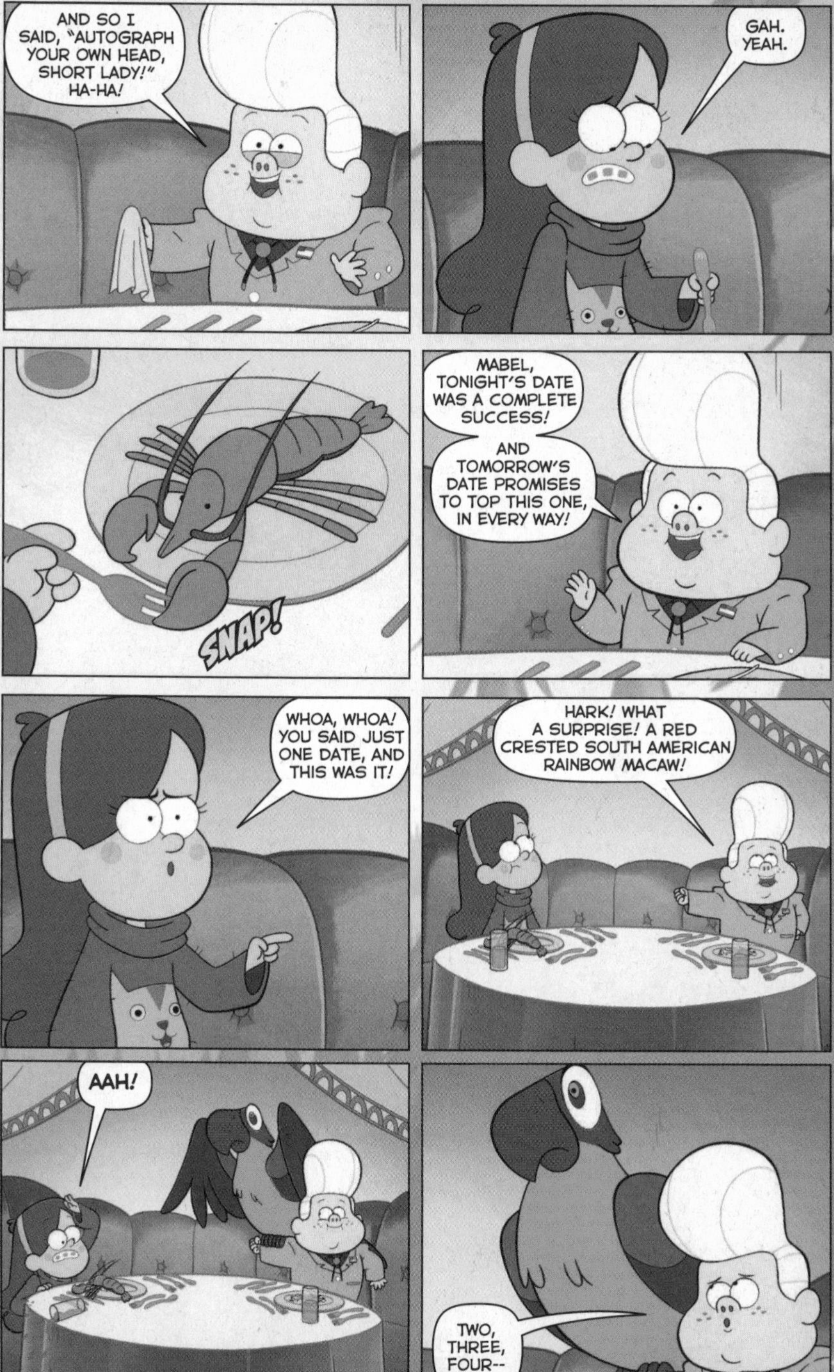
AND SO I SAID, "AUTOGRAPH YOUR OWN HEAD, SHORT LADY!" HA-HA!
GAH. YEAH.
SNAP!
MABEL, TONIGHT'S DATE WAS A COMPLETE SUCCESS!
AND TOMORROW'S DATE PROMISES TO TOP THIS ONE, IN EVERY WAY!
WHOA, WHOA! YOU SAID JUST ONE DATE, AND THIS WAS IT!
HARK! WHAT A SURPRISE! A RED CRESTED SOUTH AMERICAN RAINBOW MACAW!
AAH!
TWO, THREE, FOUR--

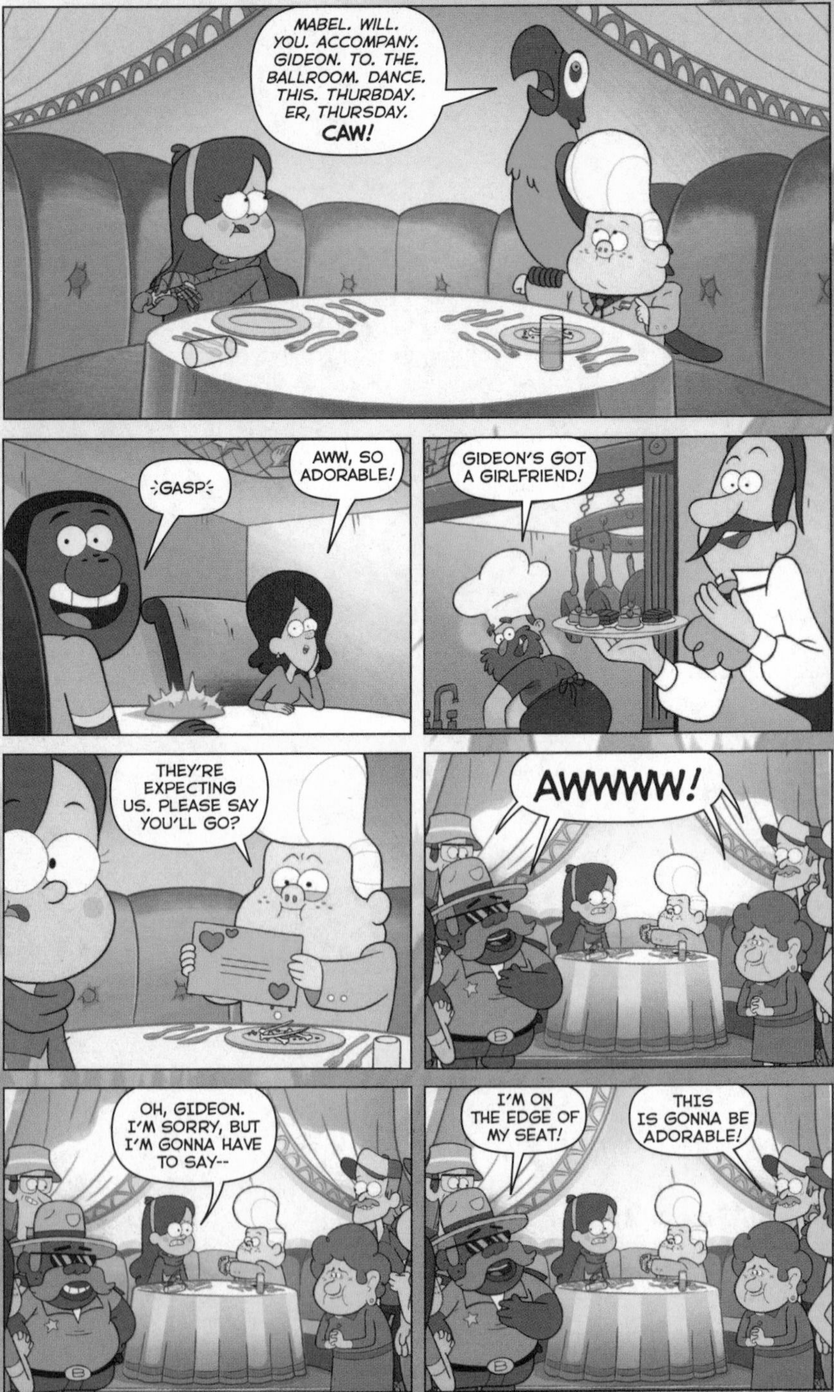
MABEL. WILL. YOU. ACCOMPANY. GIDEON. TO. THE. BALLROOM. DANCE. THIS. THURBDAY. ER, THURSDAY. CAW!
GASP
AWW, SO ADORABLE!
GIDEON'S GOT A GIRLFRIEND!
THEY'RE EXPECTING US. PLEASE SAY YOU'LL GO?
AWWWW!
OH, GIDEON. I'M SORRY, BUT I'M GONNA HAVE TO SAY--
I'M ON THE EDGE OF MY SEAT!
THIS IS GONNA BE ADORABLE!

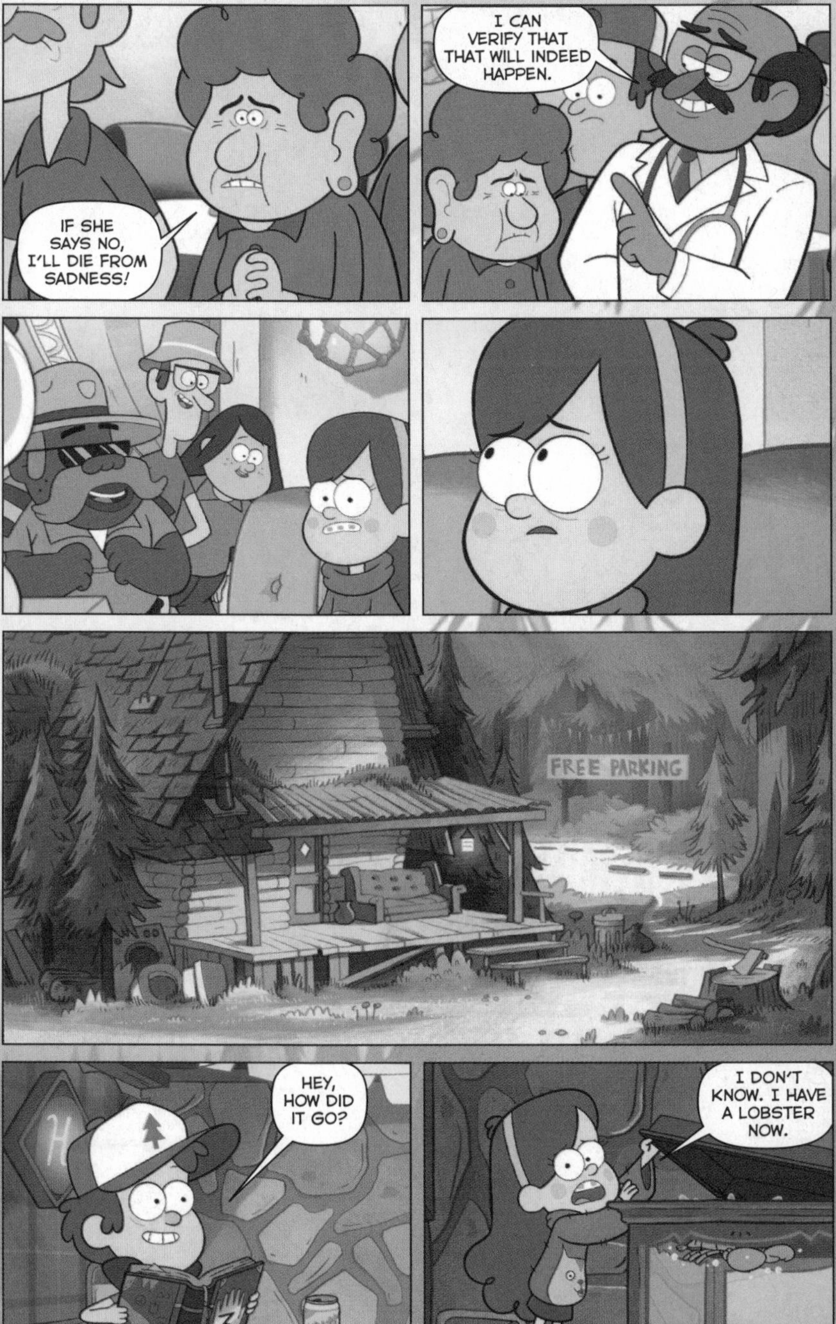
IF SHE SAYS NO, I'LL DIE FROM SADNESS!
I CAN VERIFY THAT THAT WILL INDEED HAPPEN.
FREE PARKING
HEY, HOW DID IT GO?
I DON'T KNOW. I HAVE A LOBSTER NOW.

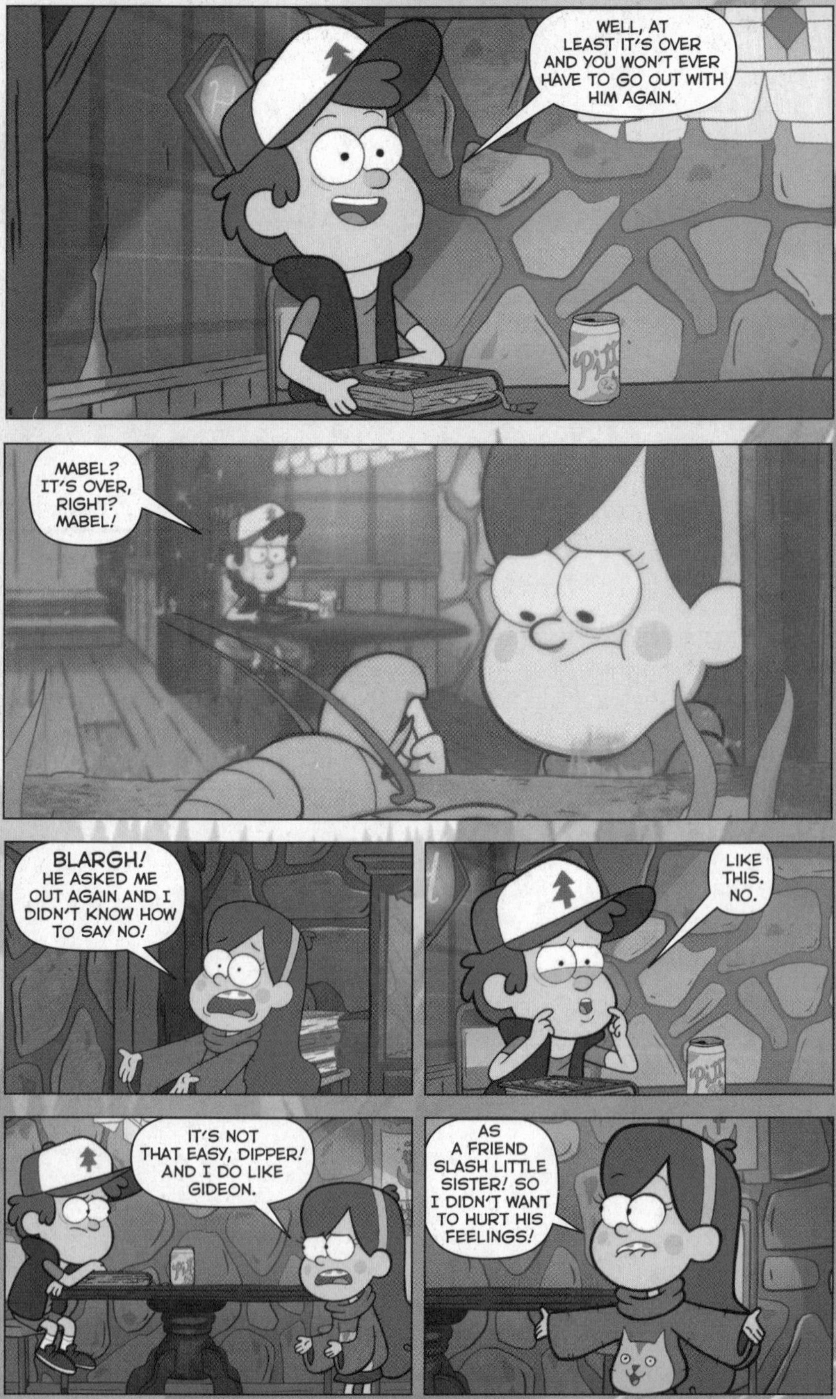
WELL, AT LEAST IT'S OVER AND YOU WON'T EVER HAVE TO GO OUT WITH HIM AGAIN.
MABEL? IT'S OVER, RIGHT? MABEL!
BLARGH! HE ASKED ME OUT AGAIN AND I DIDN'T KNOW HOW TO SAY NO!
LIKE THIS. NO.
IT'S NOT THAT EASY, DIPPER! AND I DO LIKE GIDEON.
AS A FRIEND SLASH LITTLE SISTER! SO I DIDN'T WANT TO HURT HIS FEELINGS!

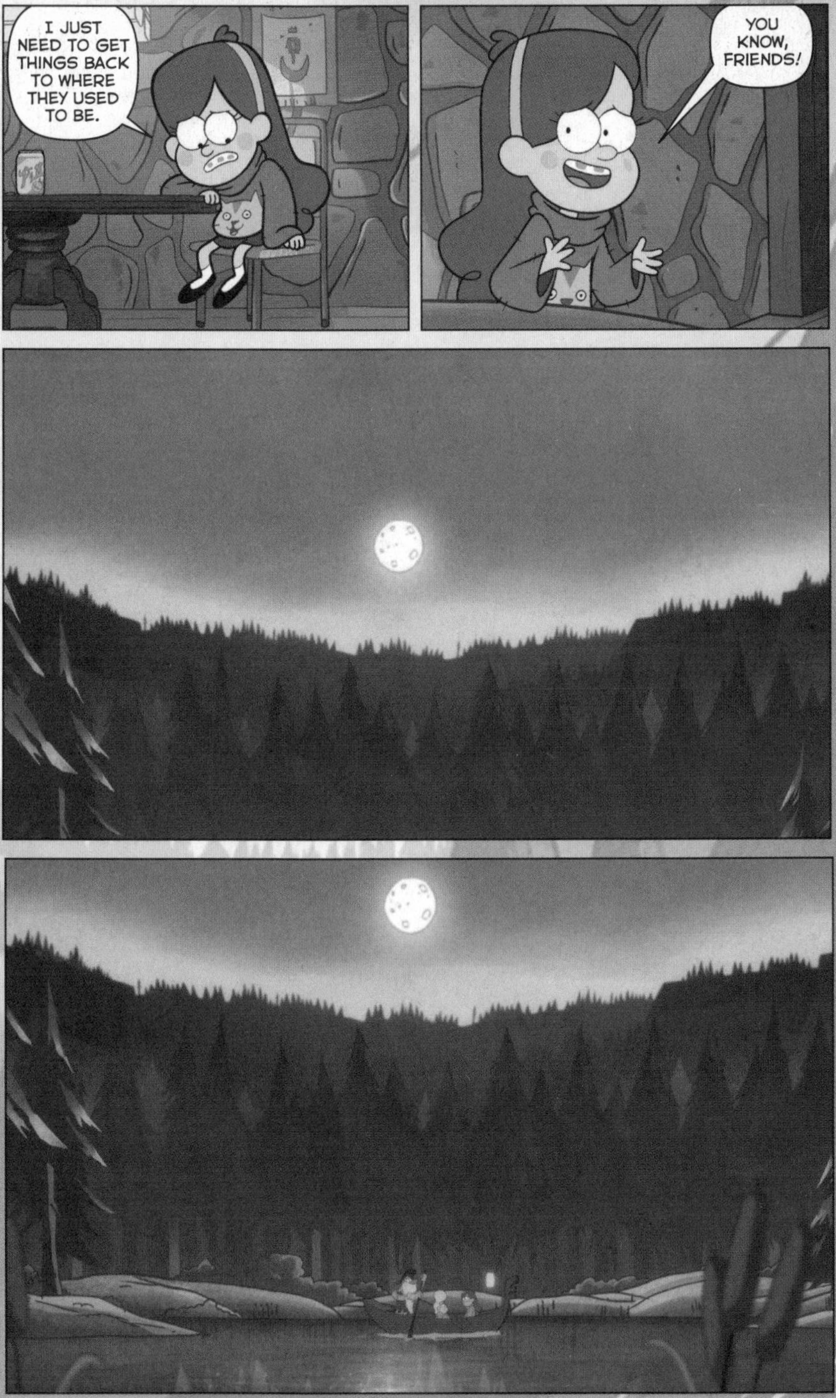
I JUST NEED TO GET THINGS BACK TO WHERE THEY USED TO BE.
YOU KNOW, FRIENDS!

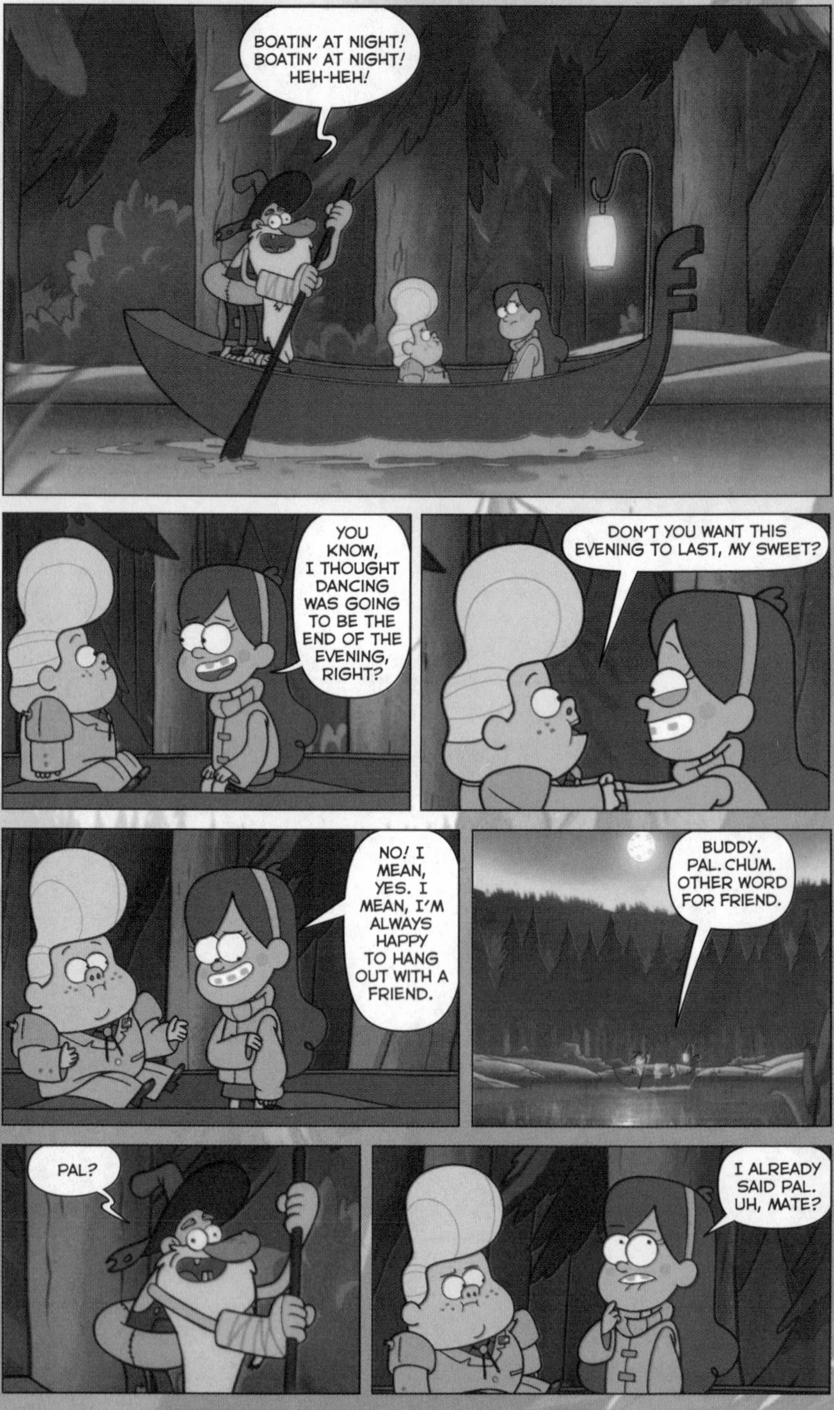
BOATIN' AT NIGHT! BOATIN' AT NIGHT! HEH-HEH!
YOU KNOW, I THOUGHT DANCING WAS GOING TO BE THE END OF THE EVENING, RIGHT?
DON'T YOU WANT THIS EVENING TO LAST, MY SWEET?
NO! I MEAN, YES. I MEAN, I'M ALWAYS HAPPY TO HANG OUT WITH A FRIEND.
BUDDY. PAL. CHUM. OTHER WORD FOR FRIEND.
PAL?
I ALREADY SAID PAL. UH, MATE?

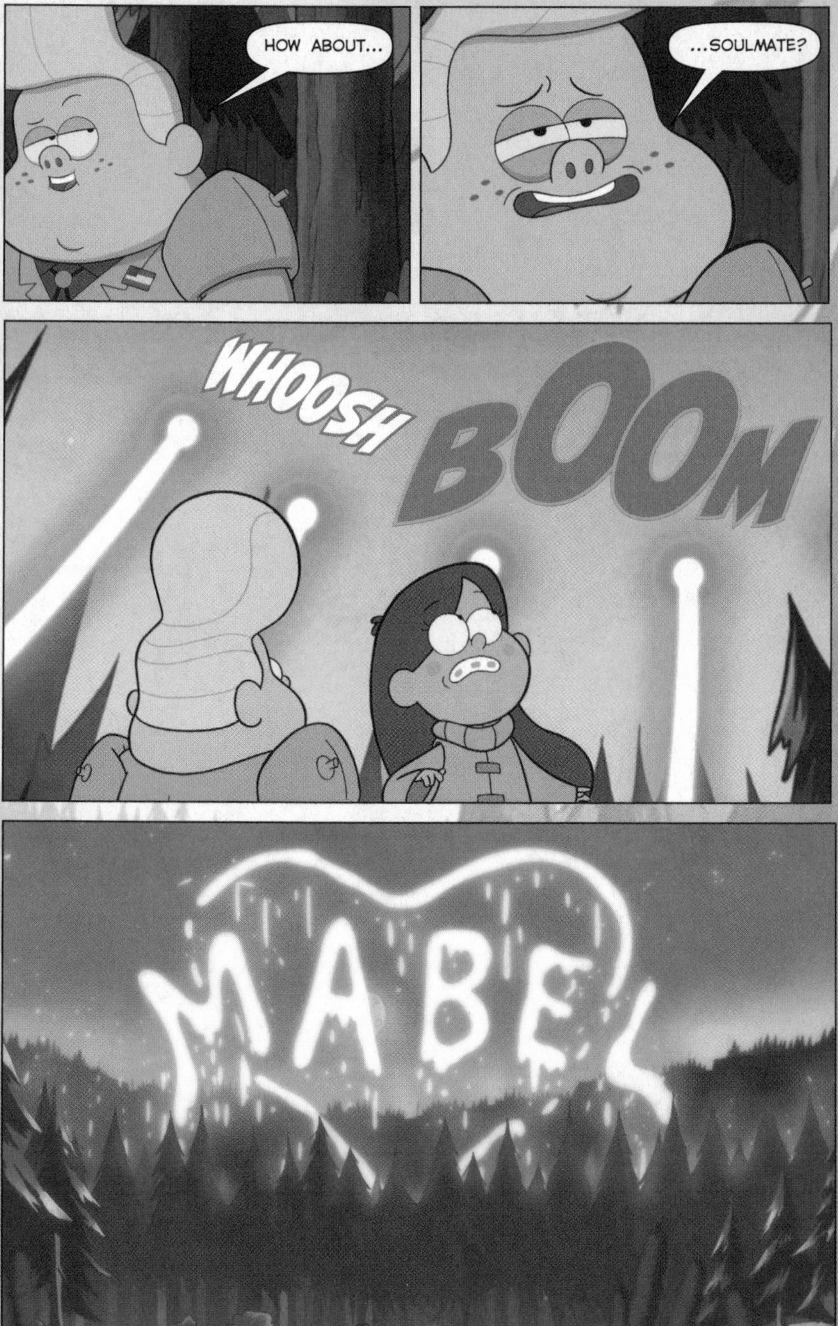
HOW ABOUT...
...SOULMATE?
WHOOSH
BOOM
MABEL

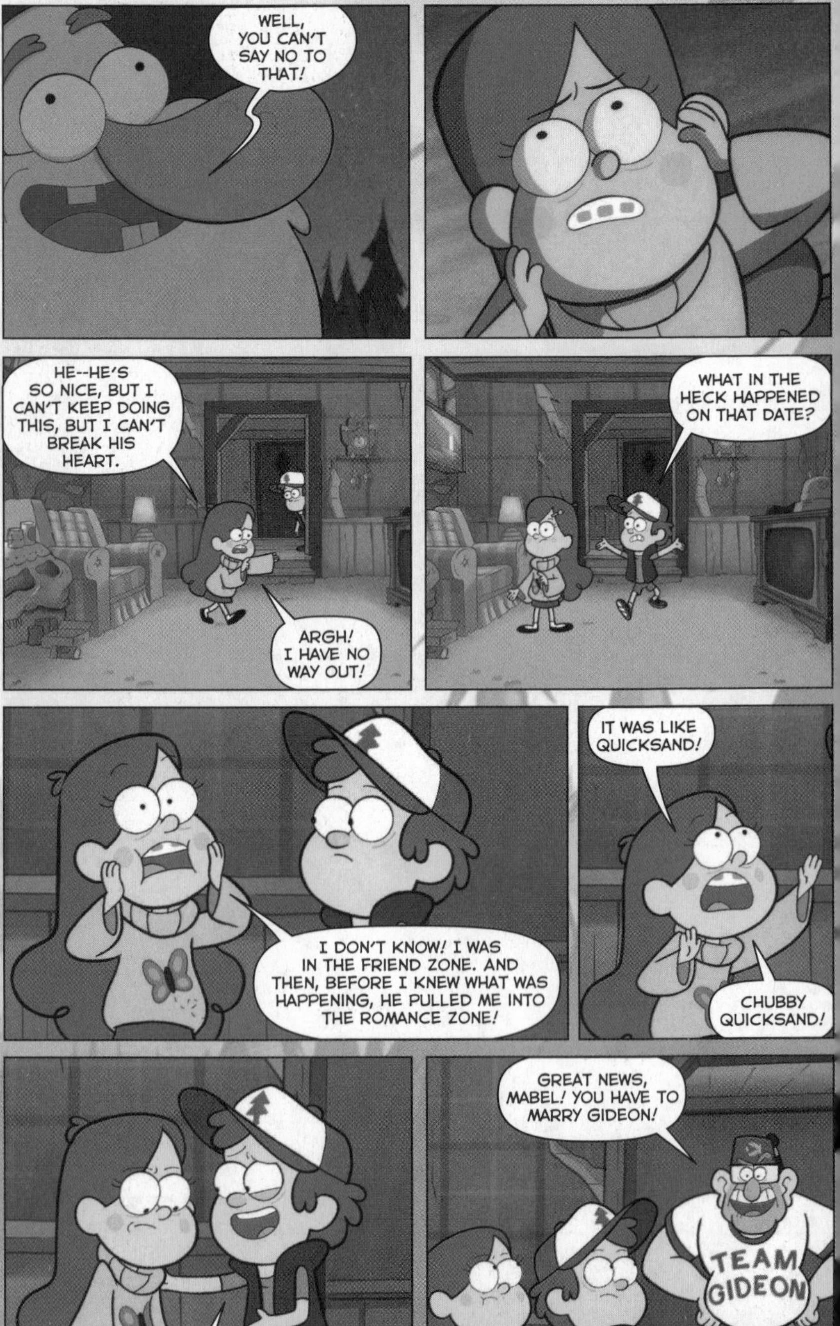
WELL, YOU CAN'T SAY NO TO THAT!
HE--HE'S SO NICE, BUT I CAN'T KEEP DOING THIS, BUT I CAN'T BREAK HIS HEART.
ARGH! I HAVE NO WAY OUT!
WHAT IN THE HECK HAPPENED ON THAT DATE?
I DON'T KNOW! I WAS IN THE FRIEND ZONE. AND THEN, BEFORE I KNEW WHAT WAS HAPPENING, HE PULLED ME INTO THE ROMANCE ZONE!
IT WAS LIKE QUICKSAND!
CHUBBY QUICKSAND!
MABEL, COME ON. IT'S NOT LIKE YOU'RE GOING TO HAVE TO MARRY GIDEON.
GREAT NEWS, MABEL! YOU HAVE TO MARRY GIDEON!
TEAM GIDEON

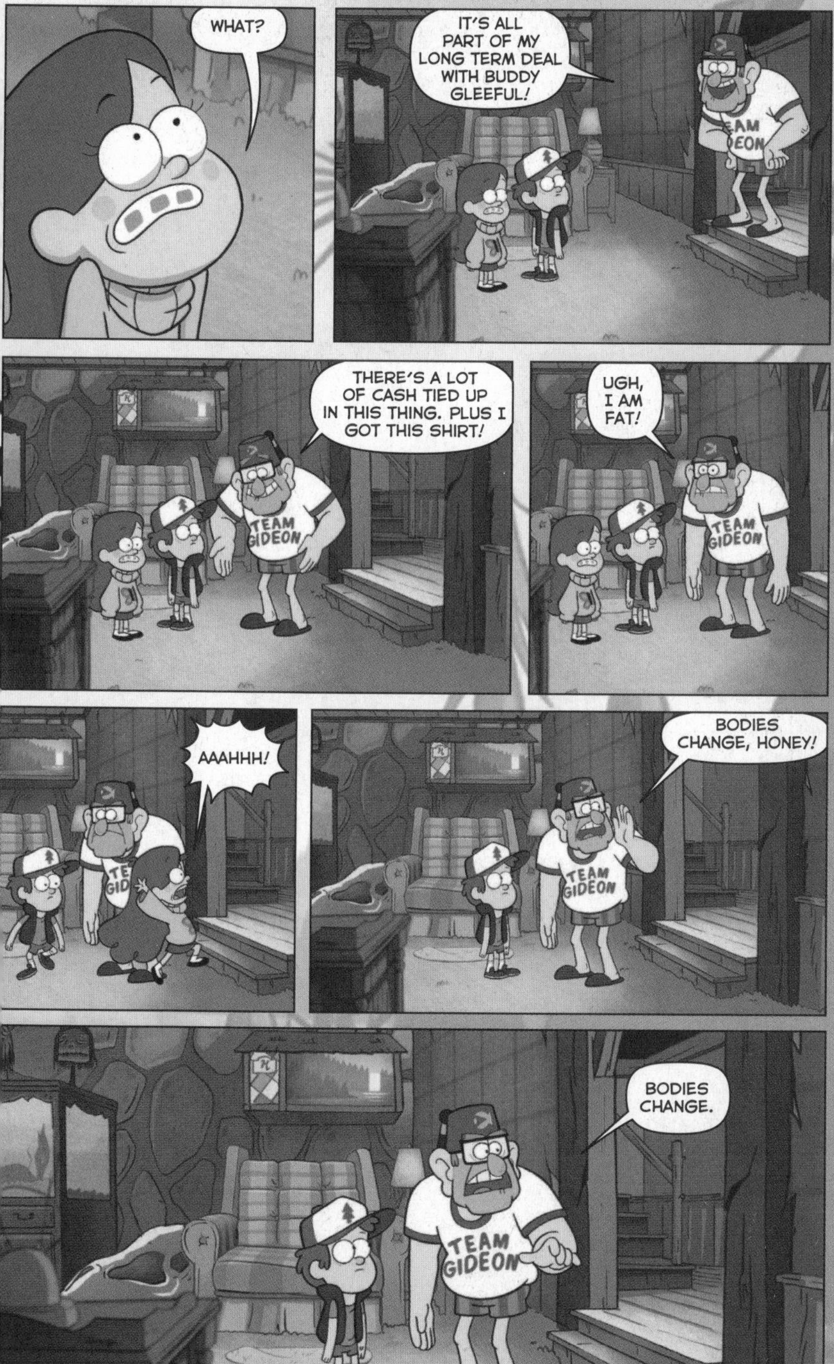
WHAT?
IT'S ALL PART OF MY LONG TERM DEAL WITH BUDDY GLEEFUL!
THERE'S A LOT OF CASH TIED UP IN THIS THING. PLUS I GOT THIS SHIRT!
UGH, I AM FAT!
AAAHHH!
BODIES CHANGE, HONEY!
BODIES CHANGE.

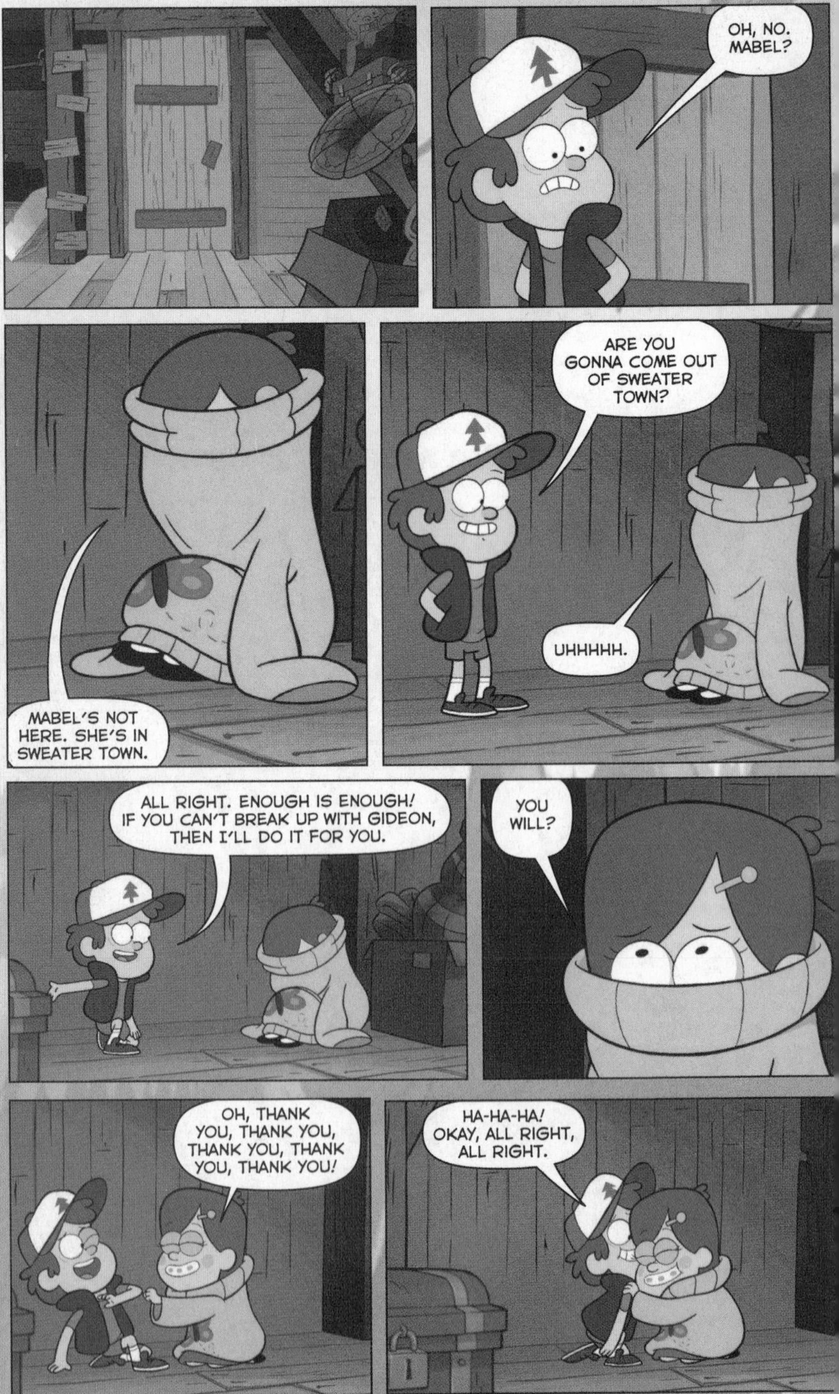
OH, NO. MABEL?
MABEL'S NOT HERE. SHE'S IN SWEATER TOWN.
ARE YOU GONNA COME OUT OF SWEATER TOWN?
UHHHHH.
ALL RIGHT. ENOUGH IS ENOUGH! IF YOU CAN'T BREAK UP WITH GIDEON, THEN I'LL DO IT FOR YOU.
YOU WILL?
OH, THANK YOU, THANK YOU, THANK YOU, THANK YOU, THANK YOU!
HA-HA-HA! OKAY, ALL RIGHT, ALL RIGHT.

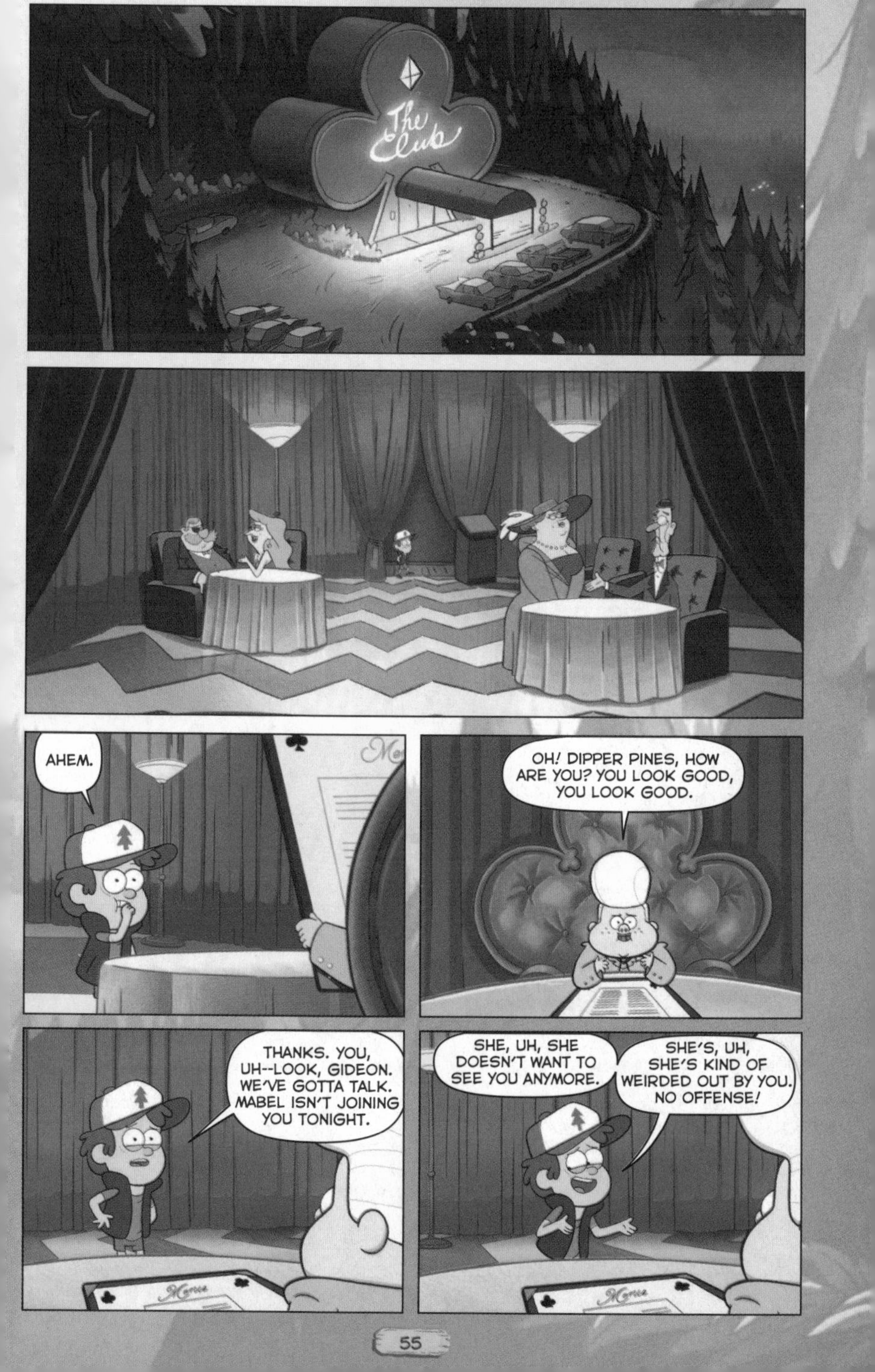
The Club
AHEM.
OH! DIPPER PINES, HOW ARE YOU? YOU LOOK GOOD, YOU LOOK GOOD.
THANKS. YOU, UH--LOOK, GIDEON. WE'VE GOTTA TALK. MABEL ISN'T JOINING YOU TONIGHT.
SHE, UH, SHE DOESN'T WANT TO SEE YOU ANYMORE.
SHE'S, UH, SHE'S KIND OF WEIRDED OUT BY YOU. NO OFFENSE!

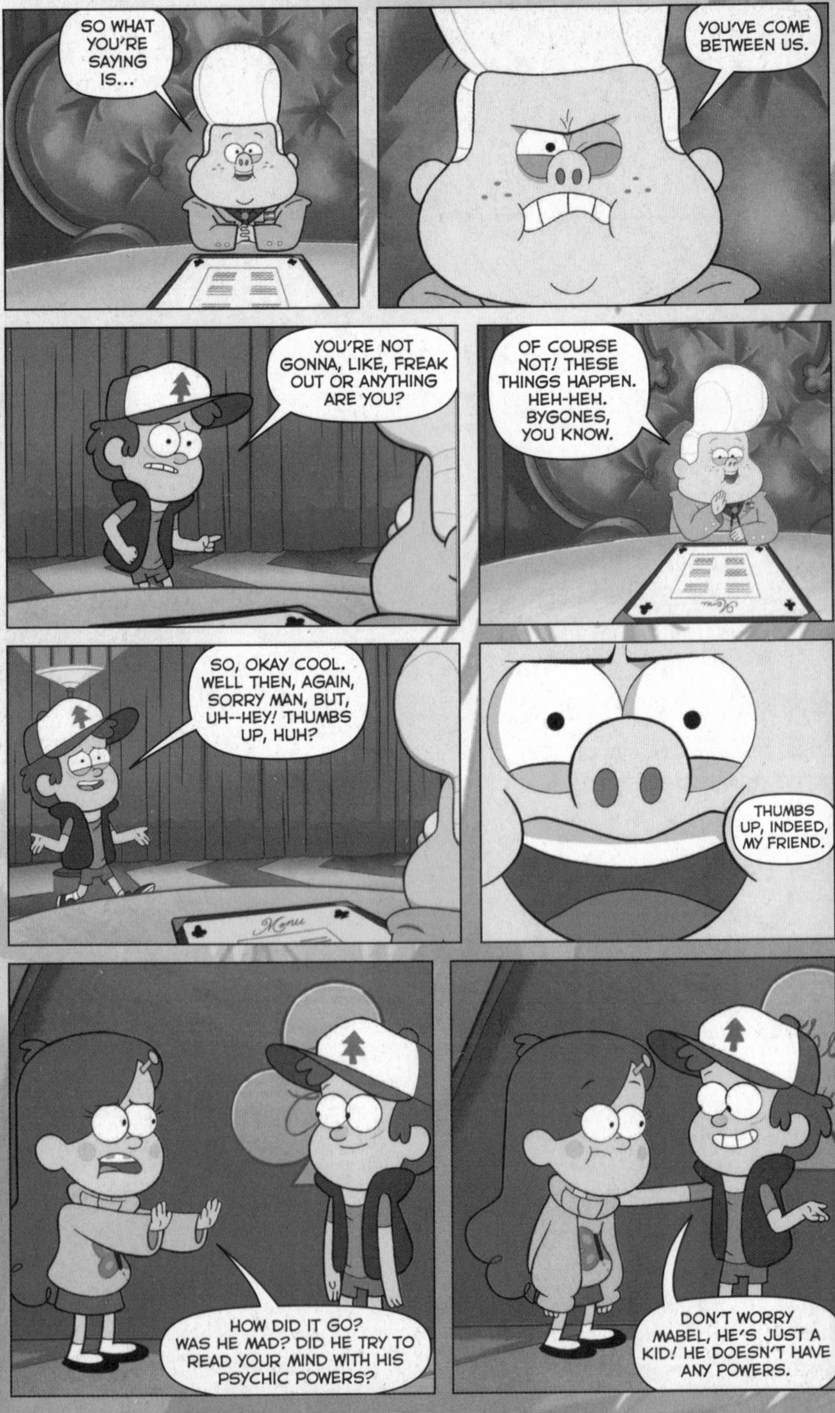
SO WHAT YOU'RE SAYING IS...
YOU'VE COME BETWEEN US.
YOU'RE NOT GONNA, LIKE, FREAK OUT OR ANYTHING ARE YOU?
OF COURSE NOT! THESE THINGS HAPPEN. HEH-HEH. BYGONES, YOU KNOW.
SO, OKAY COOL. WELL THEN, AGAIN, SORRY MAN, BUT, UH--HEY! THUMBS UP, HUH?
THUMBS UP, INDEED, MY FRIEND.
HOW DID IT GO? WAS HE MAD? DID HE TRY TO READ YOUR MIND WITH HIS PSYCHIC POWERS?
DON'T WORRY MABEL, HE'S JUST A KID! HE DOESN'T HAVE ANY POWERS.

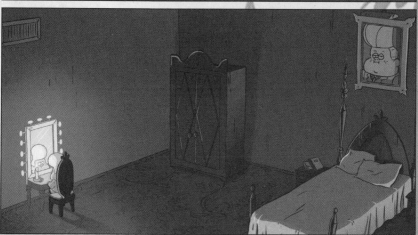

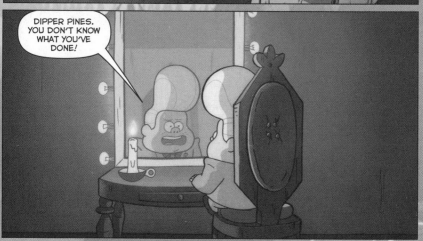

DIPPER PINES. YOU DON'T KNOW WHAT YOU'VE DONE!

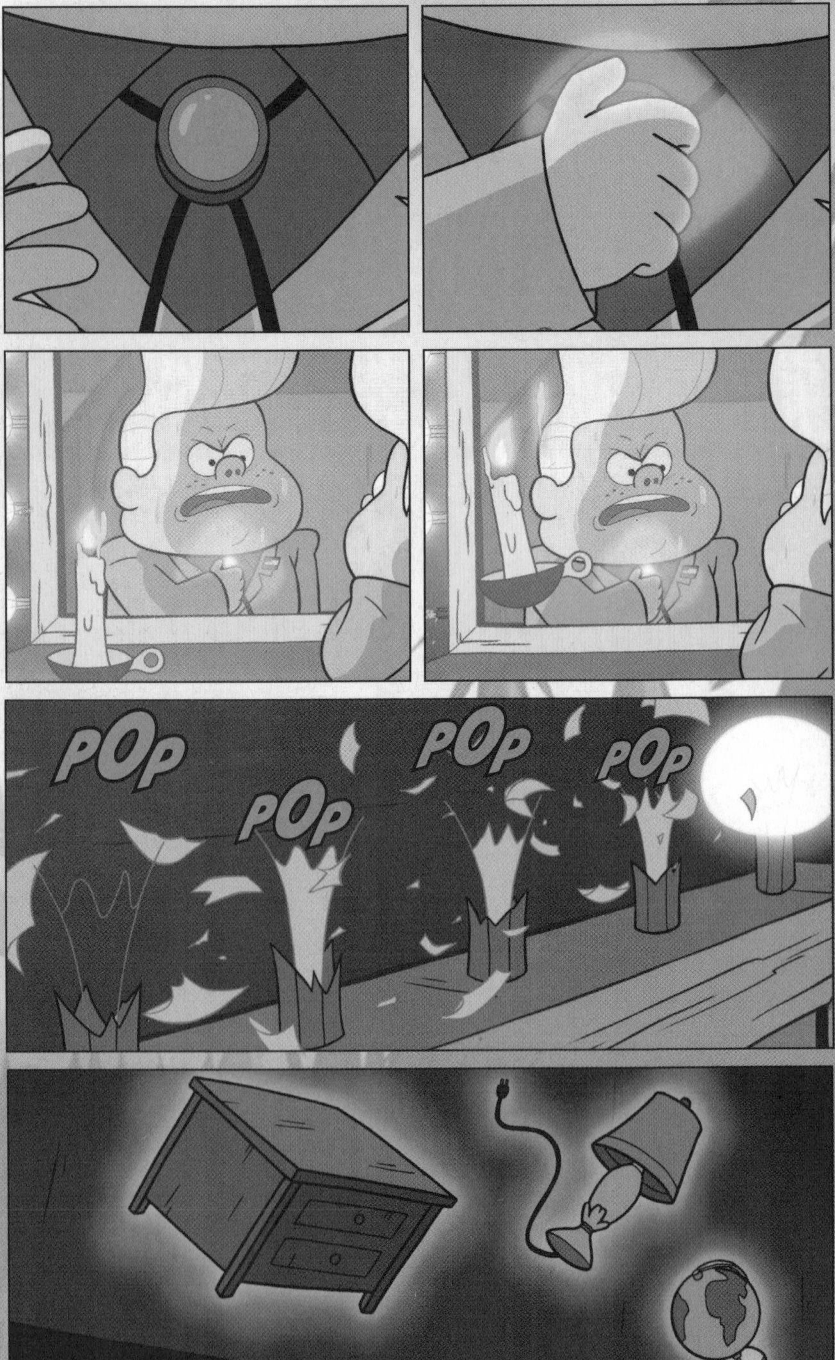
POP
POP
POP
POP

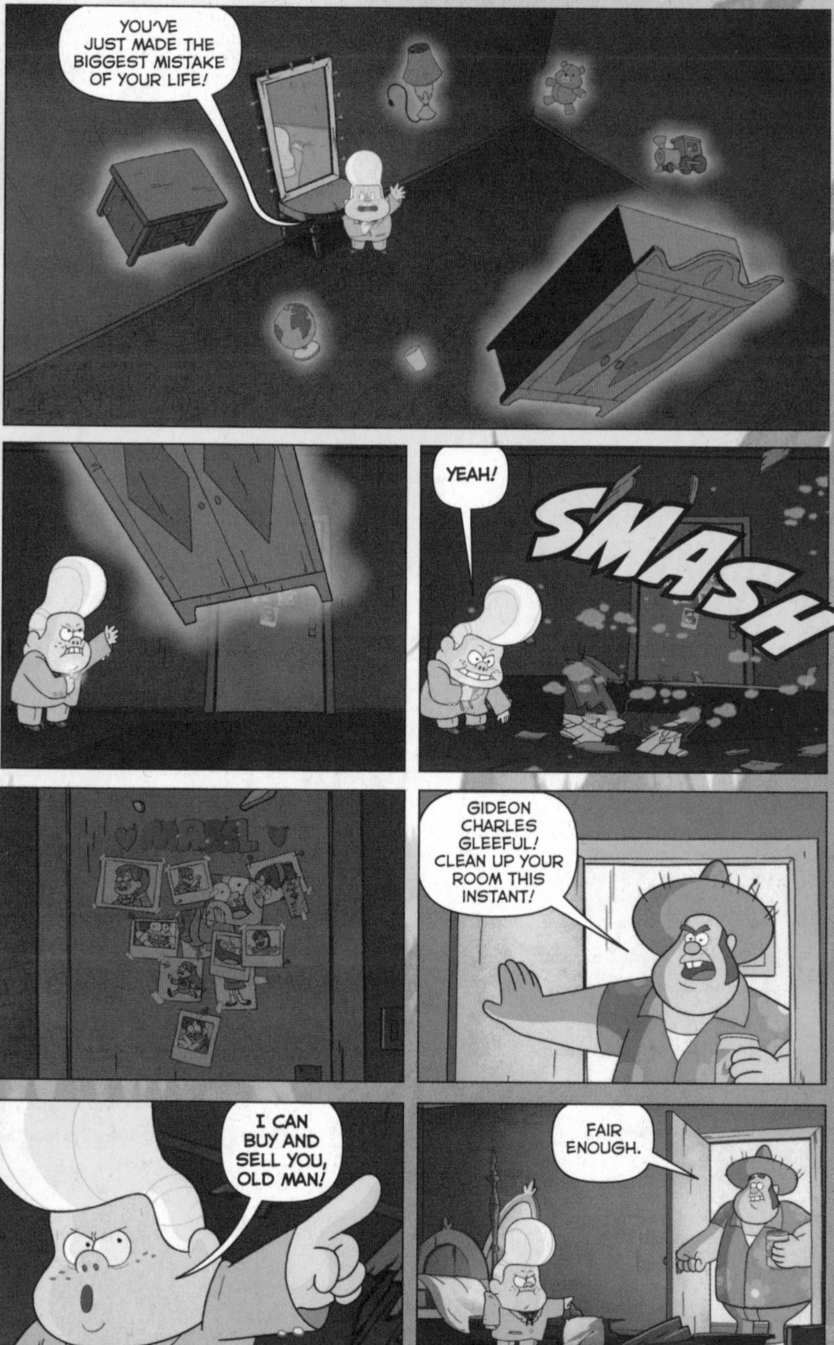
YOU'VE JUST MADE THE BIGGEST MISTAKE OF YOUR LIFE!
YEAH!
SMASH
GIDEON CHARLES GLEEFUL! CLEAN UP YOUR ROOM THIS INSTANT!
I CAN BUY AND SELL YOU, OLD MAN!
FAIR ENOUGH.

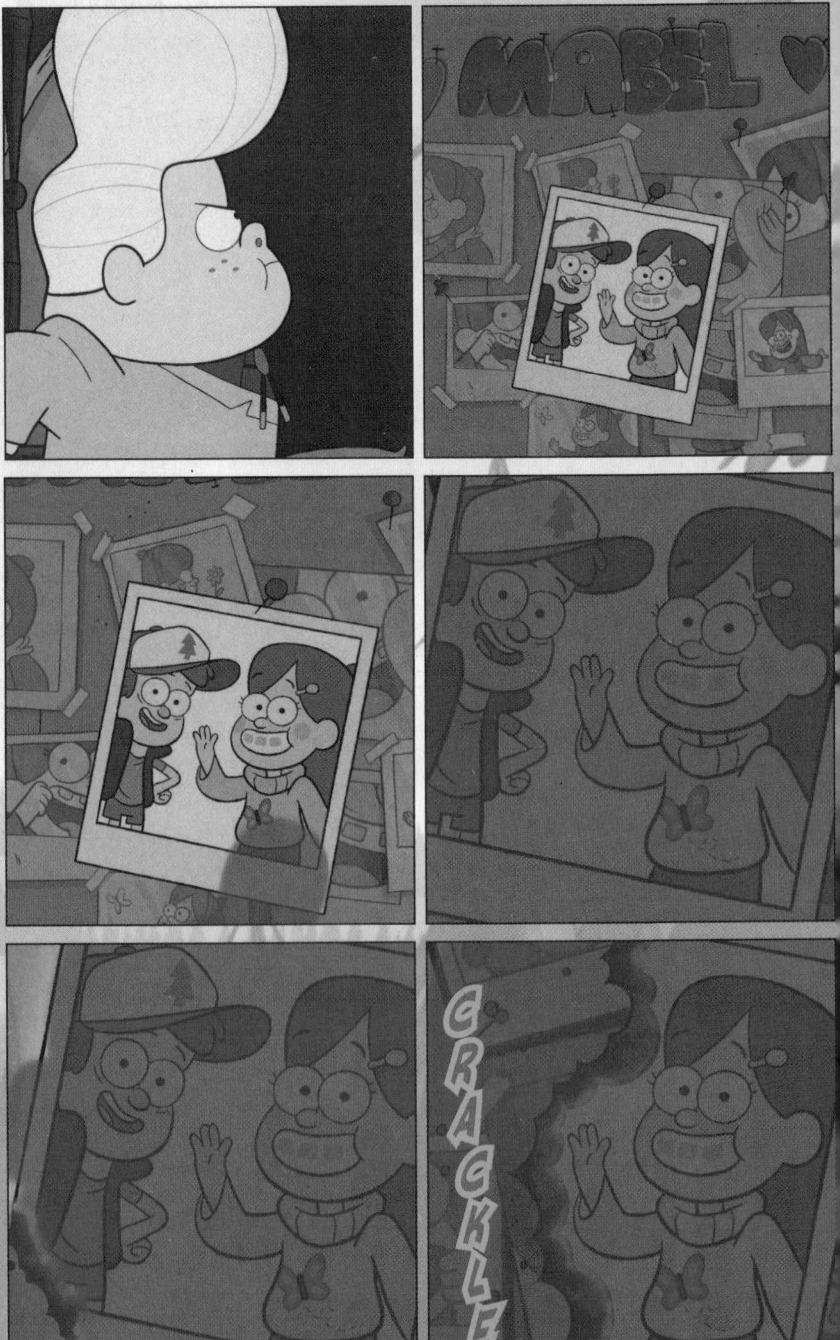
MABEL
CRACKLE

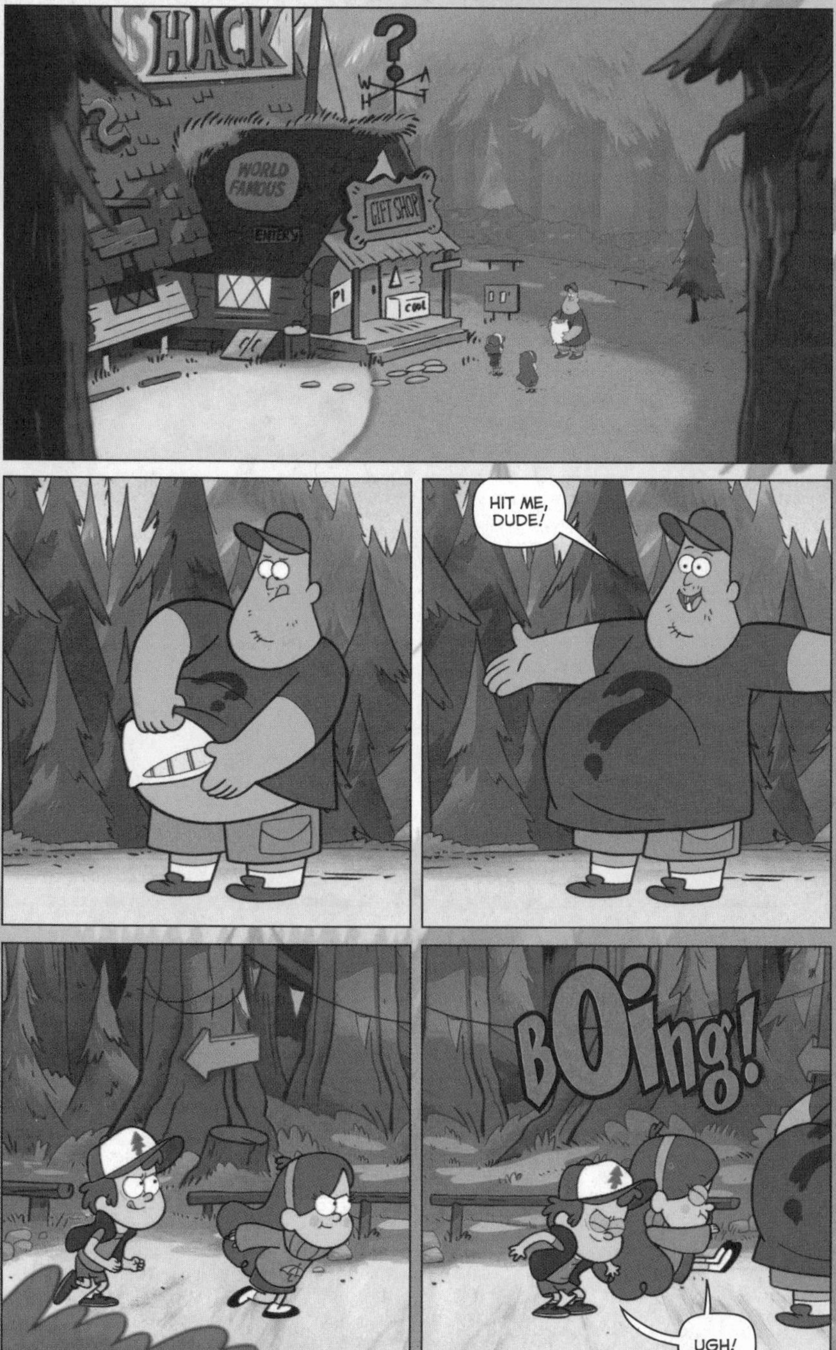
SHACK
WORLD FAMOUS
GIFT SHOP
ENTRY
HIT ME, DUDE!
BOing!
UGH!

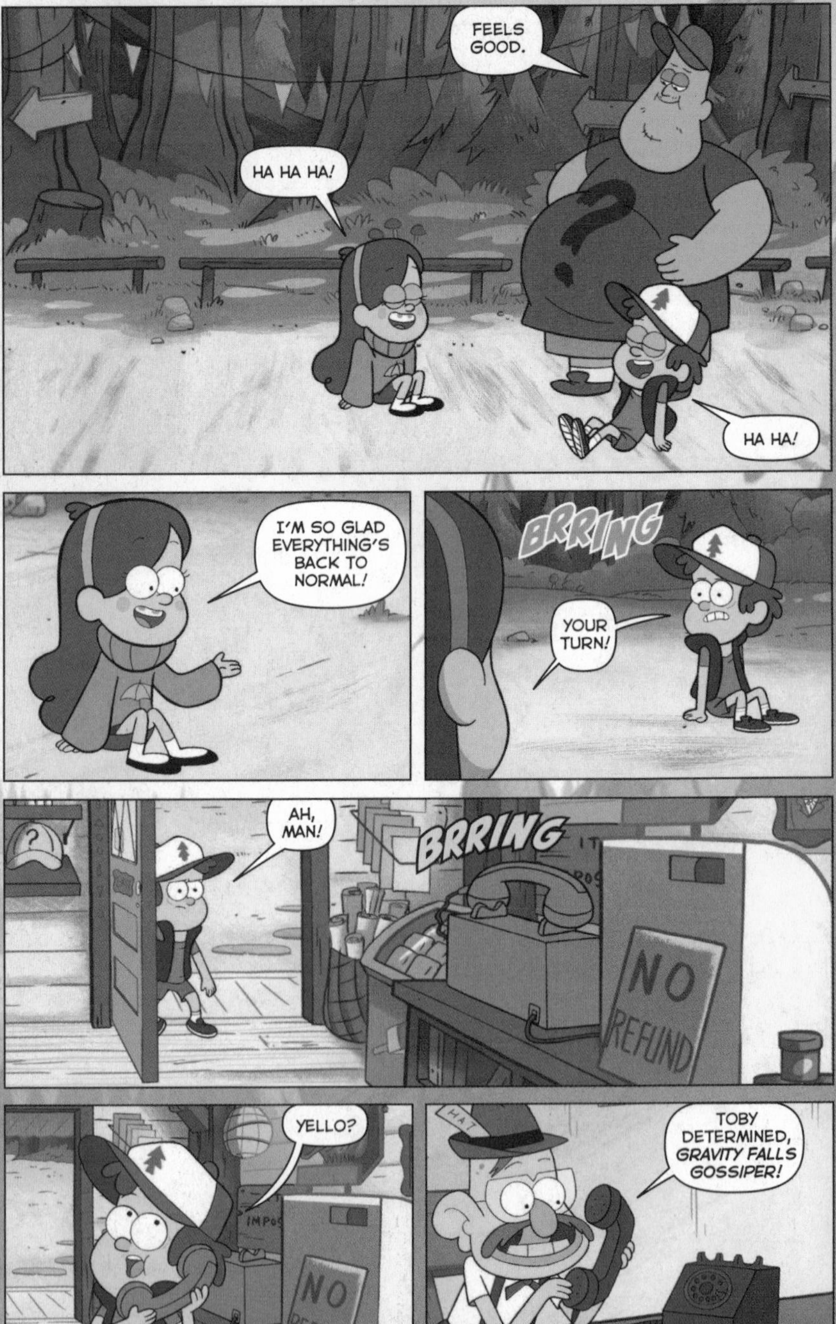

FEELS GOOD.
HA HA HA!
HA HA!
I'M SO GLAD EVERYTHING'S BACK TO NORMAL!
BRRING
YOUR TURN!
AH, MAN!
BRRING
NO REFUND
YELLO?
NO REFUND
TOBY DETERMINED, GRAVITY FALLS GOSSIPER!

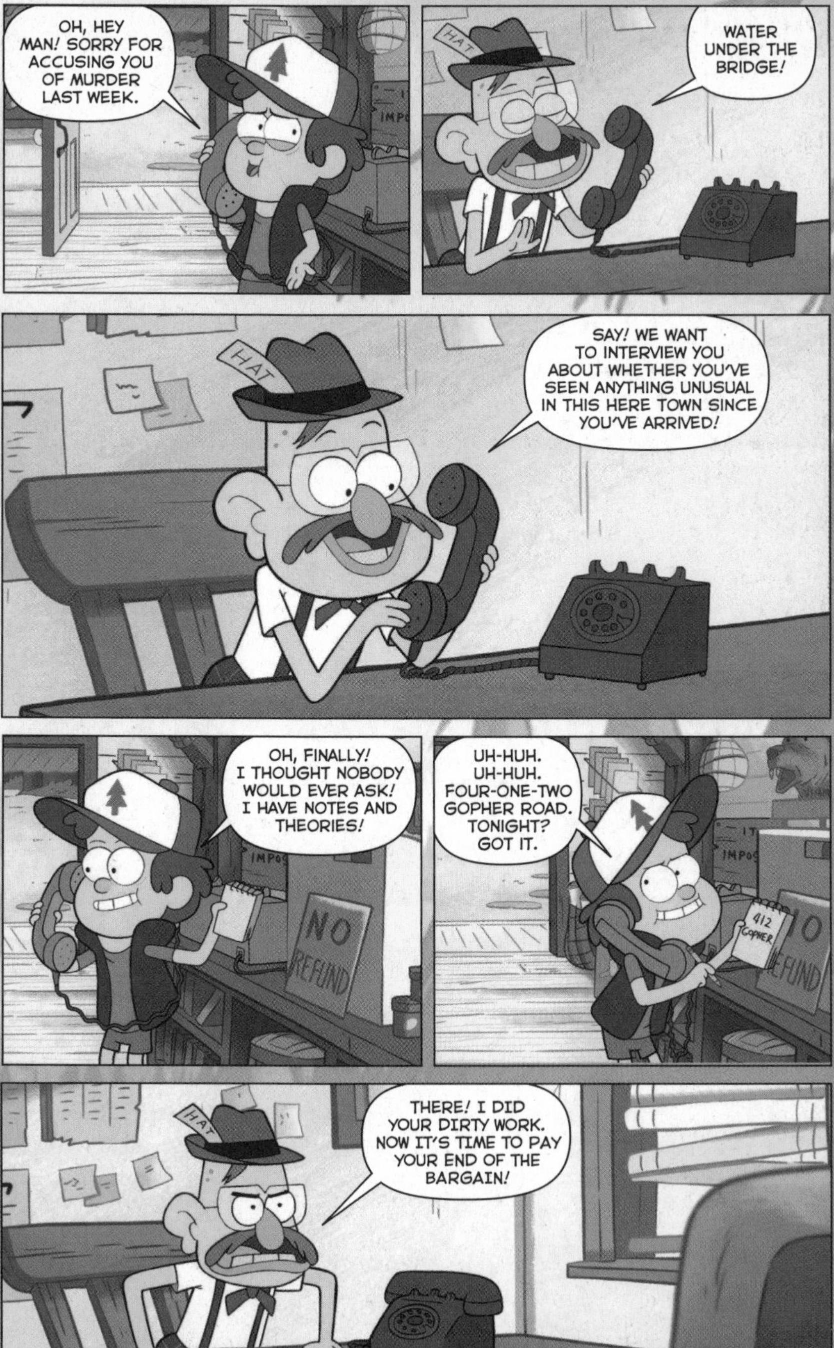
OH, HEY MAN! SORRY FOR ACCUSING YOU OF MURDER LAST WEEK.
HAT
IMPO
WATER UNDER THE BRIDGE!
HAT
SAY! WE WANT TO INTERVIEW YOU ABOUT WHETHER YOU'VE SEEN ANYTHING UNUSUAL IN THIS HERE TOWN SINCE YOU'VE ARRIVED!
OH, FINALLY! I THOUGHT NOBODY WOULD EVER ASK! I HAVE NOTES AND THEORIES!
NO REFUND
UH-HUH. UH-HUH. FOUR-ONE-TWO GOPHER ROAD. TONIGHT? GOT IT.
412 Gopher
HAT
THERE! I DID YOUR DIRTY WORK. NOW IT'S TIME TO PAY YOUR END OF THE BARGAIN!

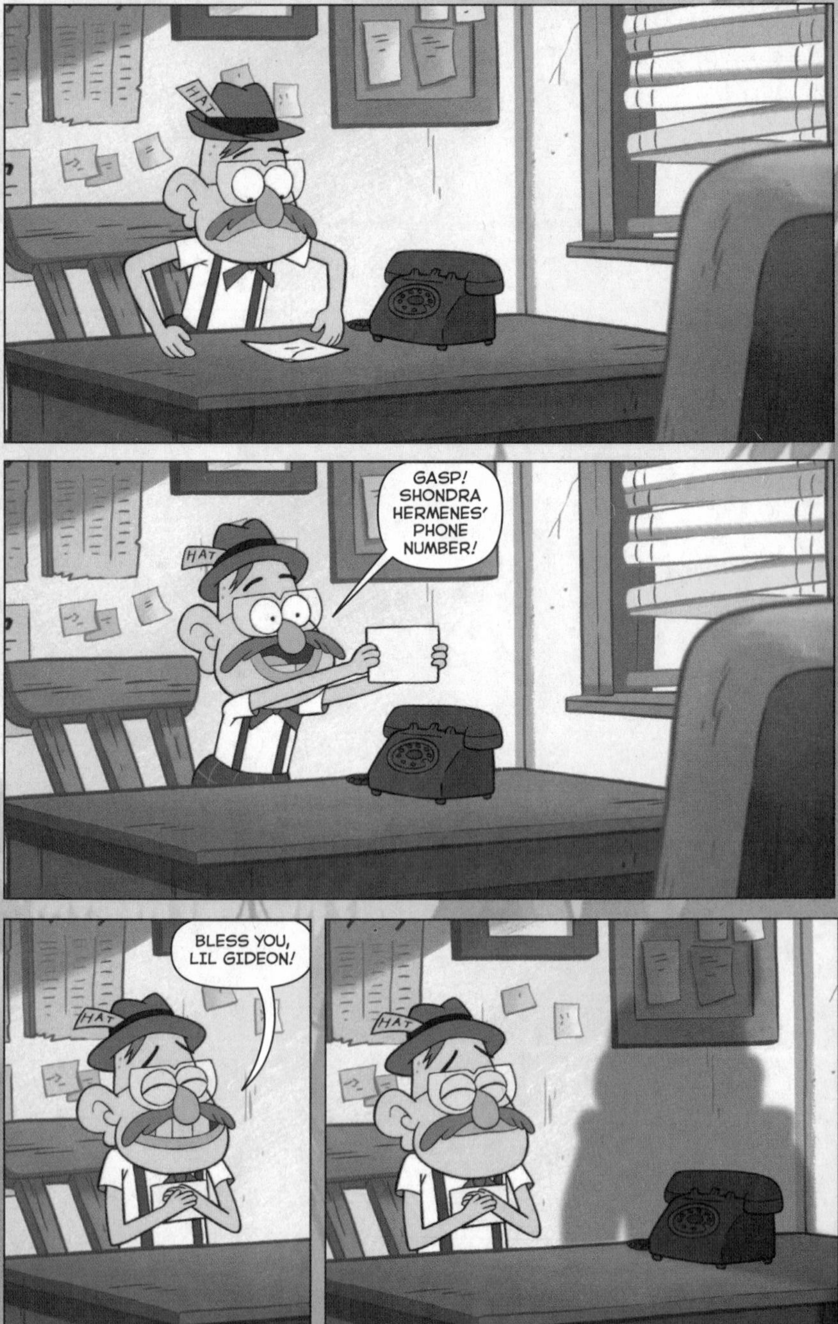
HAT
HAT
GASP! SHONDRA HERMENES' PHONE NUMBER!
HAT
BLESS YOU, LIL GIDEON!
HAT

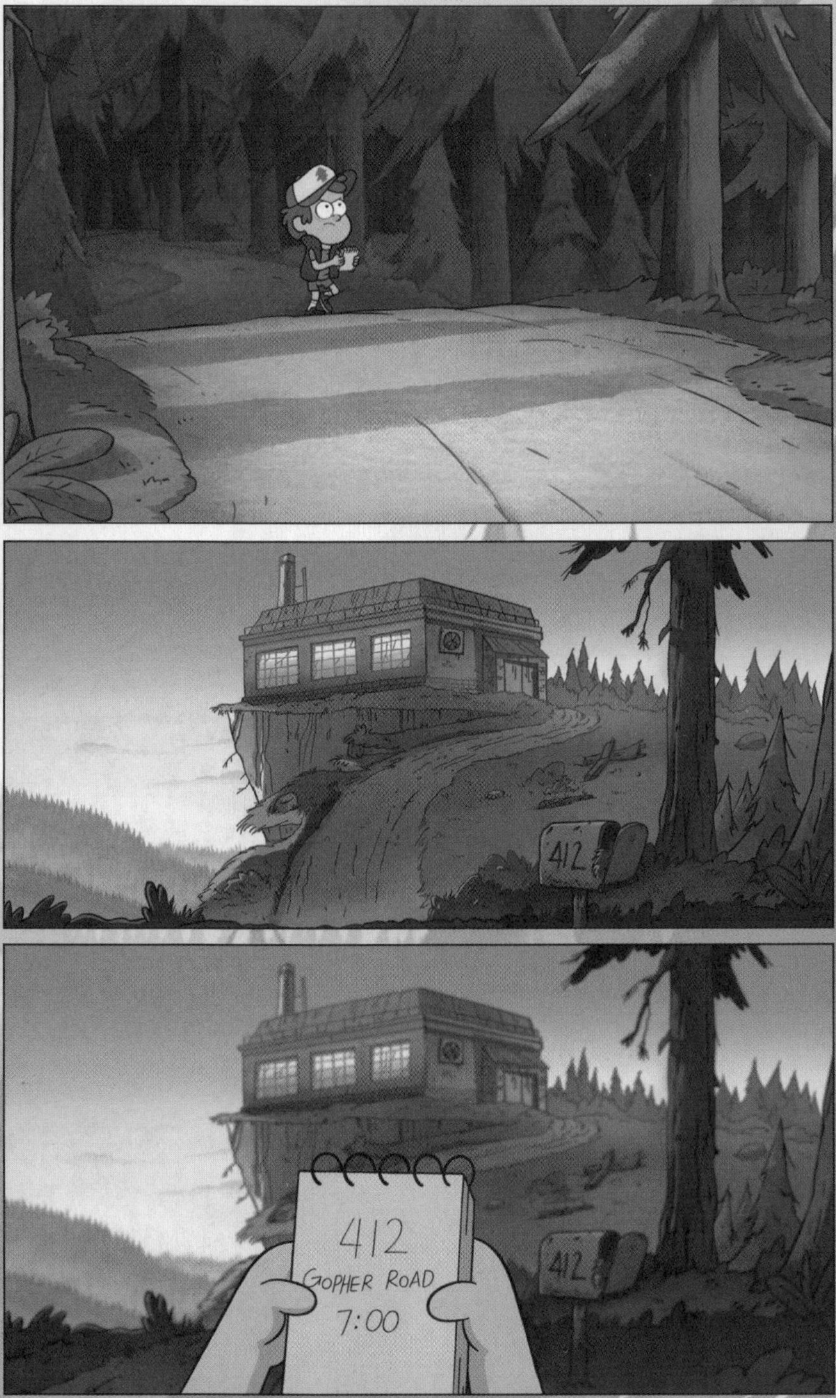
412
412
GOPHER ROAD
7:00
412

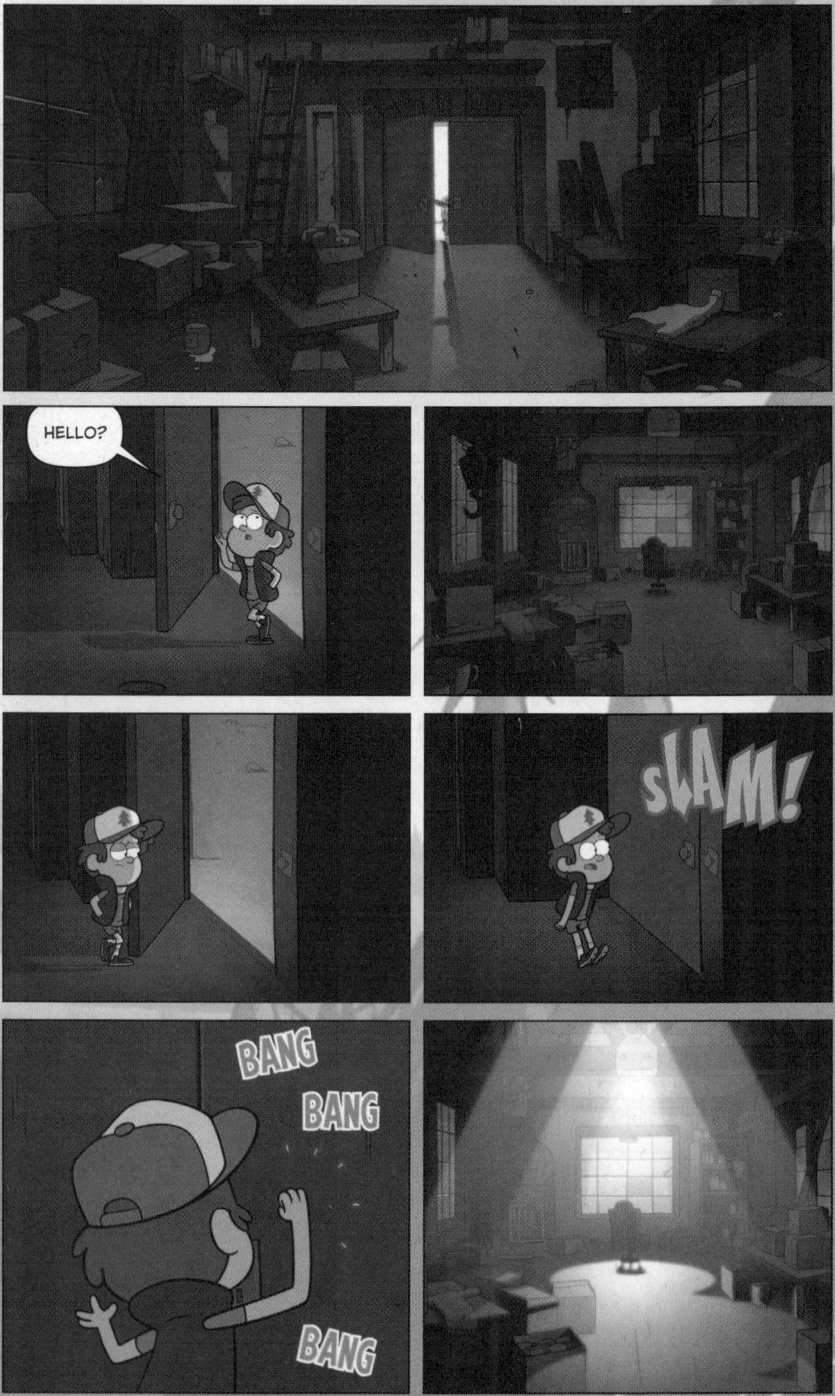
HELLO?
SLAM!
BANG
BANG
BANG

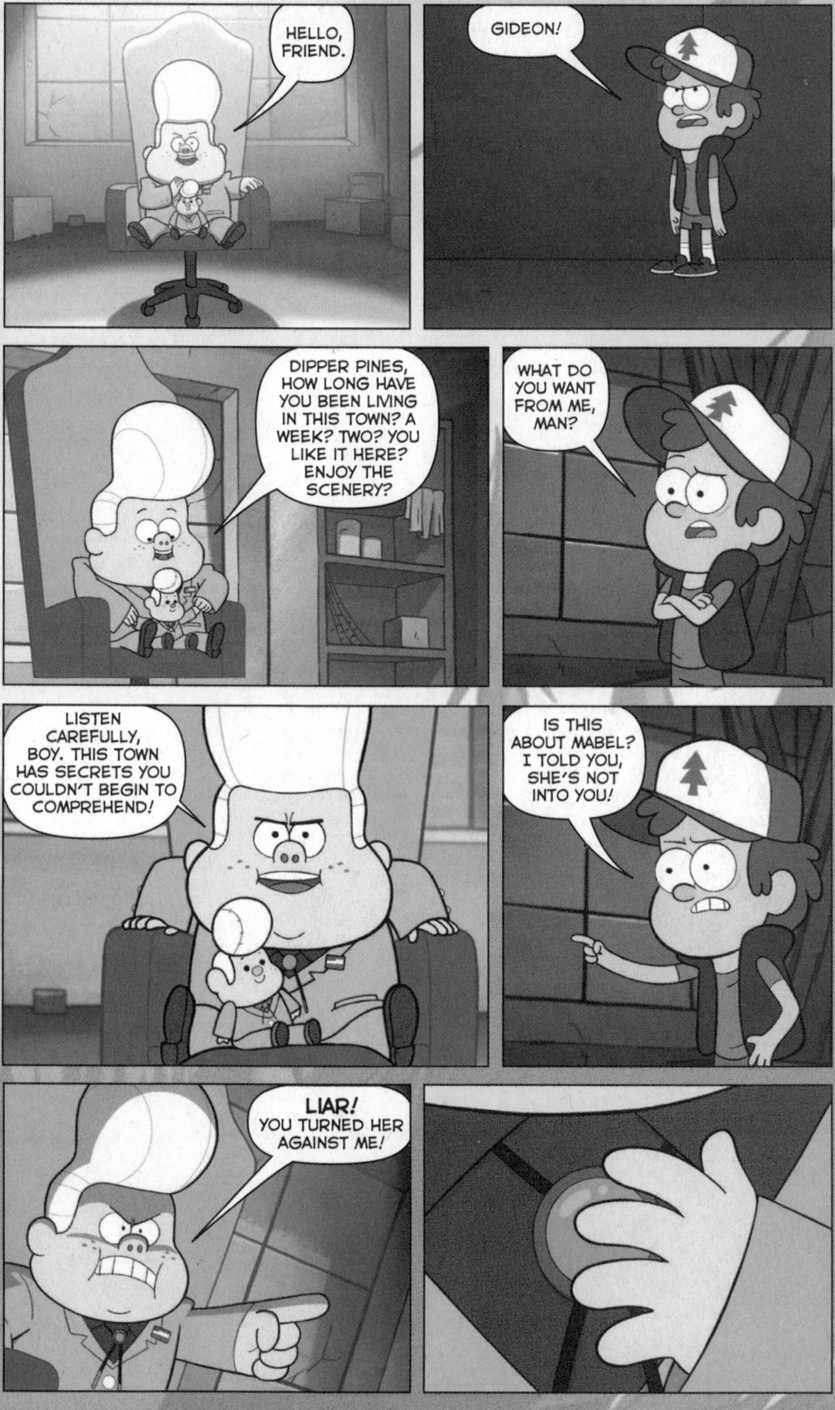
HELLO, FRIEND.
GIDEON!
DIPPER PINES, HOW LONG HAVE YOU BEEN LIVING IN THIS TOWN? A WEEK? TWO? YOU LIKE IT HERE? ENJOY THE SCENERY?
WHAT DO YOU WANT FROM ME, MAN?
LISTEN CAREFULLY, BOY. THIS TOWN HAS SECRETS YOU COULDN'T BEGIN TO COMPREHEND!
IS THIS ABOUT MABEL? I TOLD YOU, SHE'S NOT INTO YOU!
LIAR! YOU TURNED HER AGAINST ME!

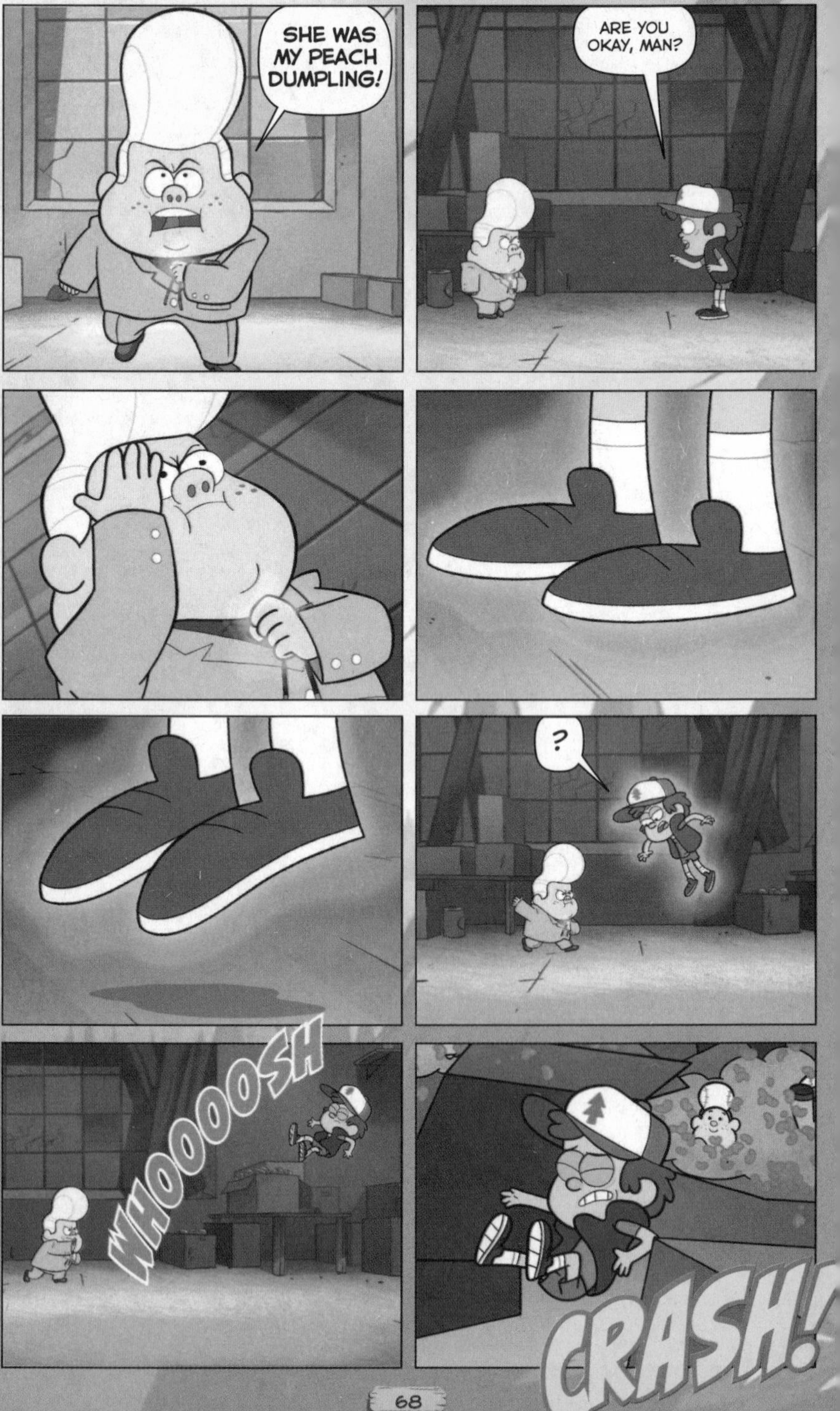
SHE WAS MY PEACH DUMPLING!
ARE YOU OKAY, MAN?
?
WHOOOOSH
CRASH!

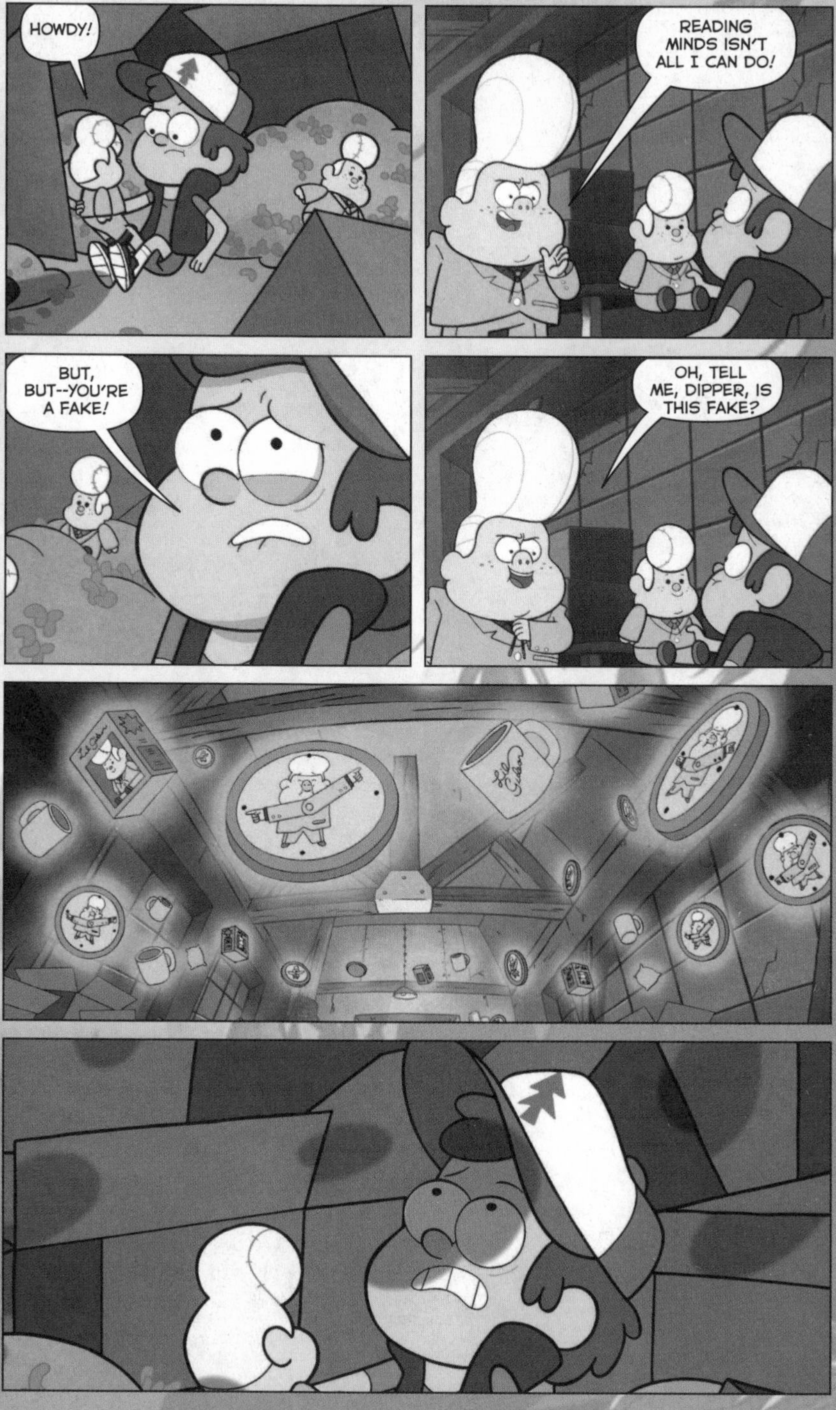
HOWDY!
READING MINDS ISN'T ALL I CAN DO!
BUT, BUT--YOU'RE A FAKE!
OH, TELL ME, DIPPER, IS THIS FAKE?

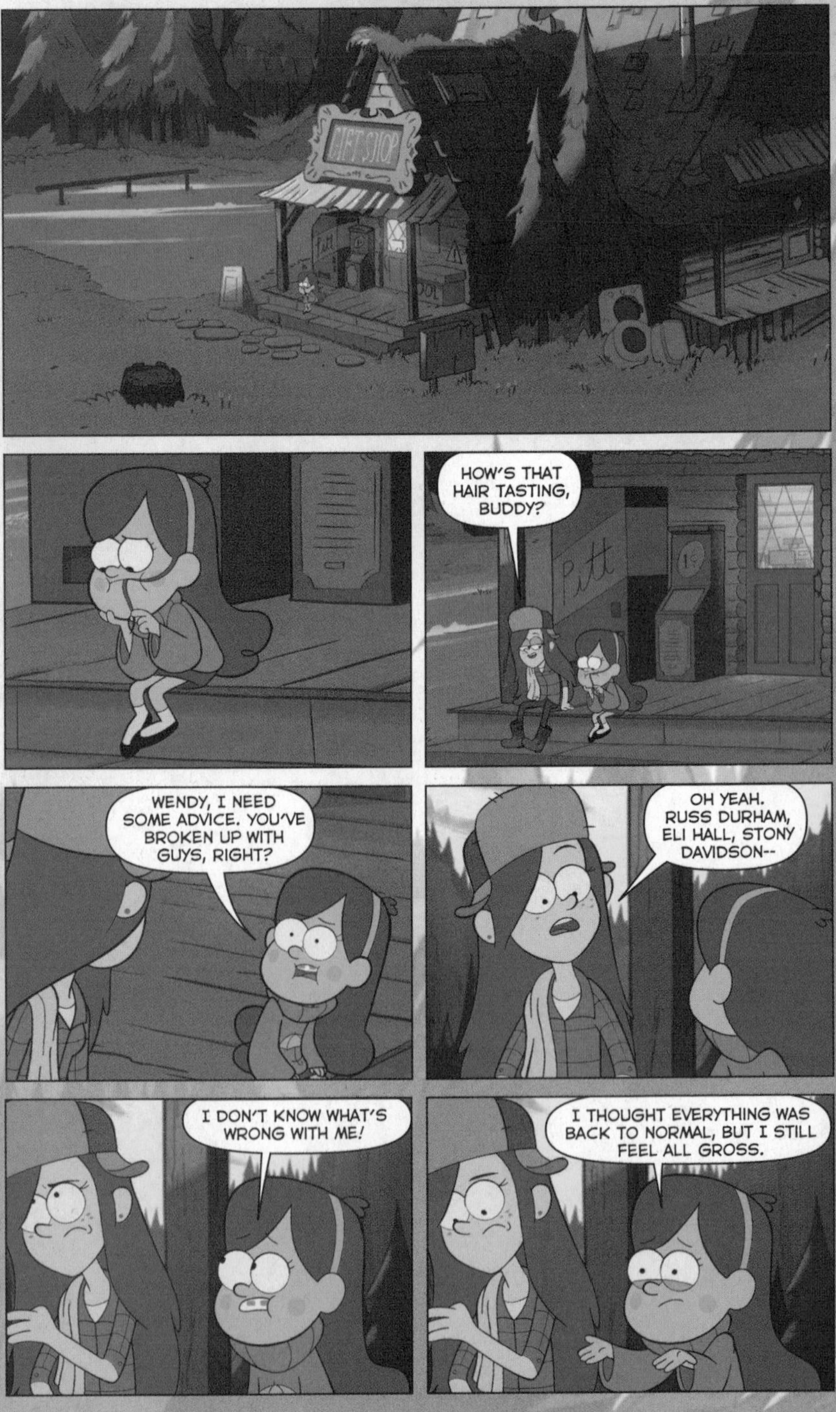
GIFT SHOP
HOW'S THAT HAIR TASTING, BUDDY?
WENDY, I NEED SOME ADVICE. YOU'VE BROKEN UP WITH GUYS, RIGHT?
OH YEAH. RUSS DURHAM, ELI HALL, STONY DAVIDSON--
I DON'T KNOW WHAT'S WRONG WITH ME!
I THOUGHT EVERYTHING WAS BACK TO NORMAL, BUT I STILL FEEL ALL GROSS.

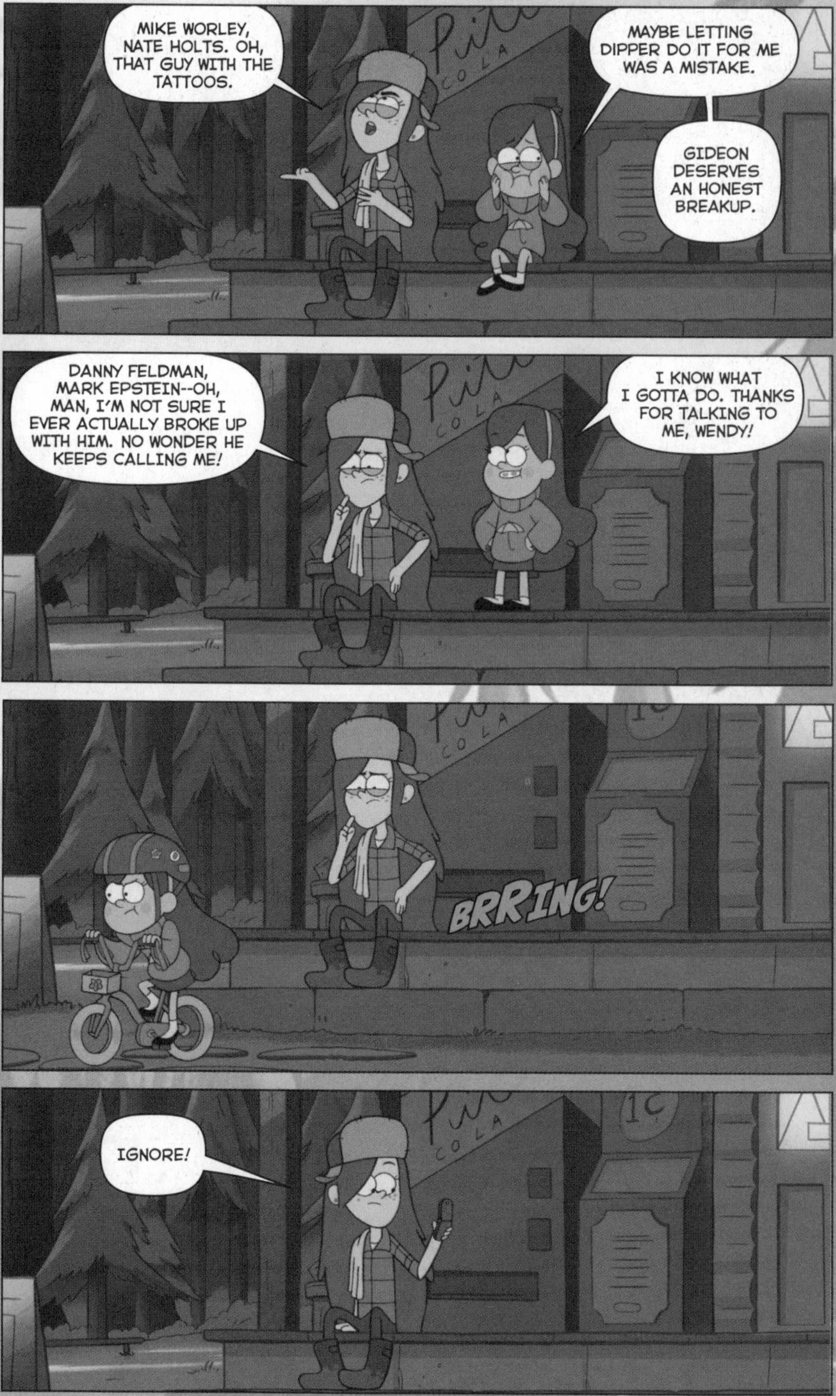
MIKE WORLEY, NATE HOLTS. OH, THAT GUY WITH THE TATTOOS.
MAYBE LETTING DIPPER DO IT FOR ME WAS A MISTAKE.
GIDEON DESERVES AN HONEST BREAKUP.
DANNY FELDMAN, MARK EPSTEIN--OH, MAN, I'M NOT SURE I EVER ACTUALLY BROKE UP WITH HIM. NO WONDER HE KEEPS CALLING ME!
I KNOW WHAT I GOTTA DO. THANKS FOR TALKING TO ME, WENDY!
BRRING!
IGNORE!

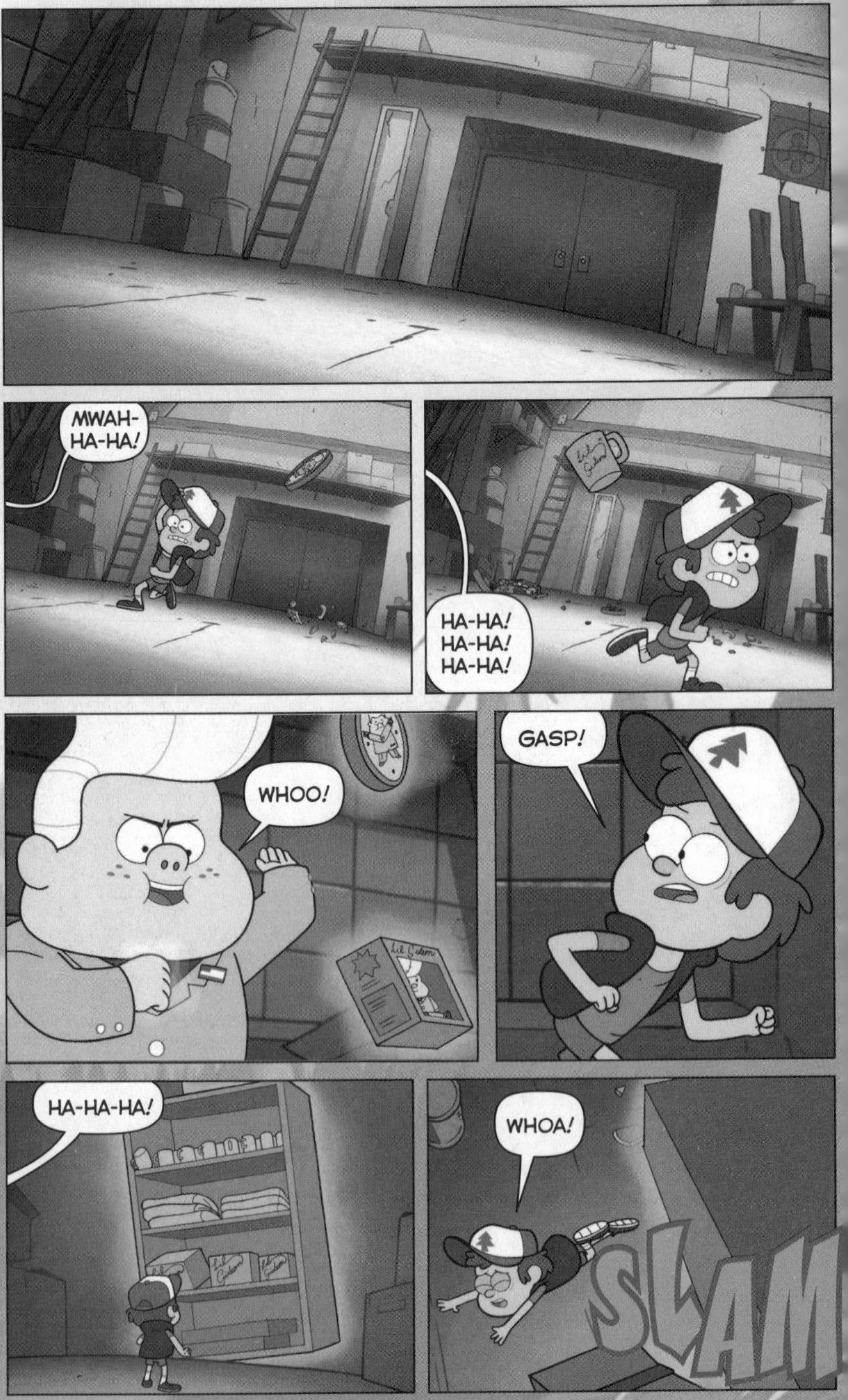
MWAH-HA-HA!
HA-HA! HA-HA! HA-HA!
WHOO!
GASP!
HA-HA-HA!
WHOA!
SLAM

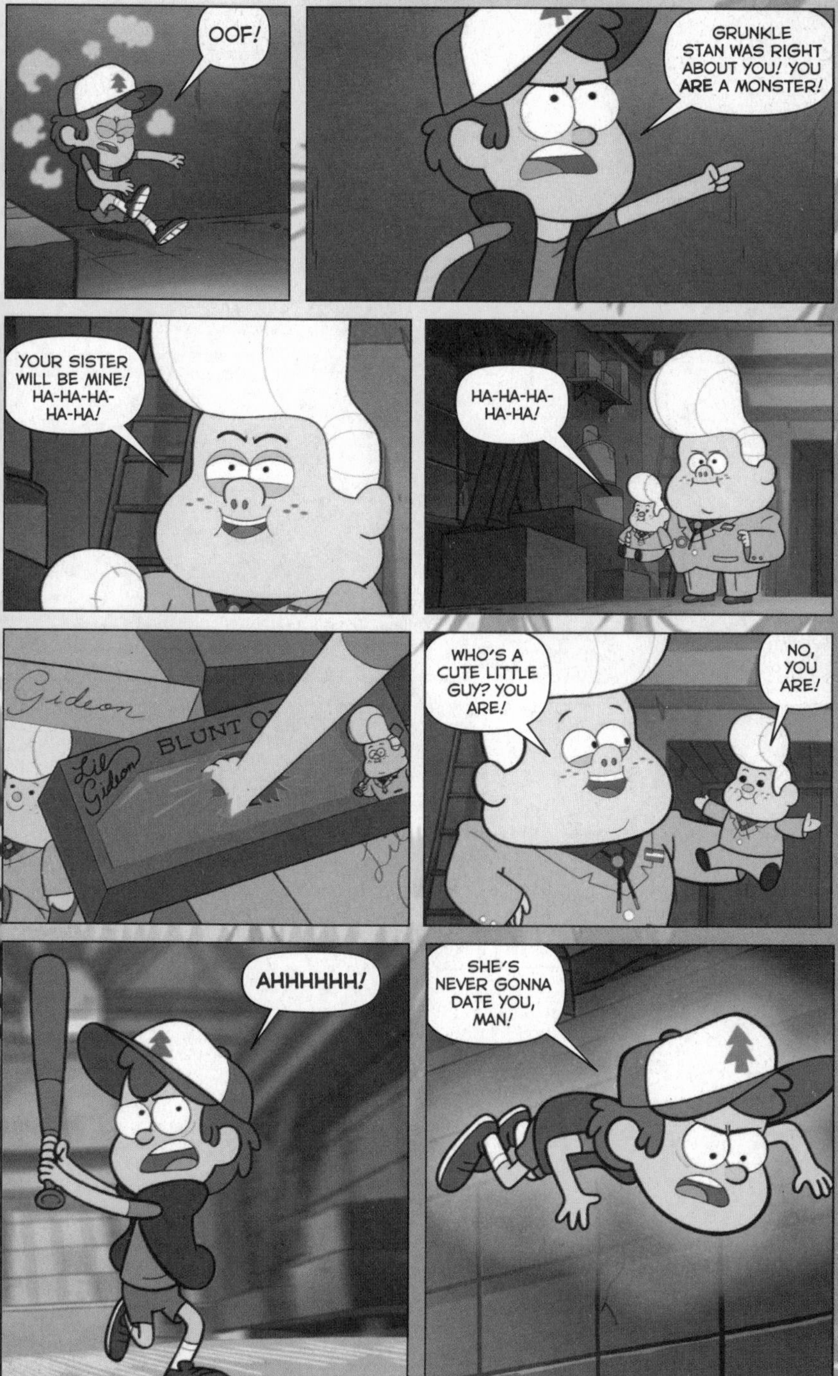
OOF!
GRUNKLE STAN WAS RIGHT ABOUT YOU! YOU ARE A MONSTER!
YOUR SISTER WILL BE MINE! HA-HA-HA-HA-HA!
HA-HA-HA-HA-HA!
Gideon
Lil Gideon
BLUNT
WHO'S A CUTE LITTLE GUY? YOU ARE!
NO, YOU ARE!
AHHHHHH!
SHE'S NEVER GONNA DATE YOU, MAN!

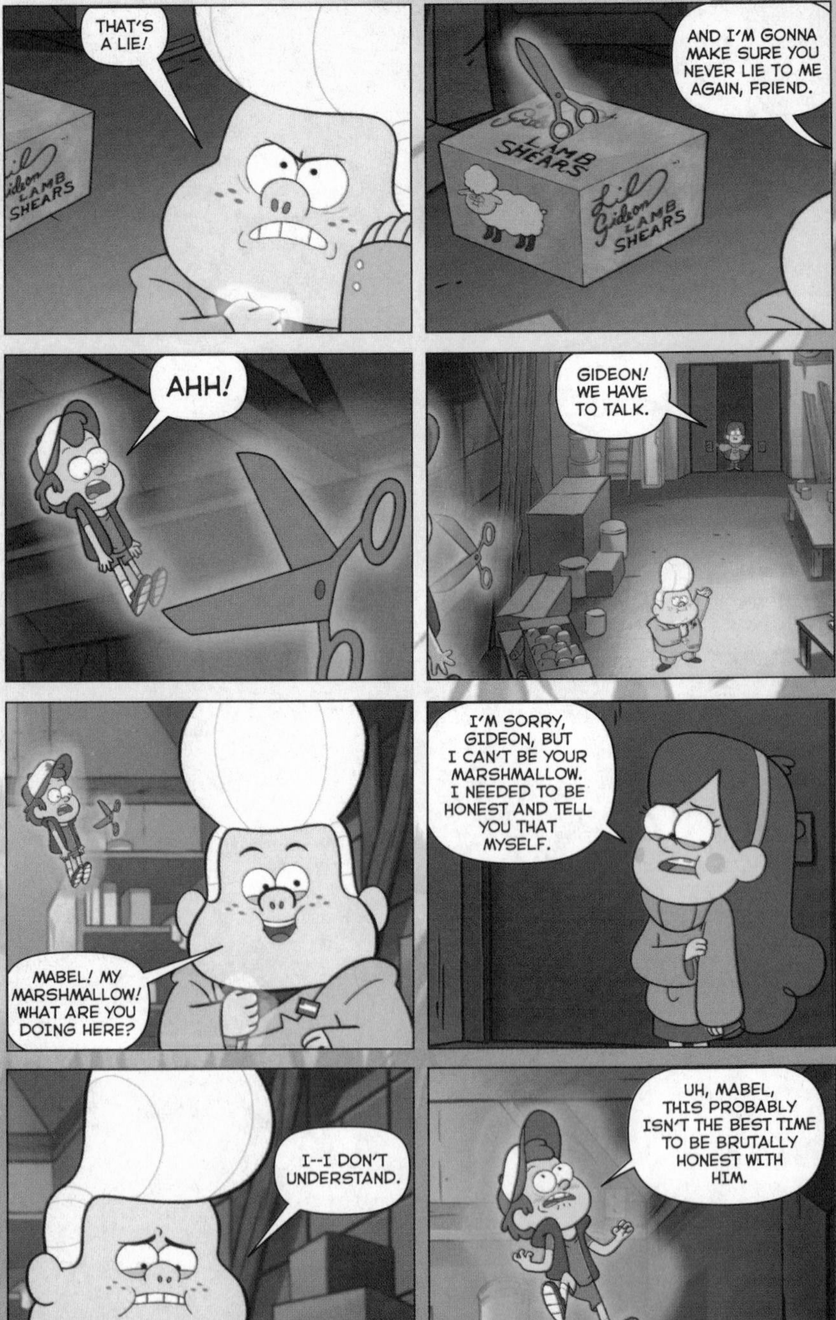
THAT'S A LIE!
Lil Gideon LAMB SHEARS
AND I'M GONNA MAKE SURE YOU NEVER LIE TO ME AGAIN, FRIEND.
LAMB SHEARS
Lil Gideon LAMB SHEARS
AHH!
GIDEON! WE HAVE TO TALK.
MABEL! MY MARSHMALLOW! WHAT ARE YOU DOING HERE?
I'M SORRY, GIDEON, BUT I CAN'T BE YOUR MARSHMALLOW. I NEEDED TO BE HONEST AND TELL YOU THAT MYSELF.
I--I DON'T UNDERSTAND.
UH, MABEL, THIS PROBABLY ISN'T THE BEST TIME TO BE BRUTALLY HONEST WITH HIM.

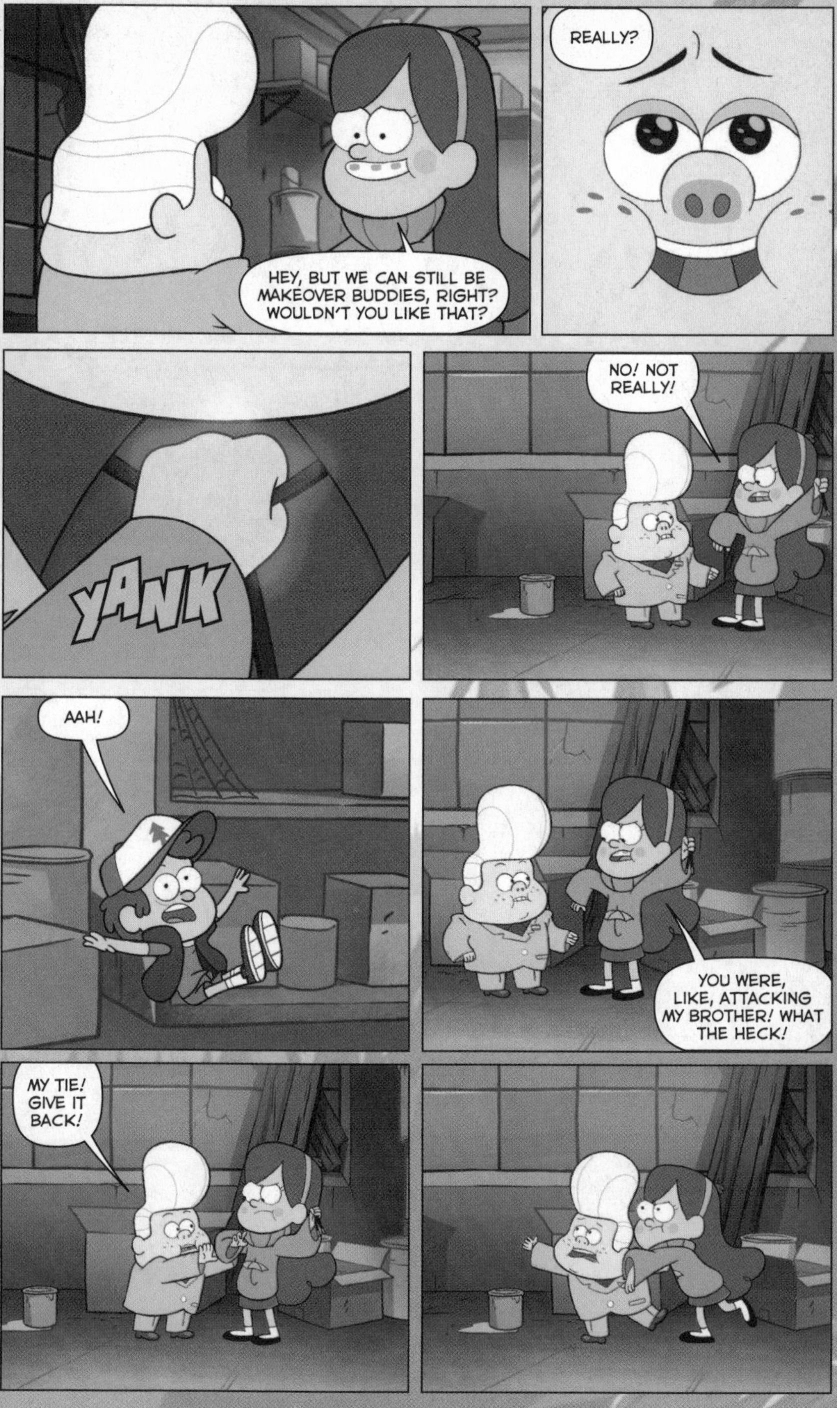
HEY, BUT WE CAN STILL BE MAKEOVER BUDDIES, RIGHT? WOULDN'T YOU LIKE THAT?
REALLY?
YANK
NO! NOT REALLY!
AAH!
YOU WERE, LIKE, ATTACKING MY BROTHER! WHAT THE HECK!
MY TIE! GIVE IT BACK!

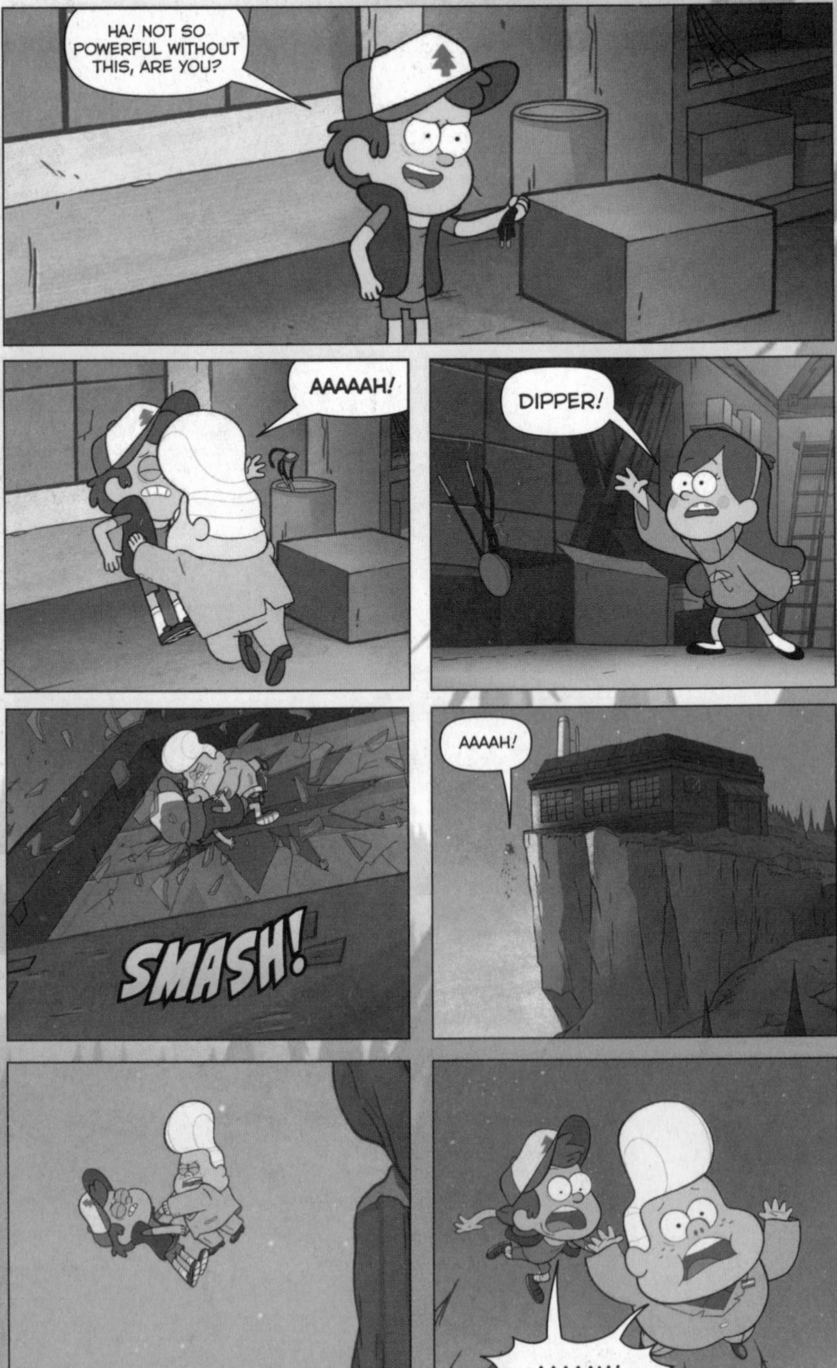
HA! NOT SO POWERFUL WITHOUT THIS, ARE YOU?
AAAAAH!
DIPPER!
SMASH!
AAAAH!
AAAAAH!

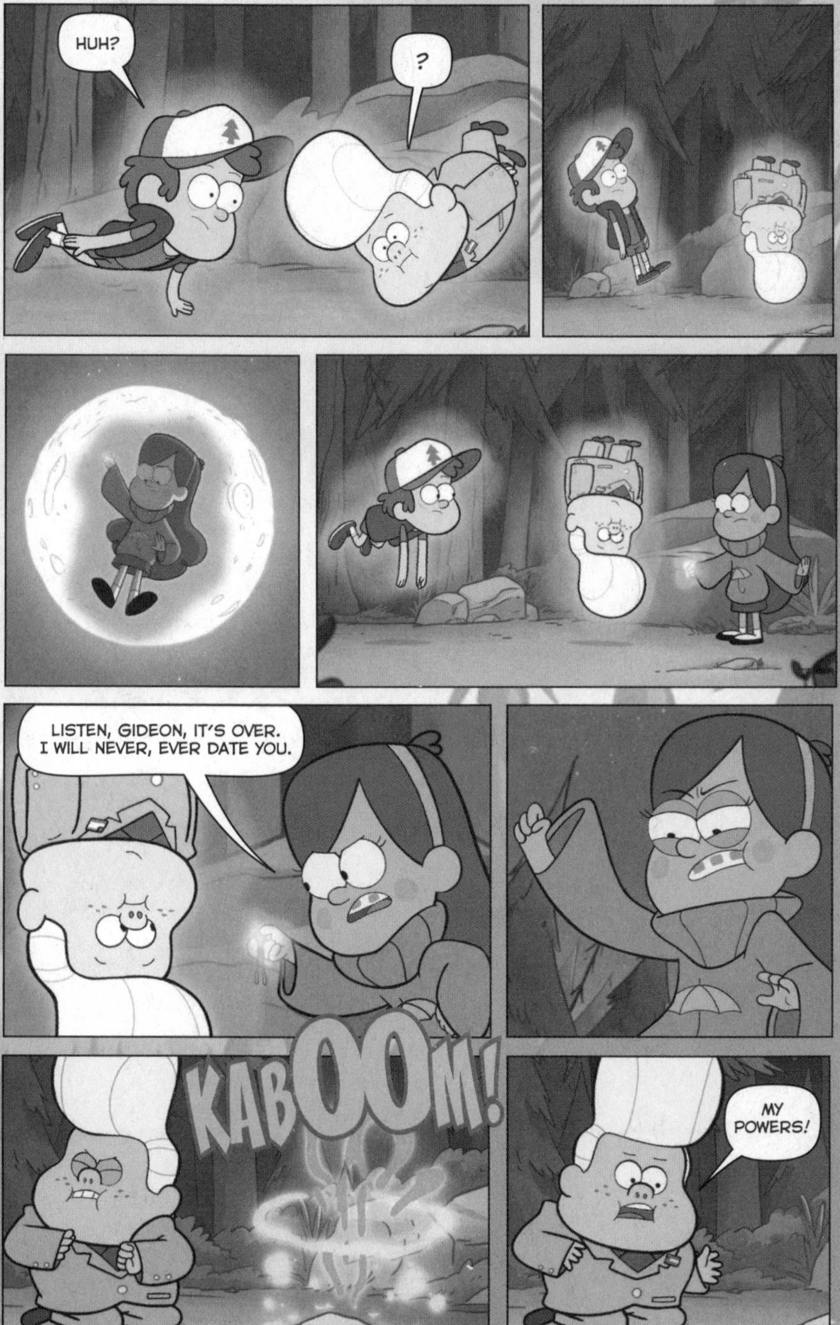
HUH?
?
LISTEN, GIDEON, IT'S OVER. I WILL NEVER, EVER DATE YOU.
KABOOM!
MY POWERS!

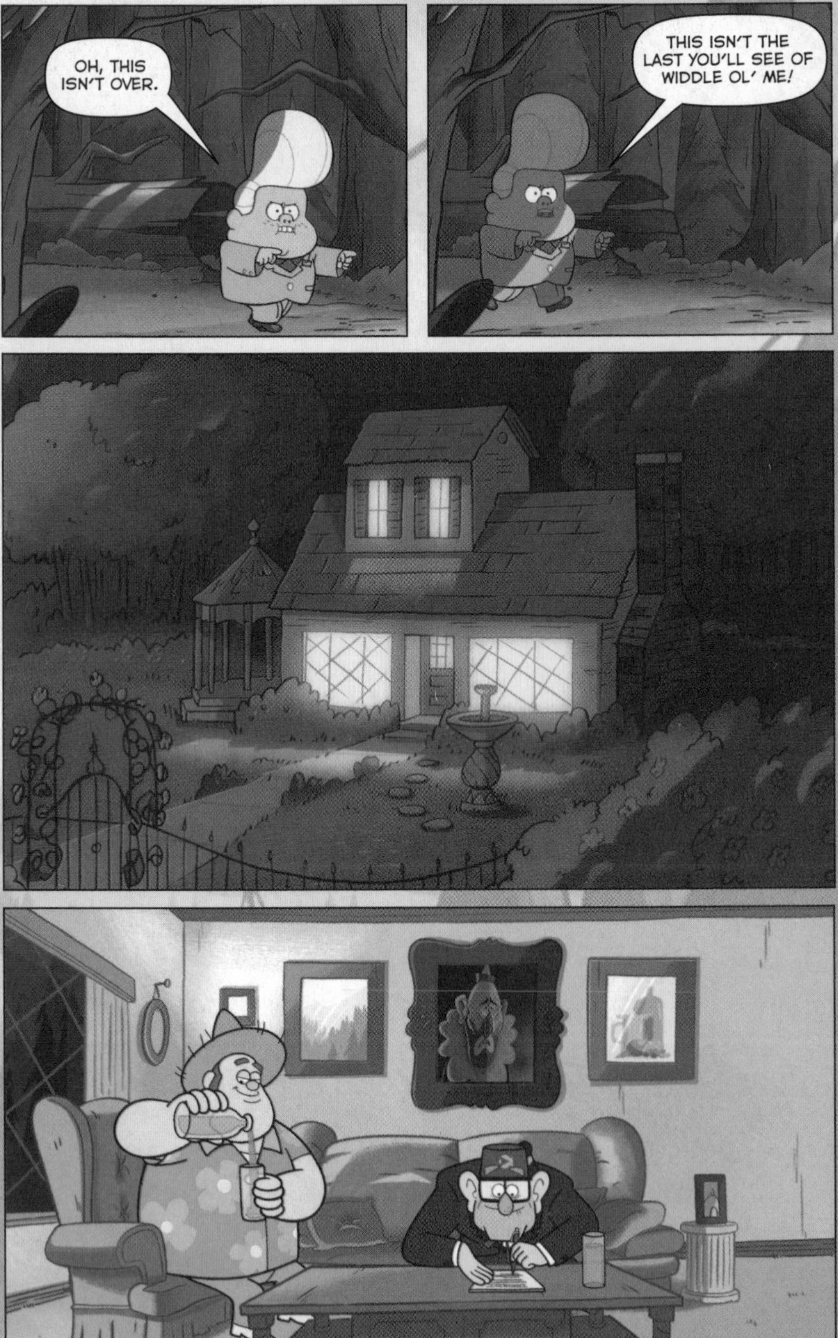
OH, THIS ISN'T OVER.
THIS ISN'T THE LAST YOU'LL SEE OF WIDDLE OL' ME!

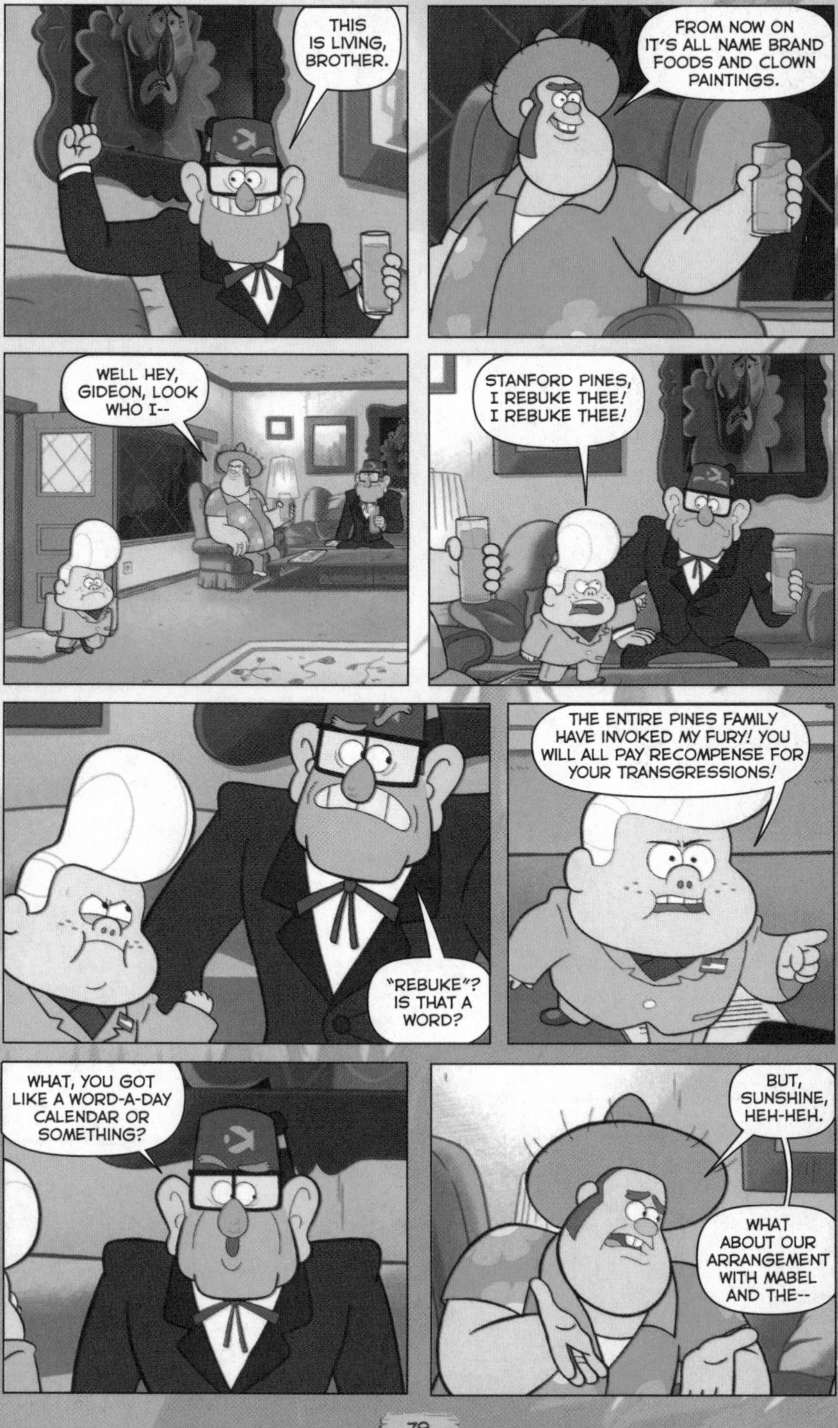
THIS IS LIVING, BROTHER.
FROM NOW ON IT'S ALL NAME BRAND FOODS AND CLOWN PAINTINGS.
WELL HEY, GIDEON, LOOK WHO I--
STANFORD PINES, I REBUKE THEE! I REBUKE THEE!
"REBUKE"? IS THAT A WORD?
THE ENTIRE PINES FAMILY HAVE INVOKED MY FURY! YOU WILL ALL PAY RECOMPENSE FOR YOUR TRANSGRESSIONS!
WHAT, YOU GOT LIKE A WORD-A-DAY CALENDAR OR SOMETHING?
BUT, SUNSHINE, HEH-HEH.
WHAT ABOUT OUR ARRANGEMENT WITH MABEL AND THE--

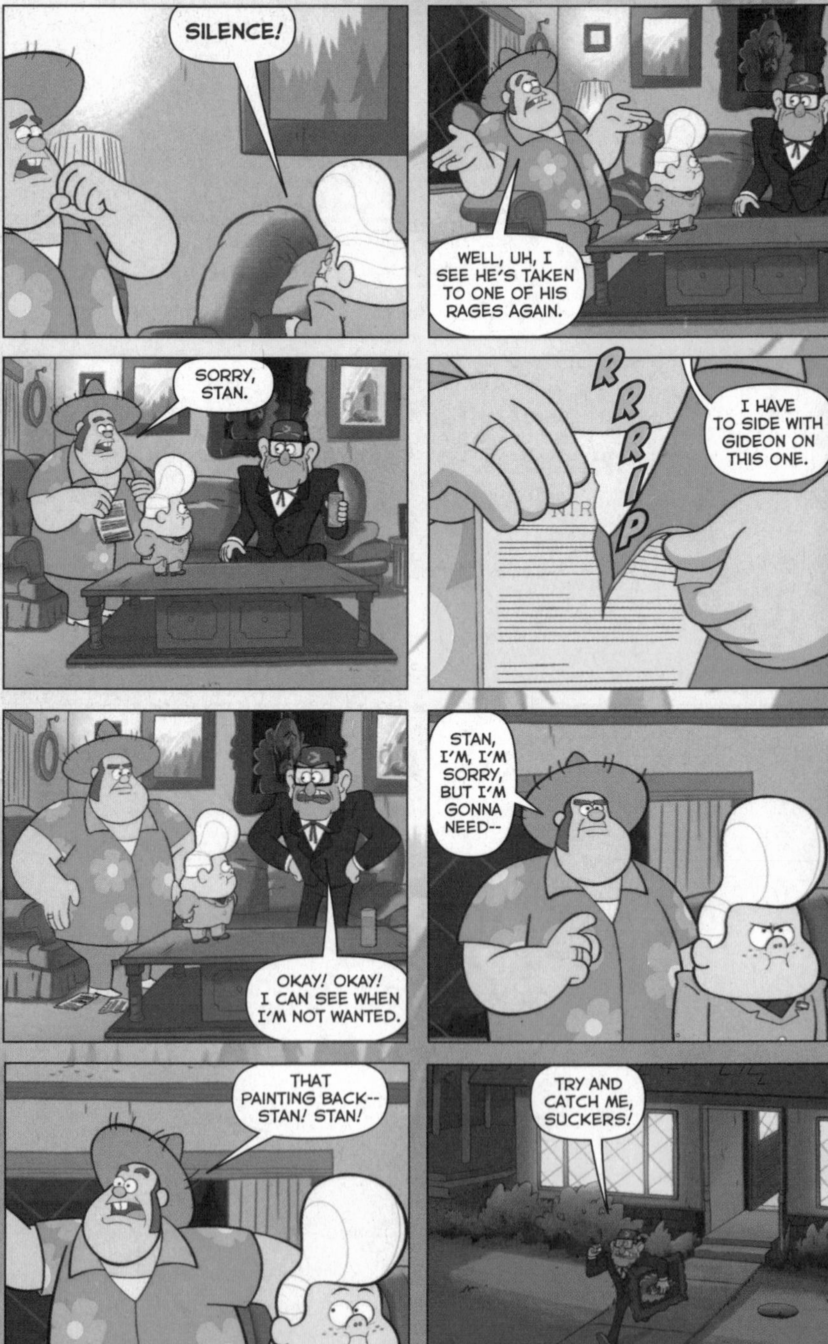
SILENCE!
WELL, UH, I SEE HE'S TAKEN TO ONE OF HIS RAGES AGAIN.
SORRY, STAN.
I HAVE TO SIDE WITH GIDEON ON THIS ONE.
RRRIP
OKAY! OKAY! I CAN SEE WHEN I'M NOT WANTED.
STAN, I'M, I'M SORRY, BUT I'M GONNA NEED--
THAT PAINTING BACK-- STAN! STAN!
TRY AND CATCH ME, SUCKERS!

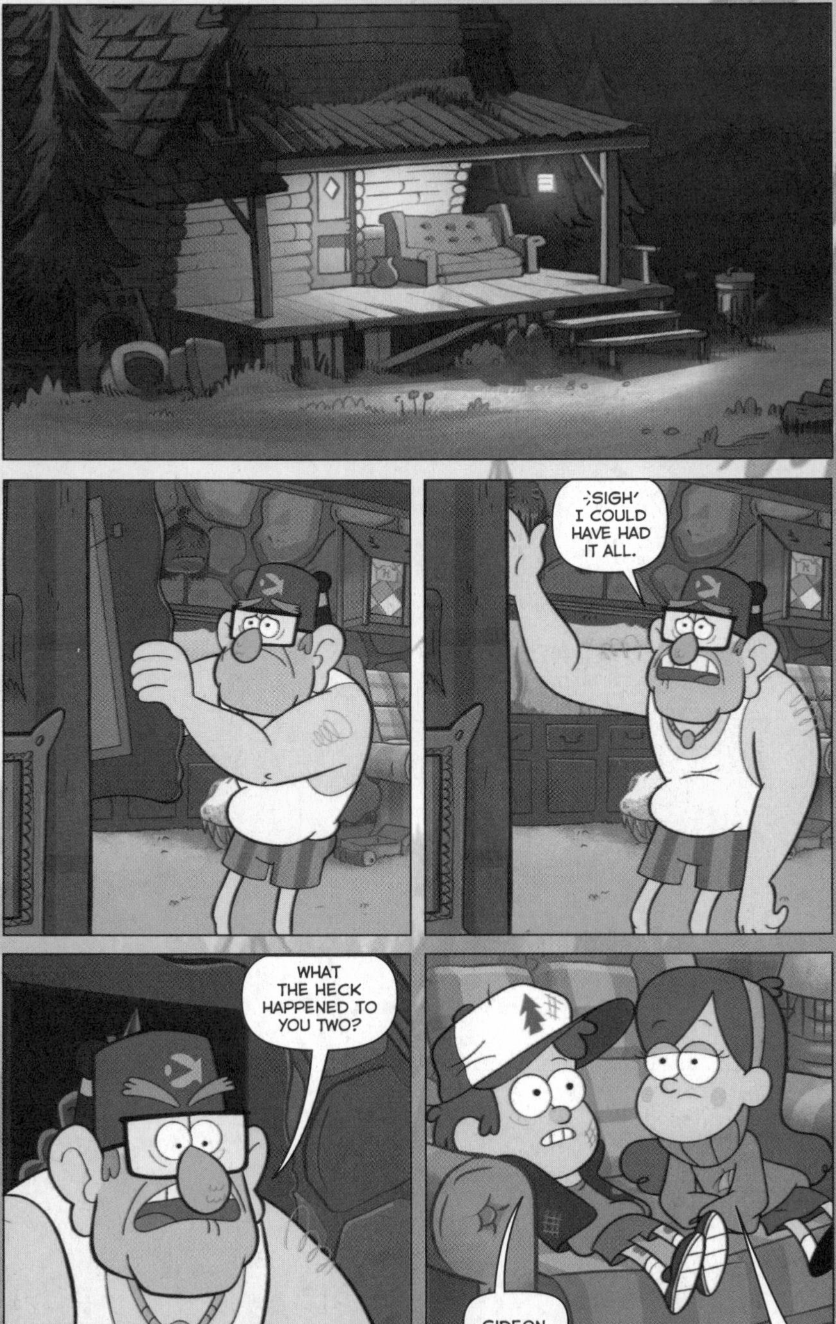
SIGH
I COULD
HAVE HAD
IT ALL.
WHAT
THE HECK
HAPPENED TO
YOU TWO?
GIDEON.
GIDEON.

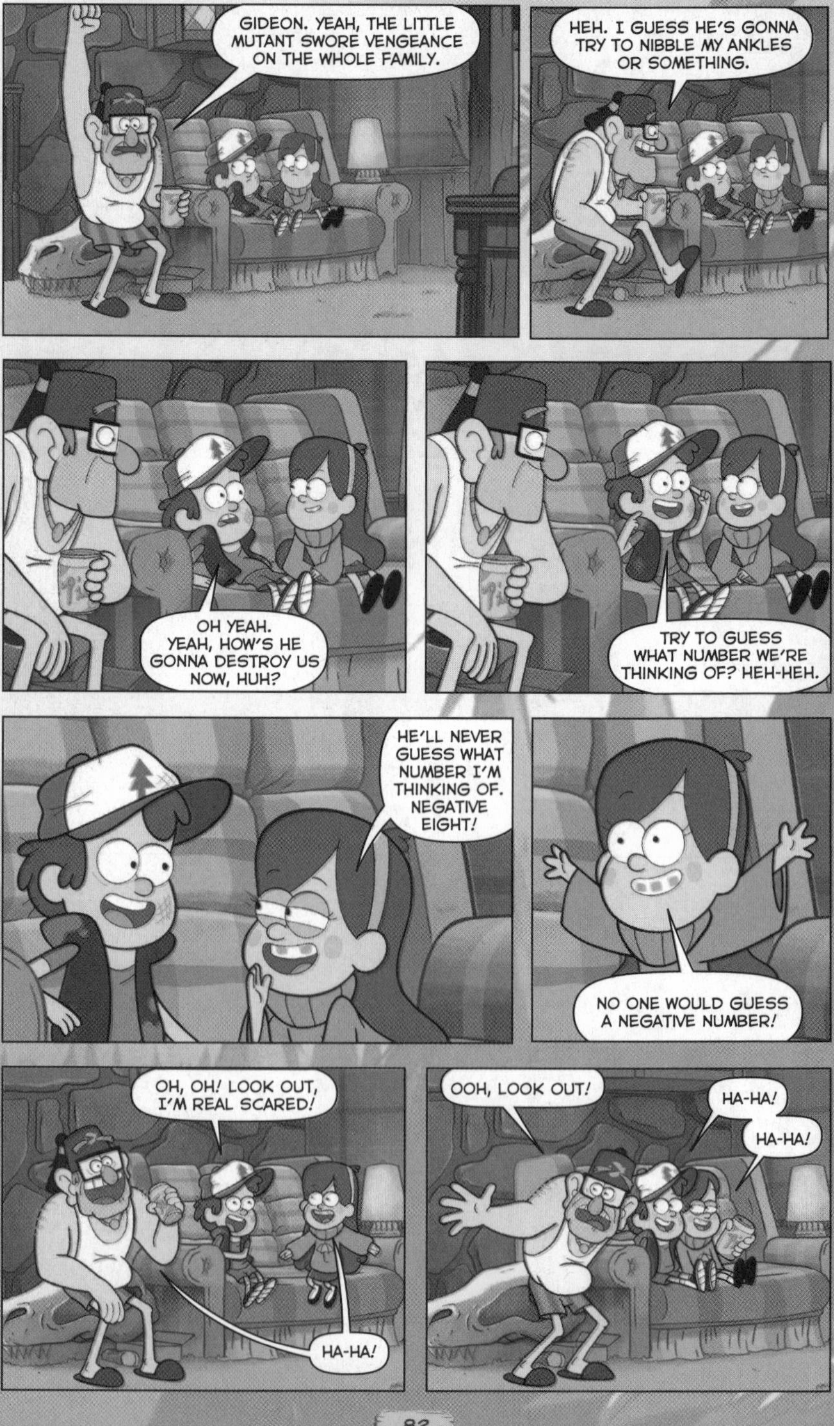
GIDEON. YEAH, THE LITTLE MUTANT SWORE VENGEANCE ON THE WHOLE FAMILY.
HEH. I GUESS HE'S GONNA TRY TO NIBBLE MY ANKLES OR SOMETHING.
OH YEAH. YEAH, HOW'S HE GONNA DESTROY US NOW, HUH?
TRY TO GUESS WHAT NUMBER WE'RE THINKING OF? HEH-HEH.
HE'LL NEVER GUESS WHAT NUMBER I'M THINKING OF. NEGATIVE EIGHT!
NO ONE WOULD GUESS A NEGATIVE NUMBER!
OH, OH! LOOK OUT, I'M REAL SCARED!
HA-HA!
OOH, LOOK OUT!
HA-HA!
HA-HA!

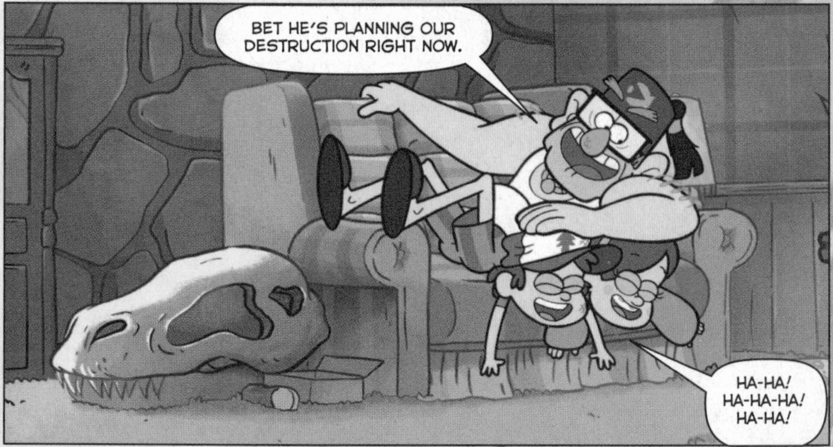
BET HE'S PLANNING OUR DESTRUCTION RIGHT NOW.
HA-HA! HA-HA-HA! HA-HA!

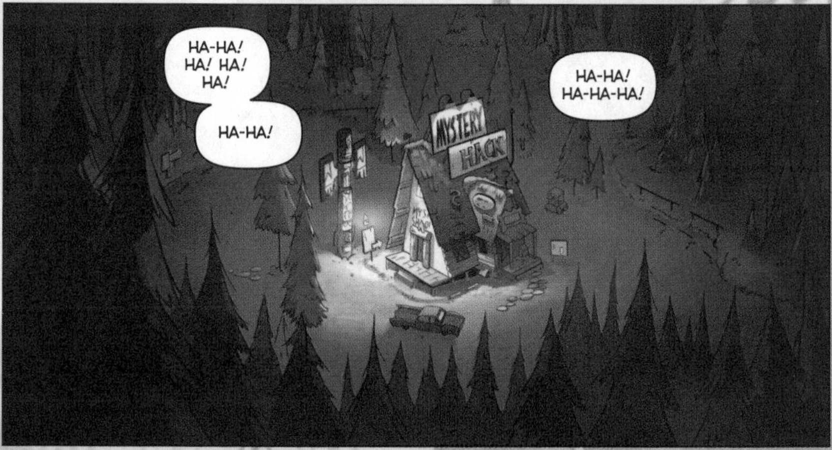
HA-HA! HA! HA! HA!
HA-HA!
HA-HA! HA-HA-HA!
MYSTERY SHACK

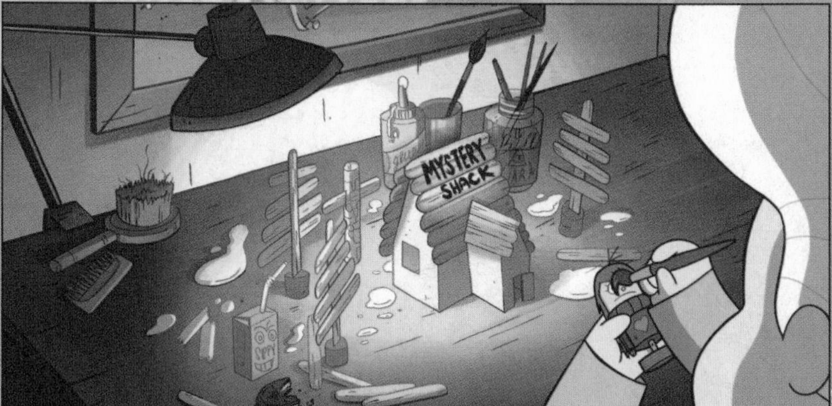
MYSTERY SHACK

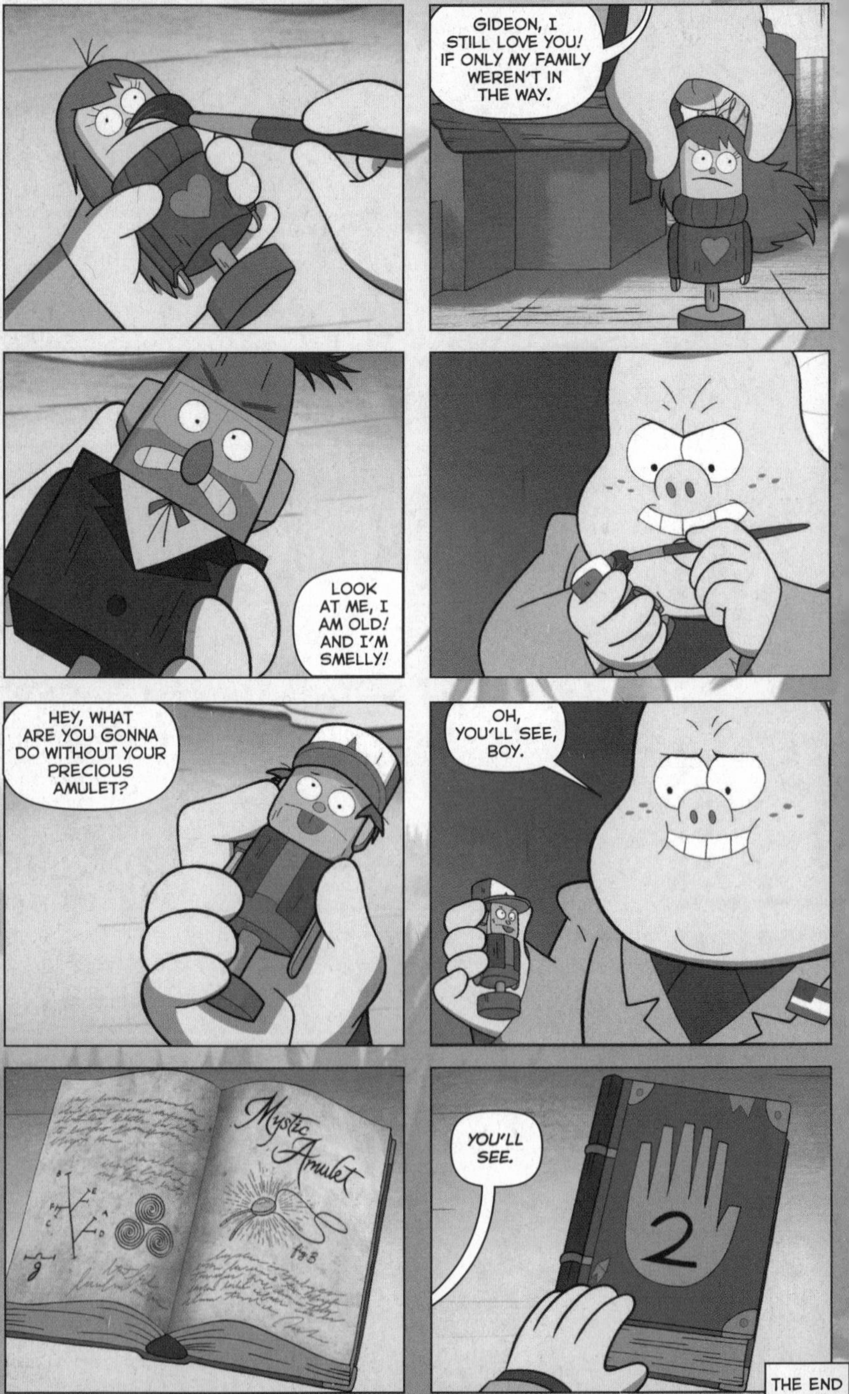
GIDEON, I STILL LOVE YOU! IF ONLY MY FAMILY WEREN'T IN THE WAY.
LOOK AT ME, I AM OLD! AND I'M SMELLY!
HEY, WHAT ARE YOU GONNA DO WITHOUT YOUR PRECIOUS AMULET?
OH, YOU'LL SEE, BOY.
Mystic Amulet
YOU'LL SEE.
2
THE END

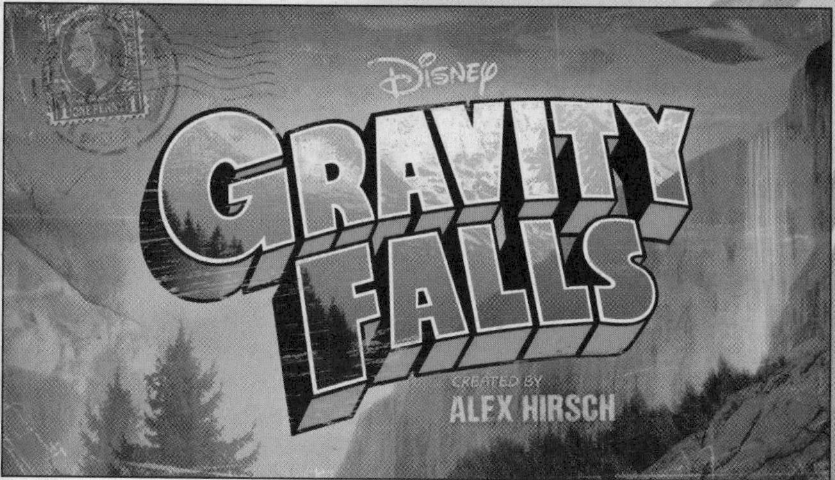
DISNEY
GRAVITY FALLS
CREATED BY
ALEX HIRSCH

THE INCONVENIENCING
EPISODE 5

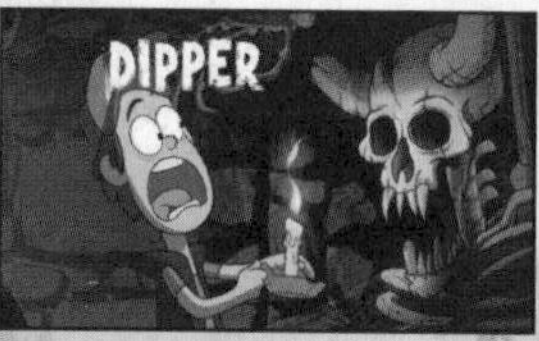
DIPPER

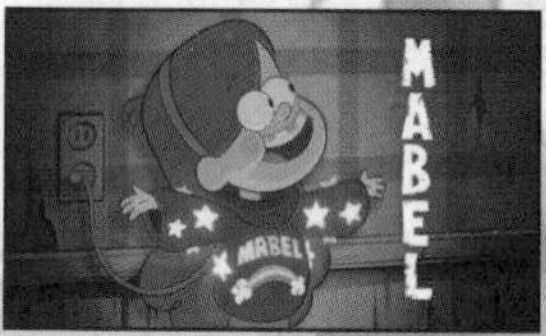
MABEL
MABEL

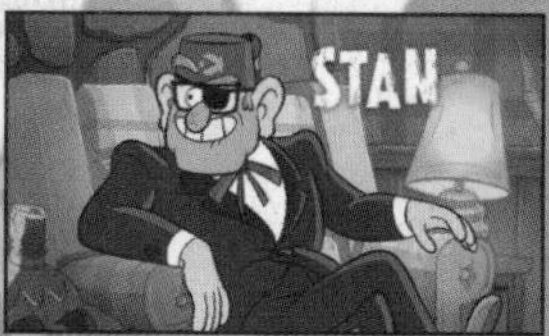
STAN

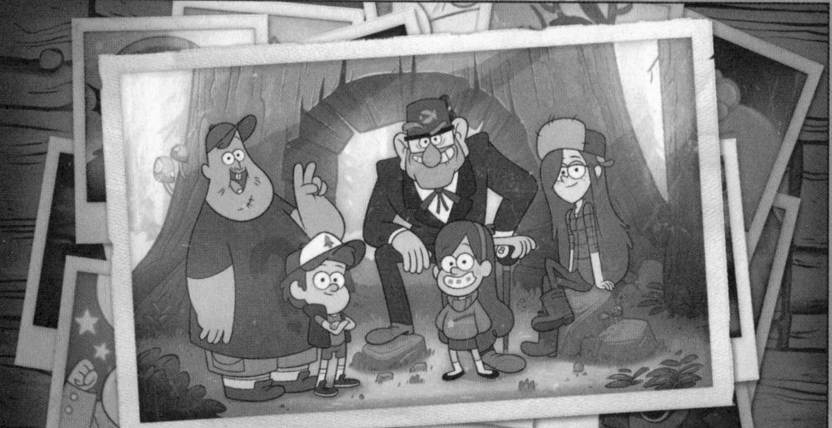

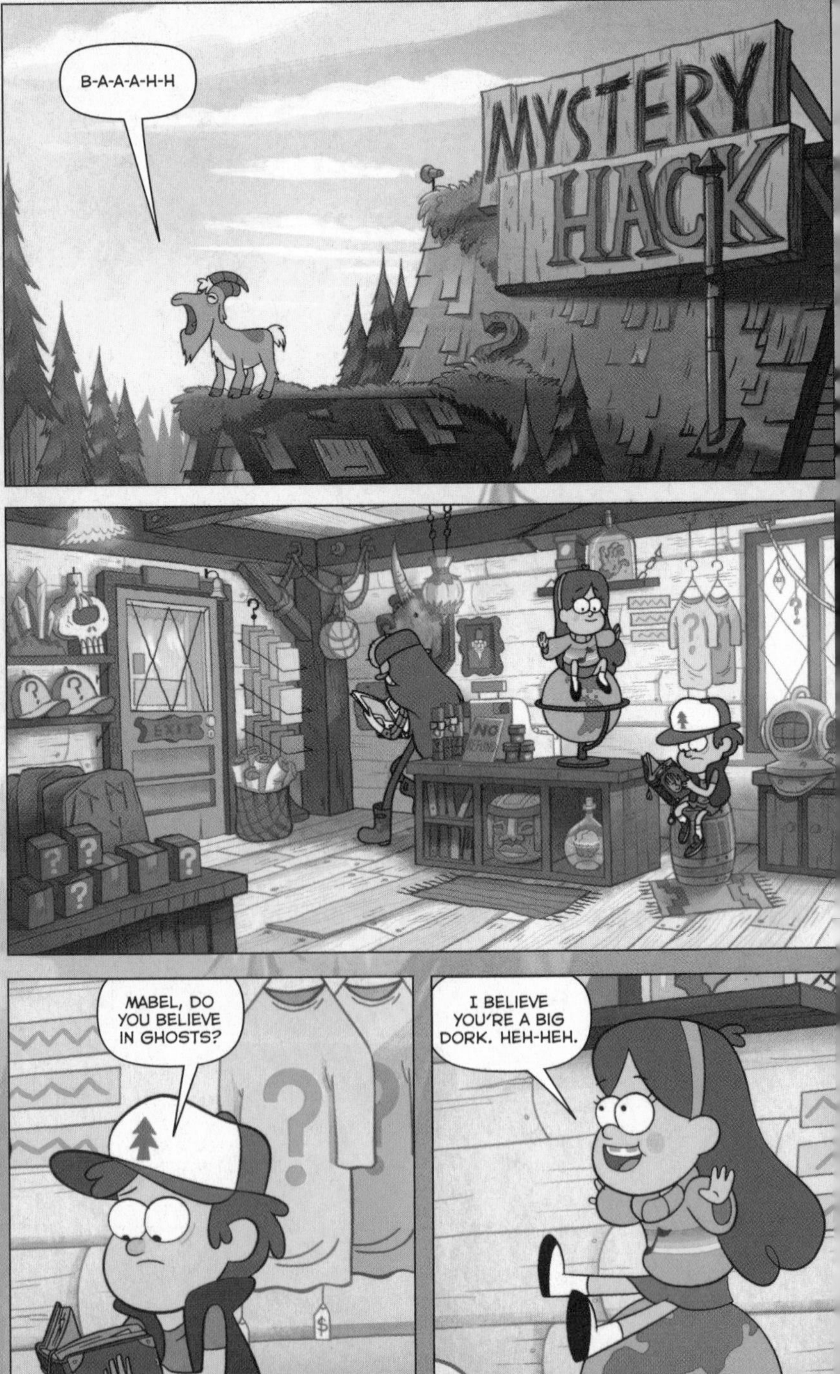
B-A-A-A-H-H
MYSTERY HACK
EXIT
NO
MABEL, DO YOU BELIEVE IN GHOSTS?
I BELIEVE YOU'RE A BIG DORK. HEH-HEH.

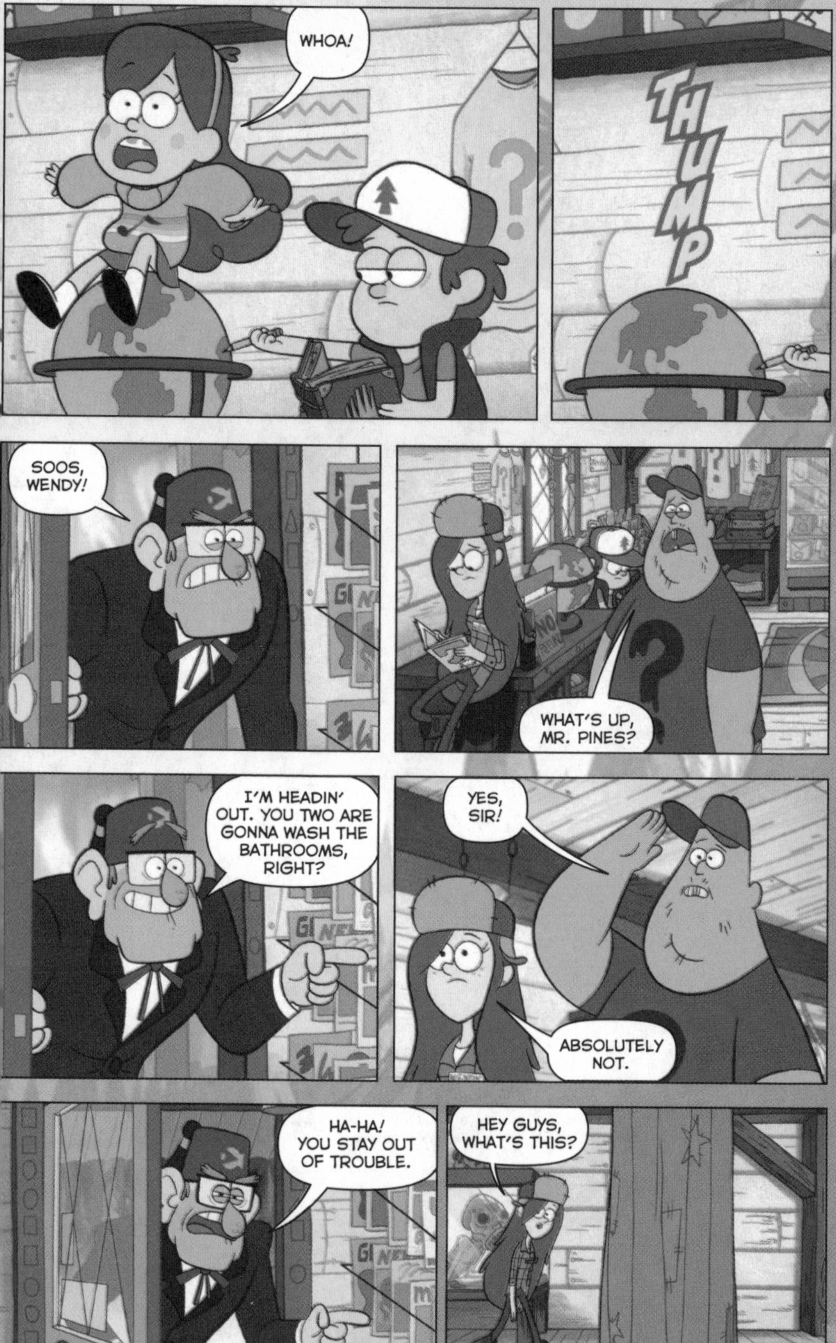
WHOA!
THUMP
SOOS, WENDY!
WHAT'S UP, MR. PINES?
I'M HEADIN' OUT. YOU TWO ARE GONNA WASH THE BATHROOMS, RIGHT?
YES, SIR!
ABSOLUTELY NOT.
HA-HA! YOU STAY OUT OF TROUBLE.
HEY GUYS, WHAT'S THIS?

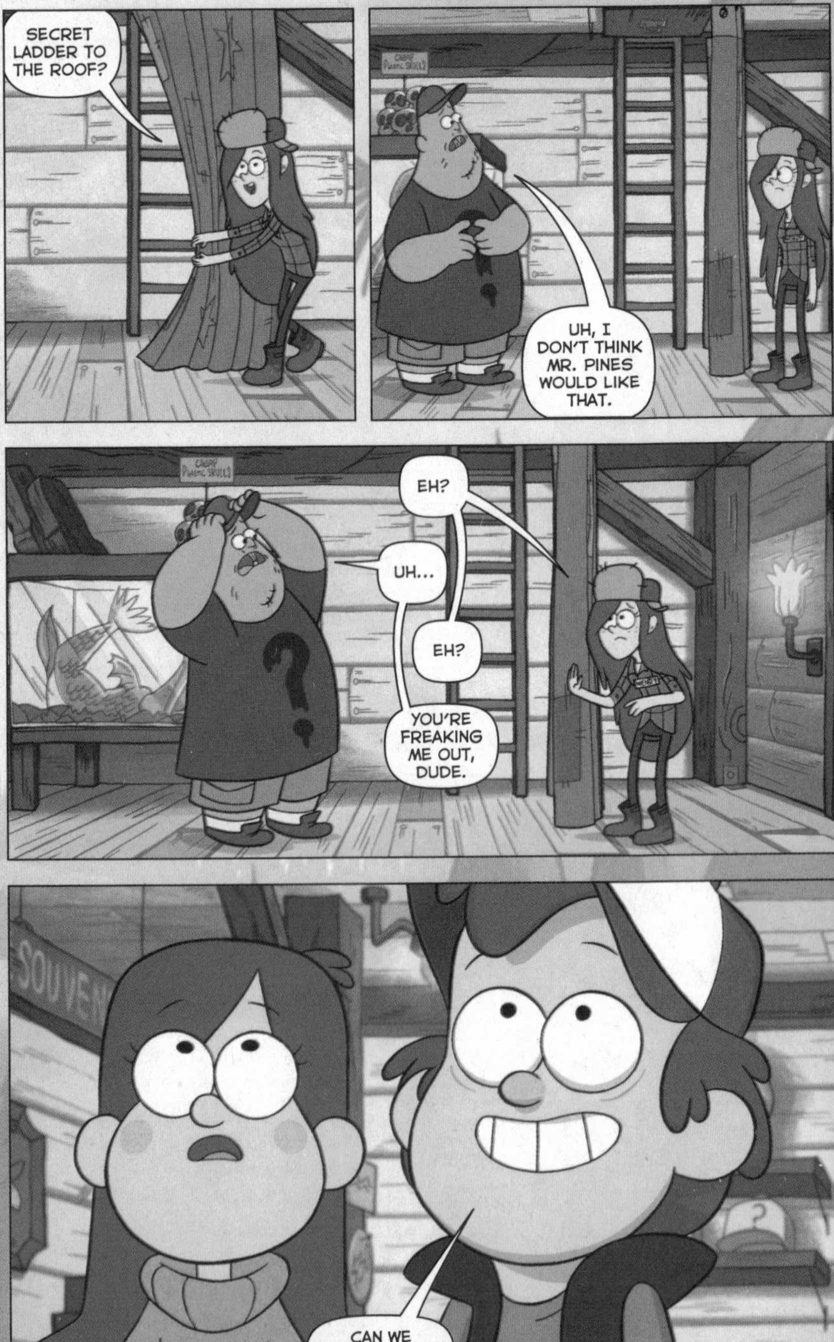
SECRET LADDER TO THE ROOF?
UH, I DON'T THINK MR. PINES WOULD LIKE THAT.
EH?
UH...
EH?
YOU'RE FREAKING ME OUT, DUDE.
CAN WE ACTUALLY GO UP THERE?

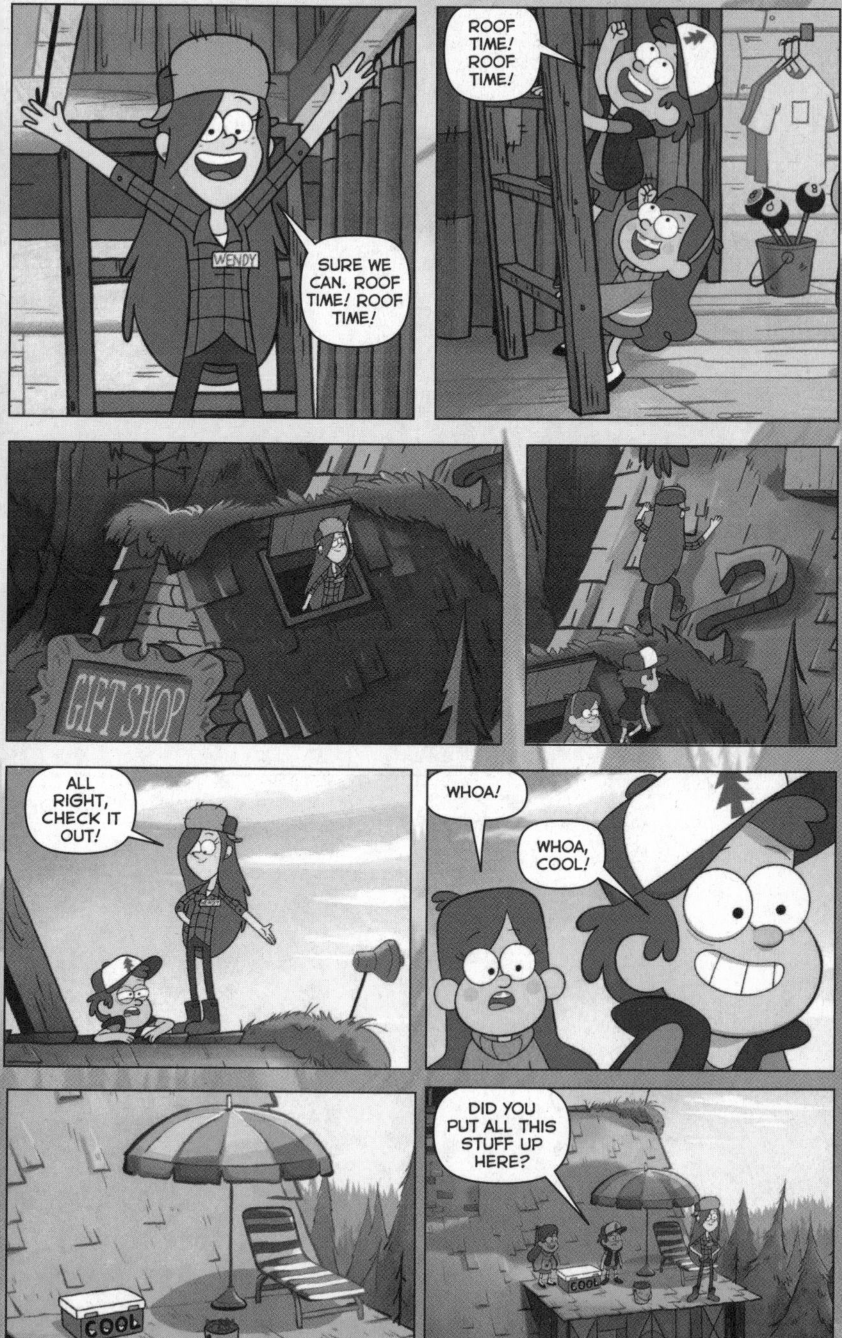
SURE WE CAN. ROOF TIME! ROOF TIME!
WENDY
ROOF TIME! ROOF TIME!
GIFT SHOP
ALL RIGHT, CHECK IT OUT!
WHOA!
WHOA, COOL!
COOL
DID YOU PUT ALL THIS STUFF UP HERE?

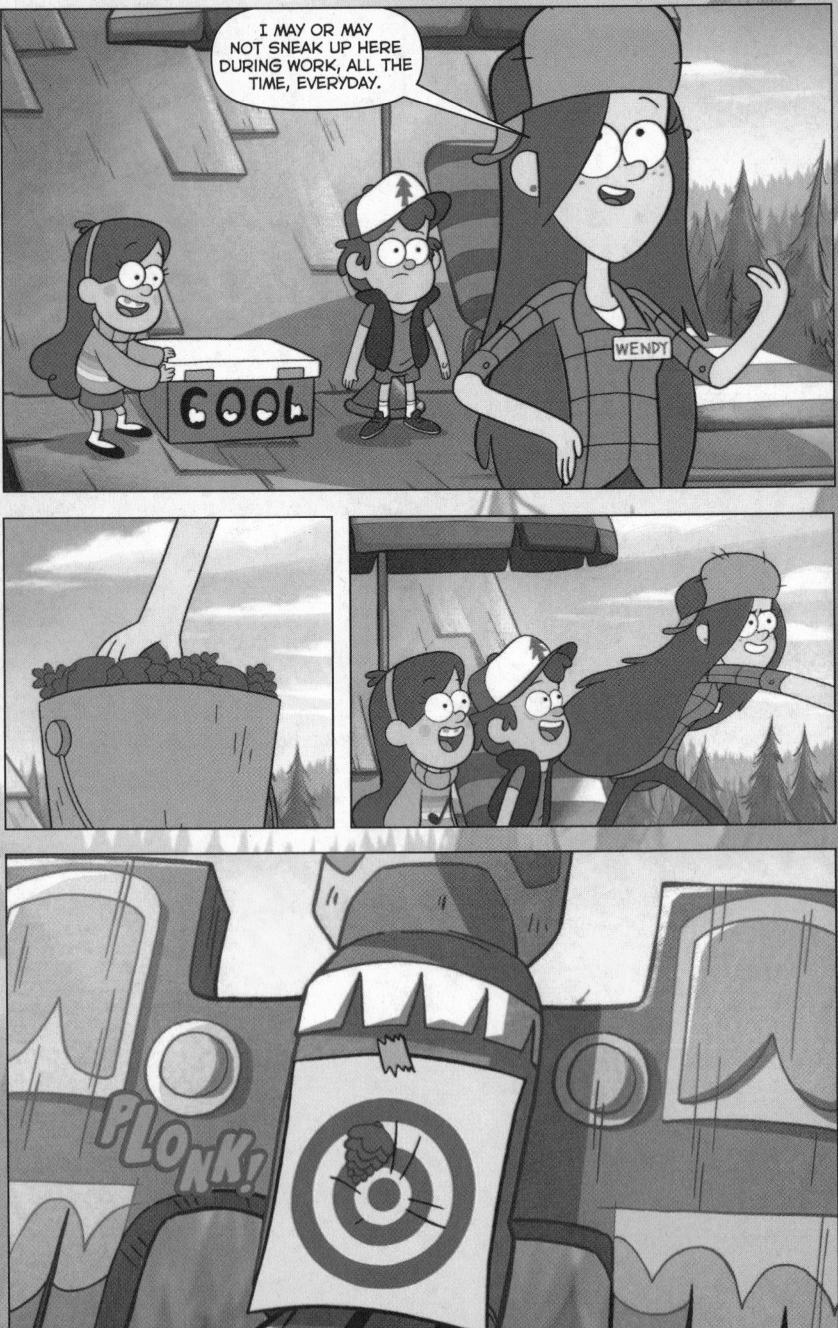
I MAY OR MAY NOT SNEAK UP HERE DURING WORK, ALL THE TIME, EVERYDAY.
WENDY
COOL
PLONK!

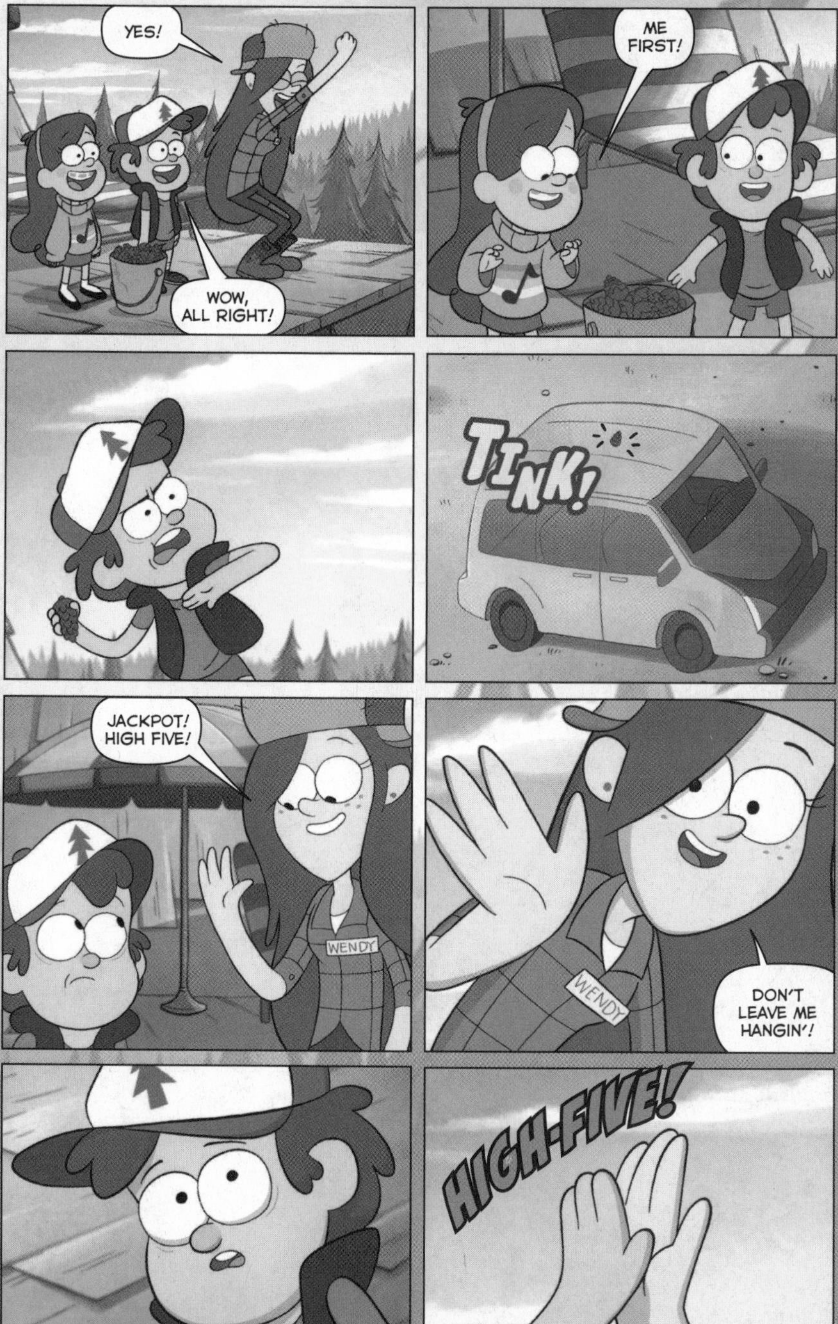
YES!
WOW, ALL RIGHT!
ME FIRST!
TINK!
JACKPOT! HIGH FIVE!
WENDY
WENDY
DON'T LEAVE ME HANGIN'!
HIGH-FIVE!

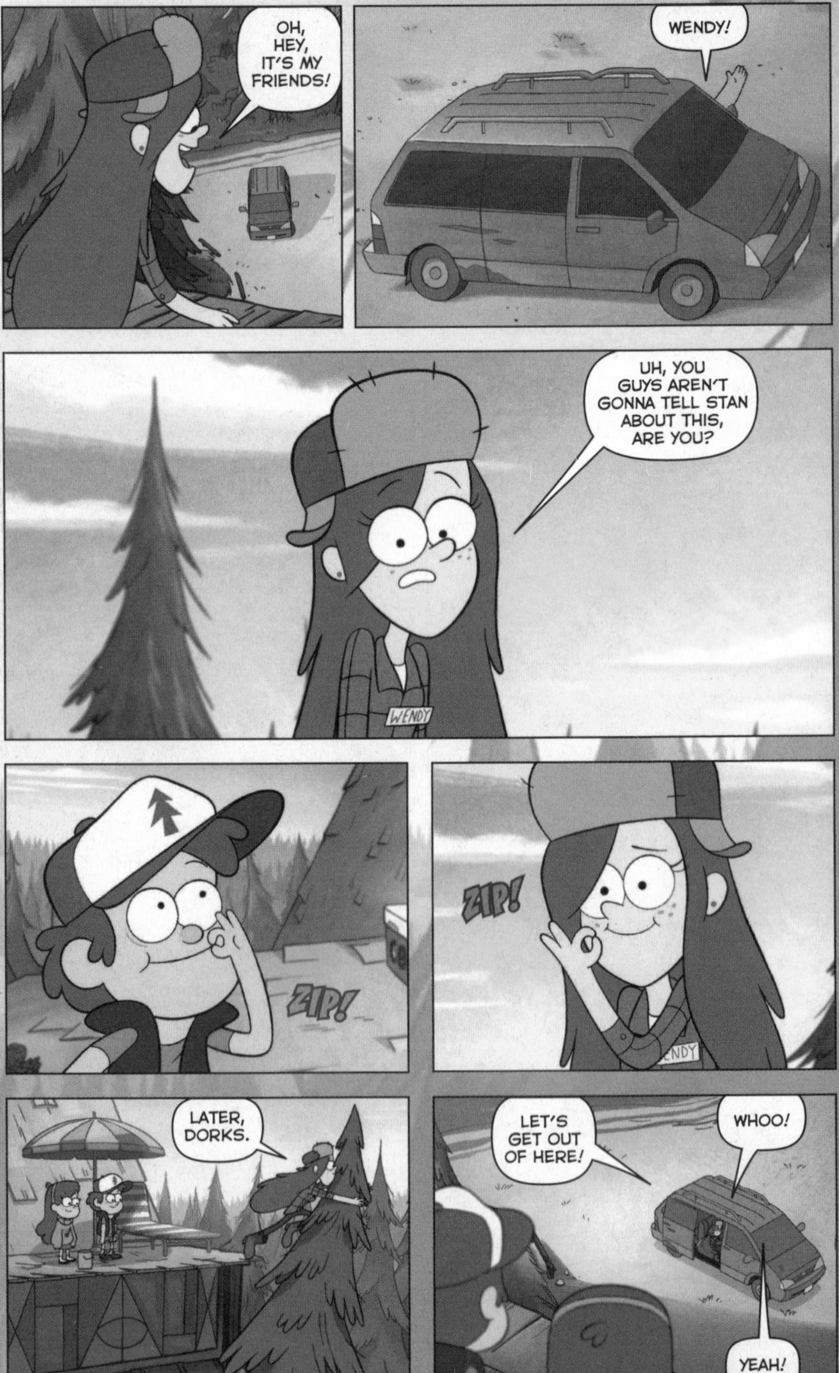
OH, HEY, IT'S MY FRIENDS!
WENDY!
UH, YOU GUYS AREN'T GONNA TELL STAN ABOUT THIS, ARE YOU?
WENDY
ZIP!
ZIP!
LATER, DORKS.
LET'S GET OUT OF HERE!
WHOO!
YEAH!

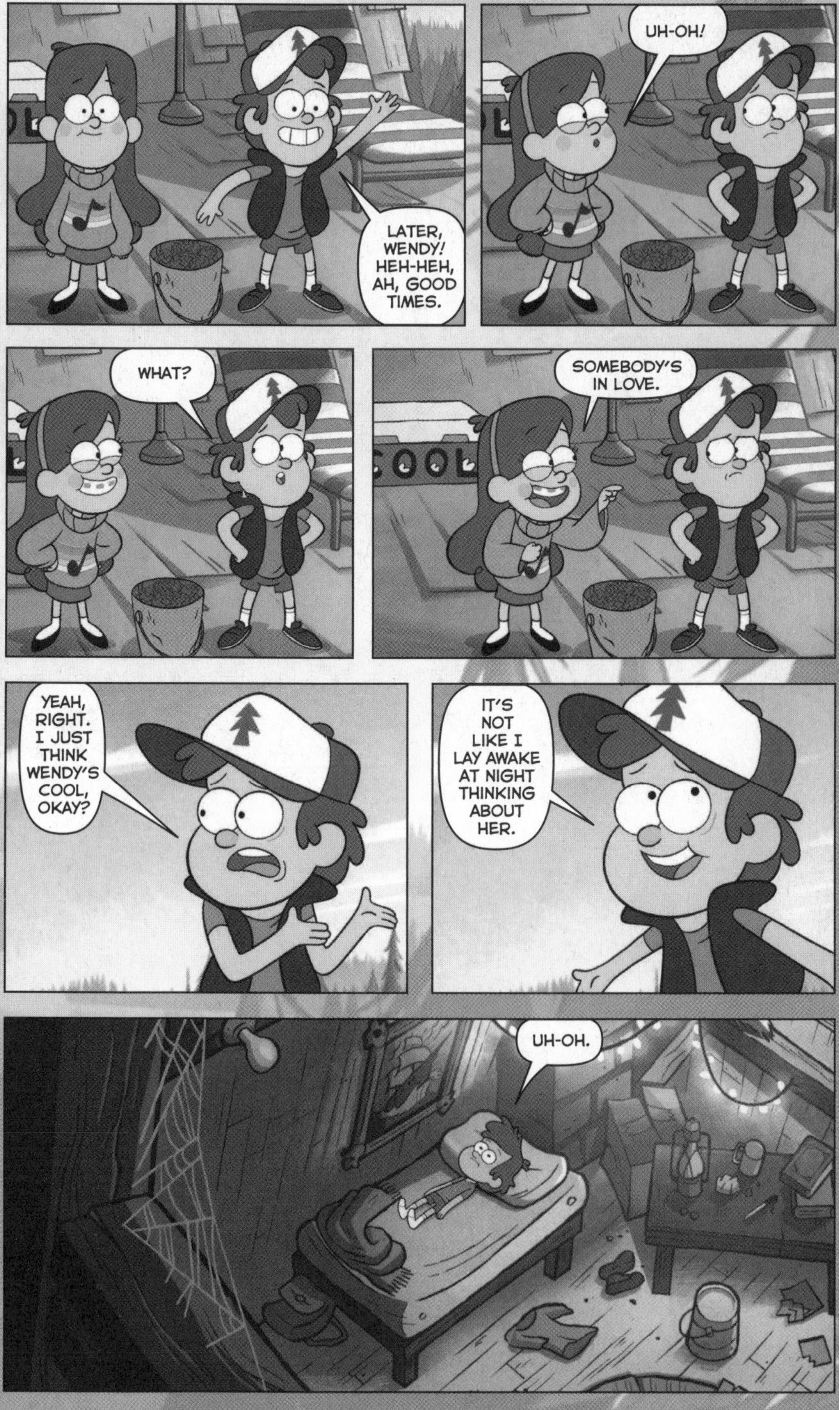
LATER, WENDY! HEH-HEH, AH, GOOD TIMES.
UH-OH!
WHAT?
SOMEBODY'S IN LOVE.
YEAH, RIGHT. I JUST THINK WENDY'S COOL, OKAY?
IT'S NOT LIKE I LAY AWAKE AT NIGHT THINKING ABOUT HER.
UH-OH.

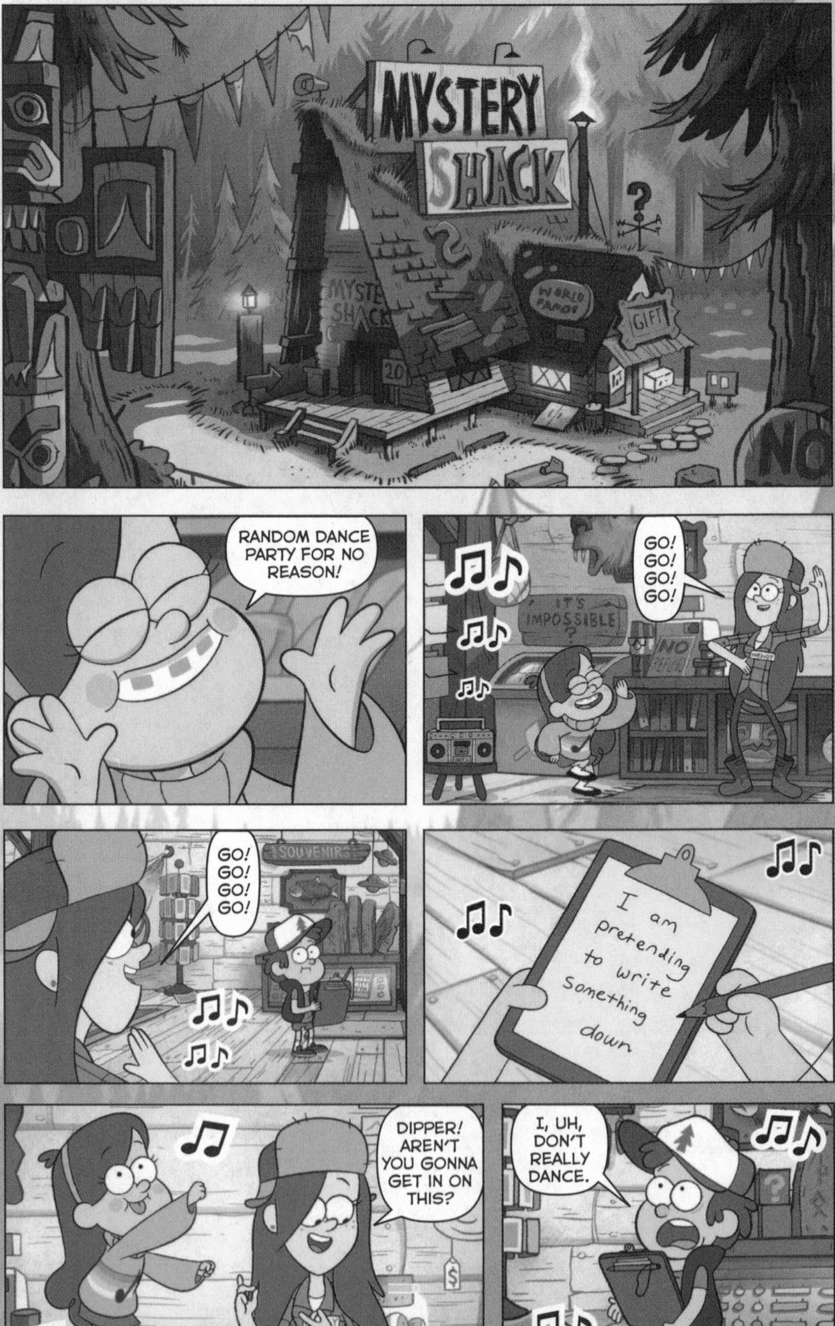
MYSTERY SHACK
RANDOM DANCE PARTY FOR NO REASON!
GO! GO! GO! GO!
IT'S IMPOSSIBLE?
GO! GO! GO! GO!
SOUVENIRS
I am pretending to write something down
DIPPER! AREN'T YOU GONNA GET IN ON THIS?
I, UH, DON'T REALLY DANCE.

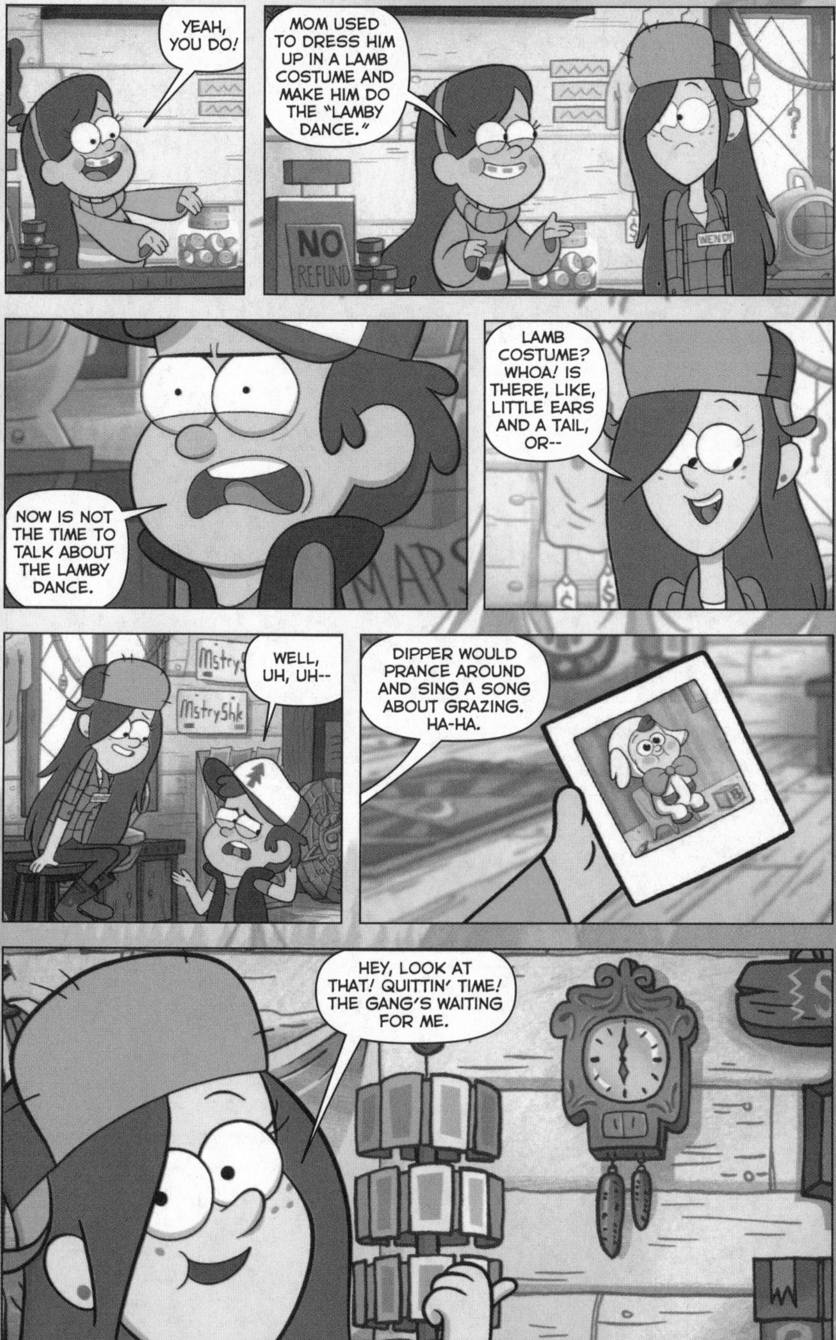
YEAH, YOU DO!
MOM USED TO DRESS HIM UP IN A LAMB COSTUME AND MAKE HIM DO THE "LAMBY DANCE."
NO REFUND
WENDY
NOW IS NOT THE TIME TO TALK ABOUT THE LAMBY DANCE.
MAPS
LAMB COSTUME? WHOA! IS THERE, LIKE, LITTLE EARS AND A TAIL, OR--
MstryShk
WELL, UH, UH--
DIPPER WOULD PRANCE AROUND AND SING A SONG ABOUT GRAZING. HA-HA.
HEY, LOOK AT THAT! QUITTIN' TIME! THE GANG'S WAITING FOR ME.

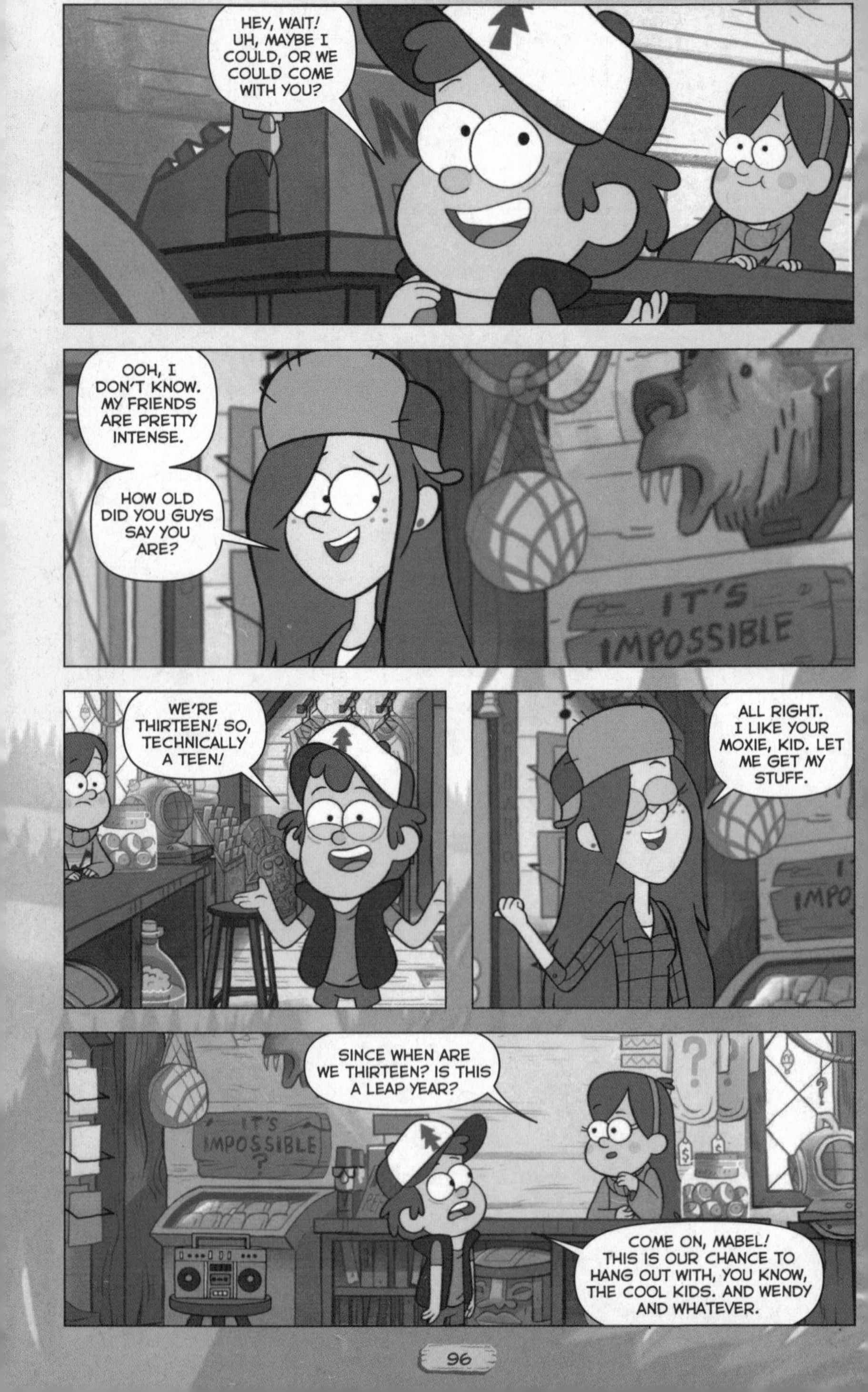
HEY, WAIT! UH, MAYBE I COULD, OR WE COULD COME WITH YOU?
OOH, I DON'T KNOW. MY FRIENDS ARE PRETTY INTENSE.
HOW OLD DID YOU GUYS SAY YOU ARE?
IT'S IMPOSSIBLE
WE'RE THIRTEEN! SO, TECHNICALLY A TEEN!
ALL RIGHT. I LIKE YOUR MOXIE, KID. LET ME GET MY STUFF.
SINCE WHEN ARE WE THIRTEEN? IS THIS A LEAP YEAR?
IT'S IMPOSSIBLE ?
COME ON, MABEL! THIS IS OUR CHANCE TO HANG OUT WITH, YOU KNOW, THE COOL KIDS. AND WENDY AND WHATEVER.

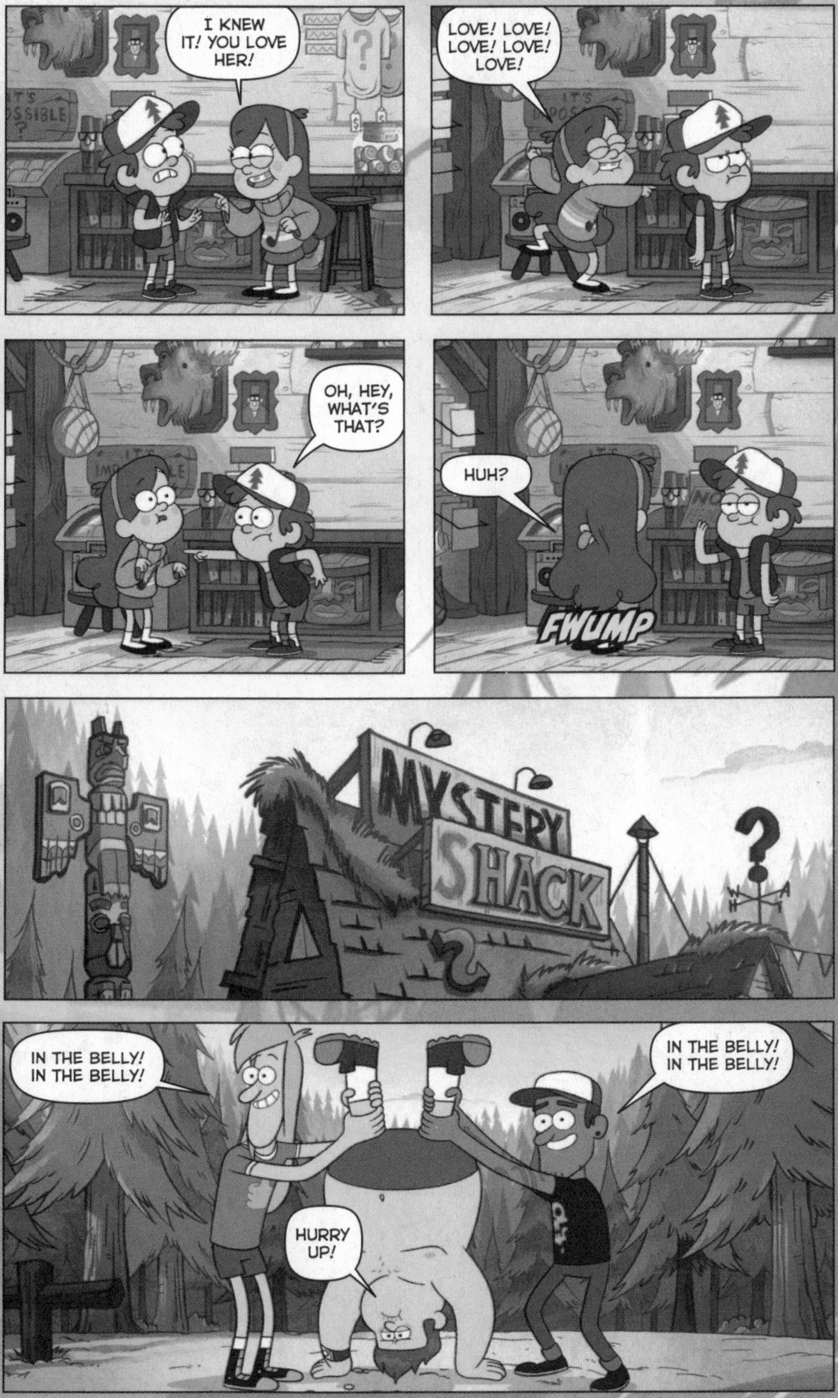

I KNEW IT! YOU LOVE HER!
LOVE! LOVE! LOVE! LOVE! LOVE!
OH, HEY, WHAT'S THAT?
HUH?
FWUMP
MYSTERY SHACK
IN THE BELLY! IN THE BELLY!
IN THE BELLY! IN THE BELLY!
HURRY UP!

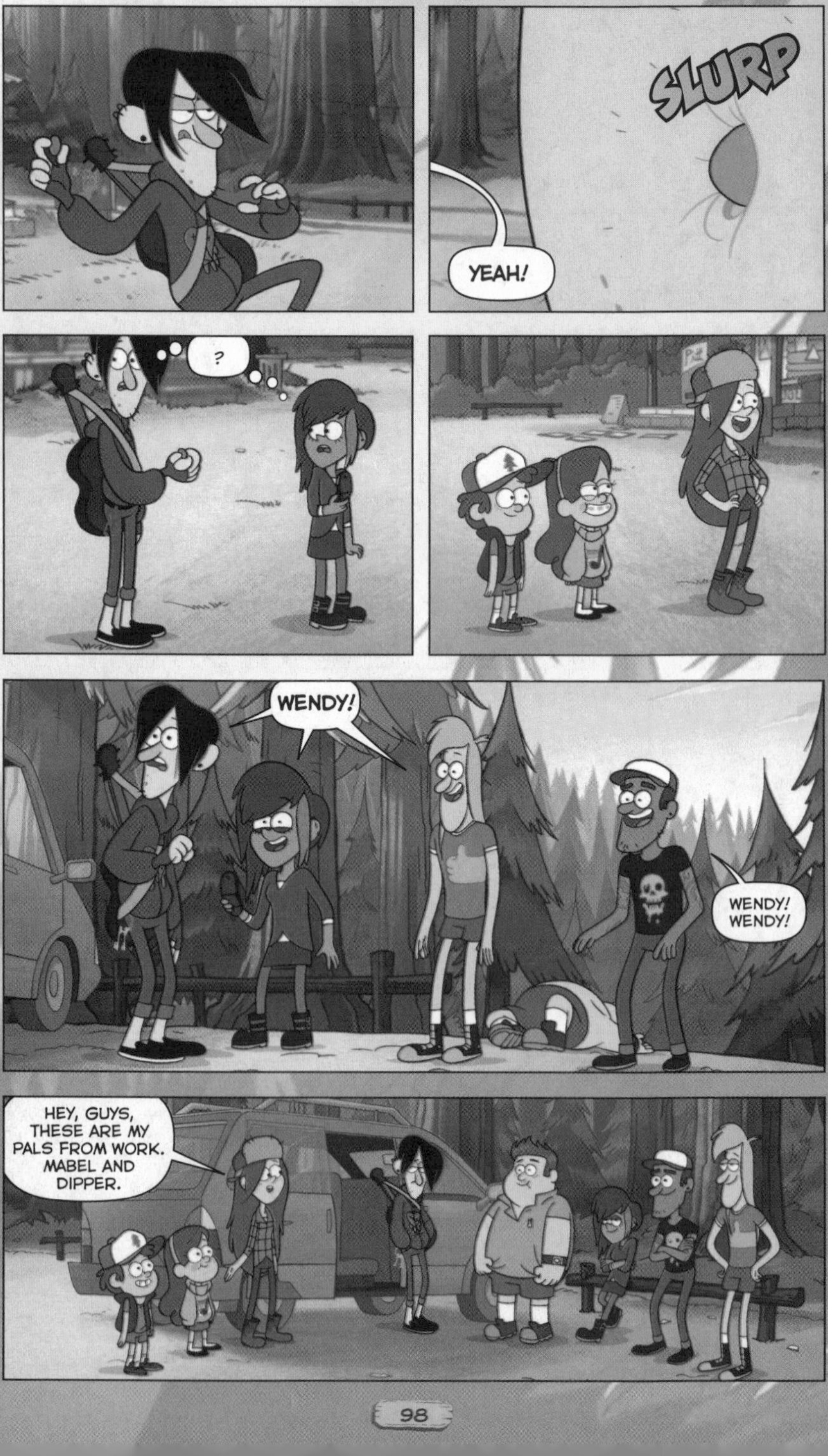
SLURP
YEAH!
?
WENDY!
WENDY!
WENDY!
HEY, GUYS, THESE ARE MY PALS FROM WORK. MABEL AND DIPPER.

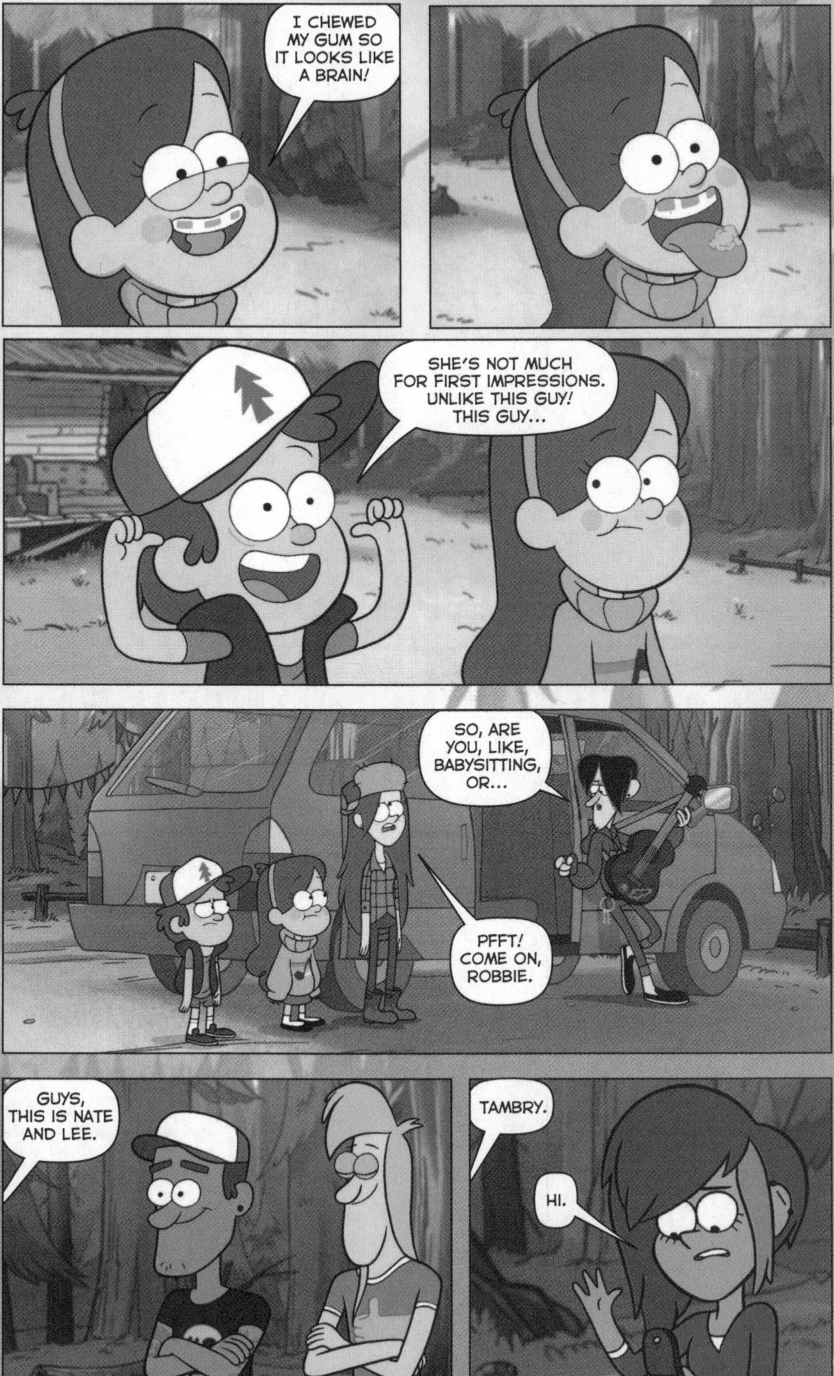
I CHEWED MY GUM SO IT LOOKS LIKE A BRAIN!
SHE'S NOT MUCH FOR FIRST IMPRESSIONS. UNLIKE THIS GUY! THIS GUY...
SO, ARE YOU, LIKE, BABYSITTING, OR...
PFFT! COME ON, ROBBIE.
GUYS, THIS IS NATE AND LEE.
TAMBRY.
HI.

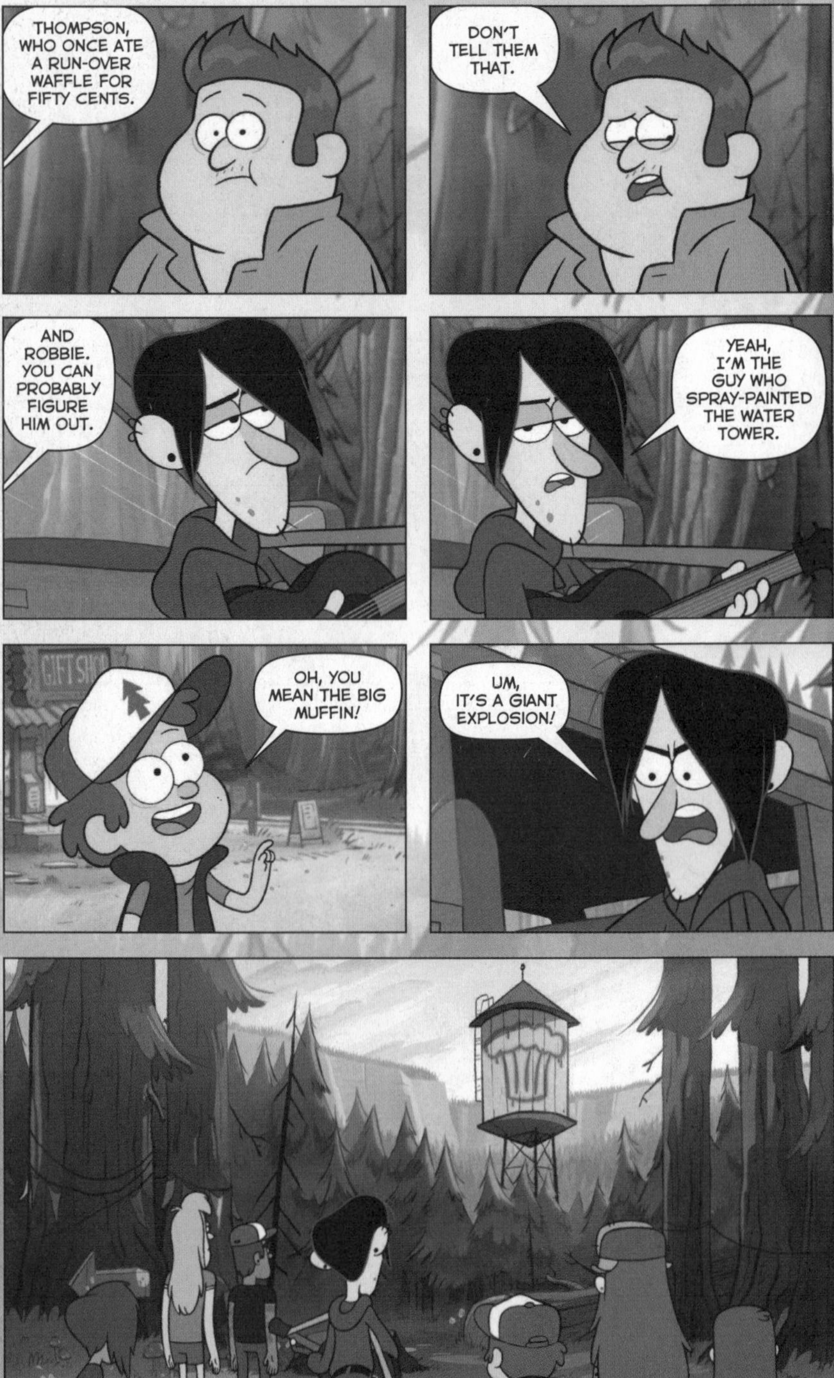
THOMPSON, WHO ONCE ATE A RUN-OVER WAFFLE FOR FIFTY CENTS.
DON'T TELL THEM THAT.
AND ROBBIE. YOU CAN PROBABLY FIGURE HIM OUT.
YEAH, I'M THE GUY WHO SPRAY-PAINTED THE WATER TOWER.
OH, YOU MEAN THE BIG MUFFIN!
UM, IT'S A GIANT EXPLOSION!

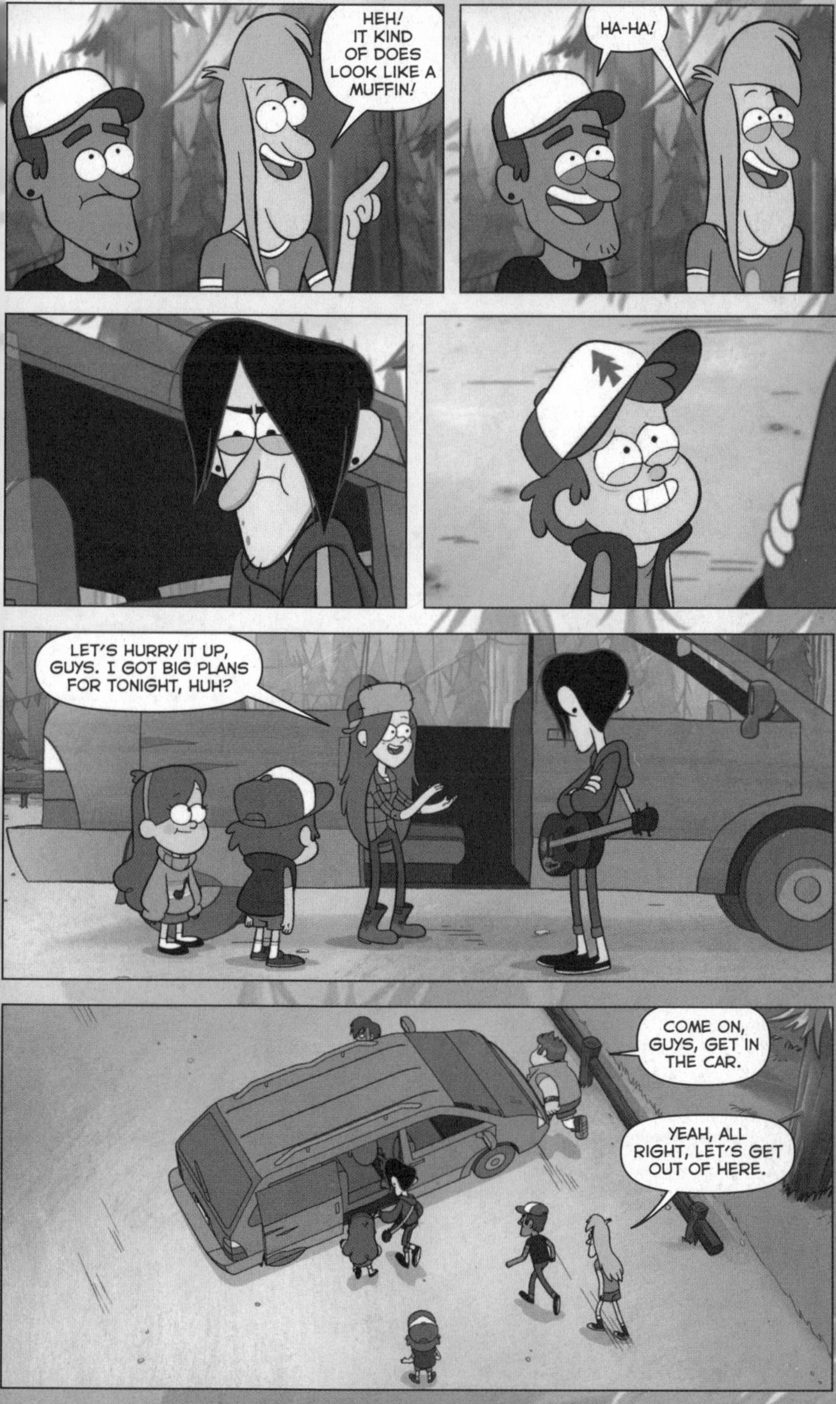
HEH! IT KIND OF DOES LOOK LIKE A MUFFIN!
HA-HA!
LET'S HURRY IT UP, GUYS. I GOT BIG PLANS FOR TONIGHT, HUH?
COME ON, GUYS, GET IN THE CAR.
YEAH, ALL RIGHT, LET'S GET OUT OF HERE.

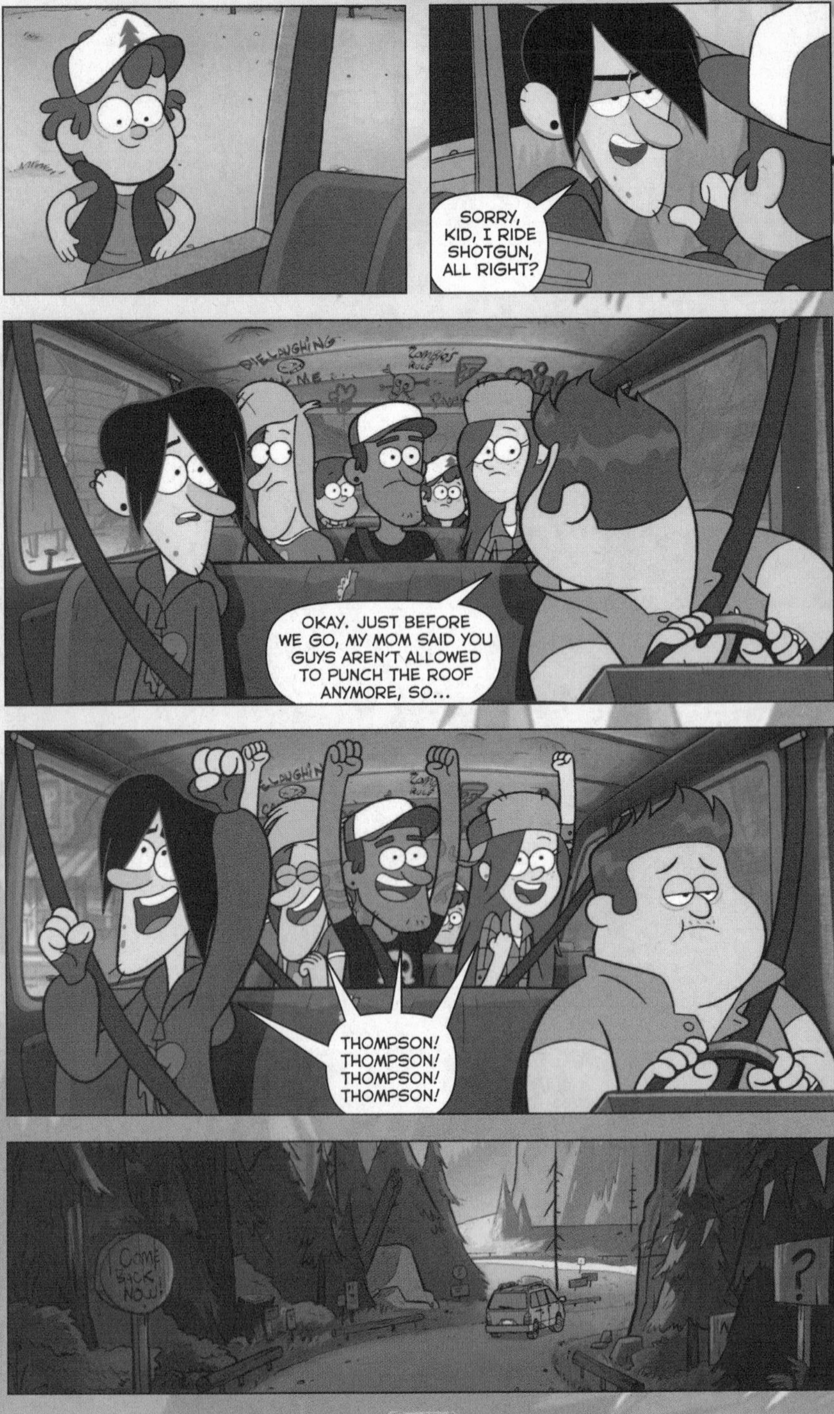
SORRY, KID, I RIDE SHOTGUN, ALL RIGHT?
OKAY. JUST BEFORE WE GO, MY MOM SAID YOU GUYS AREN'T ALLOWED TO PUNCH THE ROOF ANYMORE, SO...
THOMPSON! THOMPSON! THOMPSON! THOMPSON!

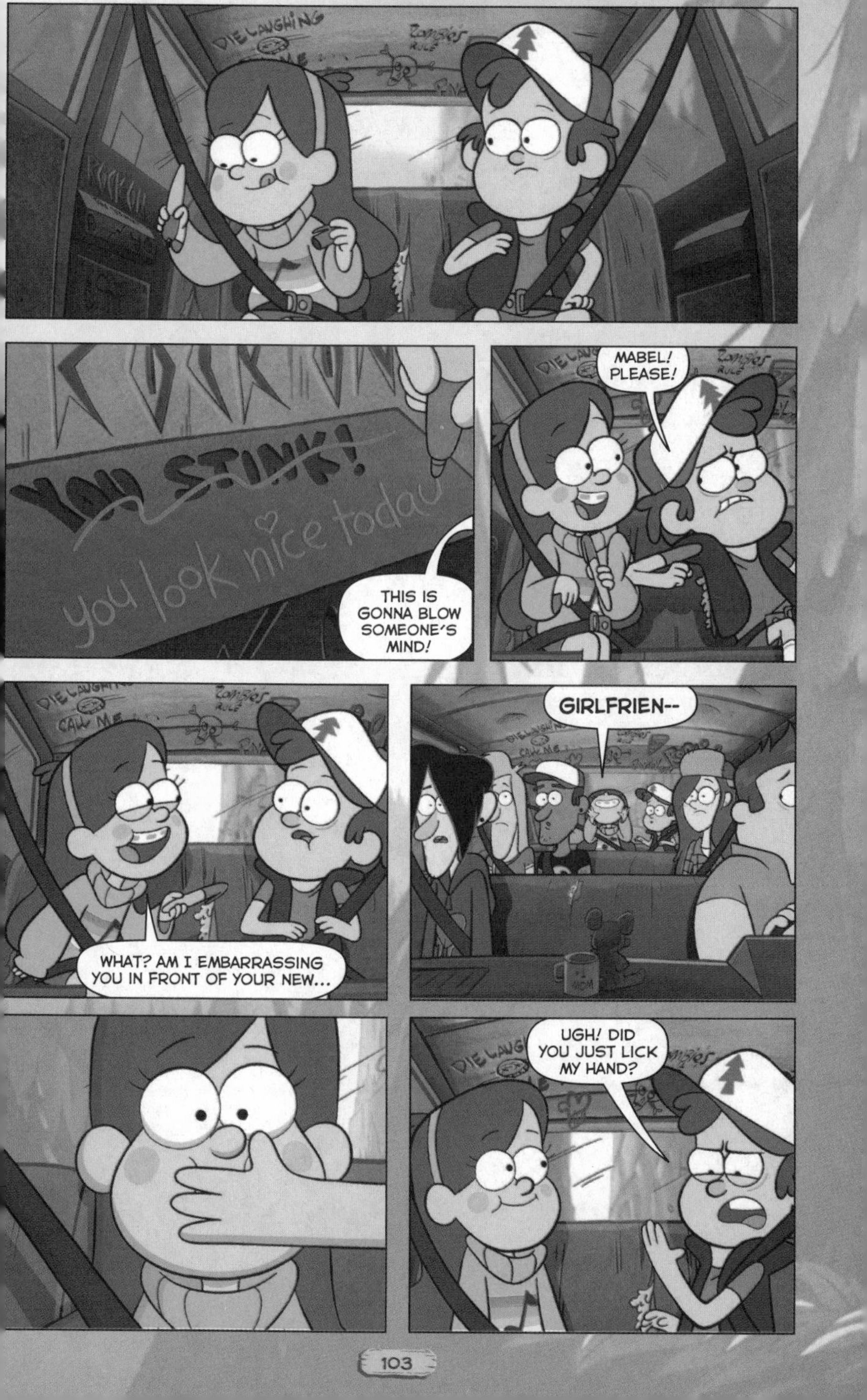
DIE LAUGHING
ZOMBIES RULE
YOU STINK!
you look nice today
THIS IS GONNA BLOW SOMEONE'S MIND!
MABEL! PLEASE!
WHAT? AM I EMBARRASSING YOU IN FRONT OF YOUR NEW...
GIRLFRIEN--
UGH! DID YOU JUST LICK MY HAND?

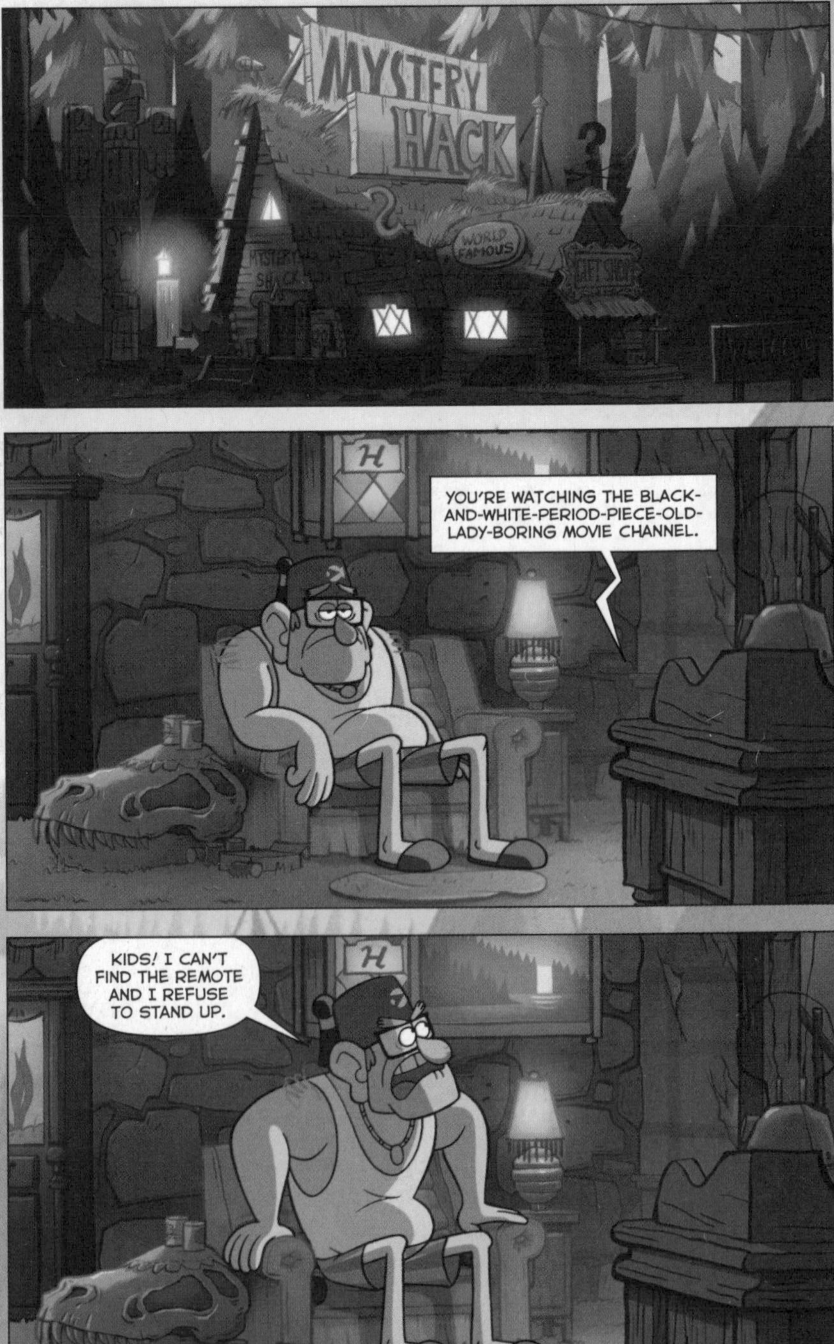
MYSTERY
HACK
WORLD FAMOUS
YOU'RE WATCHING THE BLACK-AND-WHITE-PERIOD-PIECE-OLD-LADY-BORING MOVIE CHANNEL.
KIDS! I CAN'T FIND THE REMOTE AND I REFUSE TO STAND UP.

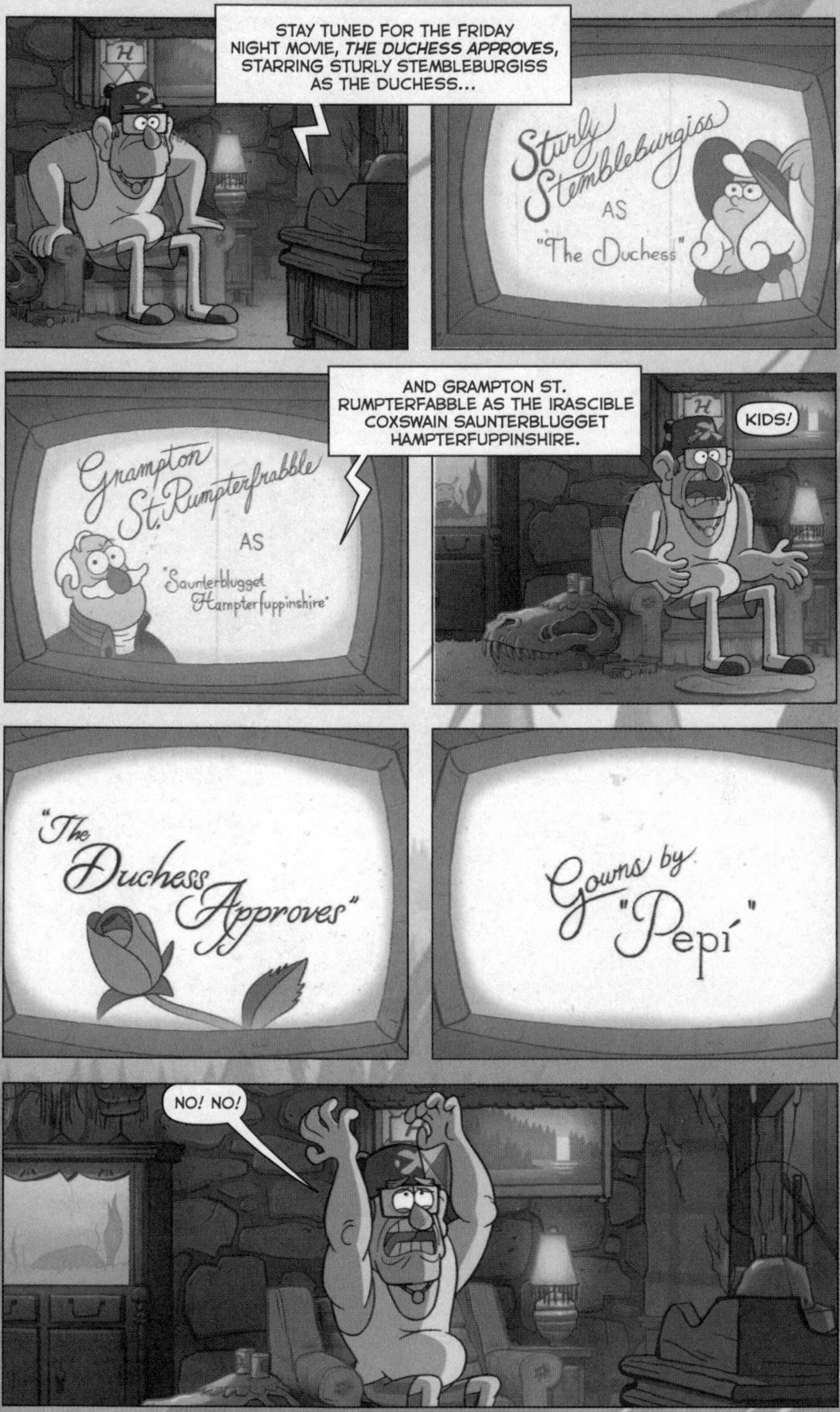
STAY TUNED FOR THE FRIDAY NIGHT MOVIE, *THE DUCHESS APPROVES*, STARRING STURLY STEMBLEBURGISS AS THE DUCHESS...
Sturly Stembleburgiss AS "The Duchess"
AND GRAMPTON ST. RUMPTERFABBLE AS THE IRASCIBLE COXSWAIN SAUNTERBLUGGET HAMPTERFUPPINSHIRE.
Grampton St. Rumpterfrabble AS "Saunterblugget Hampterfuppinshire"
KIDS!
"The Duchess Approves"
Gowns by "Pepí"
NO! NO!

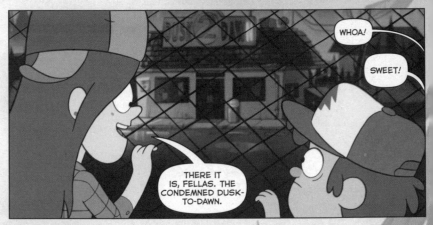

WHOA!

SWEET!

THERE IT IS, FELLAS. THE CONDEMNED DUSK-TO-DAWN.

NEAT-O!

WHY DID THEY SHUT IT DOWN? IT'S LIKE A HEALTH CODE VIOLATION, OR...

TRY MURDER!

SOME FOLKS DIED IN THERE. THE PLACE'S BEEN HAUNTED EVER SINCE.

THIS TOWN HAS SUCH A COLORFUL HISTORY!

WHAT? ARE YOU GUYS S-SERIOUS?

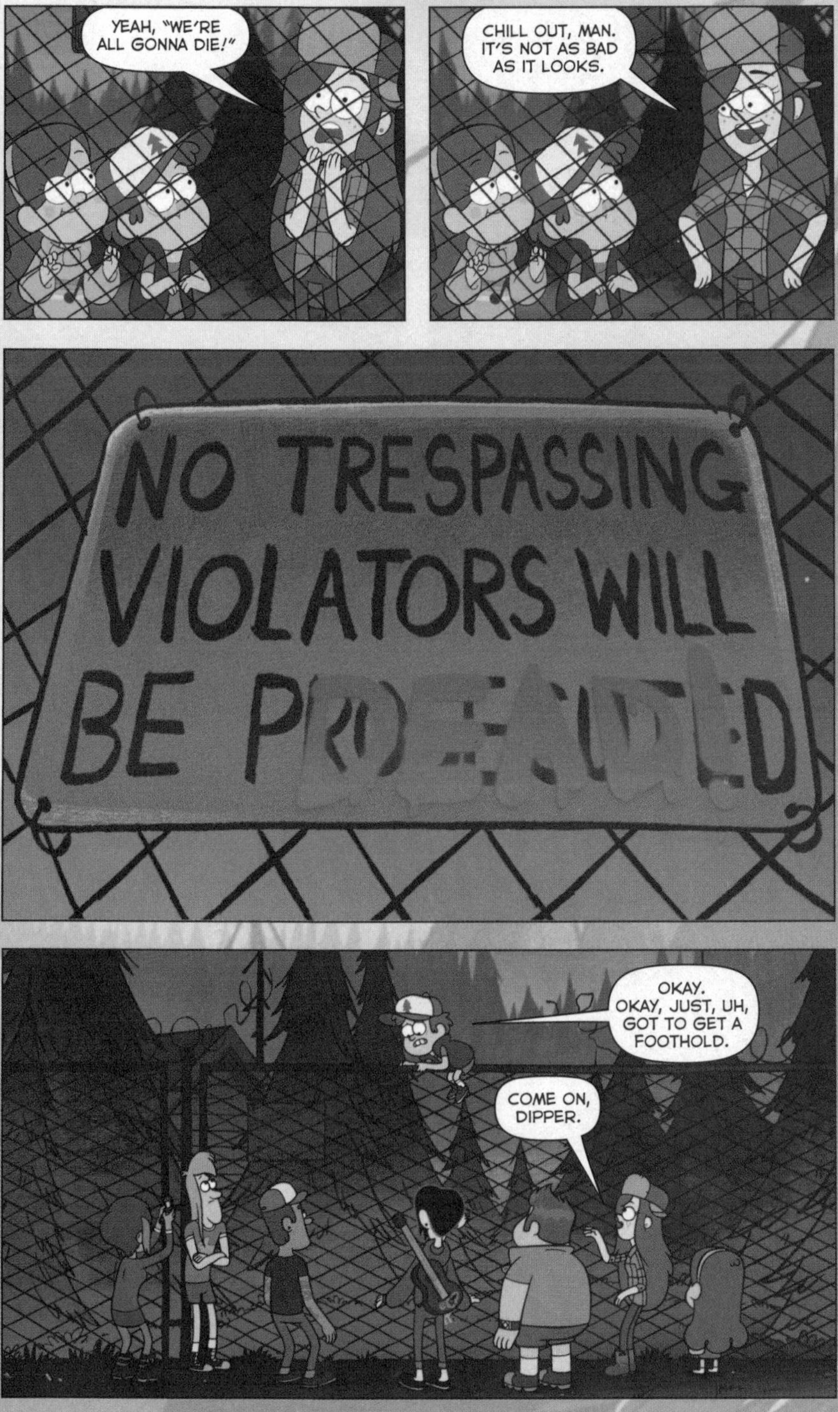
YEAH, "WE'RE ALL GONNA DIE!"
CHILL OUT, MAN. IT'S NOT AS BAD AS IT LOOKS.
NO TRESPASSING
VIOLATORS WILL
BE P
OKAY. OKAY, JUST, UH, GOT TO GET A FOOTHOLD.
COME ON, DIPPER.

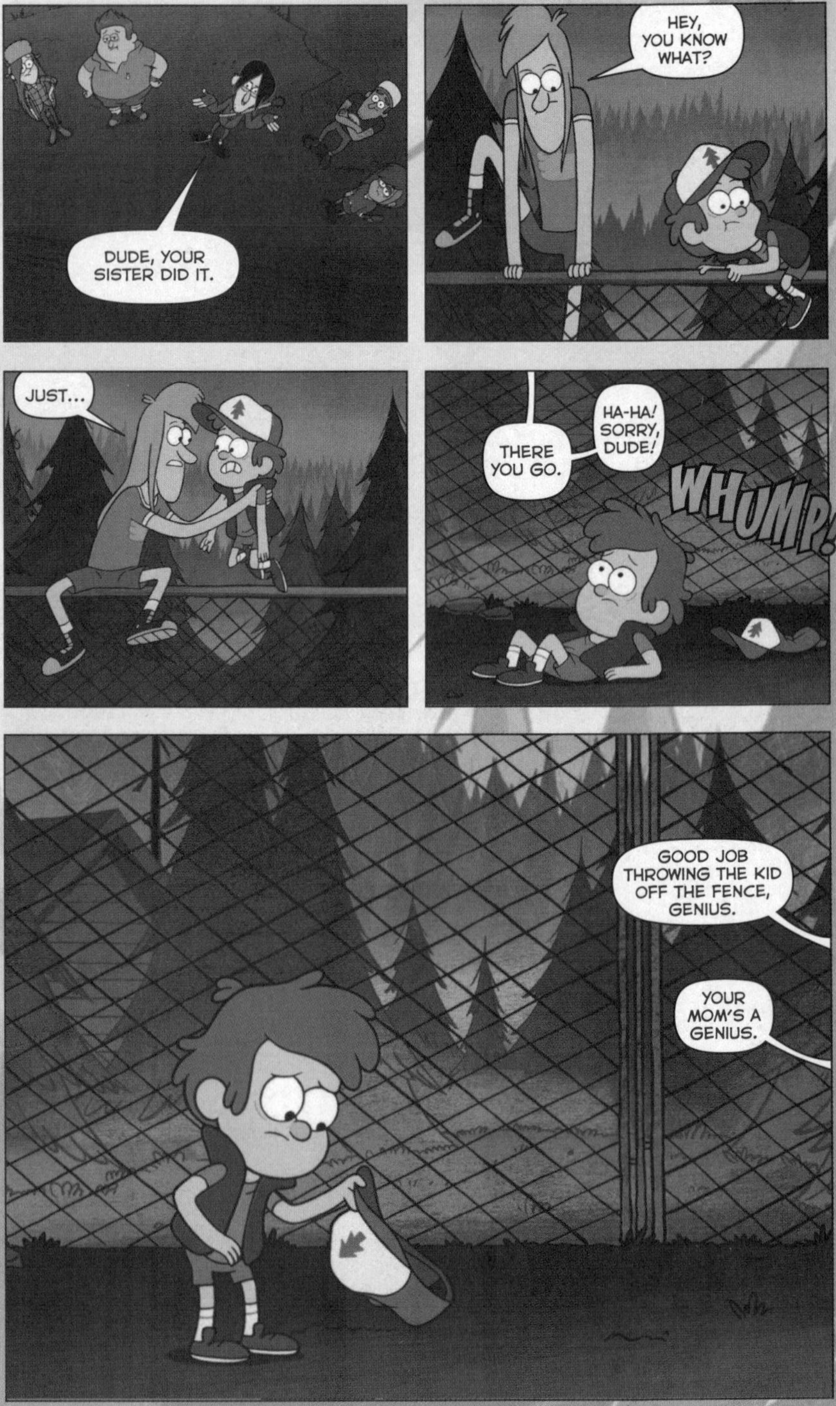
DUDE, YOUR SISTER DID IT.
HEY, YOU KNOW WHAT?
JUST...
THERE YOU GO.
HA-HA! SORRY, DUDE!
WHUMP!
GOOD JOB THROWING THE KID OFF THE FENCE, GENIUS.
YOUR MOM'S A GENIUS.

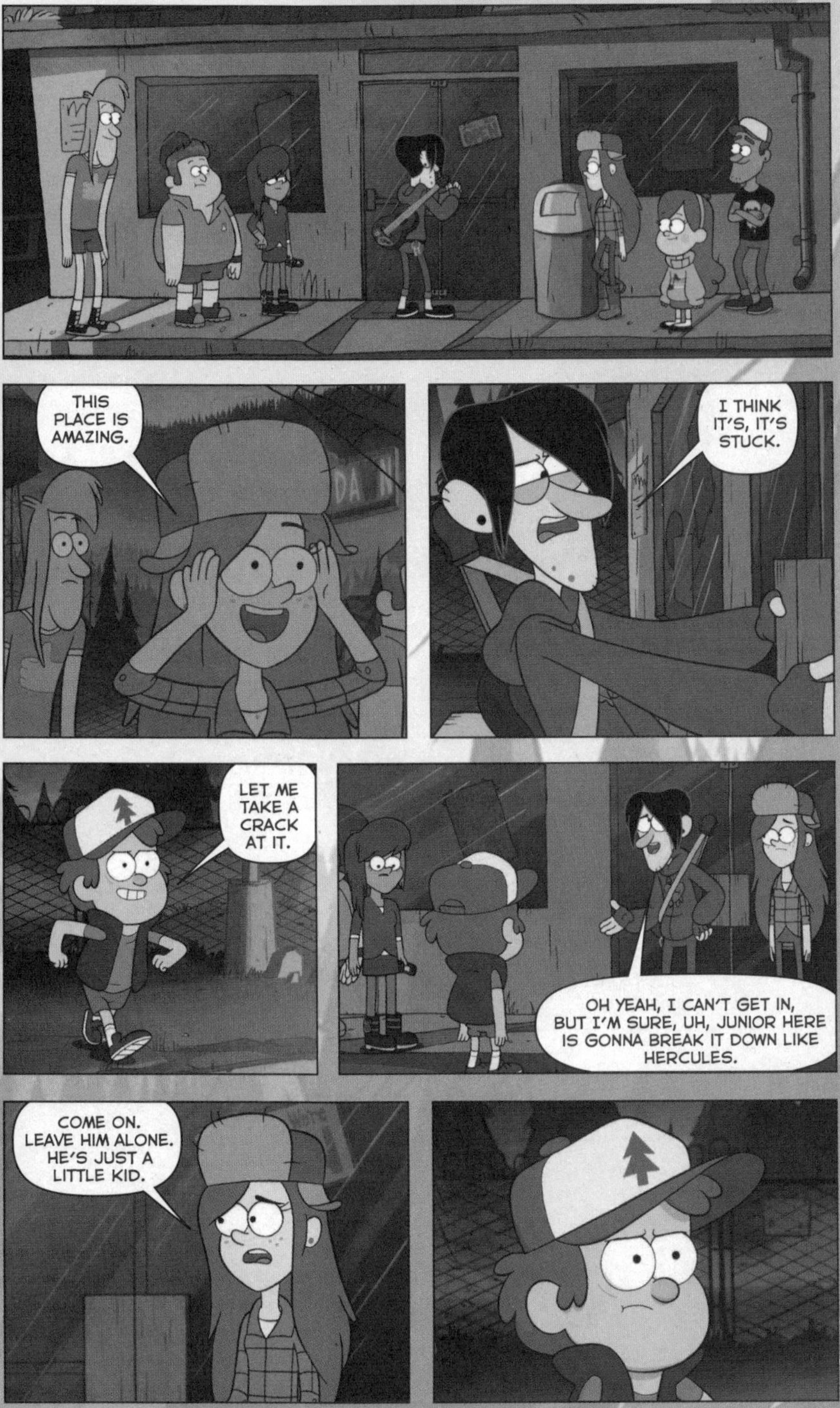
THIS PLACE IS AMAZING.
I THINK IT'S, IT'S STUCK.
LET ME TAKE A CRACK AT IT.
OH YEAH, I CAN'T GET IN, BUT I'M SURE, UH, JUNIOR HERE IS GONNA BREAK IT DOWN LIKE HERCULES.
COME ON. LEAVE HIM ALONE. HE'S JUST A LITTLE KID.

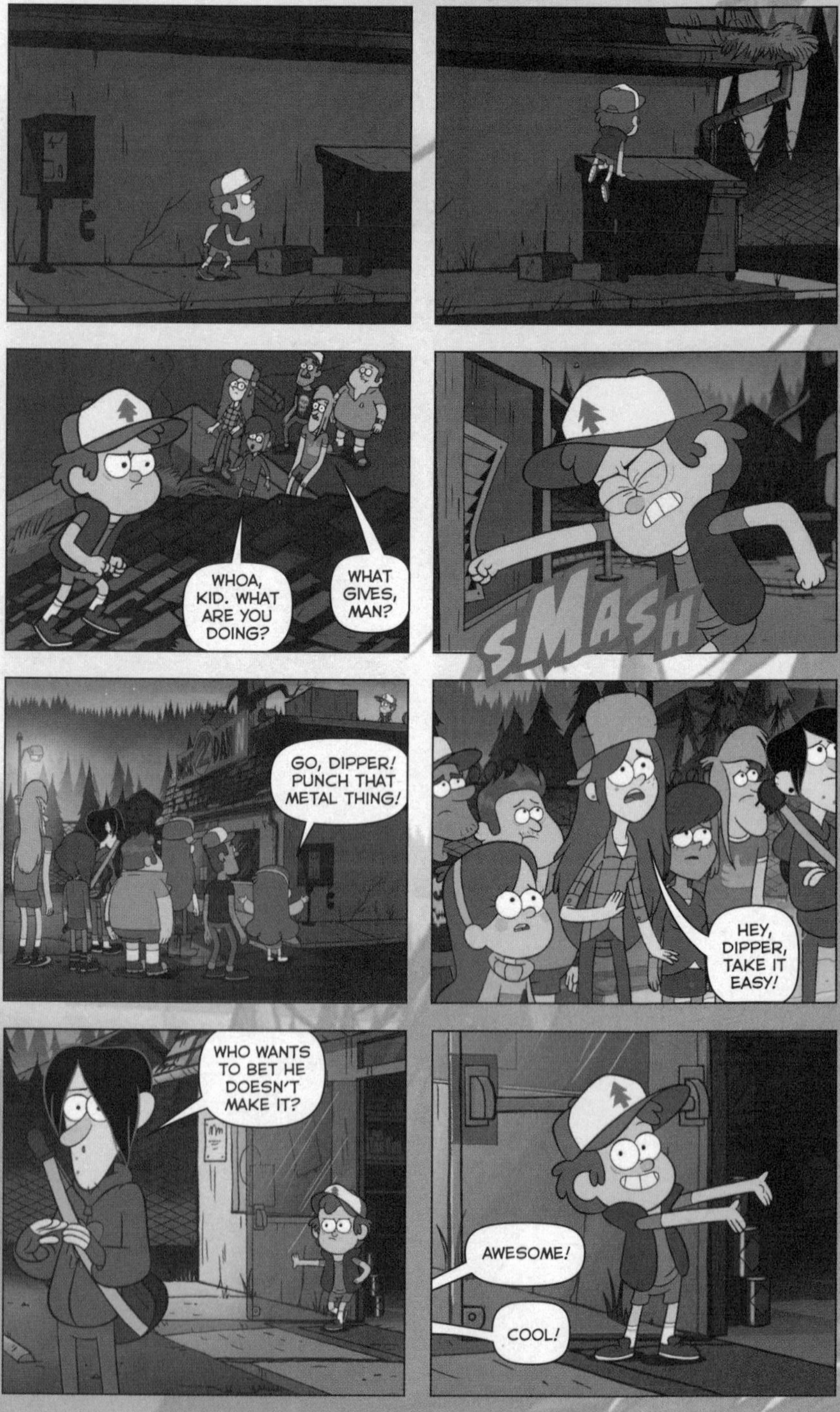
WHOA, KID. WHAT ARE YOU DOING?
WHAT GIVES, MAN?
SMASH
GO, DIPPER! PUNCH THAT METAL THING!
HEY, DIPPER, TAKE IT EASY!
WHO WANTS TO BET HE DOESN'T MAKE IT?
AWESOME!
COOL!

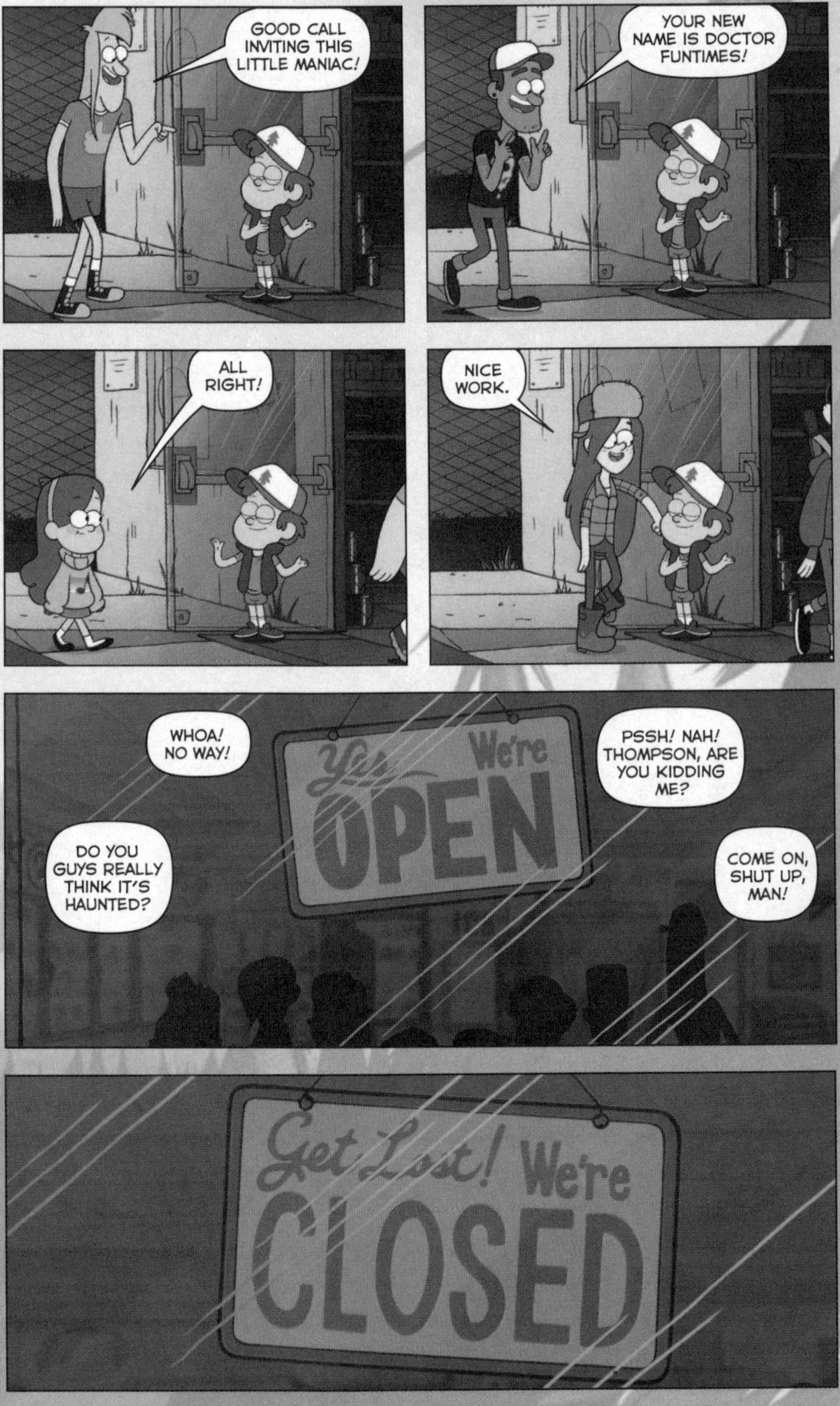
GOOD CALL INVITING THIS LITTLE MANIAC!
YOUR NEW NAME IS DOCTOR FUNTIMES!
ALL RIGHT!
NICE WORK.
WHOA! NO WAY!
You We're OPEN
PSSH! NAH! THOMPSON, ARE YOU KIDDING ME?
DO YOU GUYS REALLY THINK IT'S HAUNTED?
COME ON, SHUT UP, MAN!
Get Lost! We're CLOSED

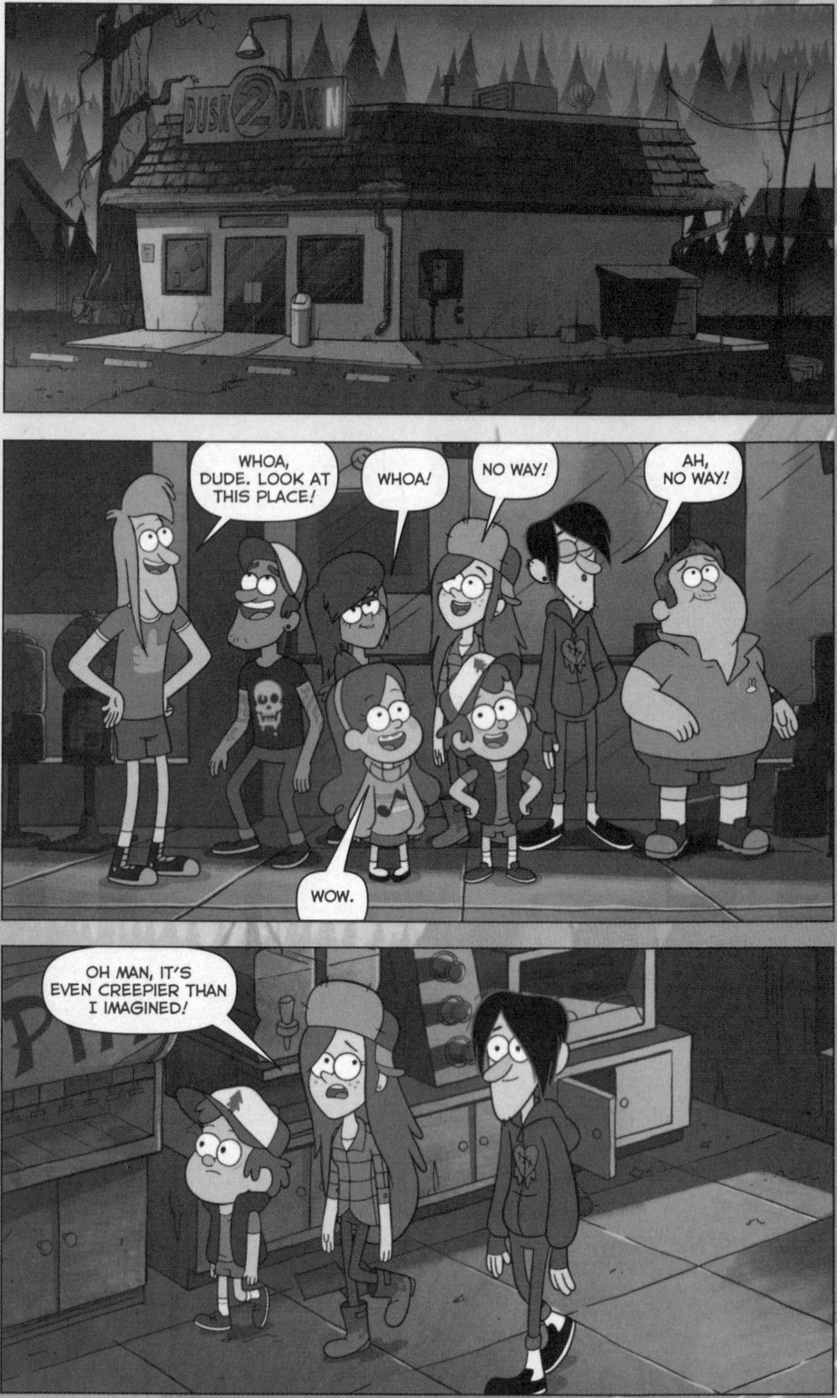
DUSK 2 DAWN
WHOA, DUDE. LOOK AT THIS PLACE!
WHOA!
NO WAY!
AH, NO WAY!
WOW.
OH MAN, IT'S EVEN CREEPIER THAN I IMAGINED!

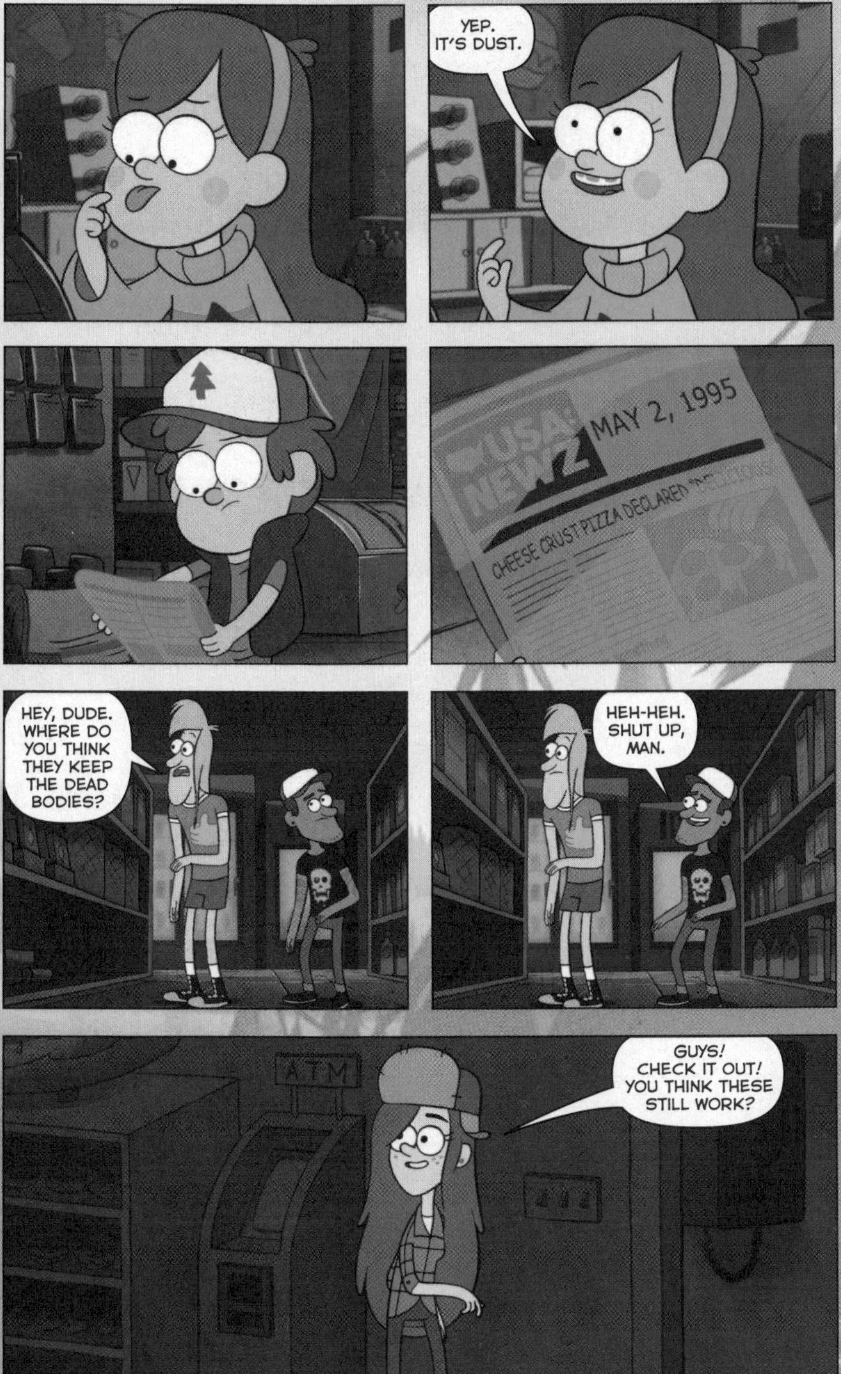
YEP.
IT'S DUST.
MAY 2, 1995
CHEESE CRUST PIZZA DECLARED
HEY, DUDE. WHERE DO YOU THINK THEY KEEP THE DEAD BODIES?
HEH-HEH. SHUT UP, MAN.
GUYS! CHECK IT OUT! YOU THINK THESE STILL WORK?
ATM

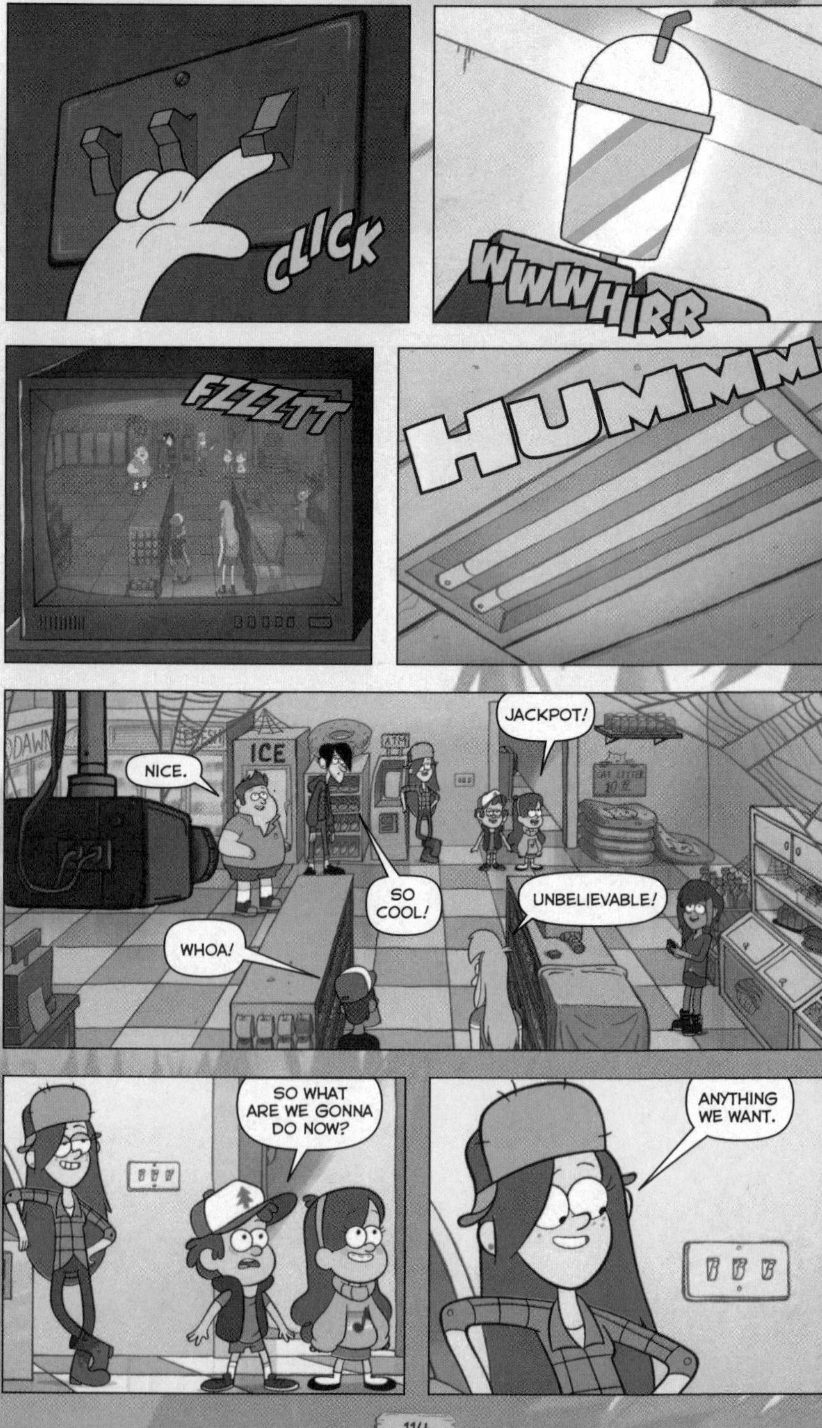
CLICK
WWWHIRR
FZZZTT
HUMMM
NICE.
JACKPOT!
SO COOL!
WHOA!
UNBELIEVABLE!
ICE
ATM
SO WHAT ARE WE GONNA DO NOW?
ANYTHING WE WANT.

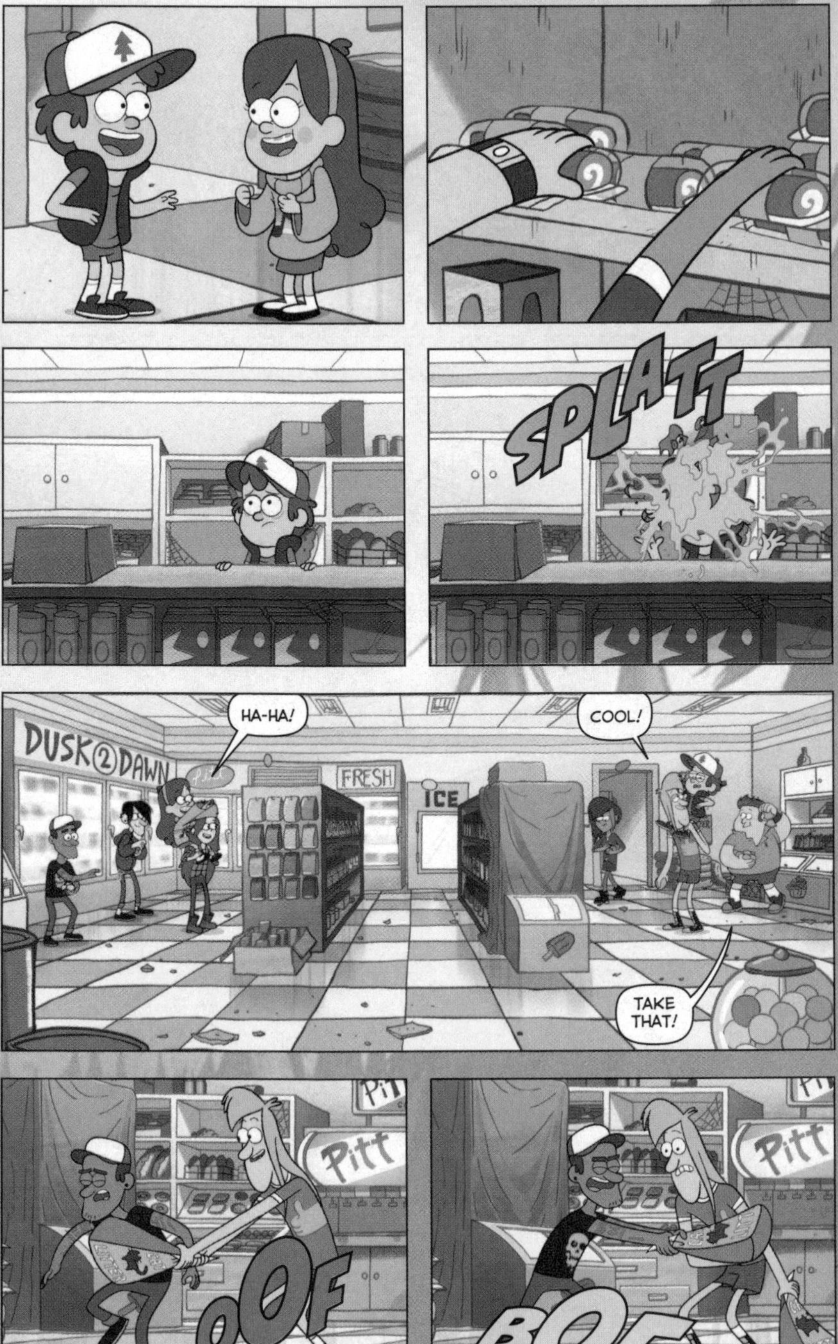
SPLATT
DUSK 2 DAWN
FRESH
ICE
HA-HA!
COOL!
TAKE THAT!
Pitt
OOF
BOFF

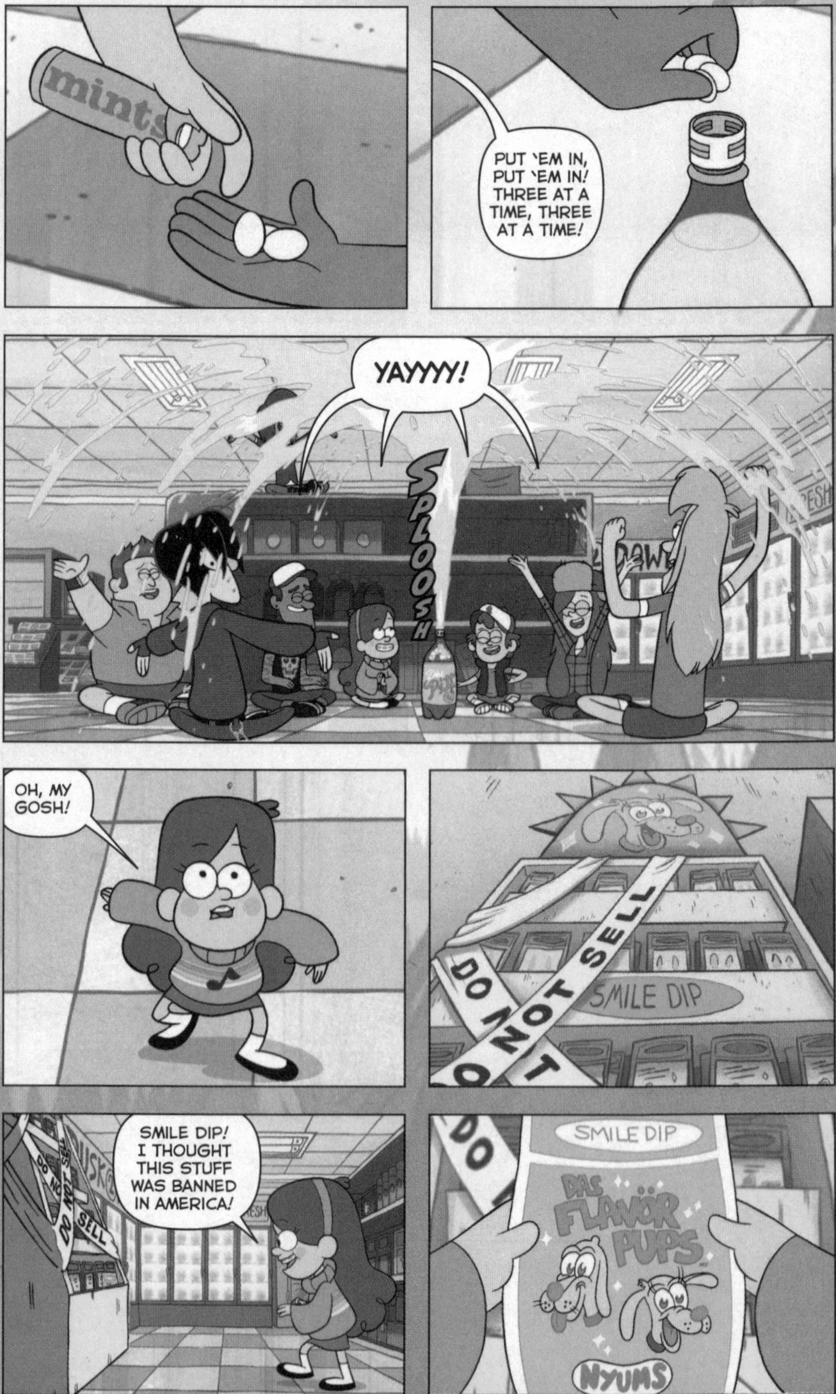
mints
PUT 'EM IN, PUT 'EM IN! THREE AT A TIME, THREE AT A TIME!
YAYYYY!
SPLOOSH
OH, MY GOSH!
DO NOT SELL
SMILE DIP
SMILE DIP! I THOUGHT THIS STUFF WAS BANNED IN AMERICA!
DO NOT SELL
SMILE DIP
DAS FLAVÖR PUPS
NYUMS

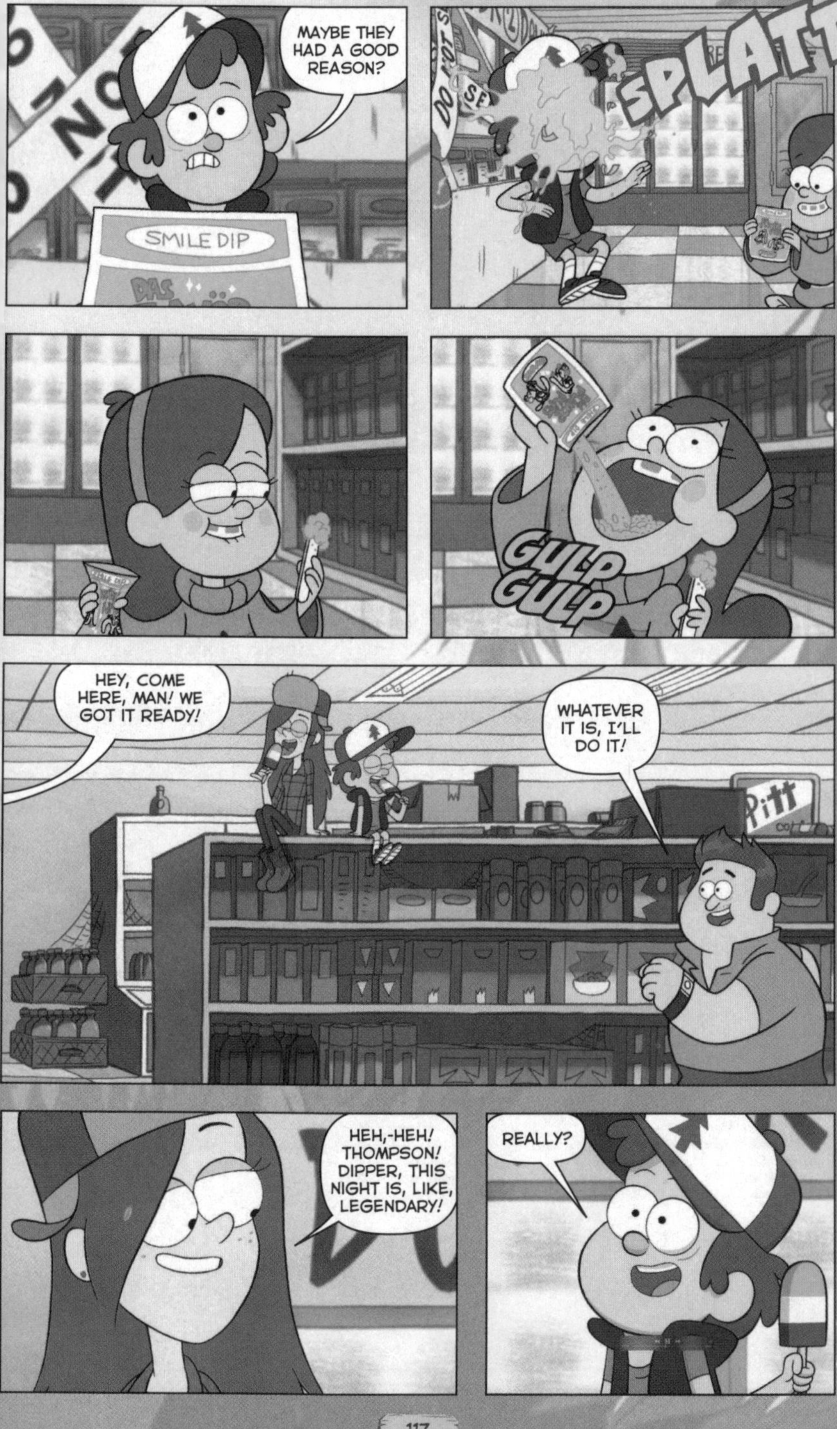

NO
SMILE DIP
MAYBE THEY HAD A GOOD REASON?
SPLATT
GULP GULP
HEY, COME HERE, MAN! WE GOT IT READY!
WHATEVER IT IS, I'LL DO IT!
HEH,-HEH! THOMPSON! DIPPER, THIS NIGHT IS, LIKE, LEGENDARY!
REALLY?

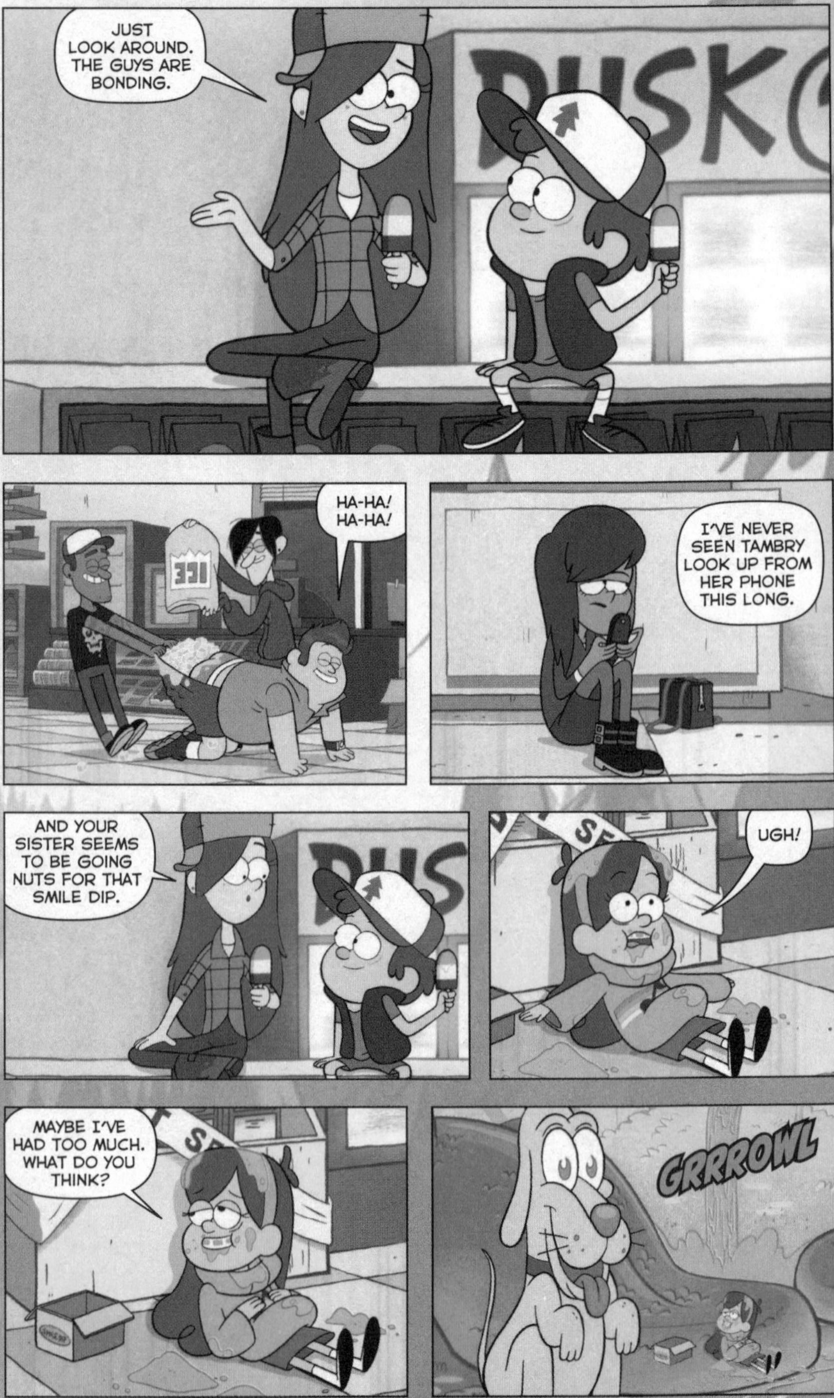
JUST LOOK AROUND. THE GUYS ARE BONDING.
DUSK
HA-HA! HA-HA!
ICE
I'VE NEVER SEEN TAMBRY LOOK UP FROM HER PHONE THIS LONG.
AND YOUR SISTER SEEMS TO BE GOING NUTS FOR THAT SMILE DIP.
UGH!
MAYBE I'VE HAD TOO MUCH. WHAT DO YOU THINK?
GRRROWL

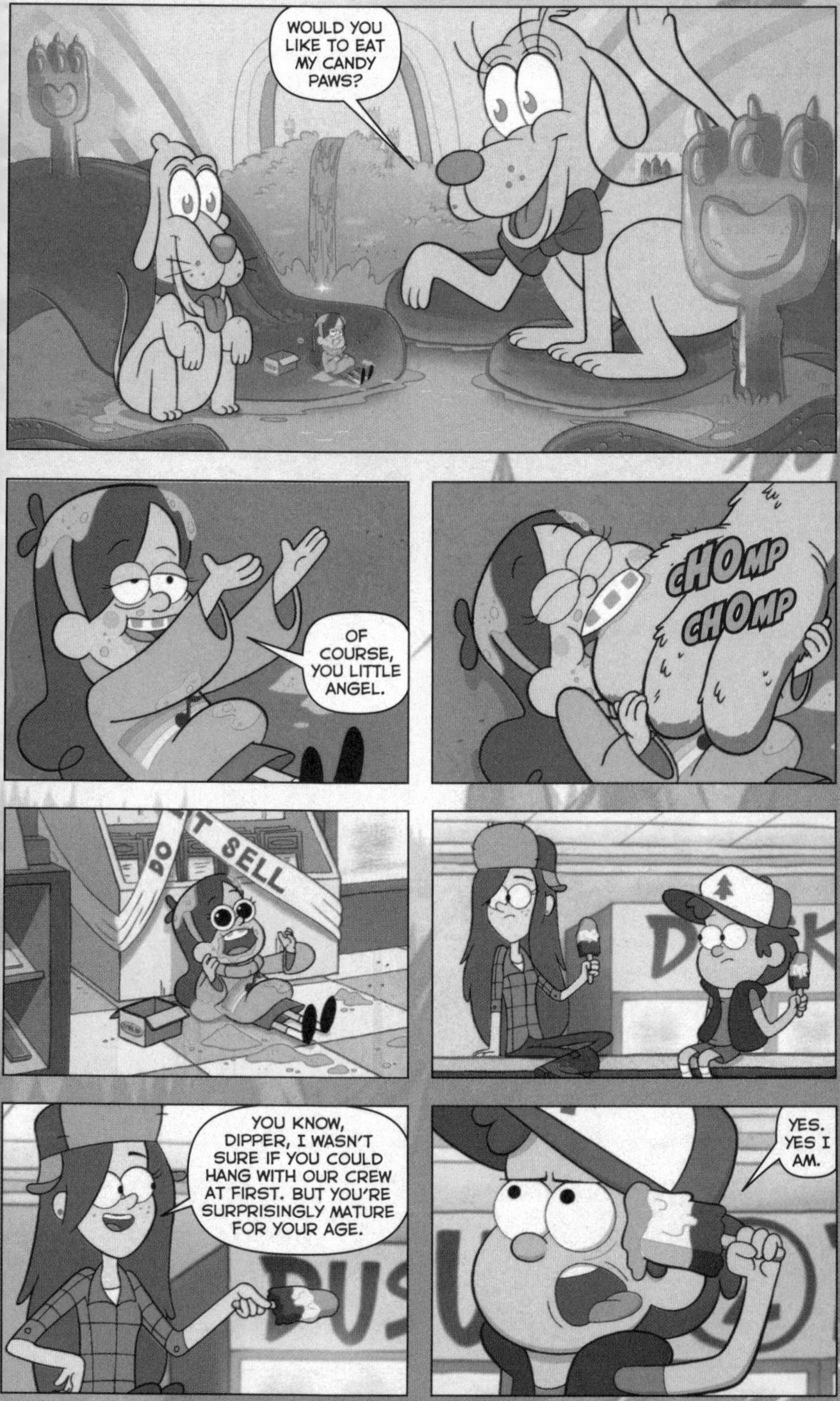
WOULD YOU LIKE TO EAT MY CANDY PAWS?
OF COURSE, YOU LITTLE ANGEL.
CHOMP
CHOMP
DO NOT SELL
YOU KNOW, DIPPER, I WASN'T SURE IF YOU COULD HANG WITH OUR CREW AT FIRST. BUT YOU'RE SURPRISINGLY MATURE FOR YOUR AGE.
YES. YES I AM.

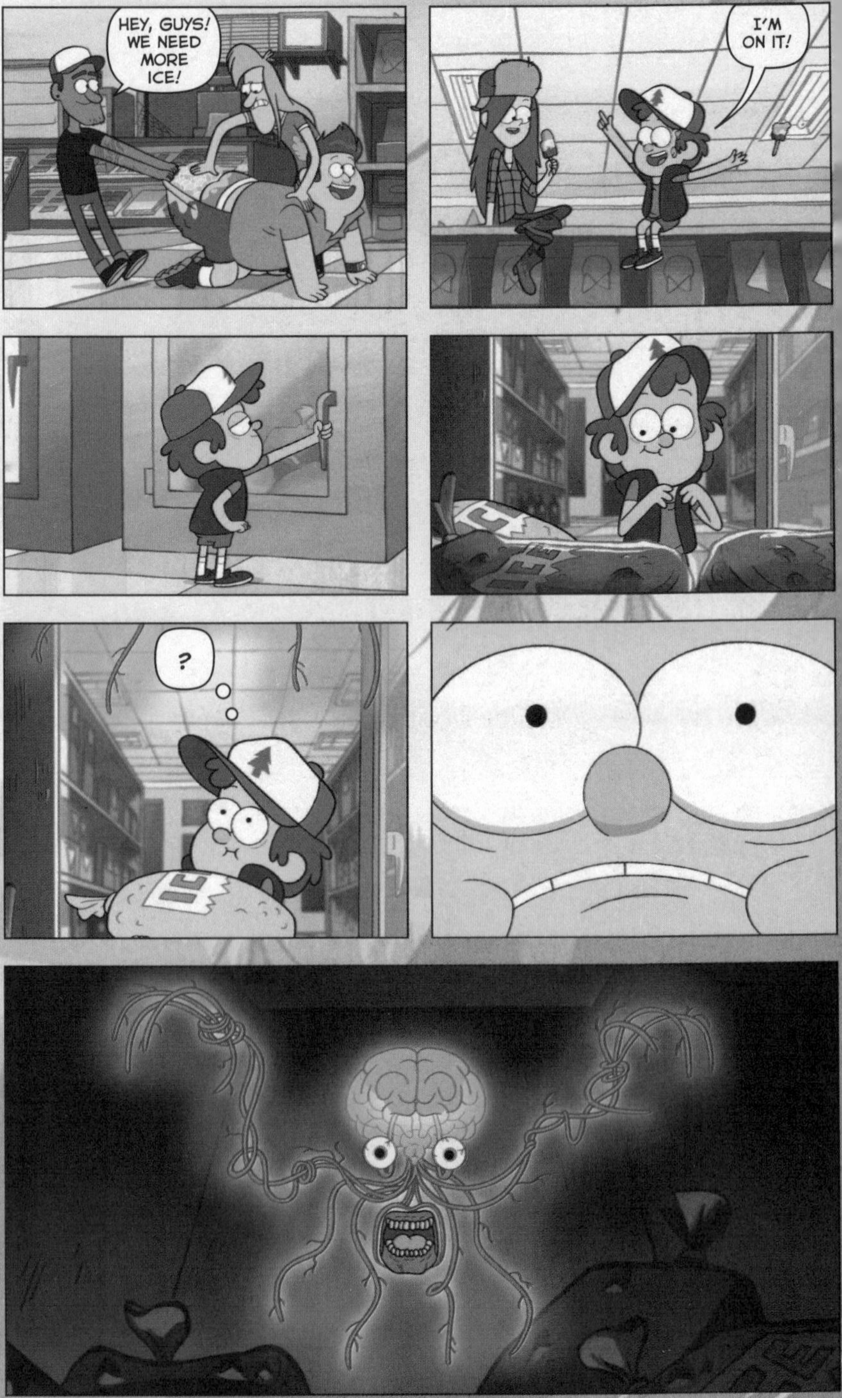
HEY, GUYS! WE NEED MORE ICE!
I'M ON IT!
?

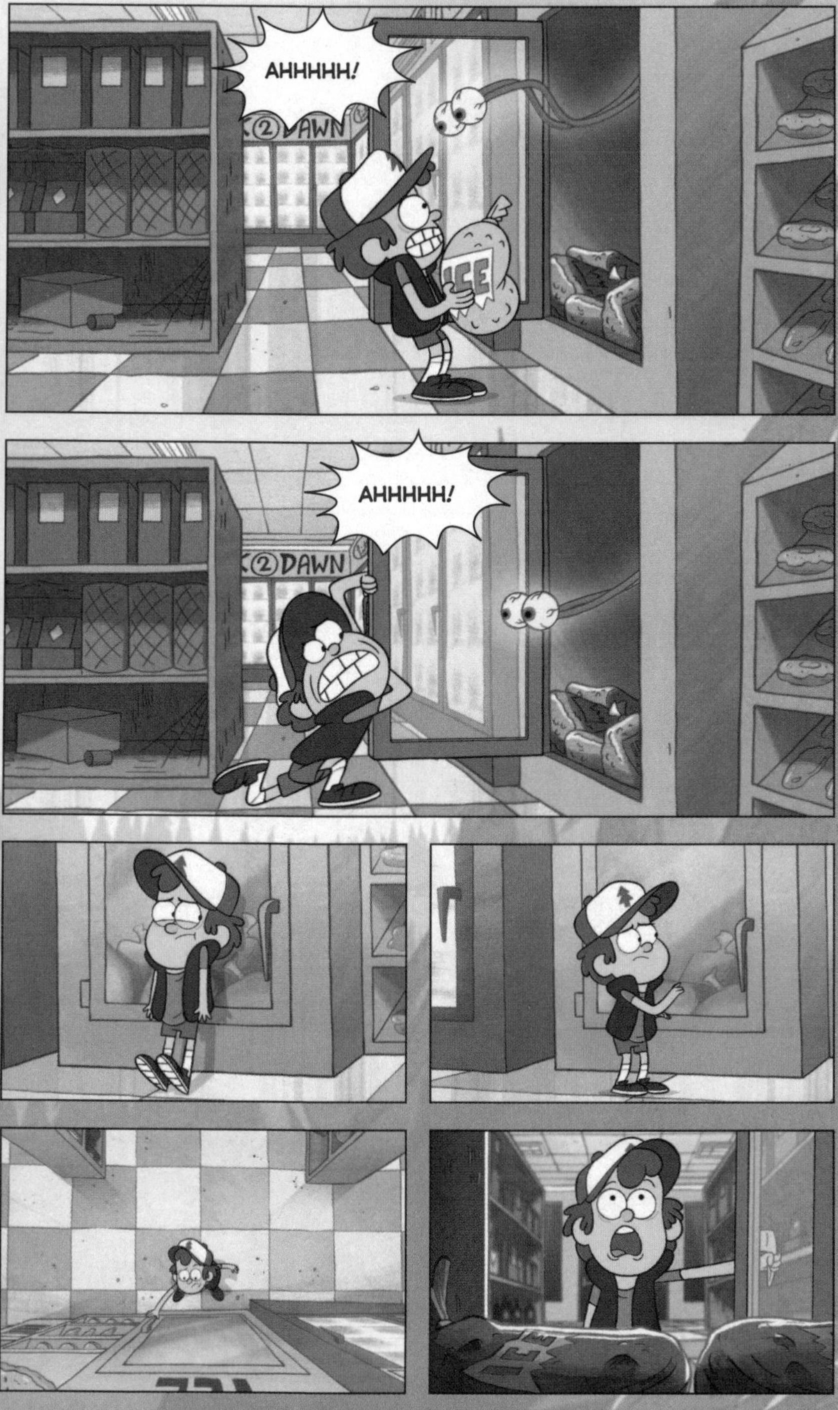
AHHHHH!
AHHHHH!

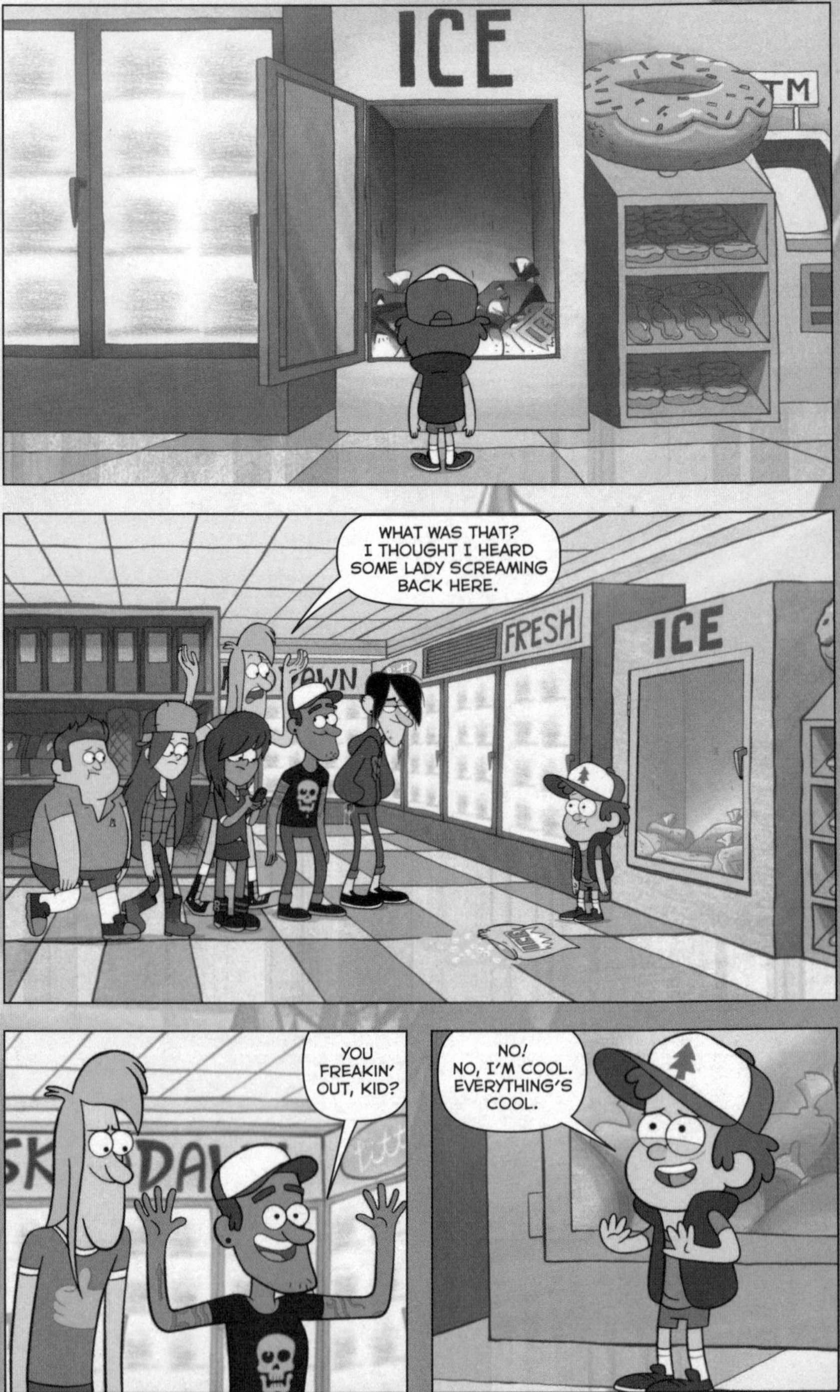
ICE
TM
WHAT WAS THAT? I THOUGHT I HEARD SOME LADY SCREAMING BACK HERE.
FRESH
ICE
YOU FREAKIN' OUT, KID?
NO! NO, I'M COOL. EVERYTHING'S COOL.

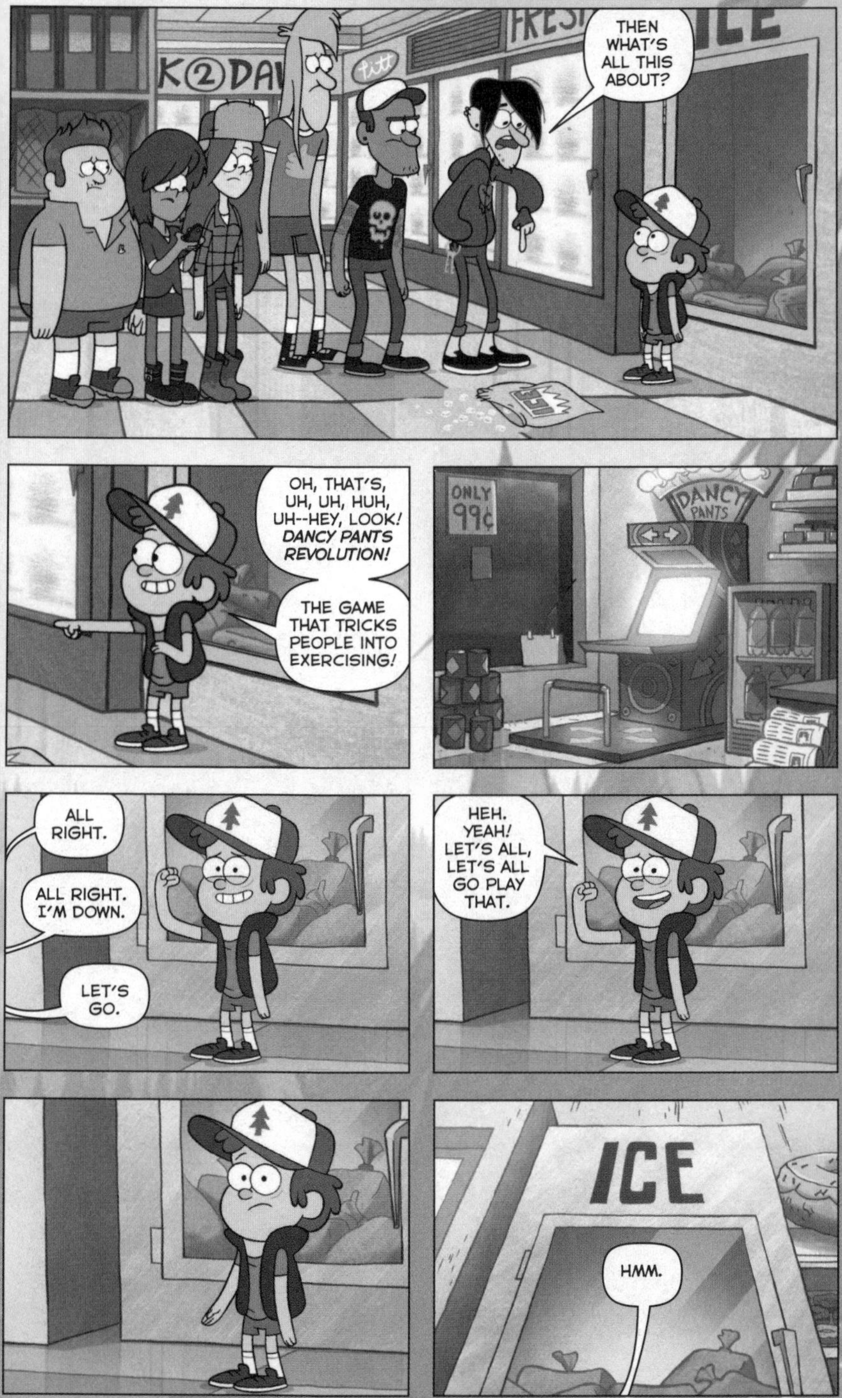
THEN WHAT'S ALL THIS ABOUT?
ICE
OH, THAT'S, UH, UH, HUH, UH--HEY, LOOK! *DANCY PANTS REVOLUTION!*
THE GAME THAT TRICKS PEOPLE INTO EXERCISING!
ONLY 99¢
DANCY PANTS
ALL RIGHT.
ALL RIGHT. I'M DOWN.
LET'S GO.
HEH. YEAH! LET'S ALL, LET'S ALL GO PLAY THAT.
ICE
HMM.

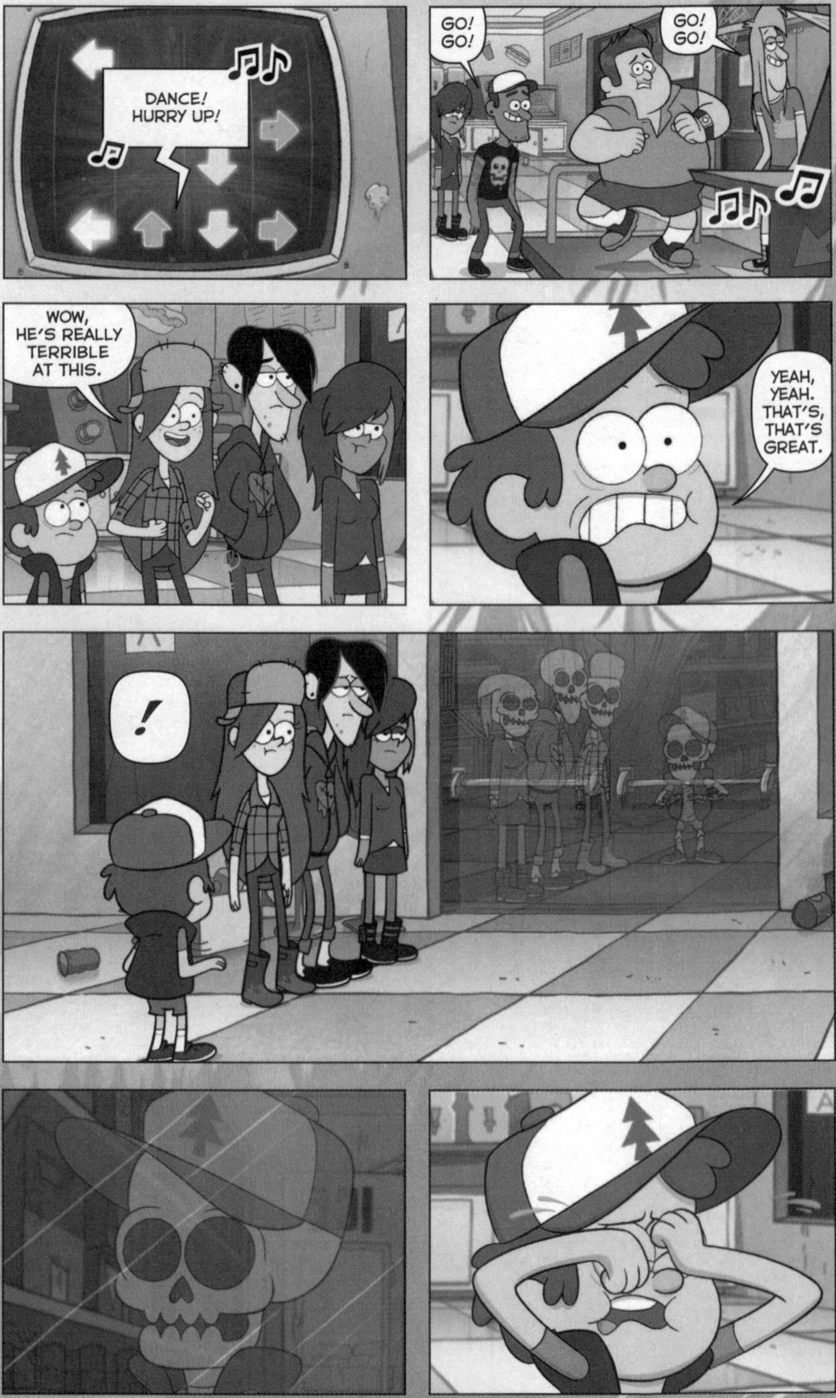

DANCE! HURRY UP!
GO! GO!
GO! GO!
WOW, HE'S REALLY TERRIBLE AT THIS.
YEAH, YEAH. THAT'S, THAT'S GREAT.
!

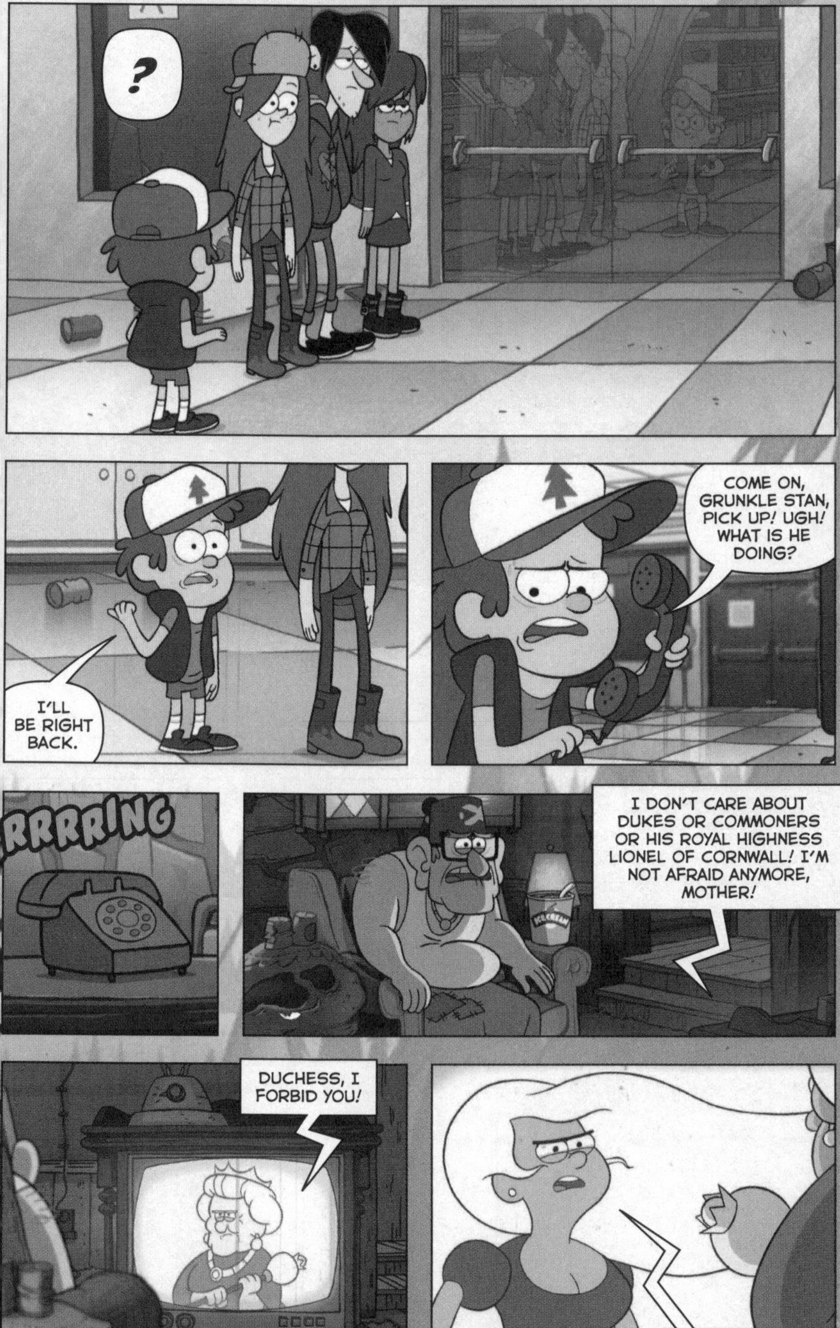
?
I'LL BE RIGHT BACK.
COME ON, GRUNKLE STAN, PICK UP! UGH! WHAT IS HE DOING?
RRRRRING
I DON'T CARE ABOUT DUKES OR COMMONERS OR HIS ROYAL HIGHNESS LIONEL OF CORNWALL! I'M NOT AFRAID ANYMORE, MOTHER!
DUCHESS, I FORBID YOU!
I MAY BE A DUCHESS, BUT I'M ALSO A WOMAN!

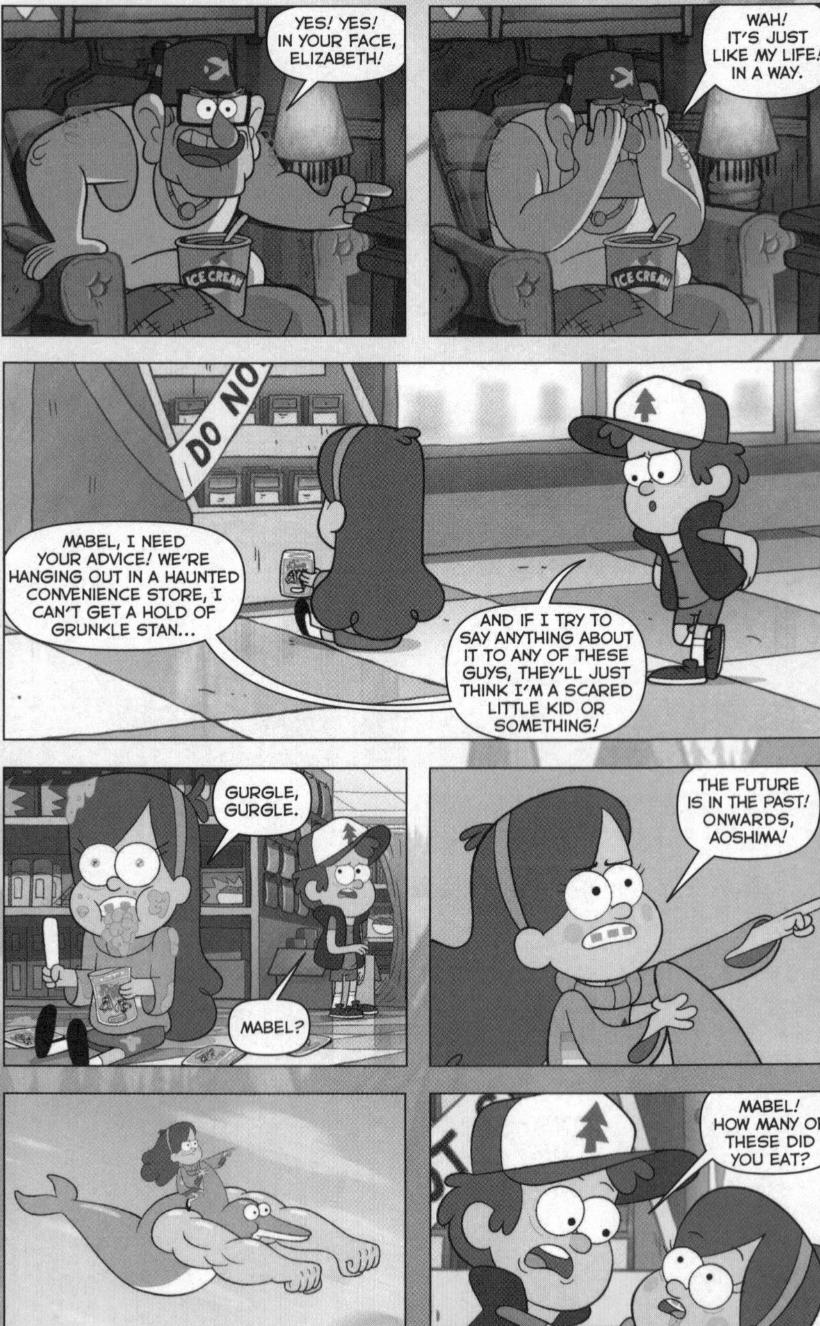
YES! YES! IN YOUR FACE, ELIZABETH!
ICE CREAM
WAH! IT'S JUST LIKE MY LIFE! IN A WAY.
ICE CREAM
DO NO
MABEL, I NEED YOUR ADVICE! WE'RE HANGING OUT IN A HAUNTED CONVENIENCE STORE, I CAN'T GET A HOLD OF GRUNKLE STAN...
AND IF I TRY TO SAY ANYTHING ABOUT IT TO ANY OF THESE GUYS, THEY'LL JUST THINK I'M A SCARED LITTLE KID OR SOMETHING!
GURGLE, GURGLE.
MABEL?
THE FUTURE IS IN THE PAST! ONWARDS, AOSHIMA!
MABEL! HOW MANY OF THESE DID YOU EAT?

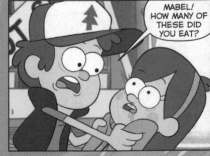

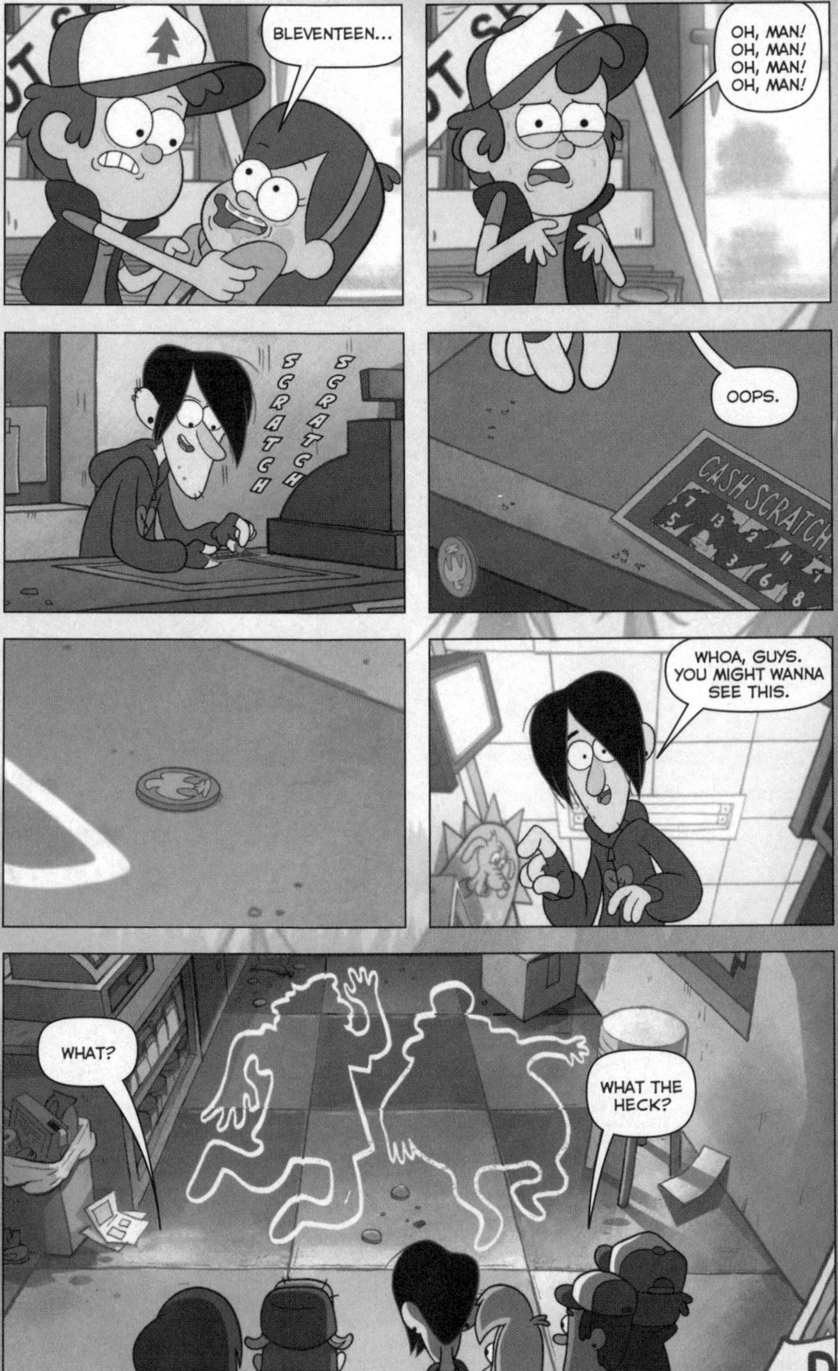
BLEVENTEEN...
OH, MAN!
OH, MAN!
OH, MAN!
OH, MAN!
SCRATCH
SCRATCH
OOPS.
CASH SCRATCH
WHOA, GUYS. YOU MIGHT WANNA SEE THIS.
WHAT?
WHAT THE HECK?

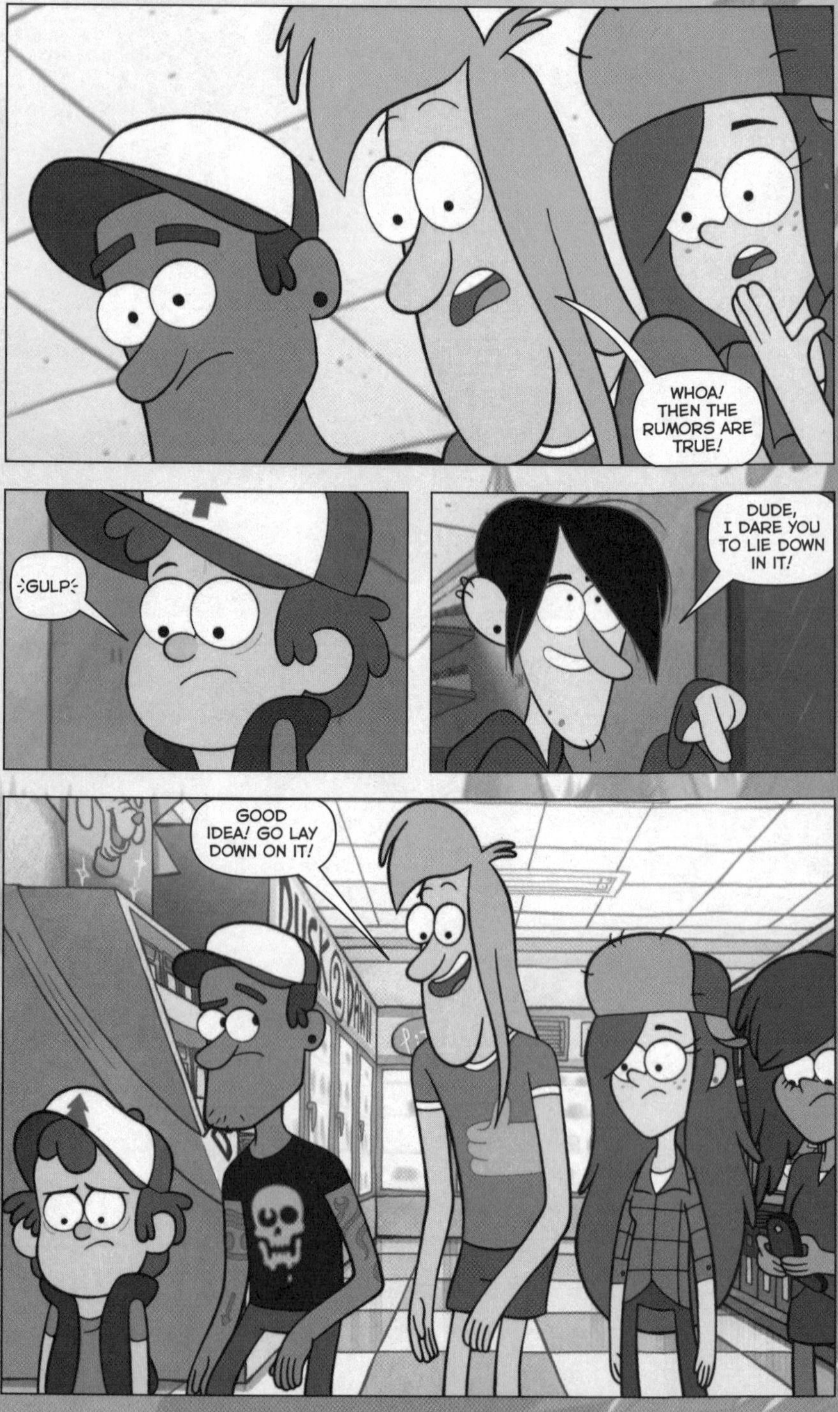
WHOA! THEN THE RUMORS ARE TRUE!
GULP
DUDE, I DARE YOU TO LIE DOWN IN IT!
GOOD IDEA! GO LAY DOWN ON IT!

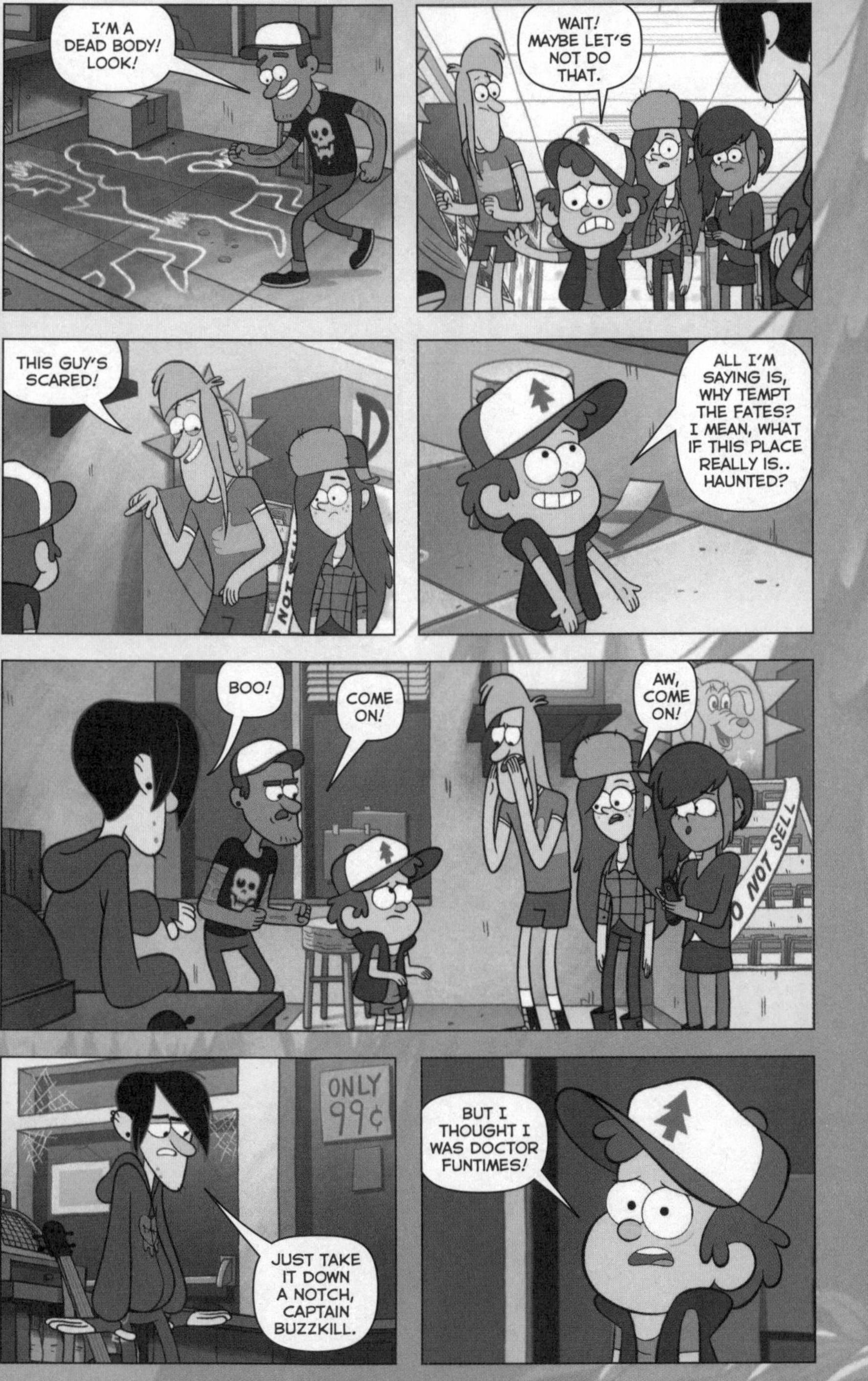
I'M A DEAD BODY! LOOK!
WAIT! MAYBE LET'S NOT DO THAT.
THIS GUY'S SCARED!
ALL I'M SAYING IS, WHY TEMPT THE FATES? I MEAN, WHAT IF THIS PLACE REALLY IS.. HAUNTED?
BOO!
COME ON!
AW, COME ON!
DO NOT SELL
ONLY 99¢
JUST TAKE IT DOWN A NOTCH, CAPTAIN BUZZKILL.
BUT I THOUGHT I WAS DOCTOR FUNTIMES!

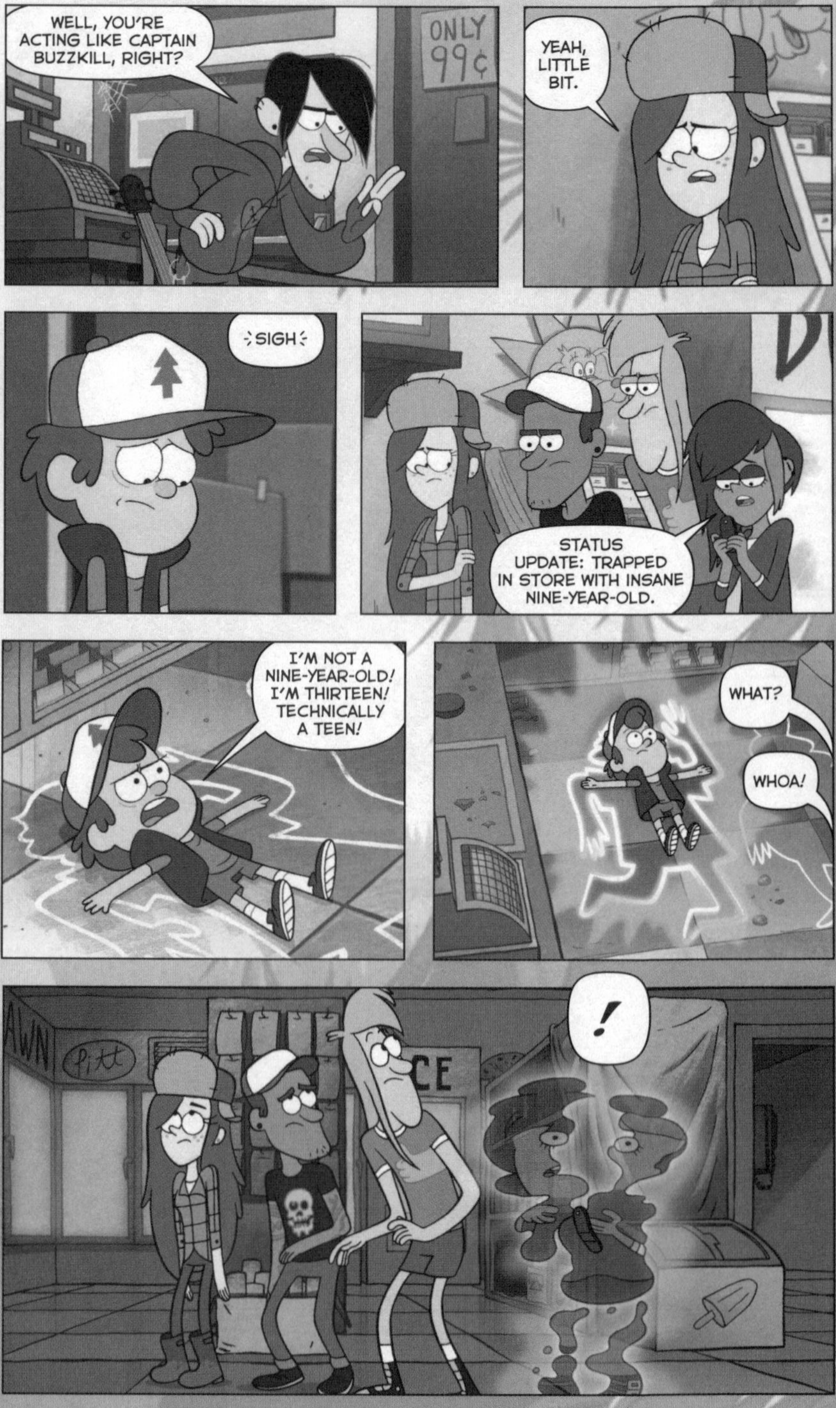
WELL, YOU'RE ACTING LIKE CAPTAIN BUZZKILL, RIGHT?
ONLY 99¢
YEAH, LITTLE BIT.
SIGH
STATUS UPDATE: TRAPPED IN STORE WITH INSANE NINE-YEAR-OLD.
I'M NOT A NINE-YEAR-OLD! I'M THIRTEEN! TECHNICALLY A TEEN!
WHAT?
WHOA!
!

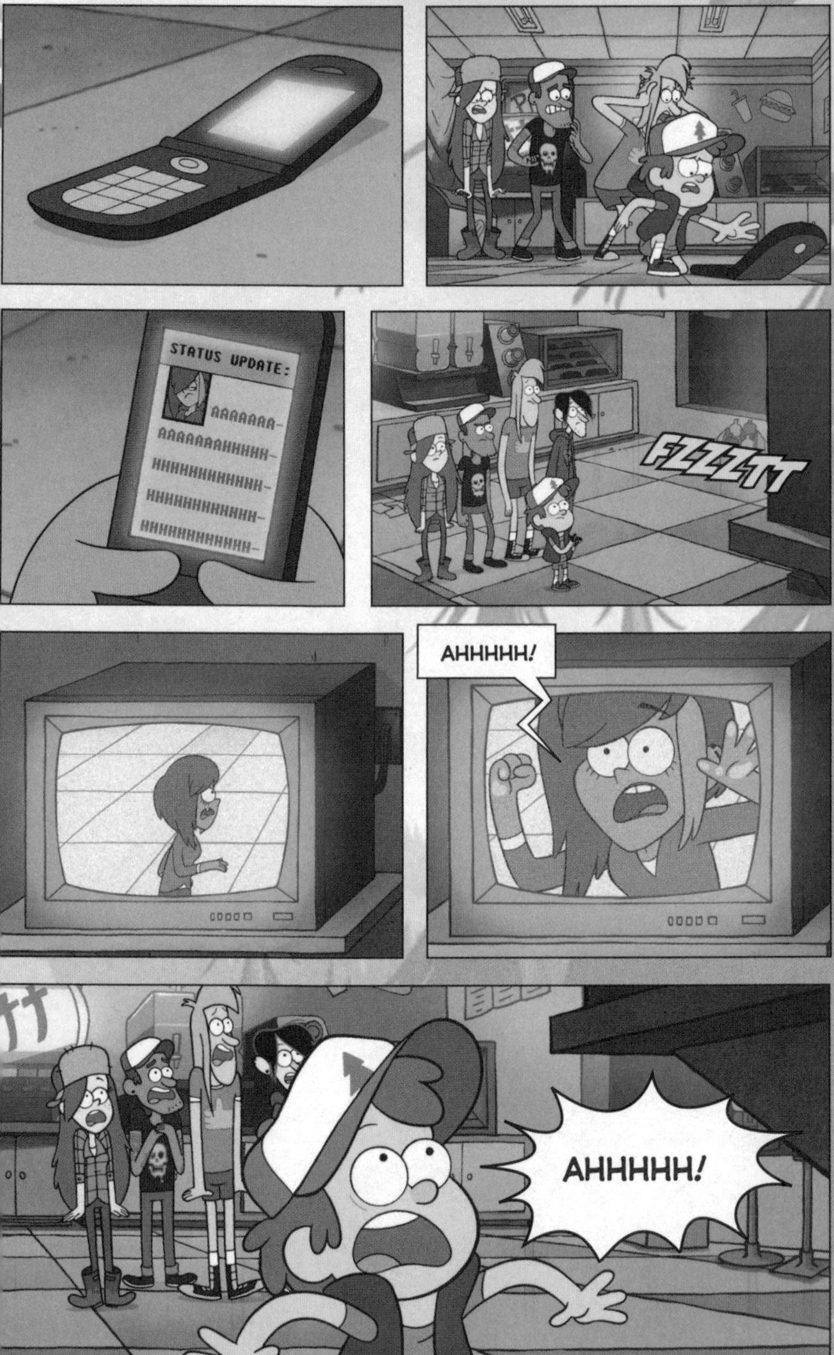
STATUS UPDATE:
AAAAAAA-
AAAAAAAHHHHH-
HHHHHHHHHHHHH-
HHHHHHHHHHHHH-
HHHHHHHHHHHHH-
FZZZTT
AHHHHH!
AHHHHH!

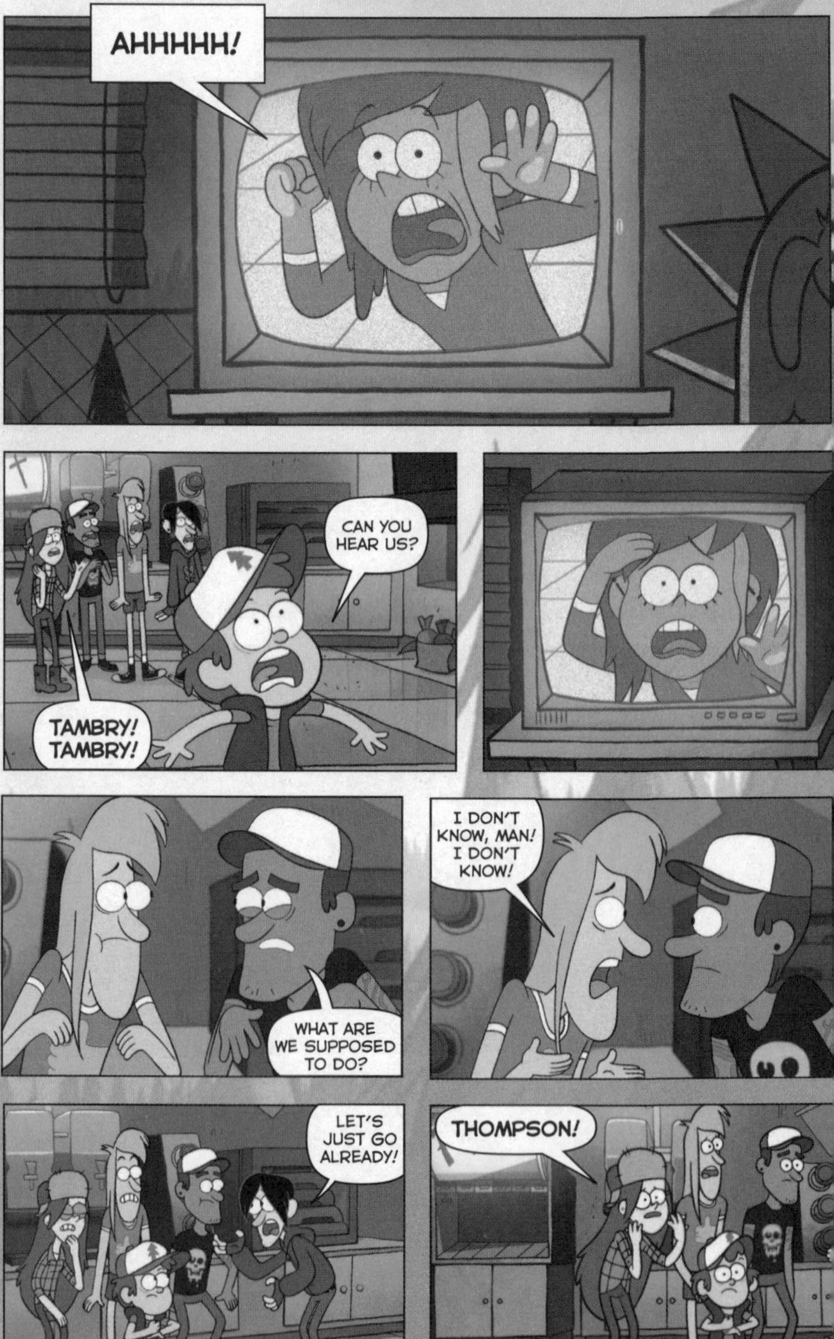
AHHHHH!
CAN YOU HEAR US?
TAMBRY! TAMBRY!
WHAT ARE WE SUPPOSED TO DO?
I DON'T KNOW, MAN! I DON'T KNOW!
LET'S JUST GO ALREADY!
THOMPSON!

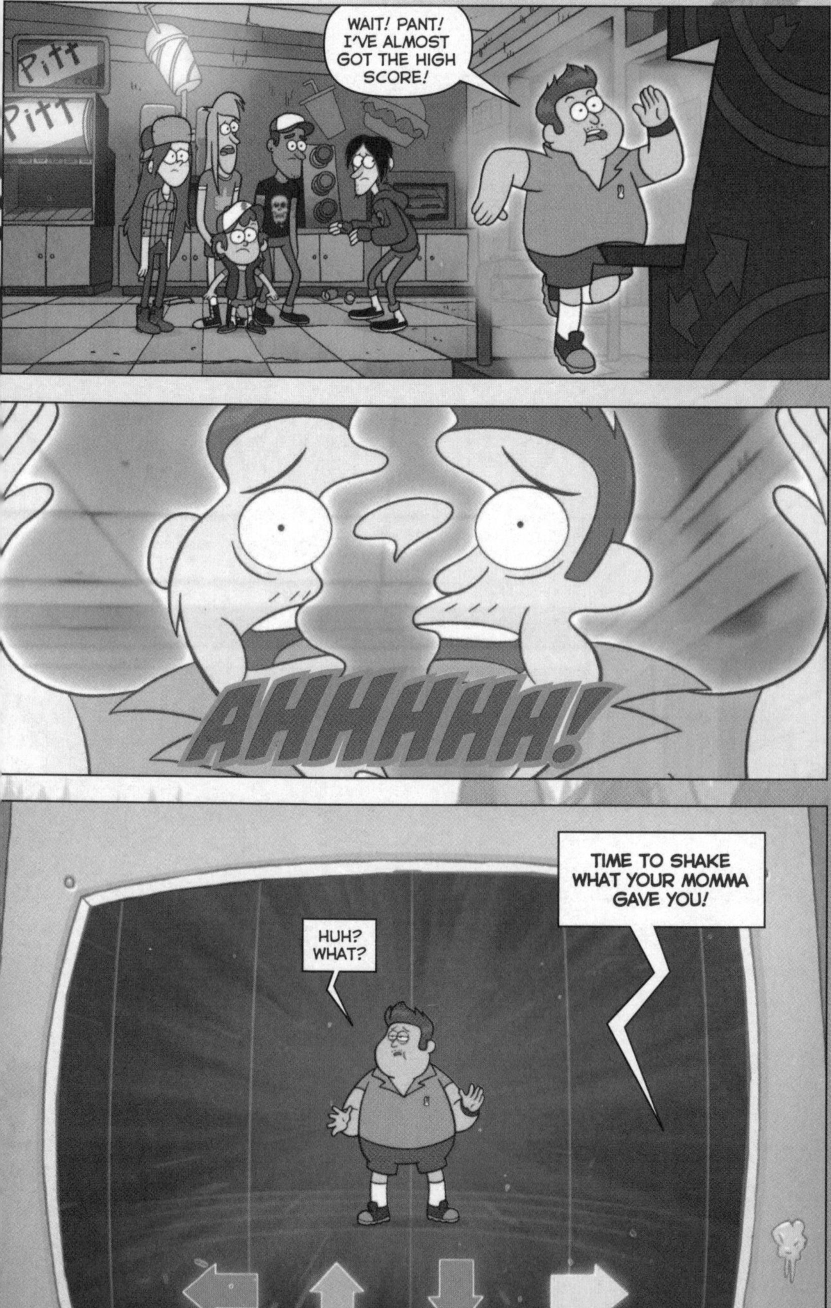
WAIT! PANT! I'VE ALMOST GOT THE HIGH SCORE!
Pitt
Pitt
AHHHHHH!
TIME TO SHAKE WHAT YOUR MOMMA GAVE YOU!
HUH? WHAT?

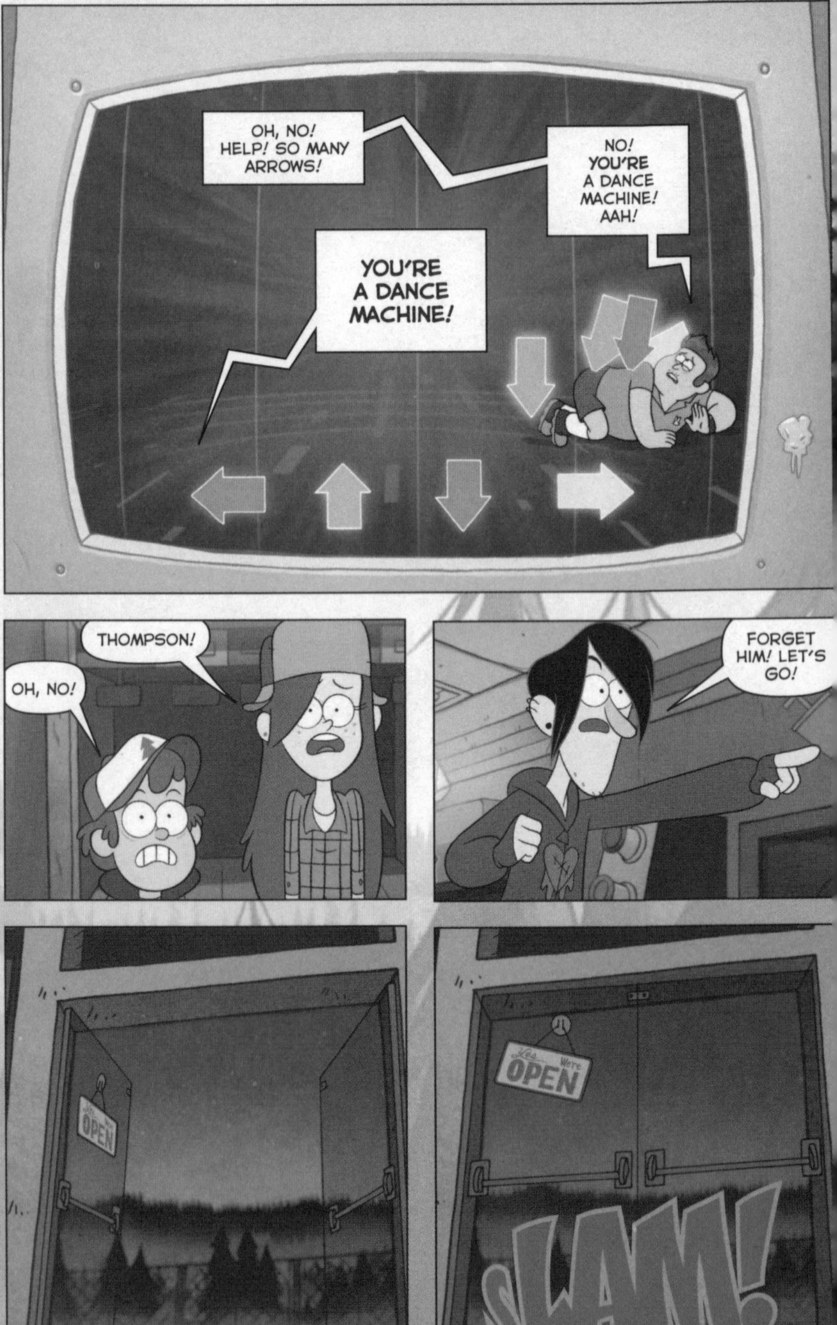
OH, NO! HELP! SO MANY ARROWS!
NO! YOU'RE A DANCE MACHINE! AAH!
YOU'RE A DANCE MACHINE!
THOMPSON!
OH, NO!
FORGET HIM! LET'S GO!
OPEN
OPEN
SLAM!

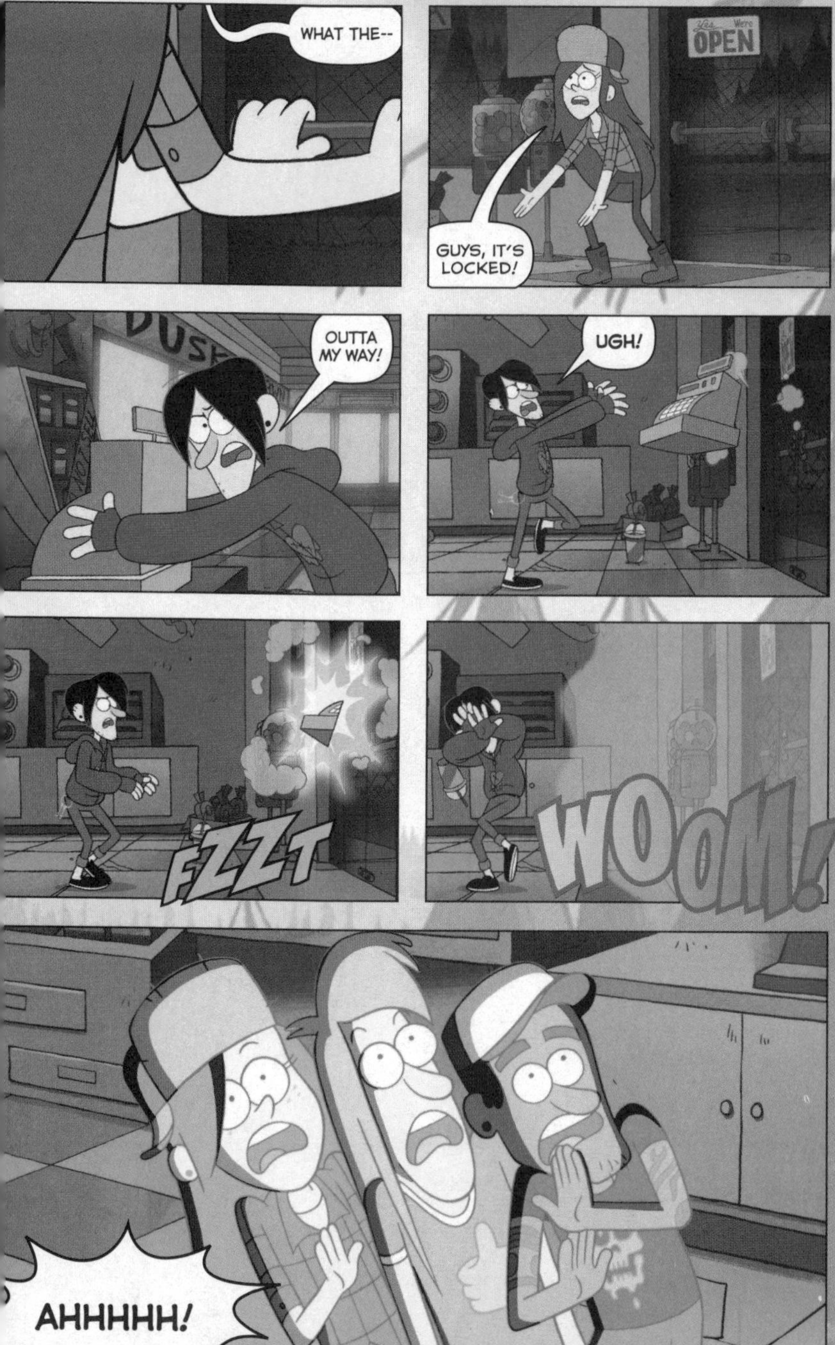
WHAT THE--
We're OPEN
GUYS, IT'S LOCKED!
OUTTA MY WAY!
UGH!
FZZT
WOOM!
AHHHHH!

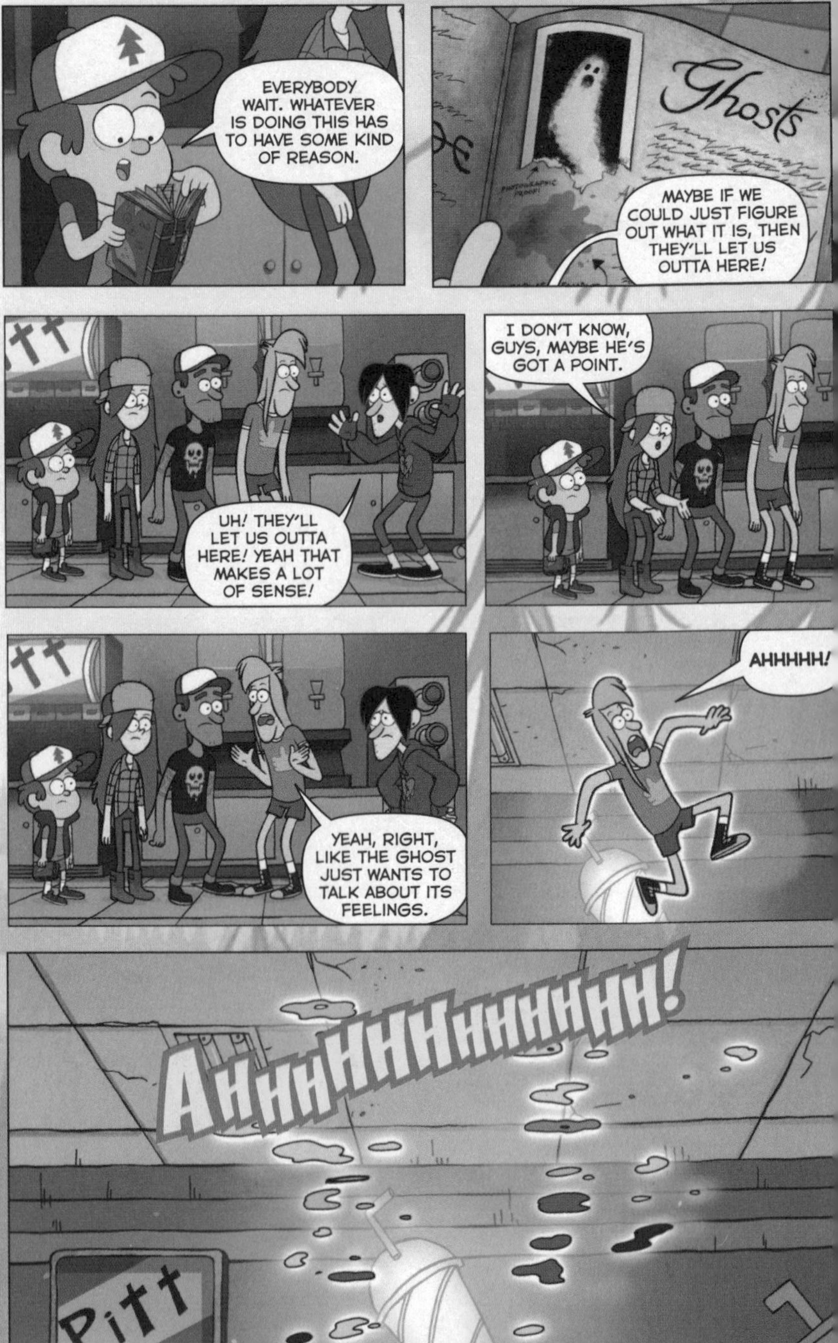

EVERYBODY WAIT. WHATEVER IS DOING THIS HAS TO HAVE SOME KIND OF REASON.
Ghosts
MAYBE IF WE COULD JUST FIGURE OUT WHAT IT IS, THEN THEY'LL LET US OUTTA HERE!
UH! THEY'LL LET US OUTTA HERE! YEAH THAT MAKES A LOT OF SENSE!
I DON'T KNOW, GUYS, MAYBE HE'S GOT A POINT.
YEAH, RIGHT, LIKE THE GHOST JUST WANTS TO TALK ABOUT ITS FEELINGS.
AHHHHH!
AHHHHHHHHHHHHH!
Pitt
COLA

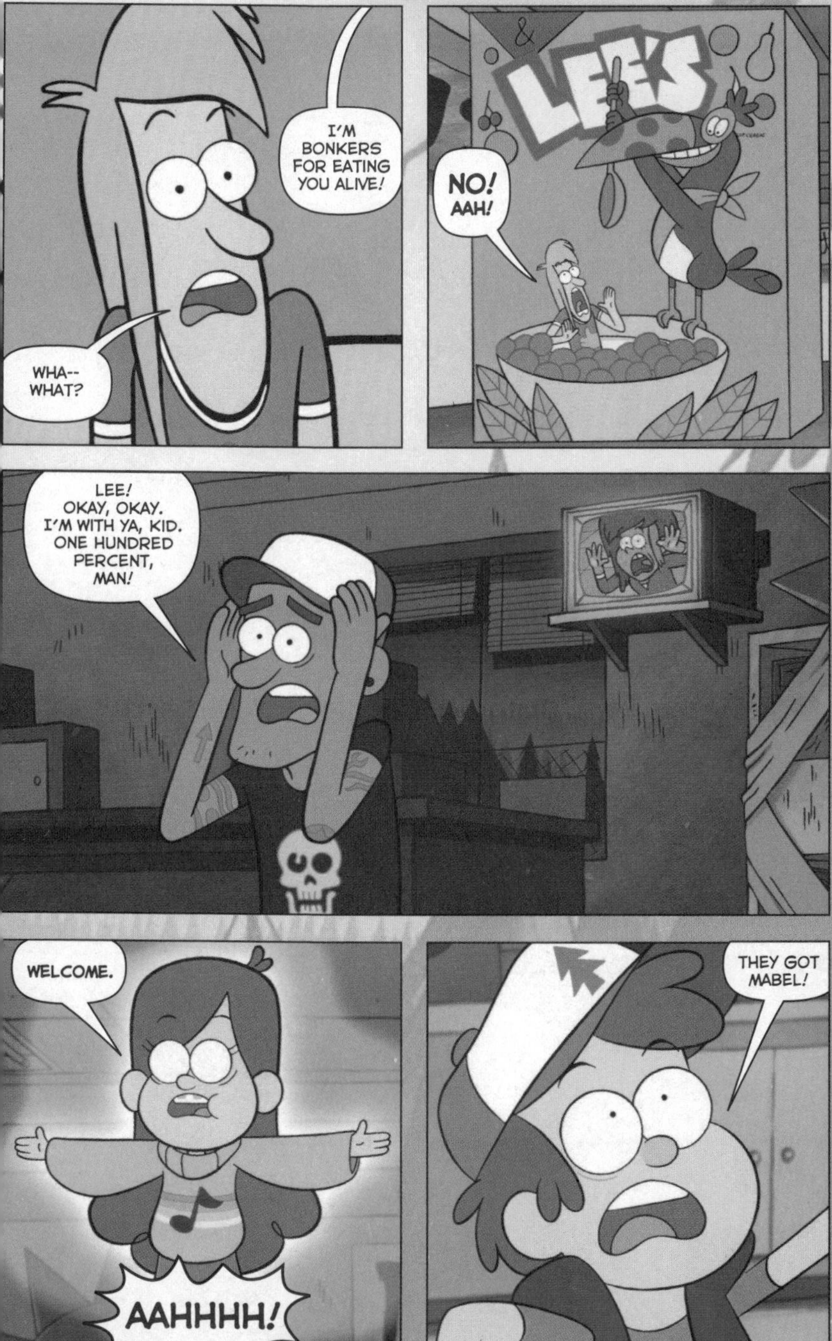
I'M BONKERS FOR EATING YOU ALIVE!
WHA-- WHAT?
LEE'S
NO! AAH!
LEE! OKAY, OKAY. I'M WITH YA, KID. ONE HUNDRED PERCENT, MAN!
WELCOME.
AAHHHH!
THEY GOT MABEL!

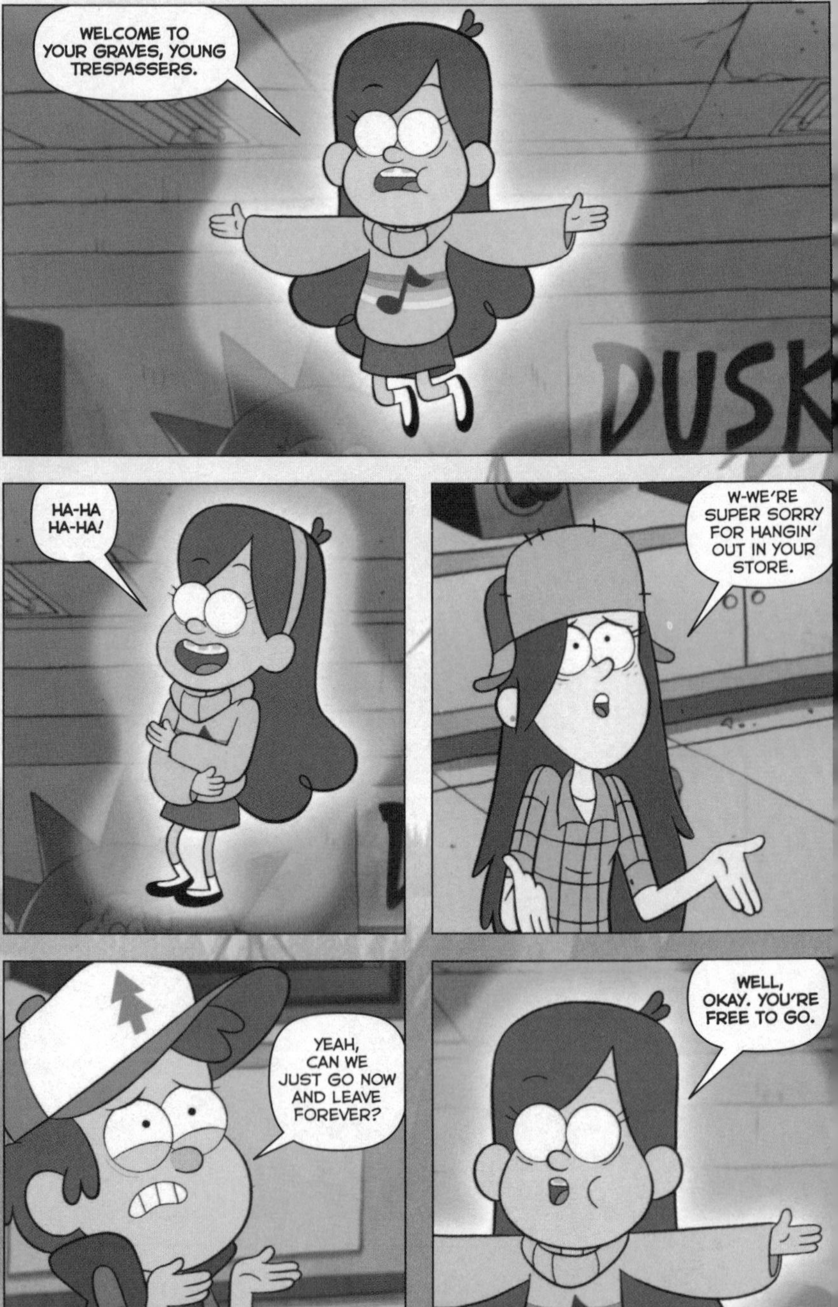
WELCOME TO YOUR GRAVES, YOUNG TRESPASSERS.
DUSK
HA-HA HA-HA!
W-WE'RE SUPER SORRY FOR HANGIN' OUT IN YOUR STORE.
YEAH, CAN WE JUST GO NOW AND LEAVE FOREVER?
WELL, OKAY. YOU'RE FREE TO GO.

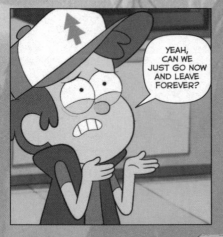

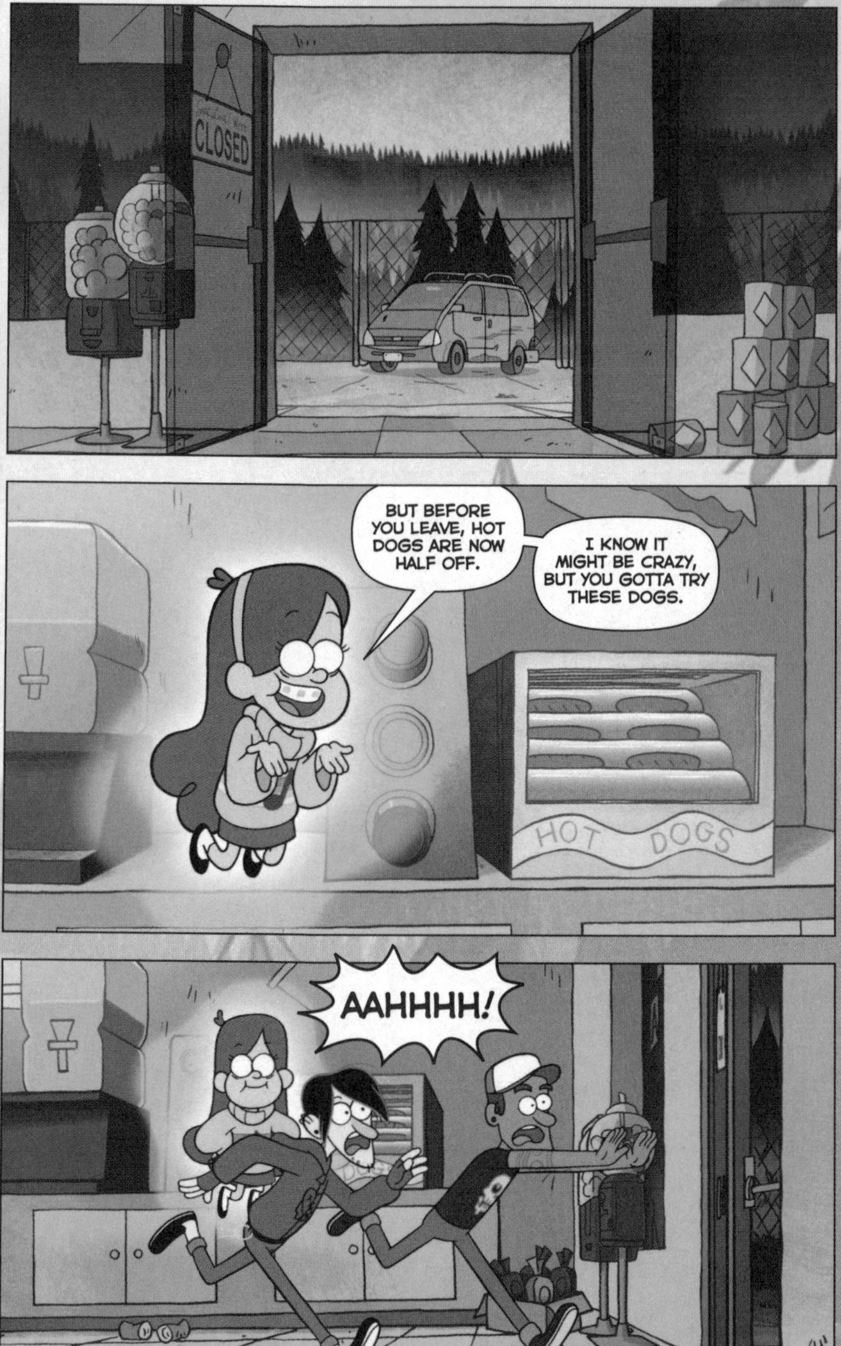
CLOSED
BUT BEFORE YOU LEAVE, HOT DOGS ARE NOW HALF OFF.
I KNOW IT MIGHT BE CRAZY, BUT YOU GOTTA TRY THESE DOGS.
HOT DOGS
AAHHHH!

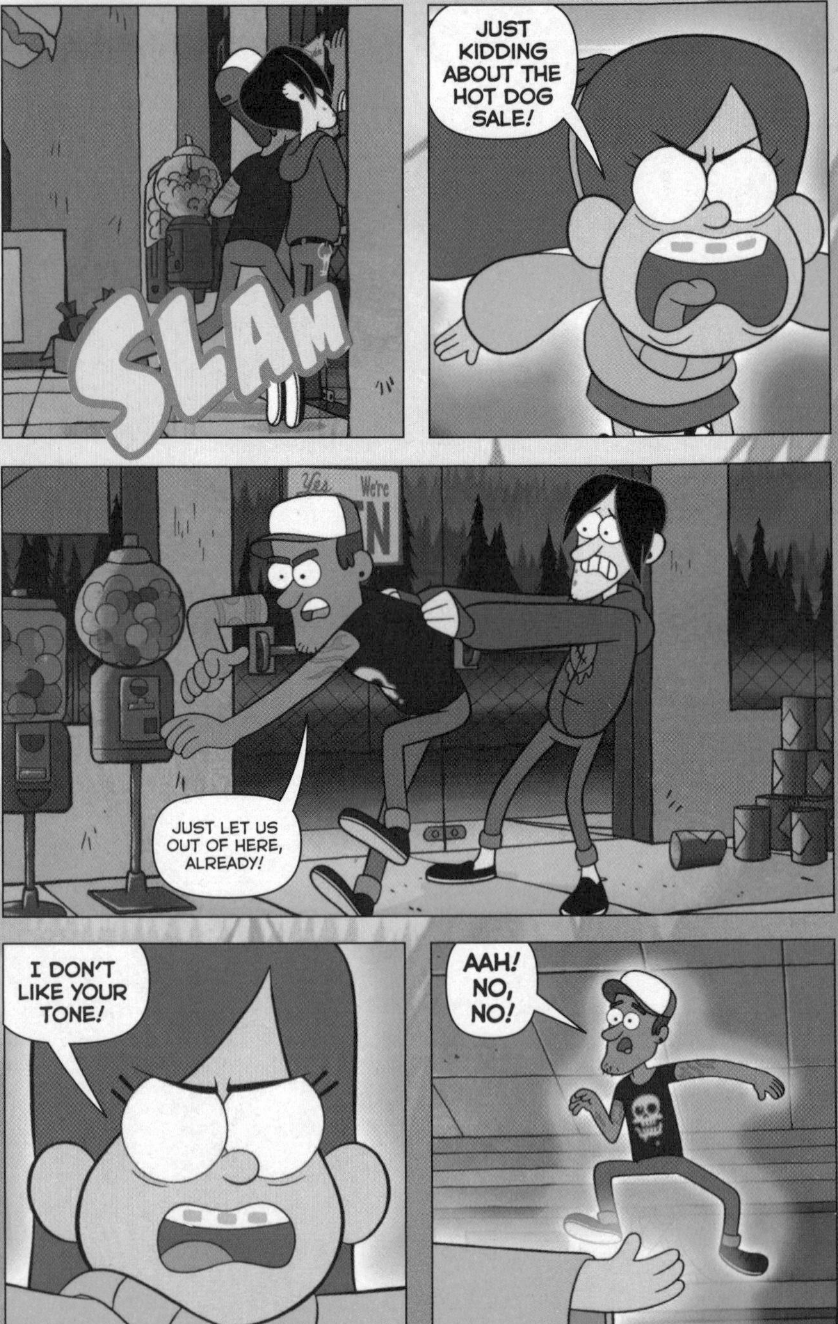
SLAM
JUST KIDDING ABOUT THE HOT DOG SALE!
Yes We're
JUST LET US OUT OF HERE, ALREADY!
I DON'T LIKE YOUR TONE!
AAH! NO, NO!

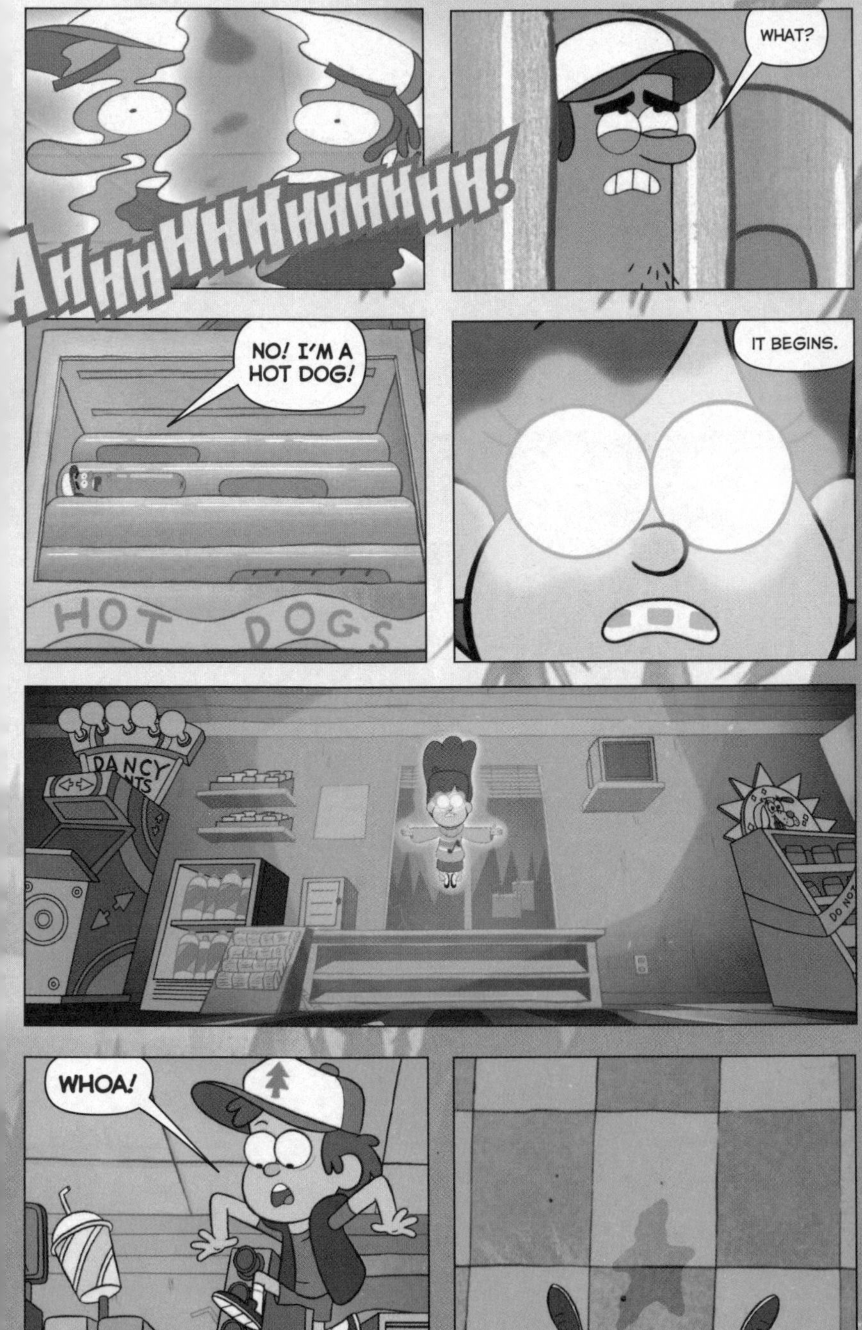
AHHHHHHHHHHHHH!
WHAT?
NO! I'M A HOT DOG!
IT BEGINS.
HOT DOGS
DANCY
WHOA!

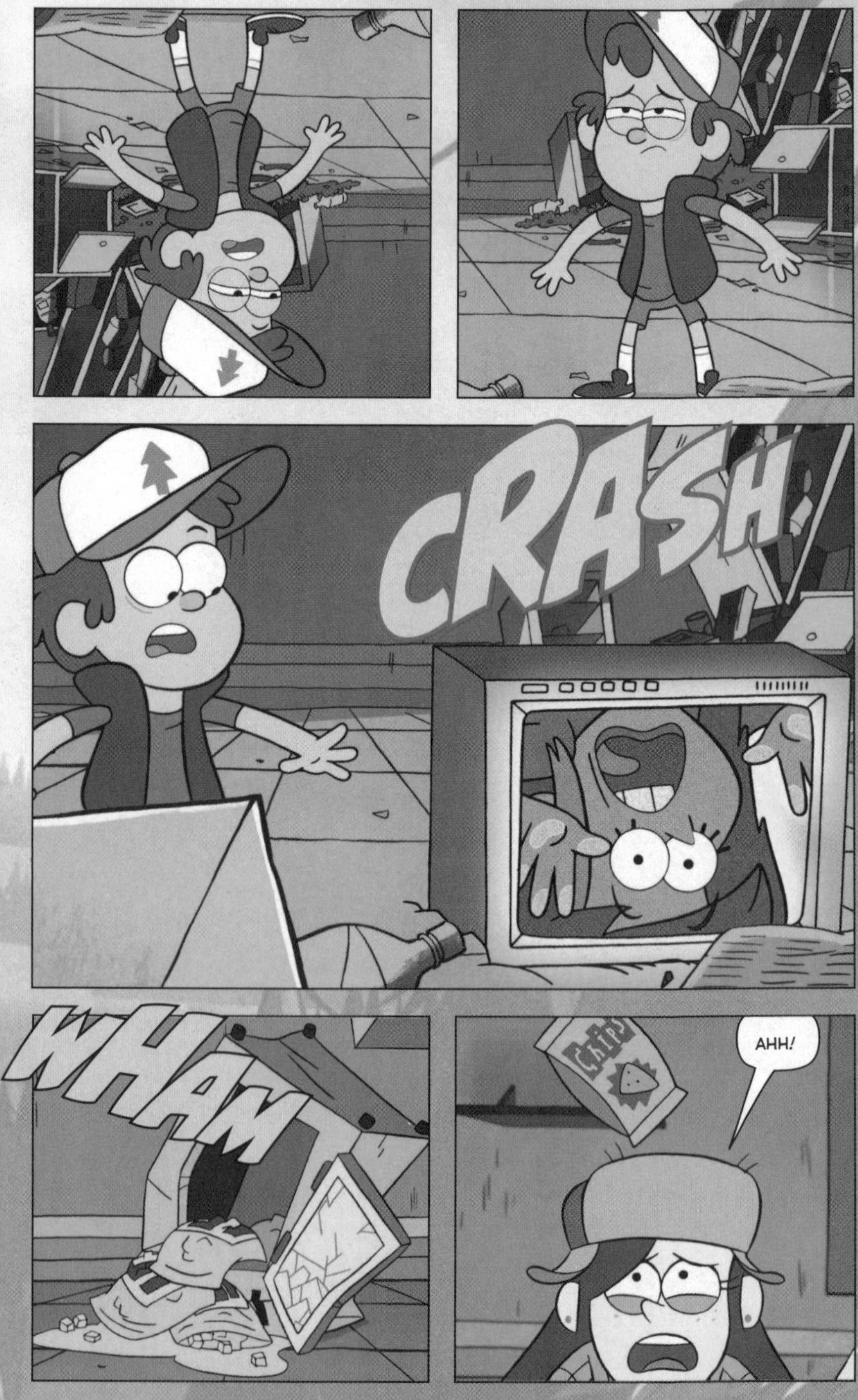
CRASH
WHAM
Chips
AHH!

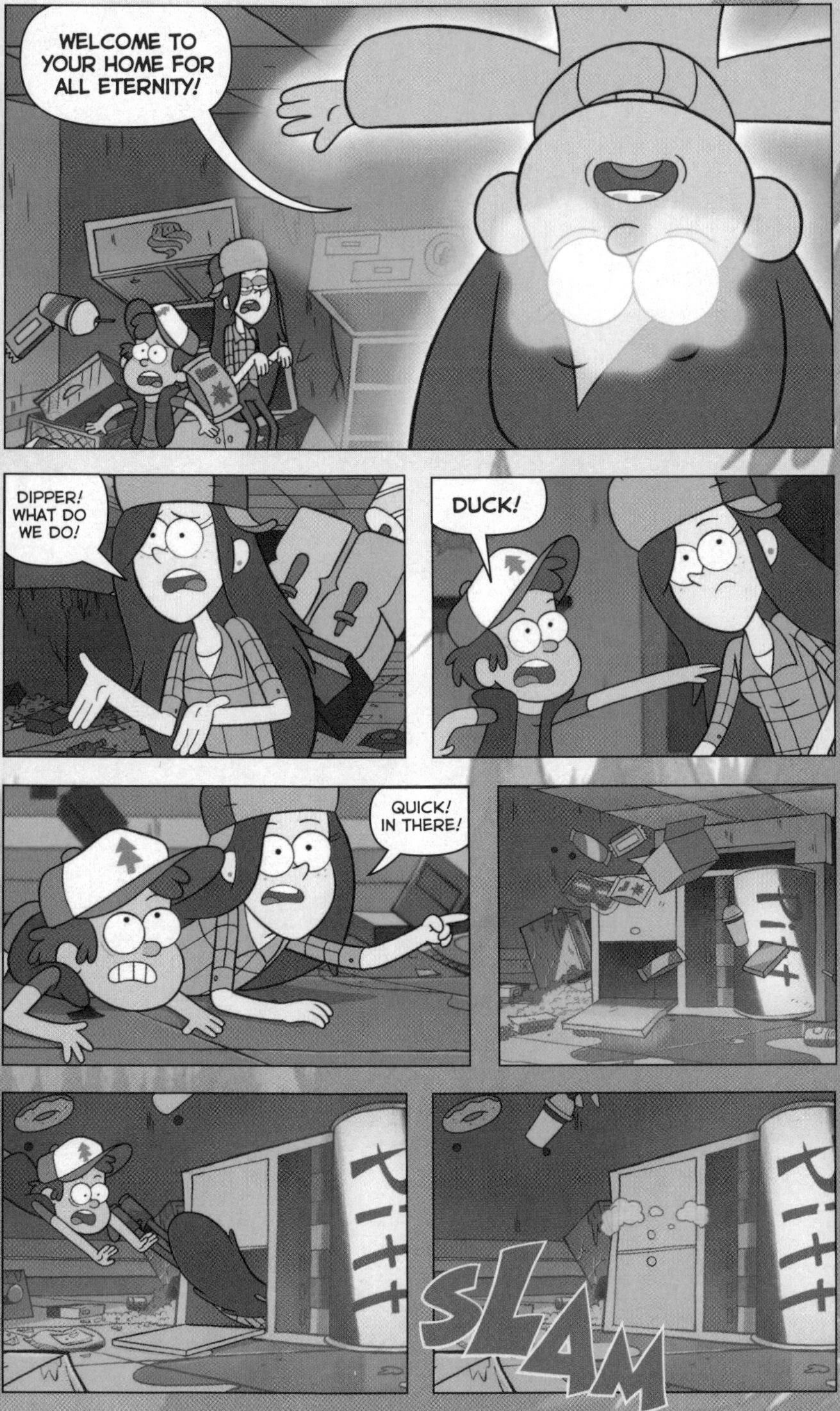
WELCOME TO YOUR HOME FOR ALL ETERNITY!
DIPPER! WHAT DO WE DO!
DUCK!
QUICK! IN THERE!
SLAM

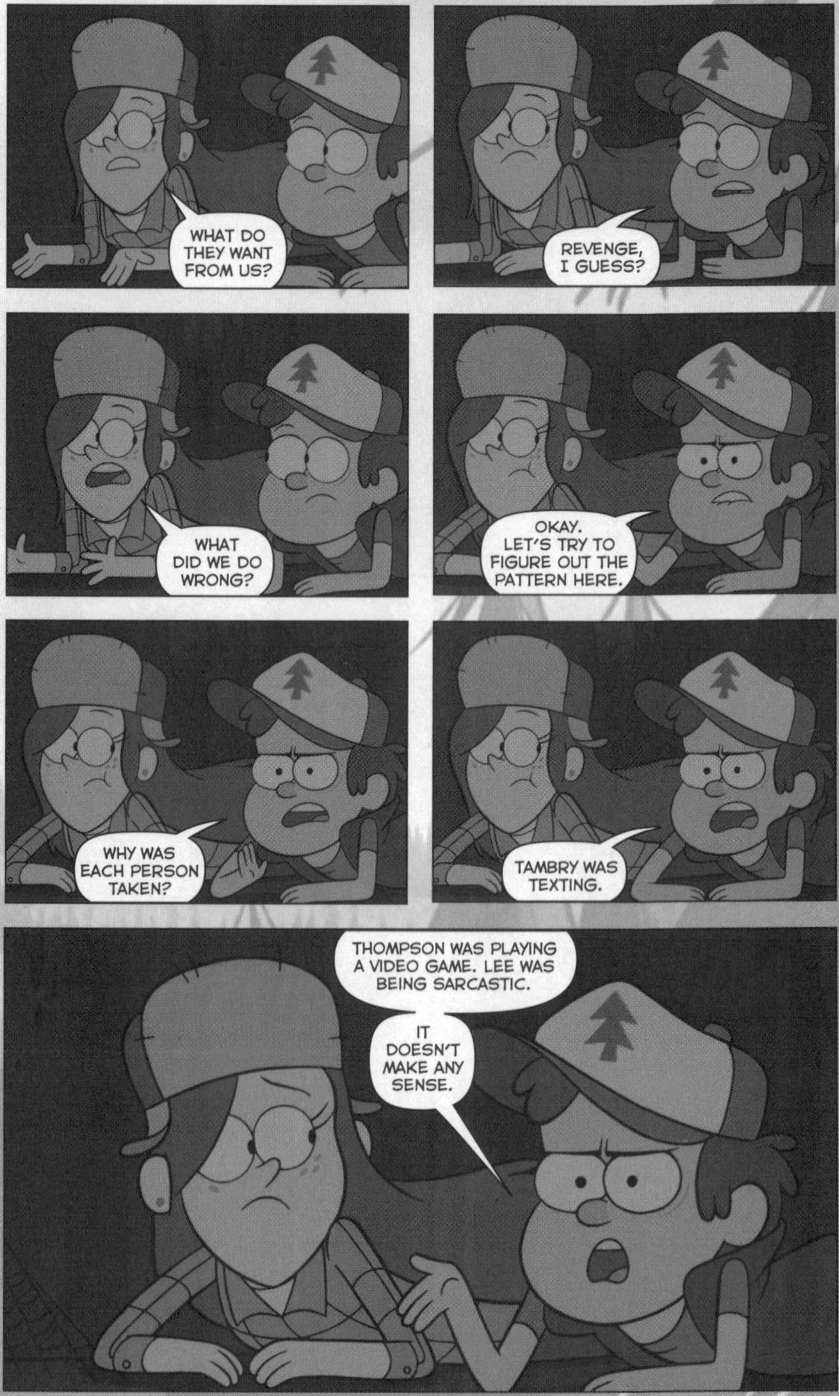
WHAT DO THEY WANT FROM US?
REVENGE, I GUESS?
WHAT DID WE DO WRONG?
OKAY. LET'S TRY TO FIGURE OUT THE PATTERN HERE.
WHY WAS EACH PERSON TAKEN?
TAMBRY WAS TEXTING.
THOMPSON WAS PLAYING A VIDEO GAME. LEE WAS BEING SARCASTIC.
IT DOESN'T MAKE ANY SENSE.

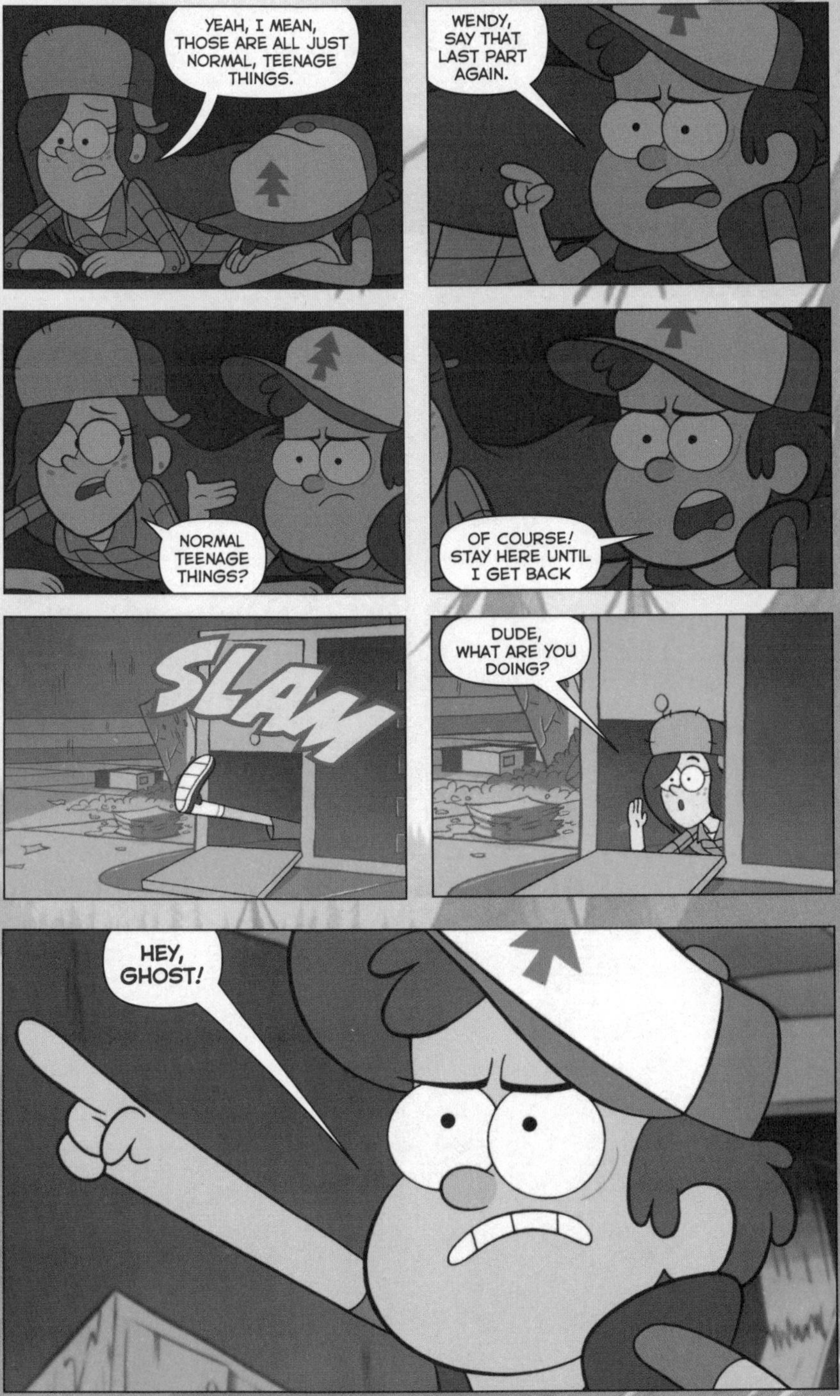
YEAH, I MEAN, THOSE ARE ALL JUST NORMAL, TEENAGE THINGS.
WENDY, SAY THAT LAST PART AGAIN.
NORMAL TEENAGE THINGS?
OF COURSE! STAY HERE UNTIL I GET BACK
SLAM
DUDE, WHAT ARE YOU DOING?
HEY, GHOST!

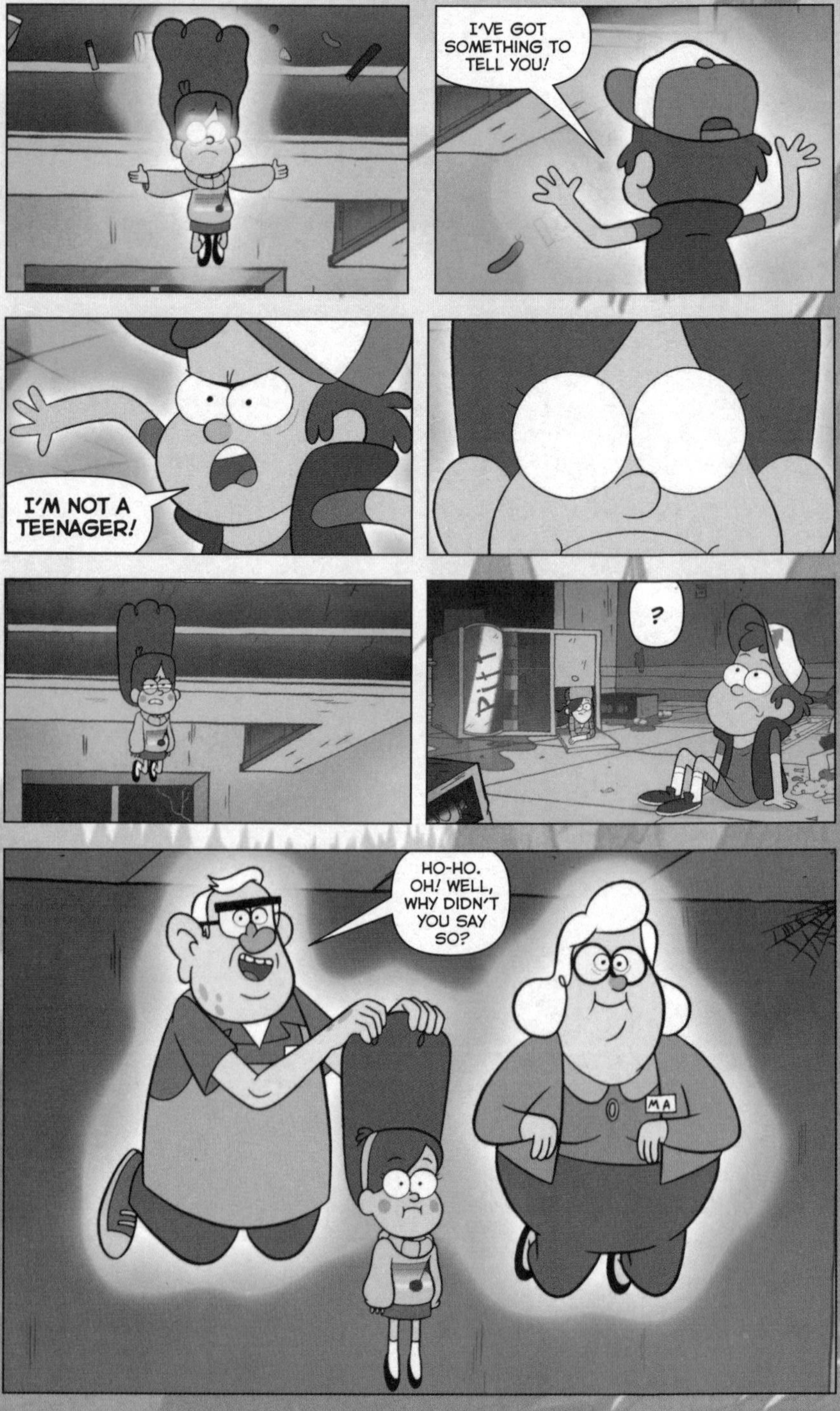
I'VE GOT SOMETHING TO TELL YOU!
I'M NOT A TEENAGER!
?
HO-HO. OH! WELL, WHY DIDN'T YOU SAY SO?
MA

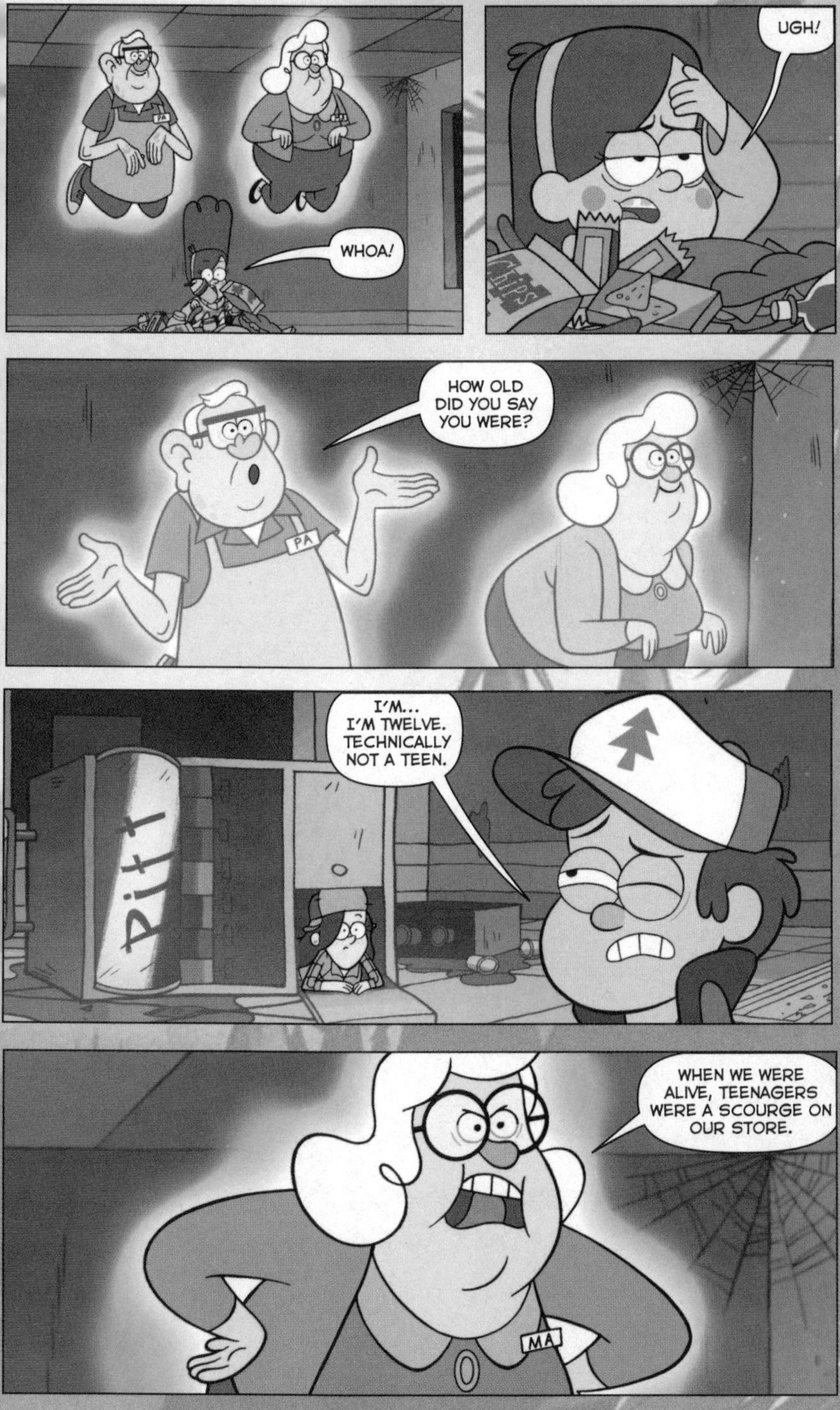
WHOA!
UGH!
HOW OLD DID YOU SAY YOU WERE?
I'M... I'M TWELVE. TECHNICALLY NOT A TEEN.
WHEN WE WERE ALIVE, TEENAGERS WERE A SCOURGE ON OUR STORE.

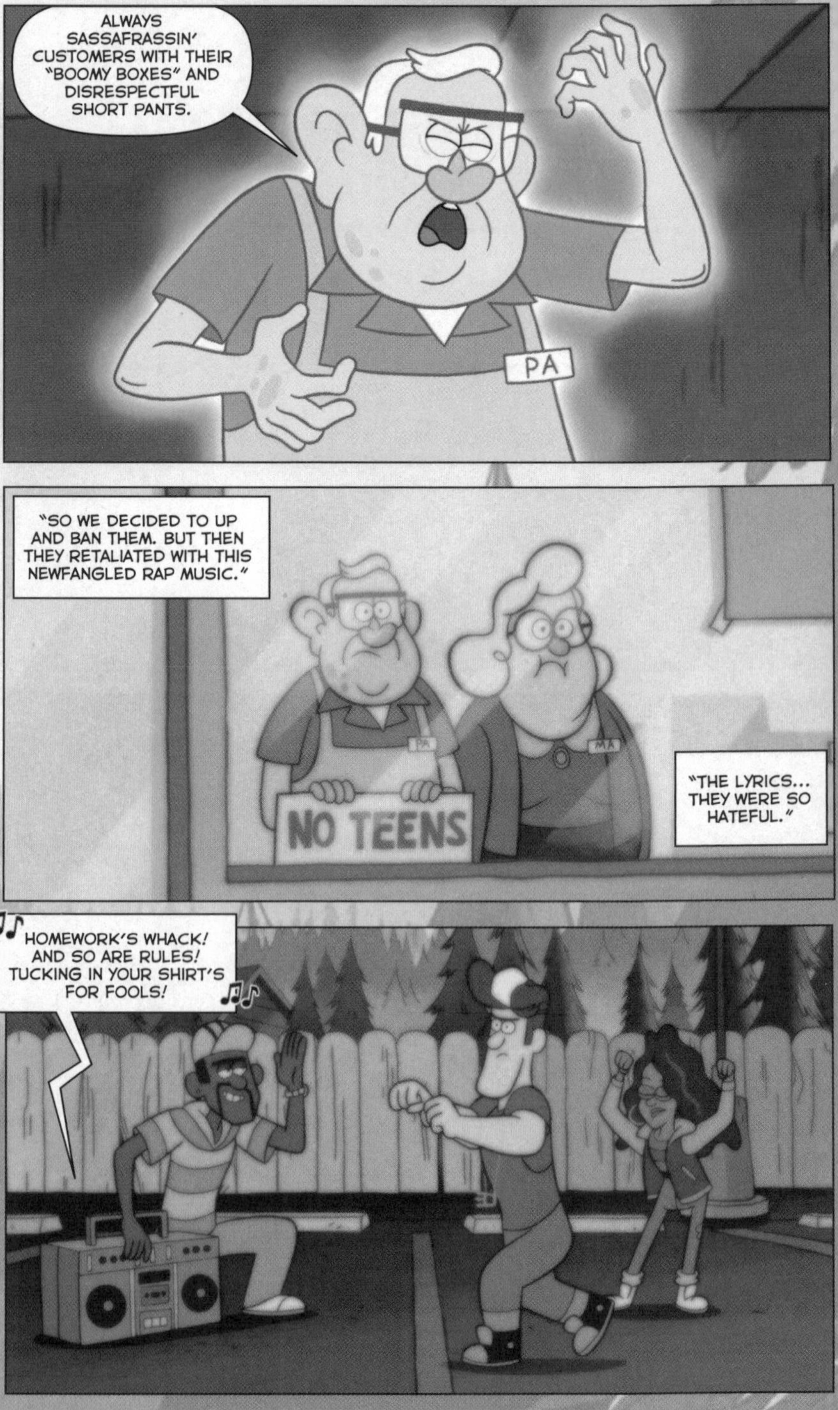

ALWAYS SASSAFRASSIN' CUSTOMERS WITH THEIR "BOOMY BOXES" AND DISRESPECTFUL SHORT PANTS.
PA
"SO WE DECIDED TO UP AND BAN THEM. BUT THEN THEY RETALIATED WITH THIS NEWFANGLED RAP MUSIC."
PA
MA
NO TEENS
"THE LYRICS... THEY WERE SO HATEFUL."
HOMEWORK'S WHACK! AND SO ARE RULES! TUCKING IN YOUR SHIRT'S FOR FOOLS!

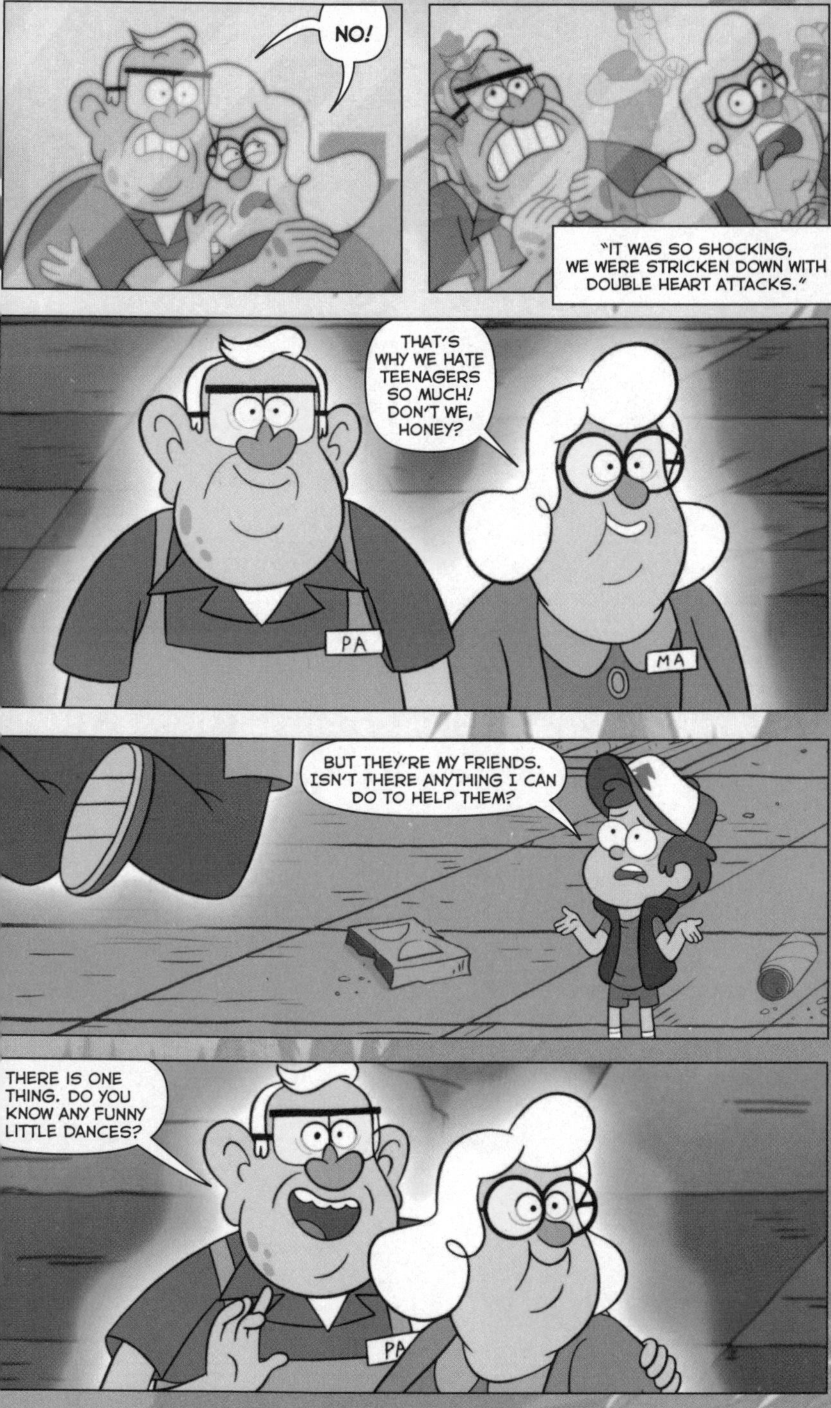
NO!
"IT WAS SO SHOCKING, WE WERE STRICKEN DOWN WITH DOUBLE HEART ATTACKS."
THAT'S WHY WE HATE TEENAGERS SO MUCH! DON'T WE, HONEY?
PA
MA
BUT THEY'RE MY FRIENDS. ISN'T THERE ANYTHING I CAN DO TO HELP THEM?
THERE IS ONE THING. DO YOU KNOW ANY FUNNY LITTLE DANCES?
PA

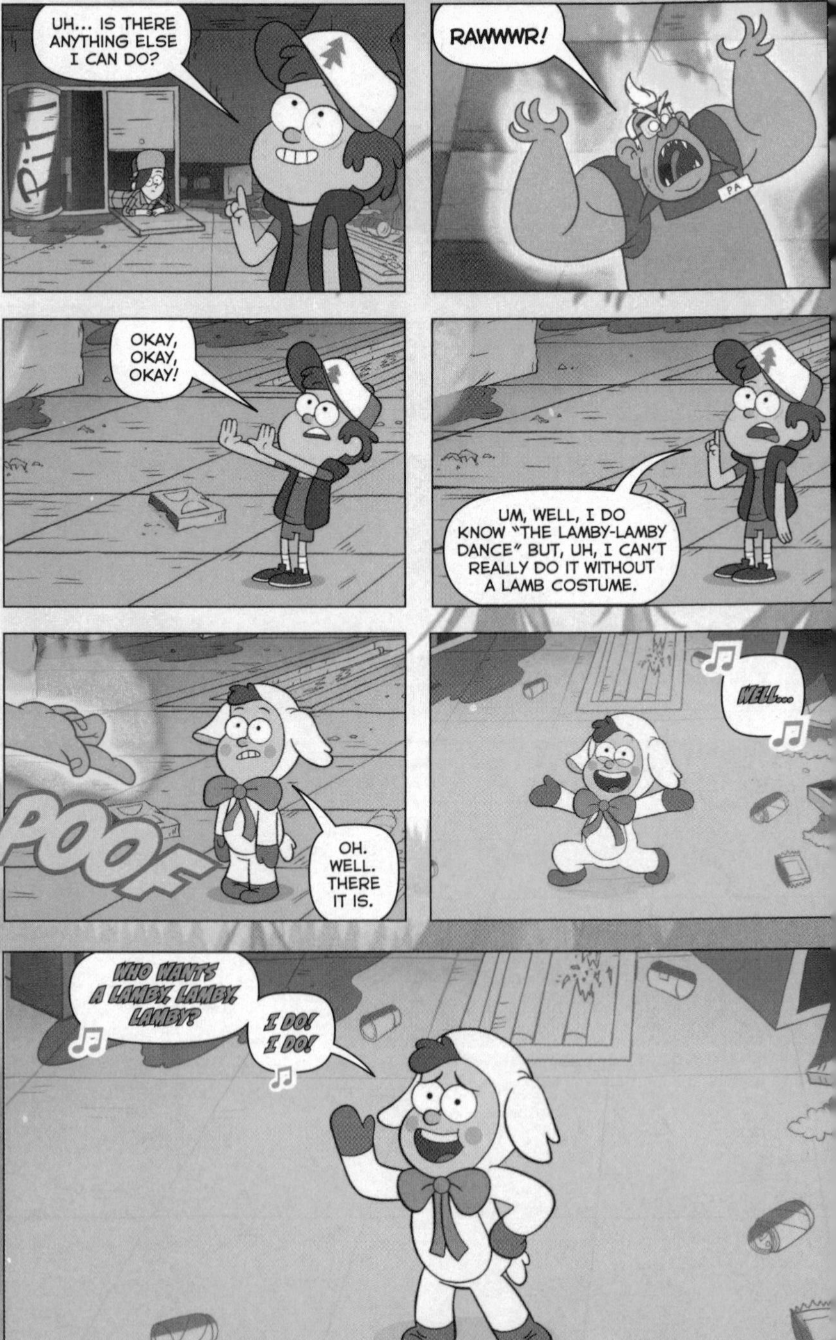
UH... IS THERE ANYTHING ELSE I CAN DO?
RAWWWR!
PA
OKAY, OKAY, OKAY!
UM, WELL, I DO KNOW "THE LAMBY-LAMBY DANCE" BUT, UH, I CAN'T REALLY DO IT WITHOUT A LAMB COSTUME.
POOF
OH. WELL. THERE IT IS.
WELL...
WHO WANTS A LAMBY, LAMBY, LAMBY?
I DO! I DO!

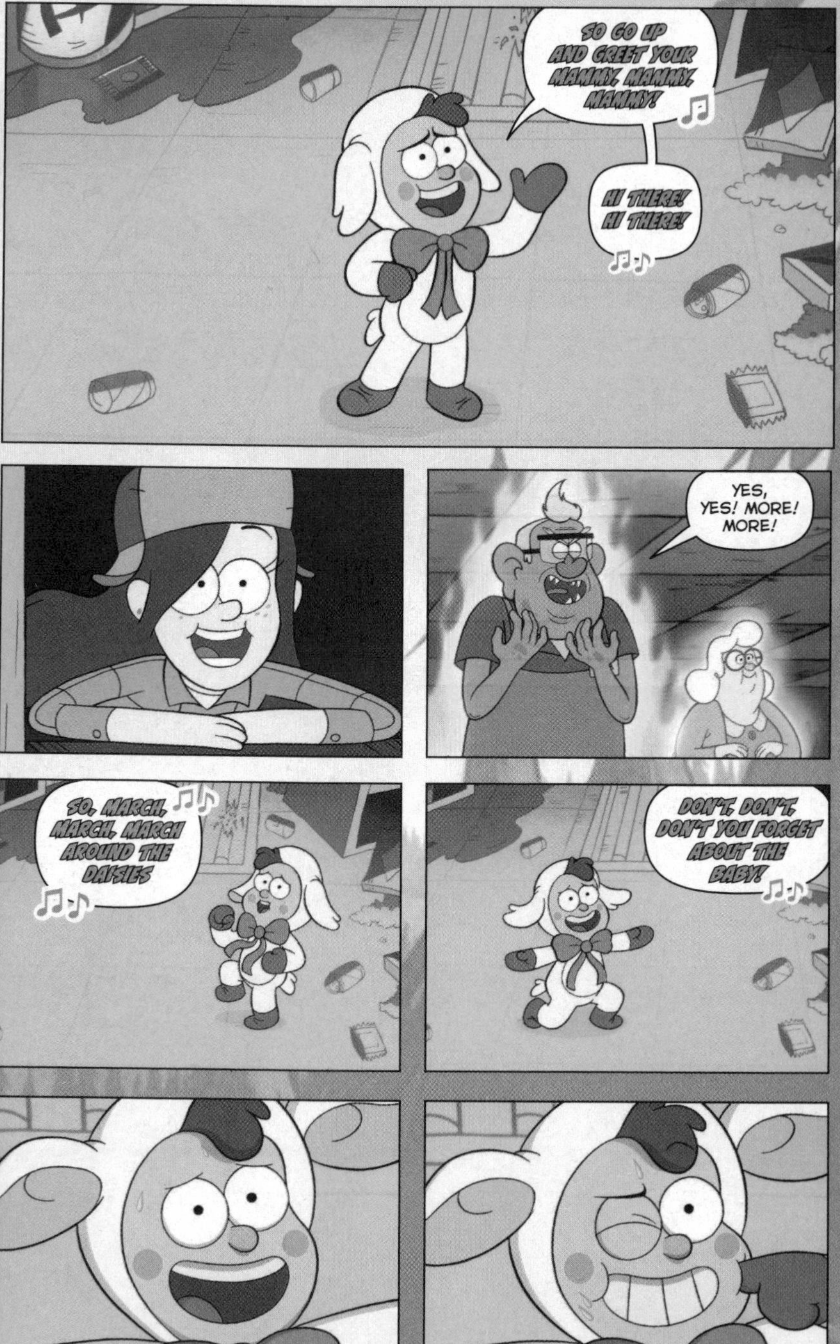
SO GO UP AND GREET YOUR MAMMY, MAMMY, MAMMY!
HI THERE! HI THERE!
YES, YES! MORE! MORE!
SO, MARCH, MARCH, MARCH AROUND THE DAISIES
DON'T, DON'T, DON'T YOU FORGET ABOUT THE BABY!

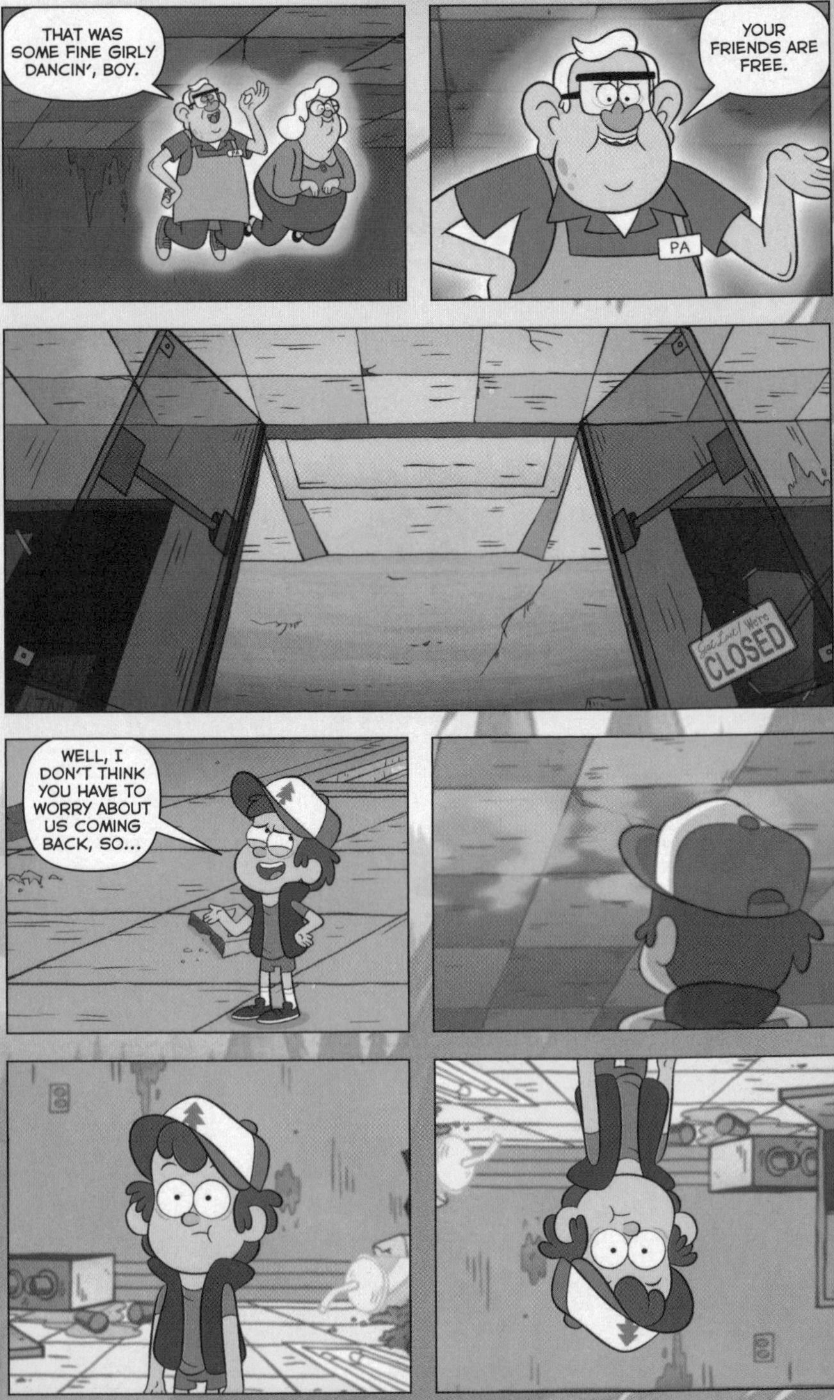
THAT WAS SOME FINE GIRLY DANCIN', BOY.
PA
YOUR FRIENDS ARE FREE.
PA
Get Lost! We're CLOSED
WELL, I DON'T THINK YOU HAVE TO WORRY ABOUT US COMING BACK, SO...

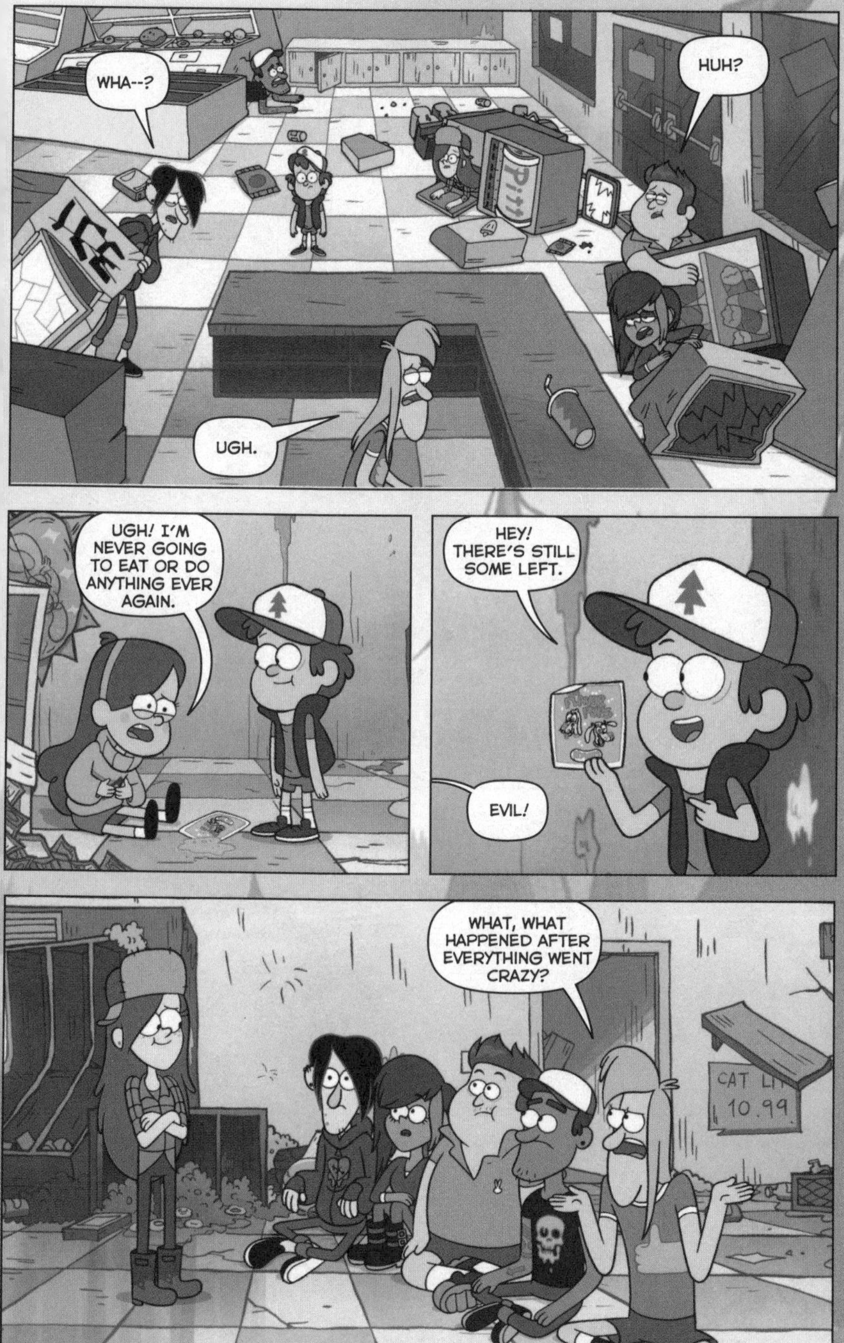
WHA--?
HUH?
UGH.
UGH! I'M NEVER GOING TO EAT OR DO ANYTHING EVER AGAIN.
HEY! THERE'S STILL SOME LEFT.
EVIL!
WHAT, WHAT HAPPENED AFTER EVERYTHING WENT CRAZY?
CAT LIT
10.99

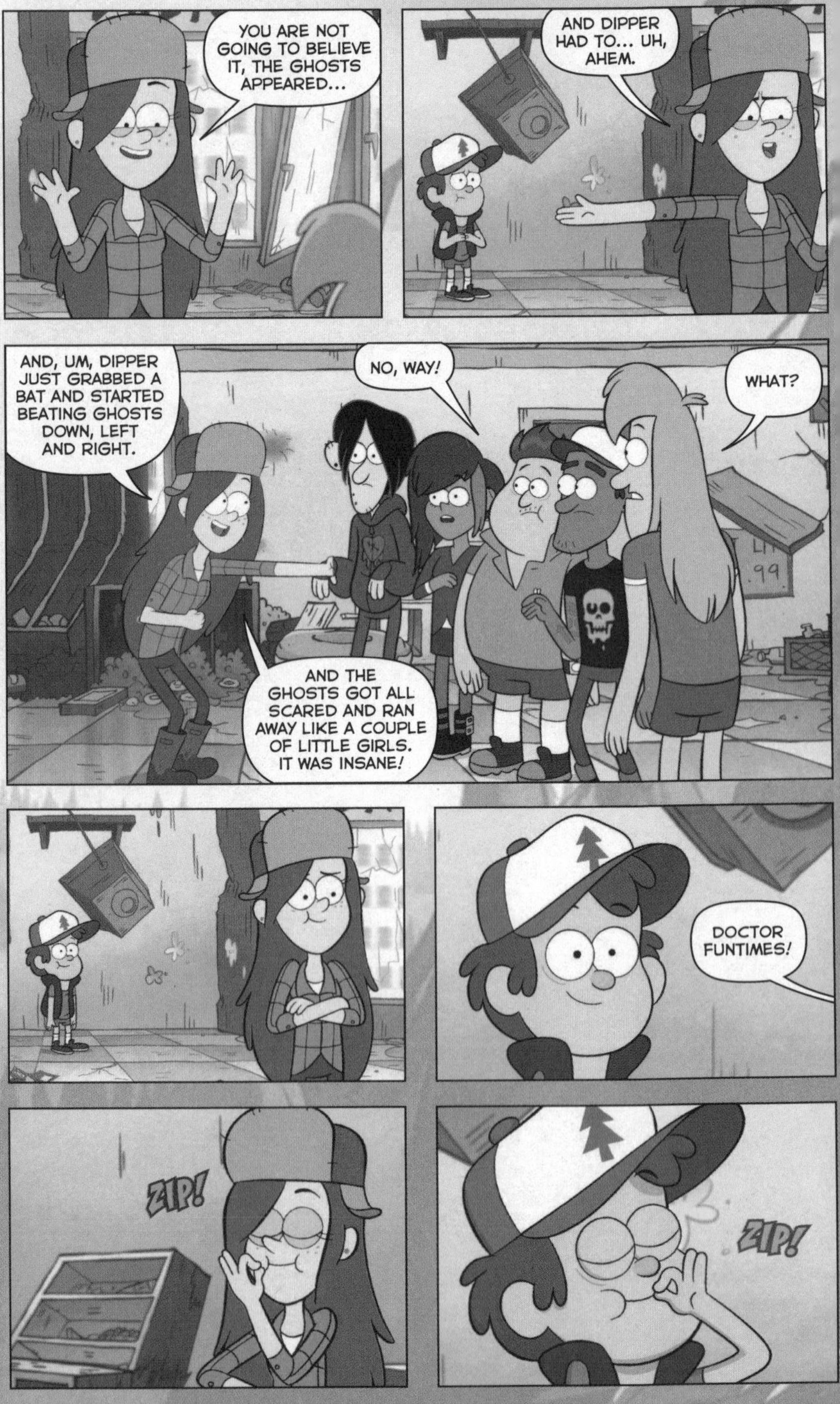
YOU ARE NOT GOING TO BELIEVE IT, THE GHOSTS APPEARED...
AND DIPPER HAD TO... UH, AHEM.
AND, UM, DIPPER JUST GRABBED A BAT AND STARTED BEATING GHOSTS DOWN, LEFT AND RIGHT.
NO, WAY!
WHAT?
AND THE GHOSTS GOT ALL SCARED AND RAN AWAY LIKE A COUPLE OF LITTLE GIRLS. IT WAS INSANE!
DOCTOR FUNTIMES!
ZIP!
ZIP!

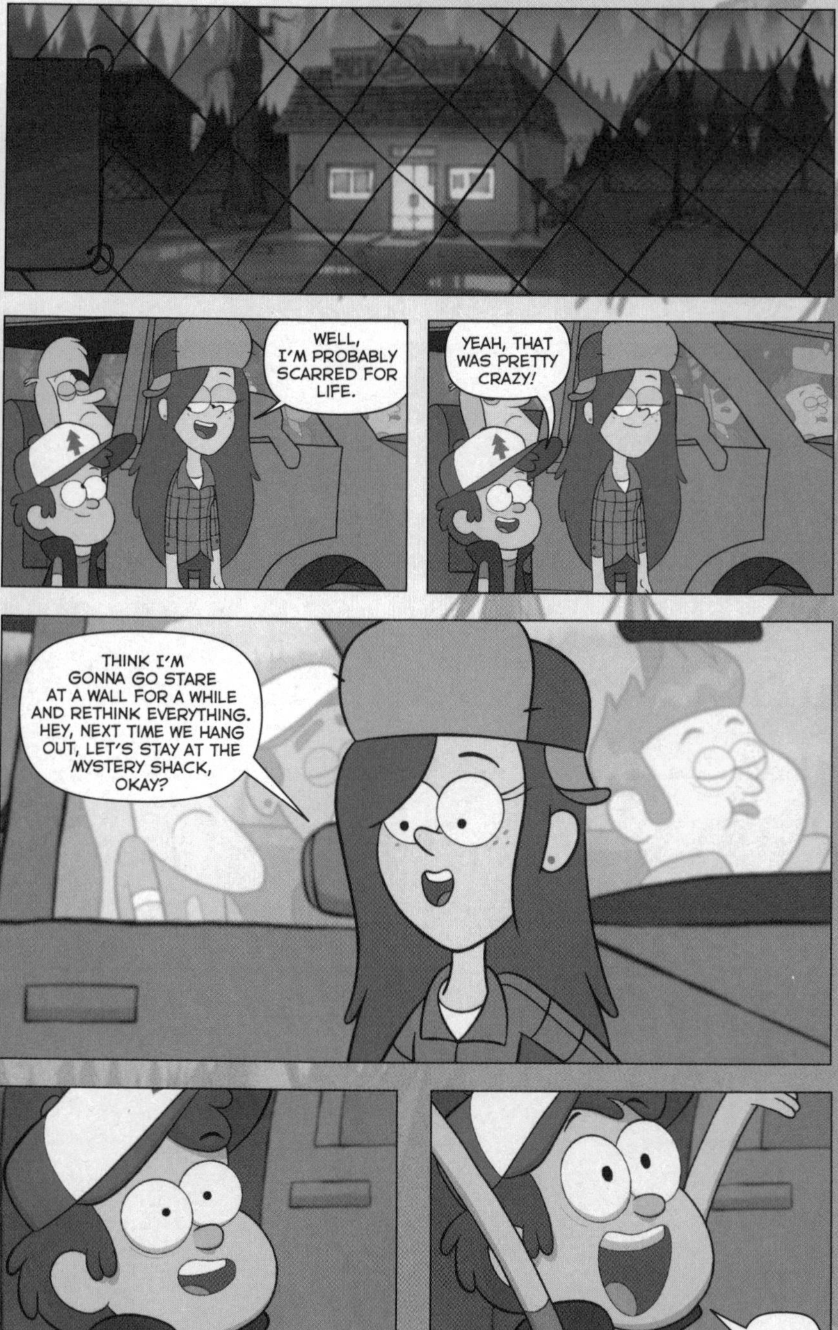
WELL, I'M PROBABLY SCARRED FOR LIFE.
YEAH, THAT WAS PRETTY CRAZY!
THINK I'M GONNA GO STARE AT A WALL FOR A WHILE AND RETHINK EVERYTHING. HEY, NEXT TIME WE HANG OUT, LET'S STAY AT THE MYSTERY SHACK, OKAY?
NEXT TIME?

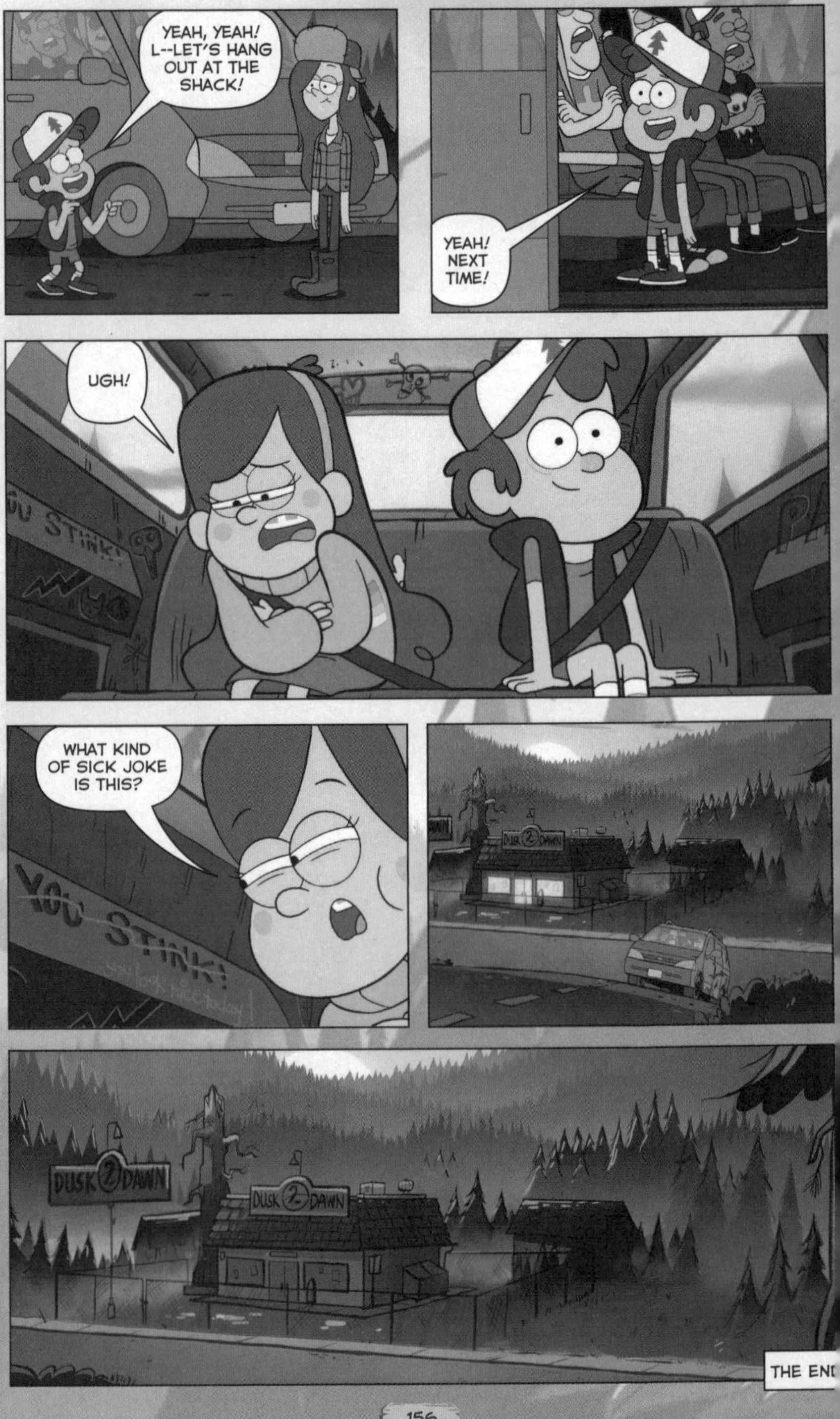
YEAH, YEAH! L--LET'S HANG OUT AT THE SHACK!
YEAH! NEXT TIME!
UGH!
WHAT KIND OF SICK JOKE IS THIS?
YOU STINK!
DUSK 2 DAWN
DUSK 2 DAWN
DUSK 2 DAWN
THE EN

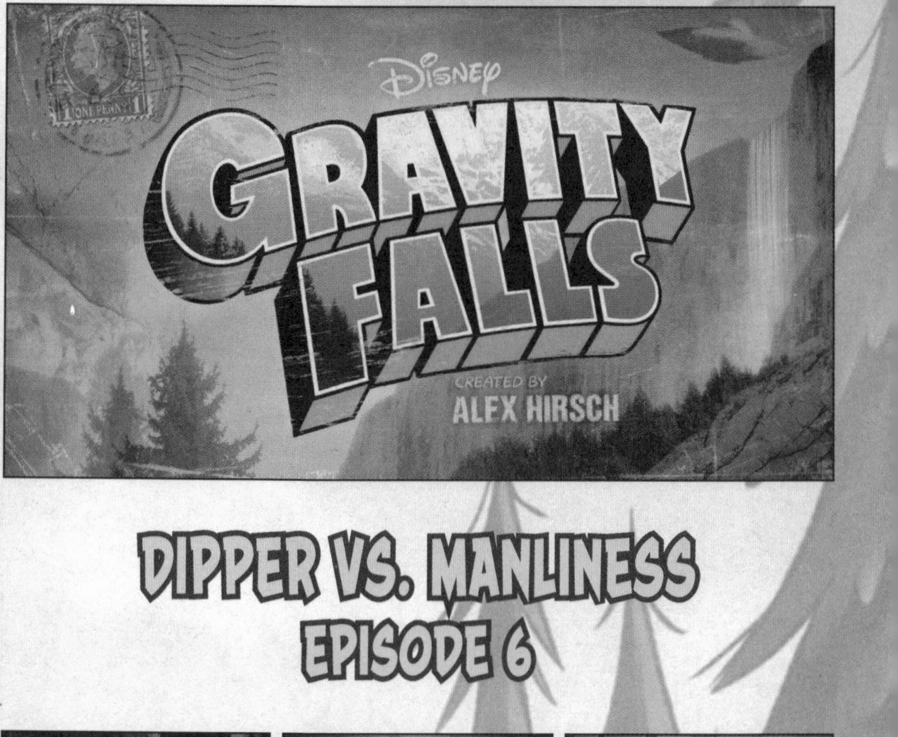
DISNEY
GRAVITY FALLS
CREATED BY
ALEX HIRSCH

DIPPER VS. MANLINESS
EPISODE 6

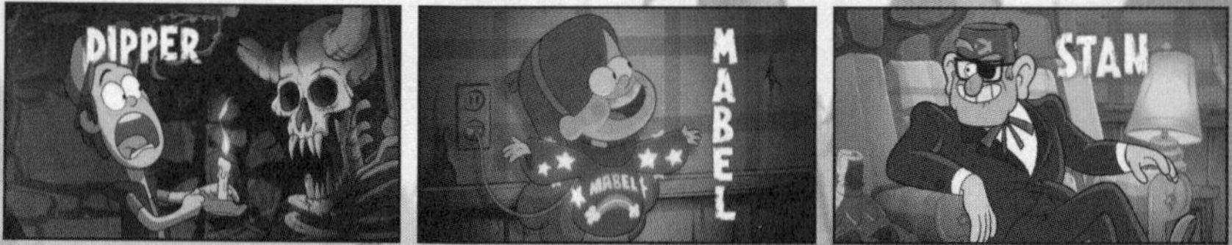
DIPPER
MABEL
STAN

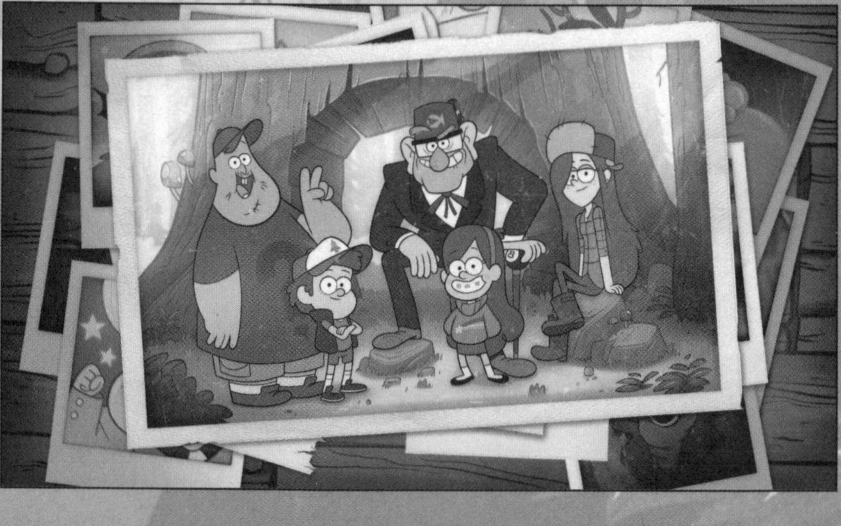

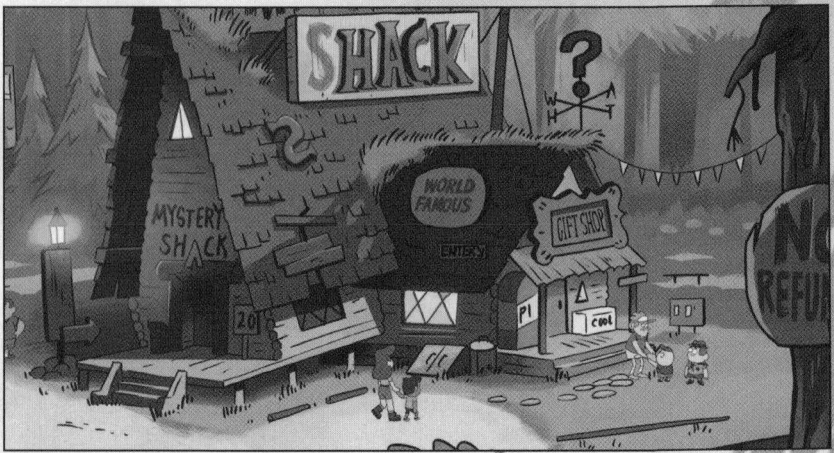
SHACK
MYSTERY SHACK
WORLD FAMOUS
GIFT SHOP
ENTRY
COOL
NO REFUN

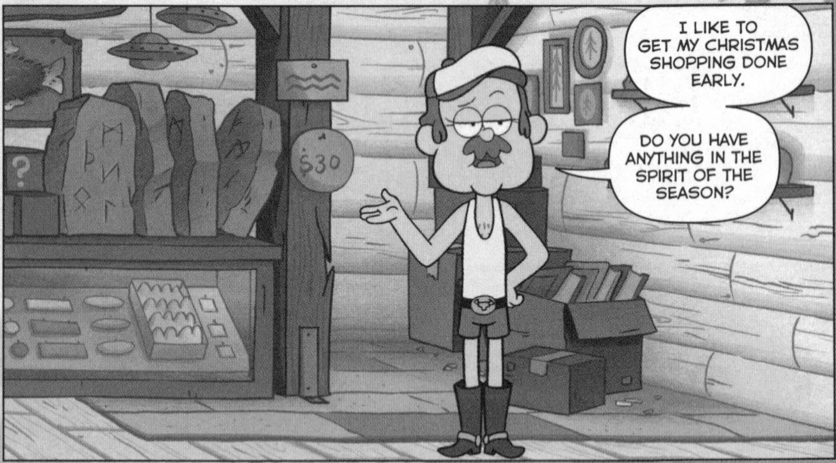
I LIKE TO GET MY CHRISTMAS SHOPPING DONE EARLY.
DO YOU HAVE ANYTHING IN THE SPIRIT OF THE SEASON?
$30

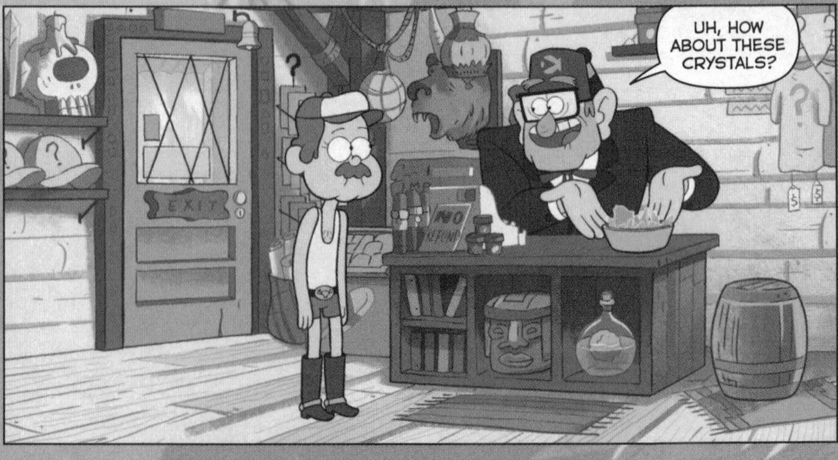
UH, HOW ABOUT THESE CRYSTALS?
EXIT

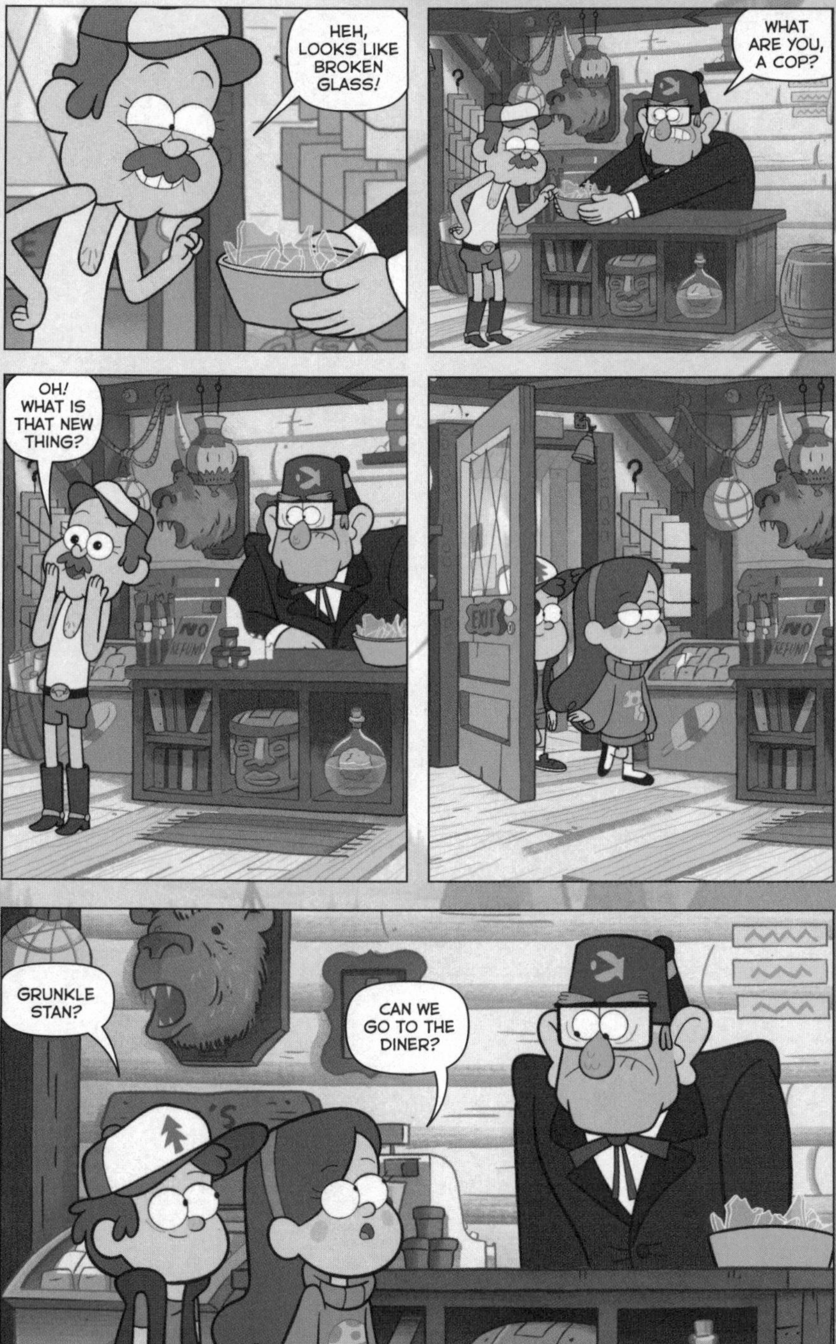

HEH, LOOKS LIKE BROKEN GLASS!
WHAT ARE YOU, A COP?
OH! WHAT IS THAT NEW THING?
EXIT
NO REFUND
GRUNKLE STAN?
CAN WE GO TO THE DINER?

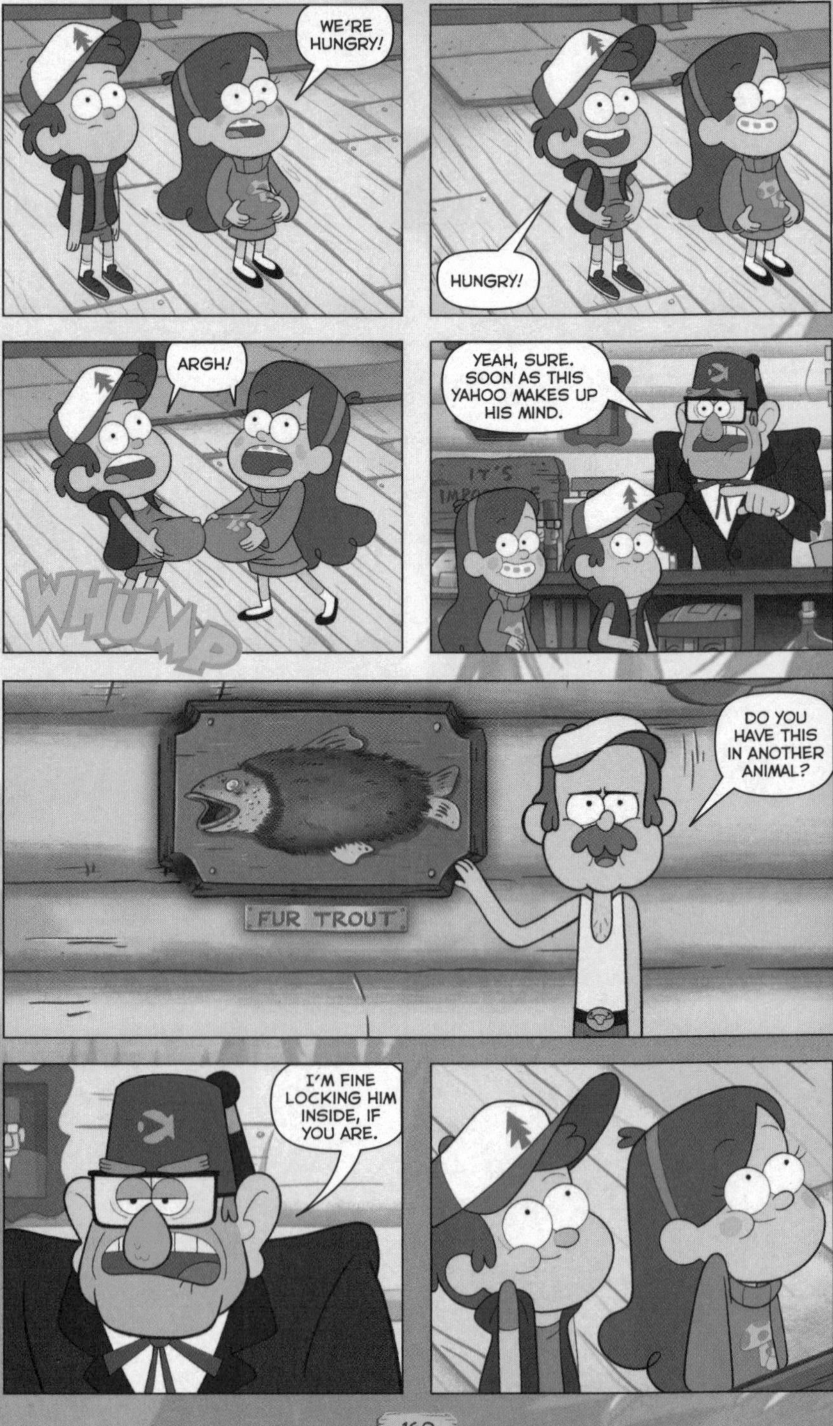
WE'RE HUNGRY!
HUNGRY!
ARGH!
WHUMP
YEAH, SURE. SOON AS THIS YAHOO MAKES UP HIS MIND.
DO YOU HAVE THIS IN ANOTHER ANIMAL?
FUR TROUT
I'M FINE LOCKING HIM INSIDE, IF YOU ARE.

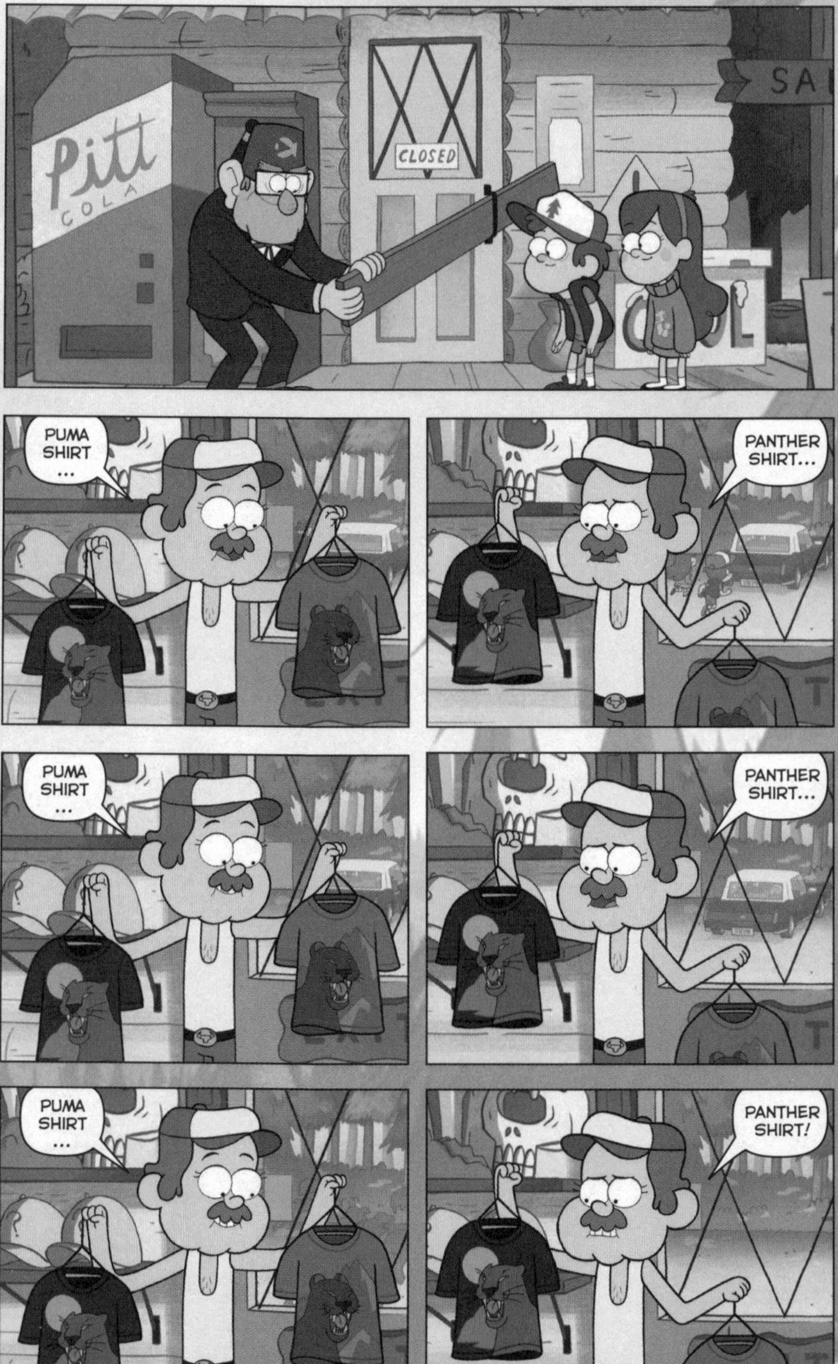
Pitt
COLA
CLOSED
PUMA SHIRT ...
PANTHER SHIRT...
PUMA SHIRT ...
PANTHER SHIRT...
PUMA SHIRT ...
PANTHER SHIRT!

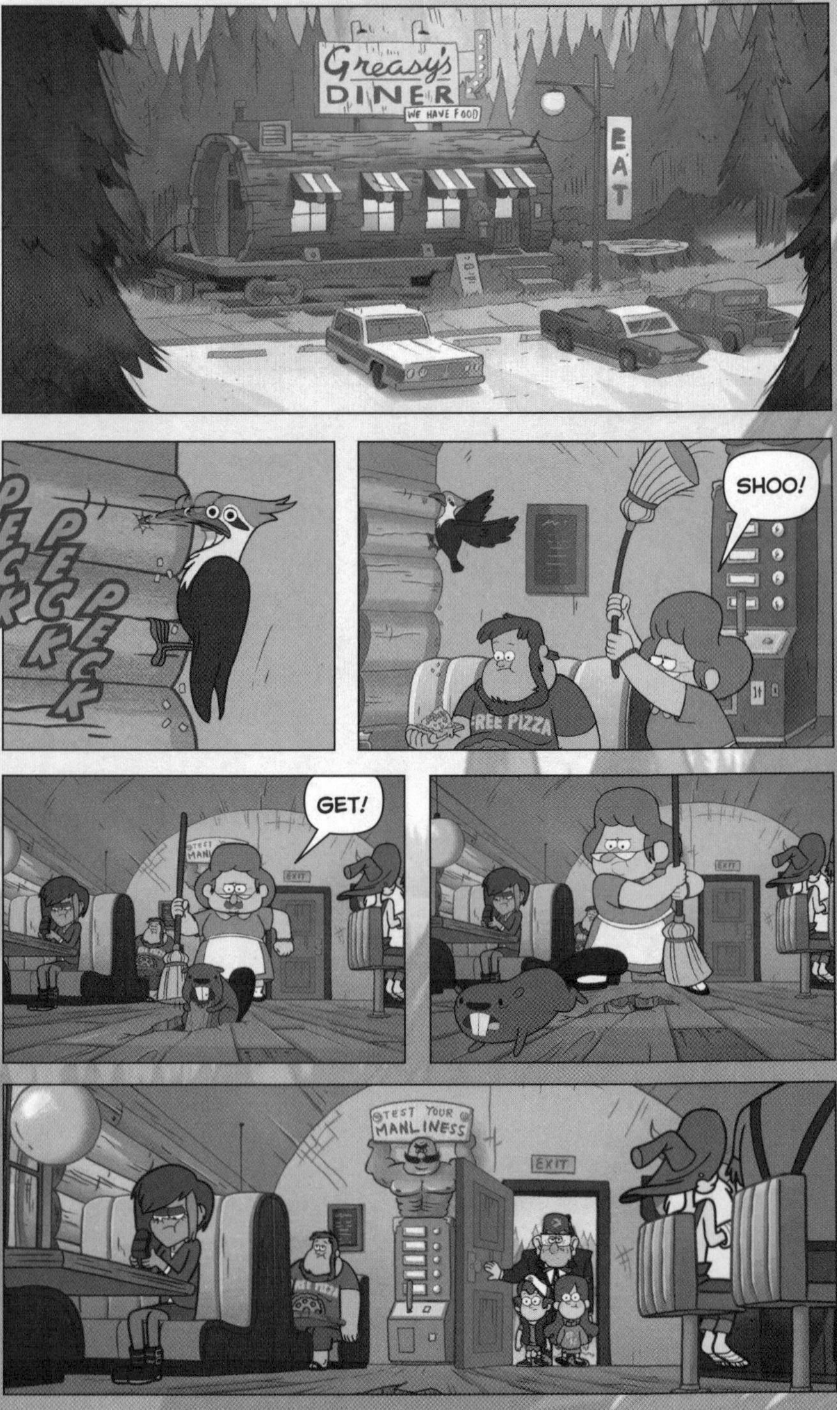
Greasy's
DINER
WE HAVE FOOD
EAT
PECK PECK PECK
SHOO!
FREE PIZZA
GET!
TEST YOUR MANLINESS
EXIT

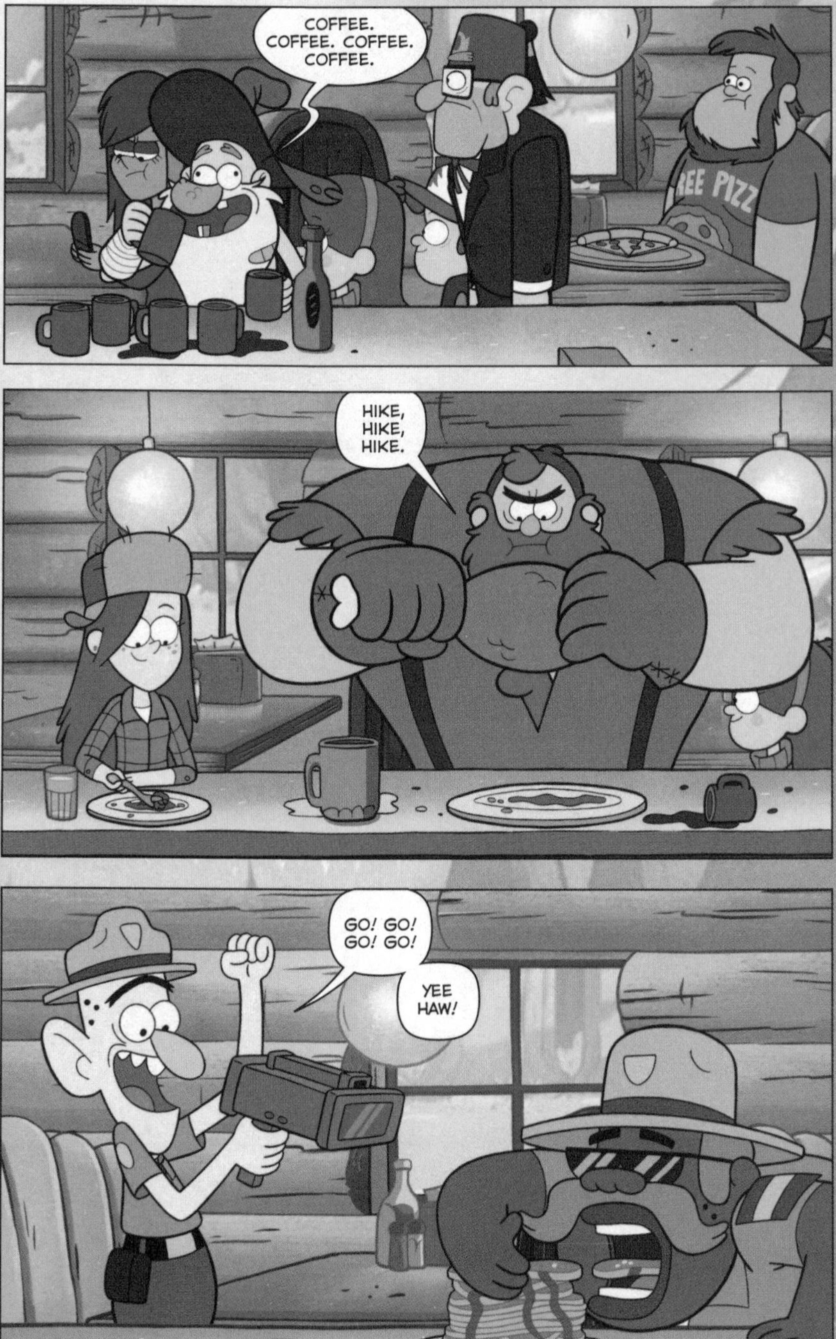
COFFEE. COFFEE. COFFEE. COFFEE.
REE PIZZ
HIKE, HIKE, HIKE.
GO! GO! GO! GO!
YEE HAW!

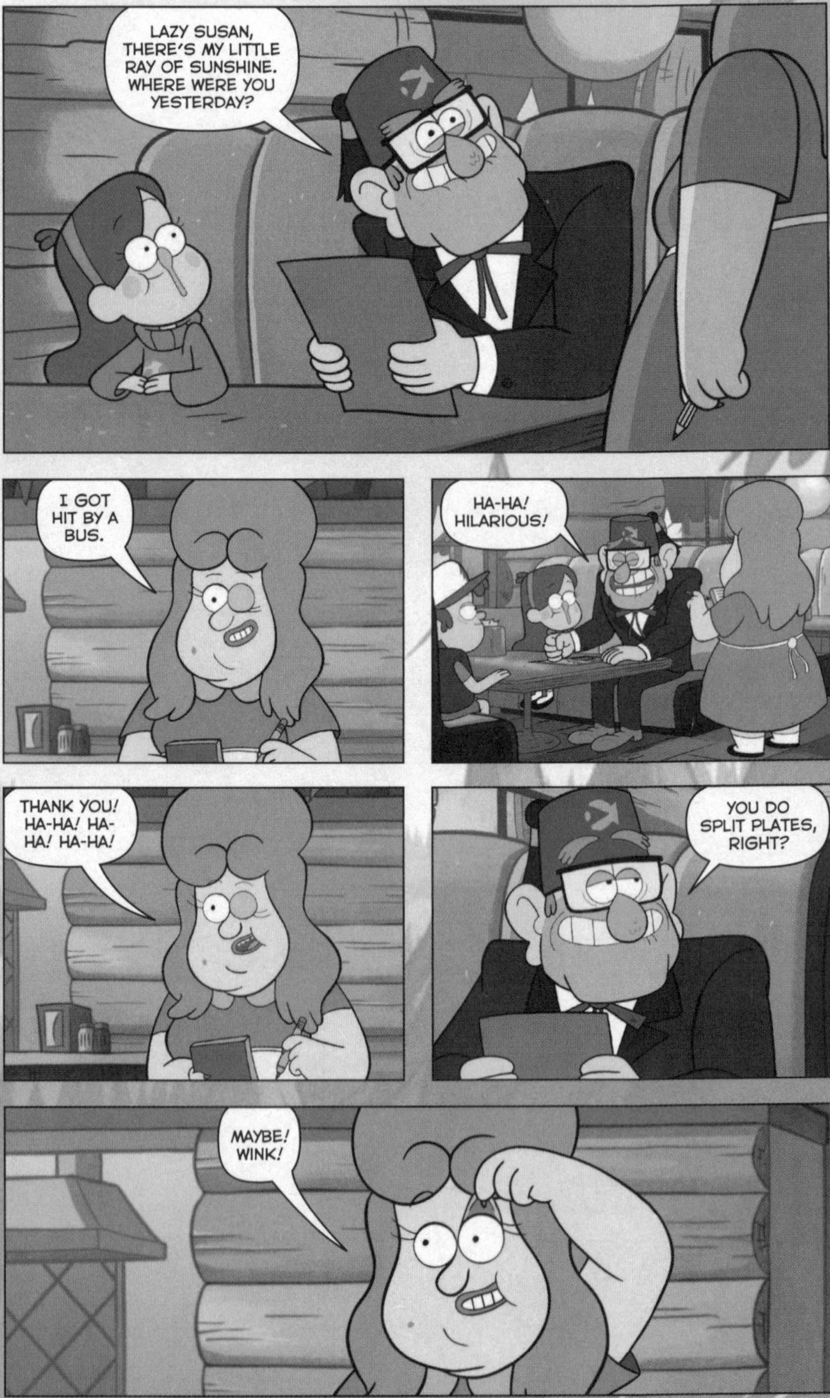
LAZY SUSAN, THERE'S MY LITTLE RAY OF SUNSHINE. WHERE WERE YOU YESTERDAY?
I GOT HIT BY A BUS.
HA-HA! HILARIOUS!
THANK YOU! HA-HA! HA-HA! HA-HA!
YOU DO SPLIT PLATES, RIGHT?
MAYBE! WINK!

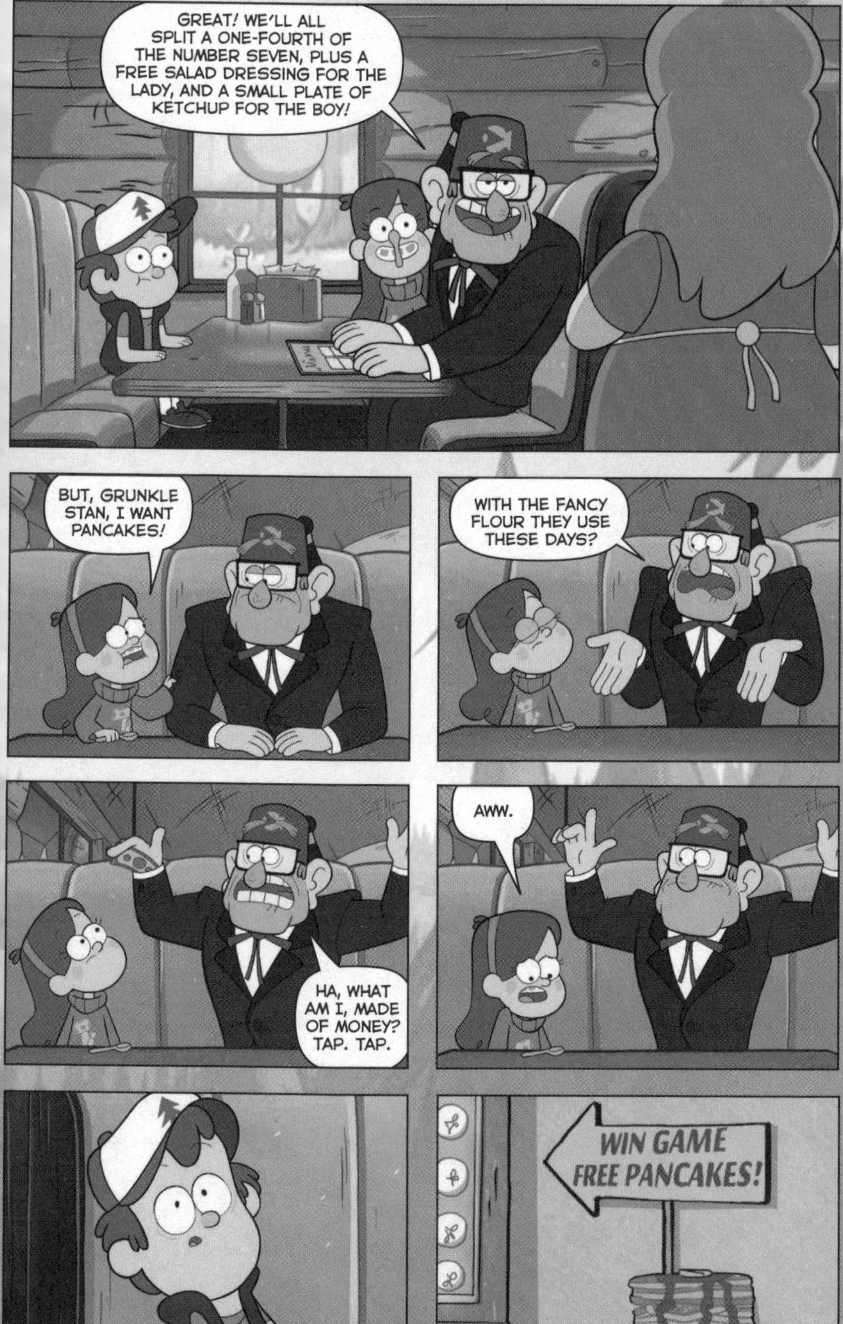
GREAT! WE'LL ALL SPLIT A ONE-FOURTH OF THE NUMBER SEVEN, PLUS A FREE SALAD DRESSING FOR THE LADY, AND A SMALL PLATE OF KETCHUP FOR THE BOY!
BUT, GRUNKLE STAN, I WANT PANCAKES!
WITH THE FANCY FLOUR THEY USE THESE DAYS?
HA, WHAT AM I, MADE OF MONEY? TAP. TAP.
AWW.
WIN GAME FREE PANCAKES!

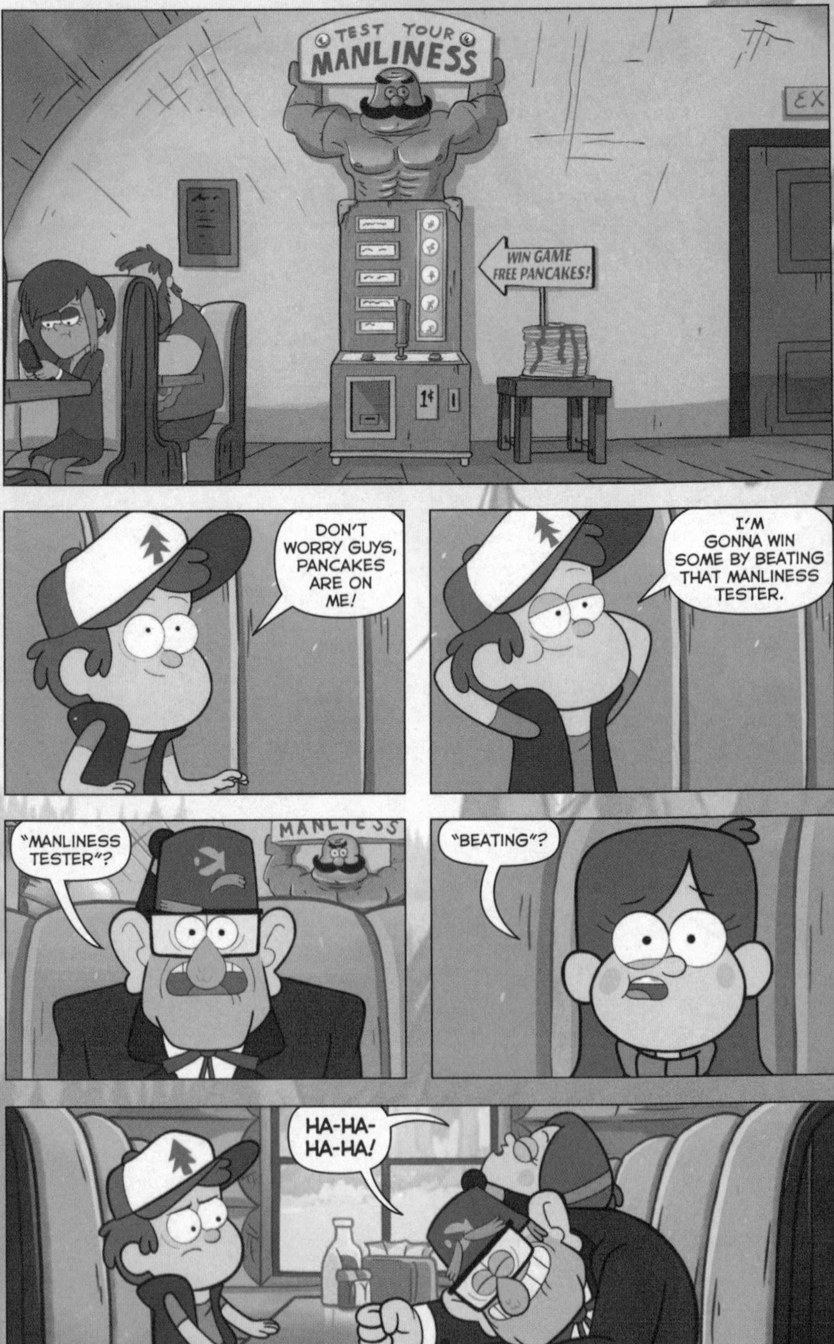

TEST YOUR MANLINESS
WIN GAME FREE PANCAKES!
1¢
DON'T WORRY GUYS, PANCAKES ARE ON ME!
I'M GONNA WIN SOME BY BEATING THAT MANLINESS TESTER.
"MANLINESS TESTER"?
"BEATING"?
HA-HA-HA-HA!

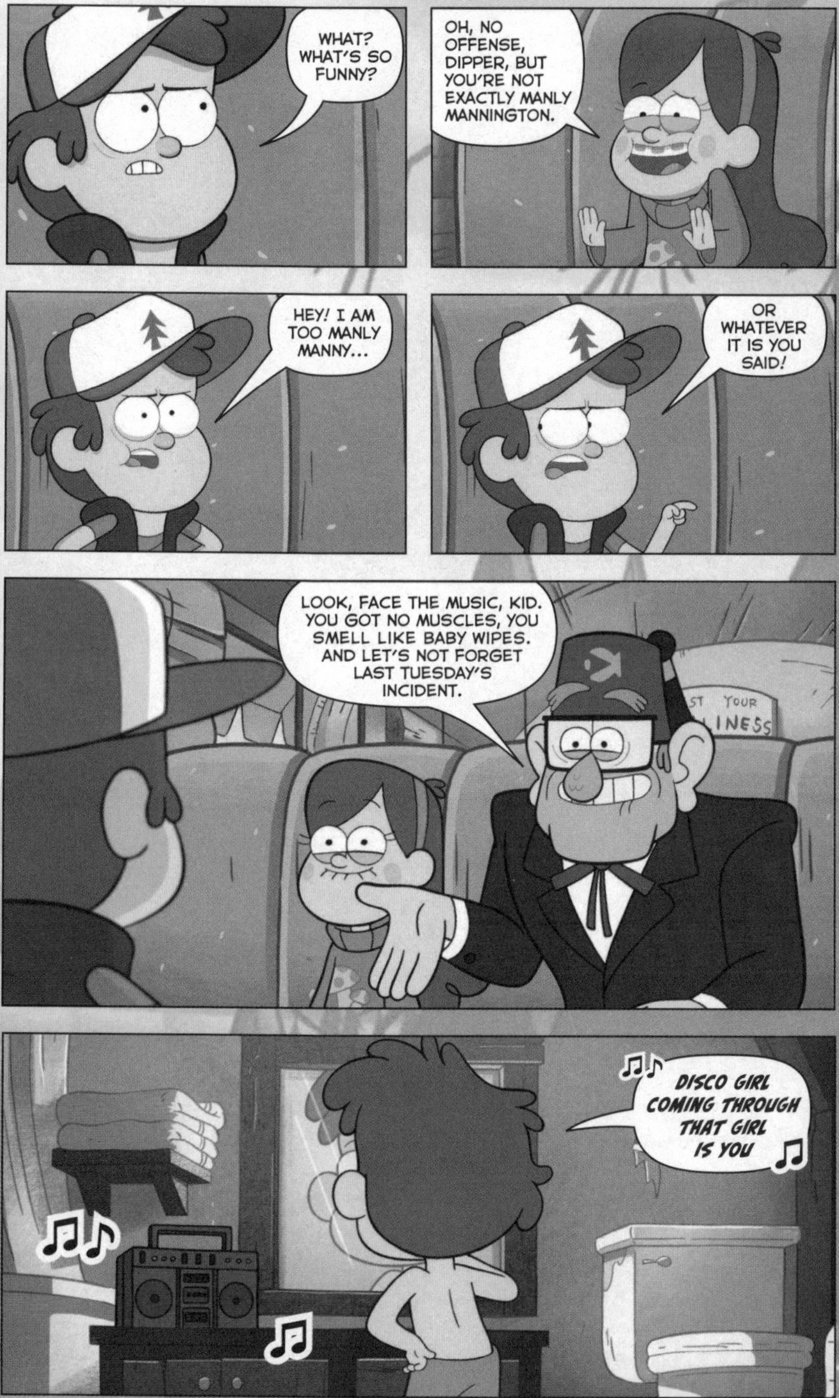
WHAT? WHAT'S SO FUNNY?
OH, NO OFFENSE, DIPPER, BUT YOU'RE NOT EXACTLY MANLY MANNINGTON.
HEY! I AM TOO MANLY MANNY...
OR WHATEVER IT IS YOU SAID!
LOOK, FACE THE MUSIC, KID. YOU GOT NO MUSCLES, YOU SMELL LIKE BABY WIPES. AND LET'S NOT FORGET LAST TUESDAY'S INCIDENT.
ST YOUR
LINESS
DISCO GIRL COMING THROUGH THAT GIRL IS YOU

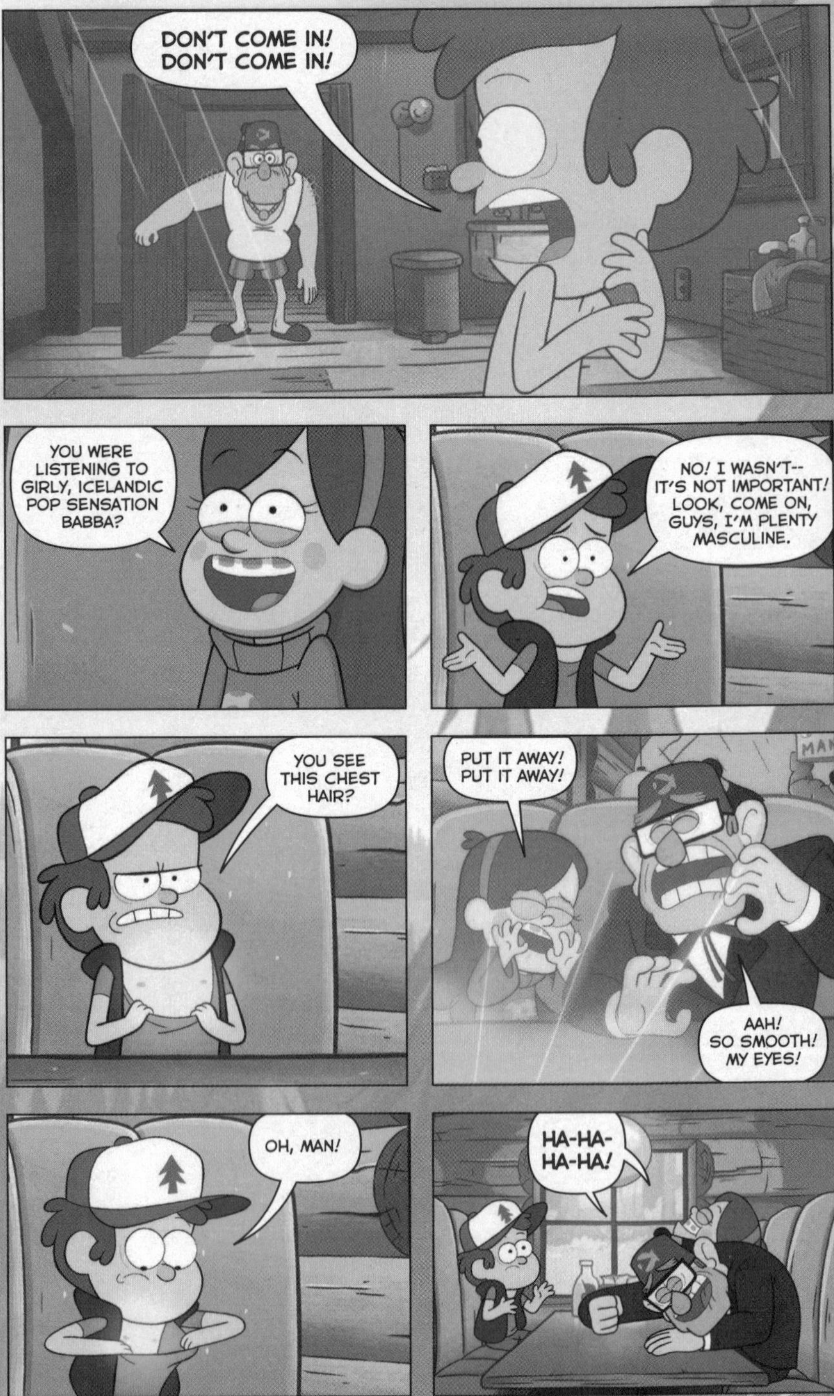
DON'T COME IN!
DON'T COME IN!
YOU WERE LISTENING TO GIRLY, ICELANDIC POP SENSATION BABBA?
NO! I WASN'T-- IT'S NOT IMPORTANT! LOOK, COME ON, GUYS, I'M PLENTY MASCULINE.
YOU SEE THIS CHEST HAIR?
PUT IT AWAY! PUT IT AWAY!
AAH! SO SMOOTH! MY EYES!
OH, MAN!
HA-HA-HA-HA!

FINE, FAMILY-OF-LITTLE-FAITH. GET READY TO EAT YOUR WORDS! AND A PLATE OF DELICIOUS PANCAKES.

ALL RIGHT, DIPPER. TIME TO MANHANDLE THIS MAN-HANDLE.

TEST YOUR MANLINESS

MANLY MAN

AND A ONE, AND A TWO--

QUIT STALLING!

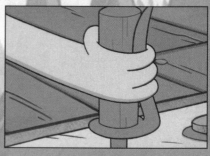

MAN

BARELY PASSABLE

MIDDLE AGED WOMAN

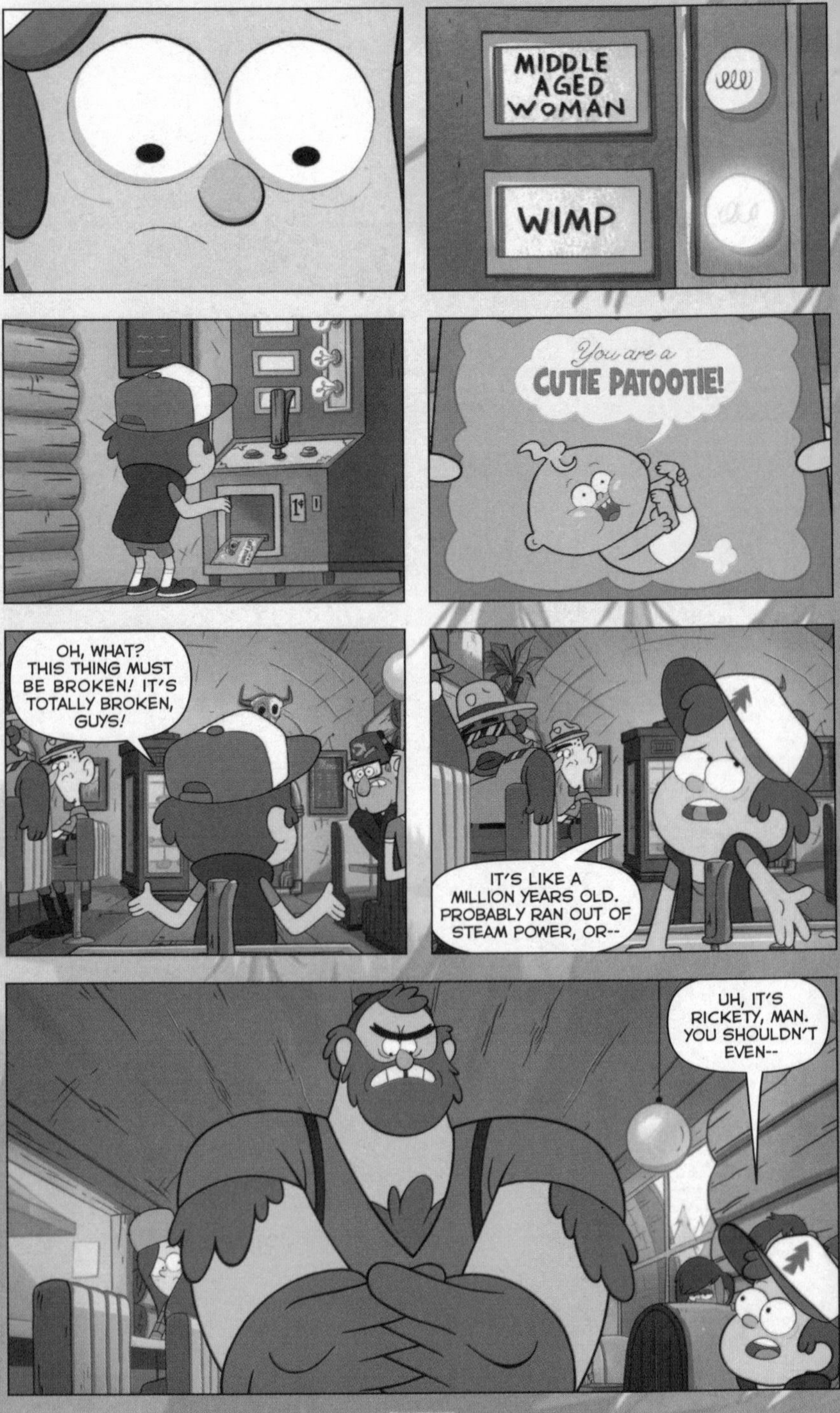

MIDDLE AGED WOMAN
WIMP
1¢
You are a CUTIE PATOOTIE!
OH, WHAT? THIS THING MUST BE BROKEN! IT'S TOTALLY BROKEN, GUYS!
IT'S LIKE A MILLION YEARS OLD. PROBABLY RAN OUT OF STEAM POWER, OR--
UH, IT'S RICKETY, MAN. YOU SHOULDN'T EVEN--

KABOOM
YEAH! PANCAKES FOR EVERYONE!
WIN GAME FREE PANCAKES!
YAAAY!
CHEER!
HA-HA-HA-HA!

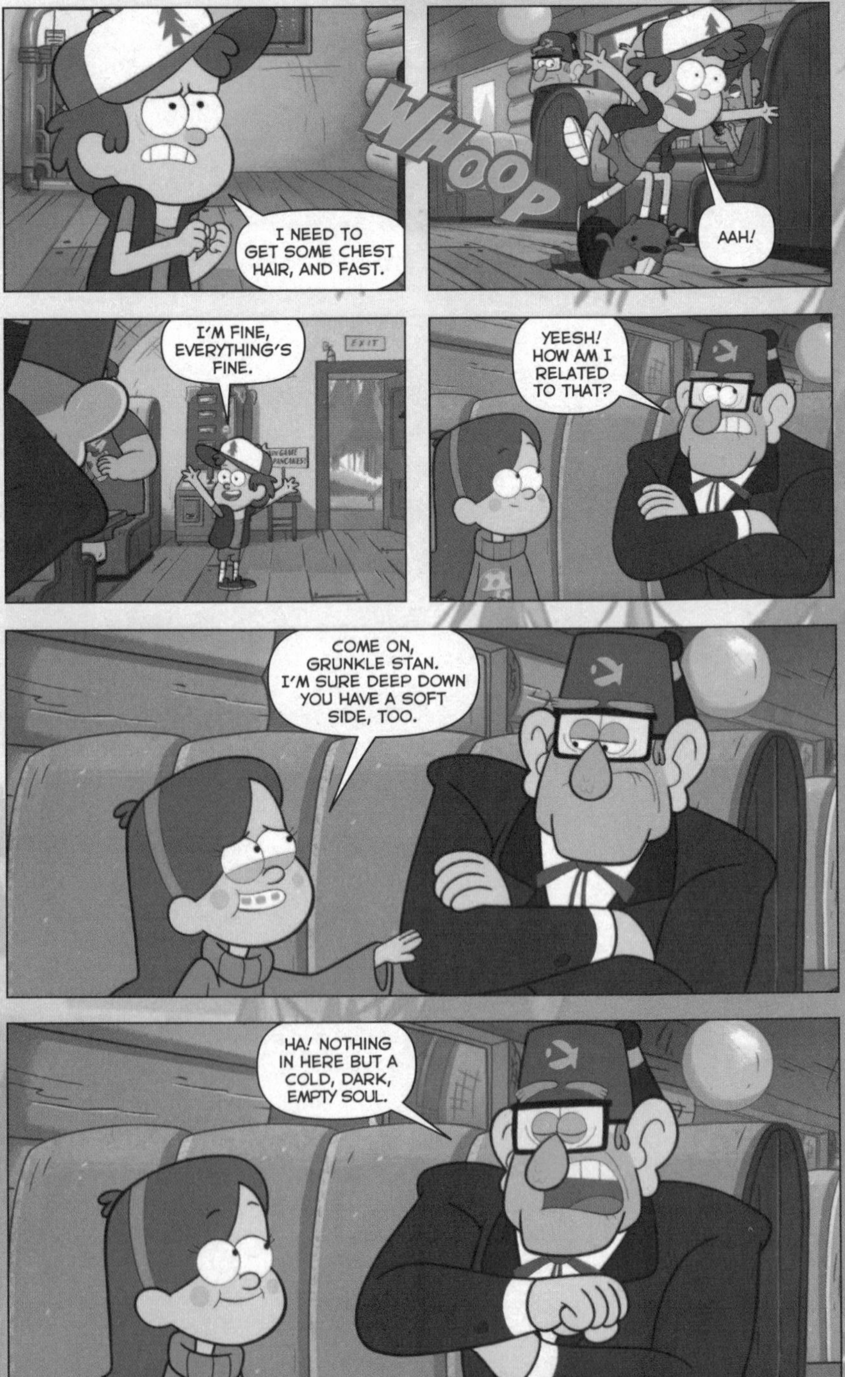
I NEED TO GET SOME CHEST HAIR, AND FAST.
WHOOP
AAH!
I'M FINE, EVERYTHING'S FINE.
EXIT
YEESH! HOW AM I RELATED TO THAT?
COME ON, GRUNKLE STAN. I'M SURE DEEP DOWN YOU HAVE A SOFT SIDE, TOO.
HA! NOTHING IN HERE BUT A COLD, DARK, EMPTY SOUL.

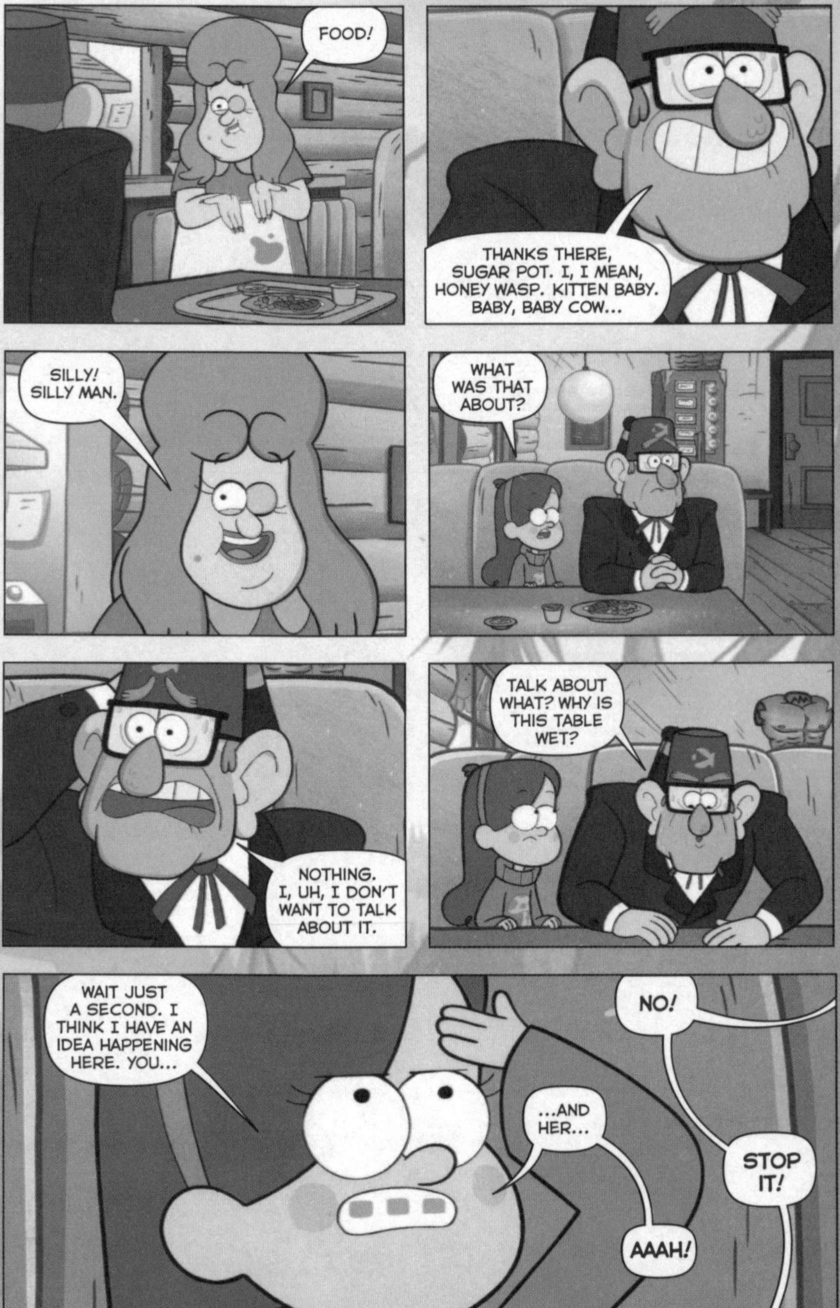
FOOD!
THANKS THERE, SUGAR POT. I, I MEAN, HONEY WASP. KITTEN BABY. BABY, BABY COW...
SILLY! SILLY MAN.
WHAT WAS THAT ABOUT?
NOTHING. I, UH, I DON'T WANT TO TALK ABOUT IT.
TALK ABOUT WHAT? WHY IS THIS TABLE WET?
WAIT JUST A SECOND. I THINK I HAVE AN IDEA HAPPENING HERE. YOU...
...AND HER...
AAAH!
NO!
STOP IT!
OH, BOY.

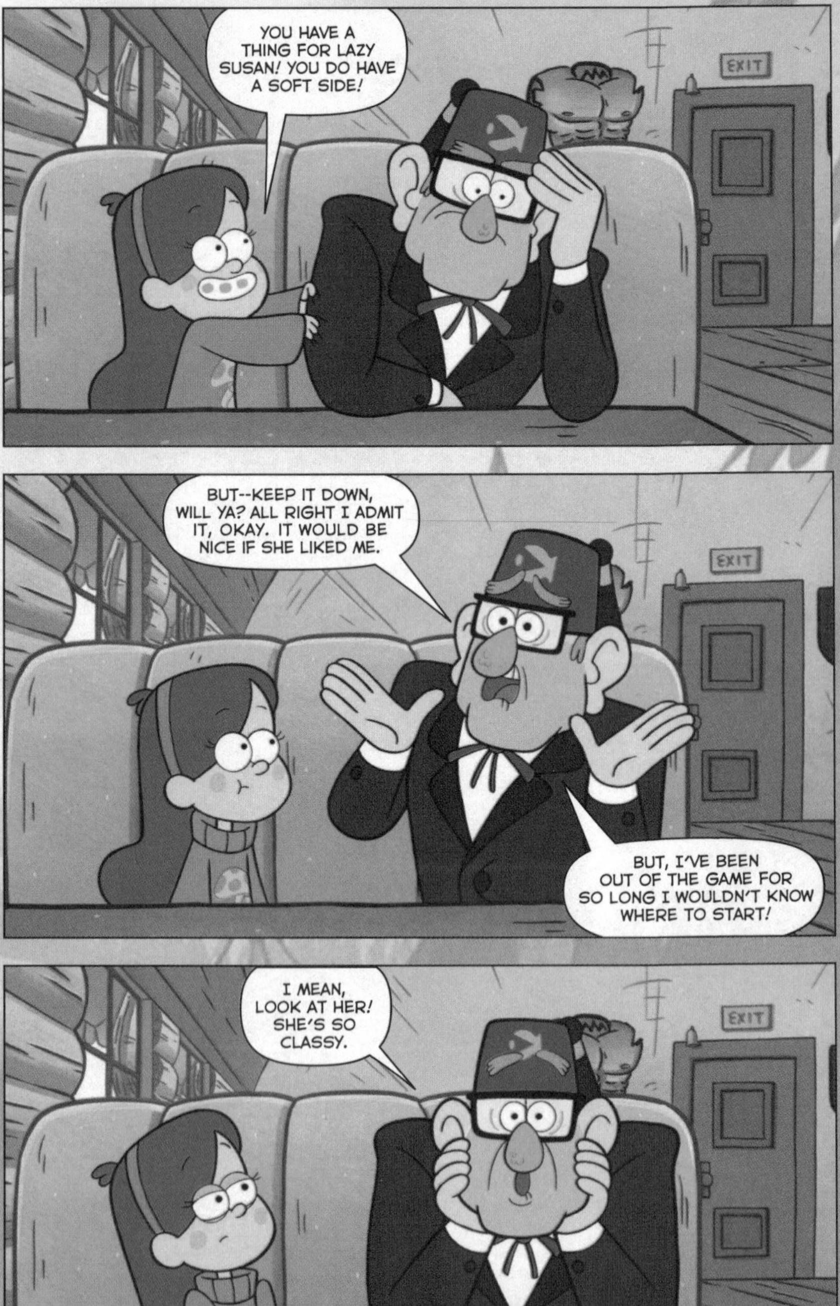
YOU HAVE A THING FOR LAZY SUSAN! YOU DO HAVE A SOFT SIDE!
EXIT
BUT--KEEP IT DOWN, WILL YA? ALL RIGHT I ADMIT IT, OKAY. IT WOULD BE NICE IF SHE LIKED ME.
EXIT
BUT, I'VE BEEN OUT OF THE GAME FOR SO LONG I WOULDN'T KNOW WHERE TO START!
I MEAN, LOOK AT HER! SHE'S SO CLASSY.
EXIT

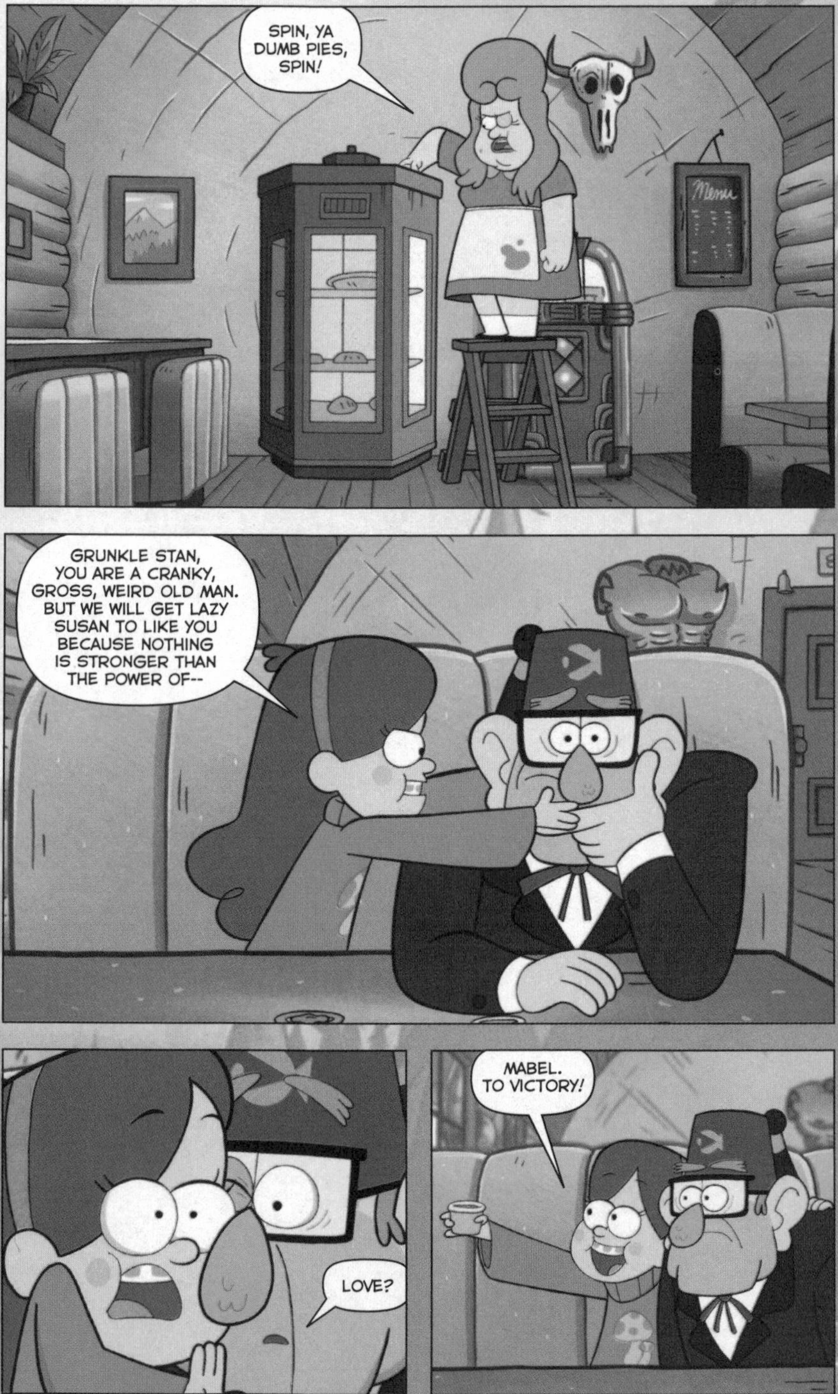
SPIN, YA DUMB PIES, SPIN!
GRUNKLE STAN, YOU ARE A CRANKY, GROSS, WEIRD OLD MAN. BUT WE WILL GET LAZY SUSAN TO LIKE YOU BECAUSE NOTHING IS STRONGER THAN THE POWER OF--
LOVE?
MABEL. TO VICTORY!

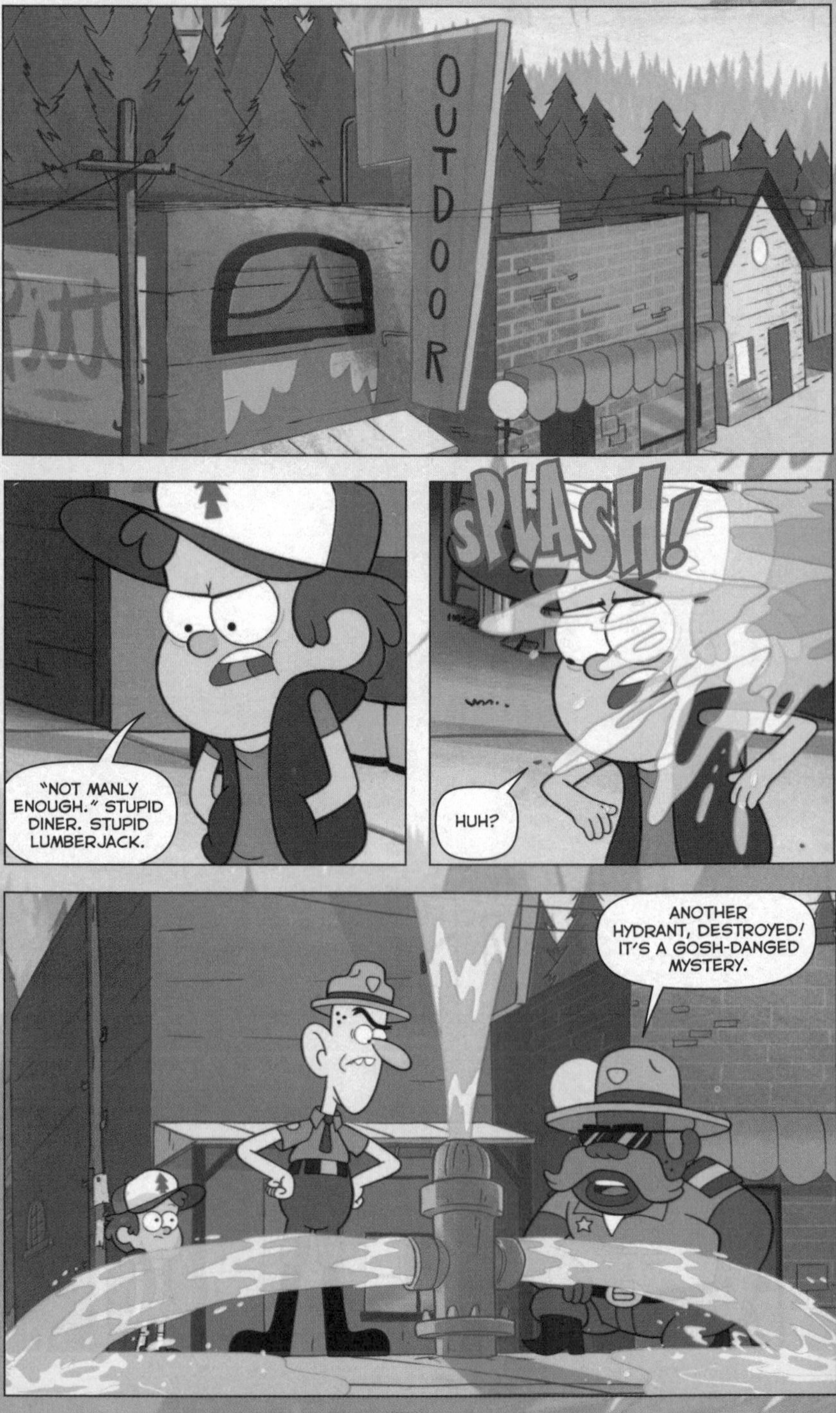
OUTDOOR
"NOT MANLY ENOUGH." STUPID DINER. STUPID LUMBERJACK.
SPLASH!
HUH?
ANOTHER HYDRANT, DESTROYED! IT'S A GOSH-DANGED MYSTERY.

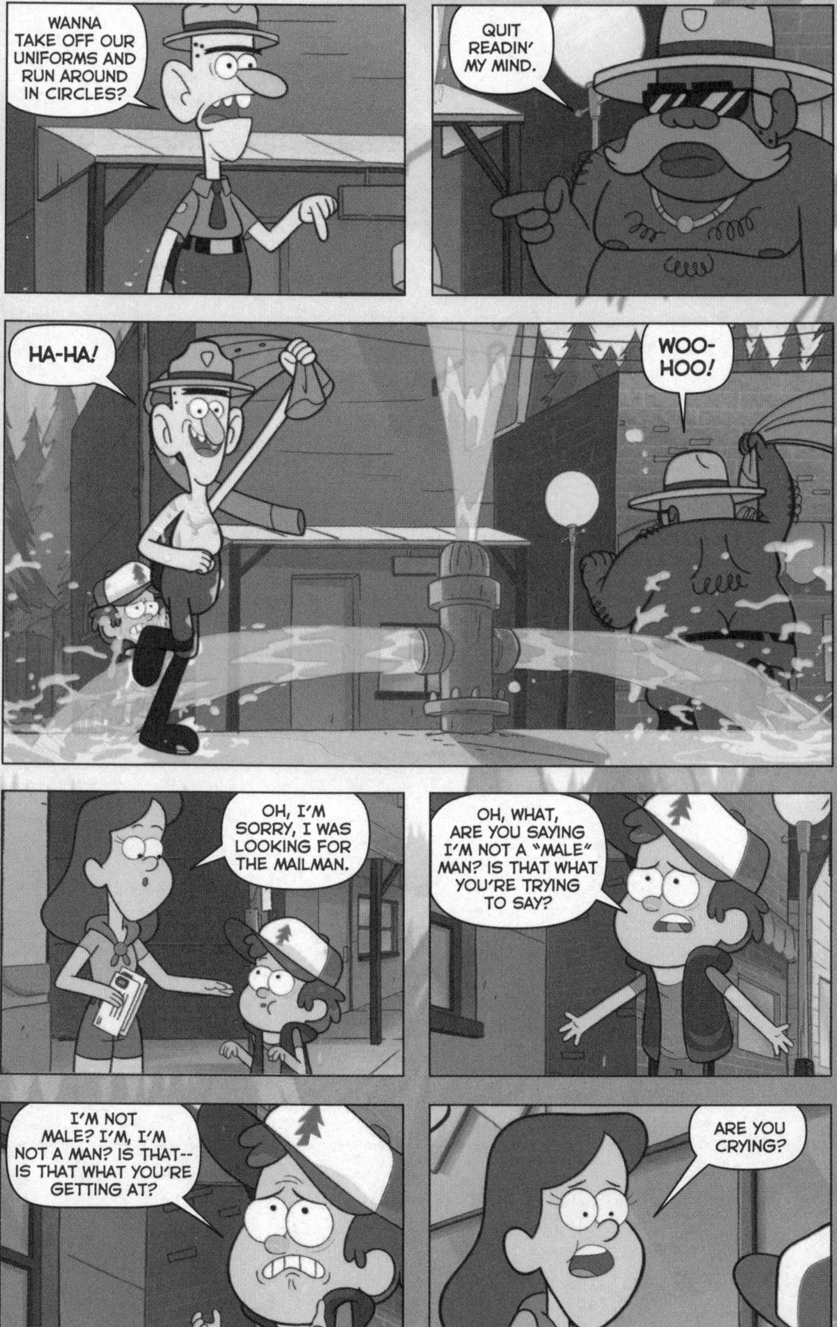
WANNA TAKE OFF OUR UNIFORMS AND RUN AROUND IN CIRCLES?
QUIT READIN' MY MIND.
HA-HA!
WOO-HOO!
OH, I'M SORRY, I WAS LOOKING FOR THE MAILMAN.
OH, WHAT, ARE YOU SAYING I'M NOT A "MALE" MAN? IS THAT WHAT YOU'RE TRYING TO SAY?
I'M NOT MALE? I'M, I'M NOT A MAN? IS THAT-- IS THAT WHAT YOU'RE GETTING AT?
ARE YOU CRYING?

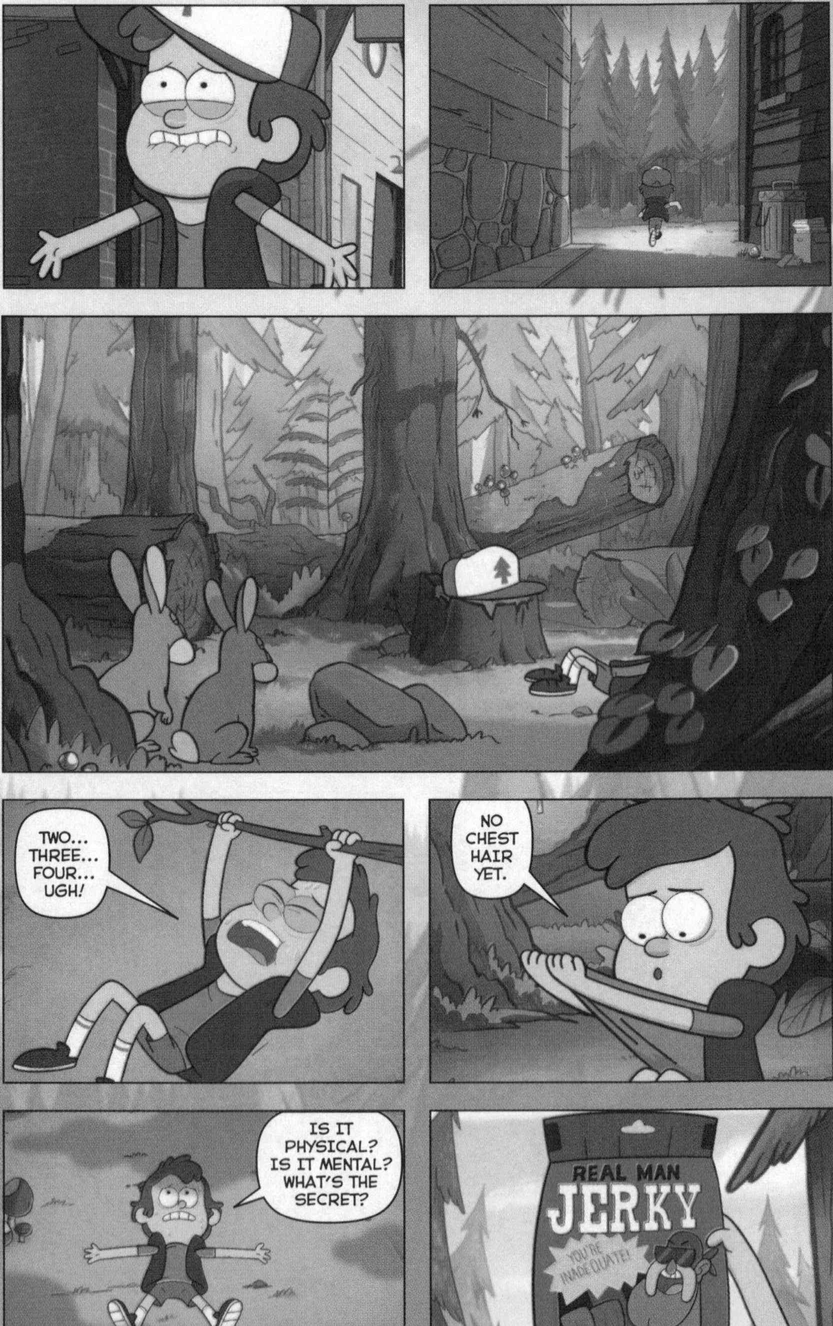
TWO... THREE... FOUR... UGH!
NO CHEST HAIR YET.
IS IT PHYSICAL? IS IT MENTAL? WHAT'S THE SECRET?
REAL MAN JERKY
YOU'RE INADEQUATE!

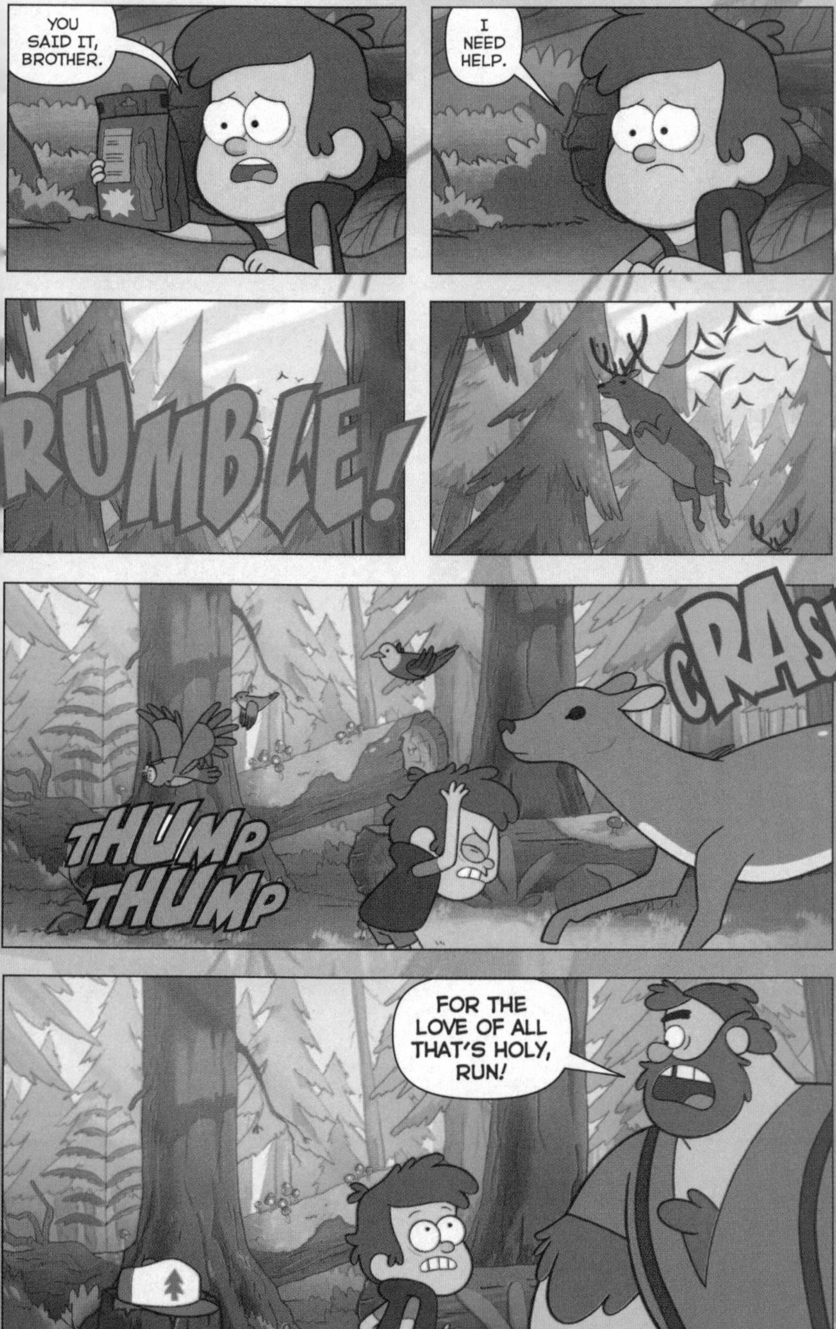
YOU SAID IT, BROTHER.
I NEED HELP.
RUMBLE!
CRASH
THUMP THUMP
FOR THE LOVE OF ALL THAT'S HOLY, RUN!

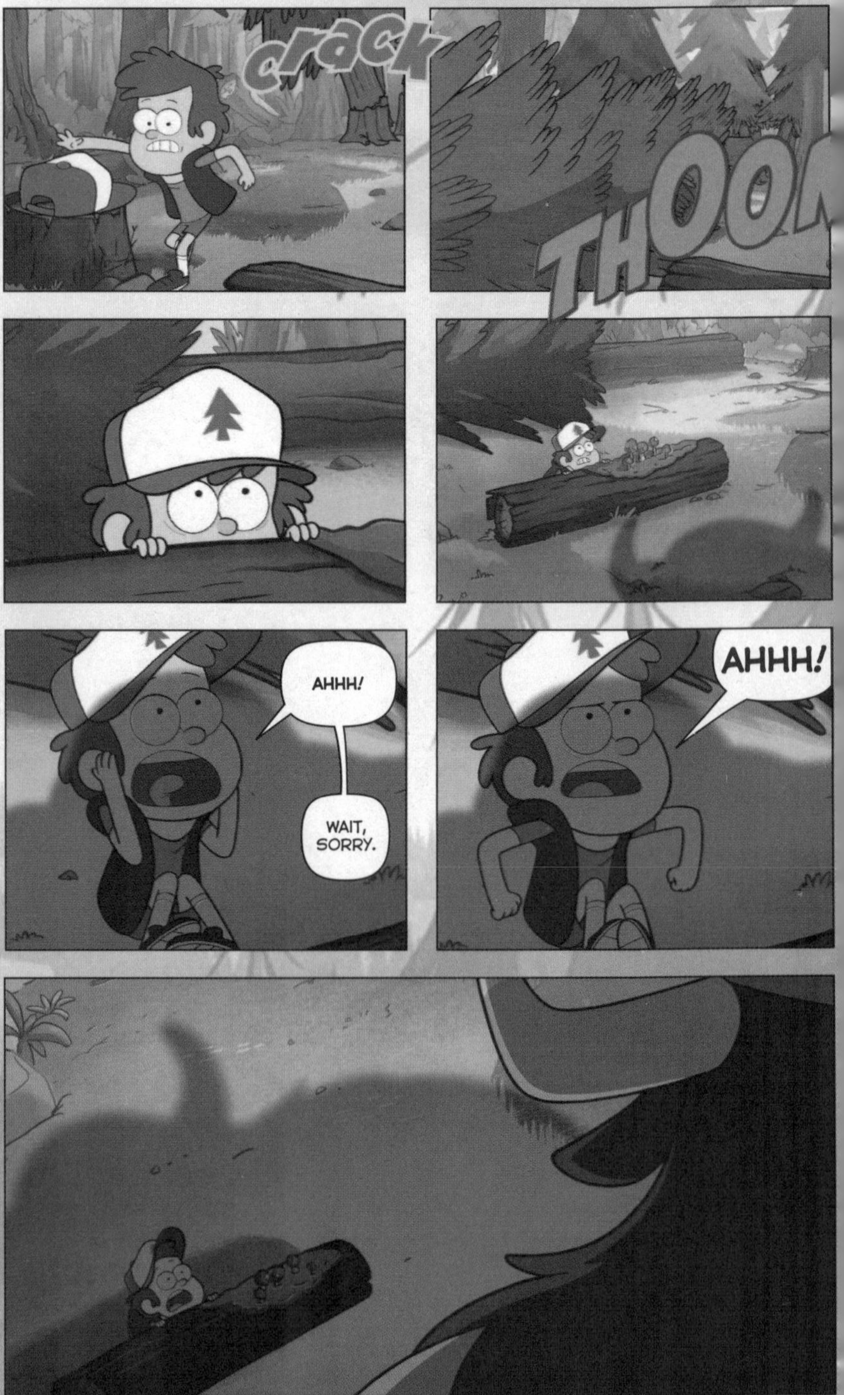
CRACK
THOOM
AHHH!
WAIT, SORRY.
AHHH!

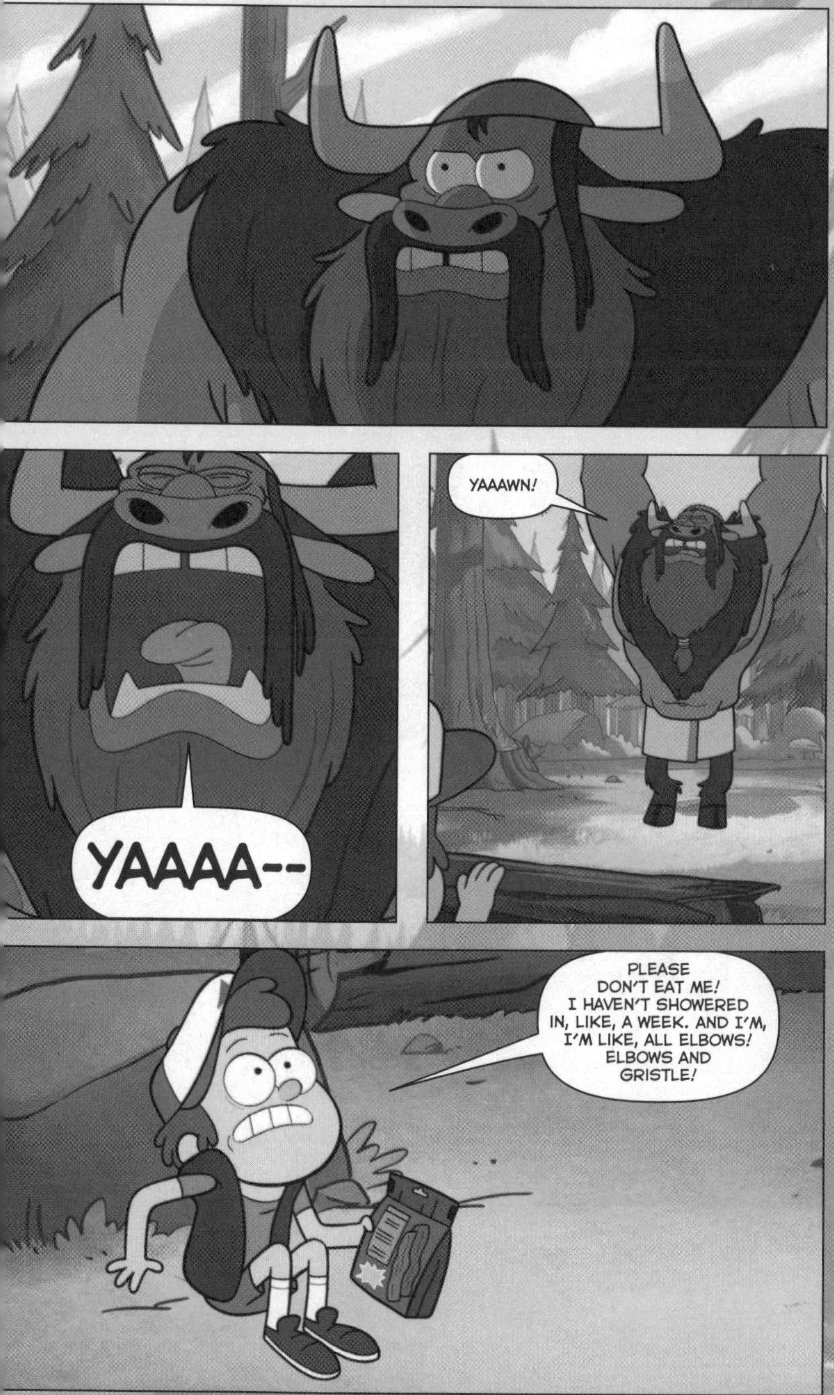
YAAAA--
YAAAWN!
PLEASE DON'T EAT ME! I HAVEN'T SHOWERED IN, LIKE, A WEEK. AND I'M, I'M LIKE, ALL ELBOWS! ELBOWS AND GRISTLE!

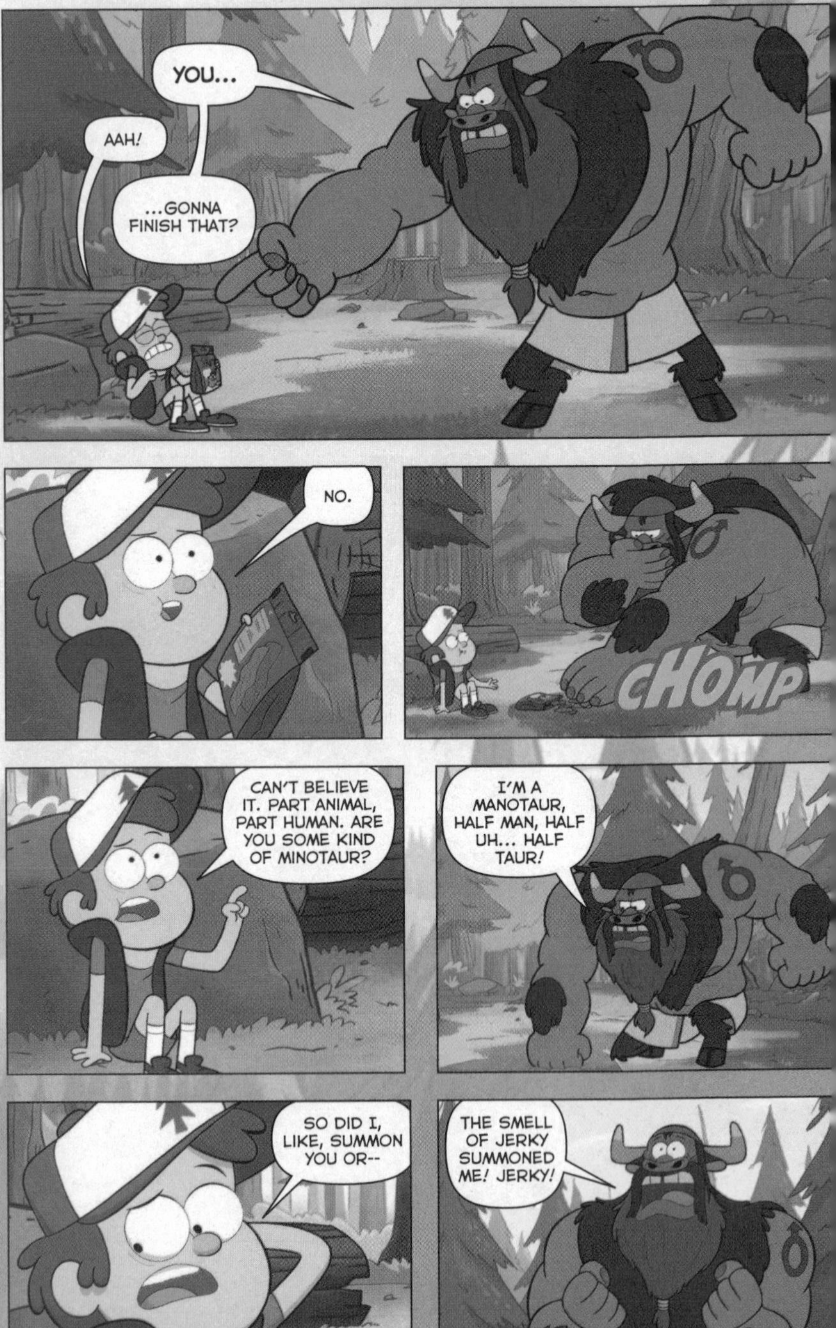
YOU...
AAH!
...GONNA FINISH THAT?
NO.
CHOMP
CAN'T BELIEVE IT. PART ANIMAL, PART HUMAN. ARE YOU SOME KIND OF MINOTAUR?
I'M A MANOTAUR, HALF MAN, HALF UH... HALF TAUR!
SO DID I, LIKE, SUMMON YOU OR--
THE SMELL OF JERKY SUMMONED ME! JERKY!

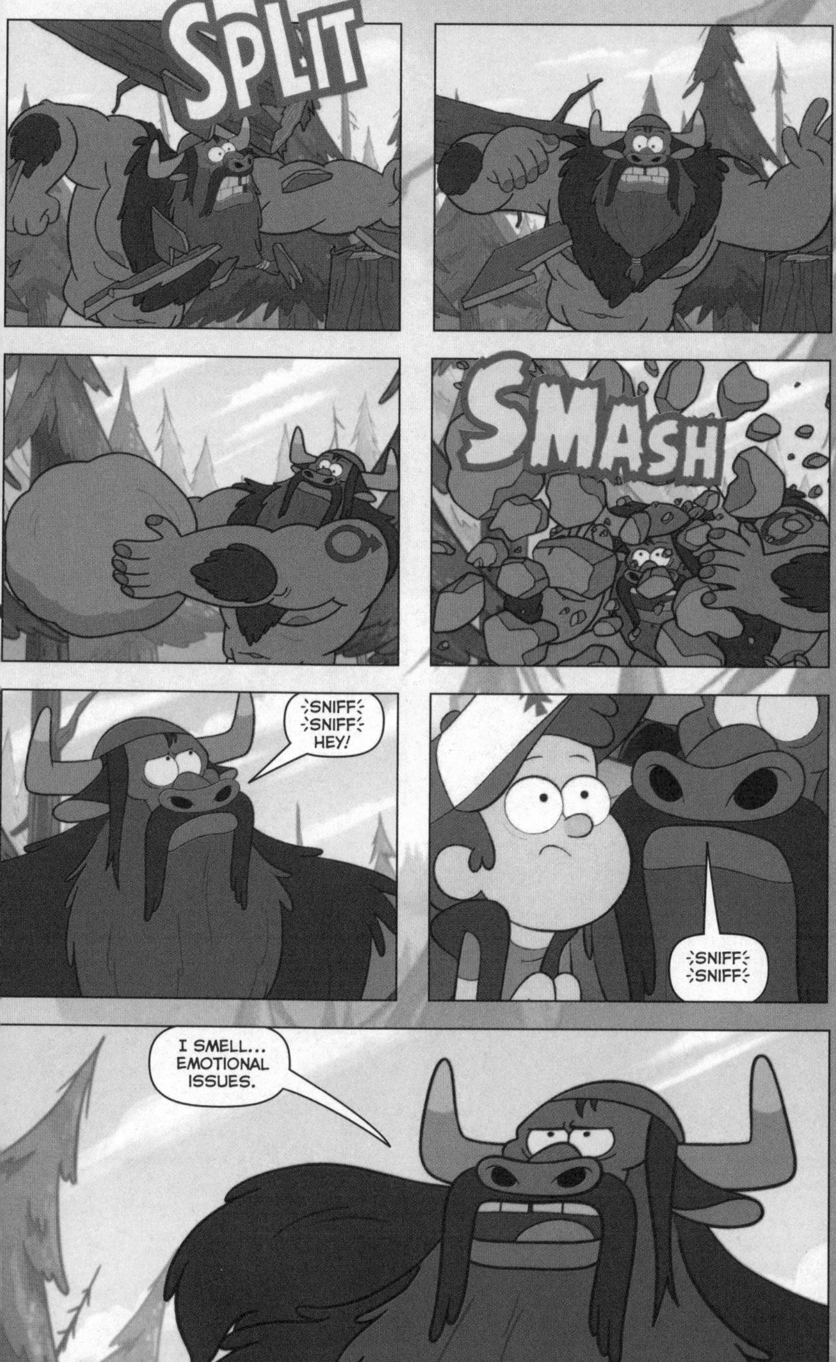
SPLIT
SMASH
SNIFF SNIFF HEY!
SNIFF SNIFF
I SMELL... EMOTIONAL ISSUES.

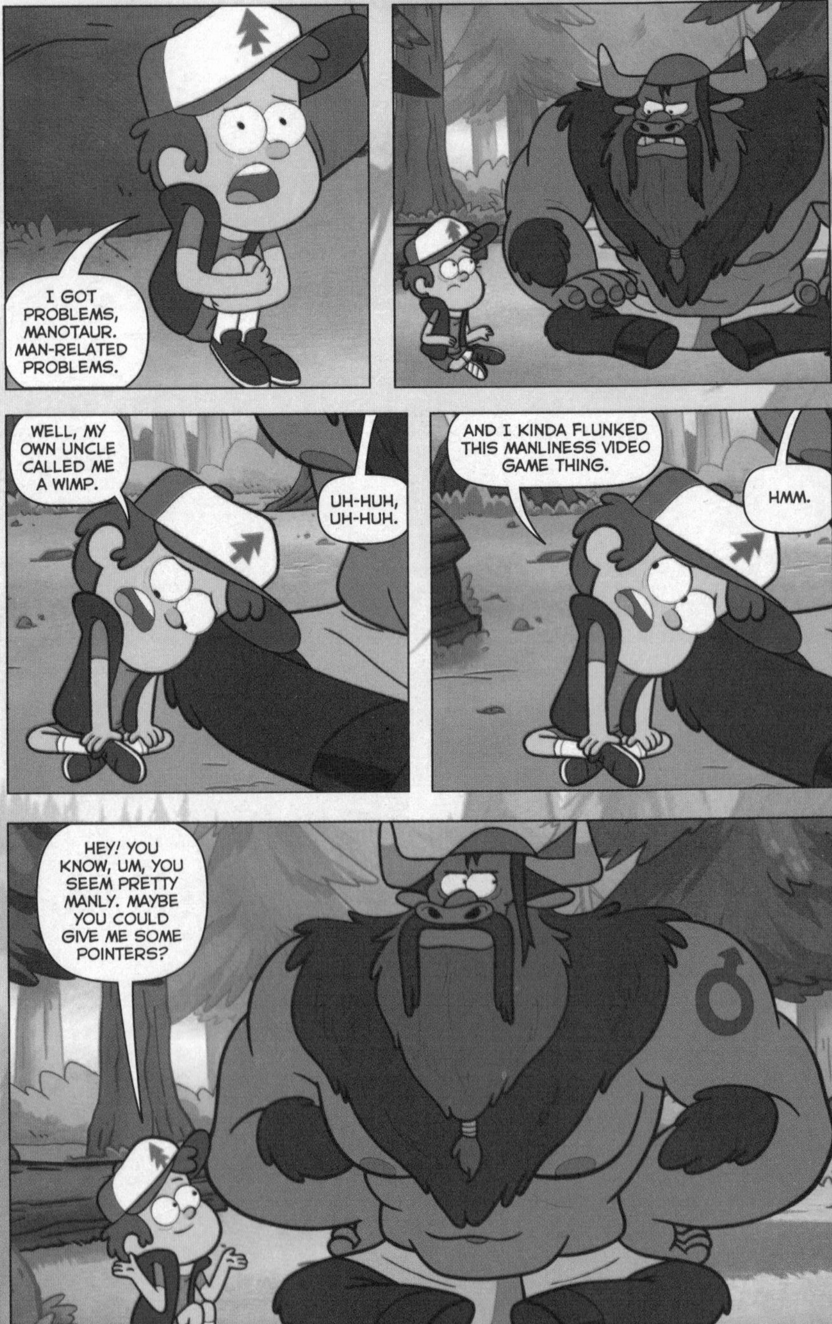
I GOT PROBLEMS, MANOTAUR. MAN-RELATED PROBLEMS.
WELL, MY OWN UNCLE CALLED ME A WIMP.
UH-HUH, UH-HUH.
AND I KINDA FLUNKED THIS MANLINESS VIDEO GAME THING.
HMM.
HEY! YOU KNOW, UM, YOU SEEM PRETTY MANLY. MAYBE YOU COULD GIVE ME SOME POINTERS?

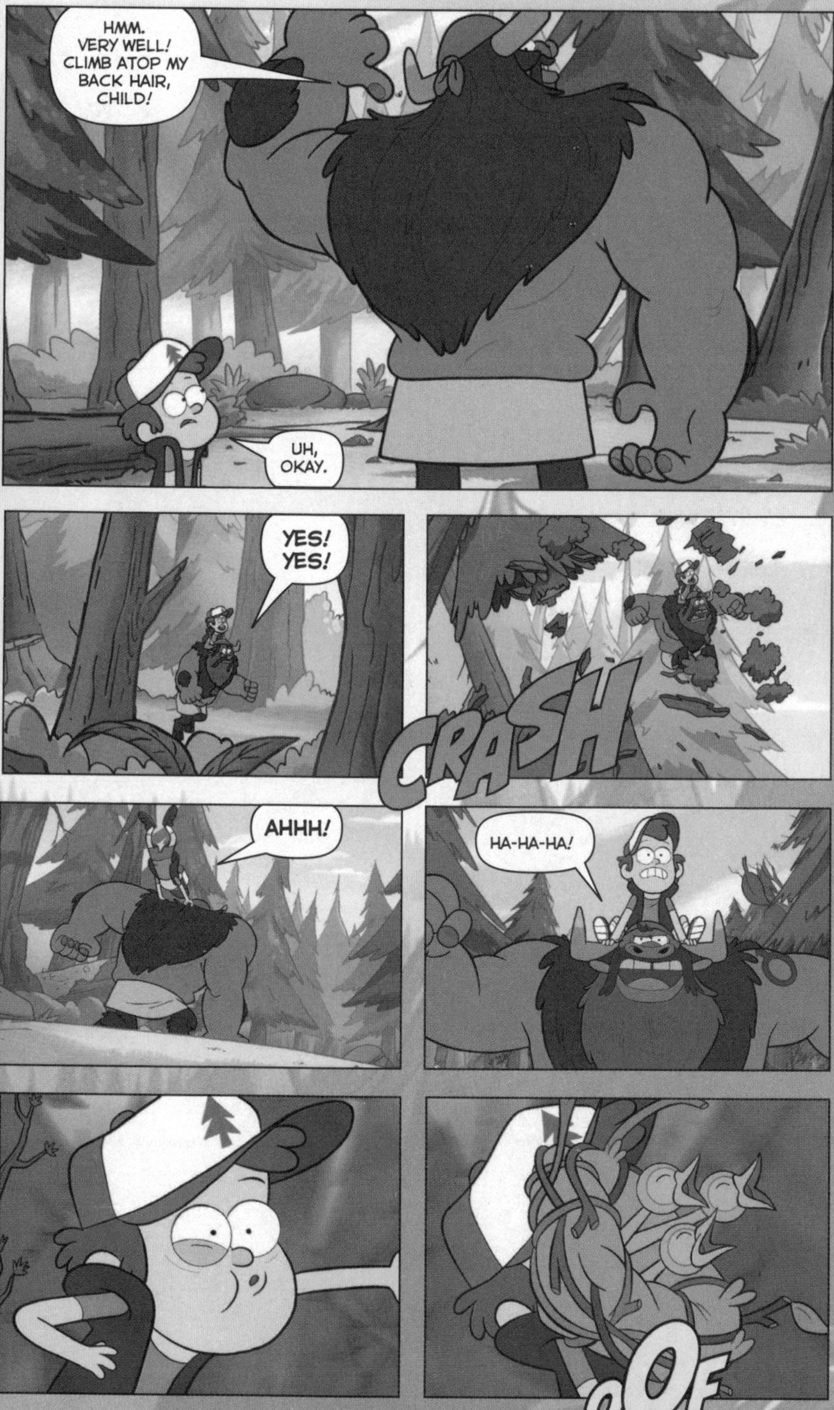
HMM. VERY WELL! CLIMB ATOP MY BACK HAIR, CHILD!
UH, OKAY.
YES! YES!
CRASH
AHHH!
HA-HA-HA!
OOF

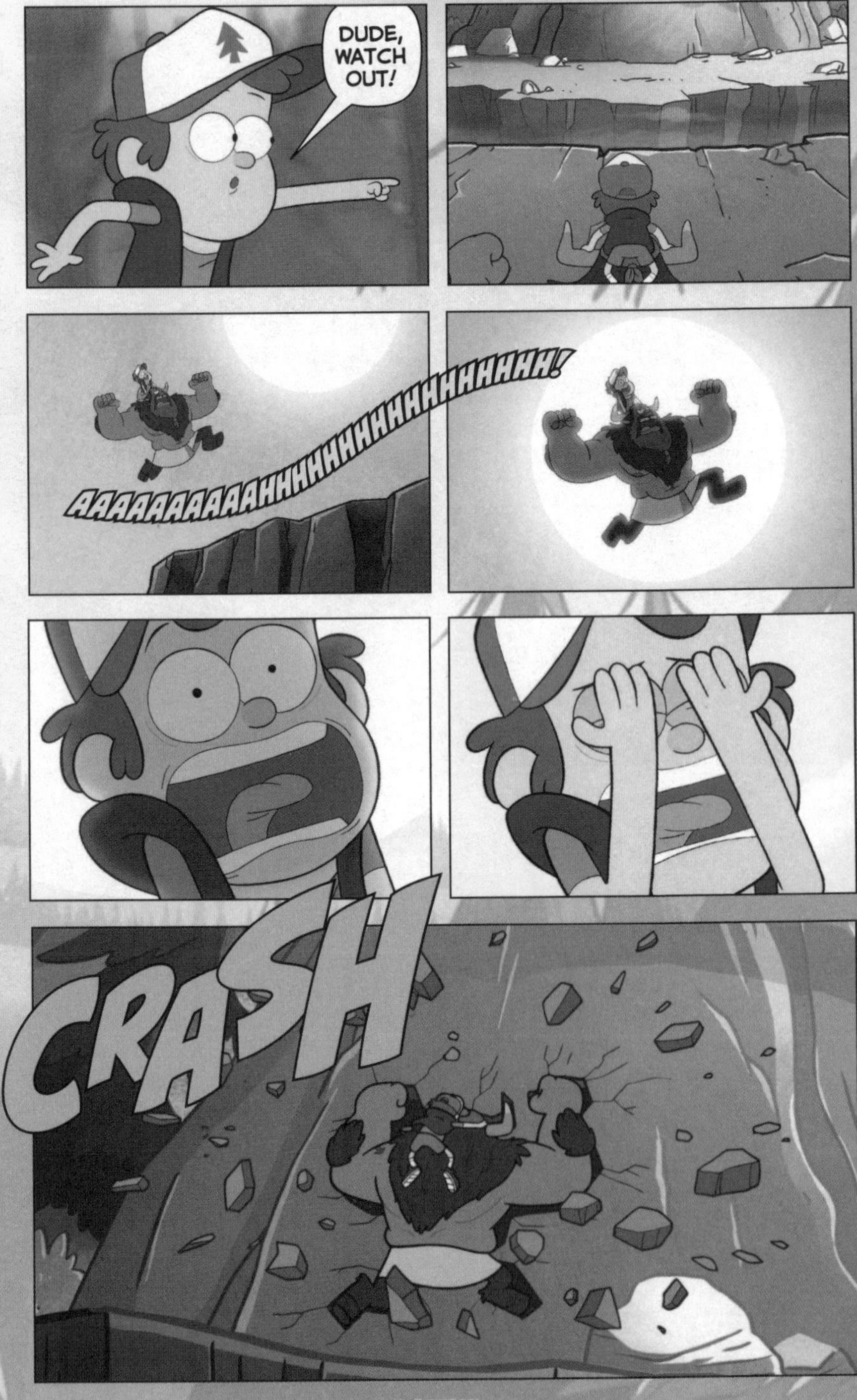

DUDE, WATCH OUT!
AAAAAAAAAAHHHHHHHHHHHHHHHHHHHHHHH!
CRASH

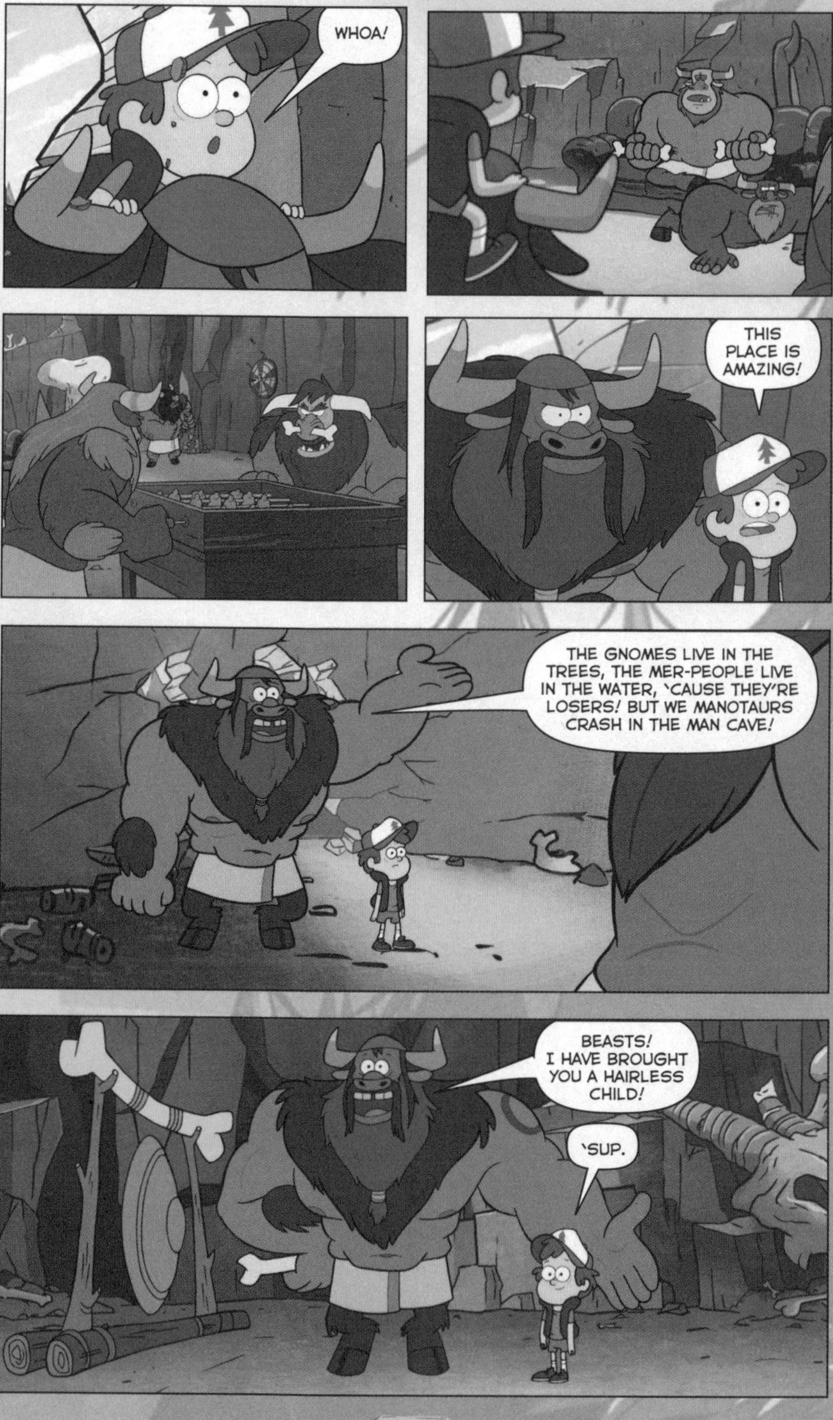
WHOA!
THIS PLACE IS AMAZING!
THE GNOMES LIVE IN THE TREES, THE MER-PEOPLE LIVE IN THE WATER, 'CAUSE THEY'RE LOSERS! BUT WE MANOTAURS CRASH IN THE MAN CAVE!
BEASTS! I HAVE BROUGHT YOU A HAIRLESS CHILD!
'SUP.

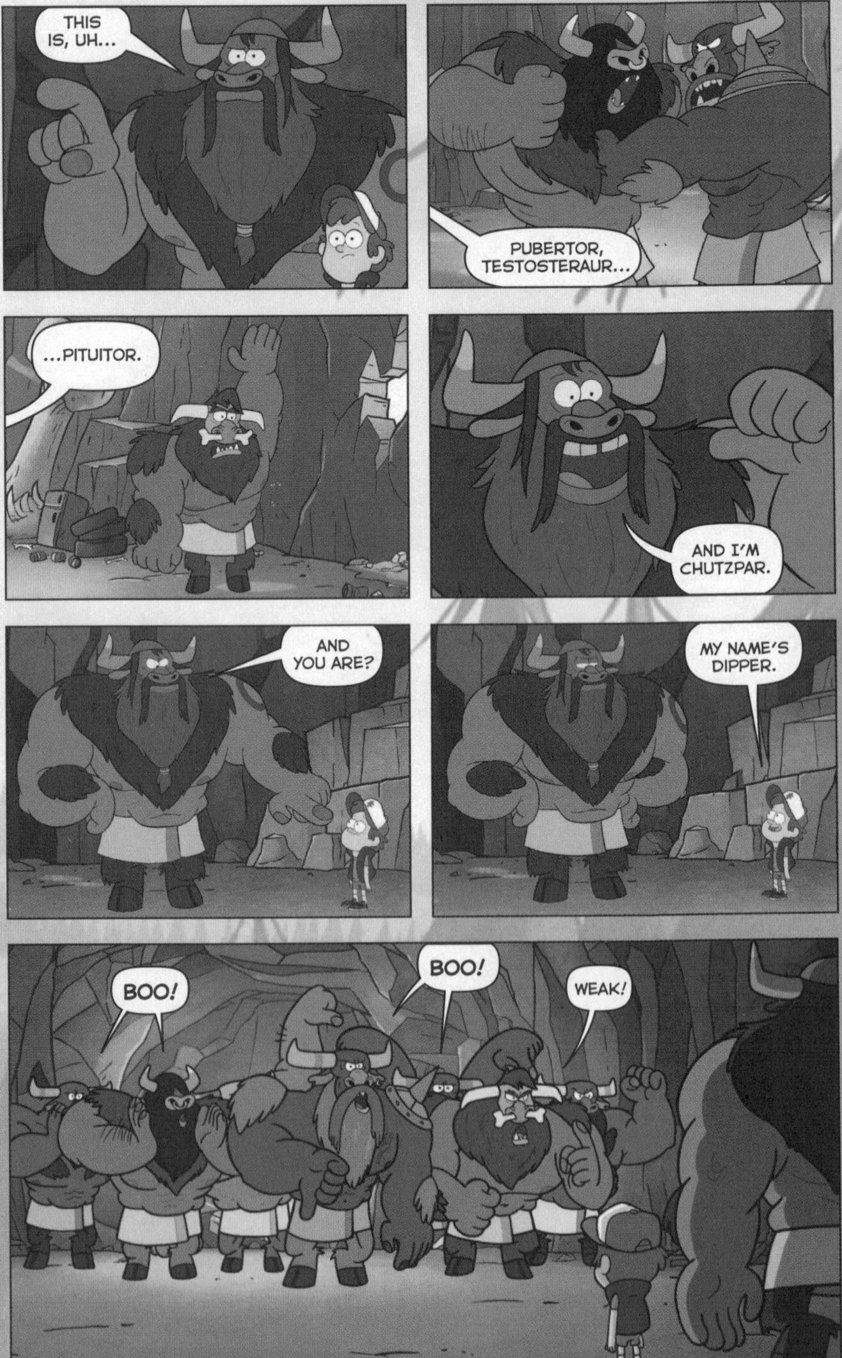
THIS IS, UH...
PUBERTOR, TESTOSTERAUR...
...PITUITOR.
AND I'M CHUTZPAR.
AND YOU ARE?
MY NAME'S DIPPER.
BOO!
BOO!
WEAK!

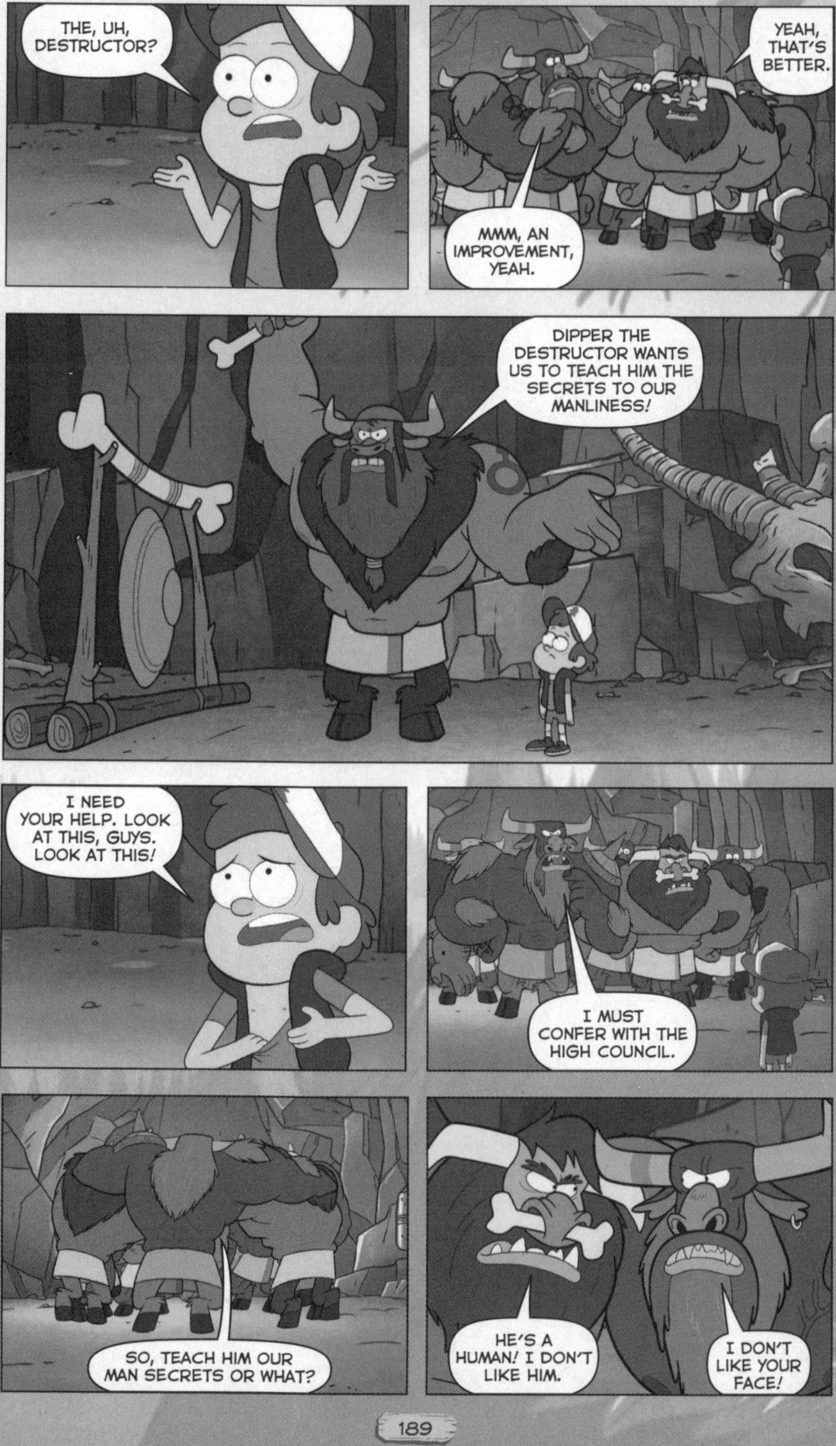
THE, UH, DESTRUCTOR?
YEAH, THAT'S BETTER.
MMM, AN IMPROVEMENT, YEAH.
DIPPER THE DESTRUCTOR WANTS US TO TEACH HIM THE SECRETS TO OUR MANLINESS!
I NEED YOUR HELP. LOOK AT THIS, GUYS. LOOK AT THIS!
I MUST CONFER WITH THE HIGH COUNCIL.
SO, TEACH HIM OUR MAN SECRETS OR WHAT?
HE'S A HUMAN! I DON'T LIKE HIM.
I DON'T LIKE YOUR FACE!

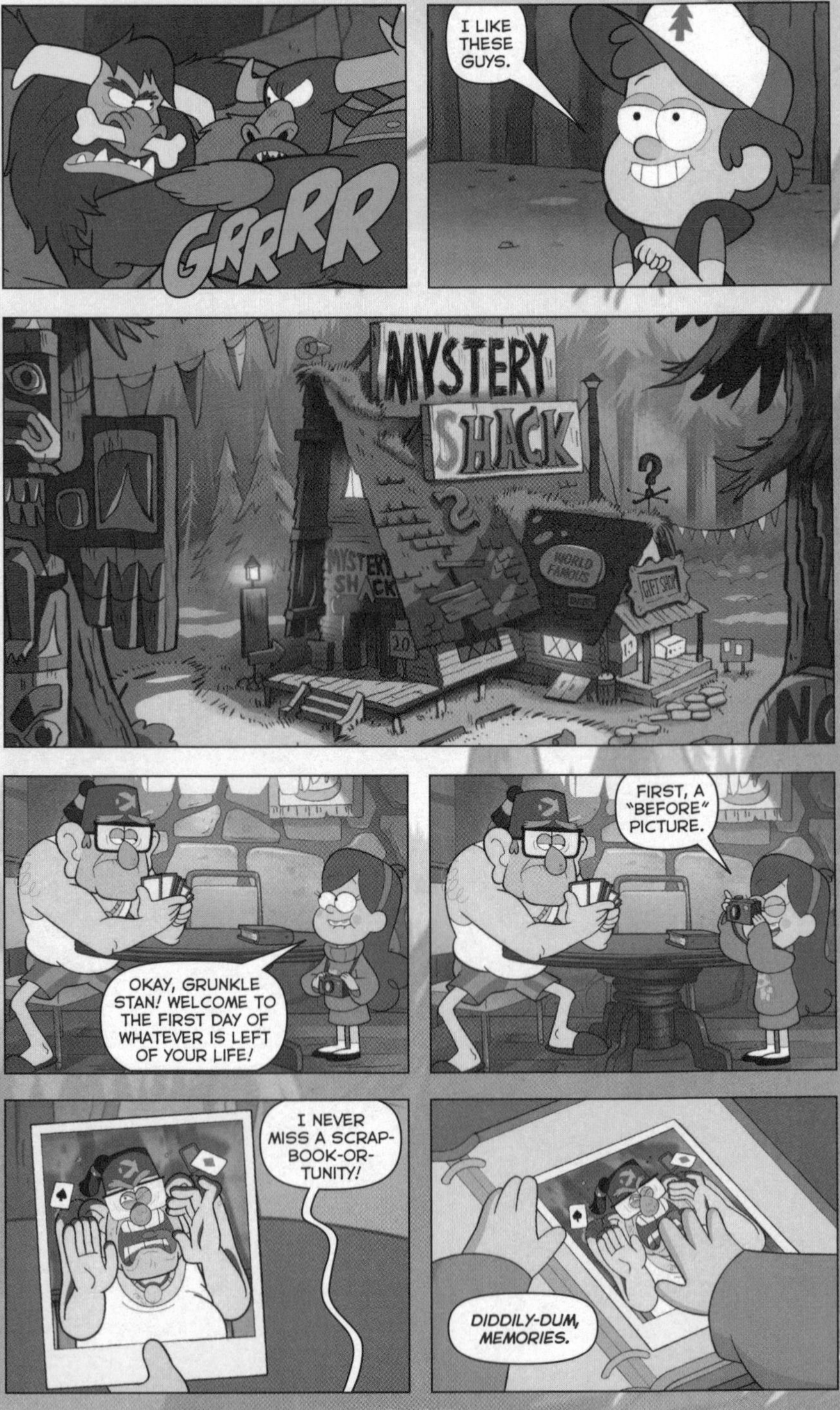
GRRRR
I LIKE THESE GUYS.
MYSTERY SHACK
WORLD FAMOUS
GIFT SHOP
OKAY, GRUNKLE STAN! WELCOME TO THE FIRST DAY OF WHATEVER IS LEFT OF YOUR LIFE!
FIRST, A "BEFORE" PICTURE.
I NEVER MISS A SCRAP-BOOK-OR-TUNITY!
DIDDILY-DUM, MEMORIES.

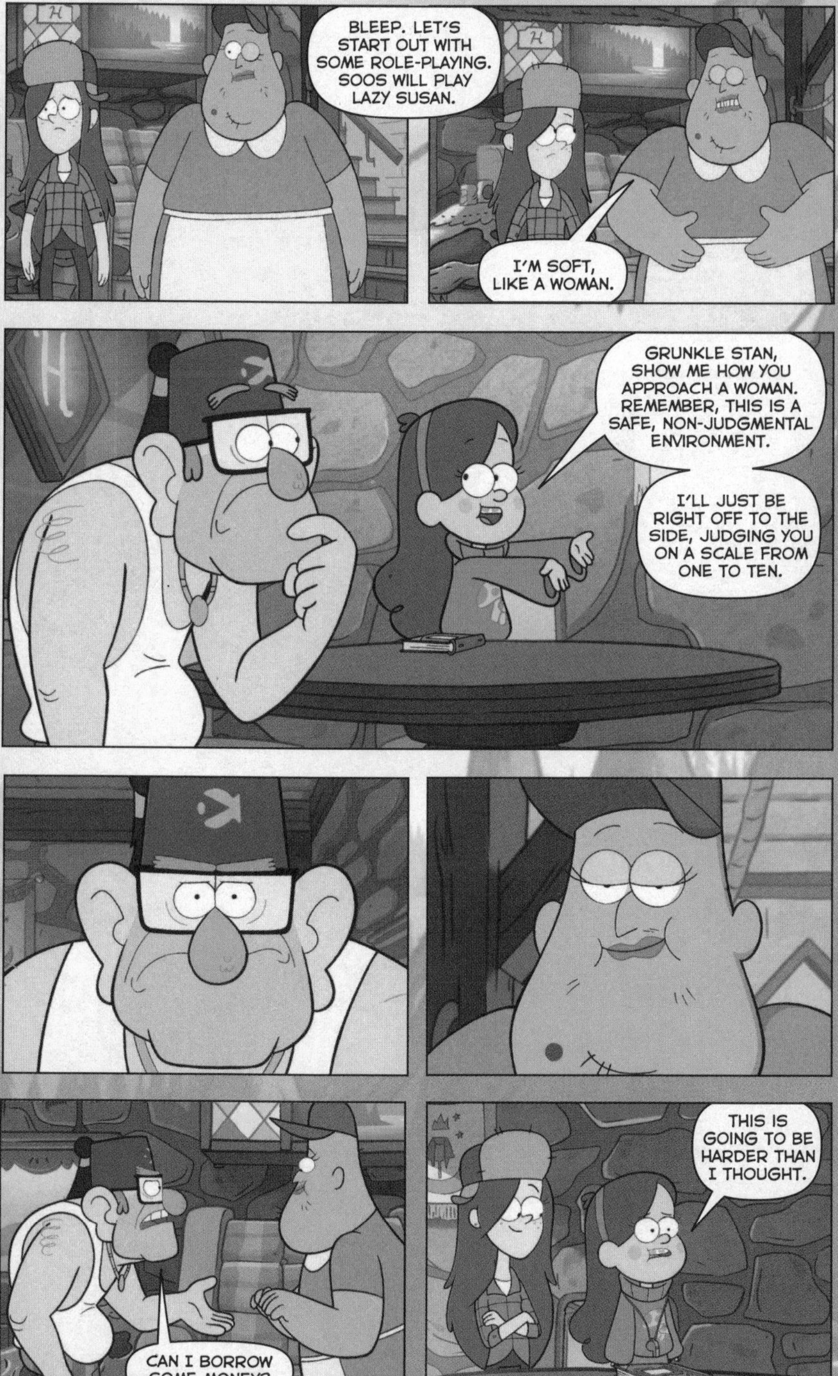
BLEEP. LET'S START OUT WITH SOME ROLE-PLAYING. SOOS WILL PLAY LAZY SUSAN.
I'M SOFT, LIKE A WOMAN.
GRUNKLE STAN, SHOW ME HOW YOU APPROACH A WOMAN. REMEMBER, THIS IS A SAFE, NON-JUDGMENTAL ENVIRONMENT.
I'LL JUST BE RIGHT OFF TO THE SIDE, JUDGING YOU ON A SCALE FROM ONE TO TEN.
CAN I BORROW SOME MONEY?
THIS IS GOING TO BE HARDER THAN I THOUGHT.

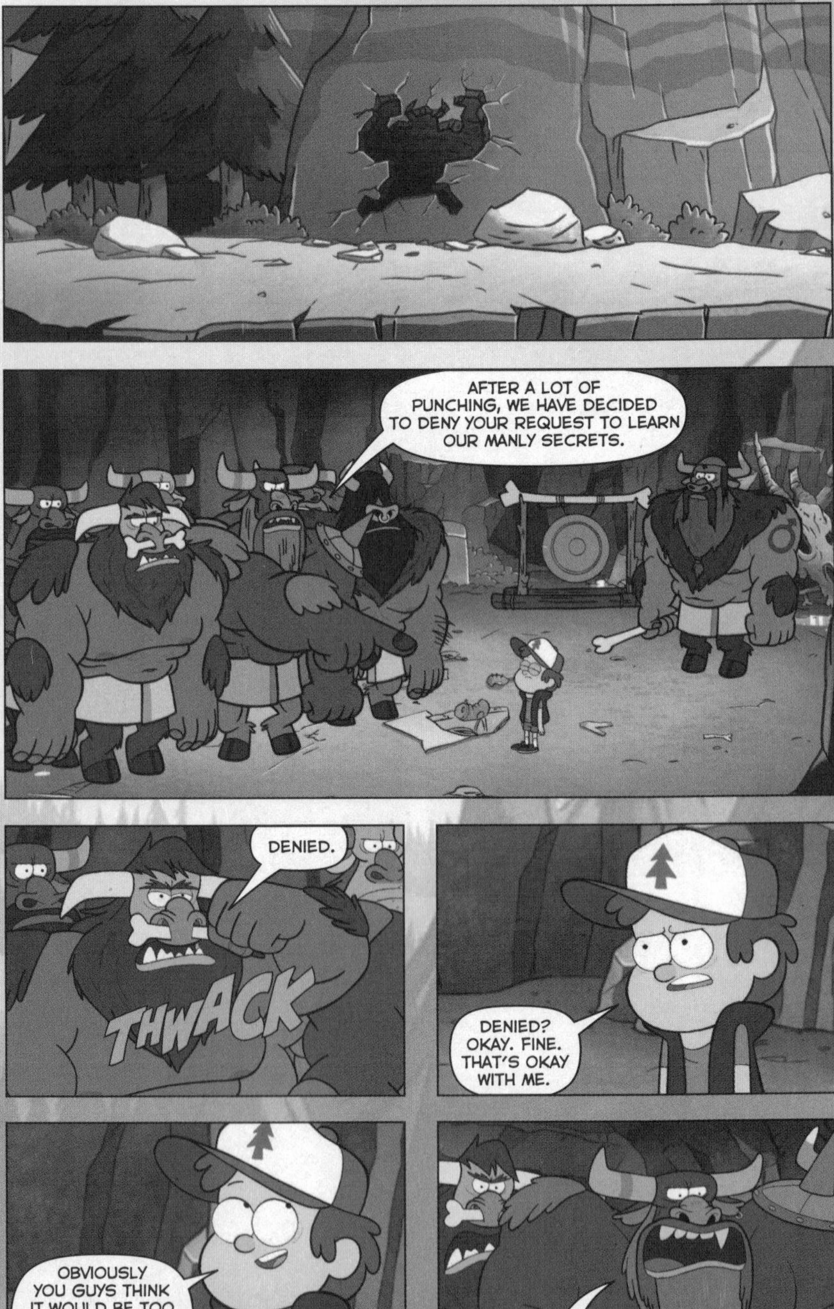
AFTER A LOT OF PUNCHING, WE HAVE DECIDED TO DENY YOUR REQUEST TO LEARN OUR MANLY SECRETS.
DENIED.
THWACK
DENIED? OKAY. FINE. THAT'S OKAY WITH ME.
OBVIOUSLY YOU GUYS THINK IT WOULD BE TOO HARD TO TRAIN ME! MAYBE YOU'RE NOT MAN ENOUGH TO TRY!
NOT MAN ENOUGH?

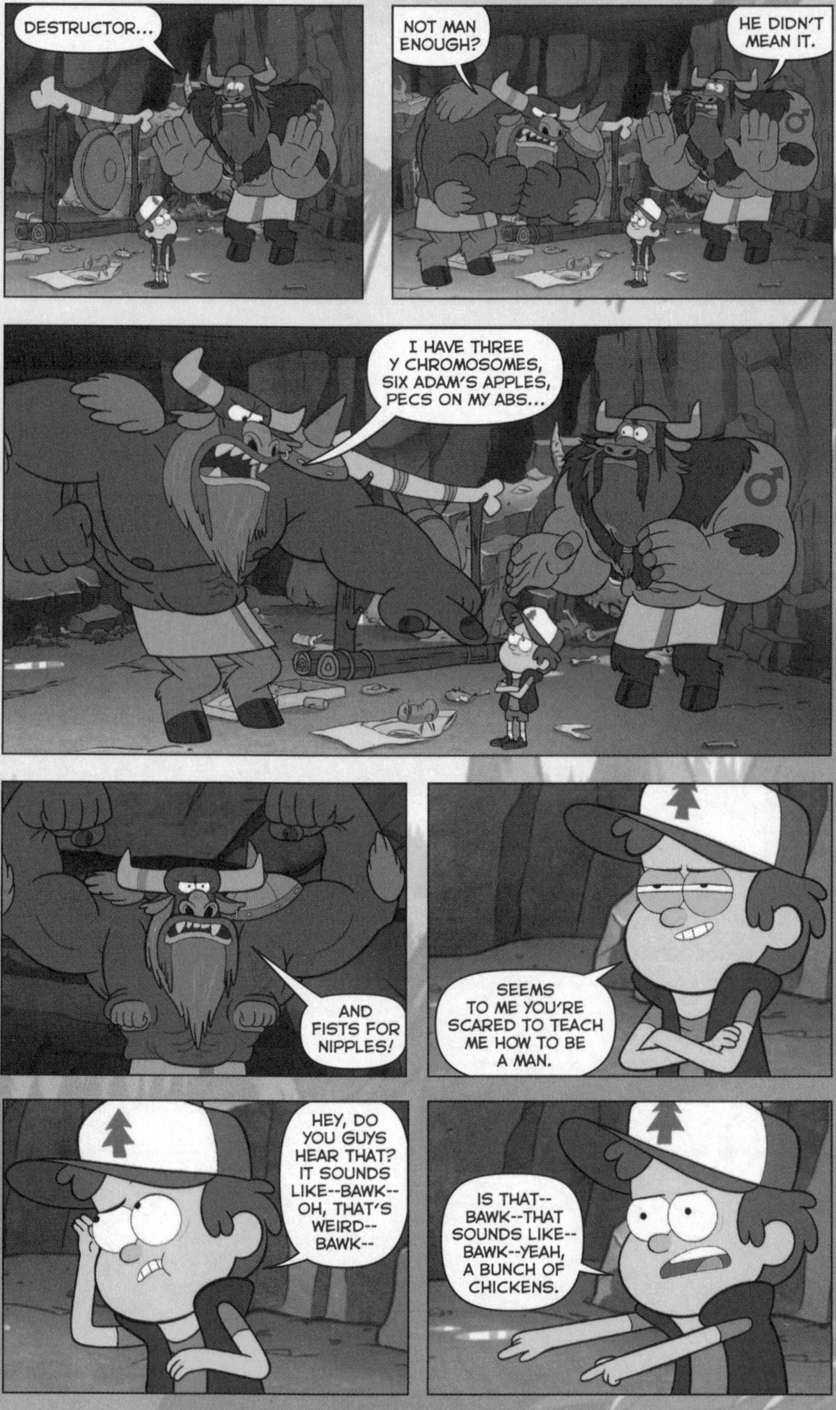
DESTRUCTOR...
NOT MAN ENOUGH?
HE DIDN'T MEAN IT.
I HAVE THREE Y CHROMOSOMES, SIX ADAM'S APPLES, PECS ON MY ABS...
AND FISTS FOR NIPPLES!
SEEMS TO ME YOU'RE SCARED TO TEACH ME HOW TO BE A MAN.
HEY, DO YOU GUYS HEAR THAT? IT SOUNDS LIKE--BAWK--OH, THAT'S WEIRD--BAWK--
IS THAT--BAWK--THAT SOUNDS LIKE--BAWK--YEAH, A BUNCH OF CHICKENS.

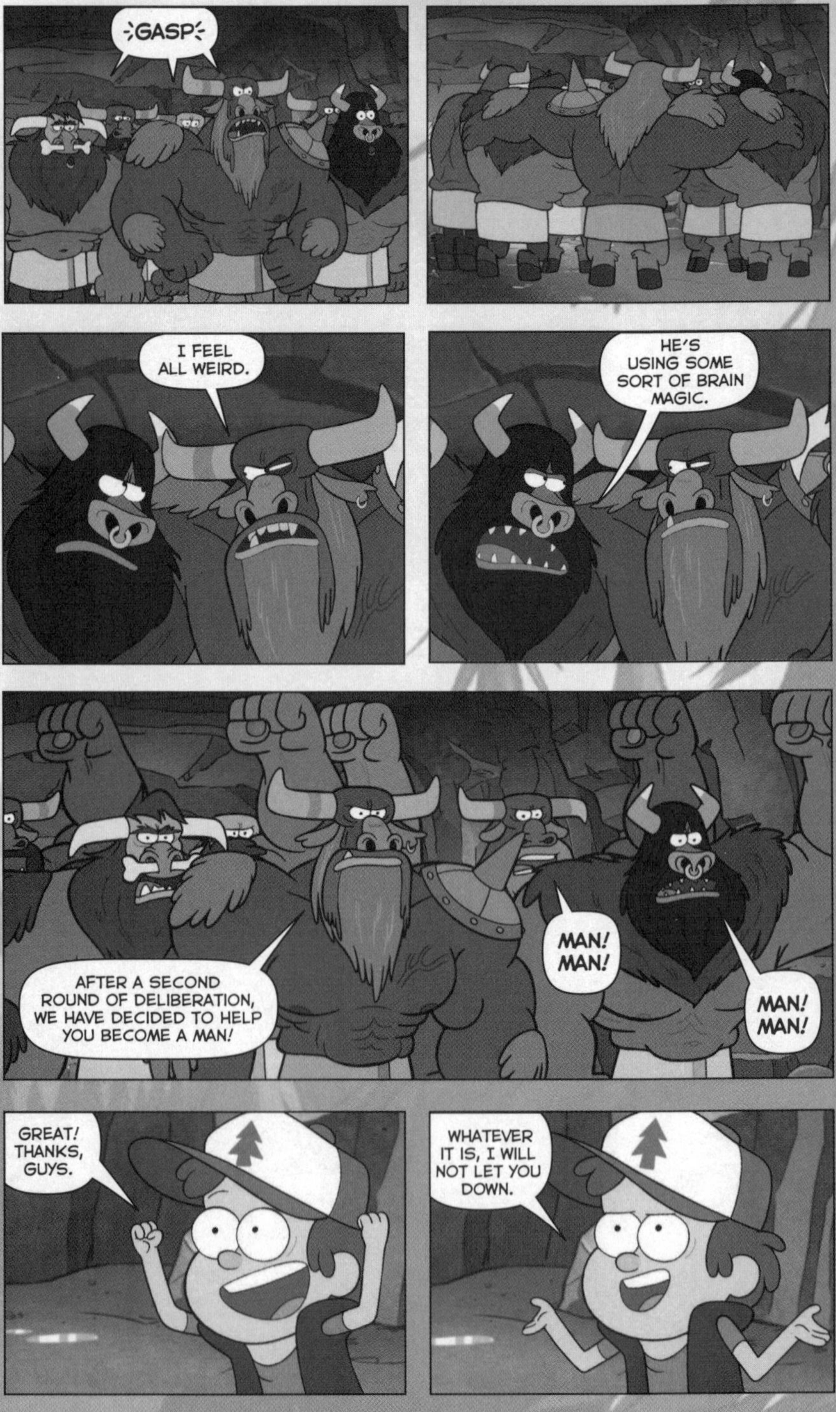
GASP
I FEEL ALL WEIRD.
HE'S USING SOME SORT OF BRAIN MAGIC.
AFTER A SECOND ROUND OF DELIBERATION, WE HAVE DECIDED TO HELP YOU BECOME A MAN!
MAN! MAN!
MAN! MAN!
GREAT! THANKS, GUYS.
WHATEVER IT IS, I WILL NOT LET YOU DOWN.

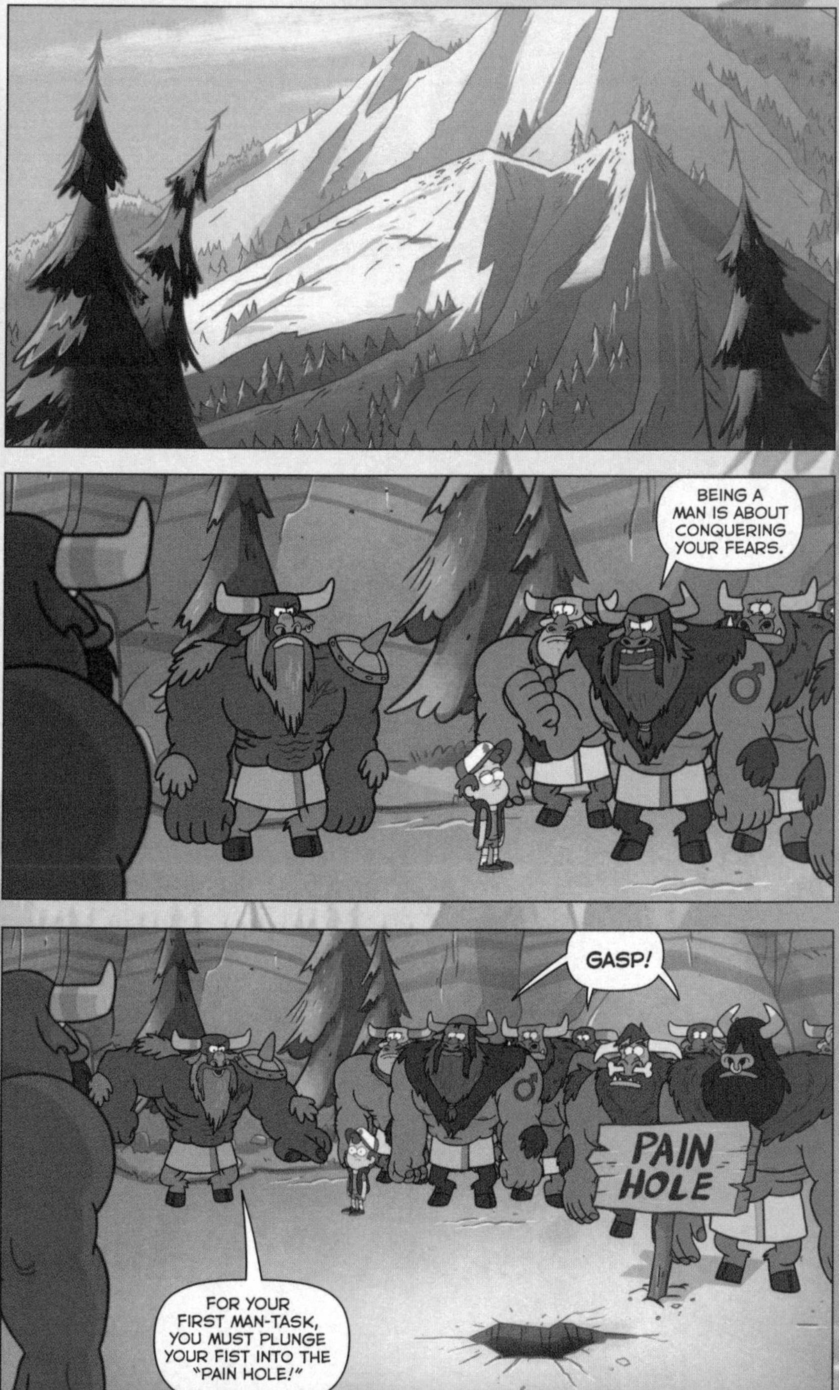

BEING A MAN IS ABOUT CONQUERING YOUR FEARS.
GASP!
PAIN HOLE
FOR YOUR FIRST MAN-TASK, YOU MUST PLUNGE YOUR FIST INTO THE "PAIN HOLE!"

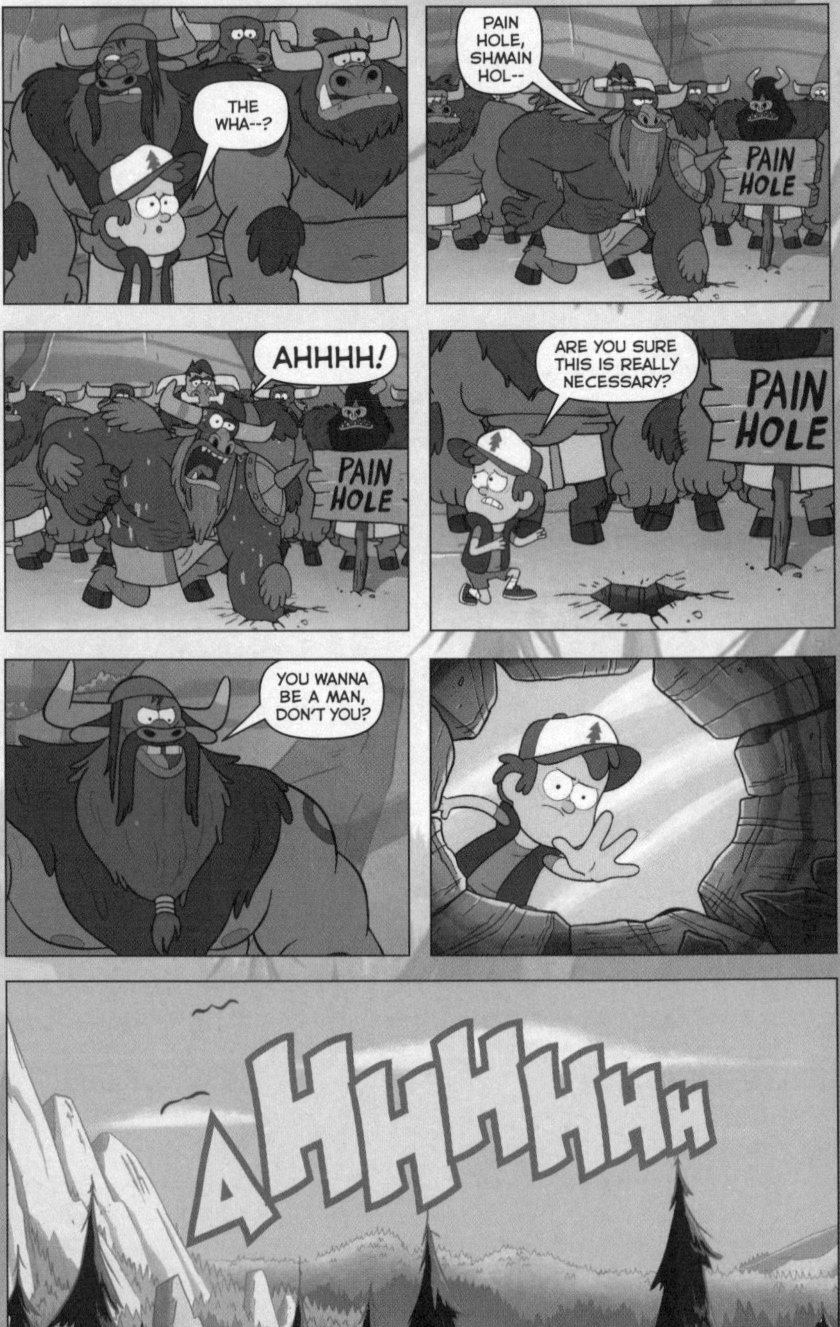
THE WHA--?
PAIN HOLE, SHMAIN HOL--
PAIN HOLE
AHHHH!
PAIN HOLE
ARE YOU SURE THIS IS REALLY NECESSARY?
PAIN HOLE
YOU WANNA BE A MAN, DON'T YOU?
AHHHHHH

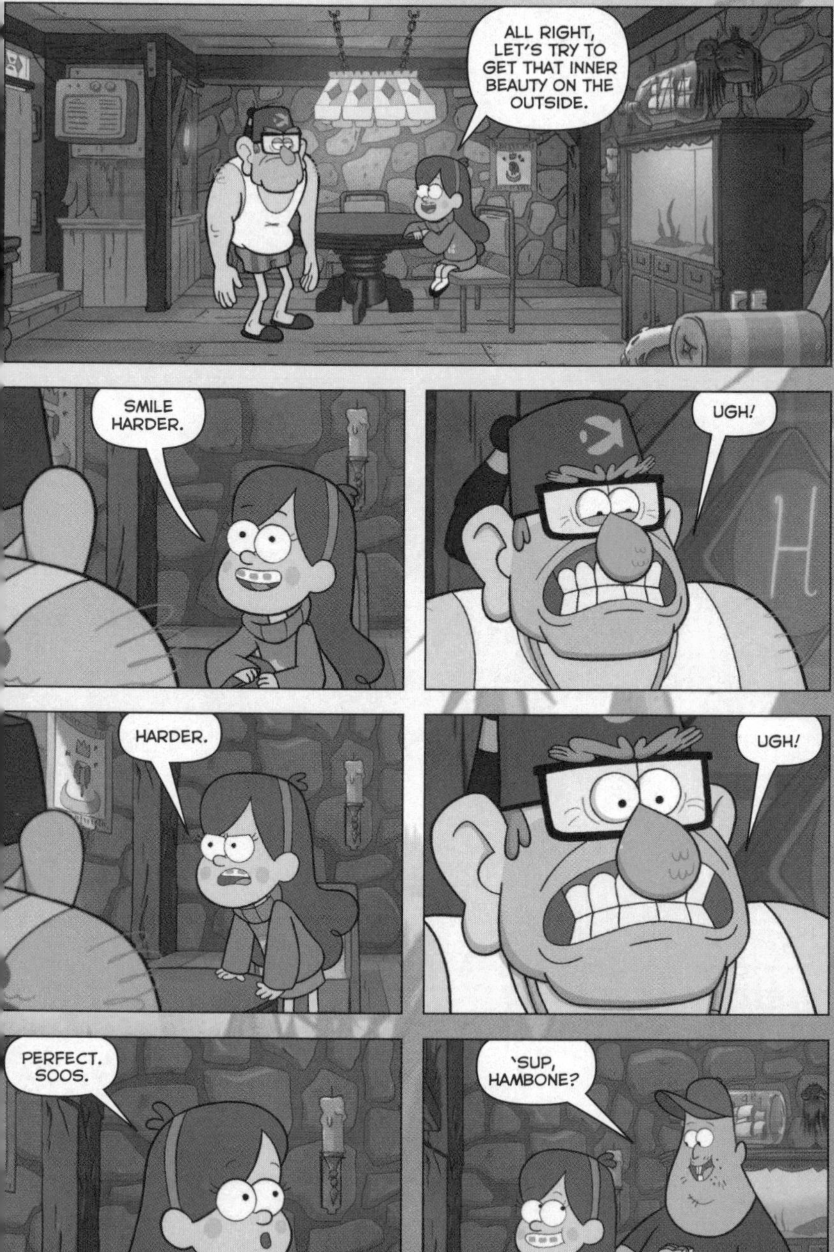
ALL RIGHT, LET'S TRY TO GET THAT INNER BEAUTY ON THE OUTSIDE.
SMILE HARDER.
UGH!
HARDER.
UGH!
PERFECT. SOOS.
'SUP, HAMBONE?

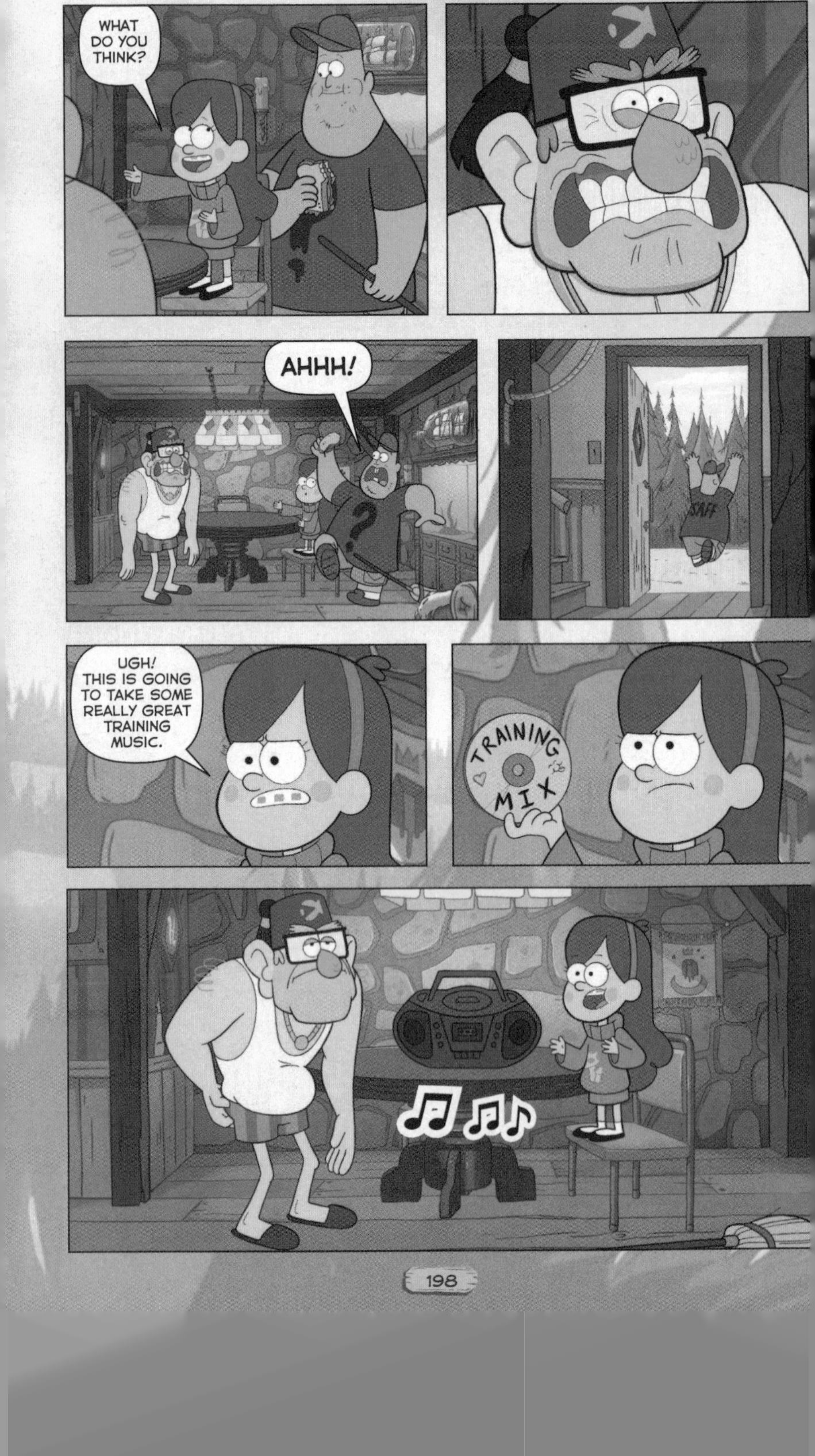
WHAT DO YOU THINK?
AHHH!
UGH! THIS IS GOING TO TAKE SOME REALLY GREAT TRAINING MUSIC.
TRAINING MIX

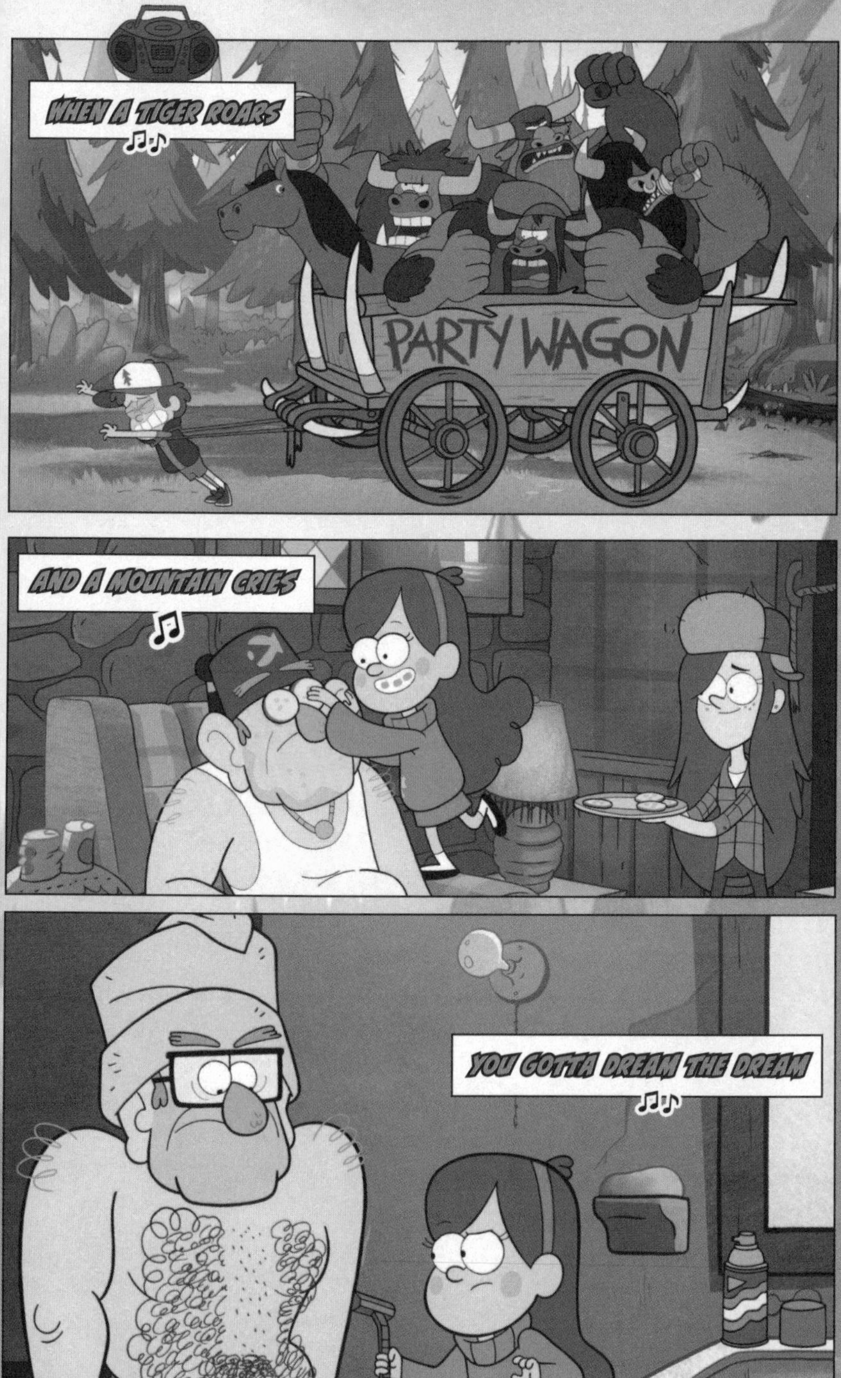
WHEN A TIGER ROARS
PARTY WAGON
AND A MOUNTAIN CRIES
YOU GOTTA DREAM THE DREAM

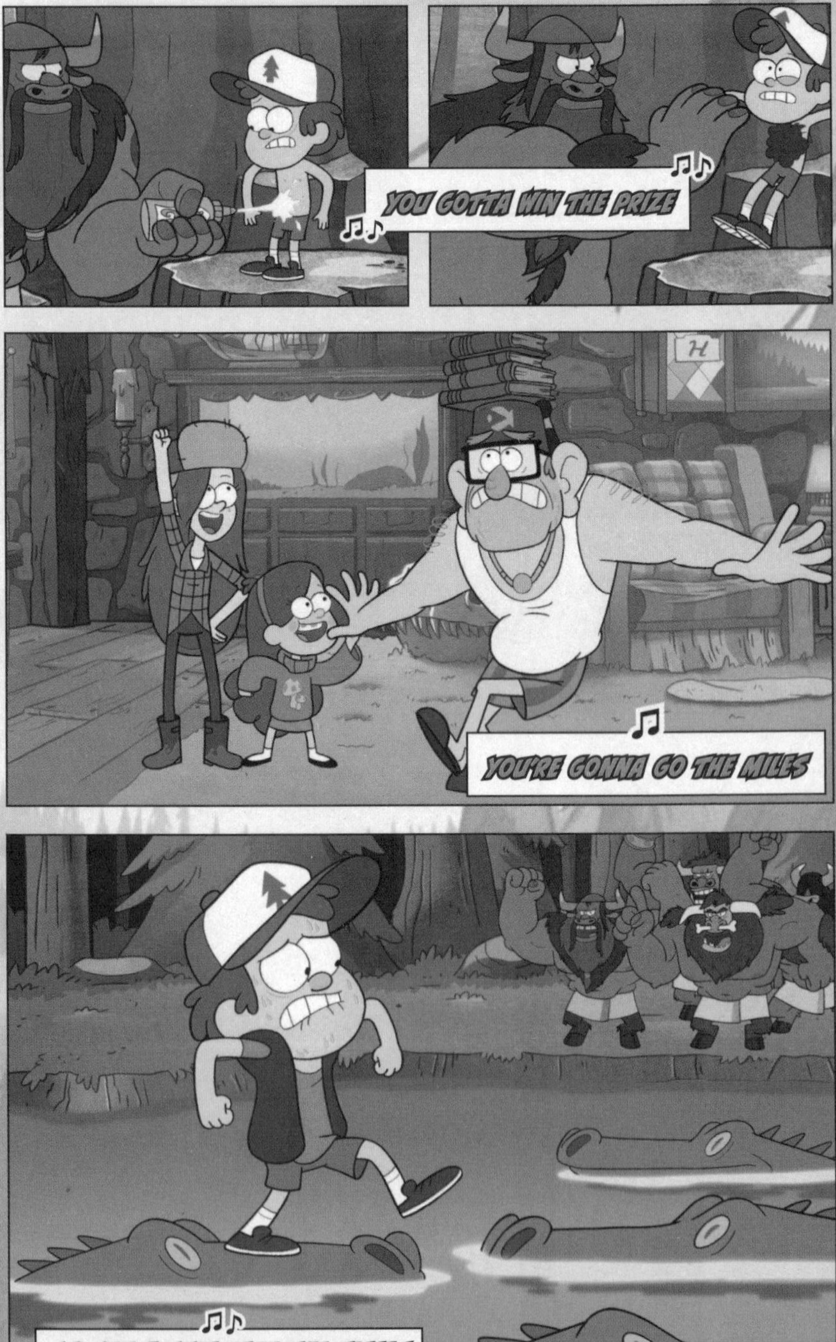

YOU GOTTA WIN THE PRIZE
YOU'RE GONNA GO THE MILES
YOU'RE GONNA FACE THE TRIALS

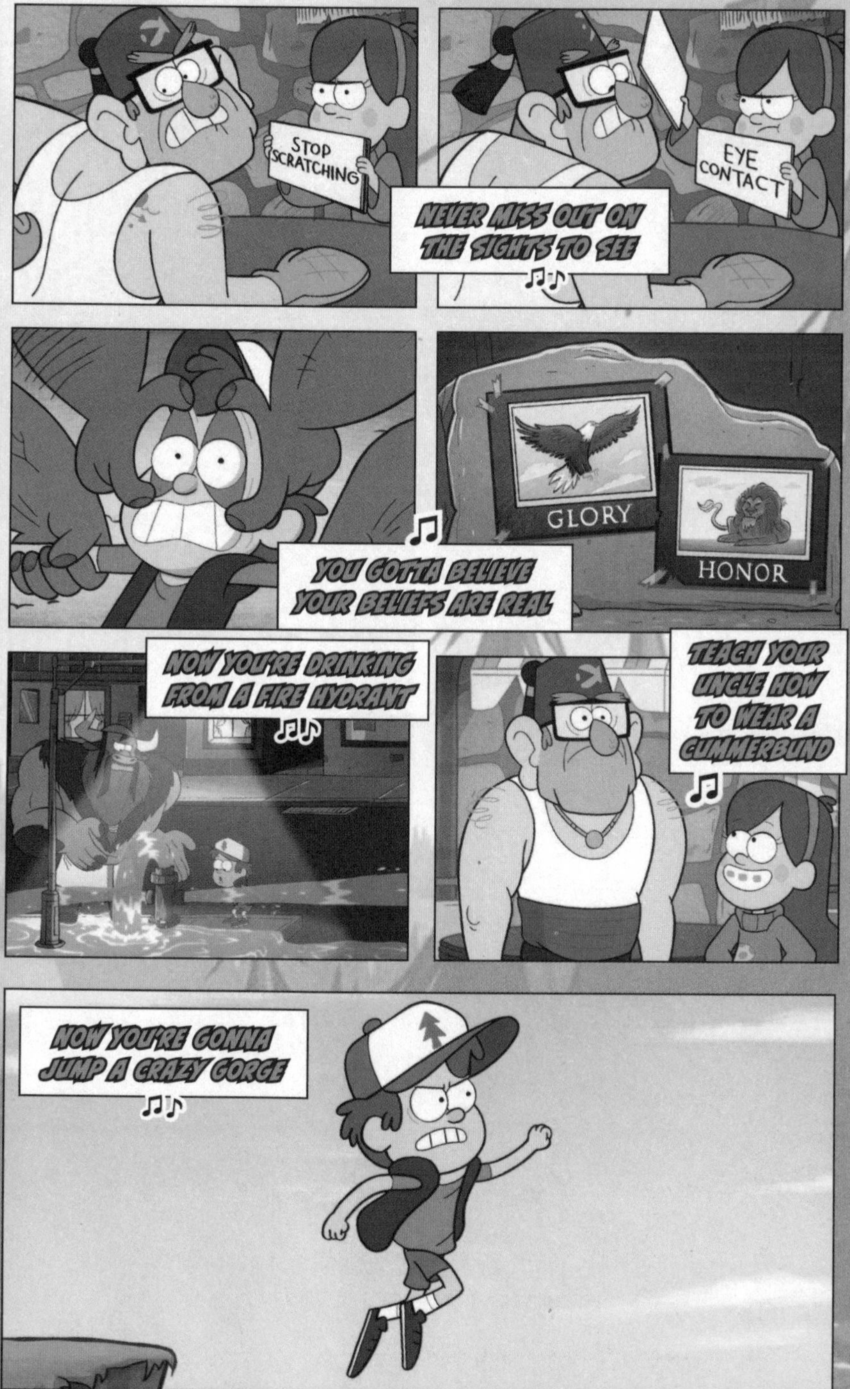
STOP SCRATCHING
EYE CONTACT
NEVER MISS OUT ON THE SIGHTS TO SEE
YOU GOTTA BELIEVE YOUR BELIEFS ARE REAL
GLORY
HONOR
NOW YOU'RE DRINKING FROM A FIRE HYDRANT
TEACH YOUR UNCLE HOW TO WEAR A CUMMERBUND
NOW YOU'RE GONNA JUMP A CRAZY GORGE

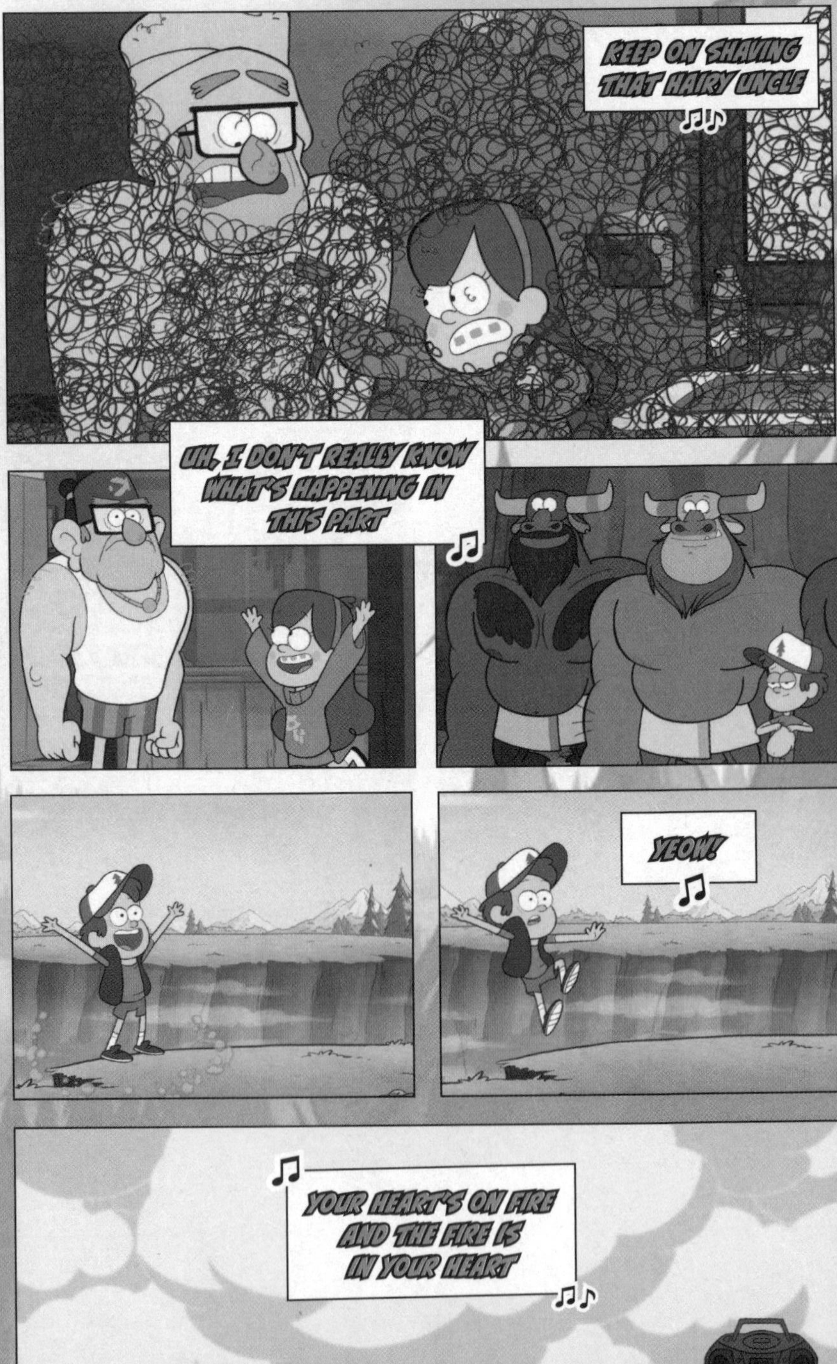
KEEP ON SHAVING
THAT HAIRY UNCLE
UH, I DON'T REALLY KNOW
WHAT'S HAPPENING IN
THIS PART
YEOW!
YOUR HEART'S ON FIRE
AND THE FIRE IS
IN YOUR HEART

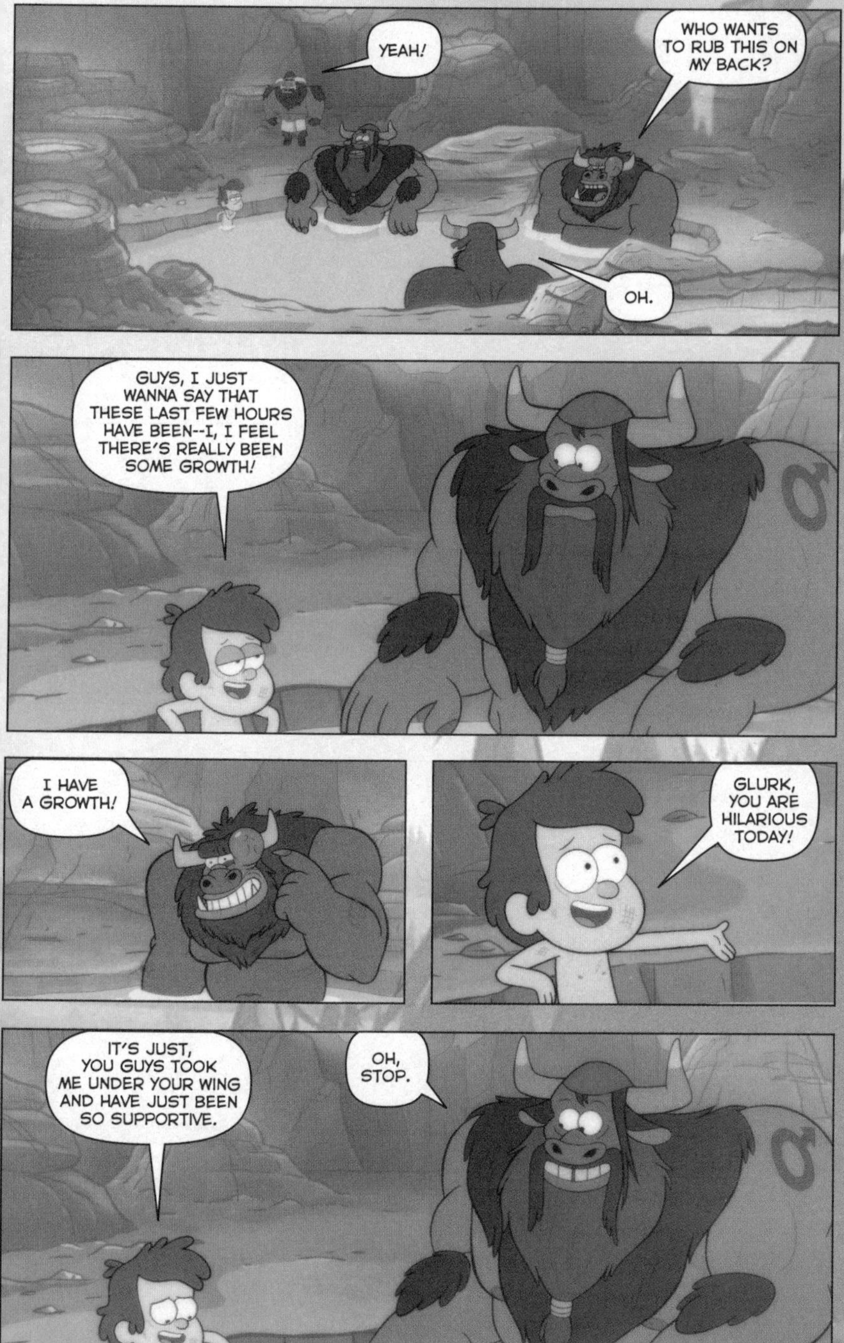

YEAH!
WHO WANTS TO RUB THIS ON MY BACK?
OH.
GUYS, I JUST WANNA SAY THAT THESE LAST FEW HOURS HAVE BEEN--I, I FEEL THERE'S REALLY BEEN SOME GROWTH!
I HAVE A GROWTH!
GLURK, YOU ARE HILARIOUS TODAY!
IT'S JUST, YOU GUYS TOOK ME UNDER YOUR WING AND HAVE JUST BEEN SO SUPPORTIVE.
OH, STOP.

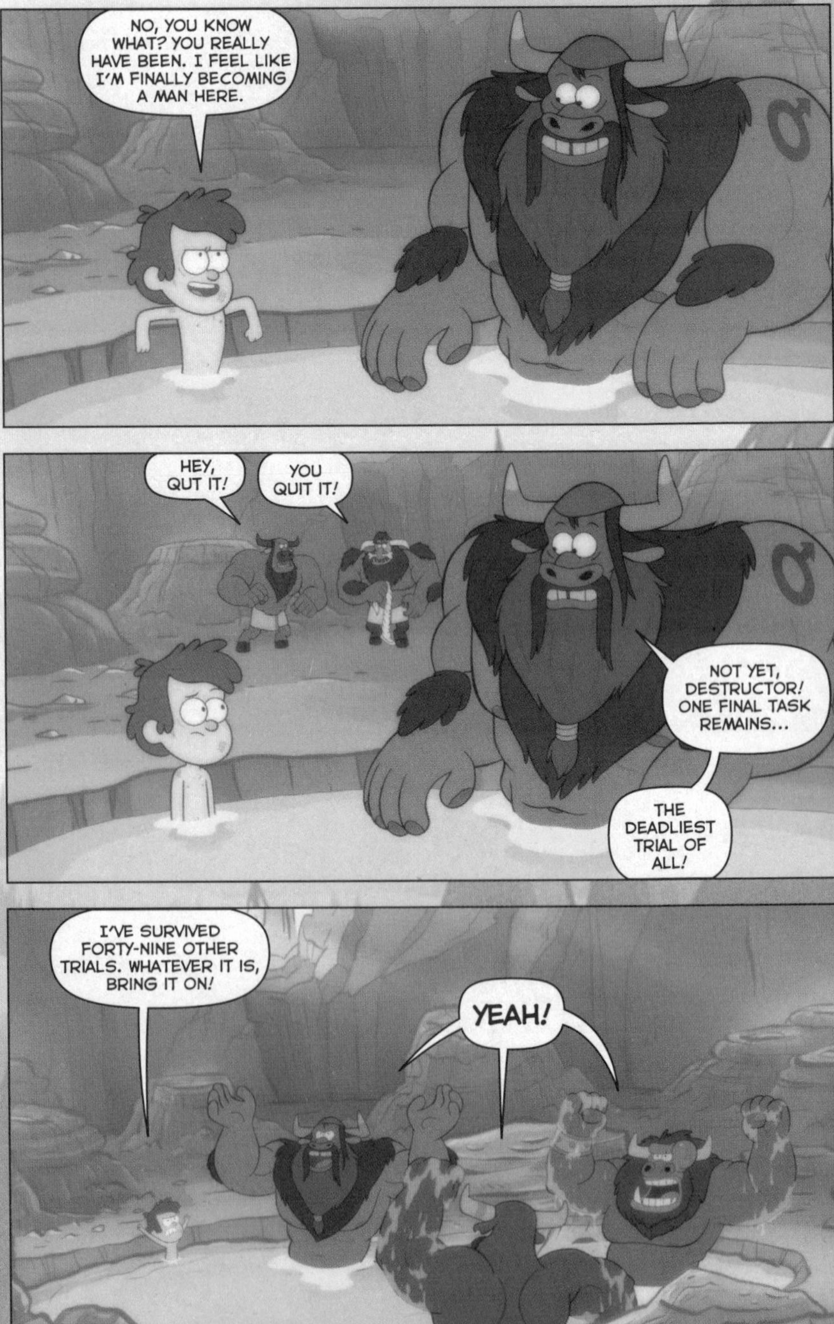
NO, YOU KNOW WHAT? YOU REALLY HAVE BEEN. I FEEL LIKE I'M FINALLY BECOMING A MAN HERE.
HEY, QUIT IT!
YOU QUIT IT!
NOT YET, DESTRUCTOR! ONE FINAL TASK REMAINS...
THE DEADLIEST TRIAL OF ALL!
I'VE SURVIVED FORTY-NINE OTHER TRIALS. WHATEVER IT IS, BRING IT ON!
YEAH!

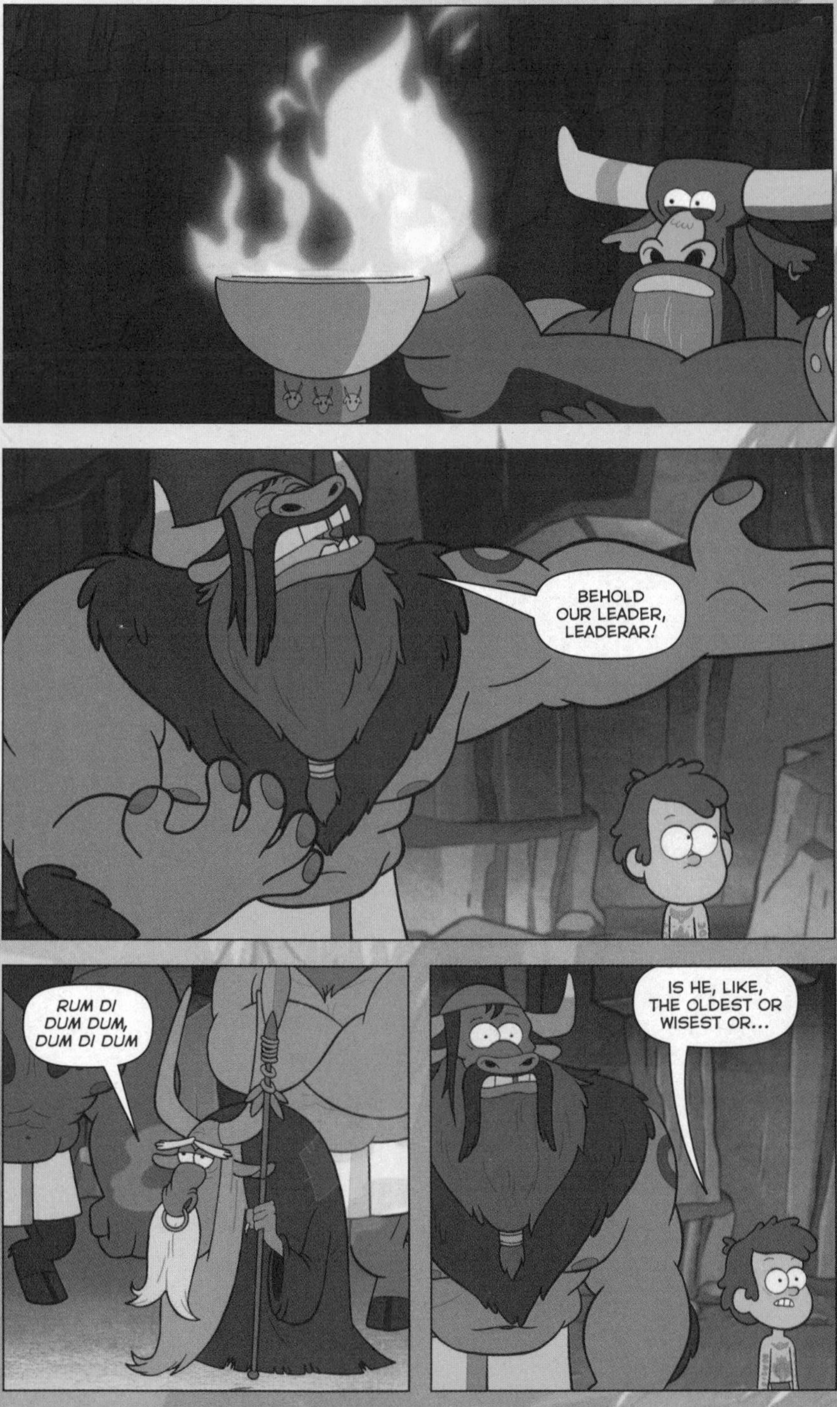
BEHOLD OUR LEADER, LEADERAR!
RUM DI DUM DUM, DUM DI DUM
IS HE, LIKE, THE OLDEST OR WISEST OR...

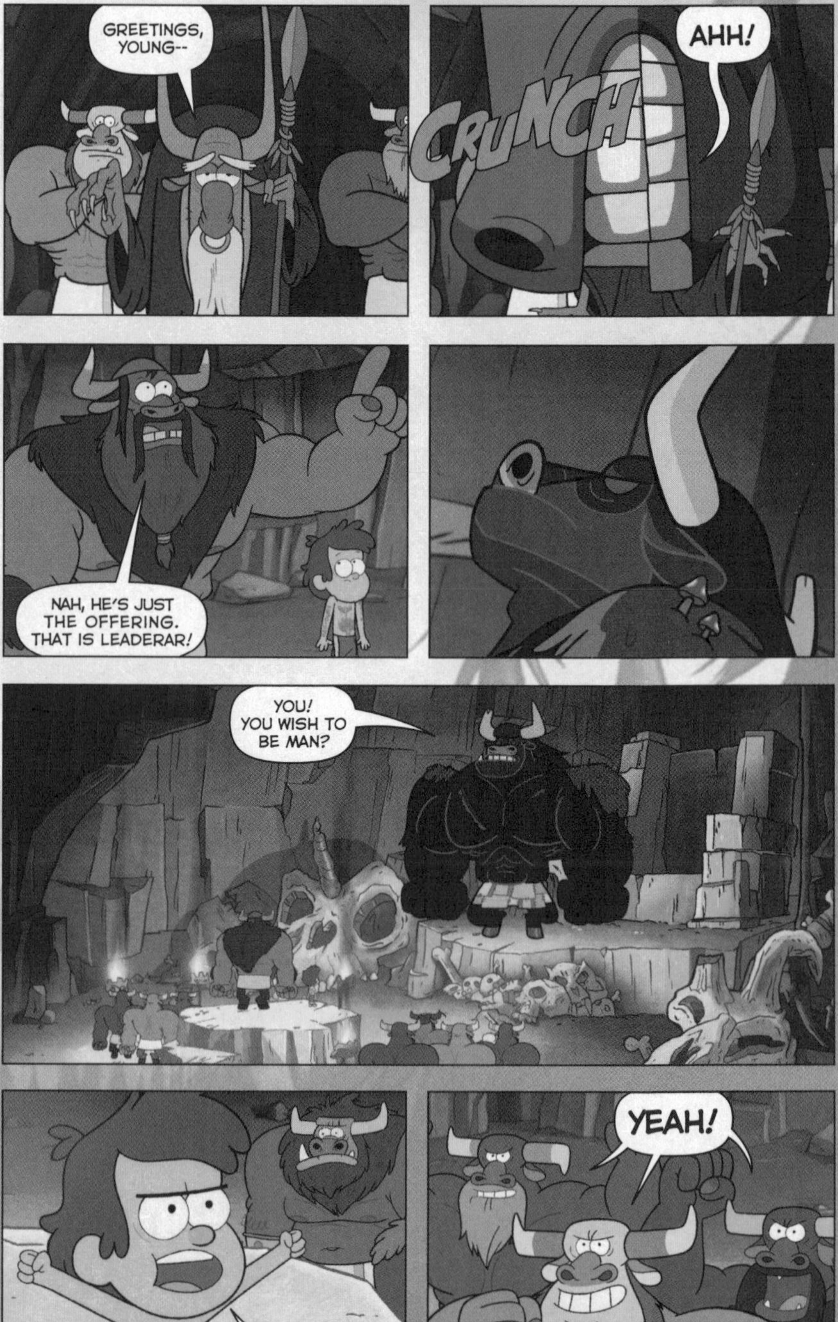
GREETINGS, YOUNG--
CRUNCH
AHH!
NAH, HE'S JUST THE OFFERING. THAT IS LEADERAR!
YOU! YOU WISH TO BE MAN?
RROARR!
YEAH!

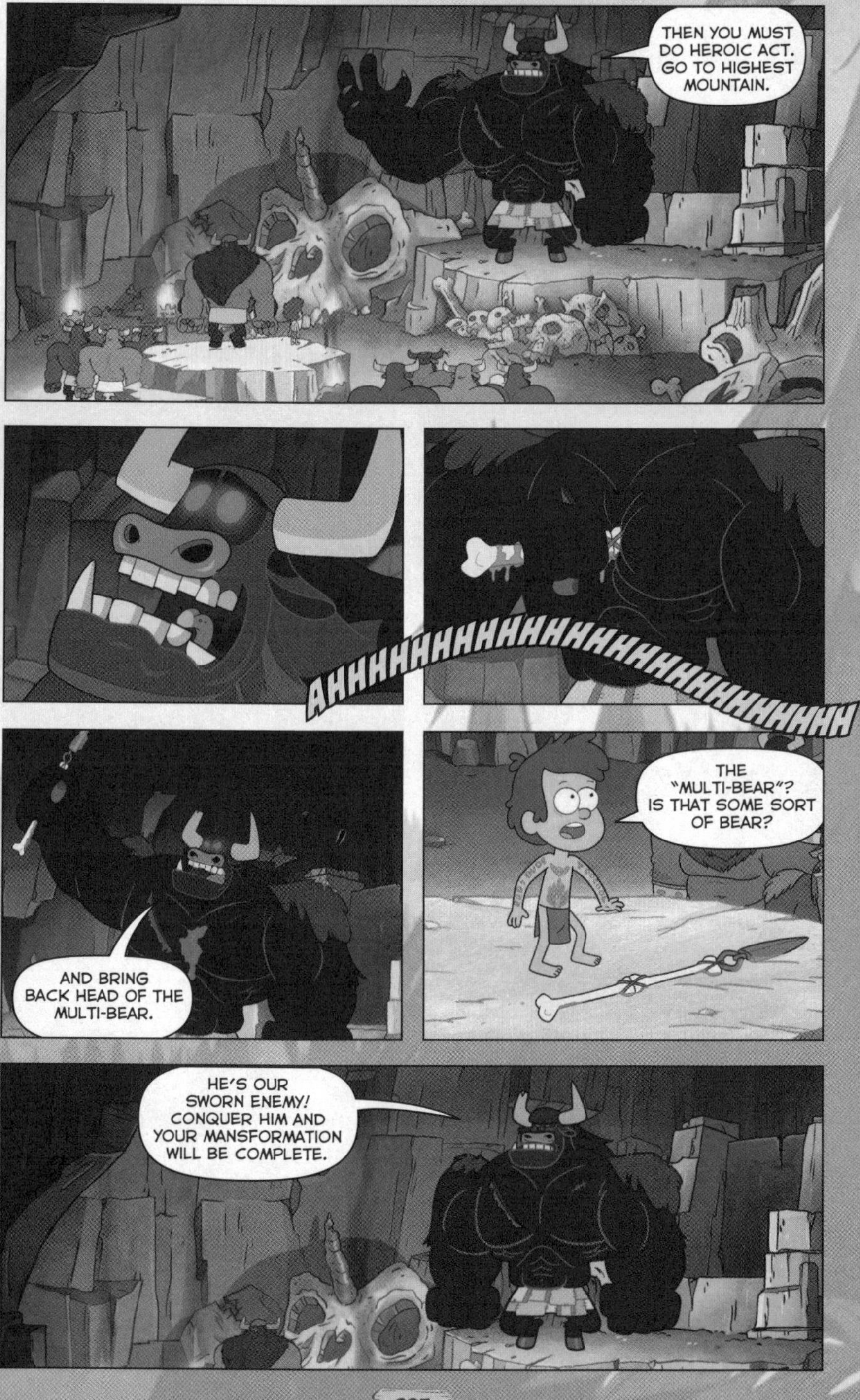
THEN YOU MUST DO HEROIC ACT. GO TO HIGHEST MOUNTAIN.
AHHHHHHHHHHHHHHHHHHHHHHHHHHHHHHHHHHHH
AND BRING BACK HEAD OF THE MULTI-BEAR.
THE "MULTI-BEAR"? IS THAT SOME SORT OF BEAR?
HE'S OUR SWORN ENEMY! CONQUER HIM AND YOUR MANSFORMATION WILL BE COMPLETE.

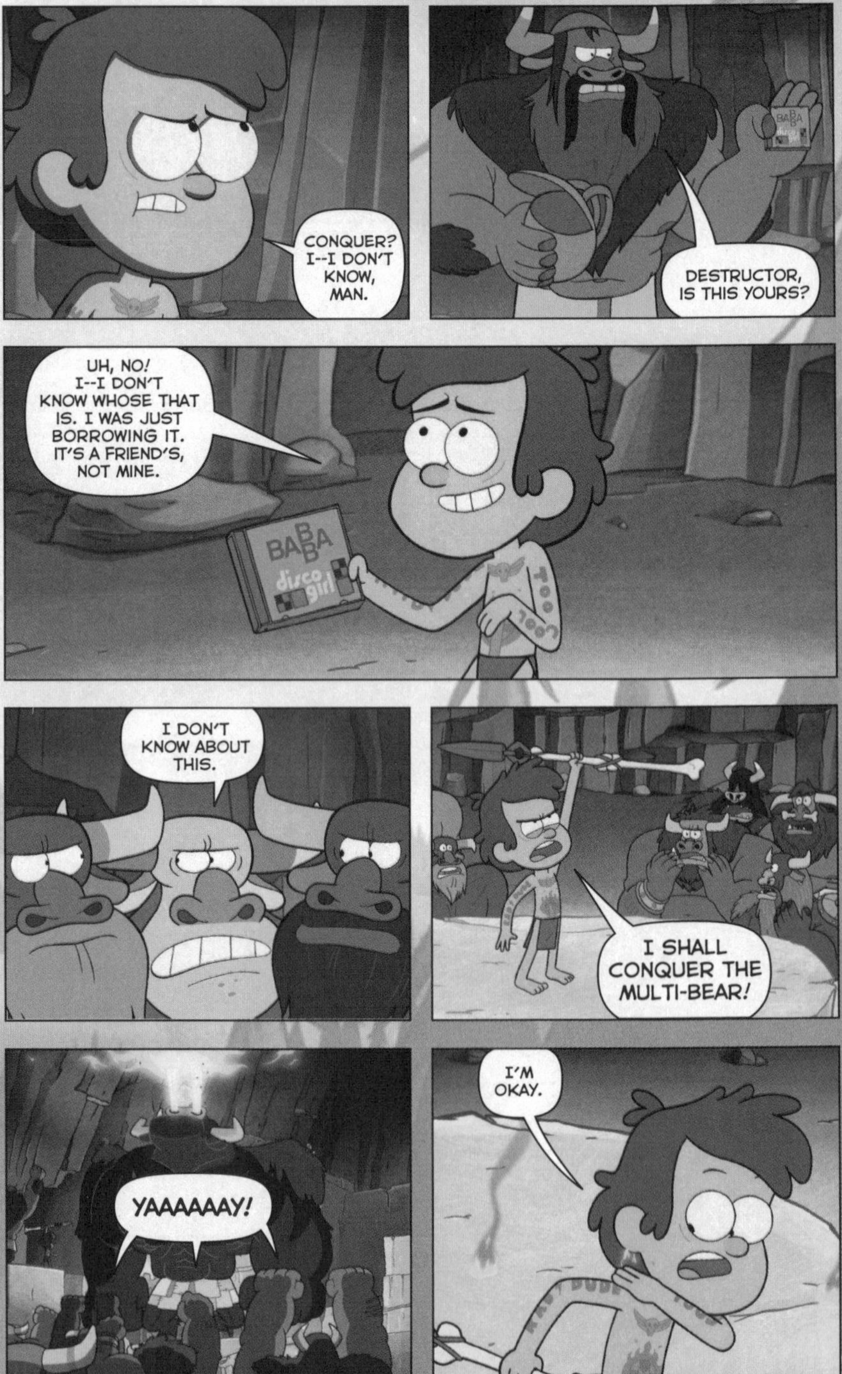
CONQUER? I--I DON'T KNOW, MAN.
DESTRUCTOR, IS THIS YOURS?
UH, NO! I--I DON'T KNOW WHOSE THAT IS. I WAS JUST BORROWING IT. IT'S A FRIEND'S, NOT MINE.
I DON'T KNOW ABOUT THIS.
I SHALL CONQUER THE MULTI-BEAR!
YAAAAAAY!
I'M OKAY.

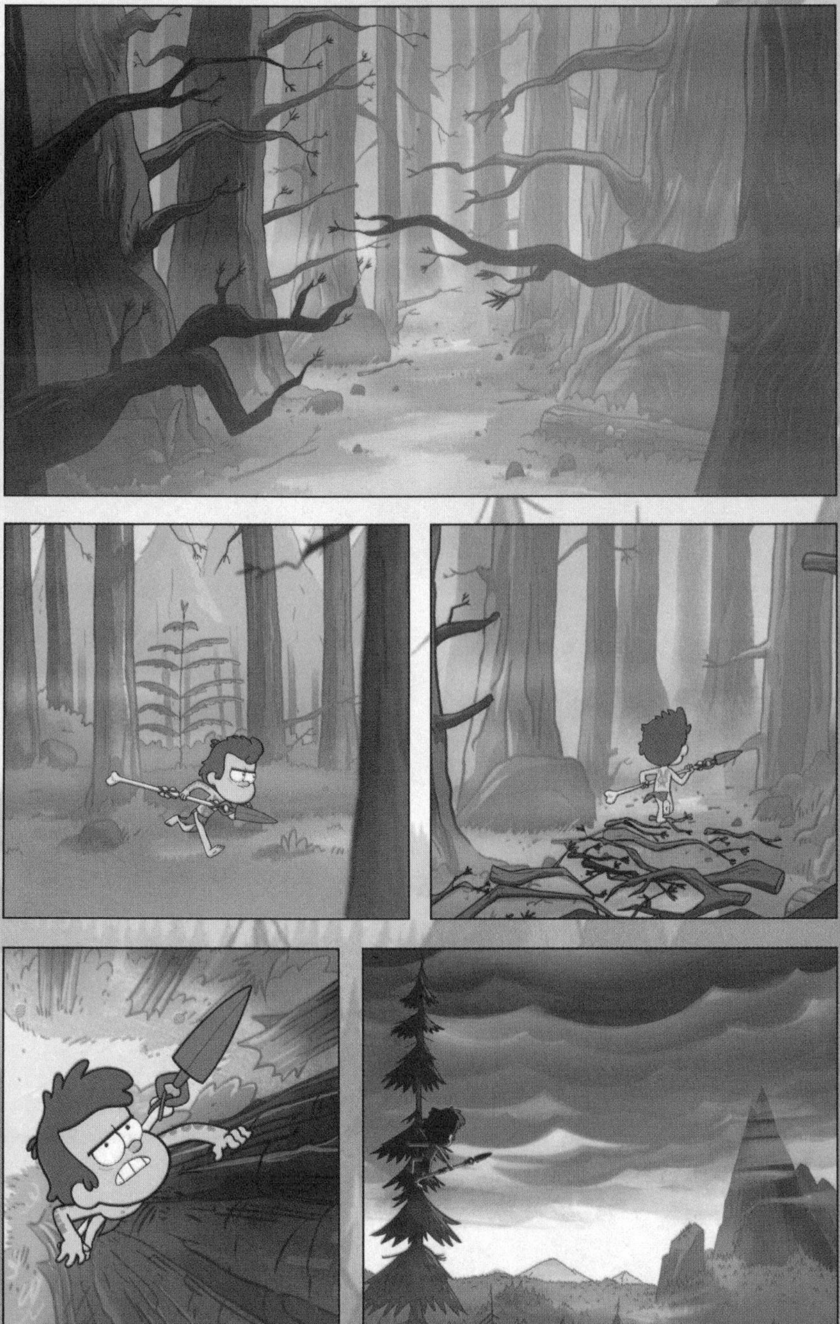

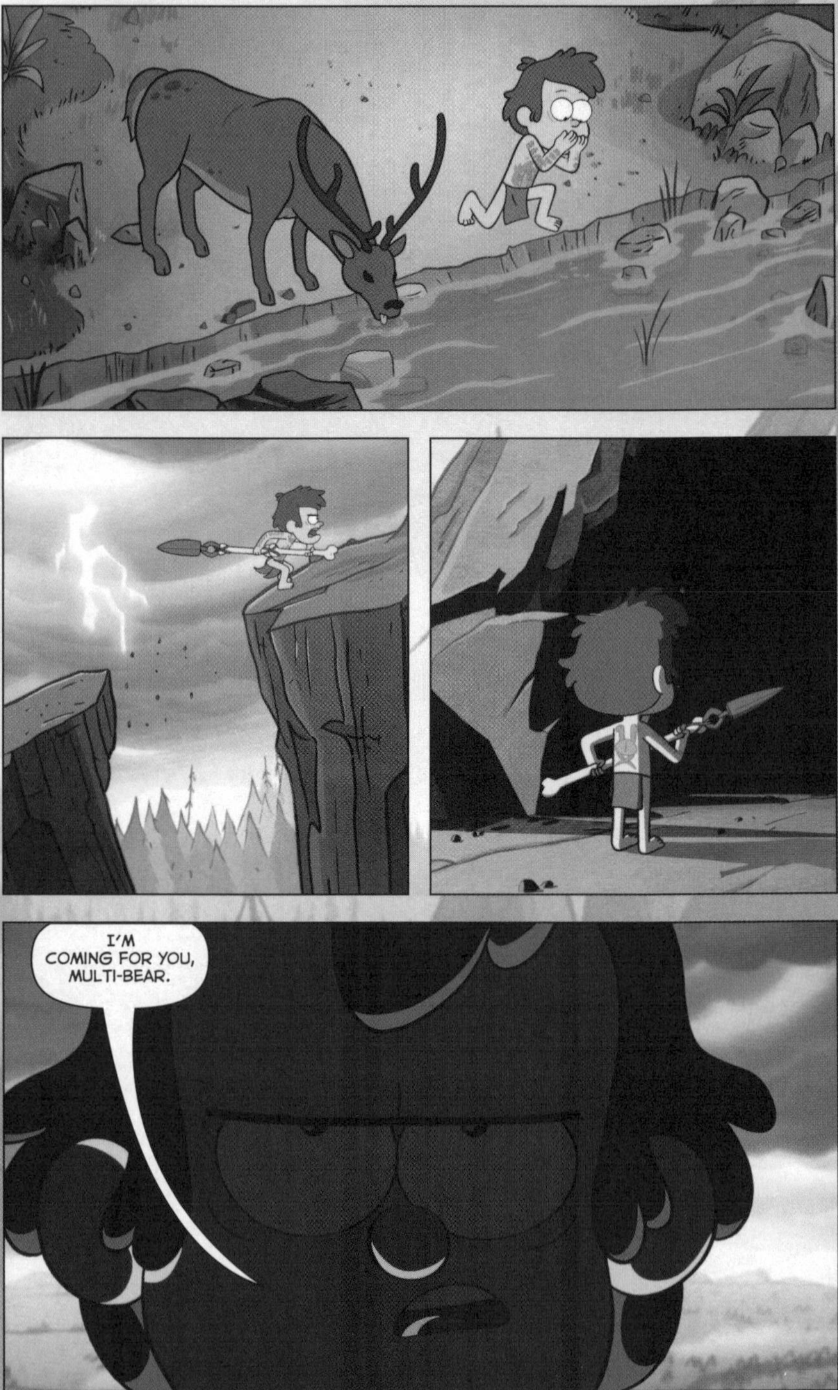
I'M COMING FOR YOU, MULTI-BEAR.

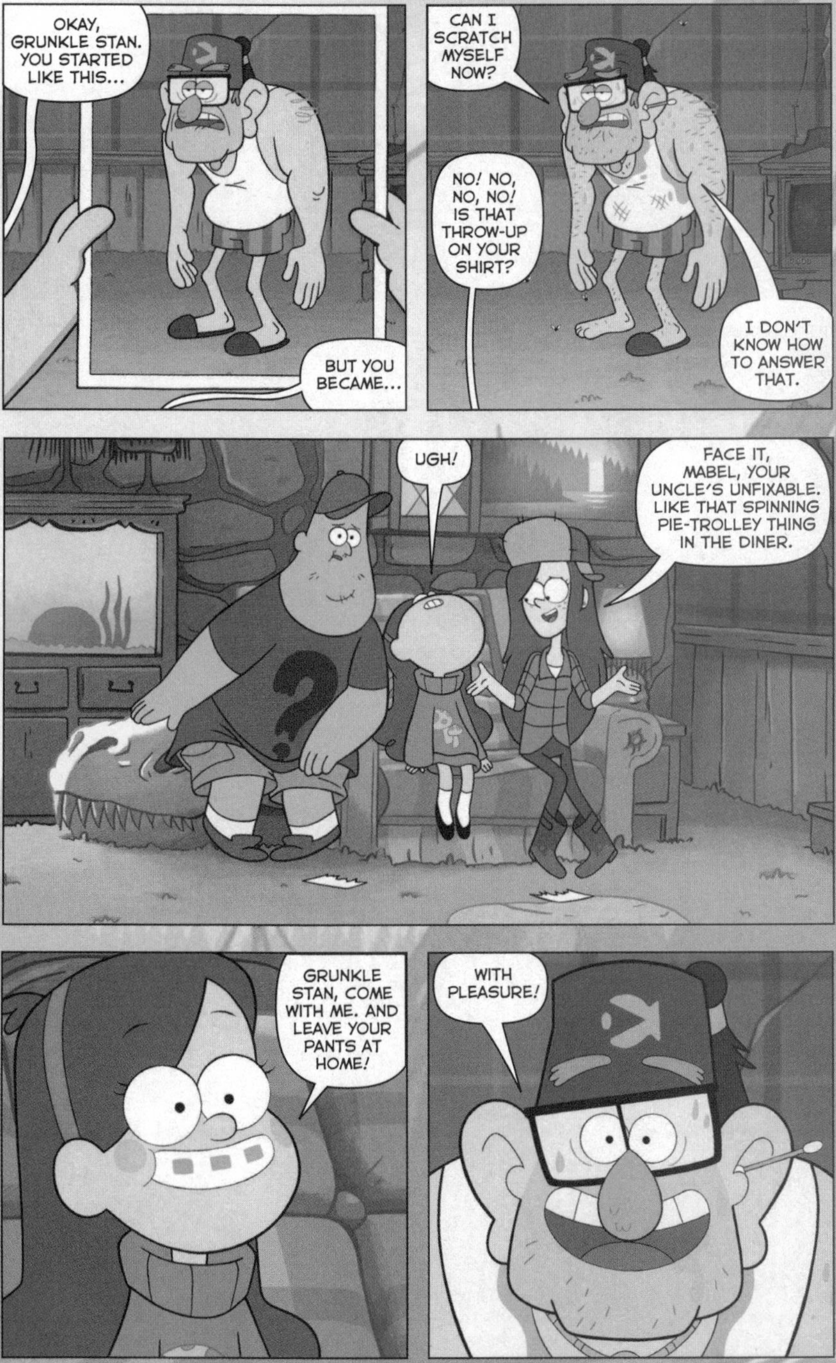
OKAY, GRUNKLE STAN. YOU STARTED LIKE THIS...
BUT YOU BECAME...
CAN I SCRATCH MYSELF NOW?
NO! NO, NO, NO! IS THAT THROW-UP ON YOUR SHIRT?
I DON'T KNOW HOW TO ANSWER THAT.
UGH!
FACE IT, MABEL, YOUR UNCLE'S UNFIXABLE. LIKE THAT SPINNING PIE-TROLLEY THING IN THE DINER.
GRUNKLE STAN, COME WITH ME. AND LEAVE YOUR PANTS AT HOME!
WITH PLEASURE!

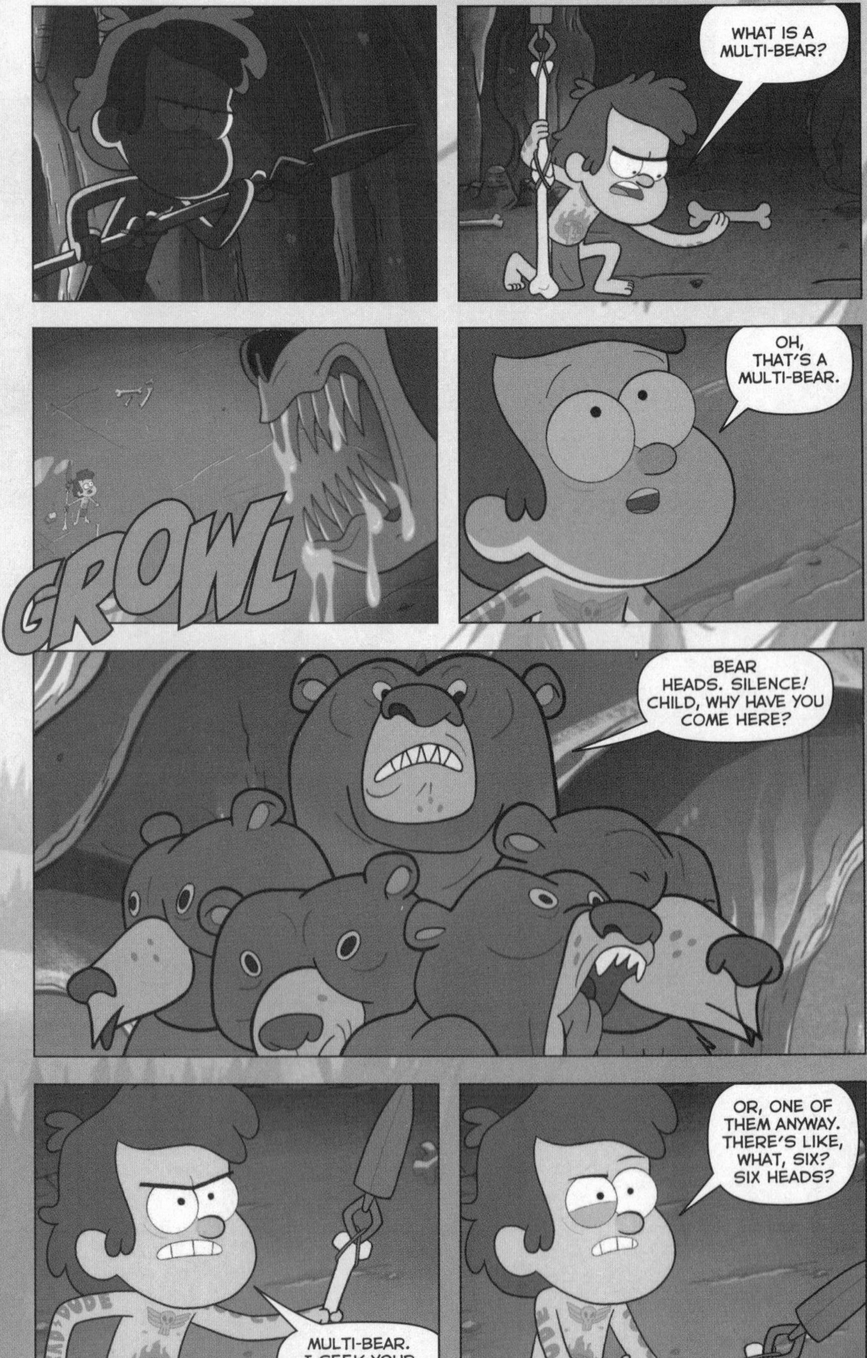
WHAT IS A MULTI-BEAR?
GROWL
OH, THAT'S A MULTI-BEAR.
BEAR HEADS. SILENCE! CHILD, WHY HAVE YOU COME HERE?
MULTI-BEAR. I SEEK YOUR HEAD!
OR, ONE OF THEM ANYWAY. THERE'S LIKE, WHAT, SIX? SIX HEADS?

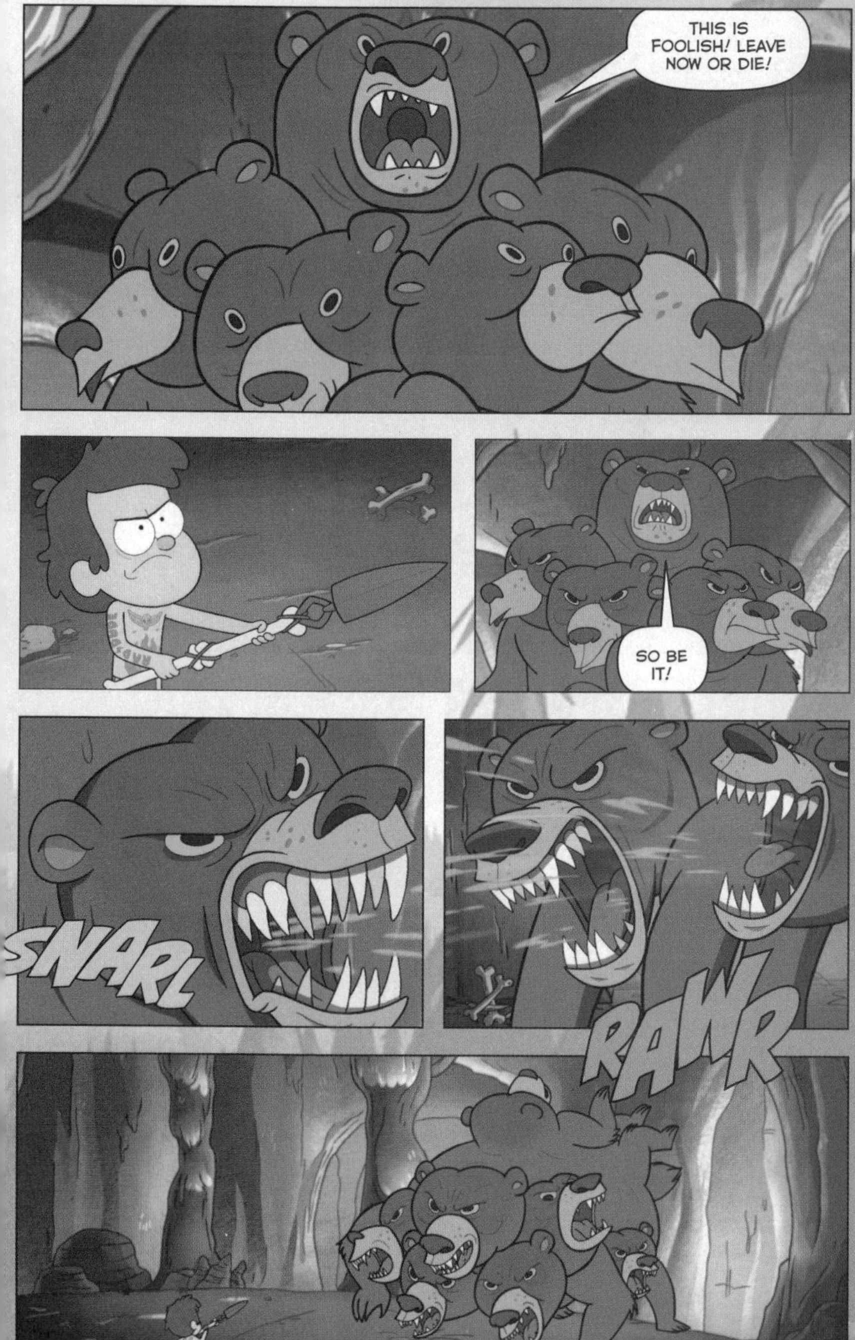
THIS IS FOOLISH! LEAVE NOW OR DIE!
SO BE IT!
SNARL
RAWR

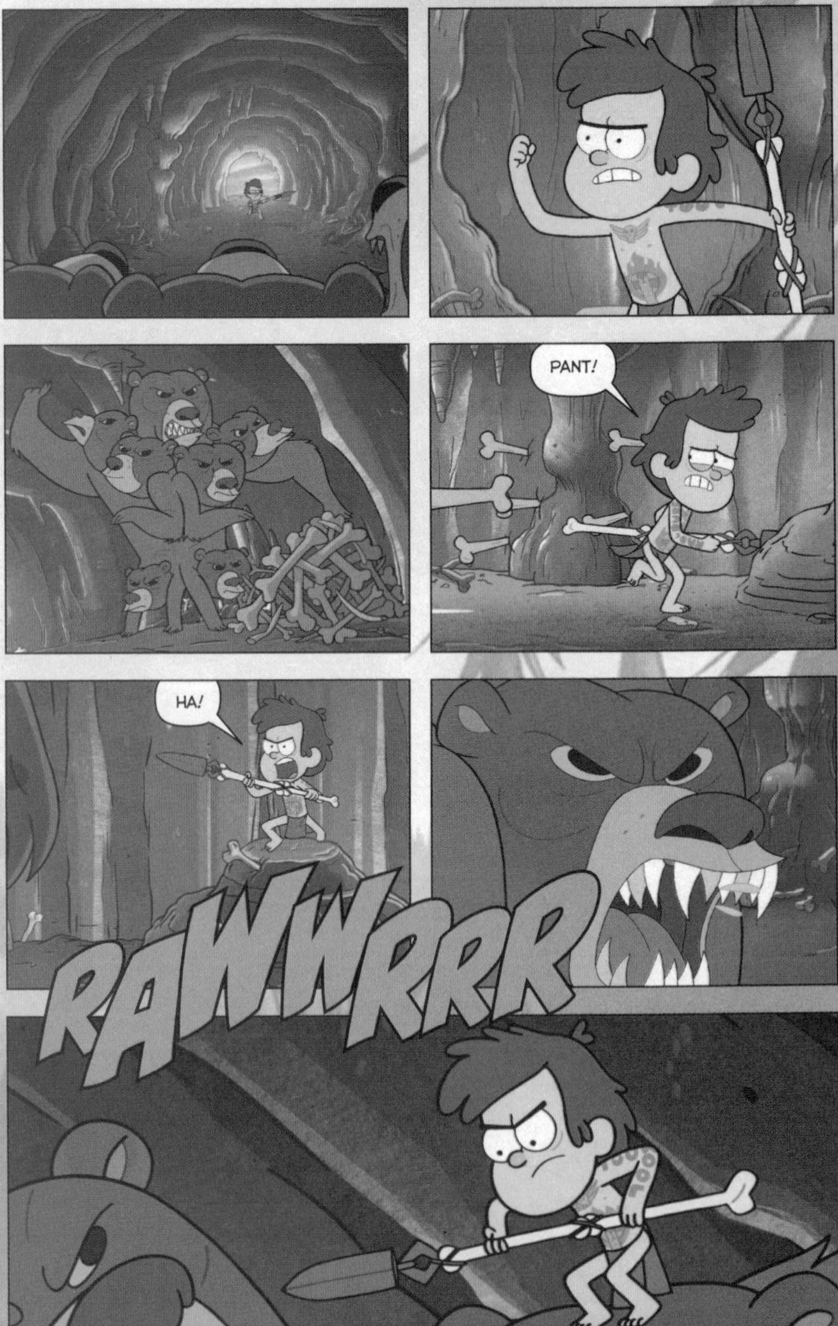
PANT!
HA!
RAWWRRR

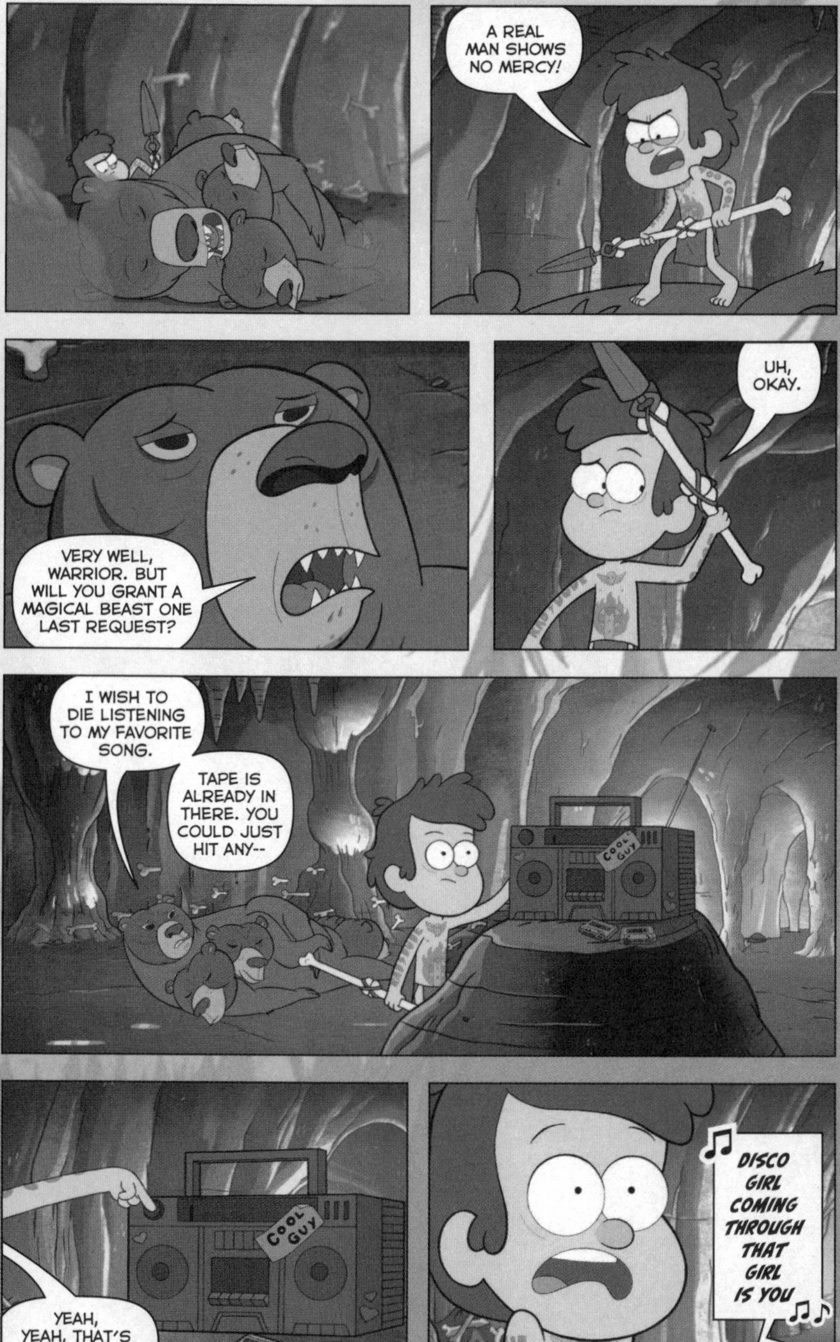
A REAL MAN SHOWS NO MERCY!
VERY WELL, WARRIOR. BUT WILL YOU GRANT A MAGICAL BEAST ONE LAST REQUEST?
UH, OKAY.
I WISH TO DIE LISTENING TO MY FAVORITE SONG.
TAPE IS ALREADY IN THERE. YOU COULD JUST HIT ANY--
COOL GUY
COOL GUY
YEAH, YEAH, THAT'S IT. PRESS AND HOLD.
DISCO GIRL COMING THROUGH THAT GIRL IS YOU

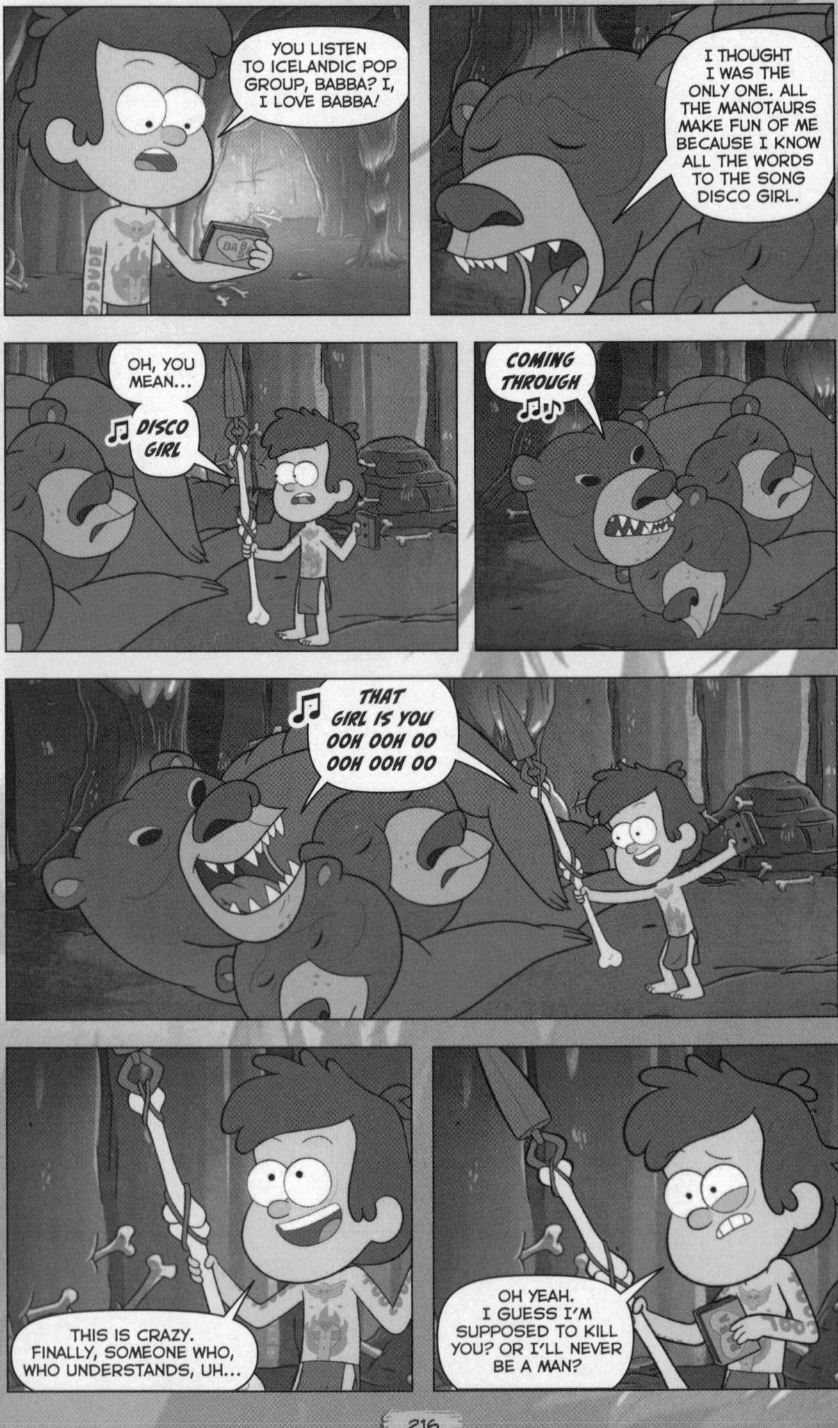
YOU LISTEN TO ICELANDIC POP GROUP, BABBA? I, I LOVE BABBA!
I THOUGHT I WAS THE ONLY ONE. ALL THE MANOTAURS MAKE FUN OF ME BECAUSE I KNOW ALL THE WORDS TO THE SONG DISCO GIRL.
OH, YOU MEAN...
DISCO GIRL
COMING THROUGH
THAT GIRL IS YOU OOH OOH OO OOH OOH OO
THIS IS CRAZY. FINALLY, SOMEONE WHO, WHO UNDERSTANDS, UH...
OH YEAH. I GUESS I'M SUPPOSED TO KILL YOU? OR I'LL NEVER BE A MAN?

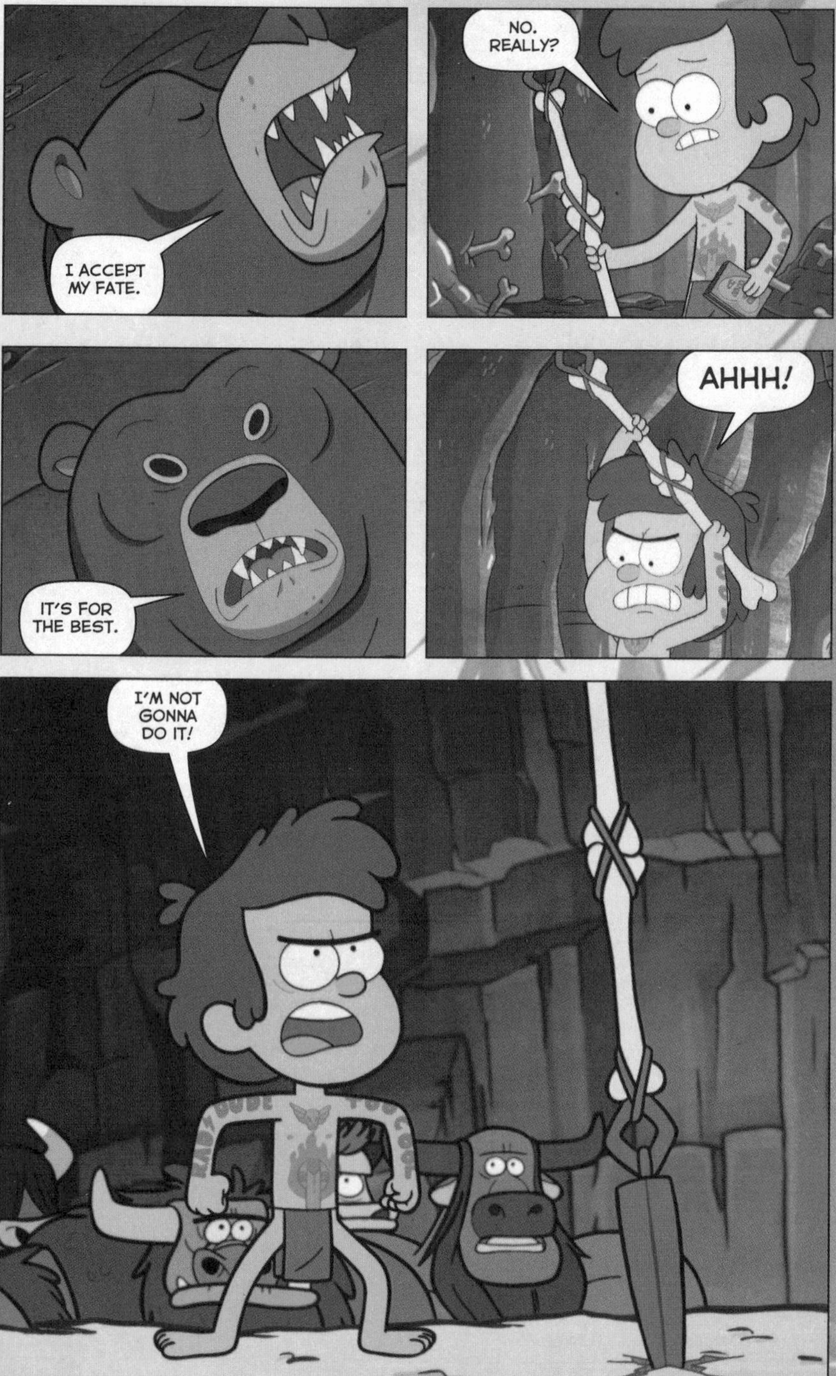
I ACCEPT MY FATE.
NO. REALLY?
IT'S FOR THE BEST.
AHHH!
I'M NOT GONNA DO IT!

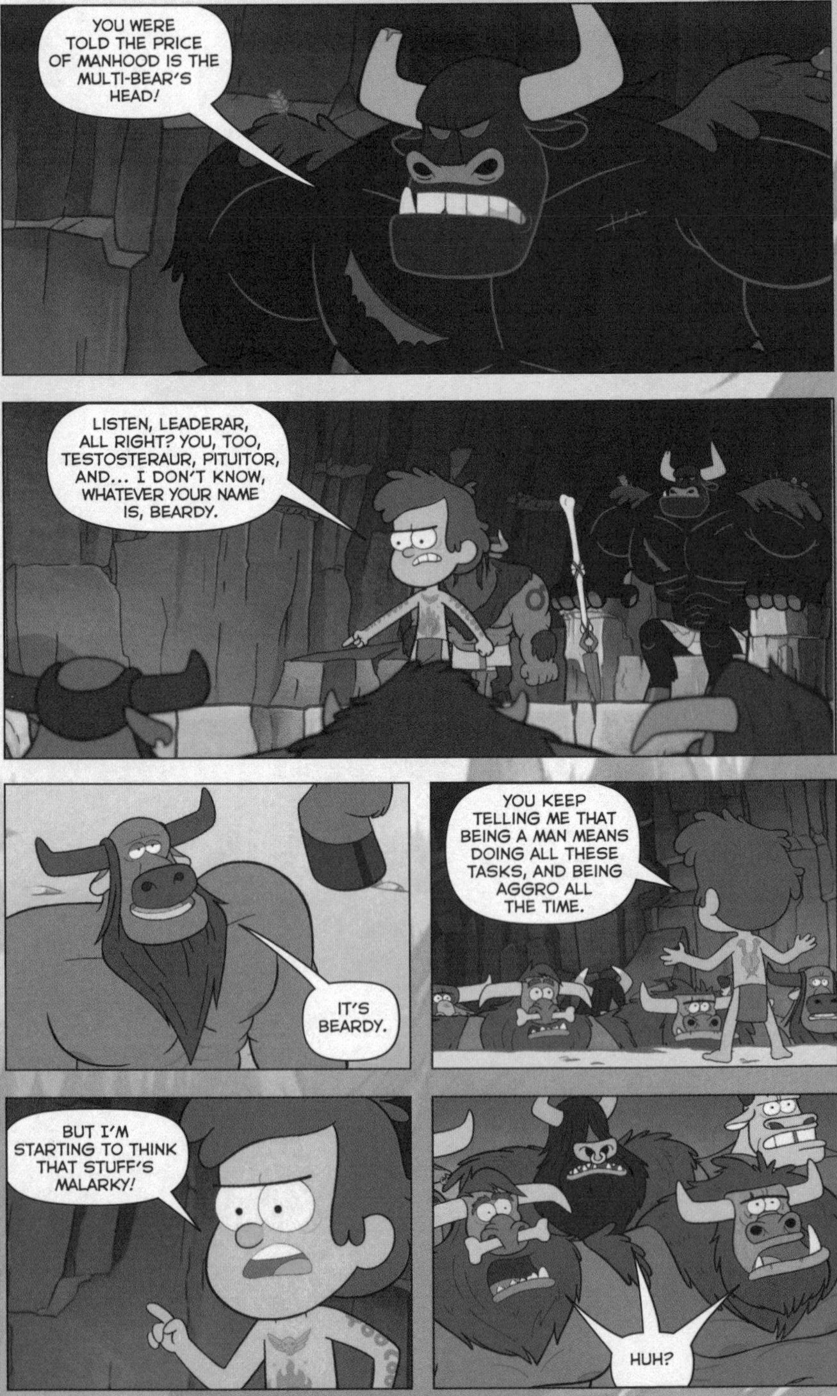
YOU WERE TOLD THE PRICE OF MANHOOD IS THE MULTI-BEAR'S HEAD!
LISTEN, LEADERAR, ALL RIGHT? YOU, TOO, TESTOSTERAUR, PITUITOR, AND... I DON'T KNOW, WHATEVER YOUR NAME IS, BEARDY.
IT'S BEARDY.
YOU KEEP TELLING ME THAT BEING A MAN MEANS DOING ALL THESE TASKS, AND BEING AGGRO ALL THE TIME.
BUT I'M STARTING TO THINK THAT STUFF'S MALARKY!
HUH?

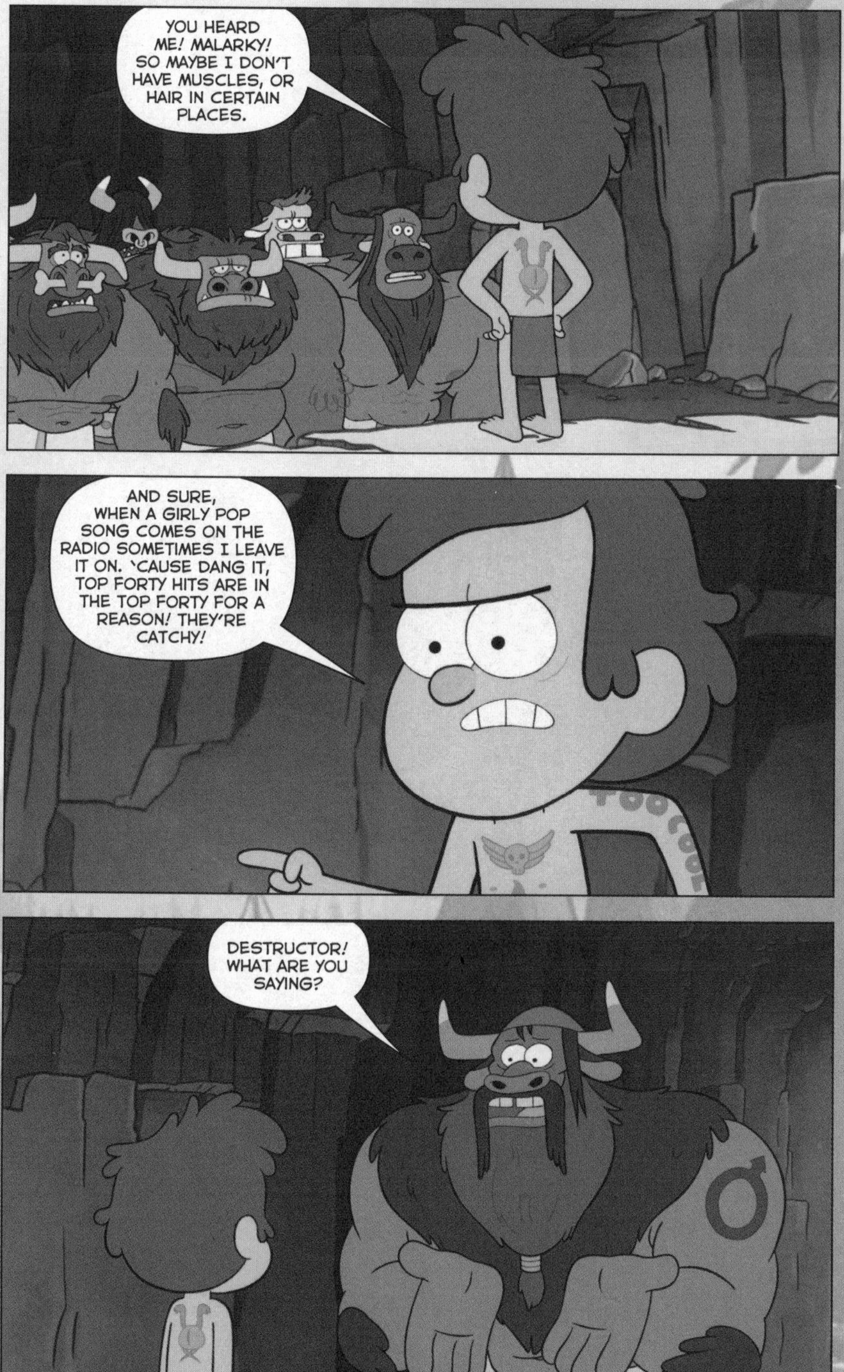
YOU HEARD ME! MALARKY! SO MAYBE I DON'T HAVE MUSCLES, OR HAIR IN CERTAIN PLACES.
AND SURE, WHEN A GIRLY POP SONG COMES ON THE RADIO SOMETIMES I LEAVE IT ON. 'CAUSE DANG IT, TOP FORTY HITS ARE IN THE TOP FORTY FOR A REASON! THEY'RE CATCHY!
DESTRUCTOR! WHAT ARE YOU SAYING?

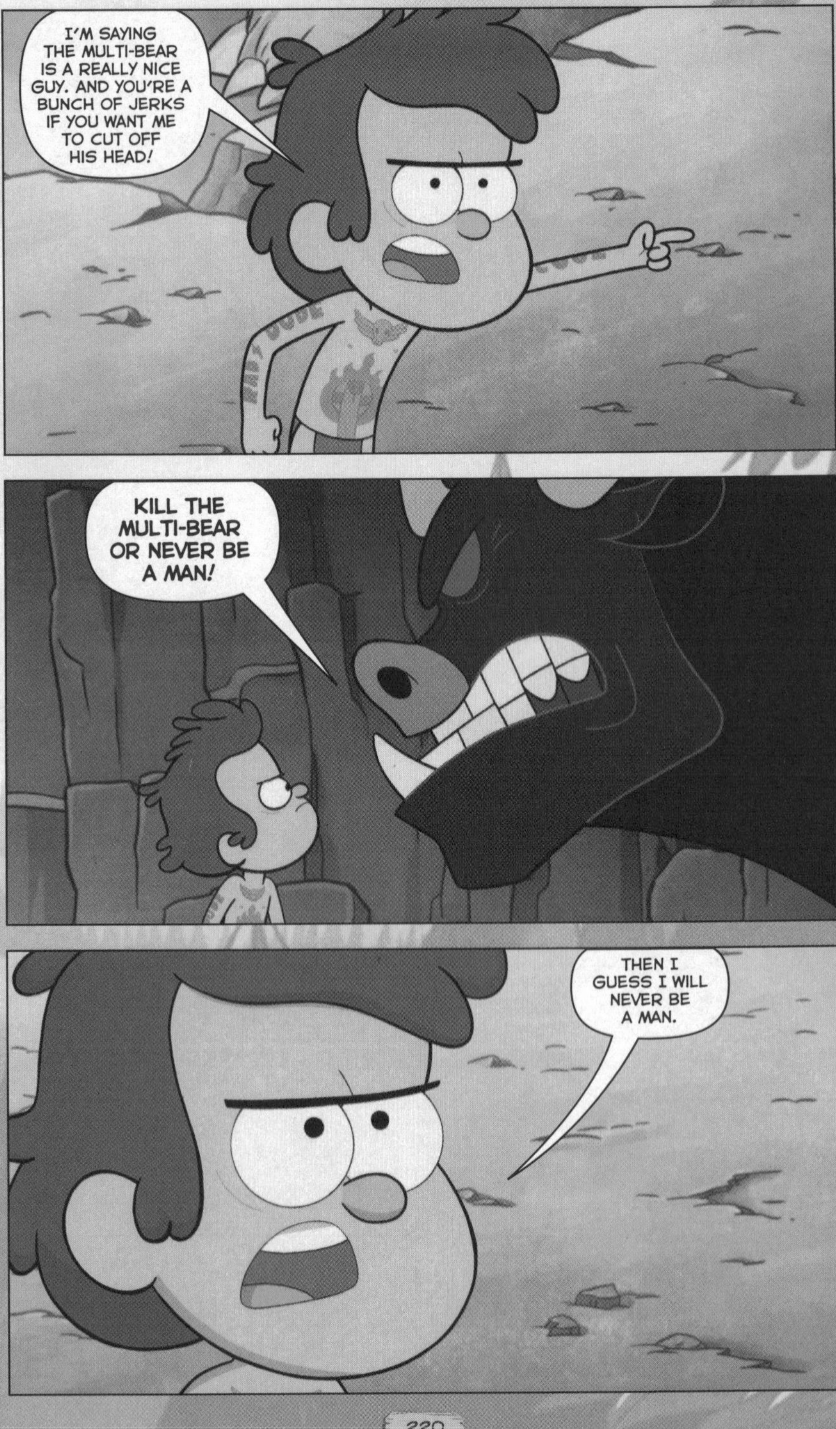
I'M SAYING THE MULTI-BEAR IS A REALLY NICE GUY. AND YOU'RE A BUNCH OF JERKS IF YOU WANT ME TO CUT OFF HIS HEAD!
KILL THE MULTI-BEAR OR NEVER BE A MAN!
THEN I GUESS I WILL NEVER BE A MAN.

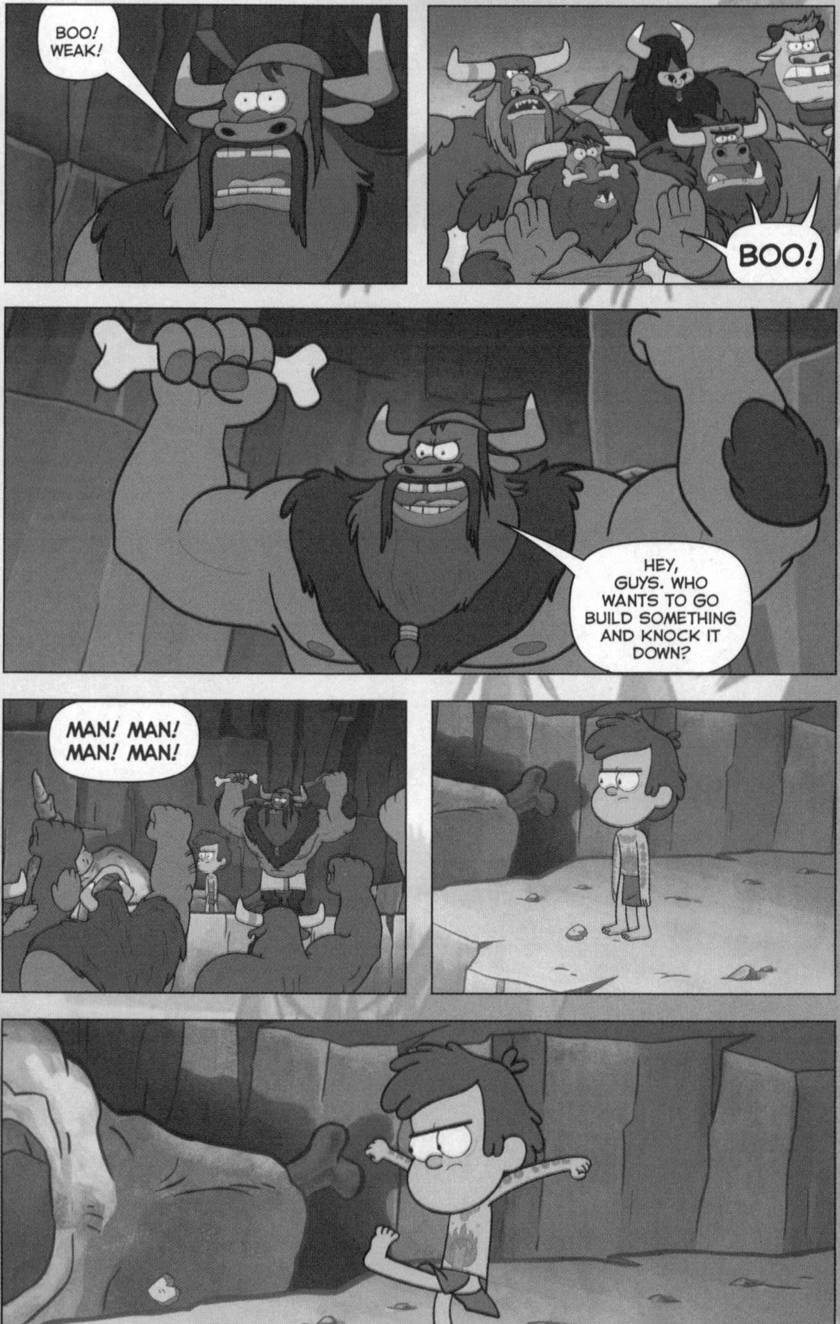

BOO! WEAK!
BOO!
HEY, GUYS. WHO WANTS TO GO BUILD SOMETHING AND KNOCK IT DOWN?
MAN! MAN! MAN! MAN!

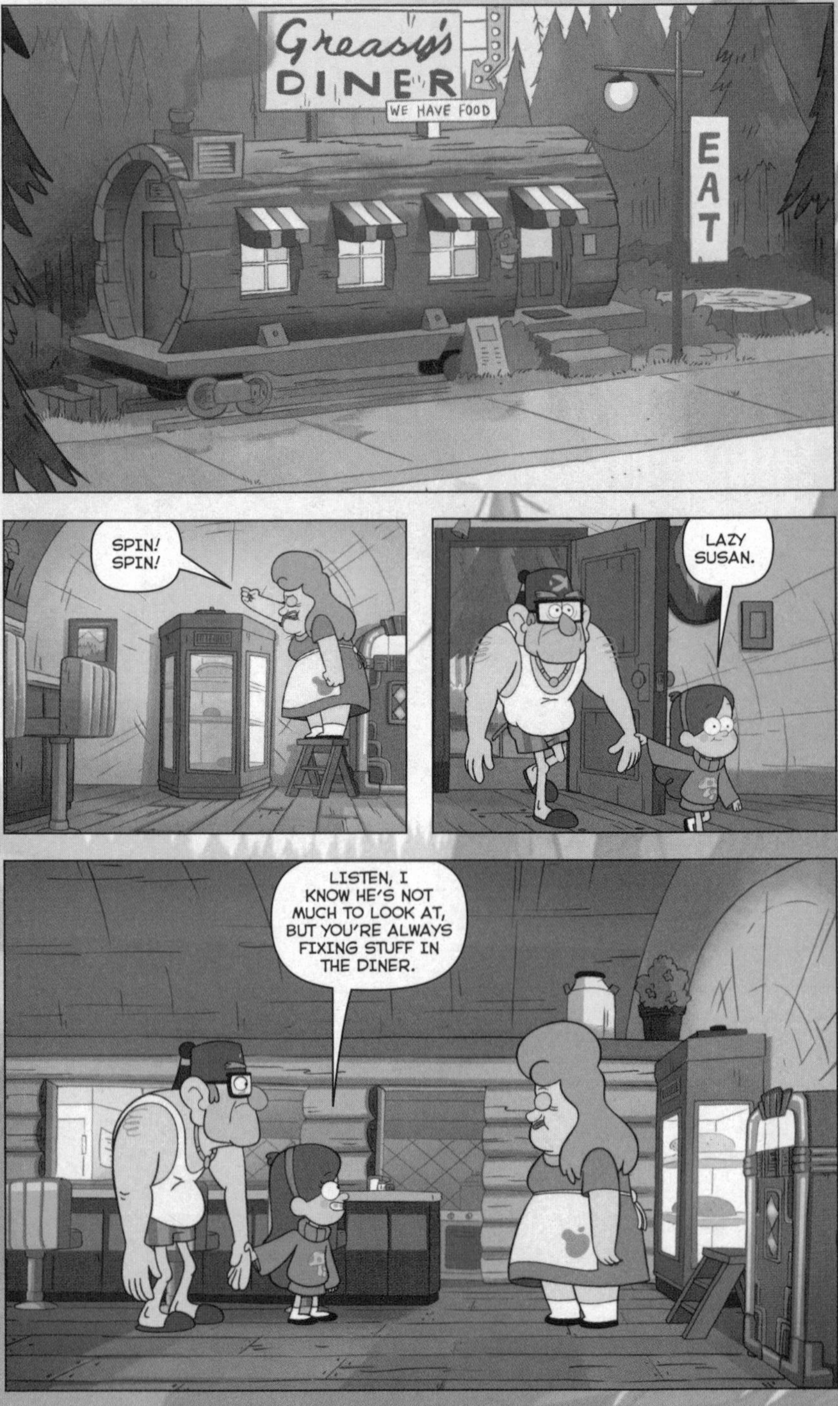
Greasy's
DINER
WE HAVE FOOD
EAT
SPIN! SPIN!
LAZY SUSAN.
LISTEN, I KNOW HE'S NOT MUCH TO LOOK AT, BUT YOU'RE ALWAYS FIXING STUFF IN THE DINER.

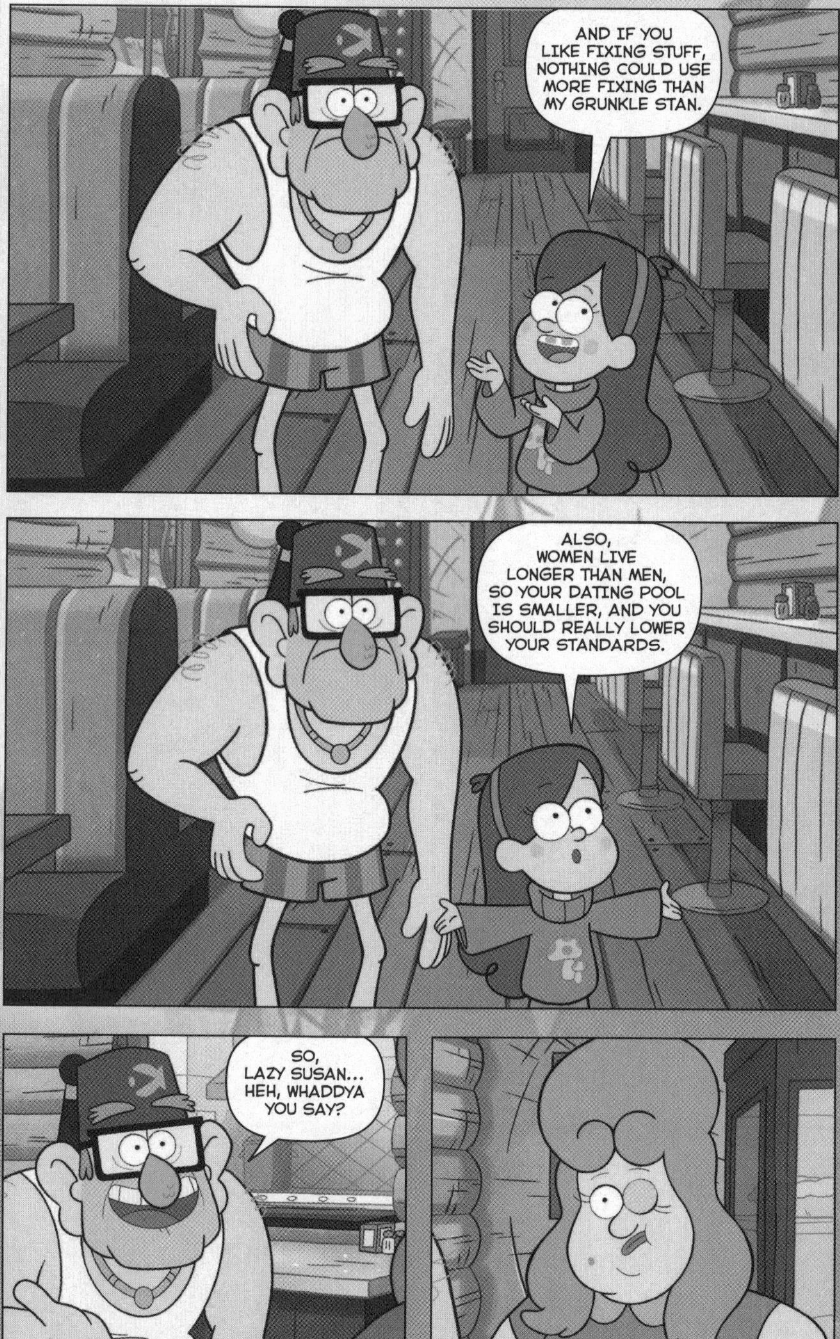
AND IF YOU LIKE FIXING STUFF, NOTHING COULD USE MORE FIXING THAN MY GRUNKLE STAN.
ALSO, WOMEN LIVE LONGER THAN MEN, SO YOUR DATING POOL IS SMALLER, AND YOU SHOULD REALLY LOWER YOUR STANDARDS.
SO, LAZY SUSAN... HEH, WHADDYA YOU SAY?

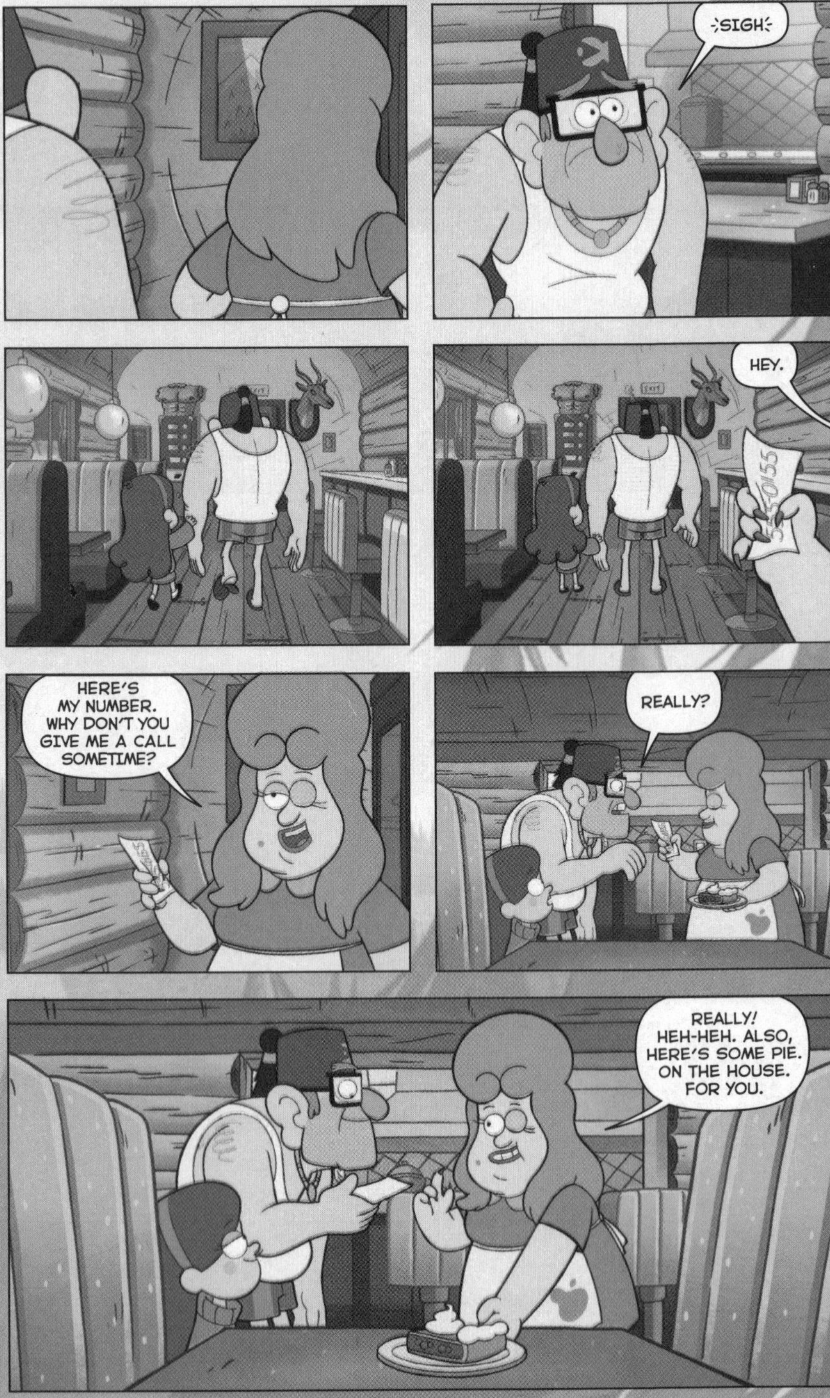
SIGH
HEY.
HERE'S MY NUMBER. WHY DON'T YOU GIVE ME A CALL SOMETIME?
REALLY?
REALLY! HEH-HEH. ALSO, HERE'S SOME PIE. ON THE HOUSE. FOR YOU.

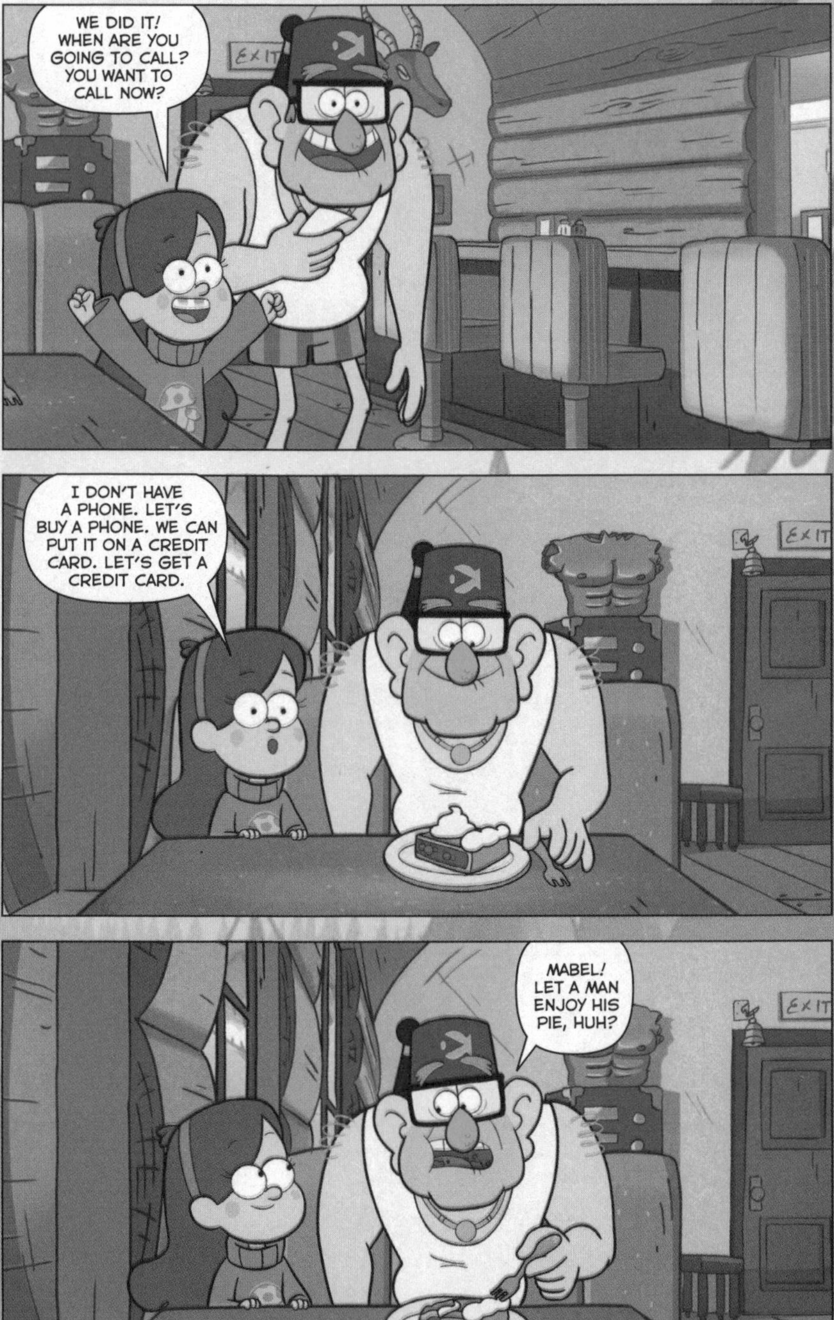
WE DID IT! WHEN ARE YOU GOING TO CALL? YOU WANT TO CALL NOW?
EXIT
I DON'T HAVE A PHONE. LET'S BUY A PHONE. WE CAN PUT IT ON A CREDIT CARD. LET'S GET A CREDIT CARD.
EXIT
MABEL! LET A MAN ENJOY HIS PIE, HUH?
EXIT

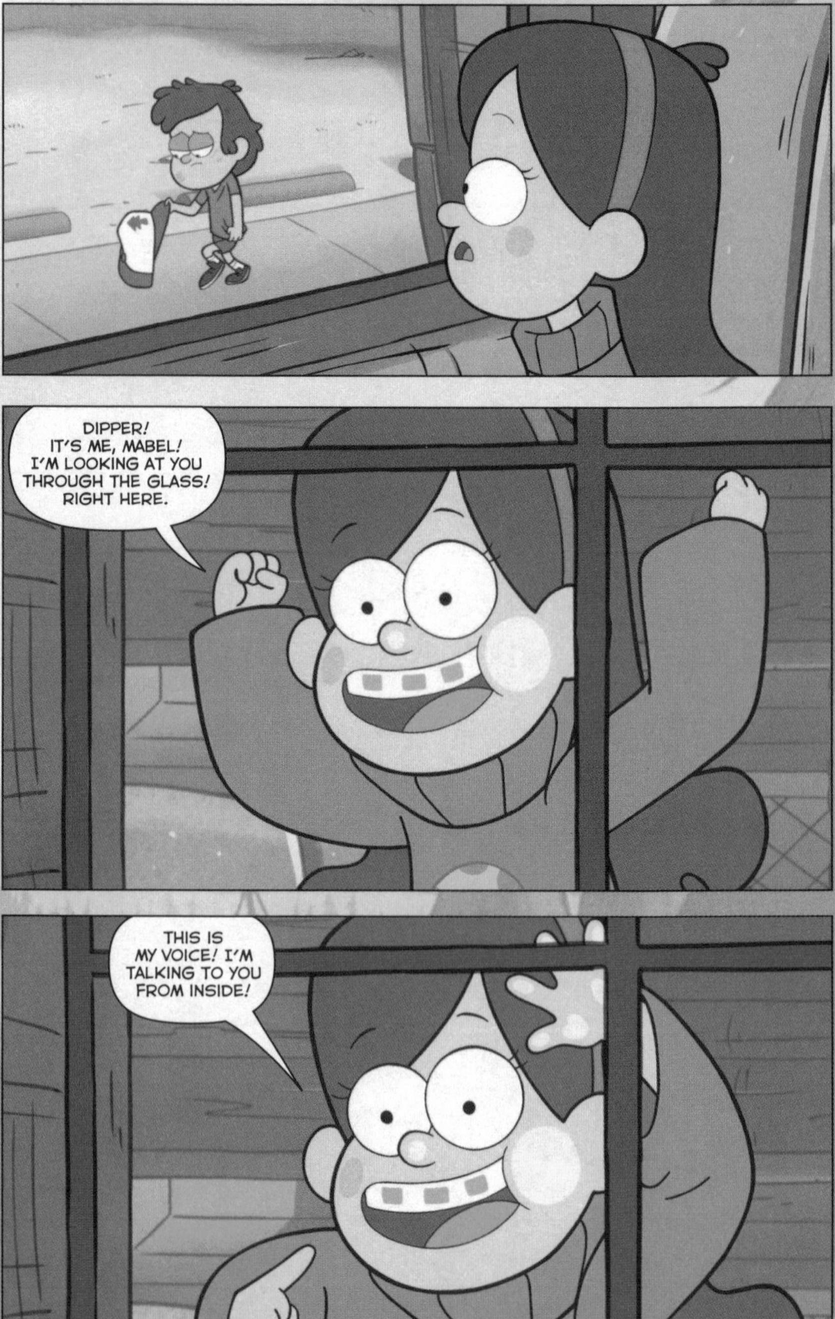
DIPPER! IT'S ME, MABEL! I'M LOOKING AT YOU THROUGH THE GLASS! RIGHT HERE.
THIS IS MY VOICE! I'M TALKING TO YOU FROM INSIDE!

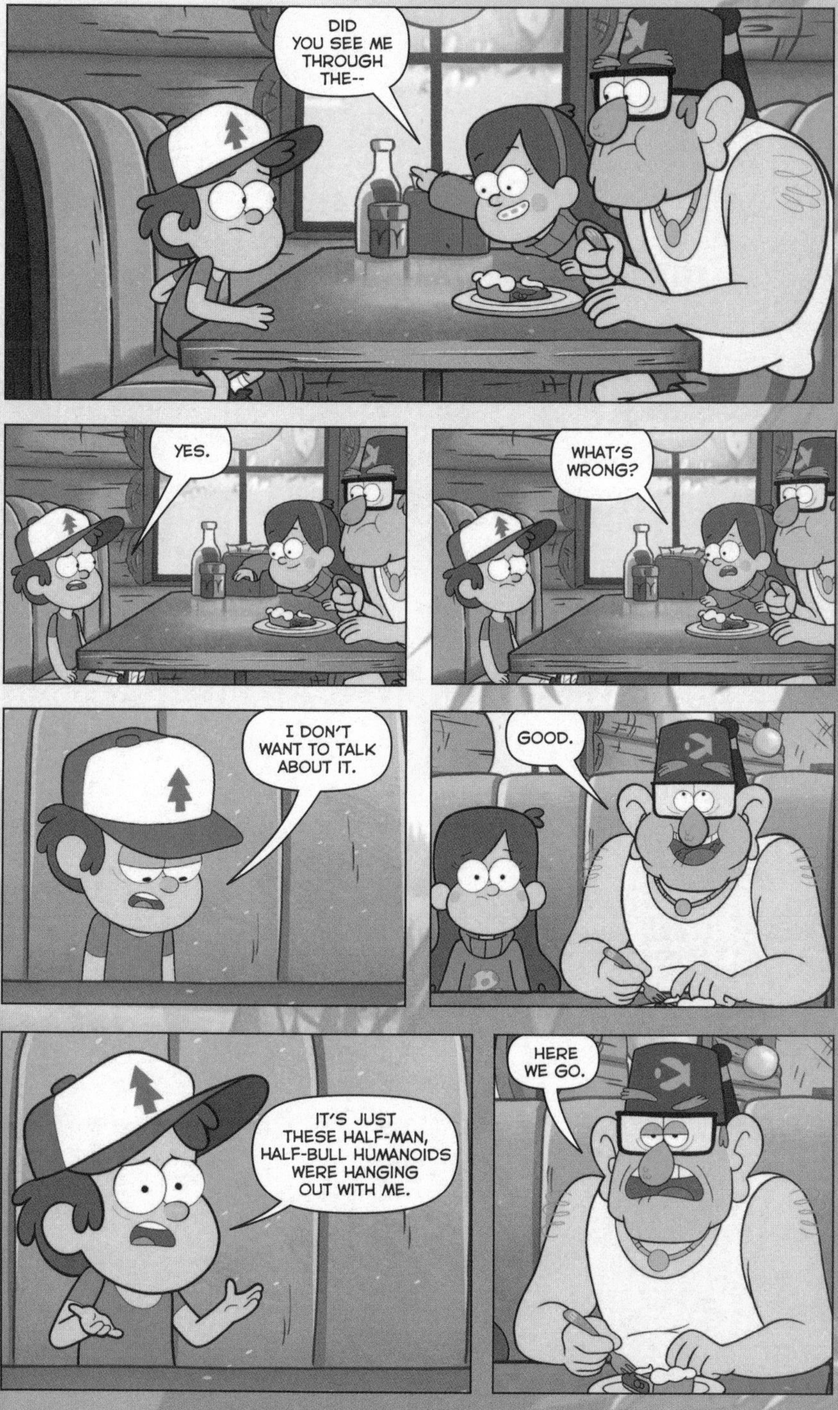
DID YOU SEE ME THROUGH THE--
YES.
WHAT'S WRONG?
I DON'T WANT TO TALK ABOUT IT.
GOOD.
IT'S JUST THESE HALF-MAN, HALF-BULL HUMANOIDS WERE HANGING OUT WITH ME.
HERE WE GO.

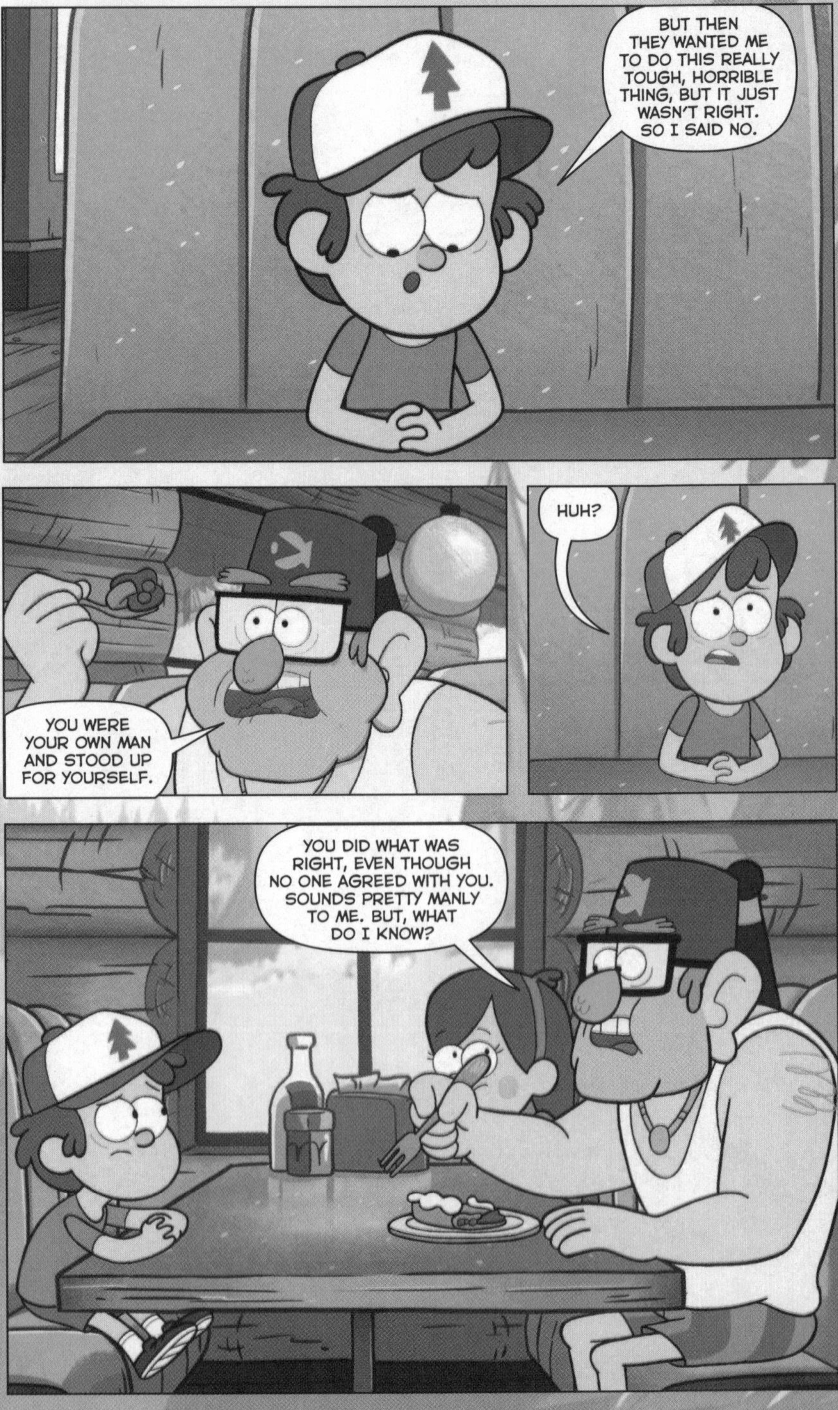
BUT THEN THEY WANTED ME TO DO THIS REALLY TOUGH, HORRIBLE THING, BUT IT JUST WASN'T RIGHT. SO I SAID NO.
YOU WERE YOUR OWN MAN AND STOOD UP FOR YOURSELF.
HUH?
YOU DID WHAT WAS RIGHT, EVEN THOUGH NO ONE AGREED WITH YOU. SOUNDS PRETTY MANLY TO ME. BUT, WHAT DO I KNOW?

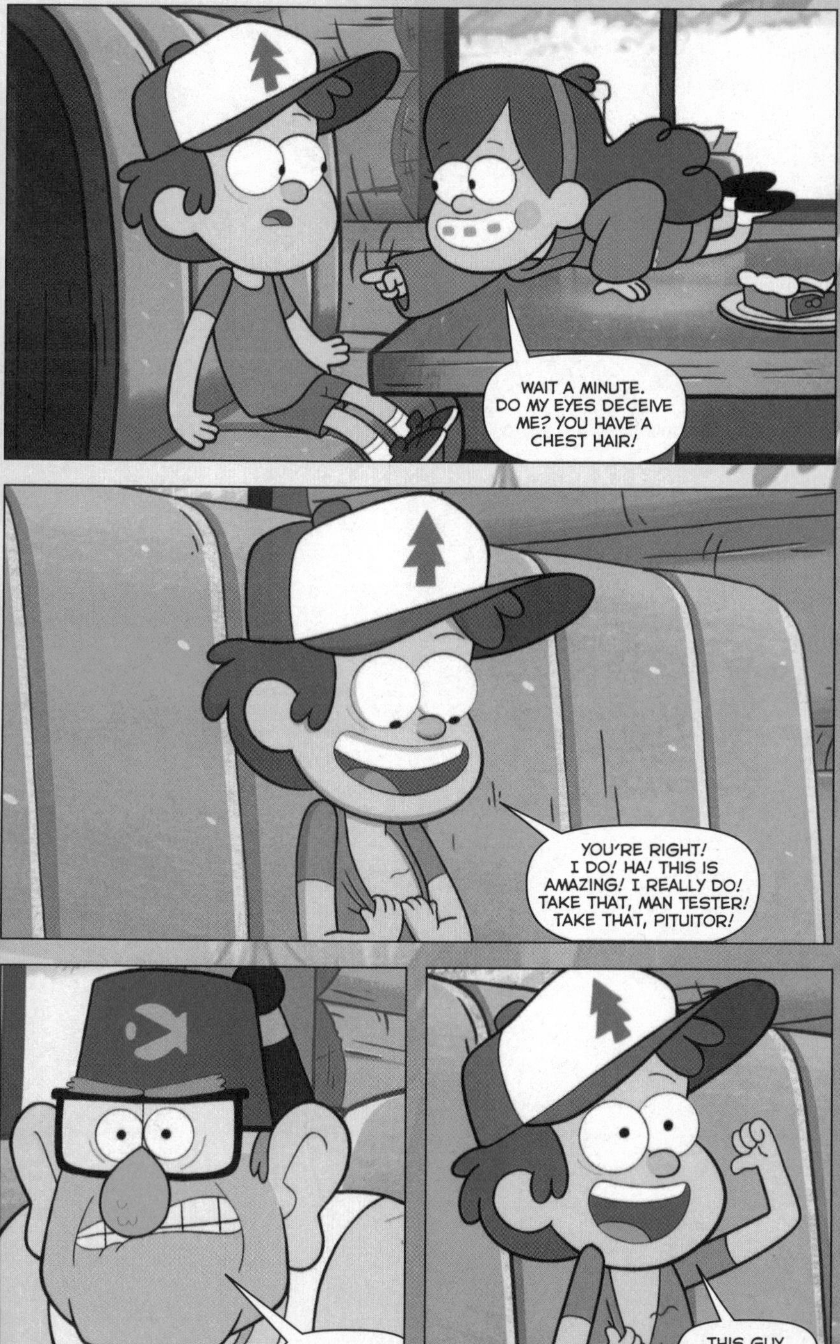
WAIT A MINUTE. DO MY EYES DECEIVE ME? YOU HAVE A CHEST HAIR!
YOU'RE RIGHT! I DO! HA! THIS IS AMAZING! I REALLY DO! TAKE THAT, MAN TESTER! TAKE THAT, PITUITOR!
PITUITOR?
THIS GUY HAS CHEST HAIR!

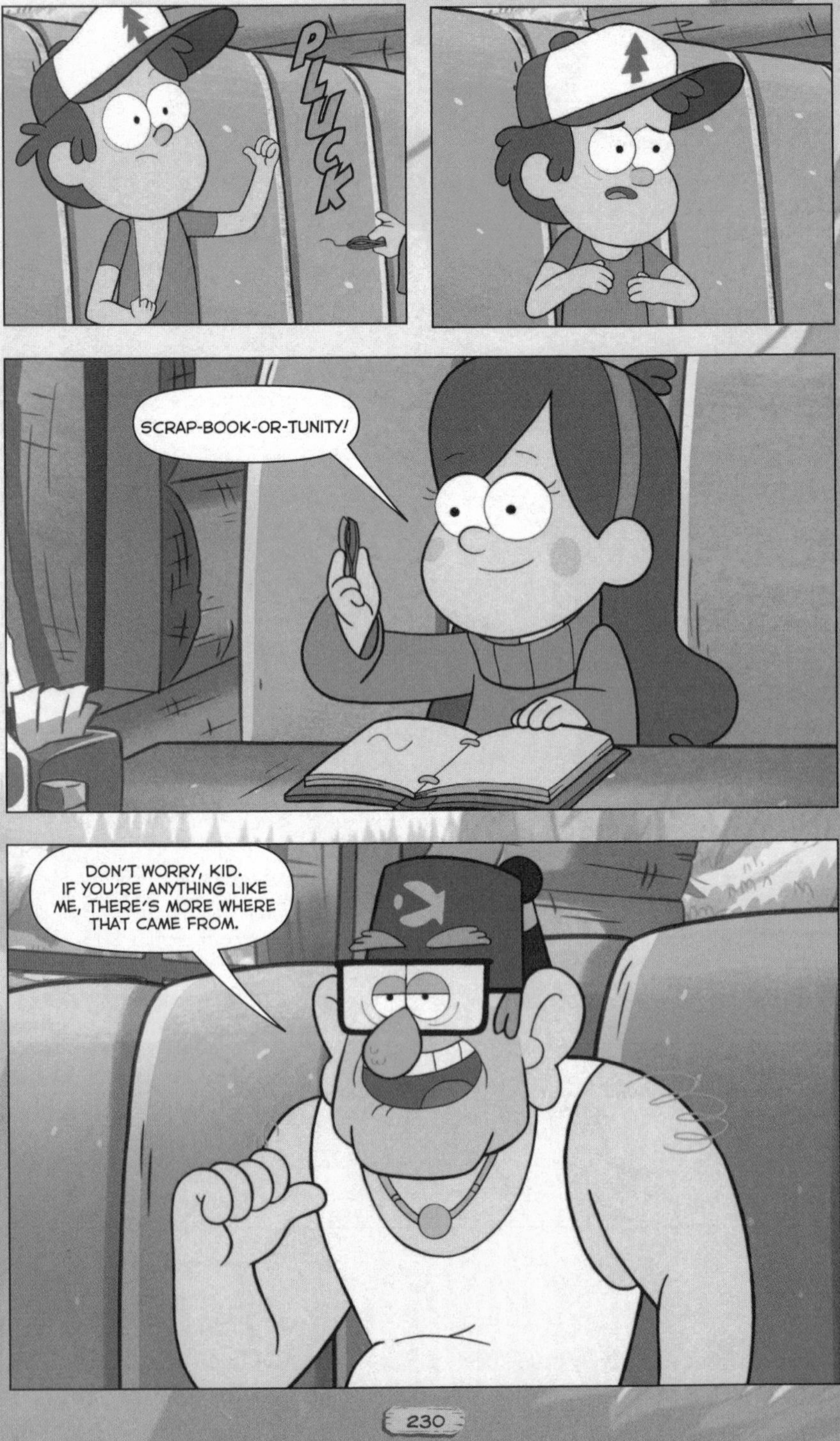
PLUCK
SCRAP-BOOK-OR-TUNITY!
DON'T WORRY, KID. IF YOU'RE ANYTHING LIKE ME, THERE'S MORE WHERE THAT CAME FROM.

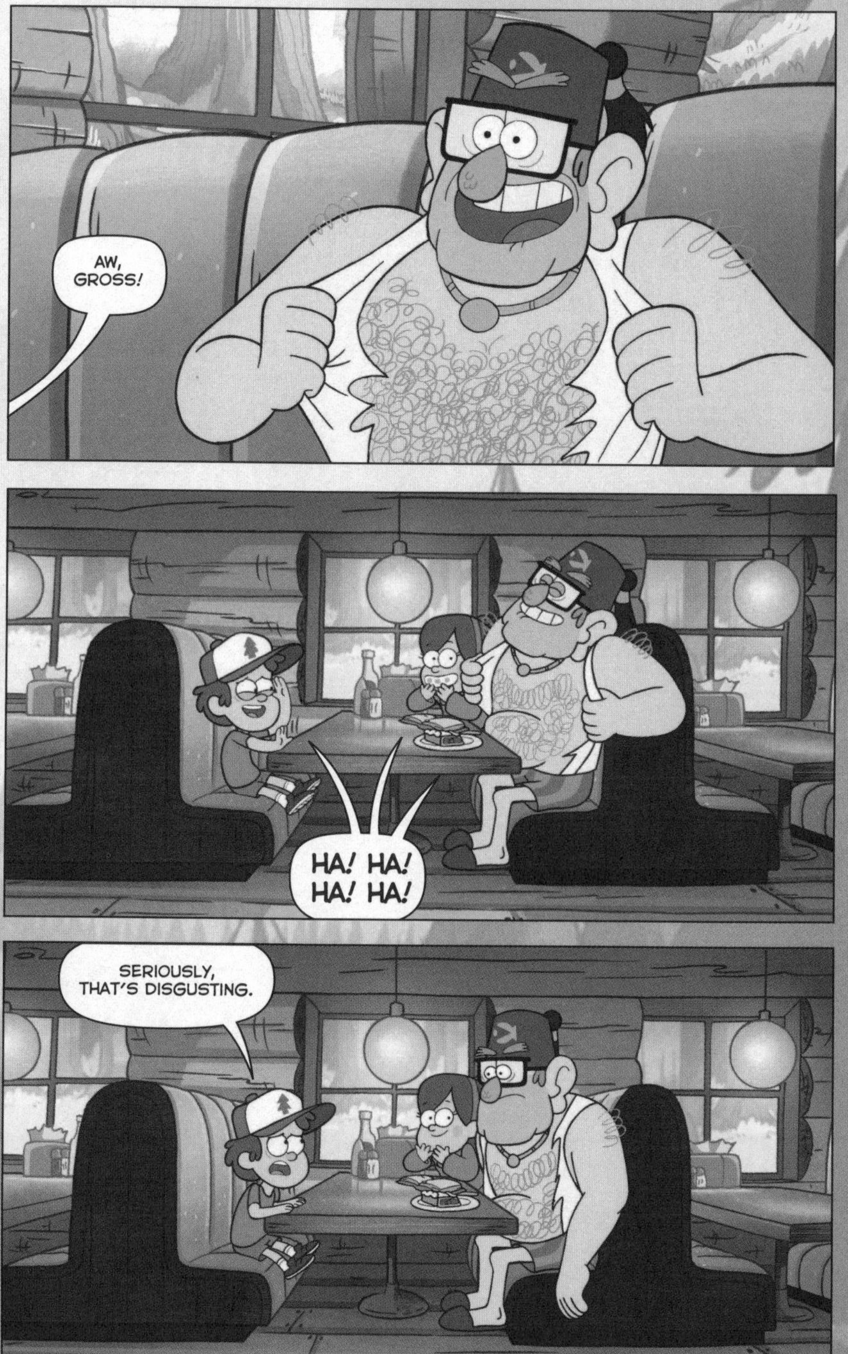
AW, GROSS!
HA! HA! HA! HA!
SERIOUSLY, THAT'S DISGUSTING.
THE END